PAUL DUCARD

THE

OTHER SIDE

OF EVIL

ISBN: 0615595332
ISBN 13: 9780615595337

Library of Congress Control Number: 2012901541
Paul Ducard, Brooklyn, NY
Author's Photo: Ayako Takahashi
Painting on the cover, "The Garden of Earthly Delights," by Hieronyimus Bosch,
courtesy of Wikicommons

For my wife and my two girls

FOREWORD

This book has been a long time in coming. Conceived in a classroom in Washington, DC, in 1993, its first few words weren't transcribed onto paper until 1996. It was only in 2000 that I first fed what I had written into a computer; and it wasn't until March of 2010, nine thousand miles away from my wife and daughter, that I brought the story to a close.

I almost hesitate to say it was a labor of love. What do I mean by that? Researching the book as some of the most fun I'd ever had. Reading everything I could get my hands on. Listening to every free podcast there was to download. But writing the book? Well, writing the book was trying at the best of times. It coincided with moving to and from multiple cities, working my "day job" for hours that only management consultants would consider reasonable, and struggling with the possibility of someone misunderstanding the person I was by reading the story I had created.

But I wanted to tell the story. The story I had dreamed up in my head reading Milton, Dante, Clavell, Eco, and Tolkien, among many others. Watching *Star Wars*, *The Exorcist*, and *Jacob's Ladder*; *What Dreams May Come*, *Defending Your Life*, and *Bill & Ted's Bogus Journey*. (I kid you not.) It was my story, but it was nothing more than a story.

It is here now for people to read and I hope they do. Read and consider that there's always more than one way to see "the truth."

A special thanks to Michael C. (you know who you are) for listening to all my ideas and reading the manuscript, for telling me where I'd gone terribly wrong. A special thanks to my wife too, who knew, although she was never able to understand just why I was writing what I was writing, that it was important to me to finish. A special thanks to my sister as well for guiding me onto a path that would ultimately make more sense than the one I was then on, strewn as it was with jumbled thoughts. Thanks to John Kelly—may he rest in peace—for teaching me Latin and founding my love for Greek and Roman history. And, without intending to sound too Academy Awards, thanks to my mother and father who gave me everything I have...aside from my exceptional luck in life.

Paul Ducard
New York City, 2012

"...[I]t seems to me that the world has always been in the same condition, and that in it, there has been just as much good as there is evil..."

NICCOLÒ MACHIAVELLI,

The Discourses

Hell hath no limits, nor is circumscribed
In one self-place, but where we are is Hell,
And where Hell is, there must we ever be.

CHRISTOPHER MARLOWE,

Doctor Faustus

1

CHAPTER ONE

Shaded from the rays of the setting sun, he stood in the archway of his apartment's balcony, watching, as the surrounding wasteland was slowly devoured by the late-afternoon shadows. From his vantage point high above the city, he could see everything that lay beyond the confines of its outermost defensive wall. As the sun dipped beneath the city skyline behind him, its fading light caught in the buildings, temples, and fortifications, casting shadows that snaked outward, until the city's entire profile seemed to stretch for miles across the dissolving plain. The inverted image gave the landscape a broken appearance, as if the horizon itself had cracked open to suck the color from the rapidly fading sky.

His apartment sat atop the city's central temple, the oldest and tallest building within the walls. At the ceremony marking the founding of the city, he himself had laid the first stone. From there, he had spoken to the weary masses gathered atop its thick, rectangular form, steeling them together into a cohesive group and inciting them to action. He'd spoken as the people's proven leader, wrapped in the armor of political invincibility, for he alone had led them from their lives of servitude to this new place. It was desolate there, when they had first arrived, but free from the injustice that had consumed their lives for so long. When the temple was completed years later, it would become a memorial to those who had died founding the city, and would be dedicated to his personal courage in leading their noble insurrection. As the author and leader of the most stupendous upheaval ever recorded, his people had honored him with a seat above all other seats, from where he could look down and see all his children, now forever assured of their place in the universe.

The energy rising from the city just below him was palpable, self-sustaining. No trace remained of the early days, when blood had washed over the city's then fragile walls. The city's vibrations murmured freedom, something the universe had never experienced, before he stepped up onto the cornerstone of those foundations that day to proclaim their new city of cities. Citizens were free to come and go as they pleased, content with the daily pattern of their lives or conspiring, perhaps, to bring about something different. Either way, they now lived and died as they wished, freed from the yoke of some malicious tyrant who dictated how they should go about it. They had the right to either enjoy or hate their existence, with no one telling them how, or when, or where. It was a hard-fought harmony and one, he now felt, was slipping through his fingers.

He turned back and gazed up at the setting sun. "Someone created that sun," he thought. "But it was not God," he murmured to himself and closed his eyes.

Word had reached him of riders intercepting a massing of newly arrived at Apsatsus. He could see the wretches in his mind's eye. Tattered and confused. Bleeding. With a desperation unlike anything any of them had ever experienced before. Unlike anything they could ever have experienced before. They'd be wild animals freed from their cages, not knowing where to go and fearing harm from every direction. And it would be his responsibility to dispel all their confusion and convert them to the truth—or spit them back out onto the empty, pitiless plains.

"They will add another inch to the miles of my alienation," he thought.

He wrapped his robes more closely around himself to ward off the encroaching chill of evening. The shadows were gone, absorbed by the invisible depths of darkness. Now, it was simply night.

⌘　⌘　⌘

Only the reflected glow from the lights of the city below illuminated the room when Gazardiel entered. He hadn't knocked. He never did. But he blinked for a few moments, trying to adjust his eyes to the darkness.

"Is anyone here?" he asked cautiously, his words scattering across the hollow space.

The room was chilly with the evening air, but sweet-scented from the incense burning in some unseen corner. As his eyes slowly adjusted to the semi-darkness, he could make out a movement across the room's open space: white linen curtains caught in the evening breezes, gently billowing in and out of the balcony doorway. A sudden fear struck him as he stood there, feeling utterly alone in the darkness.

"I am here." The voice floated in from somewhere beyond the curtains. "Is it time already?"

"Yes, my Lord." Gazardiel bowed his head.

His master was on the balcony. "Come out," he now said calmly. "You can humor me for a few minutes."

"I was worried for a moment," Gazardiel said, straightening up.

Now that his vision had adjusted somewhat to the gloom, he made his way slowly toward the balcony, hands held up before him to avoid colliding against any unseen obstructions. He chastised himself silently for being so easily caught off guard, his fears so easily sensed. He hated coming here. Speaking with him. His master. Their Master.

"Where are you, my Lord?" he asked, stepping through curtains and onto the vast balcony. Its mosaic tiles played games with his eyes in the dim light.

"You know, I enjoy the darkness," the Master said from some still-unidentified spot nearby. "I like watching the city at night. It gives me peace for some reason." His last few words were uttered in almost a whisper. As if he were listening for an echo. "I like the smells of far-off places when they come to me, borne on the winds. Especially in the evening hours, when the lands all around us sigh in relief and we can give thanks for another day."

"Sounds like you're planning a trip, my Lord," Gazardiel said nervously, still scanning the balcony to trace the spot where the Master was perched.

He sensed the presence of others there too, but could see no one. He began to sweat. The wind gave the Master's voice no direction; it yielded no clues for Gazardiel to gauge where it emanated from.

Without warning, the Master stepped from the darkness and flashed him a churlish smile. "I will be here for quite sometime to come, I expect," he said, inspecting the younger one's startled expression carefully.

Gazardiel couldn't look at him, at least not straight in the eye. The suddenness of his appearance had put him off-balance. The whiteness of the Master's teeth surprised him. They flashed brightly, even in the faint light.

"I took great interest in your orations today," the Master said without adequate preamble. "You are developing into quite the statesman."

The Master broke his gaze and made his way over to an unlit lantern hanging from the wall. Absently, he began to search his robes for a match. From the darkness nearby stepped the Master's bodyguard.

So there had been others, Gazardiel thought. There always are. Always present. "Always listening," he grumbled, mouthing the words without realizing it.

"Did you say something?" the Master asked.

"No, no," Gazardiel replied, startled that he had been heard from so far away.

"Hmm," the Master mused, continuing to pat himself down. "Your orations," he said, as if to remind himself of the issue at hand. "I wonder."

"Wonder, my Lord?" Gazardiel inquired, anxious to get the conversation concluded and the Master out the door and down to the waiting Council.

"What has gotten into you? My pupil?"

"There's no reason to mock me," Gazardiel protested, looking back from the silent bodyguard, "just because we see things differently."

There had been a time when the Master could do no wrong, when Gazardiel hung on his every word. He was their Master. Indisputable. A fortress of valor who had made their world what it was. The Master had meant everything to him. But the years had passed and Gazardiel had grown. Grown to see things differently. Taking the lessons he'd learned from the Master and making his own way. He simply saw things differently now. Differently from the way their Master saw them. And now Gazardiel had little left, but venom, barely veiled, a weakness he understood he needed to overcome, if he were ever to lead. But he so hated coming to his place. Whatever civility he had been able to muster when he stepped out onto that balcony was gone in a flash.

"Mm. Indeed," the Master said, continuing to pat down his robes.

The bodyguard stared at Gazardiel without expression.

"Wasn't it you who had taught me that even an entire people can be blind, when they are incapable of but one vision?" Gazardiel continued, becoming very aware of his feet planted firmly on the floor. He needed to hold on for a few more minutes.

"An 'entire people,' you say?" the Master asked, producing a small box of matches from some hidden pocket. "And how do you define an 'entire people'?" With squinting eyes, Gazardiel's master studied the tip of the match recovered from the box. Once satisfied, he struck the match and applied the crackling and sparking tip to the lantern's beaten wick.

"We have to draw the line somewhere," Gazardiel continued, annoyed that the Master was paying more attention to the lantern than to their conversation. "Why not here? Why not now?"

"Why not tomorrow or in a thousand years?" the Master retorted, seemingly unable to get the wick alight. "That is the problem with your argument. When will it ever be the right time to say, 'No more. We shall have no more?'"

"I don't wish to argue over this with you again," Gazardiel said, pausing slightly before finishing with, "my Lord".

He shot a slightly nervous look back over at the bodyguard. No expression. None at all. He was forever watching. Gazardiel rebuked himself for not having been better prepared. Weaknesses were not to be betrayed in the Master's presence. Ever.

"My views are my views and there is nothing you can say to make me believe otherwise," he declared.

The Master frowned as the smoking tip of the match sputtered out and the wick remained unlit. He pulled another match from the box and began to carefully adjust the wick, winding it up and down.

"Well, then. Perhaps I gave you too much credit," he finally said, breaking off some of the wick's burnt liniments. "But I ask you, Gazardiel, as a politician, do you not always have to be in the mood to discuss politics?" He smiled at the expressionless bodyguard.

"There's no point in lecturing me. This city is done with your politics," Gazardiel replied quickly and forcefully. "You may have built this place," he added, gesturing down to the city below, "but, unlike you, it has changed." He could feel his blood rising. "You sit in Senate chambers all day, grumbling over the speeches of other members, complaining about the meager progress we make. And when you're done complaining, you come up here and sit all night, night after night, poring over what you think you've accomplished, lamenting how no one lives in the old ways."

Gazardiel's heart raced. He was speaking now as he would never speak in chambers, ever loyal to the formal and proper proceedings of the house. But it was weakness that had led him to this spot. Out on the Master's balcony.

"Breathing in the air, admiring the night sky or whatever other damned thing it is you do up here," he continued, hurtling on relentlessly. "Leaving this city to rot right beneath you. And you're not even aware that you are the cause of the rot you blame everyone else for!"

A line had been crossed, but Gazardiel knew he would not stop to heed his own warnings. At least, not on this subject.

"Your 'philosophy' or whatever you choose to call it, is eating this city up from the inside out," Gazardiel said heatedly, straightening up again and flashing a look at the silent bodyguard once more. "When will you come to terms with the fact that Man is not what you think he is? That Man is the virus that infects our body? This city? When will you reconcile yourself to the fact that this is not your city anymore?" He breathed heavily, flush with his churning emotions. "When will you realize that your time is over? Yours is no longer the voice they hear. *Our* time has come."

"Bravado," the Master quickly countered, "is all I hear these days."

He modulated his tone only slightly as he continued to examine the unlit wick. He squinted. To Gazardiel, the Master's eyes didn't seem as they once were. Old and bleary now, not clear and sharp as they used to be, when Gazardiel had been a novice. And had respected him and his accomplishments. Gazardiel shifted his defensive stance to absorb the verbal blows he anticipated. Body language, he had learned, was nearly as important as the message itself. The Master had taught him that. But Gazardiel found himself growing increasingly annoyed as the Master continued to play with the lantern, now lit, alternating the light on the balcony from dark to light, dark to light, with each turn. He found his temper rising. Another weak point. He could hardly contain himself. Seconds ticked by. Then finally, the Master blew out the lantern flame with a dissatisfied look and began searching for yet another match. Gazardiel felt his temper straining to its outermost edge.

As the match was struck, the flickering flames threw the deepening lines of the Master's face into relief. Gazardiel remembered seeing those same lines, less prominently etched, as a boy. How very expressive of wisdom they had seemed to him then. "How long will it be until I am smart enough to have lines like those?" he had asked himself as a boy. He was grown now. Gazardiel knew his face remained unmarked, unlike the Master's. But was he as wise as the Master? Had the Master ever been wise? Do not confuse wisdom with age, Gazardiel quickly thought, trying to shake himself free from this moment of broken concentration.

"It is time we speak of political options, my friend," the Master finally said, breaking the silence. "Speeches will no longer resolve issues."

"Speeches in the hallowed chambers of this city have always resolved issues. You saw to that. And to our impasse on Man, my Lord, there is no issue worthy of further discussion. There is only the will of the people and the situation of my motion to the Council," Gazardiel snapped, startling even himself with his sudden intensity. "This is what you continue failing to see. I may come up here as your former novice, but I will not work with you in compromise. Not on this. The bill will stand. Man will end. Here, at least. Though you have told me otherwise, you do not work in options. You work in absolutes. You refuse to consider seeing our points—anything, in fact—in any light other than your own."

"Did I not teach you that there is no difference between someone who sees nothing and someone who sees only himself? I question your motives, Gazardiel." The lantern had been re-lit but, again, the Master had fallen to playing with the wick. "What do you, Gazardiel, hear in the voices of the people?" The Master turned to look at him now. "What do they tell you that they do not tell me? Or perhaps, more accurately, what do you, Gazardiel, hope to gain from the message you hear? In the legislation that you foist upon the Council, as if they know you like I do."

The Master's last words were choked with clear disdain, the first time Gazardiel had seen real emotion in him on this point.

"I give the people a fresh perspective, a more powerful tool to shape their city," Gazardiel said, his voice faltering a little under the Master's intent gaze. "I offer them a chance to seize their future. Or at least take it out of the hands of those who are unworthy of directing its course. You can only offer them more of the same. The bill will change all that. For good." Gazardiel's argument sounded unconvincing, even to his own ears.

"You are looking to undo a rule of law that makes up the very fabric of this city," the Master replied. "Something that has worked to make this city what it is, even what you, in your perverse way, seem to want it to be. But I know better. With your coalitions and backroom deals, you look to cement your own position, Gazardiel. There is no brave new way. I know this. The Council knows this, though they follow you like the slippery serpents they always have been. Only you will not admit it, at least, not in public, and that is what really makes me wonder."

The Master tossed the burnt match stub up and over the balcony's rail.

"I will worry about the Council," Gazardiel replied somewhat sheepishly. He wasn't sure he really wielded the kind of control he was suggesting he did. But it was necessary for the Master to believe that he, Gazardiel, was supremely confident. "You can think what you want to, but you cannot stop this from happening. The bill will pass."

Gazardiel was done talking. He was almost sure forthcoming events would bear him out.

"I see." The Master clasped his hands behind his back and looked at his bodyguard.

Without so much as a signal being given, the bodyguard acknowledged the Master's command, turned, and withdrew, leaving them alone on the balcony.

The Master turned to look out over the city once again. "I see," he repeated.

Fresh scents came in on the wind. Gazardiel stood there. Idle. Unsure. This was surely further weakness on his part. He'd come to collect the Master. He wasn't entirely sure it was appropriate for him to leave without fulfilling his charge. The balcony's mosaic-tiled floors seemed to dance now under the flickering lantern light, much as the city's lights danced their way over the balcony. It was so distracting.

"I have been appointed to oversee an inquiry into your party," the Master finally said. "I thought you might like to know."

"'Appointed?' 'Inquiry'?" Gazardiel inquired disdainfully. "What promises did you make this time? Who appointed you?"

"Call it what you will. It does not matter. It is happening."

"What do you intend to do?"

Gazardiel could not help but be worried. The Master had done this before. It was his constitutional right to do so, though any inquiry had to be approved by a vote of the Council. The Master had gotten to them before he could.

"I will do what has to be done. What I see fit to do," the Master said. Now *that* sounded final.

"What do you intend to do?" Gazardiel repeated, his nervousness inducing laughter this time. A sign of weakness. Again.

"What has to be done," the Master repeated, turning back around to face him. "We need to go. You are here to escort me down. The Council will be waiting for us and we should not keep them waiting longer than is necessary. You, of all people, should know the rules."

The Master walked over to the lantern, opened it, and blew out its flickering flame.

CHAPTER TWO

The distant object that had barely broken the horizon the day before took shape, becoming clearer to the tired mass of travelers moving slowly forward. Silhouetted against the more fluid lines of the white-capped mountains that flanked its sides, this object, a tower, pierced the sky's translucent blue with its clean, sharp point.

Though it still lay many miles away, the turmoil and sense of disorientation the travelers had suffered from over the past several days began to dissipate. In their passage across the arid and featureless wastelands, the future had ceased to be a concern. But for the revolutions of the hot sun above them, time had ended. What happens tomorrow is irrelevant when there is no understanding of what's happening today. Few spoke. No words of substance were uttered. One woman kept mumbling to herself, "Utter end, utter end..."

But with the appearance of the needle-like tower in the mountains, the travelers found a renewed strength. Now there was a purpose to their toils. The slog over sands, the spine-filled shrubs, and the scorching heat morphed into a kind of push forward. A momentum. A passion. Pressing onward with a sense of purpose, the thick layers of dread that had hung like a cloud over the group in the preceding days suddenly lifted. The desert no longer ate at them. No longer was the shuffling of tired feet and weeping the only sounds to breach the silence that held them together. In the fading light of day, with the snowcapped mountains and the strange needle-like tower before them, the mood lightened.

Their horsemen escorts told them to halt for the evening and helped them again with the business of setting up camp. The horsemen distributed food sparingly among the group, but as the evening shadows approached, there was the feeling among its members of enjoying a banquet. Campfires sparked to life and the mountains glowed, backlit by a low-riding sun dipping toward the horizon. Long fingers of soft pinks and oranges sprang up and began to stretch across the fading sky toward them. Finger-like clouds encircled the highest mountains and stretched across the range. The many threads of light turned into shadows that lived with them, and the whole camp was soon enveloped in their cool, darkening grasp. Peace settled over the tired, dirty camp. Now snuggling in what might be their last night of the march, each anticipated step of the next day meant revelation of all the answers that had gone missing since their arrival in this place. This strange place, incomprehensible to them all.

It felt as though a friendly hand were reaching out to them over the many miles from the tower in the mountains. In response, sparks from their fires sprang up into the night sky and danced in the blackest of black nights, floating up and away toward the darkening mountains. It soon became difficult to distinguish the campfires' sparks from lights visible in the mountains. The waves of heat released from the ground in the early evening distorted the mountains' distant lights and carried them higher into the surrounding desert air than the tongue-licks of their fires. The sky was filled with the tiny dots of red-hot light, mixed with the wavering strings of mountain lights. Many thousands, millions, billions of lights. Something was there before them. They all came from below the darkened outline of that tower. In the mountains.

⌘　⌘　⌘

The group had come together only days before. They began washing up sporadically on the banks of an unknown river, in an unknown place, as if dragged and deposited there by an unknown will. Men, women, and children materialized on the riverbank, confused, disoriented, soaked to the skin, and overcome by hunger. Crying and shaking, they dragged themselves ashore. Some, in a state of delirium, tried wading back out into the fast-moving river, but strong currents picked them up and pushed them right back on the shore, mud-covered and shivering and colder than ever. No answers to their predicament anywhere in sight.

Grim-looking men, clad in black, chainmail and armor, brandished swords and whips, looking on from the heights of the riverbank. Watching the growing crowd as they fumbled on the shoreline. Sneering at them. These men didn't speak; they only shouted as they cruelly dragged people up from the banks of the river, herding them together with the punishing crack of their whips. People huddled together in wet packs and cried as one. Total strangers, holding onto each other for protection and comfort. Looking for loved ones in vain. Trying to make sense of what was happening. Where they were. The cries were individual, disconnected, but they rose up, nonetheless, in a single wail from all along the river's edge. At this place. The soldiers waited for more to wash ashore.

When enough people had coagulated on the shores, organized squads of soldiers began separating the frightened huddle, shouting and cracking their whips as they herded them in groups from the muddy edge of the river and funneled them up over its marshy banks. Threats and abuses poured out, punishment for lack of compliance meted out quickly, violently, and without regard. Two men who rushed the soldiers were cut down, their broken and bleeding bodies left lying at the feet of the wet and startled mass of people, before the soldiers dragged the bloody remains to a pit of burning pitch and threw them in. Fire consumed the bodies, along with those of others similarly dispatched. Screams rose and fell like crashing waves. Piercing, panic-stricken screams.

But there was nowhere to go. Trapped between squads of angry soldiers and the pitiless river. Terror took over. Rapid looks from left to right and all around. Shaking, shaking. They couldn't stop shaking. Several people were singled out at random and beaten brutally until they crumpled to the ground. Others clawed at them as they were beaten, trying to pull them back into the protective circle of people. Total strangers. The soldiers did their work sternly and without compassion, moving the groups of people into successively larger groups farther and farther away from the river's edge. More people washed up across the bank, soaked, stunned, and shaking. They were left there for the next squad of soldiers, waiting now behind them, as the crowd moved forward and out of sight of the river's edge. It was a never-ending scene. The next round of waiting soldiers would drag out the next bunch of horrified arrivals, retched up by the great cold river. The clear-blue-sky day took no notice of the chaos.

A large, walled camp, dotted with fortifications, weapons, and rank upon rank of black-clad soldiers, surrounded the entire scene. While some of them awaited their turn to seize the masses on the riverbank, others corralled the collected groups of shuddering, wet, and crying people into metal-framed chutes. Penned in like animals they were, powerless, and trapped. One of the shuddering group was pushed into one of the open pens. A holding pen. The soldiers who had dragged them from the river stepped aside and began to prepare their baggage. They were going somewhere. Supplies and horses were gathered and outfitted. The group huddled together in their pen, clutching one another, shaking, and hoping that by hiding within the group, they would be less noticeable targets.

More and more people were pushed into the holding pen until it could hold no more. People were crushed together as the gates closed behind them. Perhaps a thousand of them mashed into the crowded space. Standing in the mud and waiting. It had only been a few minutes from the riverbank, but a lifetime seemed to have gone by.

Soldiers began shouting orders, their horses snorting as they reined up. The front gate of the pen was suddenly flung open with startling violence. The group recoiled in horror as the horses plowed in. Fleeing the careening animals, people trampled over each other, trying to move as far to the rear as possible. But there was nowhere to go. Too many people crushed in too small a space. With rallying cries, the soldiers dragged them cowering from the pens and out into the open. Moving them forward and out. It became a stampede once the back gates were opened and more mounted soldiers began pushing people up from the rear. Children were mashed into the mud, adults struggling to pull their limp bodies out of the deadly path of the masses. They quickly hurried forward into the open and rallied into a single rough traveling column under the direction of the merciless soldiers. Small supplies of water were thrown to the group.

"Take these!" yelled one soldier, tossing satchels of water into the air. He appeared to be the leader. "You're gonna need 'em."

The other soldiers guffawed.

With ferocious shouts and bullwhip cracks to urge them on, the column quickly began moving forward. In no known direction. To no understood destination. They simply moved to avoid being whipped or trampled over by the horses. Other soldiers mounted up and fell in on both sides of the column. After passing through the heavily gated outer wall surrounding the riverbank camp, the column set out into an empty and rolling plain. Glancing back at the fortification's gates closing behind them, the column could see the holding pen filling up again, and abuses raining down on the next group being formed. Just like before. Just like it had happened with them. Only a few moments earlier. A conveyor of horrors. Shouts rose up from the soldiers manning the several thousand yards of wall traced up and downriver. Another shipment out of Apsatsus.

⌘ ⌘ ⌘

Setting a relentless, breakneck pace, the leader dragged the column forward from astride his horse. Always in the same direction. Day and night. Toward the rising sun. The landscape was bleak, with no water or significant vegetation in sight. Scrubs here and there, but little else. Where once trees had stood, now only burnt, mangled stumps erupted from the soil. Hard gravel, hot sand, and dusty earth were all they had to walk on. Rough rocks and dust, as the column dropped through unexpected crags in unexpected places. Waves of billowing heat, rising up from the ground, sucked at them. The soldiers gulped down much of the stored water taken from the riverside fortress. Bringing up the rear was a pack of dogs that had joined the column almost as soon as the group left the fortress, jogging along, unperturbed by the heat and the pace. Snapping and biting at the heels of the stragglers. Sometimes, fighting among themselves.

During the infrequent intervals when the column was actually permitted to rest, all were strictly forbidden from talking. A few people whispered to each other as the eyes of the watchful soldiers moved over them, up and down the line.

"Hey. You. Do you know where we are?"

"No, I don't," said a man in the crowd.

"I was on my way to work as usual and suddenly found myself swimming in that river, pushed along," volunteered another.

"Same thing happened to me!" said a third.

No one could explain what had really happened, but the accounts were nearly identical. They were just there. They had just arrived. From wherever they had been before. Leaving whatever they had been doing earlier.

The column started up again. Stragglers who could not keep up the savage pace were pounded with fierce orders and cruel blows. Some were ridden down in the dust swirling around the column. Several were cut down. A few were abandoned where they had collapsed from exhaustion, left to die in the empty and barren land. All alone. Except for the dogs that quickly picked up and tore at what had been left behind.

Those who attempted to escape were quickly recaptured and dealt with. Some were cut down as they ran. The open desert left them no place to hide. The soldiers chose one recaptured escapee who had managed to elude detection for several hours to make an example of for the rest of the column. Brutally beaten, bleeding, and moaning, he was tied to a set of heavy spears, arms stretched wide and feet strapped down low. The soldiers writhed around below him, throwing rocks at him and betting on who could hit what was left of the man's bleeding face. Shouts of protest from the crowd were met by angry jeers from the soldiers and the cruel crack of their whips. When the man was all but dead, he was taken down and thrown to the dogs. As his body was ripped to pieces and his screams rent the air, the soldiers could be heard laying bets on which dog would come away with the largest portions. Those among the crowd who cried at the sight were whipped. Those who stood firm were whipped too. No one attempted to escape again.

⌘　⌘　⌘

The next day, the column came out onto a landscape of rolling hills and sharply cut ravines, a place that seemed to have been a riverbed once, but was nothing but dust and debris now. Dust-covered faces streaked with tears, spit, and blood looked out on the rolling wastes. Exhaustion and heat had begun to overtake more travelers, as their meager water rations dwindled to nothing. Children fell first, but were quickly picked up and carried by the younger adults. Those who could no longer make their way fell into the arms of others, who dragged them along as far as they could. The pace was too rapid and when nothing more could be done for them by their fellow travelers, the exhausted simply fell out of line, easy prey for the soldiers who used them in their games of torture or set upon by the dogs following the column. A hot, constant wind licked the open stretches. Windstorms came, and the clouds, engorged with dust and debris, bit all the harder into the column's watering eyes and sand-flecked faces. Covering up, the soldiers set a harder pace, their brutality only increasing with the frustration of not getting to their destination faster.

As the fourth day dawned, one of the soldiers, a member of the squad that had scouted several miles ahead the previous evening, returned alone, breathless and bleeding. He choked down some water and reported to the leader.

"You cut each other down, didn't you? You worm!" the leader shouted, his sudden burst of fury surprising everyone.

It was the first time the column had witnessed dissension among their cruel masters.

"That's not what happened," the soldier explained. "They came for us. They were waiting." The battered solder looked around at the others. "They're coming for all of us!"

The leader slapped him hard in the face. The rest of the soldiers began murmuring angrily among themselves, ignoring the column for the first time since they had begun their slog. After several minutes of argument, the leader pulled back on his horse, reared up, and shouted orders.

"Double-time this mess!" he screamed.

Soldiers drew swords as the column moved out at its new, faster pace. Running a now disordered and ragged race, the soldiers shot constant, nervous looks at one another and broke into sporadic, heated arguments. Something was coming for them and the sense of fear grew within the entire column, soldiers and travelers alike. The column surged forward, even as some of the soldiers peeled off, fleeing on their own and leaving the people to their suffering for the first time since arriving at the river.

It finally came for them in the early evening hours on that fourth day.

⌘ ⌘ ⌘

They erupted from the nearby hills, plunging down the slopes, their sand-and-brush camouflage streaking off their shoulders under the momentum of their charge. Hooded horsemen. Shooting arrows off the backs of their horses and swinging curved swords. Their blades' edges glinted in the fading sunlight and their arrows rained down on the black-clad soldiers, paralyzed by the sudden attack. Fear erupted. The column broke up. The travelers ran in all directions, fear of the oncoming horsemen overcoming their fear of the soldiers' beatings. Who was going to beat them now? The eerie clang of arrows and spears echoed in the surrounding ravines. Horses and men screaming, the sounds reverberating from metal to bone, helmet to feet, as blood sprayed the hot, ashen ground around them.

But this new, fearsome group targeted only the black-clad soldiers, who fell hard to the dirt and sand. Some of the travelers picked up the fallen soldiers' discarded weapons and beat their wounded, black-clad bodies as they lay writhing. Others lunged forward to snatch whatever food or water the soldiers might have been carrying as provisions. Some of them broke from the column and huddled together in whatever cover they could find, watching the ambush. Horseman to soldier. Bloody, but brief. The leader fell, shouting orders, three arrows through his breastplate. His horse, now riderless, running wild, zigzagging nowhere out into the dust. Leaderless and unable to rally against the sudden onslaught, the soldiers who had not been felled fled. The horsemen finished off wounded soldiers who were still moving. The rest were systematically cut down where they stood. No quarter was given. None at all. There was no glint of celebration in the raider's eyes. At least, nothing like the cruel delight of the black-clad soldiers the travelers had witnessed in the previous days. Some of the hooded riders dismounted and began picking through the dead soldiers' equipment, even while the fighting continued. Others rallied the now disoriented groups of people who had run. A core troop quickly assembled the column again and after shooting two of the dogs that had remained snarling over the bloody remains on the field, pushed the column forward. Or rather, backward. This time, in nearly the opposite direction from which they had come. Toward the setting sun. The cruel black-clad soldiers were gone. Dead to the last and left to rot in the waning light of that fourth day.

⌘   ⌘   ⌘

The hooded horsemen carried food and water for all. Saviors. After the column had distanced itself from the site of the brief battle, it was allowed to rest, eat, and drink. The horsemen dismounted and dispensed first aid to those who were wounded and care to those who were ailing. They erected horse-drawn stretchers for those who were too grievously injured to walk, and provided solace to those who were unable to compose themselves, broken down by the whole ordeal. The unexpected humanity of these riders allowed some of the horror of the preceding days to subside. Many began to return to the reality so recently ripped from them by the river, the dust, and the cruelty, demanding an explanation for their situation. Where were they? Who were those brutal soldiers? Where had the horsemen come from and where were they all going? Unthreatened, the horsemen did little more than continue to distribute food, water, and care, providing no more information than the brutish guards they had just cut down.

As the clamor of demands began to reach a shrill pitch, one of the horsemen remounted his animal and spoke. "All of you! Calm. I cannot explain, if you do not permit me to speak."

The incensed shrieks dropped to a low grumble.

"We are of the City of Dis, Gehennites, riders of the plains of Tartarus. We are its horsemen, its protectors. If you want to continue to survive, you will do as we say," he said, pointing around to the other horsemen. "But do not misinterpret our kindness as weakness. Anyone who jeopardizes the safety of the whole group will be left out here in the wastelands. Tartarus is a cruel place, as your last several days' journey has already taught you only too well. Those of you who cooperate will be taken to our city, a place of safety. Be patient. Once we reach our destination, you will learn of your fate soon enough."

New questions now punctuated the air. What was Dis? Who or what were Gehennites? Where was Tartarus? Where were they being taken? And once they arrived, who exactly would they be safe from?

Refusing to divulge anything further, the speaker rallied the other horsemen and ordered them to move out. People scuttled together as they were herded into a column once again. But this time, cared for, fed, restored, and revitalized, the column quickly formed and the mass fell into a marching rhythm despite the questions and protests raised. Some stayed behind, ignoring the warnings, refusing to continue without being provided further explanations.

"You may not live to regret your decision," the leader warned. "I've implored you to follow us and see things through. But if you will not be convinced, take these weapons, some water, and these shelters."

As if on cue, the horsemen immediately dropped the stated items to those unmoved by the leader's pleas.

"If you change your mind or find yourselves at the edge of desperation, follow the setting sun. You will find us if you just follow the setting sun."

The leader shouted out his orders sternly. The rest of the column went quickly on its way, only some looking back over their shoulders as they moved ahead.

⌘　⌘　⌘

The column traveled easily by day and rested comfortably by night. Gradually, the air became cooler and drier. Almost cleaner.

The horsemen kept to themselves, providing food, water, and aid to the others whenever needed, but never providing any further indication of where they were going or what was in store. Later, they crossed a river, though it was not as vast as the one from which they had emerged just days ago. The horsemen had pontoons ready and after locating a particular crossing that only they seemed able to identify, they accompanied the column as it was floated across. Some in the column panicked at the idea of heading back into the water, but as soon as the first few made it across the river safely, the others were emboldened enough to attempt it themselves.

The land around them was expansive and brittle to the touch. Not a tree, a bird, a wisp of life did they pass. Just the dust kicked up by the column, their feet dragging, and the hooves of their escorts' mounts. At night, it was black as pitch, the opaque and silent darkness broken only by the fires and conversations of the column and the more muted exchanges between the horsemen.

Far off in the distance, a mountain range became visible. It grew closer as the days passed. Soon, a tiny interruption in the approaching mountain range came into view. A tower. In the mountains. From the horsemen's sudden change in behavior at the sight, their elation was palpable. Where they had been stern, but friendly earlier, they were now clearly excited by what could only be assumed as their impending homecoming. As for the travelers, they could only speculate over the significance of this sudden change of mood. They approached their destination, regardless, unable in their ignorance to decide what they should anticipate. And whatever that destination was, the horsemen followed what seemed to be their time-tested pathway home, alert to the now designated coordinates in an apparently featureless land. This tower in the mountain must surely lead them to Dis, whatever Dis was.

As they made camp that night, campfires sprang from what appeared to be another column several miles away. Many of the travelers became frantic once again, apprehensive that the nearby encampment marked the presence of another group of black-clad soldiers coming to reclaim this column as their own. Scouts could be seen setting out to reconnoiter the other camp.

Anticipating their concern, the leader reined in his mount and spoke. "I'm sure you will all have noticed the tower on the horizon we're approaching. You can take heart from the knowledge that this place is our final destination. That is the temple tower of Dis."

A murmur arose.

"I am sure each of you wishes that this march were over," he said, as he looked at each of the travelers nodding in agreement.

Regardless of the perennial enigma of their situation and their half-fearful anticipation of it, nearly any conclusion to the march seemed preferable to one held indefinitely at bay.

"And tomorrow, your wish will be granted. Tomorrow, we shall reach Dis."

A shout arose from the horsemen around them, but the column, unsure how to respond, looked around at their cheering saviors, only half-heartedly following with some muted cheers of their own, clueless as to what they were cheering for, but at least aware now that their ordeal in the wastelands was coming to an end.

"As for the campfires nearby, do not be afraid," the leader continued. "Our scouts travel back and forth only to exchange news. It is another column of travelers like yours. Like you, they are anxious to reach the end of their journey. But unlike you, they come from a place far more terrifying than your riverside rally point. Tomorrow at dawn, they will join us for the conclusion of this unpleasant passage upon which you have all unwillingly embarked. Soon, we will all be home."

With this, the leader turned his horse and rode off to meet with horsemen of the other camp.

The column was hushed and anxious that last evening. What had the leader meant by "home"? Wherever they were headed, it was not the "home" each of them had known. Whether they could ever get back to their lives again was still uncertain. This strange place had disoriented, horrified, and beaten them down. And now it teased them with uncertainty. Most lay sleepless, listening to sounds floating across from the other camp several miles away. Even across the distance, the shouts and cheers could be heard quite clearly. Their bonfires burned high into the evening sky, sparks dancing on the wind. The celebrations seemed completely out of place in a world filled with so much horror and fear of the unknown. On what strange journey had these others embarked that they camped with so great an inclination for revelry?

At dawn, both groups marched close in toward one another. Continuing the merriment that had echoed out across the wastelands the night before, the other column was visibly happy. They seemed to know one another well, and many were even on friendly terms with their horsemen escorts. Their jovial mood was startling. Some were on horses themselves. Some were well provisioned. Others walked in silence, as if weighed down by some heavy burden. The columns did not merge, but now moved in parallel lines toward the tower in the mountains. One column, quiet and apprehensive; the other, jocular and overcome with elation. Toward the mountains they moved. To the temple tower of Dis. As the distance closed in the late morning, speculations regarding the mountain range and the nature of the looming tower ended, for the City of Dis was truly, awesomely enormous.

CHAPTER THREE

Days of watching the mountain range, with its arrow-like tower moving closer and closer, now converged in a sense of wonder. This was, indeed, a mountain range, but the city *was* the mountains, if that were possible. The familiar features of buildings, temples, and towers gradually stood out within a huge encircling mass of walls and courtyards ringed out below them. The peaks and valleys of the approaching city skyline, gathered together to present the illusion of a mountain range, with the temple tower rising up from among them and piercing the sky. Awestruck by the sheer magnitude of the metropolis, both groups lapsed into a contemplative silence.

Although they began passing successively larger settlements filled with people going about their everyday work, each traveler's focus lay on the massive battlements of the mysterious city before them. As they approached, the sheer height of the surrounding walls drew the eye so that they were all anyone could look at.

Built from many gargantuan chunks of solid rock, placed together in wide, singular cuts, the walls stretched many hundreds of feet straight off the ground. The sheer size of the segments indicated that their mining and their placement into the fortifications had involved engineering feats. Every hundred feet across the top perched a metal-armored battlement, like a metal-capped canine tooth set in an already forbidding grip of teeth. Several of these sharply pointed teeth were further reinforced with fortified towers protruding even higher into the sky.

The thousands of buildings that made up the city behind the fanged walls stretched over hundreds of square miles. As far as the eye could see in every direction, as high as one could look. The top of each of those many heights swarmed with birds that flew in circles through the haze and morning light, searching for morsels on the ground far below them. Each edifice was unique in design and characterized by a spark of mad architectural genius. But none compared in size with the massive central tower that, with its own lookouts, rose as a giant sentinel atop the well-protected mounds before it. With a literal jungle of buildings and towers and skyscrapers spread over miles, it was hard to make out the mountains upon which this miraculous city must have been originally built. An apparent mountain range of buildings had been erected over the mountains themselves.

Many thousands of people inhabited the villages that were spread throughout the land surrounding the city and leading right up to the outermost walls. The closer the columns got to the walls, the larger and denser the encampments became. Towns, nearly cities themselves, speckled the sides of the great walls, hugging them like a baby does its mother. There was no end to their stretch. As far as the eye could see. As the travelers moved up toward the city walls, shops, apartment buildings, open markets, civic areas, and other establishments could be seen in full operation. Barter and trade. Craftsmen and grocers selling their wares. Donkeys braying while pulling their loaded carts of produce from the outlands and into the villages closest to the column. Herds of sheep tended by shepherds and their dogs. Children running through the makeshift alleyways of the endless stream of commerce at every turn, always shadowed by the mountainous city walls behind them.

So busy were these people that the columns escaped noticed at first. Since tens of thousands milled about, who would notice a few thousand more? But as the columns drew closer and the villagers looked up from their daily routines, they attracted the attention of an increasing number of onlookers. Their interest in the arriving columns was a combination of both curiosity and longing. Some sent up cheers to the astonishment of the travelers, tossing food and clean clothing into their midst and asking them to accept their offerings. Not knowing what else to do, the people in the columns shook hands with their benefactors and obliged. Water and wine were handed out, along with other foodstuffs, and before long, the columns were nearly engulfed by the thronging crowds. Their approach had become a party and as villages farther down the line became aware of their arrival, more and more flocked to see what, or rather, who was approaching the city's walls. The horsemen seemed uneasy, but did not intercede. With stern, yet friendly shouts, they managed to make moderate progress toward the walls.

On all the battlements stood vigilant guards, dressed in the same shade of gray as the wall itself. They blended in nearly completely, making it difficult to judge their numbers. Given their elevated position, it was also impossible for anyone standing down below to target them. As these guards surveyed the surrounding outlands, one would cast an occasional glance at the mass of travelers and the crowd of onlookers approaching the city walls. They surveyed the scene without emotion.

At a signal from one of the horsemen, two of the massive teeth suddenly creaked and jumped back from their position. To the travelers, there had been little indication that these two slabs, these two particular teeth, represented the city gate. Slowly, these slabs moved backward into the city. When they were nearly twenty feet back, they began shifting behind the wall slabs closest to them, thereby opening the way for the travelers' entry into the city. Far above the gate doors stretched a massive walkway from which more gray-clad guards, armed with crossbows, peered down at them. None of the wall guards showed the slightest hint of welcome. Their countenances were fierce and angry, as if they were sickened by the arrival of these strangers. Those from the villages outside the walls did not move any farther. They eyed the gray guards' pointed arrows warily, but continued to wave the columns into the walled city. There in the archway, boarded across the main walkway, was a bronze placard that read:

TAKE ONLY HOPE WITH YE INTO THE CITY, LOST FAR FROM THE EYES OF GOD.

A greeting or a warning?

As the gates closed behind them, the newly arrived realized that they were standing in a massive open intersection. Avenues and streets radiated out from this point, up through the city's mountains of buildings and out across the rear of the walls, as far as one could see. Everything was carefully planned and well organized. People walked and horse-drawn conveyances, packed with passengers, filled the many broad thoroughfares nearly to the point of breach. There were bakeries and clothing shops. Outfitting stores and whole markets full of nothing but fruits and vegetables. Shoe repairs and newspapers for sale. Looking up into the city, one could see more fortifications swell up from behind the massive outer walls. Rings of walls, in fact, sectioning off whole areas of the city. At the next closest wall, also gargantuan in size and strength, guards could be seen drilling along their own solemn posts. The city was clearly prepared for the newly arrived, though it had escaped no one's notice that among them were city guards searching for any villager who might have illegally attempted entry.

The avenue along which the travelers continued to make their progress was lined with what appeared to be soldiers who had cleared the way of all obstructions. Behind them and all along the avenue were thousands of people, so effusive in their welcome that the greeting the newly arrived had received in the villages beyond the walls seemed mild by comparison. Moving at a more measured pace so that the crowd could enjoy the apparent parade, the procession of weary travelers made its way up the avenue, before turning slightly to the left and moving up and farther into the city and closer to the second ring of walls. When they finally reached its gateway, the second wall's gates opened exactly as those of the first wall. The crowds from within the first wall passed off the travelers to the crowds waiting behind the second one. Again, the newly arrived stood in an open intersection with broad avenues leading off in many directions. This time, however, they moved off to the right, the avenue climbing at the same slight angle toward the central temple.

In the next few hours, the procession zigzagged its way across avenues stretching perpendicularly to walls enclosing vast living spaces. The city's populace, out to greet the travelers, grew thinner and thinner at each new level. Each successive wall became smaller in size and increasingly ancient in appearance. Pockmarked and burnt in some sections, it was evident that these inner walls had witnessed violent times. Patched and repaired now, they no longer provided the protection the city needed. Not like the outer walls.

Through six sets of walls they progressed, each hewn from a single rock and each gate designed in much the same way as the first massive gate had been. The seventh wall was very different, though, a colossal section of masonry held together by the combination of mortar and time. These walls and their gates had clearly been damaged at one point and then rebuilt, holes filled in and burnt-out passageways repaired. Though massive in its own right, the seventh wall's gate came down like a drawbridge unlike the many sliding doors of teeth, now stacked many miles behind and below them. Once inside the seventh wall, the wide avenues the newly arrived had come to expect disappeared. The living spaces of this part of the city were crisscrossed with much smaller streets, radiating out in spiderweb-like patterns. It looked more like an older, ancient city than one that had been properly planned and engineered. Few, if any, of the inhabitants here paid the new arrivals much attention. Those who did were prompted more by curiosity than anything else. From that point on, progress slowed considerably as the travelers now navigated much smaller and narrower streets. The city itself grew increasingly crowded with buildings, more densely packed than ever. Looking back down toward the main gates, the newly arrived could see the streets spanning outward down the city's layers. Far away, the giant gates of the first wall were closed shut. But as the newcomers moved up to the city's apex, a still more formidable walk lay ahead, spanning yet another latticework of buildings running around that central tower.

Once inside the eighth wall, the cityscape changed again. There was a maze of streets at this level, and it was impossible to tell where each of them led. The passage was so narrow and allowed so little light to penetrate, it was as if the travelers were making their way upward through intersecting tunnels. Most of the buildings flanking the clutter of streets in this part of the city were ancient beyond all reckoning. People stuck their heads out of windows and doorways to see what was happening outside, but didn't seem particularly interested in the proceedings. Here, no crowds gathered to see them.

Navigating the darkened maze for hours, the newly arrived finally reached the ninth wall. It stood before them like a giant inverted pyramid, its top high enough to be barely visible from below. Guards wearing red uniforms patrolled its heights, peering over the edge at the tired-out crowd collected below them. Crossbows and bolts at the ready, these guards exchanged a few terse words with the lead horseman. Several moments later, a wooden gate, badly scarred and partially burnt, opened and the horsemen directed the procession to cross into the next part of the city, slowly and in single file. These gates, barely held together by their many layers of repairs, were not prepared to accommodate so many people at once.

Crossing over, the travelers stood in a large amphitheatre, gazing at the expanse of green grass that stretched in every direction and seemed overpowering in its appeal after their days in the desert and the laborious climb up through the city, flanked by stone structures. The sweet fragrance of vegetation floated gently around them, but to the newly arrived, it packed the force of a punch in the face, when compared to the base smells of the deserts and the odor of civilization in the city below them. All around stood large stands of trees, miniature forests almost, intersecting intricate, but well-designed parks. Arrangements of gardens, bushes, flowerbeds, and fountains spotted the grounds flanking the walkways. The travelers felt they had been pulled from the flaming sands and dropped in the middle of the lush and verdant. The incongruity of the present, juxtaposed with the last several days they had endured, moved some to tears. Stretching before them was a long, tree-lined stone gravel path leading up to a colossal archway that towered several hundred yards ahead. The horsemen looked around with wonder, as if they themselves had never laid eyes on the place. The lead rider overcame his own rapture, dismounted, and prodded the other dismounting horsemen and the newly arrived on down the pathway. A group of five white-robed people stood before the archway, their stance protective, not menacing. Waiting for them.

Unexpectedly, the horsemen bid the group farewell and nodding to the five, remounted. They reined their horses around and urged them back down the path and through the gate. The ninth gate. The group watched them go. Almost forlorn. To see their silent saviors depart. They had come from nowhere and pulled the travelers from the depths of despair, provided them food and water. Led them out of the desert. And none of the travelers knew the name of a single horseman.

As the gates closed back up behind the departing riders, the group of five white-robed people approached. Three of them were women. Two were men.

"Come this way," they said in very mild, but encouraging tones. "There is nothing to fear here."

Bidding them to follow, they led the newly arrived through the domed archway. Within the archway was a great marble vestibule rising up a hundred feet. Paintings of the sky spread out across the ceiling, merging into a depiction of the mountains as the travelers moved closer to the far end. It was as if they still stood outside, looking up into the city on the mountain. Passing through to the other side of the dome, they looked up as one at the temple tower standing before them. The beacon of the city.

"You may take rest in the dormitories of this temple. If you are injured, you will be treated. Rest today and tonight in preparation for tomorrow's events," one of the two white-robbed men said.

"Clean yourselves and worry not for any reason," continued one of the white-clad women. "You have many questions and we have many answers. But you must be patient." She smiled at the newly arrived.

Few smiled back.

"All will be explained in time," she reassured them.

"Meanwhile," said the other white-clad man, "take rest and enjoy your time in this most sacred of places."

No one knew what he meant, but for most, obtaining answers to the queries crowding their minds was now secondary to recovering from the ravages of the last several days. Other white-clad people of the temple directed them inside to the lodgings that awaited them. Some of the weary travelers continued to peer upward at the tower before them. It had called to them across the open and empty lands and guided them to that very spot. Looking up at the tower's apex, none could make out the contours of its top in the fading afternoon light. There was only a radiant brightness that burned the scene into the minds of those who looked upward, as if mesmerized. No one had taken note of the temple tower as the travelers made their way through the city, the excitement and confusion around them sucking up all their attention. Although it stood so large before them now. And so exposed. Yet it was so quiet and hidden where it stood, as if it could decide when it wanted to be seen.

⌘ ⌘ ⌘

The Great Hall slowly filled with the warm and muffled murmurs of the weary, but recuperating travelers. The massive edifice that now sheltered them all was the city's central temple. It was one of the first permanent structures to be built in the city, a symbol of unity and community for a people possessed of little but cohesion. The central temple had marked a new life for the early founders, declaring their existence to the universe at large within its hallowed halls. In the temple's warm and outstretched arms, the newly arrived gathered together, to be educated, enlightened, and led. About the Great Hall hung a curious air of enchantment, unequaled by any that surrounded other edifices in the city and only faintly mimicked by the sprawl of buildings that had grown up around it. Quite unaware of the history and purpose behind the structure that now served as their temporary dormitory, few of the newly arrived knew what to make of it. But for the people of the City of Dis, this was the center of their lives.

The hall was cavernous, but magnificent in decor. For the once-ragged bunch, there was an abundance of finely embroidered divans to rest on and long oaken tables stood laden with every kind of food and blossom imaginable. Sprawling rugs in jewel colors sectioned off the vast expanse of beautiful white stone floor, creating an ambience of warmth and relaxation in a place that otherwise might have felt ecclesiastical. The huge room was bathed in a soft light that poured in through the many towering windows lining the walls, enveloping the travelers in an aura of comfort and calm.

All were now clad in white linen and had been fed well. They had awoken to a fine breakfast. The meal over, they had been brought to the Great Hall to prepare themselves for what lay ahead. Some of the newly arrived spoke with one another, but the majority kept to themselves, looking up into the eves of the massive room and carefully watching their hosts, who stood observing things quietly. Those who had celebrated their arrival from the outlands with song and dance several nights earlier, continued their revelry, oblivious to the other group from the river watching them from across the space of the hall with a mix of interest and curiosity. These other new arrivals from the outlands now received visitors from the city's existing inhabitants. Sometimes, these meetings would erupt into spontaneous shouts and tears or hugs and kisses, drawing smiles of amusement from the white-clad hosts. The reunions of joy found a natural place in the halls of the ancient and beautiful building.

⌘ ⌘ ⌘

Apprehension engulfed the entire room when a young man entered through one of the large doors set against the back of the hall. He was closely followed by an entourage of robed escorts who carefully scanned all of the new arrivals with piercing eyes. The young man crossed the room with a commanding stride and stepped up upon a low platform positioned under the largest window. All eyes were fixed upon him as the rest of his escort lined up behind him on the platform. His startling entrance had silenced everyone. After scanning the room himself for a moment, he requested everyone to take a seat wherever they were most comfortable. Then he spoke.

"I am Gazardiel. I am here to tell you what will soon happen to you all. There is no cause for alarm. You are safe here. As soon as I leave, you may sit down to this afternoon's lunch, spread out before you there," he said, indicating the tables of food lining the walls. "Later in the week, each of you will be processed and provided access to the grounds of this mighty and noble temple. As you undoubtedly already know, it is the central temple of the City of Dis. But before you are permitted to enter its most sacred areas and participate in our city's life, you must undergo an orientation."

Gazardiel paused, always curious to observe the reaction of the crowd which, following a tumultuous and horrendous journey, now found itself in a lecture hall full of monk-like professors brandishing the prospect of examinations. As the murmur of conversation died down, he continued.

"We shall start with the basics," he said with a thin smile. "Those of you who do not yet understand or haven't already guessed, you are dead."

A shout rose from those so recently pulled from the river. They turned to one another, some with expressions of horror, others with looks of solemn satisfaction. Gazardiel's escort took several steps up and surrounded him protectively on all three sides.

"There is little point in crying, little point in shouting," he continued in a raised voice. "You have come to the end of your lives as you knew them. Meet that end. Understand it. The sooner you come to accept the fact that one life has passed and another has begun, the sooner this new world will make sense to you."

It was a monster of a statement, shocking to the core, not just in its finality, but also in the awareness that there was nothing else to know. Those who had come from the outlands made no comment, but looked over at their compatriots from the river. These people understood. Their passing into the afterlife had been difficult too. But they now had the benefit of experience none from the river could know. Their own realizations were far behind them. Those from the outlands understood that the shock of death itself was often simply too much to bear. But they also knew there were things far worse out there than death.

"Of course, you must all be wondering where you are, if you are, in fact, dead," Gazardiel went on. "The answer is simple. For many of you, much of your lives was spent contemplating, philosophizing, and, perhaps, killing one another in order to gain a greater understanding of where you sit right now. Your senses do not deceive you and there is little point in forcing yourself into denial. You are in what many of you know of as the afterlife. And while this is a simple way to define where you sit now, you will soon come to discover that it isn't any easier living this life than it was the previous one."

A smug look crept over Gazardiel's face before he continued. "Odds are that more than half of you never accepted the idea of an afterlife. When men and women first started arriving in this hall, there was never any doubt in their minds as to where they stood. Times were simpler. Most importantly, gods and superstition abounded and these people fully expected to come to an afterlife, an underworld and what have you, when they passed. The transition was easy." He smirked again. "Or, well, an easier one.

But with the rise of more organized religions, the underworld was quite arbitrarily split between a place for the good and a place for the evil. Still, the transition was not difficult, as there still remained an afterlife to believe in.

"Today, Man's earlier blind acceptance of religion and superstition has been considerably eroded. Time has passed and Man's understanding of the universe has evolved. With DNA, nuclear fission, and super-string theory serving as Man's new gods, there is far less room for the old dogmas of the past. As a result, many of you will continue to doubt your present existence for years to come. Ironically, those of you who followed and believed in your fantastical religions and superstitions may find it easier to accept that you're now in what you came to know in life as 'Hell.'"

Gasps poured from the crowd. Many began to bawl. Others yelled, claiming they were in the wrong place, disputing the apparent judgment just passed upon them. Gazardiel's escorts moved in closer, hovering around him. How many times had he seen this situation? So often. So much effort expended on making them... Man...comfortable. He would change that. He *was* changing that. He listened for several seconds to their protestations and objections, his face an impenetrable mask, unmoved by the sudden burst of anger and emotion. When he had had enough, he raised his arms and with a terrifying roar, bade his audience to be silent. Regaining his composure, he dropped his arms to his side, clasped his hands behind his back, and began to slowly pace the platform.

"In the next several days, you will find that this place you called 'Hell' is the only place you will ever want to be in!" he shouted. Gesturing to those who had arrived from the outlands, he continued, "Those of you who have come from the City of God know this better than the rest. You risked the last existence you may ever have to come here. To you, my friends," Gazardiel said with a bow, "rest assured that whatever sacrifices you undertook to get here were not in vain."

A sad expression crossed his face and he bowed his head. "Each of you, take food and water and rest. All will be explained. And you will take great heart in the knowledge that will soon be imparted to you. Even though some of you have lived many Earth lives here in this existence, I am certain that you remain ignorant of the true history of the afterlife. The history of Heaven."

Gazardiel looked back at those who had fled the City of God. "You older ones who suffered so much to escape the City of God! You know my words to be the truth. Mix with these newly passed," he said, pointing to the sobbing group of travelers from the river. "They have only just come from the Styx and have had no more than a taste of the retribution that would be upon them, had they not been saved and brought here. Share your knowledge with them. Tell them of your struggles and your sacrifices, all endured to reach this single place, so often cursed in the world from which you came. Tell them what Heaven *really* is."

Scanning the whole room again, Gazardiel continued with a hint of a sneer. "Our leader will soon arrive to teach you the true history of the universe and the power that mankind really holds in this Heaven. Listen to what he has to say. Don't dismiss it, just because you have been taught he is a liar. Listen to what he has to say, because he is the only one who will ever tell you the truth."

Gazardiel scanned the crowd one last time, before stepping off the platform. Pathetic, he said to himself. These mongrels of God. And our master's supposed salvation.

Circling the young angel, his escorts parted the crowd as they walked back to the great door through which he had entered. As the doors closed behind them, a shout rose up again in the room. Slowly, following Gazardiel's instructions, the jubilant refugees, the ones who had come from the City of God across the outlands to Hell with gratitude and cheer, began to mingle with those just arrived from the Styx. The river. All equal now, in the eyes of Hell. The din slowly turned into a buzz.

⌘　⌘　⌘

It took the better part of a week to process all of the new arrivals. Each was invited to be interviewed before a committee of white-clad men and women, like those they had met on the first day, as they entered the ninth gate. During the interviews, these Caretakers, as they were known, explained their roles as guardians of the temple. They deposed each person, carefully collecting facts about their lives, family history, and significant defining moments in life. It was more psychology than interrogation. Everything was gently solicited and diligently transcribed and catalogued in the temple's records. While the interviews were conducted with thoroughness, questions were posed only at a pace each of the newly arrived was comfortable with. When they were on or around the temple grounds, the Caretakers answered general questions about the temple, providing assistance and emotional support to those still suffering from the ordeal of reaching Dis and notifying each of the newly arrived when it was his or her turn to be interviewed. With the Caretakers serving as intermediaries, help of any kind was always provided.

The newly arrived were well cared for during the weeklong processing session. Three times a day, they ate together in the Great Hall. Food of every variety was provided and the guests lacked for nothing. During each meal, the Caretakers would re-cite aloud to the assembly some of the life stories gleaned from the interviews, ensuring that the identities of the interviewees remained confidential. The newly arrived were required to clean their individual place settings and maintain the tableware they used during meals. Simple, but comfortable apartments were pro-vided on the temple's many floors. Individual apartments gener-ally housed between eight and sixteen people; each person was allotted his or her own bed. Each apartment had several bath-rooms and every one of these was fully stocked with common amenities anyone would expect to need. The newly arrived with families were given larger suites and often housed within a single apartment. Those children who had arrived on their own, unac-companied by a parent, were removed from the group. As they had yet to endure the many trials and tribulations experienced by those who were biologically senior to them, they were taken to other temple facilities, specifically designed to orient children and place them in citizens' homes. For them, the transition into this new society would be very different.

For the most part, the newly arrived were allowed to spend their time at leisure. When they were not being interviewed, the temple and its grounds were at their disposal. Three faces of the temple looked onto courtyards. Though the newly arrived had been assured they were not prisoners within the ninth circle of walls, these areas were secluded from the surrounding cityscape. The sounds of commerce and its many sweet and acrid smells floated up from the city and over onto the grounds. But no one, other than guards and Caretakers, was permitted to pass through the gates to the area beyond. Fields were available for games. Running tracks and benches ran the length of the walls under squadrons of tall old trees. In the center of one garden lay a central pond where the newly arrived could swim, go boating, or simply spend their days at leisure on its banks, observing how their new world functioned and wondering what reality lay down below in the city—beyond that ninth unscalable, ivy-covered wall.

The higher floors of the temple housed a formidable library containing many millions of books. Within seemingly endless sections lay books in every language from every age and about every topic imaginable. The temple library put even the greatest libraries of Man to shame. Dark hardwoods were everywhere, accented by marble busts of authors, philosophers, and writers. Windows, rivaling those of the Great Hall, shed light upon the huge reading areas and lounges, where anyone could take up their books and allow more cerebral pursuits to occupy their minds. Quiet, secluded corners were available for reading or simply reflection. Only those areas of the temple above the library were off-limits. The newly arrived were told that in the apartments above, in the highest eves of the temple, resided the Master. And they would meet him soon enough.

⌘ ⌘ ⌘

On the morning of the seventh day since their arrival in the city, the temple bells began to ring and all the newly arrived assembled once again in the Great Hall. One of the four main arms of the hall housed a theater of sorts, laid out with rows of well-worn benches. The Great Hall's burning candelabras were placed among the benches and on the theatre's stage. The faintest scent of incense floated down from the belfries. The late morning light suffused the room with a relaxing warmth.

The calm was shattered as the footfalls of the newly arrived echoed across the marble floors and their loud, pointed conversations reverberated throughout the hall. When all had been seated and the collective tumult of their voices and gestures quelled by curiosity about their new situation, another bell sounded high above in the eaves of the temple. The one they recognized as Gazardiel proceeded into the hall from a door behind the stage, this time without his protective escort. He took up his position behind a podium of immense size that was located at the center of the timeworn, darkly stained stage.

"I trust you all find yourselves comfortably rested and recovered after this past week," he said, looking around the room at some nodding heads. "You have become familiar with the temple and been nourished within its rich grounds. But your long days of leisure will now be given over to study. Today, you truly begin the first day of your new lives, for today, you take your first step toward learning the Truth, something that has invariably eluded each of you all through your lives." Gazardiel paused to let the significance of his words sink in.

"For the next phase of your days here, you will spend your time learning. This is not a process by which you will be taught what you should think or how to go about it. There are no tests and no one can fail. The lessons you learn here are for your benefit, your edification, your enlightenment. What we will teach you is the Truth, the Truth about yourselves, the Truth about the world as it is, and the Truth about what you are doing here within this hall. Your whole lives have been filled with speculation about life, its beginnings, and its ends. When you were children, you learned from teachers, whether at home, in the classroom, or out in the world. Your teachers taught you what they themselves had learned from their experiences and you shaped your lives on the foundations they had helped lay out for you. Today, your classroom has moved to the space within these walls," Gazardiel said gesturing around the room. "The lessons you will learn here, the knowledge that will be imparted to you, will not only introduce you to the society that awaits outside, but will give you a clearer picture of the universe than any of you have ever seen. I envy you for this, for today will begin *the* most important lesson of your existence. Today, the road that you embark upon will be, for the first time in all of your lives, the road of true knowledge. 'The Truth.'"

The crowd stirred. What could possibly be so important that each person would apparently awaken the next day with insight far exceeding the bounds of a single day's experience? The truth, he had said. In Hell. They were dead and the road before them unclear. What reason did they have for not expecting the next day to be filled with more horror than the road just traveled?

"I understand your hesitation. I do. But you have been kept in this temple and with good reason," Gazardiel continued. "The world outside the walls of Dis is not the world you knew. Gehenna, the land upon which Dis was built, and the rest of Heaven are very different from anything you might expect. It takes time to understand the magnitude of effort needed to craft the civilization into which you will soon be sent. Like the worlds from which you have all just come, this city was forged by millions and millions of individual efforts. But unlike the worlds from which you all have just arrived, the results of these individual efforts have been collected to focus on one single objective: freedom. Freedom to live in harmony. Freedom to live in peace.

"What is 'freedom,' you ask?" Gazardiel inquired, continuously scanning the faces of the crowd. "Such a nebulous concept. So subjective. What one sees as freedom another interprets as tyranny. Here, freedom is our ongoing design and has only been gained through the sacrifices of untold billions. Freedom is very personal to us. It is well defined in the context of our past. A past you don't yet share with us. Despite our successes, we, as a city, Gehennites, as our citizens are known, are forever striving to make our freedom more tangible and attainable. A reality. Something more objective. We, as a city, can never be satisfied with what we have, when we also have the ability to make it better. In this respect, our city is very unlike the worlds from which many of you have just arrived. Here, those who govern do so with the faith of the people they serve truly instilled in them. Make no mistake, though. We do not live in a utopia. Such fantasies are as impossible to realize as the attainment of perfection itself. There is no such thing as perfection. But the adoration of perfection and the will to make life for the common all a more perfect place is a virtue valued here above all else. Every Gehennite strives for it. It is within this equation that your importance lies, for every group of the newly arrived represents the next generation of freedom."

It hit Gazardiel hard to speak to these men and women about this subject. They were not worthy; nor would they, in all likelihood, ever be. But it was his duty to make their acquaintance, no matter how unappetizing the prospect appeared to him. Once his bill passed, this would be but an unhappy memory of what was once Dis. Gehennites would be pure. But for now, all eyes were focused on him and the murmurs that had filled his previous pauses were now absent.

"In order to understand where we come from and how we have gotten to where we are, it's necessary for you to first understand the history of the world of which you are now a part. Make no mistake. You and you alone can determine whether this place will be your home or merely another stop in your travels. For some, this new world may prove uninhabitable. It is highly structured and organized. For others, it is not structured enough. But for most, it is a fine and noble place. For most, it is the Heaven that Heaven once was. That Heaven should be. You will make your own decision and only you can make this a world in which people wish to continue to live."

Gazardiel paused again as the crowd soaked in the import of his words. They had a choice. They could stay or they could leave. How many would leave? Not enough of them. We find so few, but they cost us so much, he thought.

"Your lecture will be provided by the Master," he continued. "Gehennites know him as 'Master,' not because of the power and authority he wields in Dis, but rather, as a token of our appreciation for his many and noble deeds in making this city and its people. I call him 'Master,' as I was once his student. I learned from him in much the same way that you will. What I learned, I hope one day to use to help govern. What you learn will be the foundation for your new lives. Without the knowledge of the past, you can neither appreciate the present nor anticipate the future. What the Master will teach you in this time will be the most valuable information any of you have ever acquired, regardless of whether you were a farmer, a garbage man, or an astrophysicist in your former life. Take careful mental notes of what he tells you. Mark his words well."

Gazardiel was finished. He had done what he had to do. Another group to add to the city's rolls. They sickened him. Man had eaten up the city's resources since he first began arriving in Dis. Man didn't appreciate the sacrifices needed to make Dis a city that accommodated his special needs. Up to this point, only fear of the unknown had kept these people from revolting. He scanned their faces to pick out the potential troublemakers. He could tell from experience. While they were now subdued, comforted by the Caretakers' grace, people could go only so far, before demanding to know their rights. The two groups that had existed days ago were now gone. The refugees from the City of God had mixed with those coughed up by the river. This would calm some of them for now, but experience told Gazardiel this lull would be fleeting.

Those recently pulled from the river were completely unaware of their great fortune at being washed up upon those banks on that day and at that time. Intercepted by those horsemen. From the agents of Heaven. The blood of many patriots had cast in stone the rights they would soon inherit. They would benefit from that sacrifice without being asked to make any sacrifices of their own. People died each day to further secure those rights. The rights of every Gehennite. These people would not understand and, in the next few days, would be given all the rights they would ever have again.

CHAPTER FOUR

"What were you thinking?" the Master asked resentfully. "You could have done me the service of letting me know to my face instead of having me find out this way."

"It was not meant to be an insult. You are *a* leader of this city but you are not *the* leader," Maalik pointed out. "We understood long ago that the Senate made the laws and that the rights of all angels would be inviolate."

"And men!" the Master nearly gasped. "Do not forget Man Maalik. Man is the reason for all this," the Master objected, waving his arms around the empty Senate chamber. "His Man brought us here and we should continue to honor that fact. Man led us to freedom."

"Yes and no," Maalik said, rubbing his eyes and sitting down on nearest bench. "Either way, the Senate will hear Gazardiel's petitions. The time is right for us, the duly elected legislative body of this city, to consider whether Man will have to fend on his own going forward. Man has had enough time to season."

"Man is not ready, Maalik, you know that as well as anyone. And excluding Man from this place was *not* the bargain we made... when I was in a position to make such bargains," the Master said insistently. "I have counted on you to live up to your word. Do not give me reason now to doubt you, your character, and your resolve. We have known each other far too long."

"Don't get carried away. I have done nothing that would constitute a violation of my resolve or my word," Maalik retorted. "The city will remain as the city was founded: based on equality. But in order for the city to be what we all dreamed it would be, the issue of Man must be properly debated and reconsidered. Like any other issues of importance."

"Man has progressed these many years," the Master pleaded. "You have been witness. He sees things now that only a few thousand years ago would have spooked him into catatonic state." The Master sat down on the bench besides Maalik, visibly more at ease. "He is coming to understand. He is progressing. Do not abandon him to God now."

Maalik looked at the Master gravely. "Gazardiel's bill *will* go to the full Senate. As the Protector of the Senate Council I have a sworn duty to uphold the laws of this city and the procedures of this Senate. If, by the weight of your arguments, you cannot defeat the bill in the normal course, it will become law. Man will no longer be admitted to Dis."

The Master paused for a few moments, thinking. "I have told Gazardiel that I have exercised my right to investigate his party."

"What would have possessed you to do that?" Maalik asked in exasperation. "Investigations are only warranted where allegations of sedition have been leveled. That was part of the bargain too, I might remind you," Maalik rebuked.

The Master looked down to the speaker's podium on the floor of the Senate. "I had to say something," he said in a whisper. "I could not be perceived as being weak. Especially not to Gazardiel, he has vexed and hurt me so with this petition." The

Master looked up. "I could not be perceived as rolling over on this."

"No one thinks you are rolling over and no one thinks you are weak," Maalik replied in a soothing voice. "You're reading too much into this. The Senate believes Man has had his time. It is not an indictment of you. It is recognition that things must change."

"Maalik, I cannot tell you how this has affected me," the Master said, his face now twitching with emotion. "I feel I have been brushed aside in the very city I established, my voice no longer heard or respected. I know it is small of me to complain but I gave up power, when I had it, so that that power could be shared with all Dis' citizens, not just those with the providential benefit of luck or possessed of villainous skill and cunning. And certainly not just those who had the benefit of being born in Heaven," he said, looking around the Senate chamber, intimating all of Heaven.

"We could not relive the past," the Master continued. "*That* was the notion that drove me. Drove me to give up everything in order to give it to everyone else. Sacrifice for the greater good." The Master sighed. "But now I am faced with possibility that all that I have done to make this place what Heaven was meant to be was done in vain. I will not give up my right to fight for what I believe is right."

"You are revered here for your sacrifice. Every day," Maalik said with affection. "We all agreed. *You agreed* that your sacrifice was necessary to prevent another abomination." Maalik put his hand reassuringly on the Master's shoulder. "No one is denying your right to speak. You will have your time on the Senate floor to make your arguments, just like any petitioning Senator may. You will be heard and your points of view carefully assessed. If, by your words, you persuade us or if we vote to pass the bill, it is no matter. Either way, the system for which you sacrificed yourself would have worked the way it was meant to. A thumb in the eye to God and for the benefit of all Heaven's citizens."

"Not *all*. Not for much longer, at any rate."

"Well, I...," Maalik sputtered.

"Thank you old friend," the Master interrupted. He looked to Maalik wearily but with a smile. "No. Really. I know you work hard to keep me happy when I am nothing but an old grouch." Maalik cracked a smile himself.

"Man is what keeps me up at night," the Master continued. "Keeps me motivated to take on the next great thing. From my perspective, Man is the only thing that has prevented God from overpowering our walls and taking away our liberty. Without Man we would have fallen long ago. Without Man we would all be God's unwilling slaves...or worse."

"I know Man means a lot to you," Maalik said, shaking his head. "More than I could ever imagine. But things change. And to resist change is to be as God was. As God *is*."

The Master smiled. "You are right." He stood. "Perhaps, then, today will be my last oration. I will have to make it a good one."

Maalik smiled. "You tell the story so very well."

Then the Master suddenly frowned. "I exchanged words in anger with Gazardiel last night. I must rectify things before the bill comes to the floor," he said as he placed both hand firmly on the bench before him. "I may disagree with him but I will trust in the sanctity of this Senate and obey the will of the people," he resolved.

"You are, indeed, a master," Maalik replied. "Gazardiel will, no doubt, be in the Negates Hem gardens, preparing himself for the coming arguments and vote."

"In much the same way his old master used to prepare to speak with the Senate."

"Come," Maalik said, slapping the Master on the back, trying to lighten the mood. "Let's get something to eat and drink and reminisce about the good old days."

"Were there ever such a thing," the Master replied.

CHAPTER FIVE

The Master entered the Great Hall. The crowd of newly arrived sat silently watching his approach. There was nothing to suggest he was in any way different from any other person sitting among them. Nothing fascinating, nothing outstanding. Caretakers flanked him as he made his way through the crowd. He peeked over their robed shoulders at the assembled crowd with a strange smile of satisfaction. Gazardiel stepped forward to assist him as he approached the stage.

The Master appeared in the peak of good health. His posture was upright and disciplined, his head held high, his chest thrust out. Yet rigid as he may have appeared, on his face was a gentle look of concern for those he gazed upon. A look of care and humility, as though he had braced himself to receive the complaints of all those assembled there. He carried a large book, frayed and tattered around the edges. He clutched it as if it were a crutch, supporting him on his way to the podium. Around his white robe was tied a plain-woven belt, from which hung a leather pouch. He also wore a small silver dagger, ornate and glittering in the Great Hall's morning light.

Once upon the stage, the Master approached the podium where he rested his heavy tome. The slap of the book's bindings on the well-worn wood echoed through the vastness of the hall, startling people who now snapped to total attention. No one spoke or breathed, as he gingerly opened the book, placed a hand on each side of the podium and, with a sigh, began to scan the crowd over the top of his nose, as if he were a professor preparing to lecture a class. As his eyes moved over the silent crowd, the Caretakers left the room, carefully closing the doors behind them so as not to make a sound.

"This is what I have to say and what I have to say is this," the Master began. "You are here. Some of you against your will, others with all the will you possess. This, for all intents and purposes, is the afterlife, Heaven, Elysium, Nirvana, whatever you might have called it in life. It does not matter how you were raised, in what religion or country you grew up. It does not matter whether you are tall or short, fat or thin, smart or dumb. It does not matter whether you believe in Heaven or Hell. You are here. Some things are true, whether you believe them or not."

He looked down at his book for the first time. "It is my well-appointed job to teach you the true history of Heaven. Believe me when I tell you that it will not be easy for many of you to understand. I will teach you how things developed here, going by your earthly calendar, several billion years ago. Time, you will find, is different here. Chronology, as you are accustomed to knowing it, means very little. But if you must have some measure to go by, as Man usually does, consider one minute here as the equivalent of a year on Earth. Not that space-time is different in this place, but here, as you will soon find, you cannot die. That is, old age, sickness, and disease will have minimal effect on you. Only those of us who have been here since the beginning can age, that too, at a rate far slower than anything your minds can now comprehend. When I delve into our history, I will describe myself mostly in terms that you might all perceive as relevant to a thirty-something-year-old.

Today, I would appear to you as, perhaps, a forty-something-year-old. So, in the span of several billions of Earth years, I have aged enough to look approximately ten years older, by your estimate." The Master looked up. "I have not gotten any better-looking, if that is what you are wondering."

The crowd sniggered at his attempt at humor.

He smiled and cleared his throat. "But these things are of little consequence to us here. What is important is that death does occur here. That is, you can be killed at the hands of another and, before my story is done, you will hear about the deaths of many millions. So then, no great mysteries are solved. Where we go from here is as much of a mystery to us as it was for you during your life on Earth. Suffice it to say that this is your second life, your afterlife, and you will learn to live it with the utmost care, because it is the only one you will get." The Master took a sip of water. "No great mysteries solved," he repeated, almost to himself.

"There are other physical boundaries, of course, that you must learn to deal with. This place, this city, which we called Dis, built in the vale of Gehenna, but now more often known as Hell, is not boundless, no matter what the earthly theologians may say. They are wrong." The Master peered over the podium, as if over a pair of reading glasses. "If there are any of *those* among this group, you were wrong. Dis is simply a part of Heaven and the City of Dis has some definite boundaries. To orient you, areas surrounded by walls are protected by the city's guards. There are, of course, areas where no walls exist and where the deserts, outlands, plains—collectively named Tartarea or Tartarus—abound. At least on this side of what was once the Acheron, but I will get to that. All of you, in one way or another, have seen some of these places, but not all. There are cities and there are farms. There are suburban areas and there are vacant areas. This is Heaven. All around us is Heaven, of which Dis is only one small part.

"After we are done here today, when next you are in the library," the Master said, pointing upward into the temple, "you will find yourselves being allowed access to sections previously declared off-limits to you. These areas have information on Tartarea, Gehenna, Elysium, and the rest. I will leave it to you to take the time to explore the geography of your new world. There are many floors of information, thousands of square feet filled with the combined knowledge of Dis and its many angels."

The Master's use of the word "angels" was not lost on anyone.

"That said, your task today is to learn your history. The history of Heaven and Hell. To make the informed decisions that will establish the rest of your existence here, you should first learn the events that shaped the heavens, for they are not like anything you have ever heard before. If after your study session, you decide that you wish to stay with us here in Hell, you will be permitted to do so, subject to our laws. If, on the other hand, you wish to see what the rest of Heaven is about, you may request an escort back to the Apsatsus fortress on the River Styx, from where some of you have recently come. From there on, you will be on your own." He looked up from the book for a moment and into the crowd. "Not that I would recommend that particular course of action," he continued. "If you wish to do neither, you will be permitted to leave the walls and live out your new lives as you see fit. Be warned, though, that giving up Hell is not a decision to be taken lightly. Ask those in the many towns built around the city's walls. Once you leave there are precious few ways of earning the right to return. Most important for you to keep in mind is that your decision is yours, as Gazardiel has told you," he said, glancing over toward his young aide. "But no decision will be made until you have endured this time with me."

He cast his eyes back down, as if embarrassed about what he had to say next. "For I am Satan, God's Lucifer, once the simple Ahriman, and I will be your Master, if only for this short time."

⌘　⌘　⌘

"God's reign had existed across time," Satan began. "As far back as any could remember, He had dominated our world and our lives. But 'time' is perhaps an inaccurate word to use. The word 'time' connotes something very specific in your minds, no doubt. Take 'we are running out of time' or 'the times, they are a-changing.' Colloquial though they are, these both denote the movement of time and the change time brings with it. Time almost inevitably carries with it a sense of growth, invention, and evolution. In short, progress. Even if that progress ultimately reveals itself to be 'regress,' the movement of time means a forward movement from some arbitrarily fixed point, established as a reference to provide a tangible form of measurement."

Satan looked around him, curious as to how many he might have lost in the opening paragraph of his lecture. "But we did not understand time in this way," he continued. "There was no fixed point from which we could measure anything. And when I say 'we,' I mean those of us who grew up and lived in the City of God. When viewed in the context of modern notions and theories of time, time truly had no meaning. And God wanted it this way. What I mean is, no one could actually remember a Heaven where God was not present. No one could recall a Heaven where anything was ever any different. It just was. He, God, just was. No one had the ability to take any measure of the movements of the universe through space, to determine if we had evolved from something that once we were not. There was God and there had always been God. And with brutal efficiency, God made sure this was the only available state of mind." Satan flipped through the pages of the book open before him. "But we will get to that later.

"Like any other being, we came from some form of union between mother and father. We grew in experience as we grew older, and we died when our bodies could no longer sustain a life force. But having said that, I have to admit there were no birthdays to celebrate, no memorials to the living. Only memorials to the dead. What we knew, or rather, what we were permitted to know, was that life had always been the same and no one was able to change it from what it had always been. We had always lived with God, under God, and for God. Until my ascent to God's Order of the Seraphim and my subsequent fall, nothing had really changed."

The Great Hall was filled with silence, its occupants flush with a mix of rampant and irreconcilable thoughts, no doubt. Satan took a deep breath before continuing. "It makes no difference to me how you conceive of the abstractions of time. Billions of years in the heavens and no one in Hell or Heaven can explain all the nuances. Take my word for it. Leave time behind, my friends. In a manner of speaking, of course," he said with a smile. "It is not necessary for you to dwell on it now. You will either become enamored by it and pursue it to all ends or it will remain blissfully abstract for those of you not wanting to challenge yourselves in that way. For our purposes here, be satisfied in knowing that by teaching you the history of Heaven I am breaching God's Word, not just for the message of my story, but in that history itself is a study of time. And since understanding time is so dangerous from God's point of view," Satan said, pausing for a moment as he leafed a page over in his book, "well, you can see the criminality in my act.

"So," he said rubbing his hands together, "let us begin. Let us begin with something many of you already understand. Perhaps it is just a common ground, so let us call it 'religion.' It does not matter whether you were Christian, Muslim, Jewish, Buddhist, Hindu, Druid, or whatever in life. I think of these monstrosities as stunted faiths, in which I bear many names and many faces. In all instances, under whatever name, I seem saddled with evil. Not only the evil that has befallen Man, but all the evil in the universe.

"I do not blame you for your misconceptions," Satan continued. "I would blame you for the rather bad portraits, however. Red simply is not my best color."

The crowd laughed. Laughed aloud with Satan. Gazardiel did not share their mirth.

"There were no answers to the questions you had about the world. Throughout existence, Man has sought a logical explanation to an illogical set of circumstances and mystical forces were the most accessible and reasonable explanations for things that had no clear answer. The natural progression of this instinct led you to the simple ideas of 'good' and 'bad'. Legends and myths belonging to all of Mankind's cultures are rife with stories of interactions between good deities and bad ones. In the complex and abundantly polytheistic religions of Man, these issues were resolved with little difficulty. When bad things happened, bad gods were the cause. When bad people did things, it was because they were infected with the ill will of evil gods. As there were so many evils in the world, a different god was created for nearly all of Man's misfortunes. These hosts made war among men, brought pestilence, and heaped fear atop it all. Man, the spawn of the good gods, the gods of health and happiness, was constantly afflicted with the minions of evil.

"Those of you of the monotheistic stunted faiths struggle even more. Your all-powerful god, with total power over the universe and the lives of Man, begs questions of inconsistency. Surely if the god possesses such indescribable power, he must be perfect. No being can come to possess such power, if he is anything but perfect, right? But if this god is perfect, how can there be so much evil in the universe? Does the god render himself both wholly good and wholly evil even if evil defies perfection? That is, unless, of course, you believe in the existence of a perfect evil."

Satan laughed quietly to himself. The room was silent, but for the settling of so many souls.

"So if the god is wholly good and loves his people, something else must be the cause of the evil, which is operating under the license of the god. Something else who authors all the pain, horror, and anguish of life. This frustrating question, 'How could God allow so much evil?' pervades many of the stunted faiths. For generations, Christians, Muslims, and Jews theorized, argued, and killed each other over whether God perpetrated these great evils or whether He allowed another being to do so. These three — Judaism, Christianity, and Islam, the worst of the stunted faiths — transformed me into that author I mentioned a moment ago. The personification of these evils; the head evil god, as it were."

Satan paused to sip from his glass of water and meditate for a moment. "Even now, I do not think God necessarily meant things to happen this way, but I am quite sure He is happy with the outcome. His design, while well planned, was not flawless. But blaming me for the ills of the world made your love for your God that much easier. It was black and white, so that even the daftest of the daft could understand.

"But let us not stray too far," Satan said, glancing at Gazardiel. "Let us keep to my intended purpose." He looked back at the book before him.

"Before I begin with this history, you must first understand God's motivations and how we have to come to this point. Many a man has said that to know history is to understand the present. While as a general precept, I have found this disposition to be true, I am afraid it is necessary for us to start in reverse here today.

"None of you fully knows where you are. What is 'Hell' and why has it acquired the reputation for which it is so infamous? In part, and to my personal amusement, the early scholars of the stunted faiths were closest to the truth about Hell. We, who lived in Heaven since the beginning, were God's servants. We did His bidding and obeyed His commands. But when we came to disagree with God, we were thrown out of His city and banished from His presence. Hell thus meant being beyond God's sight. But where they say that God will ultimately prevail and Hell and my rule, in particular, will, some day, falter, well, there we move into the realm of fiction."

Satan paused for a moment and looked up from the podium. "Let me diverge once again, if you will indulge me. Why would I fight against God, if I knew, by some law of predetermined fate beyond my control, that I was bound to lose? I mean, really. Let us take Christians as a simple example. They have always been in a pickle, I would say. How could what they call the 'Passion of Christ' have been, in any way, effective in saving Man from damnation, when they are dependant on a Second Coming to wholly vanquish the evils of the world? Few people are quite that stupid," Satan said, shaking his head in disgust. "Short of an eighth-century Catholic Church bishop.

"But getting back to my point: yes, we are far from the eyes of God here. Both literally and figuratively. And when I say that, I mean something quite different from what your theologians meant in life. My descriptions of God, my retelling of conversations and events, will be difficult for some of you to accept at first. Difficult, because I will turn God, the spiritual and incomprehensible concept, into a flesh-and-blood being. Someone you can talk with and, though not in most instances, reason with. Someone with eyes, who cannot now see us. God has done His work well in making you believe He is something beyond human comprehension, beyond the meager abilities of Man's reckoning.

"I tell you now, many of you will not believe me, believe my story. You have been told I am a liar. Someone who will do anything to take your souls. This is true. I do, indeed, take you from God, not to deprive you of Him, but to deprive *Him* of you."

Satan shot another glance over at Gazardiel, busy whispering to some Caretaker and unaware of the Master's attention.

"You have been persuaded to believe I foment chaos and disorder," Satan continued. "This is also true. Out of chaos, something uniquely potent is derived: creativity. And God does not want you to be creative. He wants you to be subservient. He wants you to obey Him without question, even if it means your own bitter and sticky end. So you see, I tell the truth about myself. And if you cannot believe me, my side of the story, then do not. Go to the City of God and see for yourselves, for there is no better understanding of something than when you have learned it firsthand. Suffer the consequences."

The hall remained very silent. More of the new arrivals were paying attention now.

"In being created in God's image, you were imbued with many attributes. Yes," Satan paused, "that part of the mythology is true. Too true, but we will get to your powers of reason later. Take me at my word when I say that your power of argument is what I cherish most in you. If you have lived long enough, you will understand that in any argument, each party is more interested in establishing how valid their argument is than in weighing the proof that exists in the argument itself. And it is there where I hope to make an impression on you. Where I hope to relay the real image of Heaven and Hell. And you should be skeptical, for in each retelling of the past, the inconvenient or embarrassing elements are discarded or passed over in silence, while the glorious elements are oft repeated, until we believe in worlds that never actually existed. I need to be persuasive enough to make a good enough argument, to show you all the elements. To make you consider the possibility that God is not who you think He is and that Satan is not what God says he is.

"Do not worry too much now about your ability to discern what is right. Even those with the greatest minds are capable of the gravest wrongs. But if you listen attentively, consider my words with an open mind, you will see that your decision about the path you choose in this afterlife requires the greatest of great care. Consider my argument. Take your time. That is all I ask. For it is better to choose the right path, making slow progress, but getting farther along, than making speedy headway down the wrong path.

"Here, our path is clear." Satan's eyes strayed to Gazardiel again. "Here in Hell, we rule ourselves as we see fit and for these past many thousands of years, we have done so democratically. In life, when good things happened, you thanked God, or Allah, or Krishna, or Buddha, or whoever, sure they were rewarding you and keeping a close watch over you. When bad things happened, you cursed your plight and feared you were being punished for some transgression only the gods themselves had the divine authority to understand. Some of you attributed the ill-fated aspects of your lives to me, lurking over you and bringing evil upon your head so as to tempt you into relinquishing your god or his word.

"Any way you look at it, you spent a lifetime humanizing—or demonizing—your life's experiences. You interpreted the nature of these events and transformed those experiences into the will of another higher power, beyond your control. You did this, because it gave meaning to things that defied your understanding. It is easier to attribute a cause to an event than to continue in life, not knowing how or why something happened to you. Call it luck, call it fate, call it destiny, call it religion. Call it what you want. In the end, it all turns out to be the same thing. In the end, everyone winds up here.

"Here, you will soon learn, is where your deepest fears were true all along. Here you will discover that there was no grand celestial reason for the comings and goings of your life. God was no clock smith, turning the wheels of the works of the universe in some grand design. God was not looking over your shoulder, or trying to teach you lessons, or waiting for you to evolve into a greater being so as to reach understanding. Understanding is anathema to God. God made a program and He called it 'the Universe'. Into that program, He added Earth, space, water, animal, and Man. Man was, in fact, designed to be something that He, God, was not. That is, Man was invested with the power of two lives, one earthly and one heavenly. Really, when you look at it in that way, God is inferior to Man, as God has nature to thank for His immunity from fear. Man must use his brains and develop his mind and body. Succeed on his own in order to overcome fear. This power given to Man was designed to give God something He lacked here in Heaven. Unquestioned belief. God was able to simultaneously create the classroom and the student, if you will, when He created Earth and Man. A student who would learn what God wanted him to learn: to serve God. In the end, the program grew beyond His control. But even so, this loss of control proved incidental to God's purpose for the universe and His designs for Man. In His program, He made very sure that you would come to believe in Him so that He could make use of your talents."

Satan shifted position before taking another sip of water. The birds chirped outside and dust motes danced in the descending beams of the morning light flooding the Great Hall.

"Germinating from the seeds God had planted, the classroom developed stunted faiths. You created them. From scratch. There was no divine order. You needed them to justify the brutality you heaped on your fellow man. Faith gave Man a means of masking his Creator's flaws in the guise of divine will. Ingeniously, by giving you the means to justify holding down your fellow man, God was preparing you to be His servant here in Heaven. The classroom He created for you was not meant to be a training ground for learning how to exercise free will. It was meant as a battleground so that you would come to believe in God's goodness and in my malevolence. The stunted faiths, in their prescribed selfish and egotistical vanity, were God's way of teaching you to conquer and destroy your own free-willed souls. To turn in on yourselves, while always being His loyal servant. In time, the stunted faiths became the strongest and most powerful ally God had in developing you.

Those faiths have brought you so far from true purity that many of you will now be unable or unwilling to understand anything else.

"But now your earthly lives are over. You have been returned to the purity from which you were created. Only some of you will see that the faith you placed in God, the learning you accumulated while in His classroom, were purposely designed to bring on your own destruction for the benefit of your creator."

No one in the room spoke. No one moved. The birds kept chirping. The dust motes continued to swirl in the beams of daylight. Satan continued to gaze at his new pupils.

"What I have to impart to you is bleak but that is not surprising. I am Satan. The Devil. 'God teaches that Satan always tells me what I want to hear in an effort to deny me my soul,' you will say. But I have faith. Faith that in time, my story, my argument, will become compelling and you will begin to listen to what I have to say. Until this point, the truth has been withheld from you in an effort to deceive you and point you in one particular direction. But when you have grown to accept me, you will begin to look at my story and analyze it for what it is worth. You will begin to see me as you would see your fellow man or woman. That is, you will see that I am flawed, that I struggle, as you do, in challenging myself to identify and correct my flaws in order to make myself better. No one is perfect, not even angels. But my self-flagellations will confuse you, as I am Satan, the great deceiver, and you will be presented with a dilemma that requires the greatest of efforts to resolve. You will hear the truth, but not want to believe it.

"Those who were, in life, unwilling to subject themselves to sponsored religion will be more readily able to embrace my truths. There will be no overwhelming, raging storm of conscience. Tormented and persecuted throughout the years as faithless and, therefore, evil, you will find the truth to be the greatest redress. Coming to finally understand that Man was wrong about God all along, and that Satan will bring you the 'God'—salvation—you sought in life. Finally, you will be able to access the wondrous brilliance of pure truth and knowledge. For you, the struggle will be over.

"But for those of you of the stunted faiths, the truth will flow unnaturally against the bedrock of your beliefs and the teachings you hold dear. You will be unable to accept the truth on its face. You will become your own philosopher, theoretician, and logician, explaining away what I tell you and denying your own access to the truth so as to hold on to the comfortable beliefs you have lived with for so long. I understand. These beliefs are easy, reassuring, because they espouse the idea that God, your creator, loves you and holds you dear. You need that love to sustain the little sense of security you have. I mean, who else loves you, when no one else does? God, right? Who does not like to be loved? Not I. Not you. How sad it would be for you to realize that the love you believed God had for you is not the love of kindness, but rather a reflection of His self-love and desire for self-preservation.

"Prepare yourselves!" Satan shouted out. "Steel your hearts! You will fight tooth and nail against all that I say, because you believe you are essential to the fabric of the universe. It is not true. Your first real revelation about Heaven will be difficult for you to accept. Your religious philosophers identified the quandary quite accurately, but settled on the wrong answer. Why would God kill, maim, and strike fear into His beloved children?" Satan looked carefully around the hall again. "*Because He enjoys your suffering.* Evil is not part of some great universal design you cannot fathom; there is no greater wisdom that God possesses that you cannot. There is a simple answer to these questions: these things happen because He programmed it that way. *Because God wanted it that way.* It was not I who held you to the fire and delivered the misery that befell you. It was God's imperfect program that damned you.

"Your parents, your schoolbooks, your synagogues, churches, temples, shrines, and mosques have spent your lifetime trying to tell you God is all-powerful and good. This was a lie. Not theirs, but God's. God loves you, but not for the reasons you think He does. What those mothers, fathers, teachers, priests, monks, mullahs, and preachers could never have possibly known was that, with my help, He designed you, built you, and bred you to be His slaves in Heaven. With each step of your lives, through His deceptions and distortions, He has made you more fully His.

So much so, that when you arrive in Heaven, you are already programmed to be part of His monstrosity, all in the name of your God. You want to know what evil is? *God* is evil."

A vibration coursed through the room like a wave racing down the shore. Struck by the audacity of his comments, many in the crowd yelled out in anger.

"Where is the proof?" one man cried out. "Why should we believe *you* to be honest and sincere? Why not God?"

"This is shameless self-promotion!" shouted a woman from the crowd. Others looked on silently.

Satan allowed the chorus of shouts to ring through the hall for a while. The guards were there. They would take steps, if necessary, to bring the crowd to order. He glanced at Gazardiel who shook his head in distress.

Gazardiel will have to be taken care of, Satan thought, now ignoring the rising din. He no longer understands. He does not grasp the importance of what I do here. These shouts of pain, of anguish, of anger, are necessary. Cathartic. Everyone has to start somewhere. Change is difficult. Change that challenges you to the core, that is so revolting that its truth requires the re-evaluation of everything most dear. That is near impossible. And that is why I am here and Gazardiel should no longer be.

Satan sighed and turned his thoughts back to the crowd. Their cries grew louder, but he would not stand for the assembly dissolving into pandemonium.

"*Curse me you can!*" Satan shouted, his voice a roar over the din. "But your curses only serve to make my point more emphatically! You can decide not to believe me without first being told the truth! Your lack of vision will help God all the more!"

The buzz of protests subsided for a moment.

"Look around you!" Satan exhorted the assembly. "You are in the Great Hall of a temple of proportions none of you has ever seen. You know you are here. You know this is not a dream. You braved the outlands and were rescued from brutal keepers. In your new environs, you have been served the finest food and drink. You have lounged for days in the gardens of this sacred place and have partaken of the knowledge that breeds within it. You have come up the city streets, safeguarded over the years of invasion, defense, and fighting by the strong walls that now protect you from yourselves, though you do not know it yet. You have been rehabilitated so that you could come to this hall and listen to me. For this single purpose!

"What do these signs tell you? That you are in Heaven? No. I have told you that you are in Hell, the belly of Hell in these hallowed grounds. If so, where are the lakes of fire? Where are your demon torturers? Were you not you taught that this place was monstrous, run by me, the greatest monster of all? These things rip at your insides, gnaw at you, because you already know that I might be telling you the truth! The Hell you were taught about exists. Believe me, my friends, it exists! But am I, as you have also been taught to believe, eternally damning your soul? That is a lie that can no longer be sustained. A falsehood to deceive you into believing the greatest lie ever perpetrated! The Hell that you are looking for exists. Mark my words. But once you have heard my tale, you will find that it has a different name. In the end, you will know it as the City of God!"

And so Satan began.

2

CHAPTER SIX

My story will, necessarily, have to be related in broad-brush strokes. It would be foolish to think that I, Satan, could give you all the details of Heaven. There are far too many facets to the story and in the end, stories within the main account that need not be told. You will learn the truth and you will divine your own opinion about Him and, consequently, me. Of course, by "Him," I mean God. You will hear me speak of Him with the greatest of admiration, then with mixed feelings, and finally with bitter resentment. Such is the way of ill-parted friends and comrades. As God's Lucifer, His fallen Seraph, this should not be surprising.

Although you are here now, it will still be difficult for you to understand "God" in the way He actually exists. Do not misunderstand me. God is great. But do not think He is beyond your comprehension. Man has a hard time dealing with God as a walking, talking being. He *is* and, in a strange way, this fact alone makes Him difficult to understand.

Unfortunately for you, mortal death does not automatically bring with it spontaneous and radical enlightenment. No understanding of the universe or ultimate knowledge is imparted to you simply for sloughing off the mortal coil. While God wanted your experience on Earth to provide you with the basic foundations for understanding, He was careful to ensure that ultimate knowledge would be impossible for you to attain there. Whatever you come to understand from my story will require effort on your part. You must listen.

But enough of that. My story is about the creation and goings-on of the beings that existed here in Heaven before the advent of Man. There was no Man in that time and space. There were only God's angels and I was one of them. Angels, thankfully, do not trace their origins to Him. He did not create them, as you have been taught to believe. The race of angels was born before God made Himself master of Heaven. God was no greater nor was He intrinsically more powerful. He was one of us. But He withheld this truth from us. He convinced us that He had ruled us for eternity. I will explain how I subsequently discovered this to be an absolute lie.

While God did not create Heaven, He certainly did create our reality. Our city or, rather, His City and our lives were structured on His grand design. His power dominated everything that lived and breathed in His City. We had food, because He provided it. We had water, because He made it so. Commerce, protection, livelihood—we had them all, because He was a merciful and loving God. Or so He told us. Into His City, He poured all of His love. Maybe, to be more accurate, His will. The universe's most beautiful and modern civilization. We, His subjects, His angels, simply called it the City of God. It needed no further description, because it was a perfect and absolute name.

Though we did not know it then, the truth of our origins was withheld from us angels. We were there—and that was all we needed to know. Or, put in another way, we knew only as much as He wanted us to know. Everything we learned in school or at home was controlled by God through His many ministries, enforced by His Secret Police, and framed in the most positive light so as to guarantee our obedience to His rule. All children were required to study God's List, a long recitation of His exploits and an expression of His love for His City. It contained all the necessary precedents and constituted a law of sorts. It was meant to lend legitimacy to His rule, a kind of reason for being that rationalized and justified everything He did in all the right ways.

Years later, when I thought about the real purpose of God's List, it became increasingly clear to me: there would be no danger of anyone starting a revolution, if the List established beyond doubt that everything in the City of God was always, unchangeably good and that God Himself was the source of all that good. There is an undeniable sense of comfort in knowing God was there for us for all eternity. The reassurance the masses drew from such a premise served as a useful tool for God to perpetuate His rule. A master propagandist, He had no difficulty in convincing most angels who blindly believed what He told them. What He told us. What we read. What we thought. We had no reason to doubt His absolute love for us, no reason to question His intentions.

With those stupid enough not to accept God's Word, He dealt differently, using His agents or His armies to lend weight to the importance of His proclamations. While the word "revolution" did not exist in our vocabulary at the time, a very small minority of high-ranking angels understood its essence. So despite the absolute authority God's rule bestowed on Him, our highly structured world was fraught with violence. Violence against those who refused to reciprocate God's love, thereby working to undermine the fabric of His perfect society. We did not see God's ways as brutal, though. It may be difficult for some of you to understand our perspective at the time. Those who did not follow the Word of God were simply enemies. We believers feared and hated them. They disturbed our peace and aimed to divide us as a city. Those radicals who dared to openly defy His rule, who chose not to live the life of an angel, a citizen, faithful to God and His teachings, were hunted down and exterminated. And we cheered. We stood up for God, our oppressor. We loved Him. We were good citizens. Only later would I come to learn the difference between being a good citizen and a good angel.

We had enemies from outside the City's walls as well. We called them "trimmers." It was as derogatory a word as one could use to describe another being. We were told there were many of them in Tartarus, the lands that lay east of the Acheron, the Great Dividing River, and outside the immediate control of the City of God. We knew little of these trimmers. Only that they were intent on destroying everything we, as good citizens, lived for. They were reviled and regarded as malcontents, the source of all disruption. Our citizens were kept abreast of the trimmers' movements through Tartarus, though only those of us who had served in the army ever actually saw any. The City walls served as much for our protection from these villains as to display the severed heads of those who dared raise their voices against God.

The City's government was complex and outwardly representative. God ruled all. There was no doubt about that. His laws were to be obeyed without question. When you got to the crux of the matter, that, in fact, was His only real rule. But citizens were allowed their say on issues through the Senate, members of which were elected by the citizenry on a regular basis. The Senate's role was to advise God on the will of the people and to regulate the City's economy. Senators wielded no direct power over the people, but were very influential in matters of business and trade, for the City had many satellite colonies around the outer edges of Elysium, the lands immediately surrounding it to the west of the Acheron. Indeed, many subjects were colonists, dependant upon the City both for protection and for the purchase of their crops and wares.

The average angel on the street saw the Senate as his or her direct link to God and the means by which to address the rigors of life as a citizen. No senator, however, ever rose to directly challenge God's directives. In the very few instances where a divergent point of view was publicly addressed, a quick retraction inevitably followed. The troublemaker was most often relieved of his post on some trumped-up charge of corruption. Corruption was, indeed, pervasive within the Senate and most senators were merely business owners who used their positions to further their business objectives. When corruption was not a justifiable pretext for divesting "errant" senators of their official duties, they were assassinated, though such acts were publicly declared as abhorrent and contrary to the rule of law. In such instances, a scapegoat was always found to lay the blame on. Justice, or the semblance of it, had to prevail. Often, a senator whom God wanted removed for political reasons was incriminated in some dubious affair or the other. For situations that did not permit this, a dupe was easily picked from among the citizens. In this way, God was able to make allies out of enemies and enemies out of allies who, in His eyes, had lost their political usefulness. Either way, dissent simply was not tolerated. God ruled with an iron fist, encased in a public velvet glove.

His many ministries managed day-to-day matters. The bureaucracy had grown a thousand fold since its beginnings and there was a ministry, a department, a bureau, a division, or an agency to deal with every little aspect of our lives. Jobs in these positions kept hundreds of thousands, even millions of angels busy. They were working, always working. Of course, some enjoyed wallowing in whatever this simple, but highly structured world had to offer. They loved its pomp and circumstance. They trumpeted here or there and bowed and scraped as they carried out the silly and seemingly endless commands. In fact, I was one of those very angels. Just another member of a bureaucracy that grew perpetually in size for no discernible reason other than to keep angels like me occupied. Like fellow angels similarly engaged, I obeyed each commandment without question and without concern for the ultimate consequences. God's kingdom was infinite, as far as we could tell, and there was no place to escape His ever-seeing eyes. They pierced the air and were capable of finding you, even if you were, like me, a zealot buried deep in an obscure, but rapidly growing government department. Working, always working.

I was not proud of myself when, after a frustrating time in the army, seeing combat with our Lord's enemies on many an occasion, I was inducted into the Servitude of God, that is, the royal bureaucracy. A desk and regular paperwork were a whole lot safer than being out in the bloody battlefields of Tartarus. But I had been a good soldier, very handy with a sword and a spear and always interested in whatever could propel me further up in the ranks. I will explain more of that later. In a short time, with the tedium of the work weighing me down, I grew dissatisfied and more than a little scornful of its worth. In the army, I could charge into an enemy formation and take many heads. I could lead angels and felt I was good at it. In government, on the other hand, nothing worked. It took forever to get anywhere and there was always someone to set up a roadblock to impede your progress. I struggled to keep my focus on the goals that might have inspired me when I first left the battlefield and joined the bureaucracy. But they were drowned in a pile of paperwork and I felt powerless to effect any changes at all. Never, though, did I question my loyalty to God.

I was working, always working, with a blind devotion to a leader who neither gave of Himself nor allowed His subjects to give, unless it suited His personal objectives. Yet I never openly protested or rebelled against this hopeless existence. I could not. At least, not if I wanted to continue my career and make my mark on the regime. Those who showed their discontentment were labeled unbelievers and quietly culled. I could not afford to be an unbeliever. I had to work within the system and show God that I was worthy of His praise. Questions were not tolerated, because questioning any state-sanctioned authority meant directly questioning Him. Only blind obedience would do. The idea of expressing my discontentment never really occurred to me. Standing here, so many years later, it seems so strange to me now.

Let me explain my mindset with a story. It pains me to bring up the subject, but I deem it necessary. I warn you that I am conflicted, for it is something I both admire as knowledge and hate with pure venom. Let me fortify your mental images with one of mine.

I was a boy at the time. I was walking back from my classes one day, a day filled, like any other, with martial training and learning about the glorification of our City and our Lord God. I crossed one of the many public squares in the City of God that lay several blocks from my home. Because of my grandfather, whom I will discuss at length, as we proceed, we lived a good life. Part of the nobility, but not powerful in any direct way. My father, Angra, was powerful in certain business circles, shall we say. It suffices to say, we did not want for anything. I had walked through this square a hundred times before. I had played there with my friends. I had picnicked there with my grandfather. I had sat there on many occasions, enjoying the gifts God had given us. But on this day, the place was different. An angel was striding back and forth across a small, makeshift platform, erected at that spot to give him a vantage position from which he could speak his mind to his fellow angels. I do not remember all the specifics of his speech, but it certainly left an impression. He spoke of a better world, one where liberty and preservation were the cornerstones of our inheritance. He claimed to be the prophet of an old calling, where one angel believed in another, not because the latter had been given his gifts by our leader, but because angels possessed inherent gifts that were far more significant. All angels were created with these gifts and no one, not even God, could give them or take them away.

The lifetime this angel had taken to grow and live and learn was rendered void in seconds, once God's soldiers arrived at the spot. The crowd shrieked as soldiers tore the speaker from the perch that, only moments before, had put him eye to eye with our Lord God. As the soldiers began to shoot showers of arrows into the dumbfounded crowd and angels began to fall, I stood there watching from the side. Panic broke out when the fleeing crowd suddenly realized that other soldiers, wielding swords and spears, had cordoned off the square. Mothers, fathers, sisters, brothers — no one was spared. Angels fled, trampling on the angels next to them as they fell. As more and more angels fell and the seconds ticked by in chaos, it was not my feet that scampered away, bearing me off to safety. It was my thoughts that ran, round and round in circles, as I recalled the number of times I had seen the heads of insurgents perched upon the walls of the City. How many times had I heard that the individual angel did not matter, when compared to the state and our beloved Lord God! Blood ran through the streets that evening. In the center of that blood I stood, watching, as angels were cut down, mothers cried, and children fled with terror in their eyes. I stood there and watched the whole thing, focused on a single thought: where did all this beauty come from? I wanted to be that soldier, wielding that power, the power of our master. The power of God. Building the state into a more perfect creature, where nothing could undermine the people's dedication to Him, where mercy was not worth the effort.

I walked home that night, blood-spattered and loving God more than I had ever loved anything in my entire life. In preparation for my service, I challenged myself to become a master of the sword and the spear. Challenged myself to be unbeatable. When I was not at school, training, I trained myself, spending hours doing nothing but making imaginary kills. I went nowhere without a weapon. Training myself. Always training myself for the time when I would use those weapons in the service of our Lord.

I would walk through that same square a thousand times more before my own fall from grace, never once forgetting what I had learned about myself that day. What troubled times were those when the youth of society could witness such barbarism and such hatred for our fellow angel and wish only to be a greater part of it. I only wish I could speak to that boy now and tell him what true power really looks like.

I hear that several members of your party that formed at Apsatsus the other day were cut down or left to die by the City of God's soldiers. Can you visualize those outlands where they fell? What were the names of those who fell out there in the scorching heat? Did you even have time to know them? What did they do to warrant such brutal deaths? Why were they made a portion for the ravenous dogs? Why did you survive? A man was crucified, was he not? Do you see his face still? The terror in his eyes and the stench of pain emanating from him? Wear that pain now. You have already seen God's mind in all its nakedness. Remember it and remember it well in the days to come. Each of us can feel and act and be this way, if we allow ourselves to, if we forget who we are. That the angel or man or woman standing next to you is just like you. You are not slaves, though you were created for that very purpose. You are "Man" and in you, both evil and good reside. Which path you decide to take is up to you.

⌘　⌘　⌘

I am where I am today because of my family. I do not mean this in a derogatory way. What I mean is that my family raised me, saw to it that I was properly educated and cared for. That I had options unavailable to most angels. I was born into a privileged class of citizens. As a simple noble family's only son, my name was Ahriman. I will explain later how I came to be known as Lucifer and, later, Satan.

My grandfather, Zoan, had been the Marshal of God's army and every schoolchild in the City and its surrounds was taught of his successful campaigns against the trimmers who were constantly harassing the City. Through nearly incessant warfare, Zoan was not only able to defend the City from the marauders' attempts to overthrow God's great kingdom and destroy what we all held most dear, but beat them back into the outlands and quell the turbulence they had instigated within the walls. Although the trimmers had been banished to the outlands, we could not shake off our memories of the powers of evil that wished us ill. While the average citizen never witnessed any of the wars that had to be perpetually waged to protect us from this external threat, news of our great victories over the disorderly armies of trimmers constantly flowed to the City dwellers. It was through my grandfather's initial successes as a general in the field that the City was able to fortify its first great wall and bring the outlying lands surrounding the old city under God's control. As the grandson of the City's most famous general, I had a lot to live up to.

Upon leaving the army, grandfather helped set up the Ministry of Information, God's first real intelligence machine. The ministry had direct control over the City's media outlets, helping to consolidate and monitor the official news disseminated among the citizens. A personal friend of God Himself, Zoan became a Seraph of God, the highest attainable office in the land. The Order of the Seraph was the highest honor in the City. Established by God Himself, it could only be bestowed by Him upon the highest of worthies. God's angel, Gabriel, was His first Seraph, commanding the City's bureaucracy and judicial system. God was at leisure to name other Seraphim, but had reserved the honor for Zoan. Laying aside his title of Marshal, my grandfather had been admitted to the Order of the Seraph, but in deference to Gabriel, it was said, he would resign and retreat into a quiet life lived away from the public eye. Angra was born almost immediately after Zoan's resignation.

Now it is important for you all to understand some of the physics involved in the aging process here in Heaven. When I say that my grandfather aged and my father was born, you must remember what I have already told you. A lifetime here is the equivalent of billions of Earth years. The universe, the Earth, and Man had yet to be created in almost all of the time I will cover in my story.

Something else that is of import in establishing the background to my story: my grandfather's generation was by far the oldest generation alive. No one really knew how old God was, but everyone knew that he was older than the City's oldest citizen. Official history puts God at the head of the City since the beginning. But there were rumors that He had been part of an older race of beings and that as the only survivor, He had ascended the throne to lead the City. Circulating such rumors was heresy, but it was not uncommon to hear such things being said among the lower classes. They needed their mystery. It was not until sometime later that I would come to understand why my grandfather's generation was the oldest. But we will come to that.

My family lived in a huge mansion in one of the more exclusive areas of the city. For the most part, the closer you lived to God's main palace, known as the Seat of God in the old Northwest Quarter, the more expensive and luxurious were the residences and the more elevated your social and political status. Considered in this light, the slaughter in the public square I had witnessed as a boy is not surprising. The closer you are to God, the more dangerous your position. But that aside, those angels bearing the rank of Minister, Senator, Marshal, and Grand General of the army were eligible to live in some of the most magnificent palaces surrounding the Seat of God. Although not nearly as resplendent and ornate as God's many and grandiose residences, these estates often spread over many acres. Many of the wealthier families had built private walled compounds within the City to further segregate themselves from the remaining inhabitants.

My grandfather had been given our estate when he reached the rank of General. But it was not until his victories over the trimmers, years later, that our family estates were increased to the size I was familiar with. With Zoan's fame came money, and we rose in status to become one of the City's wealthier families. Unwilling to build an ostentatious home or erect walls that would isolate his estate from that of other citizens, Zoan chose, instead, to keep his lands open and accessible to the City's inhabitants. Many of the City's first public parks were built upon our family lands.

Once my father had become an angel of influence and power in his own right, however, major construction took place and a house of great dimensions was built. Shortly afterward, our family lands were walled in. No longer the patriarch of the family, my grandfather sat idly by, as my father turned the family lands into a secluded barracks.

I grew up in the central house, looking out from its many rooms over the vast acres separating our estate from the Seat of God. The City grew as I grew. The areas surrounding our family estate's walls began to brim with splendid architecture and buildings of grand proportions. God was fond of large, ornate edifices and many a time, our family would be invited to the opening of private and government buildings. Still a boy and enrolled in one of the City's more prestigious elementary educational institutions, I spent much of my time at these parties, where my father was presented to City magnates. It was at these backroom meetings, behind the scenes of the Senate, that the deals of the City were struck. While the Senate spent most of its time debating and arguing over trivial and insignificant issues thrown to them by God like bones to a dog, these backroom angels actually ran things. My father was one of them and it was as a boy, watching these meetings of generals, ministers, archangels and others of influence, that I was possessed by the great vision for the glory of the kingdom. Senators, in their debating societies, may have been elected by the citizens, but the power of the state was always really held by divine right.

We will spend no more time on my youth. Though my family enjoyed a position of prominence and I had the privilege of a better education than most, life for me was much like it had always been for the children of the City of God. You learned your lessons. You behaved. You prayed to God and asked His forgiveness. You loved your God and were beaten, when necessary. You were given proper martial training and were expected to kill trimmers on sight. Trained to hate anyone who did not love God and follow His commands. We were to be the next generation. A great generation and the one that would wipe out all resistance to God and work to make all His visions a reality. Just like the generation before us, and the generation before them, and so on.

CHAPTER SEVEN

The moment my schooling was over, I joined the army. An angel with my birthright was exempt from the requirement that all angels should serve in the army. But I wanted to follow in my grandfather's footsteps and, unlike many of my schoolmates, refused to pay another angel to take my place in the regiments. Early on in my military training, I came to understand the indispensability of subjecting oneself to stringent discipline in order to generate and maintain the virtues and glory of God. He had brought our people and society to the pinnacle of power and prosperity. No external force could be allowed to thwart our Lord's work. To fulfill His destiny, nothing could be permitted to stand in the way. These ideas were burned into my brain through years of training and fighting. I accepted them readily and grew to love the army.

My promotion to the rank of Captain intensified my desire to make the military my career. I expected Zoan to be happy, when I went to tell him about it.

"Never volunteer for anything, Ahriman," he cautioned, when he saw the mark of my new rank on my uniform. "Medals and glory are for the foolhardy. Coming back to your loved ones alive is more important than all the medals and awards you may win."

This annoyed and puzzled me, coming as it did from an angel who had been Marshal of the Armies and Seraph of our Lord God. But I accepted him for what he was. Though it would have been considered heresy, I say to you that I loved him more than I loved God. Unlike my father, always wrapped up in some shady business venture, Zoan was interested in my personal well-being. Though I did not understand it at the time, I was all that mattered to Zoan, especially after my grandmother's death.

The order and discipline of army life appealed to me. It made sense. That is not to say I was not nervous or tense before going into battle. Ever a rational angel was I. And I sought to avoid those angels who confused bravado with bravery. They spoke of their prowess, but would falter in the thick of battle. I wielded my sword, undefeated, and built for myself a reputation as a fierce fighter. But never once was I not afraid. Braggarts have never understood the difference between being afraid and being a coward.

Incidentally, it was in the battle lines that I first met Simon. I will speak much more about him in my story. We were both young. He outranked me, but because of my family's social standing, I was of a superior class. Together, we fought in many battles and lost many friends. We travelled up the ranks together, though I was always one step behind him. He struck me as the very best of what God's army had to offer. He was brave and, more than anything else, loved his angels. Although I could best him in a fight, it was he who earned the angels' love through his inherent compassion.

Crossing the Acheron at the Forks of Apsatsus one day, we were ambushed. Both Simon and I were wounded. Later, I was assigned to a different unit and we lost touch. For a while. But I will get back to that.

Zoan came to see me in the hospital when I was recuperating.

"It is not such a bad wound," he said, looking under my dressings as I winced in pain. He had peeled the bandage from the wounds, exposing them and making them bleed.

"Not as bad as it could be," I agreed. "But it was only one trimmer." I flinched, watching my stitches pull apart and bleed.

"What do you mean?" Zoan asked, also noting the blood for the first time.

"I mean one trimmer shot my horse out from under me, wounded Simon, and killed my angels. It was just that one trimmer."

I could see Zoan disapproved of my use of an expletive.

"*Outlander*," I corrected, to appease him.

"Tartaruian. Where is this Tartaruian now?" He suddenly seemed more interested in my would-be assassin.

It took a bit of the breath out of me. "He was captured. They are holding him for execution. Why do you ask?"

"It would be a terrible thing to waste an angel as bold as that," Zoan said.

I looked at him. He meant it. He was not joking with me.

"He is a trim...an outlander. He killed my angels. Nearly killed me." I was annoyed by the direction in which the conversation was heading. "Does that not mean something to you?" I immediately regretted my rebellious tone.

"Tartaruian," Zoan repeated, ignoring my tone. "He did this on his own?"

"Yes!"

"Do what is right, Ahriman." he said.

I grumbled to myself.

"How did this come to pass?" Zoan asked, peeling the bandages back further from what were now sopping wet wounds.

"Simon and I were forced to wade through a swamp in order to flank an enemy position holding down our center."

"Who ordered the attack?"

"I did," I said after a moment's hesitation. I felt stupid. I could already see where he was going.

"And you were forced to flank through a swamp?"

"I would not say 'forced,' exactly. It was the most unexpected route."

"Unexpected or reckless?"

It was not easy to argue with the founding father of our City's military and not feel some sense of apprehension. "Unexpected," I repeated fervently. My white sheets were now becoming soaked with blood.

"And you ordered the attack?" he persisted.

Now he was really annoying me. "I was confident we could run them off. And we did."

"But at what cost?"

"'At what cost'?" I mimicked him.

"How many of your angels died, Ahriman?" Zoan asked quietly.

I did not know. "I do not know, but we cut down a good many trimmers."

Zoan rubbed his chin and tried not to notice, as others whispered that the great Lord Marshal and Seraph was there to see his grandson.

"What were their names?" he asked me with a glassy-eyed look.

I struggled to comprehend what he meant. "What?" I had not understood the question.

He appeared sad. "What were their names, Ahriman? The names of the angels who fell at your 'unexpected' command?"

I did not know. I shrugged. It was all I could manage. I was in pain. The nurse came over to staunch my bleeding.

"Glory," was all Zoan said, shaking his head in disappointment.

I sulked until I was well enough to leave the hospital. I could not find Simon, but wondered whether Zoan would have leveled the same criticism at him.

Shortly thereafter, I was promoted. I sent orders to ensure that the life of the trimmer who had ambushed us in the swamp was spared, but directed that he be held in captivity. I wanted to respect Zoan, though I did not understand him. The trimmer's name was Azael, I was told. I neither cared nor thought of the name again for a good, long while. He lived a protected life, while the angels who had died obeying my command did not even get a proper burial.

⌘   ⌘   ⌘

With my promotion to Colonel, I moved into the senior-officer corps. But there was a catch in my rise up the ranks: it was less a reward in recognition of my military prowess than a way of sparing my commanders the eventuality of an awkward situation. Let me explain. My family was Seraph. That privilege alone entitled me to command soldiers belonging to all angelic ranks. But being the only soldier in the whole army who came from the Order of the Seraphim, I was both an oddity and an outcast. That is, by birth, I enjoyed rights to which very few other angels were entitled. But if I were to serve in the army, I had to put up with the possibility of being commanded by my "inferiors," in a manner of speaking. I brought honor to any unit in which I served, but my presence also generated fear that my death or injury to my person in combat would bring the wrath of God down upon my unfortunate commander. Yet I had never even set eyes on God. Most people, in fact, had never seen Him.

My promotion, "entitling" me to serve, henceforth, in the intelligence and counter-intelligence corps was, therefore, a way of spiriting me out of harm's way and easing me out of a situation that might have proved embarrassing. My days in a forward fighting unit were over. Simon was also transferred to a different unit. I assumed it was a punishment posting, until I found out that he now commanded the City's cavalry corp. I, on the other hand, sat in a field office, rather than atop a warhorse. It dawned on me that I was dangerous in ways I had not even considered when I was just a junior officer, impressing people with my skill with a sword and a spear.

This setback of sorts motivated me to progress in another direction. It was not that I disliked the idea of intelligence work. I certainly felt I could plot strategy as skillfully as anyone else and intelligence work did put one's mind to the test. But it did not have the chase I needed. The charge. The blood and gore that stimulated me in strange ways. Zoan, at least, was happy to know that my proficiency on the battlefield with a sword and a spear would be deflected, hopefully, to the collection and analysis of intelligence.

"We have always been lacking in intelligence in this army," he said, when I went to visit him with my latest proficiency report.

I was not sure whether he was joking.

"I have requested another combat command," I told him.

I could see the light dim in his eyes. "Why?" It was a simple question without a simple answer. "I would have thought you would have learned from your last go around."

"Everyone makes mistakes," I said in all earnestness.

"At least you have acknowledged your mistake. It is one thing to make mistakes in your life's endeavors. But it is quite another to take liberties with the lives of other angels."

"Many angels make mistakes in their first commands." I was fighting desperation. "And it was not a 'mistake,' as you put it. I lost angels, yes. But we won the battle, didn't we? Why can you not support me? Did you never make a mistake yourself?"

His words had hurt me. No one was perfect, other than God.

Zoan's face lit up with a look of loving appeal. "I do support you, Ahriman," he said earnestly. "It is just that sometimes, I wonder to what extent you realize that your actions have consequences beyond your own self."

He was genuinely worried, which made me angrier still.

"I only want to serve God to the best of my ability," I said earnestly.

Zoan was suddenly ill at ease. "There is nothing wrong with that," he said, "so long as you are sure that serving God is what is best for you."

I did not understand. How could serving God be anything other than the best thing for me?

Zoan sensed this question in me. "Listen to me," he said. "Ignore my words. Do what you feel most fit. Only know that I have your best interests at heart and that, in my humble opinion, you will serve the City much better as an intelligence officer than as a combat officer. The City could not stand to lose you in battle." He hesitated for a moment, as if to double-check that we were alone. "I could not stand to lose you that way."

I saw fear in him for the first time. He seemed genuinely concerned that I might die in some swamp the next time around.

"I will withdraw my request for another combat command, then." I said it with the verve only truth and sincerity could summon.

"Good! Good," he said, rubbing his hands together like a child waiting for a sweet. "Securing our City from the inside, Ahriman, is as important as securing it on the outside. More so, I would say."

I did not know what he meant. I did not care at the time. He was happy and that mattered a great deal to me. I accepted the position of intelligence officer, but never withdrew the combat request.

⌘　⌘　⌘

My proficiency reports were consistently positive, though not reflective of my personal feelings about the quality of my work. My new job caused me more frustration than I had anticipated. I collected intelligence. Sounds simple enough, but it tortured me in cruel ways. Reports of fighting in Tartarus arrived in one neverending flow and were brought to me for evaluation. I could see units moving around the map and while the outcome of my analysis could, sometimes, cause those units to move from one side of the map to the other, I was not the one leading the charge. I could see Simon on my map and noted the growing number of units he commanded. Sometimes, they included infantry and artillery. Later, quartermaster and transport. He was being groomed. I was not. Angels and trimmers alike admired Simon's prowess on the field; and it did not sit well with me that he was more successful than I could ever be. His repeated victories guaranteed that. My envy lay somewhere at the source of my need to convince myself that I was responsible for Simon's successes. After all, it was my analysis that told him where to go and how to fight, I argued to myself. I could think of no greater honor than to lead our armies to victory, like my grandfather's conquests of old.

I sat and festered, frustrated when I failed to convince the generals of the brilliance of my plans, and subsequently watched, as whole units were wiped off my maps. Squads, cohorts, legions, and armies of God's angels. They moved a few kilometers here or there, this unit taking a fifty-percent loss, while another only suffered a thirty-percent loss. What did it matter, but for the glory of God? I became absorbed. I strategized and re-strategized our army's movements, oblivious that I was falling farther and farther down the dark shaft Zoan had warned me about while I lay wounded in the hospital. Angels became nothing but numbers. From my dusty little tent, I did the best I could, gaining glory only in my own mind through my proxies. Defeats in battle were buried in silence, battles I could have won, had I been there to lead, had Simon been there to carry out my orders. I would sit at night, bathed in meek candlelight, watching the many units spread across my Tartaruian maps. Who controlled the flags became paramount to me, more so than any reality I could have witnessed in the field, for those flags served no purpose other than to justify my grand strategy, which no one was willing to recognize or praise.

I dared not vent my frustrations. How could I? God needed to keep His people's spirits high, if we were to defeat the trimmers. Violence was necessary, we were told, to secure and maintain our way of life and I believed it wholeheartedly. Failure or manifestations of it could chip away at the support God needed, that He demanded of His citizens. We had to remain united in our fight against the trimmers. On a more personal level, disagreement with my superiors would implicate me in a charge of insubordination against God, Who, in His infinite wisdom, determined who should lead His forces. Who was I to argue with that?

During the lull in fighting between campaign seasons, I would couple my sword and spear training by my collection of information from the vast network of spies God maintained throughout the City and the outlying colonies and outlands. These were not part of the intelligence chain for which I was responsible, and my activities could easily have been misconstrued as malicious in intent. But once I understood the scope of God's intelligence operations within the civilian world, a world of opportunities opened up. God was interested in nearly anything that was said about the City's wars with the trimmers; with communications among the many colonies in the outlands, construction-contract negotiations and the progress of wall building around the City; the number of common areas and markets around the City and the preoccupations of the populations of such areas, including the number of dresses senators' wives were buying; even the commitment of water to the City from the northern mountains. There was nothing He was not interested in knowing.

Going through the information for myself each day, I wondered how God was able to absorb so much and what He could possibly be doing with it all. I knew my interest in such matters and the collection of this information might be seen as a dereliction of duty, when I should have been otherwise engaged, but to my mind, at least, I was gathering and sifting through this information out of love for God. Besides, there was a spigot of information flowing throughout the army and certain ministries within the government, with little or no effort made by anyone to control or contain it. It was out there, accessible to anyone with any interest, some ingenuity, and some time to kill. Me, for example. But at least my interest was for the greater glory of God and the City, as I could keep tabs on the flow of secrets reserved for His ears. That I wanted to be like Him was not a crime. That I would use this information for my own ends? Well, that was another matter I somehow justified in my own mind.

⌘　⌘　⌘

As time went on, it became increasingly clear that I would not receive another combat command. I was to be held back, punished for something I knew was outside of my control. The City's population was war-loving by nature, but there were few angels of my rank and class willing to put their lives in harm's way. Most would have retired to civilian jobs. My failure to do so and my desire to obtain another combat command made me unique, a maverick, someone who stood out in the crowd. That was frowned upon. We were all equal servants in the eyes of God. I suspected, privately, that I was seen to have tried too hard for a field assignment and was thought to have a "chip on my shoulder." I had something to prove, but no one was willing to let me demonstrate my qualities. I had yet to prove myself as a great leader, as Simon had been allowed to do. But while people acknowledged and admired this attribute in him, they misinterpreted the same quality in me as arrogance.

I was riddled with suspicion. I imagined the generals conspiring against me at every turn, jealous of my relationship with Simon, the most successful of God's newest young generals. They could see, no doubt, that the pair of us would shortly have the power to unseat them, if we were allowed to continue. Whether Simon was aware of the challenge I was undertaking on his behalf was never a consideration. I believed myself to be his agent, though he never invested such authority in me. My fight was his fight, as far as I could see. Of course, Zoan would not have hesitated to interfere in my machinations as I had ignored his express request for me to give up my quest for glory on the field of battle. I understood his love for me and his desire to see me safe. But much as I loved him, I resented him for not supporting me in my pursuit of greatness. I was not above suspecting Gabriel himself, unwilling as I was to risk sharing God's affections, if I were, indeed, to succeed. He was God's eyes and ears, running the City in His name. Zoan had been his rival, and while it was not clear why my grandfather had taken the unprecedented step of resigning from his position in the Order of the Seraphim, I was certain in all respects that Gabriel did not want me to succeed, where Zoan had buckled. All of this, of course, was sheer delusion on my part, as I was to learn when I came home once on leave.

⌘　⌘　⌘

"I have bigger plans for you," Angra said quite angrily, "and they all require you to stay alive!"

I had been home for only one night, when quarrels began with my father following an off-hand comment I had made about visiting Zoan before coming home to see my parents.

"Are you so dense?" Angra went on. "Do you really lack an understanding of what I've taught you, Ahriman?"

"I understand the purpose of your business dealings only too fully, Father," I shot back. "Those backroom power-grabbing meetings that do nothing but undermine the true purpose of God's wishes."

"You cannot possibly be that stupid," Angra said mockingly. "Real power is not wielded at the end of a sword, but by the nib of a stylus. Surely, your endless and pointless lobbying of generals taught you that?"

He knew exactly where to stick the sharp end of that stylus. But he was right, of course. I just could not bring myself to admit it. Not then.

"You cannot possibly think that someone of your...breeding... is justified in wishing to waffle in trivialities like this City's wars?"

"Careful, Father. You are treading on dangerous ground. That could easily be construed as heresy."

"And what if it is? Your grandfather, whom you admire unreservedly—though you do not heed his wishes—committed the ultimate heresy when he stepped down from the Seraphim. Yet you do not openly condemn him. You cannot speak to me with two faces, Ahriman."

"You would know best, Father," I spat.

"Yet you strive for it," he went on, unfazed.

I was confused. I quickly tried to determine whether I cared enough to continue the conversation. "Strive for what?" I asked. "What do you mean?"

"I mean your move into intelligence gathering. You deride the education I gave you, the head for business you inherited from me. Yet you accept a position that offers you access to the most secret and useful information in the realm. I know I'm not being modest when I say this, but I do give myself credit for making you valuable beyond your years."

He said it with all the intensity I had never imagined him capable of.

"If the nib of the stylus is the instrument of power, it is knowledge that instigates its drafting," he went on.

My position did give me a certain sense of empowerment, but I had regarded it as a curse, rather than as a blessing. Eavesdropping on people's secrets was simply a way of satisfying my curiosity, not a means to any particular end. Certainly not a means to the end Angra was suggesting.

"My only means of power, Ahriman, is in my accumulation of information. Who knows what and when? How do I use that information? When do I use it? Is this not what you do each day? Each hour of your miserable little military life?"

"My interest in intelligence gathering is nothing but my means of expression."

"True, but have you considered there are other ways in which to express yourself, Ahriman? You do not need armies in order to make yourself powerful. Power is the use of information and, not unlike me, you look to that information to make your play in God's Kingdom."

I said nothing. I had never got on well with my father, but he seemed to know me in the way a petulant teenager reluctantly acknowledges his parents. Maybe I was fighting the wrong fight, in the wrong place, and with the wrong people.

Angra continued more calmly. "Let's not fight, Ahriman. Whether you wish to admit it or not, you understand your own value. Zoan destroyed this family when he left the Order. We lost our privileges, because we lost the means by which one collects, accumulates, and exercises power. You are not like him. You are not afraid of your potential. But you, more than anything else, want to be like Zoan, but for the same reasons I once wanted to be like him."

Despite my anger, I did not miss the intensity in my father's eyes.

"You and I both want to establish ourselves as an angel to be reckoned with. To have power."

Angra relaxed a bit. I was sure he could sense he had hit a nerve.

"You should submit your application to the Servitude," he said.

I groaned. "You want me to become a bureaucrat?" I asked with an almost childlike whine.

"I am confident that with your grandfather's will to action and my brain for business, you will have a highly successful career in the Servitude."

I grumbled to myself.

"Think of it, Ahriman! You could propel our family back into God's good graces!"

He had such passion, my father. He really thought I could make something of myself. And yet I hated him.

He put his hand on my shoulder, as if to give me strength. I could not remember the last time we had touched in any way.

"Out of shadows and into the light. It's such a compelling story. Zoan may have been unwilling to serve, but you will not fail as he did."

"Close by God's side and in God's ear?" I asked with my first smile of the day. It was something Zoan had said many times while speaking of his service to God.

Angra smiled. He, indeed, knew me better than I then chose to admit.

"Close by God's side and in God's ear," he repeated, reciprocating my smile.

Knowing I would never again lead on the field in God's name, I surrendered my commission the next day and entered my application with the Servitude of God. My days as a warrior were meant to be over.

⌘ ⌘ ⌘

My father grew up in a cold bath of notoriety, born of Zoan's military legend and his subsequent and unexpected abdication. Finishing his mandatory military training, Angra had spent his government career cultivating an impressive network of contacts, while actually getting very little done. Using my grandfather's name, he had manipulated those contacts and propelled himself to a Virtues, a kind of undersecretary's position within the Bureau of Engineering, part of the Ministry of the Interior. There, Angra had made the best of all possible uses of his backroom negotiating skills in granting or denying licenses to government construction-project contractors. The combination of his government and private-sector contacts would make him one of the most sought-after members of the Ministry. People needed him to get things done, but at a cost. In this way, he would build the walls around our many properties with cost only to the City, though it is doubtful whether any City auditor realized it. Angra had maintained a stranglehold on the legions of contractors he basically owned. Ambitious only to the extent that it lined his pockets, he would spend most of his time in the higher circles of con artists who masqueraded as Servitude. Outwardly sincere in his nationalistic fervor, but quietly working to undermine the state for his own gain. Sadly, this was a trend among many angels in the upper echelons of God's Kingdom. Taking his wealth and notorious reputation with him, Angra would, ultimately, retire from government service early and build his own network of business organizations, outwardly committed to the upkeep of the City's many privately operated, but publicly owned works projects.

Despite my father's nefarious dealings and dangerous reputation, my family maintained its social position, if for no other reason than the intense and continuing interest the City had in my grandfather. It was a bit of a "love-hate" relationship, really, as Zoan had been both admired for his campaigns against the outlanders and hated by those within the bureaucracy who had ended up looking foolish, as they squabbled for positions inferior to the one he had voluntarily abdicated. Despite my father's personal feelings about the issue, the act of stepping down from the Order had made my family more noteworthy than Zoan's actual elevation to the rank. There was a certain nobility of purpose in his actions that forced even Gabriel to feign admiration for Zoan's decision as a tactful way of publicly handling what might have been seen as a fall from grace. Since my grandfather's resignation, the Order had been restricted to one angel: Gabriel.

As a member of this noble class, I was afforded opportunities denied to most citizens. Good care, good schooling, good prospects. These were privileges I could take for granted. And the wanting many? Well, I did not know them. What did we care, if our bread came from one baker or another, so long as it arrived on time, tasted good, and was nourishing? Reserved for the very wealthy or the powerful elite, ambrosia flowed in our house. God personally exercised a tight monopoly on its production and distribution. My clothes were made from the finest fabrics, because it was my birthright to wear them. It was our way of life. My schooling, my induction into the army, even my positions within the army. They were all off the back of my privileged status. It was the way the City ran, the way it had always run.

It was this relationship with the Order of the Seraph, through Zoan's elevation to that unattainable rank of angel, which afforded me the honor of submitting my application to the Servitude with absolute confidence. It seemed ironic to me that despite the Order allowing me such latitude, Angra associated our relationship with it as emblematic of, if not directly responsible for, the downfall of our family. Whatever be the disgrace that Zoan was perceived to have brought upon himself or God by his actions, my application was immediately accepted, whereas those of perhaps more qualified others were passed over. My family may have been relegated by Zoan's actions to a position where they provided fodder for the gossipmongers of the noble class, but the Order was still the Order. I was placed in a holding pattern, while the bureaucratic wheels spun, attempting to find some acceptable and, of course, lucrative position worthy of my status.

With the right introductions and financial backing, an angel could go quite far in the City of God. Knowing when to speak, when to act, and when to deceive were more useful assets than brains. With my grandfather's name and my father's pull to see me through, Angra saw me as an angel possessed of the greatest prospects for being feared. Ever eager to introduce me to angels of intrigue, his vision of my potential was always something I found myself struggling with. No matter what I may have said openly, somewhere in that great, vast head of mine, physical power, symbolized by the swinging of my sword, defined the fear I could instill in others, not the nib of anyone's stylus.

"I do not understand him, Mother," I said one night, as I continued to wait for news from one of the ministries. "He comes from a line of warriors, yet feels that his entreaties in the world of business will make him powerful."

"Your father *is* a powerful angel, Ahriman." She sat watching me with big, thoughtful eyes. "There is no disputing that. That he sees greater things for you should not be a surprise."

"It is not that. He has always been jealous of my relationship with Grandfather. The power that Grandfather amassed resulted from his victories on the field, not in any business room. Father wants what Zoan achieved, but is unwilling to follow in his footsteps."

"Maybe he is unable to do so. Have you thought of that, Ahriman?"

That she was defending him was unexpected. They had, on the face of it, little love for each other.

"Have you considered the possibility that your father recognizes his limitations and has come to terms with them? That he sees in you capability he does not see in himself? That you are a mix of both the personality the City loves in your grandfather and the motivation that drives your father?"

I did not know what to say. Angra was weak. I was sure of that. The state of his weakness had never really concerned me before. But it mattered to her. For some reason.

"Use the brains God gave you," she continued, "to see beyond your own wants and desires."

"To do what he cannot do," I said it to myself, but out loud. "To do what neither he nor Zoan were able to do."

I had never been very close to my mother. She would die in an accident right before my elevation to the Order. She would never see what I had achieved. Or ruined, I guess. But no matter how I saw her or continued to see her as the years went by, she gave my vision a depth I had never considered before that evening, though she probably did not understand the nature of the kernel she had planted.

⌘　⌘　⌘

Zoan was always silent when he saw my father trying to forge a path for me through the world. I loved my grandfather and had spent as much time with him as possible when I was a boy. As an adult, I tried to treat him with the respect he deserved, though he seemed to see me as the little boy who had once danced around his heels with a wooden sword in hand. He was a wise and venerable angel, but he could not envision my future the way I could. I knew what was best for myself. I may not have known where I was going once I left the army, but I was sure that no matter what happened, I would find my way eventually.

"Ahriman," Zoan said to me one night, as I continued to wait to hear about my assignment in the Servitude. "We have talked many times about your future." He could sense my distress at having to wait so long to have concrete news about my appointment. "I am glad to see you consider these less warlike efforts to be noble as well."

"Of course I do, Grandfather," I replied. "The Servitude is just another way of serving our Lord. My devotion to God is not limited to the war spirit alone." I was proud of the fact I could say that now without gagging. "I am devoted to God and want nothing more than to make you happy."

I loved Zoan dearly and could see his eyes fill with regret when I said this.

"Is there something wrong, Grandfather?" I asked with concern.

"There are very few ways that you could do that," he replied, laying his hand tenderly on my shoulder.

"What do you mean?"

I was concerned with the change in him. Zoan had been known for his sharpness of character and dryness of wit. But more and more, it seemed, he would lose himself, forgetting what he was saying, where he had been that day, what he had done, and to whom he had spoken. He engaged a nurse who would give me periodic updates. It seemed Zoan's prognosis was not favorable. He belonged to a line of the race of angels that was more susceptible to disease, it seemed. He shook his head when he sensed my concern, as if persuading himself to say something more.

"There is something else, then?" I asked.

"You do not give yourself enough credit, my boy," he said with a smile. "You see things more deeply than most. But I am afraid what I have to tell you would only serve to confuse you, something I would rather not do, especially now as you begin work at a ministry." He paused for a moment, looked to the wall, and set his jaw more firmly. "What I will tell you is this: the society that He has built for us is not infallible. Do not be fooled. The wars that I waged were wars of aggression. Souls that I brought out with me into that outland were lost in the name of God and for little gain."

"I do not understand, Grandfather."

His guilt at the lives lost in his campaigns seemed to be an increasingly annoying preoccupation with him.

"The wars you waged in the name of God," I continued, "were holy wars, bringing our enemies to their knees. They protected us and brought us lands for our people and our City. Are you trying to tell me that there was something wrong with that? Something unjust about being a hero?"

"Yes and no, Ahriman. War is sometimes necessary," he said adamantly. "To secure our borders, yes. To prevent marauders and evil angels from harming the people, yes." He shifted restlessly, his hands shaking. "But you should not lose sight of the individual, the one, especially in a world where the individual, the one, is oft-sacrificed in the name of something greater. For each brave soul who died for God's City, a host of angels were left at home, weeping over his death. You cannot forget that what you do is for the benefit of all angels, not simply to line your own pockets with the tokens and rewards of office."

His resentment of Angra was unabashed. If he had ever spent time with my father, his message and teachings were now lost to the ravages of corruption and greed.

"Remember," Zoan went on, "you can never be greater than the affections of those who follow you. If you perpetrate great evil for the purpose of propelling yourself higher than your neighbor, it doesn't matter what kudos you receive. You have betrayed your fellow angel, a crime far worse than anything you could commit against your state. Do you understand?"

I did not want to disagree with him. He was a venerable old angel. But he was confused. My grandfather's tangents from God's teachings and his obvious, but unspoken resentment was something incomprehensible for an honorable citizen. His exploits were of phenomenal importance to God's kingdom, our home. His words were seditious. Inhabitants of the City of God were taught from childhood that the state was the highest evolution of being, taking greater precedence over any individual, save God Himself. When radicals spoke out against the government, in the Senate or on the street corners of the kingdom, I felt hatred for them, as all good citizens should. I spat in their faces and cursed their unholy sentiments. When radicals were hanged, their tortured bodies hung from the City walls as a reminder of what disobedience meant, I cheered with my friends and the crowds at their demise, celebrating the end to their incendiary, disruptive agenda. I was a nationalist. A patriot. A servant of God. Our master, our Lord, was beyond the reckoning of ordinary angels and possessed of a vision which we could only hope to share. Someone with such a vision and such power could not be held back by a system of beliefs upheld by a common angel. Those beliefs were nothing, when compared to the state and its ruler, and could certainly not be allowed to stand in the way of the greater glory of the kingdom.

Zoan's words challenged my most strongly held convictions. If any other angel had made such blasphemous declarations, my deepest ire and hatred would have been instantly aroused. But coming from an angel I respected beyond all others, they shook me so that I was torn within the very core of my soul. Do I hold fast to what I know to be true, I asked myself, or do I choose to look the other way and ignore his twisted beliefs? After all, Zoan had addressed these words to me and me alone, in confidence. He was sick. Confused. Never once in these moments of consternation did I consider the possibility that he might be right. Never once was I tempted to consider his liberalism as an alternative. I stayed true to myself. To my place in God's scheme. To God Himself. Honoring my grandfather and my family, I restrained myself.

"I will do as you say." What else could I say?

"You will do great things, Ahriman. Of that I have little doubt."

⌘   ⌘   ⌘

Accepting I would never have the glorious military career I had so longed for, I was determined to reassert myself and dig into my government role with all the zeal I reserved for my love of state and the Lord our God. He was my purpose and I could serve Him in many ways. I put aside thoughts of my father and my grandfather, determined to do the best I could, when I learned of my appointment as a Powers, an officer of sorts, in the Public Information Department of the Ministry of Information. It was a natural choice, given my service in military intelligence. I decided it was better to discount any thought of the role my father may have played in my placement. Why torture myself that way? I was sworn in with a thousand other new Powers of the Servitude.

The ministry was in charge of all state-run news sources and subdivided into various departments devoted to the collection of both public and not-so-public information throughout the kingdom. While the Public Information Department or PID was innocuous enough, molding God's public communications to His angels, the Non-Public Information Department or NID was a sort of domestic spy network. It had some loose affiliations with the Secret Police and, more than once, I had stumbled upon bits of useful information coming out of the NID during my military service. But the NID was a completely civilian operation, sanctioned only to root out subversion in the City and well positioned to provide the Secret Police with leads they needed to consider investigating.

It should come as no surprise that my learning curve in the PID was far from dramatic. In the army, I had been involved in the collection and analysis of information far more sophisticated than press releases relating to wall-construction projects, food doles, or tax assessments. There were only so many public notices of circuses I could stomach in any given week and it did not take long for my initial enthusiasm to be quashed. I was a public censor, pure and simple. And though it seemed impossible, I found things actually moved slower in the PID than it had in the army. Perhaps it was the unimportant nature of the information being circulated. Or perhaps the idiocy of the department's organizational structure. I do not know. Angra's, "Give it time, Ahriman," did not inspire me with a great deal of hope or confidence.

It did not take me long to hold the oath I had taken at arm's length. I began using my former army contacts to obtain information not generally available to Powers in my department. Information in hand, I would offer it to the ministry's senior most angels. This bypassed the concerned hierarchy and allowed me to enable PID bureaucrats, accustomed to the boring details of public life, to indulge in what would otherwise have been off-limits. NID angels were equally eager to obtain information that would, otherwise, have only been available in military or Secret Police communiqués. In a strange and unexpected twist, the generals who had once despised me for my constant strategizing and requests for command were now happy to have "one of their own" in the ministry. If an investigation was coming their way, they had someone on the inside to forewarn them, beat the inspector generals to the punch, and let them save face. It served everyone's purpose to make sure my name was often among those picked out for special commendations. I became the axis through which large amounts of information flowed in both directions. Somehow, I convinced myself this was not a lapse in morality or, worse, a betrayal of my faith in God. My work was for the betterment of His kingdom, not to bilk it for personal gain. It was diverting, but not a challenge. So it should not surprise you that it did not take long for me to start looking again for something more. The same passions that had driven my army career into the wall took over once more.

CHAPTER EIGHT

"**B**ased on what you have told me, dear boy, it seems the only way you'll be satisfied with this work is if you become the Minister of Information yourself," Angra laughingly said one night at one of his business meetings.

Some of the angels there were known to me, others less familiar. I had consented to attend, both in the hope of meeting more senior Servants, likely to act as appropriate patrons, and of collecting whatever information I could obtain. Satiating my information masters was no easy task and my family name worked to raise the expectations of those who wished to be kept in the know.

"Grandfather does not share your sentiment," I said absently, sipping a cup of wine.

It was good wine, but not as good as the ambrosia Angra constantly seemed able to procure. He was particularly annoying at these meetings, his salesman persona coming to full bore when he was in the vibe. Though I did not mention my sideline job, I was sure Angra knew what I was really doing. To be honest, I was a little ashamed of the fact I was making more of myself sharing sensitive information illegally than doing my real work. Still I seemed able to justify the morality of it in my mind. It had been my father's idea, after all, that I should join the Servitude.

"How does that matter?" Angra said, a bit miffed, but happy to allow his overindulgence in wine to dull any sense of indignation. "The only real way for this to happen is for you to run the NID. Once that's achieved," he said wiping his mouth on the sleeve of his robe, "you'll be able to obtain a ministerial position."

Angra's party agreed lethargically. They were as excited to hear about my work in the ministry as I was to tell them. One person in this crowd, though, watched me intently and quietly.

"I think you give me too much credit, Father," I replied. "Becoming a minister is no simple task. There are many older and more well-connected birds lining their nests ahead of me."

I had a tendency to say what I thought when I thought it, a failing I still suffer from. Sporadic conversation broke out over this comment.

"The Minister of Information has a rather important role, Ahriman," the quiet and observant attendee said. It was the first time all evening that one of my father's business associates had spoken to me directly.

I sensed a possible opportunity. "Your name, sir?" I asked, coming out of my self-induced haze.

"Allow me to introduce you to Jehoel," my father said. "You work for someone in the ministry too, don't you, Jehoel?"

Jehoel's eyes were clear of the wine, but he stood out from the rest for more significant reasons.

"Yes," he said, without taking his eyes off me. "The NID, in fact." He ignored all the other angels in the room. "Tell me, Ahriman, are you not content simply to use your family name to bring about the fulfillment of God design and His dream for His state?"

He assumed me to be the bored and complacent scion, living off the family. Or he knew of my extracurricular activities in the PID.

"Regardless of my family's position in society, Jehoel, and the good work I do as a rising intelligence Powers in the ministry, the bureaucratic machinery turns very slowly."

"Dragging you even more slowly along behind?" Jehoel asked.

"Yes," I replied. My lack of hesitation may have given away my true feelings.

"God's will has its ways."

"Indeed. But you will excuse the heresy, if I say that the ministry often seems bereft of our Lord's will."

"I'm not sure that's heresy," Jehoel replied after a short pause. "But your secret is safe with me."

"Anyway, one must pay one's dues, I expect," I said, baiting him.

"Then I guess you also expect a long and arduous journey, before ultimately achieving your objective."

"My father's objective," I said, nodding back to my now clearly inebriated parent.

"The head of the NID is a Thrones who reports directly to the Minister," Jehoel said, "who, in turn, reports to Gabriel. That is not an easy ascent."

The rest of the party seemed to have fallen away. There was only Jehoel and me. Jehoel testing me. I sensed he wanted to duel with words, but I was not in the mood. He was obviously not in need of anything I was looking to sell.

"I have plans," I said, noncommittal.

"Yes, I think I know."

That got my attention. I looked at Jehoel carefully. Maybe he was an actual believer? A zealot like me?

Angra finally noticed the exchange. "Come," he interrupted, bringing us back to the party. "Our meal is ready and I'm sure you'll agree with me, when I say it would be a shame to let it get cold on account of some mundane government issue."

"Yes, Father," I said.

"Indeed, Angra," Jehoel said. "Our conversation has definitely whetted my appetite."

⌘ ⌘ ⌘

I was promoted to a Virtues and put in charge of all public-information handlers. In effect, I was now the deputy of the department. My seniority in PID did not warrant such a promotion and while there were some rumblings about my unconventionally speedy progress, I was happy to ignore them. I immediately set out to reform the administrative processes, removing low-performing angels and building a merit-based promotion system. It sounds like plain common sense and, perhaps, bland, but productivity picked up exponentially. Simply put, incompetents ran the department and a shot at making a real difference temporarily disconnected me from my sideline of peddling information. I was not fool enough to cut off my contacts, but with a project in hand, I had something more constructive, shall we say, to do with my time.

But building a proper network of informants, spies, and their respective handlers turned out to be only moderately more challenging than what I had been doing before. Once the goals I had set for myself were attained, my newfound interest in my job waned again. It depressed me to realize that I would never be satisfied with what I had. That I would stray from the straight and narrow and know, all the time, that what I was doing was wrong. The plain fact of the situation was that no matter what I did, I was dealing only in information suited for public consumption. It was just too boring to hold my interest.

More out of boredom than anything else, I think, I decided to bring down the head of the PID. Though he was a good customer, I allowed it to leak out that he was in possession of classified information not covered by his clearance status. True to character, he gave me up under interrogation. I had always been very careful, however, in keeping my information clean and my sources hidden from each other—classic intelligence doctrine that I used for my personal amusement. What can I say? It was not a particularly moral thing to do, but I satisfied myself in knowing that he was a blithering slob who had come to the position through some connection he had within the ministry. When he was removed, I was promoted to a Domination and became the next head of the PID. Within what was considered a remarkably short period of time by Servitude standards, I moved from a mid-level nobody to the head of the entire department.

Again, I threw myself into the new role. I was excited to have an opportunity to shape the news and, therefore, the minds of the citizenry. I guess my situation was similar to the time I had moved flags from one end of the map to the other. Position angels in strategic places and move the information around tactically to get those angels to make my kills. In this case, the "kill" was simply getting the citizenry to see things the way I wanted them to. The way God wanted them to. But manipulating angels into seeing God the way I wanted them to was not enough for me. As head of the PID, I thought there would be more interesting things to see, for sure. Yes, I did get to see more of the bureaucracy than your average angel does. Large slices of the Servitude were working on a single, highly confidential project. But I had no clearance, as the Ministry of Information had nothing to do with this project. If possible, it seemed it was totally unrelated to information gathering. I could tell that the Ministry of the Interior was highly engaged, as well as those parts of the Servitude focusing on scientific endeavors. Even my information channels had little to offer me. Whatever this project was, it took a huge amount of administrative input to run. It required constant attention and seemed to be running off a plan that had a direction of its own.

More importantly, from my perspective, it was frustrating to know that while things of such immeasurably greater importance were happening in the echelons about me, I was unable to or incapable of finding out what was happening. Though I was in a powerful supervisory position, sensitive information, vital to the City and to God, still remained beyond my grasp. Motivated by nothing more than the desire to shed my boredom, I redoubled my efforts, both from a work product and contact point of view. If I did not make my way into the NID soon, I felt, I would be terminally stuck where I was.

⌘ ⌘ ⌘

It was about this time, while searching for someone else to bring down in the same way I had framed the former head of PID, that I met Jehoel again.

"How did you become head of NID?" I asked him one evening, when we were dining together.

Though our first meeting had been somewhat tense, we had been running into each other at regular ministerial meetings since my promotion and had become friendly. It turned out that he was not simply someone in the NID, as I had been told. He ran the whole damned thing! Jehoel was a good listener and volunteered to take time off from his wife and son to "mentor" me. I blush to admit that it was originally Angra's idea, but after a few meetings, I found Jehoel to be genuinely engaging and entertaining.

"Just like you," he said with a hint of sarcasm in his voice.

"You mooched off your father, paid off the right people, and stabbed your boss in the back?" I asked.

"Just let me know when you *really* want my job," he laughed. "At least, that way I can get out of your way first."

"I do not treat friends that way." I was serious, though I do not know if he believed me.

"How is that exactly?"

"It is one thing to treat total strangers with indifference. They mean nothing to me. Add nothing to me or to my life. But a friend is someone on whom I depend. Hitting a friend makes about as much sense as hitting myself."

"How do you know that a stranger won't become something to you as well? Add something to you?"

"Proof," I said, recognizing that while my belief was deeply held, my argument was a little too thin. "You can see an angel's worth in the first few moments. If he or she is of substance, you can tell."

"That sounds like your father."

I had not considered that before.

"I am only of minor noble lineage, Ahriman. How, if what you say is true, did we become friends, if I might be so bold as to suggest we share such a relationship?"

I laughed. He was right. "Good friends, I hope," I said, trusting more in myself this time. "You have attributes that make you greater than your name."

"Well, thank you very little," he replied with a smile. "But seriously, how did you know about me when we first met?"

I thought for a moment. "You looked me in the eye and told me the truth."

"Lots of angels do that."

"That is not true. But I could tell with you." That was it. Simply put.

Jehoel thought about it for a moment. "I guess I could tell too."

"Do not be so serious, Jehoel," I said lightheartedly. "In the company we were in when we first met, I believe it was easy for us to become friends. Look at my father's companions. Sycophants and thieves. We were the only ones there who did not care why we were there."

"Oh, I cared very much why I was there."

"How so?" I asked.

Jehoel was suddenly uneasy. "We are but slaves to the grind, Ahriman," he said. "The Servitude is our life and, thus, our friendship stems from that common understanding. So make no mistake. Whatever you may personally feel about your father, being his acquaintance has certain benefits for me that those of us who wish to rectify the evils of a corrupt world and bring to it a stronger sense of justice and fairness must have."

"He cares for no one but himself," I sneered.

"And what about you? Why are you here, speaking to me? Your mentor. To what end?"

"To learn what you have learned. To make this kingdom a better place."

"Yes, but to whose end? The people's?"

I thought for a moment. I could have said yes, but I could not get myself to lie that blatantly. I felt I owed Jehoel more, though I did not really know why.

"No."

"To whom, then?"

"To myself."

"And that is where you fail. If you are to serve God, be one of His devoted, and make a difference in this world, you need to stop thinking about things in the light of only your own ends. If you make yourself into something great, it should be for the benefit of all those around you. You mock your father and while, permit me, he is not a moral angel, I do not see why that would tempt you into his way of thinking."

"We think very differently, he and I," I said sheepishly, reflecting on my short time in the Servitude.

"Ah, but you do not. You have convinced yourself you are doing God's work while, at the same time, you flaunt the power you have been granted. Making a profit along the way. You rationalize this, somehow. In that it will bring advancement. Advancement that will put you in a better position to do what exactly?"

"Succeed. Is there something wrong with wanting to succeed?" I asked, ignoring the problematic parts of his question.

"There is nothing wrong with wanting to succeed, Ahriman. To advance, as you see it. But in thinking of nothing but advancement, you have lost sight of its purpose. Your advancement is not to suit your family or our citizenry. I sense it is only for your personal amusement that you do what you do each day, Ahriman. Not for the love of God."

"That may be true," I replied, "but why, then, is my father so important to you?"

I felt I needed to keep the conversation heading in the right direction, before I said something that really got me into trouble.

"Ahriman," he said, "he is an angel of power. To know him benefits me, because I can use that relationship to do that which he is unwilling to do himself—help others."

"How is that any different from what I do?" I asked half-heartedly.

"The ultimate aim. Mine is to do something great. Yours? Well, it has nothing to do with greatness—other than for your own ends."

I felt ashamed. I had considered Angra merely a burden, my own means to an end. Jehoel saw him as a means to everyone else's ends. Jehoel was not a flag to be moved around a map. He was an angel. A true angel.

"Help others," I repeated.

"Yes, help others. So when you are mocking your job and complaining of its limits and uselessness, selling information to the highest bidder," he said with not a little bit of disdain, "think for a moment why God made that job for you. Why He made the ministry at all. Each time you belittle its work, your work, you belittle the angels God hoped you would help through your work. What you do means something to people. How you do your work sets the standard by which other people conduct themselves."

"I feel foolish." I spoke as honestly as I could. This time, it was not necessarily a sign of weakness.

"You have behaved like a child, Ahriman. You want nothing more than to entertain yourself. This is not the army, bent on nothing but destruction and mayhem. Here things are a little different. Do no work and the people will suffer. People you know and trust, as well as strangers." Jehoel shifted his approach. "How is your grandfather? Still proud of you?"

Had I not been lost in thought, I might have been angered by his insinuations. "He is fine. Thanks for asking," I managed.

But my mind raced. I had served my time in the outlands and had been wounded for it. Jehoel could not understand my sacrifice. But the force and impact of his comments proved more powerful than my selfishness. He had made me question myself. Perhaps, for the first time.

⌘　⌘　⌘

One of my official duties as head of PID was to provide a daily status report to the Minister's Council, a collection of all the department heads working for the Ministry of Information. Separately, I was required to provide Jehoel, as head of the NID, a weekly synopsis of the information collected, collated, and synthesized by PID. It was rumored, though not discussed openly, that Jehoel had personally investigated and removed several Dominations and their immediate staff in other ministries for being involved in seditious activities. Sedition often meant aiding and abetting trimmer activities, a capital offense. I had overthrown the former PID head on specious grounds to rise to my current position, but Jehoel had earned his prominence by actually uncovering criminal acts. I would speak of the majesty of God and the good works His angels undertook. But those were just words. Jehoel embodied their significance.

Jehoel observed and controlled a significant segment of the intelligence-collecting community within the City. I took pride in him in the way a son looks up to his father. I was proud to know him. At his prompting I muted my usual complaints and started working harder to make the most of what I had achieved so far, regardless of how I had achieved it. If my work also reflected well on Jehoel, I was glad for it. For the first time since joining the Servitude, I was happy to know that I was involved in contributing to someone's successes. Not in the way I had deluded myself I was doing with Simon. I could see that now. This was something real. As my mentor, Jehoel showed me the most expedient means of collecting information and streamlining analytical processes, eliciting praise from the Minister himself on several occasions. In my heart, I credited Jehoel's good counsel for the rise of my star within the ministry.

I came to know him and his family well through the frequent visits I made to his home. His wife, Monica, was an ideal angel, who obviously cared deeply about her husband and was even more attentive to their son, Phanuel. They became my friends. They cared for me in a way I had never known with anyone else. If I visited their home, I was always welcomed. I would play with Phanuel. I would talk into the night with Jehoel and Monica. Jehoel would allow me whatever time I required, sharing with me not only his insights on the bureaucratic world, but also his personal feelings on whatever topic caught our fancy. It seemed strange to them that I did not spend much time with my own family and, for Phanuel's sake, I was careful not to denigrate Angra or reveal my disdain for him.

Considering his tender years, Phanuel was a prodigy with numbers and had an amazing aptitude for science, but the boy was frail for his age and did not possess the martial qualities required of sons of the realm. When the time came for him to begin school, he struggled with his early physical education, while simultaneously blowing every other student out of the water with his academic achievements. I could sense Phanuel's frustration with his own physical limitations. I could also see the results of other children's rage at not being able to compete with him mentally. Jehoel was a good father and never showed any outward signs of frustration over his son's lack of physical prowess. But inwardly, it ate at him. I could sense it, when he spoke of his hopes for the boy. In a kingdom that celebrated war above all else, a boy was first expected to demonstrate his ability with the sword and the spear before being given a chance to impress the world with his aptitude for cerebral feats. Brains only amounted to so much, I am afraid.

"Phanuel will be left behind," Jehoel confided in me one evening. "There's nothing I can teach him of science, or physics, or math. He is already a better mathematician than I could ever be," he said, laughing into his uneaten dinner. "But damn this City, where war means more than the achievements of the finest intellect!" he growled.

I ignored the blasphemy. "Let me tutor the boy," I said in a sudden epiphany.

Jehoel looked up. I could immediately sense his resistance.

"Now, believe me when I tell you this," I began. "You have humbled me as no other angel has. I started down a dark road, but you pulled me back from the edge. I am indebted to you for this. More than I can express."

Jehoel did not look any more convinced than he had earlier.

"But my talents also lie in places that do not involve deception and ingratitude," I went on.

Jehoel smiled.

"I spent my fair share of years in the army. I can fight well and have done so for God. I would consider it an honor, if you let me train the boy."

"I would not want to burden you with my problems, Ahriman," Jehoel said. "Phanuel will have to make do with what God has given him." He ground out the last few words.

"It is no burden," I assured him. "In fact, I would be happy to undertake the responsibility. I am certain that if I could get him on the right path from the very outset, he will blaze his own trail. He certainly does not lack motivation."

Jehoel was still uneasy. "It would not be proper for you," he said hesitantly, "with your...for someone of your class...to train the boy."

"Nonsense. If I can be your junior, can I not teach Phanuel as his senior? Besides, we are both of noble lineage."

I paused and looked at him. He was apparently conflicted by something.

"What is it, Jehoel?" I inquired. "There is no harm in me training the boy, is there?"

"No, no, there isn't," he said waving me off, as if he had just convinced himself. "You are right, of course. Monica!" he shouted out. "Ask Phanuel to come to the parlor!"

When the boy came in, he asked him, "Would you like Uncle to train you with your sword, spear, and shield?"

"Yes, Papa!" he shouted. The idea seemed to have instant appeal for him. "That would be wonderful!"

"Wonderful indeed!" I exclaimed, surprised by my own delight.

"Good. Now go get ready for bed." Jehoel kissed the boy on top of his head.

Before leaving the room, Phanuel came around the table to me and said, "Thank you, Uncle."

I looked at him and patted him on the head. I could see Jehoel in him. "You are welcome," I told him. "Be ready for me tomorrow, when your papa comes home from work. We will start before your dinner."

"Yes, before dinner, Uncle. Very clever," he said, before running out of the room.

"He is a good boy," I murmured.

Jehoel shook his head.

"You are lucky," I declared.

"Lucky," Jehoel repeated absently to himself. Then he looked at me. "He recognized in your offer a way of overcoming something he has been struggling with all along."

I smiled. "Much the same way I had recognized in you a way to deal with something I had been struggling with."

"Strangers and friends?" Jehoel asked.

"Friends," I confirmed. "I knew the minute you first spoke."

"Now that is an exaggeration!" Monica quipped, coming into the parlor. "Jehoel was just telling me how much of a brat you were, when you two first met."

We laughed. As a family laughs together, I imagined.

⌘　⌘　⌘

Working with Phanuel, I gained the son I never had. In the evenings, we would work on his swordplay and defensive posturing. I incorporated his interest in history with the rigors of combat. Though initially a bit sickly and weak, he ultimately showed great promise and later demonstrated an amazing ability to hit moving targets with his bow while on horseback.

"You are as dangerous as a trimmer with that bow and arrow," I complimented him one evening, as we worked out in a training corral.

"Do not teach him that," Jehoel said, looking up for the first time from his paperwork.

"Sorry," I said. My time in the army often made my language a bit saltier than was good for a young angel's ears.

"What else do we use weapons for, Father?" Phanuel asked, confused by Jehoel's objections. Jehoel gave me a look. He was the boy's father. Not I.

"Let us continue, Phanuel," I urged. "We have much work to do."

I wanted to train the boy, but I also wanted to make sure I recognized what was appropriate and what was my own. I did not want to overstep any bounds and knew Jehoel to be more sensitive than I was to these matters.

Discovering skills he had not known he had gave Phanuel an instant boost. Yes, he still struggled with some of the physical aspects of combat, but his sponge-like ability to soak up tactics and strategy ultimately propelled him to the forefront of his class. With time, he outgrew his boyhood weaknesses. He may not have been a strapping angel, but he did have the necessary skills now to get him past his military boards and proceeded to advance immediately to the junior-officer corps academy, something unusual for a citizen from Phanuel's social background. Jehoel, now being considered for the position of Minister of Information, seemed conflicted by his son's desire for army life.

"You would be better suited to the laboratory than the battlefield," he told Phanuel one night.

"I will do my duty," he replied, looking at me, "and come back to do the work you wish for me, Father."

Jehoel had caught Phanuel's glance in my direction. While he was undoubtedly impressed by his son's academic achievements, he continued to harbor mixed feelings about my training the boy to kill.

"He is a good son," I said, when Phanuel had left and we were alone.

"Good for you. Not as good for me," Jehoel sneered.

I left it at that. I did not delve any deeper.

⌘　⌘　⌘

Throughout this time, I continued as head of PID. Jehoel helped me evolve sufficiently to see my job as one of substance and I knew that my good work was of benefit to the City and God's realm. Yet I felt completely unfulfilled at the end of each day's work. My good fortune under Jehoel's counsel was not enough to quench my desire for further advancement. Living in an affluent section of the City's Northeast Quarter, I would come home every night and brood over what I could have done that day to better my chances of promotion. I wrote constantly in journals, shaping my theories as to how I would lead the realm to greater glory in the eyes of God. I became a virtual hermit, absorbed in my thoughts, neglecting even Zoan. I went to see him only when he summoned me. I felt I was slipping back down some path I did not want to tread. I became despondent and began thinking that if ever I was going to make the plays I had in mind, I needed to do something soon. What made it all the more difficult for me was the fact that I could not share my thoughts with Jehoel. I would have to stretch myself farther, aim higher. Simply submitting a good report or showing up at a function tailored in my father's and grandfather's name for the social elite was not enough anymore.

When Jehoel was promoted to Cherubim and Minister of Information, my hopes soared.

"The higher you rise in government, the more information you are privy to," he said to me when I congratulated him. The more information you are privy to, the more like God you are. Even though each citizen is supposed to be striving to be more like Him, no one ever truly has the ability to reach this goal. In this very odd way, God is always assured of the citizens' devotion." He looked at me. "You will stay with me, then?"

"Of course I will." I was surprised at his question.

"There is no automatic promotion, Ahriman," he said quite seriously. "The best angel for the job gets the head of NID. You understand that, right?"

"I understand," I said, a little taken aback. I did not expect him to throw the title at me, but I had also not expected him to warn me to brace myself for bad news.

"The position will remain open as long as I need to make the proper inquiries."

"I understand."

Now I was annoyed.

⌘　⌘　⌘

Not a single newspaper, placard, or herald's report was issued without my censoring it. In God's name, I determined what they read and heard, what they were supposed to read and hear. But my influence ended there. A PID official having access to classified information was considered a breach of security. Most certainly, the PID was not entitled to NID information. Though this rule was never strictly enforced, any such information in the hands of the PID was officially deemed a crime. So when information came across my desk that fit the established criteria for potentially being a state-security issue, it was my obligation to turn it over to the NID with all haste and move on. No investigation was to be conducted by the PID of any further leads in this direction. Any attempt to do so could result in a forced resignation, with potential charges being leveled against the culprit. Only the NID could investigate. If a legitimate issue were found to exist, the head of the NID, in consultation with the Minister, would bring in the Secret Police and devise a course of action.

As Minister, Jehoel recreated a firewall between the PID and the NID that had earlier existed only in principle. He was lauded by many in the upper ranks of the Servitude for stemming the massive and clandestine flow of classified information throughout the ministry. I was happy to respect this firewall, so long as I knew that Jehoel was considering me for the position of head of the NID. It would be of no consequence, once I was promoted. But as Jehoel continued to defer his decision, my dissatisfaction grew.

This indecision on his part came at the wrong time for me. I was already running out of my head with my work. This just made things worse. I was faced with real situations, where I received information that fit Jehoel's newly revised criteria and burned with envy as I was forced to turn the case over to the acting head of the NID, some buffoon Jehoel had worked with previously. The fact that I had to make my reports to this oaf made matters that much more difficult. I began making personal and, when rebuffed, official offers to assist in NID investigations. My requests were all turned down.

"You are in the PID for a reason," Jehoel grumbled at me one afternoon. "Only God Himself has the power to change the course and direction of your career."

I did not know what he meant, but was sure he was keeping something from me. I felt doubly betrayed. Both Jehoel, my friend and mentor, and the system were cheating me. I began to slip back onto the miserable path he had pulled me away from. I began to burn for a way out.

When I failed to impress the ministry with my skills and talents as a leader and a patriot, I began to unleash my frustration on my staff. I hounded them day and night to retrieve information that I would be compelled to share with the NID. The meatier and juicier the lead, the more I wanted it. It seemed logical to me that the more cases I rooted out that ended in an investigation, the greater the likelihood of my securing the NID position. My efforts proved in vain.

"Yet again, you have neglected your responsibilities," Jehoel said to me at the Minister's Council one day. "I find your work product consistently lacking, Ahriman. You seek out cases, inappropriate cases, at the expense of your staff and at the risk of burdening the NID, I might add, while failing to complete the job for which you are responsible."

"But, Minister," I protested officially, "I have brought more leads to the NID than ever before."

"Your job is not to turn over leads," Jehoel replied, irritated. "Your job is to censor public information. Period!"

"Then make me the head of the NID!" I shouted.

I was completely out of order. Amused, other Council members murmured among themselves.

"This is not the place or time for this," Jehoel retorted sternly. "My decision will not be rushed. Your impatience is getting old. You seem utterly oblivious to the fact that by constantly complaining, you only draw attention to your disappointment."

He sat back in his chair. I could hear his next words even before they left his lips.

"Consider this a formal reprimand. It will be marked in your record of achievement. If you fail to properly undertake your responsibilities to this Council again, you will be removed from office and your commission in the Servitude discharged. Either you do good work as the head of the PID or you do not work here at all."

I was shocked. Whether I would be technically eligible for the NID position with a formal reprimand on my record was now a real concern. I went over it in my mind again and again, but could not understand why things were turning out this way. Surely, it was obvious to anyone who knew me that my talents were more suited to the detection of sedition, not to deceiving the public. In addition, my family name and social position would make it embarrassing for me to be passed over. In a world where your lineage and birthright meant more than your ability and devotion, I was relegated to a position that left me in a limbo, without the rewards of either.

I tried speaking privately with Jehoel about the matter.

"Are you deliberately trying my patience, Ahriman?" he yelled. "I have told you there is nothing I can or am willing to do. You have proved yourself to be an excellent handler and censor of information. But blame it on me, yourself, divine intervention, or whatever you like, I will do nothing to assist you in your efforts to obtain this promotion. My decision will be made on the basis of merit and merit alone."

"I do not understand this!" I yelled back at him. "You know, I know, the entire damned ministry knows that I have a hold on the largest network of spies and informants in the entire kingdom. The information I retrieve is used by nearly every ministry in this government. My contacts bring me sensitive information from around the entire realm and from within the very fabric of the government. And then I have to turn it over to someone else? What sense does this make?" I screamed. "What sense does it make to force the handler to turn over the information to a third party whom the spies do not trust? Explain to me the sense in purposely trying to create a product that is inferior to the one we all know I am capable of making?"

"Ahriman," Jehoel said, "sometimes you have to accept things the way they are. I am sorry, but you are trying to work against a system that feeds on its own inability to change. The system is how it is and nothing you can do will change that. What makes sense to you doesn't matter. Why can't you see that?"

"What I see is someone unwilling to do what is right for right sake!"

"What you and I think is right is irrelevant. It's what *He* thinks is right that matters."

"Surely, you cannot believe that!" I shouted.

I had come full circle.

In a rage that went so deep it gave him an air of unnatural calm, Jehoel replied, "That is blasphemy, Ahriman. You know and I know it's not what I believe that matters. God matters! You can't make yourself what you want in a system that is built to exclude you from it. Can't you see? All that God wants is to make things His way. He isn't concerned with your spy network, your career, or your ambitions in life. He is concerned with Himself and Himself only. You either work within the system or you don't. It's that simple."

"The only way to get anything done is in the system."

"Ahriman, you've been working outside the system since the day you set foot in this place! No more will I listen to your warped arguments about how breaching ministry protocol is not a breach of the law. You can fool yourself, but you're not fooling anyone else."

"You know what I mean," I pleaded. "I need to move on."

"There is a time and a place for everything, if you just look for it," he said enigmatically.

"This is about Phanuel, isn't it?" I muttered.

"Leave him out of this!" Jehoel snapped back. "It has nothing to do with Phanuel."

I had hit a nerve.

"I think it does."

Jehoel took two rather deep breaths. "Think very carefully about what you're about to do, Ahriman. If you decide to go that way, we are done. Listen to me now. You will not become the head of the NID. Someone like you cannot take that position. Things will be done as I see fit and no other way."

"Now you're talking sedition!" I shouted. "We are all lead by God's vision."

"Call it what you will, but I refuse to allow you to take me with you when you burn." He paused for a brief second before continuing, as if regretting his words even before he had uttered them. "No, no," he said, shaking his head. "I won't help you, Ahriman. Not this time. And I'm going to tell you this once more. You will not get the head of NID. If you so much as make a single move again toward getting yourself involved in the NID, I will personally see to it that you never work again in this government. I will also see to it that you are brought up on charges of dereliction of duty and receive the maximum sentence for your crime. Do you understand me?"

I mumbled "yes" and left. What else could I say? There was no way out. I felt ruined. The ministry would not get me where I wanted to go, no matter how hard I tried. And, as for Jehoel, he was not a friend. Not anymore.

CHAPTER NINE

No matter how I tried to wrap my brain around it, I simply could not see the wisdom in a system that worked only to keep me down. I had failed in the army, but that had been nothing like this. I could have continued on my way in the army, not getting what I wanted, yes, but making a career out of it. Slowly progressing. There was always some war waiting to be fought. The ministry was different. It was a constant battle, but there was never the satisfaction of a kill. When I had killed during my career in the army, that was it. Our foes were dead. When I killed in the ministry? Well, no one cared, except some doddering bureaucrat who did nothing useful with the information I had obtained for him. Where was the glory? Where was the meaning? After much reflection and not without the greatest of regrets, I turned to the only avenue I knew I still had open to me: my father.

Angra's connections, whether I chose to agree with them or not, were powerful and controlled parts of the City in ways I simply did not know or understand. They were not gangs of thugs posted at some dangerous street corner. They were far worse. Affluent and influential. But they were not noble. This distinction between my father and his connections made Angra a bit of a celebrity. The son of a Seraph had pull. And it meant that when he wanted something done that was, say, unsavory to a zealot like me, he knew where you could get your bread buttered so long as you were willing to pay the price. These people could pull the strings that had been perpetually beyond my reach in government. Jehoel had admitted as much to me when we first met. No, Angra could get me farther along my way than I could manage on my own and, irritatingly, he knew it.

⌘ ⌘ ⌘

The Northwest Quarter, specifically around the Seat of God, was a place I considered a boring wasteland of villas, crusty old estates, and high-class brothels for the ultra wealthy and powerful. But it was where I grew up. Where my mother and father continued to live. Walking its streets, knowing that soon, I would be asking Angra for help, I could not help but feel sad. I looked up to the towering Seat of God before me. Each quarter had its own palace that served as the beacon from which God could see all His citizens. But the Seat of God overlooked the entire city. Citizens got their bearings by it when traveling through any quarter. Seeing and feeling God's presence. From the balcony of my apartment in the Northeast Quarter, I could see the Seat of God commanding the skyline. At night, with nearly every window lit up, it was my beacon. A reminder of what I could achieve, if I put my mind to it and people stopped holding me back.

Angra was, no doubt, happily conflicted over my dilemma. He wanted me to fail, as he despised my grandfather's influence over me. And yet he also wanted me to succeed, so as to further his influence over whatever he conceived as being important. He feigned disappointment when I finally overcame the knot in my stomach and came home. He began working himself into a good bottle of ambrosia as I sat there and stared a hole into the fountain at the center of the peristylium.

"I knew we would have this conversation one day," he said, fumbling with the bottle and his glass, "for no matter how righteous you are, in the end, it is pointless to fight the system." He looked up from the bottle. "You cannot make things happen without the right connections."

"You know," I said, "you have spent so much of your life screwing people for the sake of gaining power and influence, I wonder, sometimes, whether you even remember who you are."

"Who I am?" he said with a loud belly laugh. "Surely, you must be joking! I know myself better than you can ever hope to know your own self." There was arrogance in his voice as he declared, "I am the angel that makes things happen. I am the angel that can break the grind that you find yourself in. If I choose to." He pulled the cork out of the bottle with a sudden pop. "Remember. *You* came to me." He eyed the cork. "And it didn't take you long, did it?"

"What are you talking about?" I asked, willing myself to care.

He poured himself a drink. "It didn't take you long to hit that wall again."

I turned away in disgust. "It is not like it was in the army."

"Oh yes, it is," he said, drinking down his first glass. "I am talking about your grandfather, though you don't want to listen. That angel you spent so much of your life trying to emulate. It didn't take long for his accursed name to block your path."

I could not answer. I wanted to say it was my fault. Angra would never understand the relationship I had with Jehoel. I hated Jehoel for feeding me to the wolves, but even in my semi-deluded state, I still would not believe that whatever had happened between us had anything to do with Zoan.

"Zoan!" he spat, with a total lack of affection or regard. He poured himself another drink. "Everyone loves him. The savior of the City, the father of its armies, killer of trimmers," Angra said with mock theatrics. "Loved and beloved by everyone— except those who know him best. Stepping down from the Order was the single most stupid act any angel has ever undertaken." He considered things for a minute. "But he must have had something on God, something that allowed him to be left alone with his estates and his family and his fame. Untouched."

Angra was lost in space now, washed in tired visions of hatred.

When he came out of his haze, he powered down his ambrosia. I looked at a glass nearby, wanting a drink nearly as badly as I wanted my sodden father to stop speaking.

"From the first, I was thwarted by Zoan and his self-righteousness." He looked at me and took another slug of ambrosia. "Just like you." There was almost pity in his eyes. "I recognized Zoan's curse right away. It's taken you a lot longer, though, hasn't it? Trusted in your friends, did you?" he said, suddenly changing his tone. "Trusted that you could do something to make a difference? Stupid boy! Trusting in a system that doesn't work and, I would venture to say, still harboring some trust, despite the failures it has brought your way."

I did not respond, but sat and stewed. "Why did you push me to the ministry, then? Was it to see me fail? I was already unhappy in the army. If that was what you were aiming for, I did not need another nudge."

"On the contrary," Angra said. "You've achieved all that I was hoping for. You're just too shortsighted to see *what* you've achieved. Look outside your own little world for a minute, Ahriman. Your position in the ministry gives you access to information ninety-nine percent of angels do not have. Information that is valuable to many."

"I have already been down that road. And you said little then. You were looking to see me fail. It seems pretty clear." I was sure of it.

"Never!" he shouted unexpectedly. "I was looking for you to learn!"

"The system is not meant to be used that way."

"Oh, come off it already, Ahriman! The system is broken. No matter how much wonder you have for God or His government, you will never be anything of consequence, if you work within the system." He took another drink. "Zoan's grandson or not."

I sensed an opportunity. "You said Grandfather must have something on God. What is it?" I was happy to deflect the focus of Angra's temper.

"I've spent so much time trying to find the answer to that question, boy," he said suddenly, far off again, but finishing off yet another glass. "But no matter whom I pay off or whom I reward with some largesse, I've yet to figure it out. He is a moral angel, your grandfather, no doubt." He gargled through his next drink. "Like you. But only on the outside. What's he got on God? Whatever it is, it was enough to save his own neck. Your perfect grandfather."

"But he loves God! It is evident in what he stands for."

"He's a fake," Angra said, swirling around the last dregs of his next glass. "Listen to him. He has no love of God. No love of country. Talk to him and ask him. He will tell you nothing directly, but you can tell. So deranged is he that he's consented to suffer a burden of silence in order to protect us. Us. The angels who have the least reason to love him."

"I love Zoan and I have every reason to love him."

Angra laughed heartily again. "Fool yourself, if you want to. Had the same situation been presented to me, I would have chosen differently. No one refuses God and walks away, unless whatever he possesses is incredibly powerful. I would have used it," he said, making a fist, "and made myself powerful too." He finished the bottle of ambrosia and looked at me sullenly. "And whether you'll admit it or not, you would do the same."

⌘　⌘　⌘

"Without power, there is no order. Without order, there can be no state." Gabriel spoke out very clearly from the podium of one of the City's most populous gathering places. I stood there with Zoan among the crowd. My grandfather liked to listen to Gabriel whenever he spoke in public, though he made no similar efforts to attend events where God made His personal pronouncements. God spoke so seldom to His people. But Gabriel was different. And I guess I could understand why Zoan would want to attend.

The Northwest Quarter of the City may have been where the Seat of God and the Senate were situated, but it was definitely not the place usually chosen for a public address. Too dangerous. Too many angels too close to the center of government. But it did not really matter where the crowds were addressed. They would cheer, regardless. They were intimidated, paid, or urged too well in the right direction. The words were carefully chosen and always the same: God was responsible for protecting His people from whatever evil lurked outside. "Make your state powerful and you make yourselves powerful." God's agents stood in the crowds watching. The crowd. Us. No one knew where they stood. I did. Zoan did.

"You are only as good as your word, my boy," Zoan said quietly and almost inaudibly.

"What was that, Grandfather?" I was not sure he had even addressed his words to me.

"I am sorry that you had to find out this way. I'm sorry that I am the cause of your life's angst. But I am an angel who believes in the individual. That the 'glory' God speaks of is not to be found in Him, but in His people. In each and every one."

I quickly shot a look around at the crowd. At the soldiers. I was shocked that he would choose to utter such blasphemies in public.

"Grandfather, be careful," I whispered, trying to hush him.

Gabriel continued with his speech, completely unaware of our presence.

"They will do us no harm. I am Zoan, Seraph of God, remember?" he said sadly. "But I am also an angel who thinks the state should work for the benefit of its citizens, not the other way around. 'Be powerful for the state,' He says. What is power if you use it to no good end?"

"Grandfather," I pleaded. "This is not the time or the place."

"There is no better time," he said. "Look around you. The people look to me. To their hero. What better time is there than now?"

"There are agents all around us. We will be arrested!" I gasped, looking around at every eye trained upon us.

"You have grown up under God's rule, as agreed. In doing so, you have allowed Him to get what He wanted. His revenge. You were raised in a society conceived of and built by God. I have watched you become His soldier and now His Servant, coveting power, like He says," Zoan said, gesturing up to the spot where Gabriel spoke. "What a world, where I see my own grandson raised by the rule of God rather than by the rule of reason!"

"Please lower your voice," I said, trying again to quiet him down. I knew he was growing unstable, but I had not been prepared for such a public outburst.

I charted a path for us out of the crowd. It was little use. People were already looking at us.

"It couldn't have been any other way, Ahriman," he said, looking up at Gabriel again, as we hurried through the throngs.

Zoan seemed so weak. Weak like I had never seen him before. "Your grandmother, your father...our family..." He could not finish his sentence. "You swear allegiance to Him. That one," he said, pointing up at Gabriel, "and the filth He spews. Spews from the mouth of the one our entire nation fears with such love."

"Listen to me," I said, grasping him tightly by the arm and forgetting myself. "The angel you refer to is my master and will always remain so," I said in a voice I kept down with difficulty. "The angel you refer to is your master too." I checked myself. "You are lucky your blood pumps through me this day, as it spares you your life!" I spat out.

He watched me, emotionless, as I literally dragged him out of the crowd.

"You know not to bring this to me. Yet you take this moment, of all possible moments? Why? Why do you force me to play this game with you?"

I did not expect an answer. I was too infuriated. But it was like yelling at a child who knows he has done something wrong, but does not quite know what it is.

Once down a side street, I stopped, straightened myself up, and released his arm. He stared at me blankly and his look hurt me to the core.

"I am going to make it, despite you!" I growled. "I am going to succeed. And I will take great pleasure in knowing that, at least, I can share in that part of God's revenge."

I did not know what I was talking about, but I knew my words would hurt him.

I walked away. Gabriel was not finished and I am sure that my sudden departure had caught many eyes. I hoped God would forgive me for my rudeness to His one true Seraph. At least, Gabriel was loyal.

Father stood in the doorway of our house as I approached. He must have read the anger in my eyes.

"He told you something, didn't he?" he asked with a tantalizing look.

"No," I said, after thinking for a moment. "Not anything I understood, anyway." I paused for another moment, swallowing hard. "You were right. About him."

"I had the same conversation with him years and years ago," Angra said with a twisted smile. "A traitor to our state and a coward for giving up what he believed in most."

It took a lot for me to admit that my father was right. It was such an unnatural and contemptible feeling.

"Come with me, boy," he said, patting me on the shoulder and handing me a glass of ambrosia as we walked in through the front door. "Let's see what sense we can make of your mess."

⌘   ⌘   ⌘

Very little could be done directly. God's power over the generals, ministers, senators, and various orders of angels was indisputable. He kept things this way to maintain order, to keep a proper grip on the government, the army, and the people. Whoever. Interfere with this system and you were as good as gone. The Secret Police would come for you in the night. Take your wife, your children, your dog. Never to be heard from again. Play the system correctly? Make points with God and push someone else out of your way? Get rid of such individuals on your own, the way I did at the PID? That was how you got where you wanted to go.

At least, that is what Angra told me. He opened my eyes. Put me in touch with a number of carefully placed angels of influence. Quickly, I came to understand that the information I was gathering in the PID was little more than noise. Noise purposely propagated by these angels, former government officials, to throw the likes of me off and down the wrong track. They lived in a kind of brotherhood, operating just on the cusp of government control, but with only their own collective benefit in mind. If something came up that was truly of interest to the state, they took full advantage of it. Soaked whatever money and influence there was. Making themselves look good in the process. If something came up that was subversive and illegal, they took full advantage of that too. Only, in such cases, someone else was framed, was made to take the blame. Again, making them look good. It was amazing. Either way, they came out on top. They made money and accumulated power by donating land to the poor, while hanging the cheated rightful owner out to dry.

Angra was home among these angels. As a child, I had seen them only as my father's friends. As a despondent government nobody, it only took one meeting to see them as salvation.

CHAPTER TEN

I met my father and an angel named Mastema in a café some blocks from the Senate house one afternoon. Mastema was a well-known, but infamous figure, having made his way through the Ministry of Information himself, with a well-deserved reputation as a hardliner. He was an alumnus of the very position I now held and had presided over the PID during a span of years that had unofficially seen great civil unrest within the City. Later on, his many investigations as the NID head had led directly to the purging of several ministries. At the conclusion of a very public trial, over fifty angels were executed for sedition and some twenty-five others damned and banished to the outlands. Mastema was respected and feared. A true civic leader.

But that was only his public persona. He had retired early to the public sector, maintaining his grip on the largest and most valuable stable of contacts, informants, and spies in the realm. Tunneling into both legitimate and, shall we say, competitive enterprises was his specialty and he made huge profits from both endeavors. Many of the informants I had thought I owned were actually on Mastema's payroll. Jehoel must have known this, but had left me shrouded in delusions of my own making, nonetheless. He knew I was harmless, a little fish swimming in a big river, as Mastema was my true, but unknown master, picking and choosing what pearls I got and what dead ends I came up against. You had to be impressed, no matter how you measured your loyalties to God. In a game of big stakes, Mastema was a player to be reckoned with. Next to our Seraph, Gabriel, Mastema was probably the most feared angel in the realm.

"So. Your father tells me that you are looking to make your way in the government," Mastema said now, pressing himself into the café seat. He watched my father reclining on the far side of the table.

"Indeed I am," I said hesitantly. I had not had the chance to introduce myself. With a lump in my throat, I continued. "I was hoping that with your help…"

"Why should I help you?" Mastema interrupted abruptly, looking me straight in the eye. He let the silence between us build up till it was palpable. He expected an answer.

"I…I am an angel who can get things done."

My father stifled a laugh. Mastema did not share his amusement.

"Surely, someone with your background understands that I don't trust you, if I don't know you."

I hesitated for a second. "Fair enough. But if one half of what Angra has told me about you is true, you already know more about me than I know about myself." Indeed, this was truer than I really wished it were.

"Do you trust yourself, then?"

I thought for a second. "No."

"I know you're motivated, Ahriman," Mastema said, still staring into my eyes. "That can be dangerous to an angel in my position."

"True, but it depends on what spurs my motivation. You know that I push my people to do good work, but that even in this dedication, I find my position boring and deficient for my purposes."

"So what?"

"So you know I am not frivolous."

"Mm."

"And you know that I am an angel who takes care in his work. That is not something an angel in your position can afford to be missing."

Mastema smiled for the first time. "What else?"

"You know my father and the noble birthright he gave me."

"I'm not interested in your pedigree, boy," he said, reverting to his original stance. "You could be of the highest noble birth in the realm. It means precisely nothing when it comes to understanding loyalty."

I scrambled to think. Who was this angel? This was someone looking for a blood oath, not a bureaucrat's proficiency report. In an unexpected way, I realized Mastema would judge me on my own merit and ability, not on the basis of where I came from, the people I knew, or the circles I socialized in. Here, I was the commodity. My devotion meant nothing.

"Look, Mastema," I said. "My noble birth is not what makes me who I am. You have come here, knowing that I am an angel who can get things done. Fine. But what you did not know until today was that I have the will to disregard the rules to achieve a higher purpose. That I will not allow rules and regulations to come between me and my destiny."

Mastema perked up.

"Power is everything and, sometimes, to gain that power, you have to do the wrong thing for the right reason." I paused for moment. "You would not have agreed to meet with me, if you had not already sized me up and realized I am of some value to you."

Mastema looked at my father who smiled and nodded, as if acknowledging a lost bet. I made a brief mental note and tried to bury any anger.

"Surely, you understand that simply by my giving you information, the kind of information you want, at any rate," he said, looking back from Angra, "I create a situation where you have leverage over me?" Mastema's face softened.

"I understand."

"Do you?"

"What sense would it make for me to make a move on you?" I asked, regaining some of my self-control. I had promised myself at the beginning of the meeting that I would not lose my nerve. I was teetering on the edge of doing so. "With such a well-informed friend and mentor, I would be a great fool to think that I could stand to gain more from betraying you than by befriending you."

"I can be a very good friend," he said, reclining in his seat for the first time. "But we must first have an understanding. I understand you to be a determined angel. But I am unsure if you have the stomach to go down the road I'm offering you. In your determination, you have worked mostly within the system's limits. Yes, a few indiscretions here and there."

"'Here and there,'" I repeated. "I have used powers God gave me as His servant to do harm to others. How does that amount to nothing but an indiscretion?"

"That is to be expected," Mastema said. "The system wears you down. It's designed that way. But unlike most angels in your position, your indiscretions were motivated by boredom and self-flagellation, not greed. And in the world we live in, that almost makes you revered."

I was not impressed.

"Nevertheless," he continued, "you've come to the great dead end. That's what God wants. That's what the entire system is designed to do, especially for angels like you who are driven to more. You come to me with what you see as renewed determination. It's new. It's blasphemous. It's intoxicating."

He was right. I felt a little queasy.

"I'm someone well equipped to help you, yes. But now you look to gratify your ends, the ends that you had trained your sights on, until now, from *within* the system, in ways you will not be able to retreat from. It isn't easy to jump from one side of the line over to the other and then back again, even for someone as determined as you are. Don't fool yourself into thinking you can. Determined angels have both qualities and failings. On the one hand, they will stop at nothing to *achieve* what they desire. But on the other, they will stop at *nothing* to achieve what they desire." He leaned forward and looked at me again. Deep into my eyes. Again. "So do you see how serious I am, when I ask you if you understand?"

My devotion to God and His state had buoyed me throughout my brief career. Now it was that very same devotion holding me back from what I wanted most. To stray from "the true path" would mean never again fully returning to its fold. I would be giving up something I had held dear. Angra hated Zoan for having done the very same thing and I was a bit surprised at myself, when it took me only a second to decide.

"I'll swear by whatever you want me to in order to gain your confidence." I said it and meant it. If I had only known what I was truly saying, maybe I would have given it more thought. "A life with no evil," I said, smiling at my father, "is a life bereft of virtue."

At this, Mastema took my hands.

Angra remained unmoved, but watched intently, devouring the fact that his rebellious and hateful son was falling into the very web he had fought so strenuously to avoid.

Looking directly into my eyes, Mastema said, "I want you to swear allegiance to me, as your father had done before you."

"I swear my allegiance to you," I replied.

"I want you to swear to me that in exchange for my fellowship, you will give yourself fully to me," he demanded.

"I swear that you are my overlord," I replied.

"I want you to swear to yourself, on whatever you consider sacred, that you will live up to your allegiances and that you will do my bidding without question."

"I shall."

"Like in any other organization, the more you achieve, the higher up you will go. The higher up you go, the more power you accumulate. The more powerful you are, the more you can shape the City as you see fit."

In my heart, on my soul, as I could no longer swear on my honor, I agreed.

Mastema lingered for a moment, searching my eyes and, through them, my heart. Surely, he could see through the window of my soul and read what was written there: *This angel will betray me*.

"Good," Mastema said, finally releasing my hands.

Angra leaned over and patted me on the back.

I wanted to strangle him. He had finally got what he wanted.

"That's taken care of." Mastema resettled himself in his seat, seemingly pleased with the outcome of events. "I'm going to give you something big right away. I'm going to allow you to decide what to do in exchange for a particular favor. You have never had direct access to this information; so it will surprise you."

I swallowed hard. One never knows just how to react in these situations. Should I be thankful for being thrown what this angel surely considered to be nothing more than a bone? Or should I be graver in my response to the implied importance of the information? I opted for the latter.

"You know my background and my experience in rooting out troublemakers," Mastema continued. "This situation, this information, rather, concerns something that might be regarded as nothing short of rebellion. Since the purges, I have not heard of a conspiracy as organized and focused as this one. If it's what I believe it to be, the information I refer to has the potential to propel you far. If my information is correct, this plot involves some of the most high-ranking officials in the Ministry of Information. If the situation is not handled with the utmost sensitivity, it could lead to a serious black eye for God and his newly evolving plans."

I did not understand what he meant, but did not, frankly, expect to.

"If maneuvered cleverly, this situation will almost assuredly bring you into God's good graces."

I could not fathom the significance of the matter Mastema referred to. I had been Director of the PID for many years and had gone to great effort to uncover as many plots, conspiracies, and schemes as possible in the hope of seeing my own star rise. But never in the course of that time had I encountered anything as significant as the situation I was being told about. I looked to Angra for elaboration.

"Mastema is right, Ahriman," my father said. "I initially got wind of this matter through my own networks operating among the construction crews of the south wall. One of my agents came across information that would later lead Mastema's people to discover a cell."

Mastema shot Angra a foul look. Apparently, my father had said too much.

A moment later, my new mentor continued, "If you remember, several weeks ago, you received information that a group was meeting in secret."

While his knowledge of my personal business might have astonished me an hour earlier, it now seemed inevitable that Mastema had something to do with it.

"You took this information," Mastema continued, "and, much to the Minister's chagrin and indignation, made waves about running the investigation yourself." He looked at Angra. "Though the boy may not remember which set of waves I'm talking about."

The two smiled together at my expense.

Mastema looked back at me. "By doing so, you drew attention to the cell. As a result, they completely shut down operations. In short order."

Suddenly, I felt silly. In my desire to achieve notoriety, I had compromised the very investigation I was clamoring to participate in. Perhaps Jehoel was right about me.

"Don't feel too bad," Mastema said, noting my dismay. "Without making mistakes, how could we learn?"

"I guess," was all I could say. I felt so utterly stupid, it was all I could manage for the last several minutes of the conversation.

"Well said," Angra laughed, gesturing to the waiter and ordering a bottle of wine.

"Ambrosia," Mastema said, intercepting him. "I think the occasion calls for it," he added with a cocked smile.

Then he turned back to me. "You won't do that again," he continued. "Wipe it off your mind. You know better now. And there was an upside to all this."

I thought for a moment. "There is a leak within the ministry," I ventured. "And it could well be at the Minister's Council level, given the few people who have access to such information."

"Right," Mastema said with quiet satisfaction. "He's not as stupid as you suggested, Angra."

My father shifted uneasily in his seat.

"We don't know yet who is involved," Mastema continued. "It could simply be someone selling information, looking to make a quick buck with..." He paused and looked at my father.

With the greediness of a child ripping into a gift, Angra was busy opening the bottle of ambrosia he had just been handed. No point in including him in the conversation.

"...let's just call them my competition," Mastema concluded, clearly annoyed with my father.

"But it could also be someone ensconced in the cell's operations," I said, ignoring the pop of the of ambrosia bottle's cork.

"Yes. That is a possibility," Mastema said, focusing his attention back on me. "If that's the case, it seems this unidentified person—or persons—has only limited control on the south side of the City."

"How did you come to that conclusion?" I asked.

"Let's just say that's information you don't need to know. What's important is that once I saw the cell's response, I terminated your communication with the contact."

"You were prompting me with information only to turn it off, once an actual investigation began?" I asked indignantly.

"Don't you understand yet?" Mastema asked, impatience creeping into his tone. "If word leaked out, it means someone in the ministry doesn't want the case investigated."

"But they have already initiated an investigation."

"Ahriman, that's what we want." Mastema was exasperated now. He repositioned himself and motioned for me to lean over, closer to him, so that there was little chance of being overheard. "The only way to flush them out is to see where the investigation goes."

"Yeah, at my expense," I said, clearly unhappy with my unwitting role in the whole affair.

"What we were doing *for* or *against* you is irrelevant for our purposes now," Angra piped up suddenly. "What you should be concentrating on is the fact that Mastema has changed the course of the inquiry to fit your needs."

I felt like telling him to get back to his bottle. I think Mastema felt much the same way. Shushing my father, Mastema continued.

"The manner in which we were using you is, indeed, irrelevant. Had you performed your duties as the PID head, as you're supposed to, we might never have been able to set up the operation."

"That is why you consented to take me under your wing," I concluded.

Mastema picked up his freshly poured glass of ambrosia and leaned back in his chair. "I have decided you will be the one who goes in and roots out the cell."

The café was noisy. I'm sure Mastema had factored that into his choice of venue. No one even noticed us or overheard Mastema telling some bureaucratic lowlife that he was to circumvent all official routes to uncover an insurgent group bent on overthrowing the City of God.

"How am I to do that?" I asked feebly.

Looking back on it now, I felt like a child learning to walk. Up until that point, I thought I had seen and experienced enough to understand how things really worked. I had considered myself experienced, a veteran versed in the ways of Heaven. But in those few moments, as I sat there looking at these angels, the usual whirl going off in my mind, the scheming that made me the angel I was came to a halt. In a crowded bar, teaming with the City's residents, my mind was silent. For the first time in ages, my mind was silent.

"While you were being skinned by the Minister, my contact was able to make headway. But he is only a contact and I need him elsewhere."

"So tell me what I need to do," I said almost apologetically.

I gazed at my glass of ambrosia. It gazed right back. It was as inert as my mind.

"You're going to take a leave of absence."

This shocked me into attentiveness. Any time off, and I would be looking at another cycle before being considered for promotion. Then again, after my last run-in with Jehoel, promotion seemed unlikely, anyway.

"My contact will set you up. From there, it's up to you," Mastema concluded.

The silence in my mind ended and the whirl began once again. I made some quick calculations. How much of my career had been spent analyzing data and putting it into meaningless reports for some uncaring bureaucrat to take to a meeting and present those results to someone else who cared even less? How many times had I been rewarded for meaningless work? How many assistants to an assistant did you need before you realized that nothing was getting done? How many committees? Meetings? Brainstorming sessions and project managers? Here was an opportunity to make something change. I knew how to handle operatives. I had been doing it throughout my pathetic career. But now I would be the operative, wholly outside the constraints of the bureaucratic system and the very law that I had sworn to uphold.

"Now comes my part of this little deal," Mastema said, sensing my excitement. "I could have chosen someone else, but the fact is, I don't have anyone with your background and access. Your father coming to me with your problem was the obvious answer." Mastema leaned in to me again. "What I want from you is a book."

"What are you talking about? What kind of book?"

"I will get to that," he assured me. "You do realize, don't you, that our little bargain will be very lucrative for you, but will work to my benefit as well?"

"I worked that one out for myself, thanks," I said saucily. "But a book?"

"It may seem of little significance to you, but if my information is correct, this cell may be harboring an ancient book of inestimable value. No one really knows what it contains or where it came from. Or even what it looks like. But it is believed that it has powers beyond comprehension."

"Fine," I said, not wanting to seem too distracted by something so valuable to him. What would the book mean to me?

"You take down this cell and I get the book," Mastema said a little brusquely, marginally annoyed at me already. "Period. You take the glory and I get the rest."

As Mastema took his first sip of ambrosia, Angra was already ordering another bottle. I looked at my untouched glass. The exchange was unexpected. A book. Was my career really worth nothing more than a book? What could Mastema want with a book? Even if it was important, how could it possess such power?

"What you have to give up will be well worth the potential gain in the end," Angra said, somehow able to read the question in my mind, despite his impending alcoholic haze.

"Okay. I will do it," I said.

Mastema took my hands again in the same manner he had taken them before. He asked me, yet again, to swear that I would execute this operation and bring him the book in the end. Again, I swore to do so.

"You're dismissed, then. You will be contacted."

I looked at both angels as they began speaking in low tones with one another. Wholly ignoring me. As if we had not just concluded an important conversation. An important deal. As if I were not there at all. I got up to leave the café. As I reached the doorway and looked back to their table through the smoky air, I could see my father mouthing out, "If he only knew what he's got himself into." Mastema just laughed and I stepped outside into the daylight.

CHAPTER ELEVEN

A week later, I was granted a sabbatical from the PID. Though I had requested a leave of absence, a sabbatical allowed me the additional advantage of a government stipend for "research." No one actually expected you to research anything, but it did allow me to save face to some extent. When I had opened the letter, I was not sure whether Jehoel had taken pity on me and arranged for a less public exit or whether Mastema was truly that influential in the ministry.

I went to see Jehoel before I left. We had a short, terse conversation. Since our last meeting, Jehoel had grown increasingly distant, almost to the point of being unfriendly. I regretted the fact that our long friendship had come to an end and even went so far as to acknowledge the inappropriateness of my behavior. He accepted my apology with what was, clearly, skepticism and I felt it best to leave things well enough alone for fear he might take a greater interest in the purpose of my sabbatical than was healthy for me. I asked after Phanuel. Jehoel offered me his best wishes, but that was all.

A week later, Mastema's contact in the cell got in touch with me. Cyrus provided me with a full set of credentials, identifying me as a construction specialist transferred from the Northern District to work on the dilapidated southwestern walls. I was to be the foreman of a work crew. It was a good cover. As foreman, I did not have to demonstrate any real expertise in the field. It was widely known that construction specialists had cushy positions, with a rank and status admired by the common citizen for its relatively attractive pay and exemption from actual physical labor. Having already perfected the art of enjoying a sinecure, I surprised even myself at how quickly I fit in. Unexpectedly, my biggest issue turned out to involve deflecting constant, nagging questions as to why I had been demoted from my earlier responsibilities working on the northern walls.

"Bad attitude," I always replied with but a hint of sarcasm.

⌘ ⌘ ⌘

Much to my chagrin, I found myself commuting to the edge of the Southwest Quarter each morning. It was dirty, unkempt, and dangerous. And those were the quarter's more positive features. Few respectable citizens ventured there. For me, it was a bit of a shock, as I had spent almost all of my life in the Northern District and, if leaving the City, had traversed it through the main gates in the Southeast Quarter. It shocked me now to discover the appalling conditions of these sections. It was even more difficult to believe this was, indeed, part of God's City. Far from the administrative and cultural heart of everything, the Southwest Quarter decayed at the expense of the City's protection.

Years ago, God had begun a series of public-works projects to reinforce and even rebuild parts of the southern areas of the City walls. The implementation of these projects necessitated, however, the expulsion of thousands of residents from some of the poorest neighborhoods. Ejected into the outlands, most settled right outside the very walls they had once depended on for protection. These settlements below the walls made the City appear twice as large, when approaching the main gates from Elysium. Tired clusters of ramshackle dwellings, hardly more than slums, teeming with crime, hunger, and malcontent, heightened the dangers posed by decaying walls. The purpose of the wall was as much to hold the City in as to keep its former residents out. At some point, God had lost interest in His community-building efforts, handing them off to a minor official somewhere within an obscure ministry. In the end, the walls were strengthened, but it had become quite clear to the people of the Southwest Quarter that God had abandoned them in favor of more pressing interests.

In contrast, Mastema was a virtual hero in the Southern District. Though he had made himself a notorious and feared figure in the ministry, as a private citizen-business owner, he took it upon himself to ensure that the utilities of the Southwest Quarter remained intact and its people were fed. He was their savior. Their primary patron. Water and sewage had always been issues of abiding concern in the City. Rabid arguments, degenerating into fights, continued to be played out in the Senate over the subject of access to the Great Northern Forest's water. Maintaining the aqueducts that fed the City from the Acheron was a lucrative business. Through Mastema's connections and sponsorship of public-works projects, he had elevated himself to celebrity status. His tours through the Southwest Quarter and the cheers that serenaded him resembled a victory parade. The neglected poor would show up in the tens of thousands, hundreds of thousands, perhaps. No doubt, this level of adulation made many in the government quite uneasy. But Gabriel was seemingly willing to overlook Mastema's popularity in exchange for his secret funding of wall construction. And God was apparently content with him keeping the people happy, while the City took credit for keeping trimmers out.

"This work is shit," one angel named Deven told me one day, as we toiled in the morning heat.

The teams had grown to love me, as I worked alongside them out in the sun. I suffered as they did and availed of few of the perks my position entitled me to. Whatever I had, I shared with them. And they accepted me readily.

"Why is that?" I now asked Deven, as I sized up the stone we were about to lift into position in a rather decrepit section of the wall. "It may be miserable and hot, but at least, it is unpleasant."

The angels laughed.

"Always sarcasm with you," Deven remarked. "Tell me again how you got here," he said, winking at the angels looking on.

"Sarcasm," I replied.

They laughed.

"Why is this work shit?" I asked again.

"Think about it," Deven said. "When was the last time trimmers attacked this section of the wall? Actually, come to think of it, when was the last time trimmers attacked the City anywhere along the wall?"

It was a reasonable enough question.

"We hear about trimmer attacks all the time, but when was the last time any of us actually saw a trimmer?"

"I've seen my share of outlanders," Cyrus piped in. "But that was during my days in the army."

I shot him a severe look and he quickly shut his mouth.

"There are attacks on the wall all the time," I said, turning back to Deven and carefully toeing the government line.

As head of the PID, I knew that few, if any, trimmer attacks had ever been confirmed along the walls. Trimmers had lost interest in directly attacking the City long before I even joined the army. More often than not, an "attack" amounted to one of the hovels constructed against the City walls going up in flames after being singled out for some Secret Police raid. Once that information hit my desk, it was quickly converted into a trimmer attack. The City would rally behind God. He was doing the right thing. For all of us. More taxes would be collected. The conspirators would be caught and beheaded, their heads later adorning the walls at the site of the fracas. The people would suffer. Until the next attack. That was what I was paid for. That was my job.

"Ah, you're a believer," Deven said.

Cyrus looked more skeptical.

"I am a believer," I affirmed.

"And yet you're here," Cyrus observed.

I looked around at the team. All had stopped work to listen in.

"We are all God's servants," I said. "Some of us are here to serve Him by building His walls. Others are here to fight for the City and for God's Word. Still others are here to sit in the Senate and represent us citizens in God's eyes."

"Oh boy!" shouted Deven. "Here's a side we haven't seen!"

"Well, that is who I am," I said. "Sarcasm and all." I leaned in closer and lowered by voice. "One thing the Southwest Quarter is not lacking, Deven, is soldiers." I nodded to a heavily armed Wall Watcher approaching. "I would keep my thoughts to myself. Unless you would rather be spending your days in a City jail. Or worse."

Deven quickly shut up, but probably too late, I thought.

"Let's get back to work, boys," I shouted, as the Wall Watcher walked by with his weapons and armor clanging along.

State security forces were omnipresent in the Southwest Quarter as, unsurprisingly, the City's unofficial history recorded many uprisings that had sprung from there. Theories in higher political circles posited that the state of the infrastructure made it easier for trimmers to infiltrate this part of the City. The thought that a citizen could actually rise up without some sort of illicit external instigation was inconceivable to your average angel. You did not necessarily have to love God. If you feared Him, that was enough. Those of us in the ministry knew better.

We went back to work.

That is how my days went. We would repair part of the wall. Day by day. Build a guardhouse. Take rest where we could, when the heat of the day was at its height. Talk to the locals. Watch, as City soldiers stalked among us.

Building, bantering, and avoiding the soldiers. That was it. For a time. For a very long time.

⌘ ⌘ ⌘

"You will find that tapping into your anger with the system will aid you in presenting yourself as a convincing anti-government radical," Mastema told me one evening after summoning me to a quiet and nondescript restaurant near the City's main gates.

We were alone, but for the establishment's manager who frequently shot us looks of concern as he peered out the windows and up and down the street.

"But these people are crazy," I said, ignoring Mastema's comment and slapping a file folder down on the table. "Are these files the right ones?" I asked in hushed tones.

"What do you think?"

"I am impressed that you got your hands on Secret Police files," I said genuinely.

Mastema was pleased with himself. "It's easy to steal something that doesn't officially exist," he quipped.

I had no doubt he could access nearly any information he wanted.

"So why am I here?" I asked, focusing on the meeting at hand.

"I hope you're ready," he said, assuming what I had come to know as his serious expression. "Because tomorrow night is the night."

"I am ready."

"I like your confidence."

"I am sure I can convince a bunch of crazies I am the real deal. All I have to do is think like a bureaucrat. That is crazy enough for nearly anyone."

Mastema did not laugh. "Whether they are crazy or not, I would urge you to approach this matter with a little more gravity. This may be your only opportunity."

"I am ready," I assured him. "I read the files." I patted them with my hand. "I understand their aims. I have my story down." I turned it on him. "I just hope you do not leave me hanging," I said, thinking of my forged credentials.

"You worry about your part and let me worry about mine."

"We will see, then."

It was important that he believed me to be confident. My only real concern was a double-cross. Mastema was careful to make sure his lines of communication were clean. Angra, on the contrary, was careless. Tapping into my own little network of spies, at least the ones I was sure were not on Mastema's payroll, I came up with nothing. Nothing to show the people mentioned in the Secret Police file were anything short of crazy. I had no choice but to trust in Mastema.

"Just remember, there is almost as much risk in not asking enough questions as there is in asking too many," he said.

"I got it."

"I hope, for your sake, you do."

⌘　⌘　⌘

Cyrus led me through the Southwest Quarter after work the next day. We said little. Cyrus had proved himself to be a bit too open-mouthed for my liking; so it was just as well. We circled and backtracked many times to make sure we were not being followed. After what seemed like hours, we reached an innocuous building in which I was to meet the cell's contacts. Once inside, I was presented to a group of three inquisitors and told to refer to them as "Fallen," as if that were a proper name. Cyrus left me at the door with a pat on the shoulder.

I was questioned for several hours about my background, career, and political inclinations. I was well prepared. I had studied the Secret Police and NID files provided to me by Mastema's people. It was all rather bland really. If I had heard one story, I had heard a thousand. The cell was bent on overthrowing God. The only real note of interest was the group's unique claim of working toward re-establishing a democratic state. *Re*-establishing. That is, they rejected the fact that God had created the universe and Heaven and believed something had existed before Him. Not a movement so much as a cult, it seemed to me.

My own cross-examination of informants had prepared me for the many questions and by wedding my training and experience with my true vitriol for the system, I nearly convinced myself I was a dissident. Their questions were largely open-ended and designed to accommodate a considerable gray area, in the event, no doubt, I turned out to be a snitch. They gave nothing away. I gave what I calculated to be enough for them to recognize my interest, but not enough for them to suspect I was too eager. I was betraying God by conspiring to join a secret society dedicated to His downfall. What could be more dangerous than that?

I left the meeting feeling it had been all too easy. There was no mention of a book. But then again, why would there be? To the extent it existed at all. Whatever their persuasion, I prepared myself to absorb as much about the cell as quickly as possible.

⌘　⌘　⌘

I heard nothing for a long while and my life as a construction foreman became much more real than I had ever anticipated. The days were long and the work difficult. No one noticed when Cyrus left the crew. People did notice when Deven left the crew. I did not know what to make of either situation. So I articulated nothing more than my state-bound devotion to God. I did my best to strike a careful balance between the reality of my situation and the developments that had pushed me into this increasingly self-destructive lifestyle.

I had long since decided it was too risky to continue commuting to my actual apartment in the Northeast Quarter. So I took the apartment my foreman's stipend enabled me to afford in the Southeast Quarter, near the City's main gates. I returned to it every night to shed the weariness of the day's toil. It disgusted me a bit to admit to myself that I was purposely making myself suffer the discomforts of this place. Every night, I sighed as I reached the façade of my building and undertook the long ascent up the staircase to what I considered a hovel. Though I hated the place, I consoled myself in the knowledge that it was far more comfortable than the camp tents in which I had spent so much of my time as a soldier. I also reminded myself that the incongruity of the relative splendor of my real home and the grime and dirt that my work involved would have played too much on my mind as I lay in my bed at night, staring at the Seat of God. Besides, I could risk breaking my cover by going to my real home every night. To play along with whoever was watching, I varied my route to my rented home every night. I did so on the assumption that those keeping an eye on me would find my concern for my safety quite natural in the light of my recent contact with a seditious sect. So I made my new life and tried not to stand out as a loner. I was known simply as the foreman who lived on the twelfth floor, greeting those I met in the dark hallways, but never asking questions of anyone.

I had all but lost hope of getting any further in my quest, when I finally heard from the cell. Mastema had demanded an update as soon as I made contact, but I deemed it safer to make my way through the next phase without endangering myself any more than I had to. I received word, when I was reporting on my sabbatical research at the ministry, situated in a part of the City that, as a mere construction foreman, I had little business being in. Such was the danger of living a double life. On the one hand, I was expected to report back to the ministry on my status; on the other, I was expected to be managing construction teams along the southern walls. I felt fairly sure that I was being watched, but could not tell whether it was by Mastema's spies, the ministry, or the cell's Fallen. Or a combination of the three. I doubly regretted having to make my ministry reports, particularly as there was no expectation that I should actually conduct research, and I was sure any number of my construction crew and new neighbors gossiped about my periodic absences. I was also convinced that during all this time, the cell was checking on me, my apartment, my workplace, and any available information about me. I had no alternative but to trust in the sterility of my cover and while I assumed a confident stance in my interactions with Mastema, I knew it was most likely a matter of time, before someone noticed that I was really out of my element.

Fear gripped me when, returning to my foreman's apartment, I was met in my hallway by one of the three Fallen I had been introduced to so many weeks earlier.

"Are you often in the Northwest Quarter?" the Fallen asked, clearly knowing I had not been where he expected me to be.

"I was at my weekly foreman's meeting. I am a crew chief and I am required to report in," I said, not knowing whether this was true or not.

The Fallen turned and began walking down the hall.

"Wait!" I shouted after him. "Why are you here?"

"Do you really have to ask?" he said, turning around. He had a strangely blank face and I found myself seized by the absurd desire to ask him his name. "If you are still interested in what we discussed last time, be at two one five nought N Street, Southern District, Southwest Quarter, tomorrow, one hour after sundown. You will be met." He turned and walked to the stairwell. "Just make sure you are not followed," he said, disappearing down the stairs.

I stood in the semi-darkness, as the smile widened on my face.

CHAPTER TWELVE

Three members of the cell met me at the prescribed address. They did not introduce themselves as Fallen, but I believed it was understood. I immediately recognized one as an angel on my crew, but he said nothing to me that might acknowledge our connection. After being searched for a weapon, I was blindfolded and taken through a winding labyrinth of streets and alleyways. My escort did not speak to me and I could not tell how long we walked. As time went by, I noted that the sounds on the street had subsided and the smell of the ground beneath my feet had changed. It was not the same place where I had last met the Fallen. I could tell.

I rubbed my eyes for a few seconds when my blindfold was finally removed. It was a different building from the one where our last meeting had been held, but this one was just as nondescript and certainly decrepit. The smell from the house was dank. Almost like the odor of rot. No one could have lived there in an age, I thought to myself, as we walked up the steps and crossed through the dilapidated entryway. We walked through many darkened rooms and up a staircase or two. I could see that the rooms and hallways we passed were covered in debris and filth. The building had burned and had clearly never been reoccupied. God's reaction to disobedience was usually swift and order was always quickly restored.

Rats ran alongside us as we walked down the hallways, disappearing into other dark and infested corners. The house seemed to have no end, like a bad dream getting longer and darker and smellier, until it was nearly impossible to see where we were going. None of the stink or squalor affected my guides who obviously knew each turn by heart and were muttering to each other under their collective breath.

We finally came out of the building into a deep and damp alleyway. I stood confused and blinking for a moment, as even the darkened alley seemed so much brighter after the depressing passageway we had just traversed. The light of the stars above cast a gray pallor over the alley, as there were no streetlights anywhere in either direction for as far as I could see. For a few moments, I was struck by a sudden fear that I had been brought there to be killed. I wondered if they already knew my true intentions and were about to do away with me in this remote and forgotten section of the City. Someone has found me out—the thought crashed through my head and I began to sweat. But my guides did not seem to notice my sudden panic attack and they continued down the alley, as I tried as best I could to keep the banging in my ears down to a muffled roar.

We passed through the abandoned filth of the neighborhood. I wondered whether angels lived there. I saw no lights burning and heard none of the usual caterwauling that streaked across most of the Southern District at night. The streets were eerily deserted and smelled of rotting debris. We were so far into the quarter that I could not make out the Seat of God. I was as far from God as I could ever remember being. Even when I had been in the outlands, fighting the City's enemies.

When we finally reached a part of the City's walls, my guides stopped and stood silently in a line, staring at the wall. Their sudden pause caught me off guard and I waited for them to continue onward. But they stood there, staring at the wall, as if expecting something. I looked at the wall myself. It took me several seconds to realize that they look on what was, in fact, a metal door. Small, but ornate, metal carvings and welded figures adorned its outer surface. It was shaped like a giant heart, pushed into the bottom edge of the wall, severed from right to left across the center and bent ninety degrees, so that the lower portion lay smoothly on the ground and the two lobes stretching upward over our heads onto the wall. I could see no seams in its surface and wondered for a moment how it would open. The angel I had recognized earlier in the evening as a member of my construction crew stepped forward and began inspecting the door in the pale light. He examined the contours of the metal latticework, finally placed two fingers into the eyes of one of the more grotesque welded figures and one finger into its heart. Then he pushed. With a disturbingly sudden grinding noise, the ground portion of the severed heart slid into the wall. The gap revealed a featureless floor.

"You have now been shown the first step," said the angel. "You must learn to open your heart to what lies beneath the surface of things." Then he stepped back into line with the other two.

Another of the three moved to the right lobe of the door. He knelt down and, putting his hand into the dark opening in the ground, felt under the exposed edge of the door. A moment later, I heard a crack and the upright lobes of the door split in two. As the angel stood up and stepped backward to rejoin the line, the right lobe dropped into the wall a few inches, before sliding right and into the wall with a deep and muted clang. A short gust of cool air met my face. It smelled faintly of some fragrance I recognized, but could not place. In the little light we had, I could faintly make out the contours of an empty room behind the doors. I blinked for a moment, trying to clear my vision and see into the darkened chasm.

"You have now been shown the second step," said this other angel, once he had stepped back in line. Quietly, he added, "You must learn to trust yourself in opening your heart."

Finally, the last of the three stepped forward and knelt down next to the left lobe of the door. Unlike the first two, he did not search for a hidden lock, but closed his eyes and began speaking to the door. I looked at the others standing there. They stood with their eyes closed, murmuring quietly to themselves. After a few indecipherable recitations, they all began to repeat the same words, each time somewhat louder:

"Mizpah, for he said. May the Lord watch between me and thee, when we are absent one from another. Mizpah, for he said. May the Lord watch between me and thee, when we are absent one from another. Mizpah, for he said. May the Lord watch between me and thee, when we are absent one from another," they chanted.

The last remaining piece of the severed heart suddenly creaked to life and slid inward. The last angel stepped back into line with the others. The very floor of the room slid back into the wall, revealing a stairway descending into yet more darkness. This time, a great rush of cool and fragrant air hit me. It was not the cold air of a dank basement, but sweet and familiar, only so much more powerful than the last time. I felt thrown back to my childhood in that instant, as the air was released into the otherwise repugnant alley behind us. It lasted for only a moment, as the night quickly scooped up the sweet smells and carried them away across the City.

I was startled back to my immediate surroundings as the last angel spoke.

"You have now been shown the third step. You must learn to know and trust your brothers."

The three broke ranks and began making their way down the dark staircase. They gestured to me to follow them down. I complied.

⌘　⌘　⌘

The first few steps of the stairway were much wider than I had expected, much like those in God's temples that dotted the oldest parts of the City. I had to readjust my eyes to the sweet, inky darkness that enveloped me. I continued down and was startled into a consciousness of my situation with the sound of the heart-shaped door banging shut behind me. The moment the reverberations ceased, the stairway lit up as torches lining the stairway walls flamed to life.

The walls flanking the stairway were cracked and flaked with age. The stone must have eroded from lack of exposure to the air outside. From the upper levels of the stairway, I could see light and hear the unmistakable sounds of people below. It took a while before I could make out what lay at the foot of the stairs. There was a low, but persistent chanting in what sounded like a cavern-ous room below me. When I finally reached the bottom of the stairs, I stood upon a long, open landing that stretched out before me. Torches lined the hall into what my tired eyes interpreted as oblivion. Cut into the walls between the flaming torches were massive faces, the likes of which I had never seen. The carvings were clearly old, but did not match any period of antiquity that I was familiar with from my visits to the City's museums. The City had stood for untold millennia, to be sure, but looking at these sculpted faces, it seemed they had endured far greater oceans of time, worn down as they were from what must have once been a remarkable luster. They almost appeared sad, as if from the awareness that posterity was not allowed to know them, except in this dingy hallway, hidden in a labyrinth of sweaty and grime-layered back alleys.

"Interesting, aren't they?" a voice said softly from behind me.

It was not one of the three who had brought me there. It was someone else, standing in the shadows all around me.

"Who are they?" I asked, looking at the melancholy stone faces. I turned and squinted into the shadows behind me. "Who are you?"

"Fallen," he answered dismissively. "Do they interest you?"

"Of course they do," I replied, turning back to their stoic fac-es. "I have never seen anything like them." It was true.

"I do not imagine you would have seen such things before. These faces were carved a long time ago. Long before God came into being. They have stood here since the founding of the City."

"Long before God came into being?" I asked incredulously. "That is not possible." I rubbed a web of dust off the scruff of my chin. This was what I had come here for. "God made this city at the beginning of all time. Before you, before me," I said, looking back at the solemn faces. "Before the creation of the universe." I turned back to the figure standing in darkness. "Our City is eternal and its history is known to anyone who studies it."

I could make out the shape of an angel standing there.

"It is my job," the angel said, ignoring my comments, "to see to it that no matter what happens to our brothers, these images, the stone-carved heart of our brotherhood, and everything they stand for are safe."

"What makes them so important?" I asked. "I mean, their value is obvious from their age but...who were these people?"

"Oh, they are, indeed, valuable, but not in the way you might think. Our Heavenly Father would pay any price to have them," the shrouded angel said. "To destroy them."

"Why to destroy them?"

"You would not know their history, Ahriman. You studied hard and achieved much in the ways of our Heavenly Father, but you would never have read of these, for you have been taught a false history. These images are blasphemous in God's eyes, because they are the images of the true fathers of our City, the true makers of the universe."

I could not hide my surprise.

"These are the faces of those whom God unlawfully overthrew so that He could reign here in Heaven, alone, and become our Lord and master."

The angel stood by, as my mind raced. He expected this. I had not. I had prepared myself for a bunch of crazy people, to be sure. But these people *were* actually crazy. The only true history was the one God had handed down to us. The Lord, our God, had created Heaven and the universe over which He reigned, in His own way, with His angels as His faithful servants. This was different.

This was not merely disagreeing with God. This was denying Him. This was not just contradicting the Word of God. This was declaring God a lie. It just did not make sense.

"I know you are looking to see what I am going to do with this," I said to the dark angel, as I prepared myself for the next step. "You know I do not believe you, that I cannot believe you?"

"Then why are you here?"

Why was I there? For God and the good of all Heaven. Had I really lost sight of why I was there? These people were questioning God's dominion over Heaven. For carved stone, no less! Had I expected them to be anything other than crazy?

"Have you never asked yourself how you got here?" the angel continued. "Where you came from? How the universe was made and how this became the City of cities?"

I had no answer. Of course, one has questions about the past. But you do not doubt God in your questions. You accept what you were taught, because you had faith in God, faith in His Word.

"You are such a learned angel, Ahriman," the shadowy figure went on. "And you have never questioned dogma?"

"Dogma? There is no dogma. There is only the truth."

"You mean God's Word?"

"No, I mean the truth. I have come to know many things in my life, to be sure. But the scope of what you are suggesting? It defies..."

"It defies nothing," the angel said abruptly. "What is the truth? Is it what you have been told? Does that make it the truth? If it is written down somewhere for you to read, does that make it the truth? Who told you the things you know as the truth, Ahriman? Who wrote God's Word? Have you never wondered? Was the Word written by God's great hand or was it sketched by someone of flesh and blood, like you and me? You do not know and despite all your intelligence, curiosity, drive, you believe his Word is the truth. Without question. Despite what your senses, your logic would tell you, you do not question."

"I have known lies and truths. I deal with them every day," I said, forgetting for a moment that I was meant to be a construction specialist. "But nothing like this. Nothing that would make me wonder whether I am what I know, what I have always known I am."

"What you have always *thought* you were. Not known."

"No. I exist, because God made me so. Right?" I was not acting now. I spoke the truth.

"Then perhaps you have come as far as you can come tonight," the dark angel said without emotion.

My head swam for a moment. What was I doing? Wait, wait, wait! I had not come this far to throw it all out the window in order to discuss some philosophical point with someone who was clearly a madman. These were the people I needed to bring down, if I was to make a name for myself. For the benefit of all Heaven, for the benefit of God. That was why I was there.

"Look," I said, trying to get off the back foot. "If my presence here tonight proves anything, it proves that my heart is open to new things. Even things I have not seen before." I took a moment to reflect. "You cannot show me a few pieces of carved stone and then expect me to throw my entire belief system out the window. That cannot be how you recruit and convert people."

There were few sounds, besides the crackling of the torches. The chanting had stopped.

"Well, if nothing else, you have courage. *That* I must grant you," the dark angel said. "Coming down here into the bowels of your enemy, alone. With no one to get you out."

I found myself swallowing with a slight, but audible gulp.

"It is we here," he said in a louder tone, gesturing around to the surrounding shadows, "and we alone who will judge how open your heart is and where you will be allowed to place it."

He paused to see if I would gulp again. I had no doubt I would.

"No one has ever entered this room without opening their heart in one way or another," he said, unsheathing a long, curved knife. Its blade was finely polished, a fact I could make out quite readily, as it reflected the light cast down by the torches. "Your courage is a gift, but do not forget to respond with your heart as well as your head."

This was what I had wanted. This was what I had risked my life and career on. Infidels, non-believers set on the destruction of everything I knew to be true. Bringing an end to my history, my City. My God. I had to place myself in the hands of people I would have to know better than myself, but could never trust. I was a leader of spies, but I did not know what they did or, at least, how they did it. These people ate their enemies and drank their blood, some NID report had said, as a way of demanding obedience and perpetrating fear among those who might betray the cause.

"Shortly, you will be taken forward. I suggest that you reflect on what you are told this evening and prepare yourself to open your heart and mind. Remember the three steps and remember who you are."

He turned and disappeared, as if he had walked straight through the wall.

⌘　⌘　⌘

I was taken up a different stairway by two other Fallen and brought out onto another much smaller landing. Before me, behind a single long table, sat a group of twelve Fallen. Behind them, oil lamps burned, backlighting them so as to make the details of their features and expressions impossible to discern. They wore white robes, edged in gold and held tightly about their waists with a single, simple length of rope. All wore a small dagger in their belts, except the figure at the center of the table whose sword stood next to him, held up by a plain stand.

"Sit down," the one at the center requested. "I am Fallen. That is all you need know. We, at this table, wear white. White, to indicate our devotion. We are all brothers here. We are all Fallen. My brother to the left is named Fallen. My brother to the right is named Fallen. Do you understand?"

"Yes."

"Do you know why we are known as 'Fallen'?"

"I assume to hide your true identities from newcomers like me," I responded, confident I was both right and wrong. What was I meant to say? "While I have yet to understand your beliefs," I went on, "I do have some understanding of your ultimate purpose. Simply meeting here tonight is a punishable offense. Repeating what we must say is, surely, punishable too."

"You say 'yet.' What makes you think that you will ever come to understand any detail of my beliefs?" the Fallen asked.

It was a reasonable question. I had taken something for granted.

"Perhaps, then, I spoke in too cavalier a manner. I am an angel who works hard for the things he desires. I do not do things halfway. I will do what it takes to achieve my purpose. This decision is not up to me. Do not misinterpret my enthusiasm as arrogance. Once I make up my mind about something, I do what it takes to get there."

"But how far are you willing to go to achieve those ends, Ahriman? You are well known to us here," the Fallen said. "Your deceptions, your cunning. They do not pass into this sacred place unnoticed."

Silently, I cursed Mastema. My credentials had failed. All my work had been in vain. All my efforts were about to be blasted away in the few remaining moments of my life. I thought rapidly, but clearly. I had to make something up or at least die trying.

"You are right," I replied, with as full a heart as I could manage to convey. "I have been a bureaucrat working for God. I have established myself as a master of spies and I have made my life off the backs of those my father controlled, manipulated, and then disposed of. I have been an imperfect citizen, trying to make my way in life. Trying to make myself more powerful on the backs of other angels. But I have reached my limit. I have come to the conclusion that no matter how hard I try or what I do to further my position, I can never be what I want to be."

"What do you want to be, Ahriman?" the Fallen at the center asked.

"I want to be respected. I want to be known. But most of all, I want to make something happen. I want to change things and know that my labors will benefit someone in the end."

I paused for a moment, almost pleased with the fact that the realities of my life had gathered a sudden momentum in the telling and actually given my argument an unexpected power.

"I spent my years in the army trying to improve a system, a system everyone claims they want to fix, but no one is willing change," I continued, enthused. "When I entered the Servitude, I thought that inside the bounds of the law, I could make a difference. But after years of struggle and fighting to make right what so many see is wrong, I came to realize that in the society that God has created, I am just another worthless cog, upon whose desk more and more useless paperwork is thrown every day. Every day, I make one contact and break another. But on any given day, I accomplish nothing. I make no difference. Twenty people do the work of one and are content to hide their ambitions upon arrival and fall into the monotony and tedium that characterize service to God. That is the way the system works. It trains you to be more and more useless. Hard work is looked upon by your superiors as specious, disingenuous in intent. Your peers regard your efforts as a means of currying favor with your superiors, a form of ass-kissing, if you will, to achieve goals way beyond what is necessary. Eventually, you cease to struggle and fall into line, resigned to putting aside the dreams and aspirations you were once so unwilling to sacrifice, because you are wary of ruffling the feathers of some self-centered, arrogant functionary who feels it necessary to keep you down in order to feel better about himself. In the end, you wind up being what you started out hating and scoffing at. That is the system. And it has been designed that way."

I paused for a moment to let the truth of my statements sink in. I had thought these things for so long, but was unwilling to admit them openly. I loved God. I would do anything to be closer to Him. I had done things I was not proud of in order to make that happen. I bowed my head and stared at the floor.

"I can think of no greater evil than an angel worn down by life, willing to let go of his dreams and dying before his time," I went on. "When it was conveyed to me that my loyal service to my government and society was getting in the way, I told myself that I had had enough."

My words were, indeed, spoken from the heart. These were the words I had been afraid to articulate to Angra, as he dangled many sordid opportunities before me. These were the words I had forced myself to swallow in my grandfather's presence, when he clearly cared so little for my devotion to God. But most of all, these were the words I had suppressed in myself over the years in the hope that my efforts and hard work for God would pay off. Somehow. I had always thought He would take care of me in the end. My love for Him made me afraid to admit the truth of the situation to anyone, but my most inner self. To admit that the system was wrong. It was my Lord's system and I was His serv-ant. But the system extinguished any ingenuity, any creativity you could bring to it. If I fought against the system, it meant I was fighting against Him. In the end, I was unwilling to accept, even to myself, that I had been wrong all along.

The Fallen before me remained silent for several moments. The silence was deafening. My life appeared to be at stake. Never had I been faced with so imminent a risk of death. But in as much as I hated the silence, I loved it too. I felt more alive in those few moments before death than I had at any time before. Even when Simon and I were facing death at the end of a stick, buried up to our knees in a fetid swamp. It was now up to fate, the only possible escape from the outcome of my thwarted clandestine maneuvers.

"You have spoken truthfully, we know," said the Fallen who had been addressing me so far. "We have watched you from afar and been interested in your ambition and career for longer than you realize."

He stood up and made his way around the end of the table toward me. The light still did not reach his face and I could not distinguish its expression as he stopped and leaned against the opposite side of the table from where he had been seated.

"But despite these things," he carried on, "surely, you must see that your yearning for power and your efforts to do some good are at odds with one another. While one can want power to effect change, one can, just as easily, want power to erect insurmount-able obstacles in its path to ensure that change becomes impos-sible. That fine line is where we find ourselves most at odds with you."

"I cannot deny that I have wanted power from the day I set foot in Heaven," I admitted. "I never made that anything but ob-vious. And when I worked to that end, I thought that achieve-ment and commitment to the cause would be enough to propel me to stations in life where what I did could make a difference. I would be lying if I said that my ambitions were simply to make the City a better place. With power comes respect and I wish for that as well. But I am at a loss as to how to prove to you that my desire for power is meant for a good end."

I blushed for a moment. As a youth, I had wanted power to make God's City a better place for all His citizens. But as time and experience corrupted me, I found my heart changed and desired power nearly as much for the experience of leading and making the rules myself. The question was whether or not this was a bad thing in the eyes of this mysterious clandestine group.

"You had a friend once in the ministry, did you not?" the Fallen asked.

"I had many friends."

"Do not confuse acquaintances with friends. Friends, true friends, are those who would do for you what you cannot do for yourself."

I reflected for a moment.

"Those who are there for you when you need them. Those who would bend over backward to be there for you."

"I did have such a friend."

"What was his name?"

"His name was Jehoel. He was my superior and my mentor. But more than that, he was my friend," I said with genuine sad-ness in my voice.

"Why did you lose this friend?"

"I lost him as a friend when he would not help me achieve my goals. He was in a position to help me and he refused."

I could not help but feel mournful at hearing myself say this. Jehoel and his family had been my family.

"What did Jehoel think about your intentions of accumulating more power?"

"He thought it was dangerous. He thought that by making waves in the system, I would only hurt my chances of success. He had my best intentions at heart, but I could not live with his methods. I was intent only on instant gratification. He tried to tell me I was in the wrong place and, to put it baldly, by striving to make things happen in an environment where they were not meant to, I would do myself greater harm than I could imagine. I did not really realize how right he was, until it was too late."

"So what was his plan? Did he want you to wait things out and let life fall where it may or did he advise you in some other way?" the Fallen inquired.

"He never told me he had 'a plan.' He just advised me not to fight a system designed to starve the hungry and feed the fat."

"That is an interesting way of summing up the conversation, Ahriman," the Fallen said, stepping forward to approach me. When the light finally settled on his face, I found I was looking at Jehoel.

I was shocked beyond all belief. Quickly, my thoughts blurred. Mastema could not have known of this. His informants had failed to provide him with the most vital piece of information.

"It would be...an...understatement...to say I am shocked," I choked out, staring at Jehoel's face, making sure the light was not playing tricks on me.

"Indeed. You are not sure where you are or what you have gotten yourself into."

"You see correctly, Fallen."

Jehoel smiled and returned to his seat at the table. Although his features were obscured again by the shadows, somehow, I was able to discern them now through the layers of darkness.

"I have governed this council for ages and I have been able to make God love me," Jehoel said. "I have killed in the name of the brotherhood and lied in its name too. I have converted evil angels from the very system they worked so hard to create. I have become a hero while, all the time, being a traitor." He looked at me. "No, Ahriman. What I did tell you that day was this: there are other ways to make yourself in this world. You just have to open your eyes to see them. Open your heart to them. Are you as much a patriot now as you were when last we spoke?"

"Why would I be here otherwise?" I asked, as if I did not know the answer was obvious.

Jehoel smiled again and turned to the Fallen on his left. "For an angel of such intellect and ambition, he considers us fools, I think."

Quickly, I found myself reconsidering if I valued my neck. Jehoel would not kill me. He would make me his next scapegoat and win further praise for himself.

"I could have come here to bring you down," I continued. "I could have come here to make my way in the world by exposing a group of angels devoted to the overthrow of God's government. On the other hand, I could have come here for the very same reason you must have come yourself, so long ago." I scanned the darkness for anyone who might be listening. "By killing me, you will never know the true reason. But by giving me a chance, you may find that you were more of a mentor to me than you had assumed." I paused, but not long enough for Jehoel to get out his next words. "I know you, Fallen," I went on. "I know you hated the system as much as I did. I also know I was more devoted to it than you were, while, all the while, you were better than I could ever be at manipulating it to suit your own ends. I can see now that you played me. Played me just as much as the angels who kept me down. I know this excited you. You found an angel with ambition matching your own, but who was willing to throw it all aside for a chance to achieve some greater good. But I also think you underestimated me. You underestimated the lengths to which I would go to achieve those ideals. You underestimated my willingness to sell what I held dear in order to create what I thought was right. We are the same, Fallen. Only now, it is your system in which I am willing to work to make my ambitions a reality."

I was fairly certain I had not swayed Jehoel. If someone could tell I was lying, it would surely be him. Even if the power were more important than the system, I would always be a liability. The system, any system, would impose a curb on me. Restrictions ultimately meant recklessness. He knew that. Firsthand. He knew me better than anyone else.

"It is ironic, is it not?" Jehoel said after a few moments.

"You pushed me in this direction. Let me know, in your own strange way, that this was the only means by which to effect real change. And now, on the threshold of your door, as I stand willing to make the sacrifices that you yourself told me I needed to make, you act as my judge and doubt me. Perhaps you are not as great an angel as I thought you were."

A muted laughter arose from the other Fallen at the table.

"Come back tomorrow," Jehoel said, looking beyond me to the Fallen who stood quietly behind me. "Come back tomorrow and we will explore just how deeply your heart feels for your new brotherhood."

⌘   ⌘   ⌘

Over the course of the next few weeks, I gradually made points with both my old friend and the secretive people who trusted him. It still made no sense how someone as intelligent as Jehoel could be drawn into an apparently unhinged sect of stone worshippers. Yet every evening, I would meet with him and discuss my progress. The brotherhood. The system. The "Word." And how our lives had proceeded after our split. Jehoel and I outwardly rekindled our friendship. I think we had genuinely missed each other. But it was different this time. I could not trust him, for now I knew the enemy I would have to subdue. I had to act like a friend while, all the time, trying not to feel like one.

I quickly found that the best way to lie about my real intentions was to tell Jehoel the truth. He had always been able to see through me. So I needed to be careful. I had to avoid fabricating things whose veracity could be investigated so that the resultant repercussions would not boomerang on me later. I knew, despite all of Jehoel's apparent amiability, that he continued to harbor doubts about me. And have me watched. How could he trust me, knowing who I was? The best way to avoid drawing attention to myself was to do what I had always done, be the angel I had always been. I continued my second life as a foreman. I did not discuss it with Jehoel, but surely, he must have known of my arrangements with Mastema. I waited for the questions, but they never came. He either dismissed the significance of my double life or ignored it. It turned out to be his undoing.

I was so very happy to be able to see Phanuel again. The boy had become a strong, intelligent, and ambitious angel. He was now a junior army officer and, an angel to his word, worked in a scientific unit, slowly building an excellent reputation for himself. Much to his father's chagrin, Phanuel had proved to be a valuable asset to the army's research units. He appeared completely unaware of his father's dual lives. And I suspect that somewhere deep down inside, my relationship with his son held Jehoel back from either leaving me to the mercy of the cell or turning me in to the Secret Police.

Being back in touch with Jehoel reawakened many of my old feelings of regret. My home life had always been contentious and the stability of my former mentor's personal situation left me yearning. I had never had more than temporary involvements with women. My career always came first and I allowed no relationship the opportunity to grow into anything more than a passing fancy. But with Phanuel again in my life, I began to long for a son of my own. Someone I could beam at with pride and share my own life's experiences with. These thoughts clashed with the motives that drove my true purpose and it was a struggle to retain my focus on my cover and my need to learn as much about the Fallen as I could.

It was Jehoel who informed me that the Fallen were so named, because they had fallen in the eyes of God.

"Who are they?" I asked one night.

"Fallen could be anyone. Angels of means or angels taken off the streets. We do not care, so long as they are believers and loyal to the cause."

"Does that not make your organization rather open to the public? How can you be sure these angels will not turn on you?"

"We have ways," Jehoel said, suddenly looking guarded. "Some more forceful than others."

"What do you mean?"

"There is no social divide among the Fallen," he replied, purposely ignoring my question with an unrelated, but relevant, piece of information. "Each Fallen does his or her job, treating all members of the sect with respect. In this way, God cannot compete."

"The concept of rank does not exist?"

"It does to some extent, but it is not as blatant as in God's system. Some of us have what I guess you might call authority."

"So, in bureaucratic speak, it is a flat organization," I said a bit sarcastically.

Jehoel smiled. "Yes, I guess you might say that. All Fallen treat each other as they would a beloved. We are all brothers and sisters, united in our dedication to the removal of God and the restoration of the democratic regime He usurped."

"What does 'democratic' mean?" The word was unknown to me.

Jehoel laughed again. "Roughly speaking, it means government of the people. In practice, it means no one angel rules all. The people decide what is best for them."

"Do we not already have a Senate?" I asked.

Jehoel shot me an unpleasant look. It was almost a look of reproof, an unspoken comment on my apparent naïveté. I regretted my question.

"Removal of God," I repeated. It was almost too difficult to say the words out loud.

"At any cost," Jehoel said. He was quite serious.

It was such an abstruse idea. No God. It was like saying, "There is no such thing as water," or "I do not exist." But these angels were so devoted to and motivated by this nearly unimaginable end. To them, the notion of life without God meant happiness and contentment. Nothing I had seen in His massive administrative apparatus or in His elaborately structured military could ever equal the dedication and camaraderie I witnessed on a daily basis among these angels. They were united in their focus, determined in their actions, and organized in their plans and goals. They methodically scoured the remotest corners of the City for people unhappy with the system and willing to take that great step beyond into the realm of their brotherhood. "Rebel" and "insurgent" did not seem to describe their true character. But what else could I call them?

"What other means were you referring to before?" I asked, determined to make Jehoel answer the question I had asked earlier.

"Do not misunderstand our purpose as being altruistic," he said, again, with that note of discomfiture in his voice. "There are certain realities we must deal with in achieving our ends."

"Such as?" I was enjoying his tension.

"Just because we strive for a democratic state does not mean our methods of recruitment, education, and induction are any less rigorous or stringent than a military unit."

"Paramilitary," I interjected.

"Fine. Paramilitary."

"So you are not just philosophers. You are insurgents too."

"God is entrenched. You cannot displace someone by philosophical arguments alone. God's cult of personality is so strong that almost all of His people believe there was never anything else but Him. From the beginning."

"Then you are aligned with the trimmers?"

"You are confusing the issues," Jehoel replied, annoyed at my expletive.

"You are right. I am confused. You say you fight God, but I have yet to see an instance of violence. How is that achieving anything?"

"No overt violence, no." Jehoel shifted again. He was unable to look me squarely in the eye.

My interest was certainly piqued.

"Just about everyone senior here has gathered experience in God's government and His army. They were trained that way, to promote the army or God's bureaucracy. But they support these things only in their public lives. In private, they use their hard-earned knowledge to better organize members of our sect."

"So again, in bureaucratic speak, they are feeding off of God's well-honed management skills."

Jehoel laughed nervously in response. I could feel I was getting to it.

"Well, yes," he said. "But God has some pretty brutal lessons to teach."

"Yes, I suppose that is true." I was curious. "Quite true, in fact. Discipline in the army is very harsh. Discipline in the government is far less so, but psychologically, its impact is certainly more lasting." I was hoping to push him.

"I am not speaking of psychological means, Ahriman. I think you know that. Fallen who spent their careers in the military and saw combat in the outlands now protect us. They are often called upon to deal with suspected infiltrators in our midst. Or with those 'outsiders' who submit themselves, but decide not to participate."

Now I was genuinely surprised and happy, all at the same time, to hear him articulate something only hinted at earlier.

"What do you mean?" I asked innocently.

"Angels are removed." He could not get himself to say it.

Finally, after all these years, I had caught Jehoel in a contradiction that he had not been able to resolve within himself. And he had bet his life on it.

"It seems a contradiction, do you not think?" I asked, adding a dollop of recrimination to my tone, "to start a movement in the name of 'democratic' principles, but to enforce those very principles with the same brutal methods for which you profess so much disdain?" It was the truth, sharpened with a hint of contempt.

"Yes," Jehoel conceded. "But as I said, we must deal with realities. None of us are immune to temptation. We have designed these measures as a last resort."

"I see."

I did not need to push any more. A movement to remove God and supplant Him. Being involved in it meant being in constant fear that Fallen would arrive at your door one evening, having determined that you were a "reality" to be summarily dealt with. I did not know what democracy entailed, but it did not seem too far removed from God's Word. It dislodged me from the certainty of my earlier assumptions and it took everything I could muster to maintain the façade of loyalty. They might not be crazy, after all. But they were hypocrites. It seemed wise to stay as close to Jehoel as possible.

CHAPTER THIRTEEN

It took a while, but the book Mastema coveted finally came to light. I was relieved to know that it actually existed, as quite some time had passed since I had been entrusted with this mission. I was sure Mastema was getting fed up with my lack of real progress. But as it turned out, my excitement at discovering the book's existence was premature. It took quite a while longer before anyone actually discussed with me the book's purpose or meaning. I was expected to achieve a certain level of competence in the movement's fundamentals before going any farther. Then finally, Jehoel came to inform me that I had moved beyond the rank of a simple novice inductee.

How can I quickly describe what had taken so long for me to understand? The entire movement and its tenets were based on this short canon of ancient scripture—the book.

"Once you are initiated into the Fallen, you will be given a copy of the book for your own use," Jehoel said. "It is not so much a rulebook as a book of life's prescriptives. How people are meant to treat one another. How one may lead a righteous and morally upright life."

"Where does it come from?" I asked.

"When the time is right, you will be told," Jehoel said. He must have noted my exasperation at this evasion. "Patience, my friend," he said, using, for the first time in a long while, the term that would once have indicated how much I meant to him. "This is truly something you cannot attain until you have moved some distance down the right path. Only then can you share in its wisdom."

I was disgusted by the whole notion. It may well have been the source of the cell's delusions, the means by which they drugged themselves into thinking there had once been a Heaven without God, but I was going to have to swallow it. The book would make the difference between Mastema's favors and my slow, but accelerating descent into Heavenly obscurity. So I kept on. Eyes and ears wide open. Mastema had only agreed to this dubious deal so as to gain possession of one of these elusive books. If he, of all angels, cared so much about acquiring it, it must be important. But how could that be? Where the book came from, what it said, and how it possessed the power to prompt angels into risking everything for the sake of some mad notion. These speculations constantly nagged at me. In my world, the only devotion allowed was to God. There was no other and anything else was blasphemy. But in this secretive and subversive concoction of angels, the only real devotion was inspired by this little book and aimed at the brotherhood that toiled and suffered to keep its message alive.

However abstruse its meaning, the message was, indeed, proliferating. The recruits were many and diverse in both social and political stature. There were few, if any, places in the City of God, apparently, where someone could not be found with a willingness to overthrow Him. The message was everywhere. I felt a sense of shame that in all my years in the PID, never once had I come across even a whisper of what was actually happening in the City. At least, not one that I understood as clearly as I understood things now. I had truly failed God. But I would not let it happen again and kept as detailed a memory as I could of each angel who walked down those dark and torch-lined steps, gazing up in awe at those ancient and perplexing stone faces.

⌘ ⌘ ⌘

As I had said in the beginning, there was no sense of time in the way we calculate it now. When I say that I was with the cell for what felt like an eternity, in terms of the lifetime of men, it might well have been so. The point I want to make is that despite much effort on my part, I continued to feel as if I were getting nowhere. Yes, I had learned something of the pervasive nature of the movement, but simply being aware of the location of a dissident sect was not going to get me what I wanted. Besides, I still did not have a copy of the book I needed to keep my end of the bargain with Mastema. What I had learned so far was not much more than a few pages of what might be available in any Secret Police dossier and hardly what I would have considered the major breakthrough Mastema would demand.

I became recognized and respected in the cell and was given the passwords to the various locations of operations and safe houses. I was even provided regular updates regarding the loyalties of my work crews on the southern wall. But otherwise, my access and contributions were limited. I still had no understanding of hierarchy. No real understanding of how orders were passed down. Certainly no understanding of their plans and how they intended to achieve their nefarious goals. And perhaps, most importantly, no understanding of whether other cells were operating. There was no way I could expect to bring down the organization if I only took a thin slice of the pie. I needed everything at once to make this mean anything to anyone.

In one way, though, I appreciated this phase in my life in a way I had never expected I would. One of the main requirements of every Fallen was to become well versed in the operations of God's City. Each recruit studiously digested the information given about each aspect of its social, political, and moral fabric. There could be no reform without first "knowing how our enemy thinks." For the first time since I was a schoolboy, I was studying something truly academic in nature. We were not allowed to make notes on anything pertaining to the philosophy underlying the cell's existence and operations. Such information was only to be memorized. I was, however, provided reams of previously written materials on the City God had created. I taught myself the means by which each department of government functioned and the method by which each was able to implement the many commands and directives of God, His ministers, and Gabriel. I learned the archaic and, mostly, ignored rules of the Senate. How it was meant to provide "advice and consent" to God and His actions. I read about the prominent engineering works of the City, including the harnessing of great rivers that surrounded Heaven and the construction of our robust walls. Officially, of course, I was meant to ignore the reason for constructing the wall I was currently repairing, but as you can imagine, God did not desire to teach His schoolchildren hypocrisy.

Reams and reams of manuscripts were made available to me every day. Transcripts of debates within the Senate, memoranda of understanding within the many and diverse departments of government, quotas of lumber taken from the Great Northern Forest, repair bills for the decrepit aqueducts leading from the Forks of Apsatsus and the newly built aqueducts running out of the upper Acheron, legal opinions handed down by the City's high courts, administrative missals concerning construction on City parks and universities, and the many reports of God's study commissions. Each was fascinating in that it told a forgotten story. A story the general public in its apathy, as it plodded along in life, chose to ignore. Radical changes had occurred over the years and no one had even taken the time to notice their freedoms being whittled away.

"Change is the only way to make our lives better," Jehoel said one night, as we ate dinner near my foreman's apartment.

"Okay, I will play the advocate," I said, putting my utensils aside. "What is wrong with where we are now?"

"Where we are now?" he asked almost indignantly. "You and I are here tonight, because His system has driven us to such extremes that we are willing to put our lives and loved ones on the line to make something change."

"True, but change can be bad as well as good. What makes you think the change we bring about will not just be a different way to accomplish the same limited and frustrating goals?"

"Because whatever our goals, we will attain them with the consent of the people."

"There has never been the type of change you seek."

"Yes, there has."

"When?"

"That is why we are here," Jehoel said. "That is why you are with me. A conspirator. A blasphemer. A rebel."

"I do not understand."

He was skirting around my demand for a direct answer, merely suggesting he knew something I did not. I hated it when he did that.

"You would not, would you?" Jehoel said with an earnest expression in response to my admission. "You are right in one sense, Ahriman. Change is not always good," he said, picking up his line of argument. "Change was what brought us to our current state of affairs."

His meaning again eluded me.

"You see, Ahriman, God was not always God. Things have not always been as they are. God came to power like any ruler. But He came to power by subterfuge and deception."

My expression must have given me away. But I was more concerned about someone overhearing him. Rotting away in a City prison, guilty of conspiracy and blasphemy, was not the way I wanted to conclude my adventures in espionage.

Jehoel must have realized it too. "Do not look so surprised, my friend," he said in an undertone. "You did not get where you are today on merit alone, did you?"

I thought back to how I had come to run the PID and smiled.

"When you learn the supposedly legitimate ways of God's government," Jehoel continued, "you are introduced to and schooled in His truth. Not *the* truth. *The* truth is something so well guarded that merely mentioning something other than His truth could easily result in your head being removed to the City walls, without the rest of your body accompanying it." Then he grew very serious. "Have you ever noticed that under God's regime, we do not recognize the passage of time?"

"Simply using the word 'regime' is an offense that can warrant an arrest," I said.

"Pay attention, Ahriman." Jehoel carefully looked around to see if anyone was watching. Or listening. "Sure, we know how old we are and we know at what hour we need to wake up in the morning in order to get to work on time. But there is no written history of the City, no universally accepted and government-sanctioned record of the rise of God's kingdom."

"What are you talking about?" I asked incredulously. "We do have history. Every schoolchild is forced to learn it. Every soldier is expected to fight for it." I pointed at him. "And every bureaucratic is sworn to uphold it. You swore to it when you took your oath of office, just as I did."

"But where does it begin? It is a simple enough question. Where does it begin?"

"There is no beginning," I said. "It begins where it begins."

"That does not make sense, Ahriman. Think about it. What in life begins when it begins? Does existence happen spontaneously? Eh? No. Read your history books. God was always there. Our history does not begin at the beginning. It begins in the middle somewhere. There was something before God," he said, pausing for a moment and lowering his voice further. "And there will be something after God too."

"Before God, there was only God."

"You do not define a word by the word itself. God's history is how He wrote it, very well thought out, meticulously planned, and with good reason."

"How do you mean?"

"One would think God more than willing to record the grand events of His accession and achievements in power. Would that not make sense?"

"Yes, I guess it would."

"But where can you find that? In our history?" He smiled at me. "Nowhere."

He was right. But I was not willing to admit it. Not yet.

"Perhaps you should read your history again, Jehoel," I said. "The history you are so willing to reject states clearly that in the beginning, there was God. To me, that is as logical a statement as saying in the beginning, there was no God. But we know better. God was there to create the heavens, because otherwise, there would be no Heaven. God was there to create the universe, because otherwise, there would be no universe."

"Yes, you are correct in that our history reads that way. But that is nothing more than God's propaganda, designed to deflect our natural interest in our own past."

"There is no logic in that, Jehoel," I countered.

"But you said it. It is not any less logical than saying it is not."

"Where is this going?" I asked in exasperation. "You cannot say nothing exists, because everything exists."

"That is not what I am saying. We are not talking of logic in the abstract. We are talking about God. And I am saying He wants us to be devoted to Him, to be possessed of a common sense of unity, and to be dedicated in persevering in our morals and attitudes. If we see and respect Heaven this way, we must see and respect God in this way too. He gives order to our lives. Yet God does not want us to know the truth. And since the truth questions that order, that respect, every angel raised under His regime has come to see God's magnificence as something that simply has always existed and will forever exist."

"Again. Conjecture without proof positive."

"No, Ahriman. It is brainwashing. And we never even had the benefit of knowing what our brains were being washed of."

"Okay, then. Ignoring logic and taking what you say to be true on its face, what, precisely, has been washed from our collective minds? Whatever it was, it does not strike me as being particularly important. We are a great society. Flawed, yes. But largely, contented. And if we are content with the present, what possible difference could the past make to our lives?" I was not sure I meant it, but I was, after all, in a debate.

"That is the very point I am trying to make, my friend. That is what God turns our focus on, what He is betting on: removing the past from our lives and our willingness to accept what He's given us."

"That does not answer the question."

"Okay. Here you must agree with me. There are few things in life more difficult to find than the origins of an ancient and long-established custom. Right? We simply accept it as part of our lives and adhere to it completely. We may not know why or even how it got there, but it is part of us."

"Fine, yes."

"By outlawing time, God has kept us content in the present so that we have no past to compare it with!" He was excited. "Time is God's greatest ally, so long as He controls it. Otherwise, it is His greatest enemy. The passage of time act as the caustic washer of our brains. Like the water running down a riverbed, wearing away at the rock below. Time cleanses our brains, our collective memory and effectively changes the once-so-evident face of truth. Only if we are again possessed of time can we see those changes that inextricably alter the course of the universe. We asked, did we not, why God does not memorialize His accomplishments? Because only with the whitewash of time are His deeds made great."

"I think I need another drink," I joked. "Look, I grant you, long-established customs are often hard to understand. But the very idea of erasing a collective memory is impossible," I pounded out. "There are many people with as long a memory as that of God, to be sure. In fact, God depends on His people to keep these long memories in order to know why they are honoring Him and fearing Him, which, of course, is usually one and the same. It is the uncertainty surrounding our knowledge of God which results in our feeble understanding of our lives." I looked at Jehoel intently. "If I understand you, you are saying that by making us think He is something so much more than He really is, we accept Him at His word? We allow the past to disappear?"

"Yes. Exactly. And see only Him."

"No, no, no. Even if He has the power to veil the truth from us, as you say, our innate sense of inquiry into what is unknown underlies our reverence, more so than this idea that God possesses the ability to hold the actual truth, of which we are unaware, above our heads and beyond our reach."

Jehoel smiled at me and sat for several seconds just staring into my eyes.

"I misjudged you again, my old friend," he said. "I guess, then, that you are ready to see and hear the truth, after all. Then and only then will you have, for the first time in your life, the full picture of the world that we call Heaven. Then and only then will you know the truth about God."

I was not sure Jehoel had made any argument at all. I mulled it over some more as we finished up our meal. God had outlawed time to prevent us from remembering. Simultaneously, He had wowed us with His greatness, so much so that we had stopped asking the questions that needed to be asked and, instead, fallen back on God for all the answers. Whatever larger world Jehoel was seeing, I was not seeing it. And if I was not seeing it, how could I expect them to think I believed in it?

CHAPTER FOURTEEN

My next meeting with the Fallen was my breakthrough. My naïveté, as Jehoel put it, made them trust me. As the Fallen questioned me on my willingness to put aside my novice status and take on the mantle of belief, I resisted giving up the old ways. It was not too difficult to do. I fought them at every turn, with every argument at my disposal, with everything I had ever been taught. But this only made them trust me more. In fact, they appeared relieved. When I broke down and accepted the faith, I was told the truth Jehoel had given a hint of the night we had dinner together. They believed in it as much as he did. Looking back on it, I think they were excited by the prospect of converting me. I was another convert, sure. A government official too, yes. But more than anything else, to them, I was a prize. I was the grandson of Zoan, poster boy of their enemy. How easy it is, sometimes, to make others see what they want to see.

Once I had passed their tests, my access to study materials was opened wide. It was the first time I could see something mildly coherent, not simply dogmatic, and, at least, a bit along the lines of argument.

"You will be given as much time as required for quiet contemplation," I was told by the librarian, as he handed me the first few dusty pages of manuscript. "It is forbidden to remove anything from this holy place. Memorize what you have been given."

"Indeed I will," I thought to myself, perusing the first few pages. As prologue, the cell seemed to have been established about the same time my grandfather started out on his first military campaigns. The moldy papers spoke of the shortcomings of God and how the one book, presumably an allusion to this book Mastema so coveted, contained all the true knowledge needed to understand the universe. It was not a universal theory of everything. But from my perspective, any theory was worth at least some consideration. Many, many dusty pages were spent on the one book. It was the source of light, inspiring generations to live free and in harmony. It contained many oblique references to some mythical past, where each citizen was considered responsible for understanding his or her basic rights, rights guaranteed by the government and protected by civil society. It boasted a tremendous power, power that was hardly ever wielded but, when done so, wielded judiciously and with integrity. Little of substance about its secrets, however, was shared and there existed but few hints to the book's author or sources. Later documents spoke of how the book was lost for ages in some ill-defined pre-historical turmoil.

Flawed, but intriguing, I said to myself, as I carefully cultivated my understanding of the hodgepodge the cell considered history. Whether this one book actually contained the truth, was part of a concerted propaganda campaign, or merely the fictitious ranting of some madman to which generations of angels had given too much credence, its descriptions were enough to turn me into an avid reader. I became addicted to the many manuscripts available in the cell's library and sought out other books and materials that further described and interpreted the one book. More recent writings spoke of how the truth would, one day, be known and the City of Heaven regain its lost glory. It was the first time I remembered seeing a reference to the "City of Heaven". To all that lived there, it was, and would always be, the City of God. I cannot quite say why, but the tidbits of questionable and seemingly unsubstantiated history reminded me of the many arguments between my father and grandfather over nebulous political issues at a time when I was too young to understand the substance of each debate. In that strange way, I felt I was reading something about my own family history, about matters that had ultimately torn its members apart. In a way I had never expected them to, these stories filled in some of the blanks I sensed running through my life.

The amount of available reading material was actually quite surprising. That this group would warehouse so much information in one place suggested that either they were careless or supremely confident of the place never being found. Given the purported age of some of the storylines, it was likely that some of the materials were transcriptions of oral narrations. The narratives were often disorganized and frequently came off more as wild-eyed ramblings than as any organized story, let alone history. Their only point of coherence was their absurdity. Replete with gaps.

I was a bit disappointed with the questionable strength of some of the arguments. And so I began making a sort of master index for myself. How was I to take down a heretical sect of revolutionaries, if I could not even understand the philosophy underlying their arguments? That this was even necessary made me doubt the significance of their movement. It took a great deal of time to make my compilation, as many manuscripts seemed to describe the same people in the same story, but from slightly and, often, widely different angles. Most manuscripts were obviously old and many had scribbles by earlier readers etched in the margins. I could only assume that the prohibition on transcription had led many to write notes for themselves in the documents they could always return to the library. Some comments were legible, others incomprehensible. Some of the remarks were even observations on the comments themselves. Their absence of a leader, their reliance on a mysterious group of elders holed up in some remote dungeon stood out clearly as the reason for what, in my opinion, was their inability to make a major impact on the life of the City. To me, organization and adherence to doctrine were everything. Here, they did not even seem to have a unified doctrine to follow.

When the material was gathered together, the library's single message was that the old City of Heaven had been perverted into the new City of God. These documents spoke of a time when the City was small and run by a series of congresses elected directly by the people. They spoke of public works constructing housing for all citizens, and economies and markets that while small in comparison to the markets of the City of God, afforded all people work and a means of livelihood. The illustrious leaders of this City, while terrifying to behold in the eyes of evildoers, were kind and giving to those who made up their faithful constituents. Basically, peace reigned and life was good. It did not get plainer than that.

I cannot emphasize enough how totally alien this was to me. How alien it would have been to any patriotic servant of God. We followed God's Word without question. He was as true as the air we breathed. As real as the ground we walked upon. It simply did not occur to us to ask questions. Only with perfect faith did God love and protect us as His children. Only with perfect faith could we understand Him and expect His mercy. Anything else was simply unthinkable. But the very taboo etched in these letters and documents drove me, even if I was only possessed by my desire to discredit them.

⌘　⌘　⌘

Never once had I considered anything like this in my entire life. But the possibility that it could actually be true made it all the more, well, readable. Other members of the cell had similar experiences. But there was a split right down the social-class line.

Members of the social elite were more likely to have difficulties accepting the validity of these stories than the working classes. The affluent had been born into, grown up by, and owed their living to the very concepts these works challenged. We had had no previous exposure to such heretical stories, no prior preparation to grasp their meaning and, no matter what compulsions drove us to the cell now, we could not easily jettison all we had been taught earlier simply on the basis of some dusty old books propagating a history we had never known the existence of, championed by a people who harbored notions of a future that we could not clearly understand. It was not that we were afraid. We were indignant.

The laboring classes, however, the workers, traders, office personnel, and what have you, were not shocked by what they read in those tomes. At first, I attributed this response to their lack of formal education and the virtual absence of a structured upbringing. They were what their trade made them. Horse-traders were horse-traders. Laborers were laborers. Never had their lives needed to be any more complicated than that. With such simplicity of purpose guiding them, how could they understand God the way I did, especially as the lives they lived denied them the benefit of learning how to reach such an understanding? But as I talked with them and got to know them a bit in a way I had never known people of their kind, I came to discover that to many of them, these stories were not new.

Everyone grows up hearing fairy tales. Invented stories, designed to teach a moral lesson by presenting a situation and revealing through its development the mistakes made on the way to an understanding of what is right and true. An understanding often achieved the hard way. Where individuals like me were concerned, our mothers had told us stories of how God overcame evil and reigned supreme in Heaven. How faith in God, above all things, was the key to a righteous and morally upright existence. How obedience to God and His rule opened up for us a clear path, unambiguous and just. This was what we knew, because this was what we had been told from the beginning. But for the working classes, God was just there. Just another of life's burdens that had to be borne. In fact, if anything, they were taught to distance themselves from Him as far as possible. God sought His taxes; He sought His workers; and He sought His soldiers. But there was nothing beyond that in His relationship with them. God gave them nothing with which they could improve their lives. They were obedient, but only to the point that was necessary to ensure He would leave them alone. They held a stronger faith in themselves and gave no credence to the lofty words of wealthy politicians, separated from them by a vast social chasm. Policies were policies that, more often than not, interfered with their lives, whether they had faith in God or not. Their parents had raised them on childhood tales about a world where God did not predominate. These had been their fairy tales. These were their fantasy worlds.

Of course, such notions, if made public, were punishable by death. But the social standing of these angels from the lower classes actually acted as a shield, protecting them from people like me. Insulating them from the upper classes' understanding of Heaven's clearly established strata. My conversations with these angels were, far and away, the most stimulating highlights of my indoctrination. Corrupted, possibly deceitful history was one thing. These angels were real, and my own interest in the meaning and progression of their lives sometimes clouded my underlying aim of exposing them for my personal gain. I had been cloistered all my life—in my house, at the schools I attended, in the army and in the government positions I had worked in. Never had I had the will, desire, or even the opportunity to see the people who made up the other ninety-nine percent of God's kingdom. Even if their lives were mundane to them, I saw their experiences as true experiments in the natural order of things. Where my life had been chalked out for me even before I was born, these people made it up as they went along. It made me feel as if, in some way, they were more powerful than my family, with all their influence and ambitions for greater social status, could ever hope to be. The choices these people were forced to make meant the difference between life and death. One wrong decision would have a more critical impact on their lives than all the decisions I had made in my life up until that point.

I was dragged back to reality one night, when Jehoel came unannounced to my apartment.

"Ahriman, the Fallen have come to a decision. They have voted to move you into a position of power."

Even though I was a spy and thus forced to act a part to maintain my cover, I could hardly keep the expression of shock off my face.

"I realize that this is a rather quick transition," he continued, "especially since your involvement began from, shall we say, a rather unusual set of circumstances." He sounded hesitant.

As I saw it, my introduction and integration into the cell had been accompanied by an astounding stroke of luck. Why had I not been exposed? Why could they not tell that deep down inside, I was driven to destroy them?

"Why? How?" I now asked, bewildered.

"The fact is that you have taken the lessons we gave you and learned them well."

I was not sure how to respond. "I do not know what to say. I..."

"So well, in fact, that others have gauged your ability to teach."

"Teach?" I flushed. My aim had been to learn as much as possible as unobtrusively as I could. Instead, it seems, I had drawn attention to myself. "I only want to understand where these angels came from and...well...how they made their way in Heaven," I fumbled.

"I have known you for a long time," Jehoel said, "and in the short period during which you have been one of the Fallen, I have seen you shed your anger and even a good deal of your pessimism. While I personally think it is too soon to tell, the Fallen think you have come to accept the truth."

If you only knew, I said under my breath, my sinister motivations swirling in my mind.

Jehoel furrowed his brow.

"I must admit," I quickly continued, "I have learned to quieten my mind. I never really expected that. I want to believe there is something beyond what I have seen so far."

I faked a quizzical look. It was not that I did not believe what I was saying, but rather, I was laughing to myself at the conflict that burned me inside.

"But I am not ready to be anyone's teacher," I went on. "I am only just beginning to learn what you have to teach me."

"That may be true, but it does not change the facts." I could sense Jehoel's hesitation. "I am not here to ask you to teach others. I am here to ask you to spy for the cause."

There were several seconds of complete silence, while I absorbed his meaning. Jehoel watched carefully.

"What do you mean?" I was confused. Really.

"You have learned enough to begin understanding our people's true history. The ideals that we, as a group, espouse are the very ones this place lived by once, long ago. Equality. Republicanism. Inherent in these ideals is the understanding that one must make up one's own mind as to the course one wishes to take. For me to lecture you and tell you what you should think and how to go about it would be contrary to our message and defeat the very principles of our cause. We strive to give angels the truth so that they can go out and help the population wrest it back from God who had usurped it in the first place. So that they can evolve and break free of a belief system into which the notion of obedience to God in all things has been wired from the outset. We want to teach the angels they matter as individuals, and good government can only be achieved when we rid ourselves of tyrants and relearn the process of governing ourselves."

"What does this have to do with my spying? And on whom am I supposed to spy?" It was all very distracting.

"Ahriman, you have all the instruments you need to understand our movement. I think you are a natural leader, whether you know it yet or not. I have seen you in both worlds: the world of God's government, where you always strive to make yourself better, and this world, where you hunger for knowledge and take it upon yourself to help others see what you see. Now, to be truthful, you may not always do that in the most efficient and effective way," Jehoel said, shrugging his shoulders, "but the combination of those two characteristics makes you potent. You are motivated, and your charisma and intelligence make you someone people are willing to follow, willing to believe in." He paused for a moment, examining my face. "You are especially well situated to feed us information we can use to help restore what we have lost. You need to return to work at the PID."

"But how?" I asked, my voice rising to almost a shout. "Those people have no idea where I am or what I am doing. To them, I am just another nameplate on another office door. They keep me there, in part, as a favor to my family and, in part, because they do not know what else to do with me. You taught me that, Jehoel. Do you really think I make one bit of difference there? Do you really think that what I do every day makes the slightest bit of difference to anyone? At any level?" I was upset now. I had yet to achieve what I needed to return Mastema's favor. "The reason I left them," I went on, after calming myself down somewhat, "was to become part of a world where my contribution meant something. You think I can go back to that now? Reintroduce myself to a disinterested world where, after breaking my head on some bureaucrat's doorway, I find myself nowhere, and with nothing to show for my efforts?"

"You forget to whom you are preaching, Ahriman," Jehoel said, raising his voice as well. "I have been living that life, that lie, day in and day out. That pounding monotony has been mine since long before you were anyone. And you have the temerity to lecture me on living the soulless life? Unlike you, I have been willing to bet more than my career on making things change. I have put my life on the line by living in two worlds. My own family does not know me. My own wife and child think I am precisely one of those sycophantic bureaucratic cogs to whom you refer with such venom. But if the cause is to evolve, it needs a constant supply of information, the key to power. And you are uniquely positioned to do all the things you say you want to do."

"You chose me, did you not?" I asked, sitting down and rubbing my temples. "You chose me because of my access." I looked up at him.

"I chose you because of who you are," he said. "And so what if I did? If you were so dedicated to the cause, would you not have done the same thing? Are you so high-minded that the principle means more than the goal?"

"No."

"So what is it, then? This gets you where you want to be. It puts you in harm's way and makes you important overnight."

"And puts you at considerable risk," I said, looking up at him.

"Ahriman," he said angrily, "perhaps I gave you more credit than I should have. People die every day. You will die too, if they find out what you have been doing, find out what I know. About you."

Did he know about my deal with Mastema? A setup, but who was the mastermind? Jehoel seemed to think I was behind it.

"We have the opportunity now to get not just more information, but more crucial information than ever before with your connections, if they are put to careful use," he went on. "We allowed you entry with the hope that some day, you would come to the point you have already reached. On your own. So it is really a matter of whether you will help us or force me to take a very difficult decision."

Now I knew why he had not asked questions about Mastema. Working both sides. I needed time to consider how to deal with this unexpected turn of events, for in that moment, I could not quite see how to satisfy the demands of so many masters.

"So what do I do, then?" I asked dejectedly.

"You go back. End your sabbatical. Reduce the noise you used to make officially, but keep a tighter grip on information."

That perked me up a bit.

"You transmit to the Fallen what you come by. Leave the ministry out of it. The Fallen will decide whether what you provide has any value. If you bring us useful information, you will be rewarded. If not, then we will see." His face was set in stern lines.

I had no choice.

"We need to know from the others, outside the City walls. They sustain the movement. Your network is unparalleled and beholden to you. I have my orders. That is all I will say." He shifted nervously. "And that is it. Word from the outside and understanding from your connections. Do you understand?" Jehoel's threats were delivered with a smile. "You have an opportunity here to change the future. I suggest you take it."

A connection outside the walls. To trimmers. I now knew something I had not known before.

CHAPTER FIFTEEN

I found my work much the way I had left it. The information continued to come in and was edited and moved out. I was put in charge of an important project that had no clear goal, but was rigorously monitored by seniors who, themselves, had no clear understanding of its purpose. Jehoel was surely using the project as a test to see whether I could hack my new objectives correctly. Seniors sometimes threatened to intervene in my work when it was expedient for them to do so as a way of justifying their meaningless titles. But whereas earlier, I would have stewed, frustrated by the pointlessness of the work and the idiocy of my superiors, now I kept my focus and worked diligently within the system. Jehoel was pleased with the project's outcome, as the necessary volume of information was passed on, along with the absurdity that was expected.

On the other hand, things that once had been so mundane suddenly offered food for thought. What was I looking at?

Did it signify that something was happening within the City's groups of rebels? Did it have anything to do with these communications from the outside? Was it useful enough to share with the Fallen? Could they use it in any way? Would it hold Jehoel at bay and keep me alive long enough to get what I needed for Mastema? Before I became embroiled in these intrigues, I could not have cared less for my work. Now my work was a whirl that stimulated my mind every day. Looking back on it, I laugh at the peril I had put myself in without truly understanding how close to an end I had come.

⌘   ⌘   ⌘

No one in the ministry but Jehoel had a clue about my objectives. The Ministry Council, which had tortured me with endless nonsense for so long, was oblivious to my true purpose. So long as they were running a project, any project, and they had someone to suborn in the process, well, that seemed enough. What I had not been entirely prepared for was significantly greater attention from my juniors. They had immediately noticed how my interest was piqued by issues that would not have caused me to raise an eyebrow earlier, and were shocked at my conclusion that no escalation was necessary in situations that had hitherto had me howling from the eves of the ministry's main entranceway. In effect, I had converted myself from the ignorant senior manager, looking to push something somewhere for no good reason, to someone who was clearly interested in what was happening, where it was going, and when it was going to get there. Had I not carefully controlled my subordinates, I might nearly have gotten myself killed by suddenly caring about the quality of my work.

I needed to measure myself carefully. More information was not necessarily going to get me where I needed to be. I needed to get the right information to convince the Fallen that I could deliver. I also needed to carefully assess what I was actually giving them to ensure some measure of protection for myself, in case I got caught and was branded a traitor. I kept reminding myself that the longer I held it together, the more spectacular my revelations would be. There was no wrong or right. Just what kept my head connected to my torso.

Since I had toned down my usual rhetoric, the ministry officially allowed me more access without any concerns being raised at higher levels. I had been broken, they must have thought, accepting the way things were. I was on my way to becoming one of them. And as my reward, my seniors chose to care no longer what access I had. They trusted me, because they believed me to be apathetic. Trying to apply logic to this is as worthless as the work itself. I mean, how do you rationalize the following: the harder you work, the slower will be your progress; the less work you do, the more responsibility you receive. Trusting now in the stupidity of the system, vast tangles of information were soon mine for the viewing. More information, in fact, than I could ever have imagined.

⌘ ⌘ ⌘

I found it particularly interesting that the Ministry of Science and Progress had suffered some of the worst infiltrations. The Fallen were ruthless in targeting this ministry. But I could only identify these Fallen by their positions within the government. I came to know, for example, that one of that ministry's many Virtues was Fallen, but was never able to find out which one. But that was enough. Within no time, I was able to identify over a hundred and fifty angels, in and around the government, with some tie to the cell. Much the same way I had memorized the written materials I was provided, I kept a catalog in my head of all these angels. When home or even at work, I would keep lists of coded information to make sure I could reconstruct correctly what I would need when the time came. My very life might depend on how accurately I could recall all the data I was compiling. That said, I was still unable to lay my hand on Mastema's book.

I give Mastema quite a bit of credit for having stayed mostly out of my affairs, while I worked my way in. I was concerned he might consider requiring constant meetings to check on my progress and whether he was getting his money's worth. To my surprise, I did not hear from him even after I returned to the PID. I would see him from time to time around the government offices, attending meetings and socializing. He ignored me as he would any mid-level functionary. But I knew that sometime soon, he would come looking for the book. Looking for his payout.

⌘ ⌘ ⌘

There were at least two senior Fallen in the City at any given time, each one responsible for maintaining and feeding information to cells. I should step back on this point for a moment. Though I could now see an extensive network of Fallen through my renewed work at the PID, it became clear that my cell was not the only one in the City. Information coming into my cell did not always match the information I saw circulating around the City. My only guess was that it came from the outside. But who ran that operation and how they managed to maintain such tight control remained a mystery to me. Commerce in and out of the City of God was fairly constant. But it was impossible to put a finger on just who was trafficking. Whatever information did make its way in was ultimately collected by one of these two senior Fallen and distributed out the spokes of the organization. Necessary and appropriate information was sent further down the line. Angels at the bottom did not need to know the identities of angels at the top. No more than two angels knew of the right downstream contacts at any given time. The system had been perfected over the years, as was clear from the fact that no one cell knew very much about any other. Only the two hubs had anything close to an overall picture of the situation and it was logical that neither of these two senior Fallen should know who the other was. I knew Jehoel to be one, but who was this other?

Ironically, God's bureaucracy played an inadvertent, but rather useful role in camouflaging much of the Fallen's heretical activities. No matter how ruthless and meticulous the Secret Police might be, they were rather predictable. Those who rejected the Fallen initiation were often handed over to the Secret Police. It gave the latter some confirmation of a greater conspiracy without seriously imperiling the cell itself. An unspoken deal seemed to have been struck. Fallen would give up failed initiates and the Secret Police would usually be content with the offerings in exchange for the pretext these "captured insurgents" afforded of proving their competence and their indispensability to the government. Even in rebellion, it seemed, graft had a necessary role.

"In an organization this size, it is impossible to maintain total secrecy," Jehoel explained one night. "Someone is going to know we are out there. This way, the Secret Police get what they need and we dispense with those we cannot trust."

"How symbiotic!" I huffed.

"Yes, I guess, in a way."

"Not very democratic," I replied mockingly. It seemed even those who dreamed of a Godless harmony were corruptible and afflicted with a bureaucratic mindset.

When the Secret Police did strike it lucky on their own, the system was designed to prevent widespread panic among the cells. They might apprehend, at most, a single string of heretics, but certainly not enough of them to understand the complexity of the entire web. Such arrests were not discussed publicly, for there was little to be gained in revealing to the citizenry how widespread the menace was. Or how organized. Interrogations were shared with only the highest orders of angels, while the always-messy results were posted officially on the bloody walls of the City.

"The people are kept in the dark for fear they might play a part in spreading the rebellion," Jehoel said. "God focuses on the outlanders. That is the PID's real mission. It helps refocus the angels' attention."

"And directs their fears," I followed.

"Yes. God must remove from our sight all concrete evidence of actually wrongdoing, for to show His people how unhappy they are would surely hasten his fall." Jehoel's logic sounded strained to me at the time, but I was willing to go with it.

It took me a while to pass the Fallens' test, but it seems I did it in the right way. At first, I wanted to bring them everything and was reprimanded on several occasions for providing either too much information or what was considered of questionable value.

"Déjà vu," Jehoel said to me one day. He knew to expect such behavior from me. "Independently verifiable information," was all he said.

Now this is not something to come by easily, and while I had legions of sources in the City and maintained my connections in the army, there was actually very little I could share. Ironically, my behavior in those early days actually saved my neck. Had I given the Fallen something really big and important right away, they might have sensed my alternate purpose. The fact that I came across as clueless strengthened their faith in the sincerity of my intentions. At the time, I did not understand how my uselessness had proved my worthiness, but I guess not having a strategy can sometimes be a strategy in itself.

Regardless of their opinion, I personally always found something useful in the data. Say, grain stores were being moved to different districts or construction projects were engaging or being wound up along the lengths of wall. A commander might order such maneuvers to throw off the enemy's calculations; feints, as it were, designed to divert attention from the army's ultimate purpose. Bureaucrats, though, did not think along these lines. Whatever they did was motivated by the need for personal recognition and the chance of advancement. From this mosaic of little-world contests, a larger picture could be pieced together. Examining it intently, I could see certain objectives that were not immediately apparent to those in the mix. With movements of grain came the movements of soldiers. With aqueduct construction and wall refurbishment came political favors and deals being struck. I viewed all this information with an eye toward understanding the Fallen's structure.

⌘ ⌘ ⌘

It took me a while, but eventually, I was able to sort out what the Fallen considered useful from what was just plain noise. The trick lay in recognizing that the Fallen were bureaucrats, just like those in God's government. Their aims may have clashed, but their operations were, necessarily, conducted along the same lines. This deflated me a bit, as I began to imagine a time when one round of bureaucrats would simply replace another. Different mantra, same formula.

Once I had returned to the PID and started playing the part, Jehoel stopped his periodic threats and became almost thankful. Maybe even a bit proud of my usefulness. In the Fallen's thirst for information, trust that would normally have taken a significant period of time to establish was built quickly. I did not understand it. They could have obtained much of the same information from Jehoel himself, but seemed pleased now to get it from me. He was the Minister, after all. The reach of his access far exceeded my own.

"That may be true, but sometimes, what may be plain to you is noise to me. You have served a greater purpose here," he told me one day, when I was feeling particularly vulnerable.

I did not know what he meant, but was amused to have achieved a higher degree of notoriety simultaneously in the ministry and within the Fallen by working to betray them both. Soon, I was permitted to make reports directly to the council of Fallen itself. Of course, I initially objected to this development, as such direct connections jeopardized their safety. Viewed from another perspective, such a promotion escalated the danger I would be in, should Mastema come to understand that I was working both sides. In the Fallen's eyes, this only served to underscore my commitment to them. I allowed myself to be talked into it.

⌘ ⌘ ⌘

Whether he realized it or not, Jehoel's advice changed everything for me. My clear change of heart, as one Ministry Council member characterized it, brought me into ever-higher circles of power and influence. Not that I was afraid of senior government people, but I had never before been comfortable speaking with them as equals. They spoke in two ways. The first, in wide, sweeping platitudes aimed at convincing the already converted. I considered this a completely senseless exercise, but one necessary to undertake, if for no other reason than to demonstrate that you had "got it," and were capable of discharging more complicated and pointless projects. It did not matter if they knew not what they talked about, so long as they said something everyone agreed with. The second kind of speech favored by senior officials involved a fencing game, where they always one-upped each other, selecting choice pieces of information from their conversations, until they had enough to create gossip to start their own circles and direct missiles at their pre-selected targets. Walking the fine line between inanity and a firefight proved a delicate exercise, requiring little intellect, but great amounts of skill.

"The most sublime element of this truth," Jehoel said one night at one of these high-society gatherings I was becoming more accustomed to attending, "the reason such magnificent and horrible changes are possible without making those under its influence rise up in revolt is that institutions such as ours are indefinite..."

Half the crowd was oblivious, while the other half looked stunned by such a statement. The two groups whispered sense-lessly among themselves.

Smiling confidently, Jehoel continued, "...and necessarily are required and, perhaps, even suited to being defined and redefined according to the necessities of the future."

The crowd was suddenly relieved and nodded along in agree-ment. No one knew what he meant, but they all agreed.

I was suddenly nervous. "What was that?" I asked, as we po-litely stepped away to find another group of adherents.

"What?" he asked sarcastically. When he recognized the seri-ousness of my intent, he huffed, "Have you not learned anything in all the time we have been friends?"

I shrugged noncommittally.

"Speaking with certain angels," he continued, "one must know where to land the most pointed of views. If you want to make these angels yours, you must discuss issues that make them yours."

"By tossing seemingly heretical notions into their midst?"

"No. By telling them the things they want to hear in ways they have never heard them before. When angels think you know something they do not, you make your position clear to them: 'I am superior to you in the eyes of God.'" Gesturing over his shoulder, he continued, "In this one simple exchange, I was able to make six senior Virtues from a variety of ministries imagine that I was both cavalier and patriotic about my positions. Their reactions betrayed their own views on the same topic. Did you note that idiot, Haniel, from the Interior Ministry made no comment when I suggested the ministry system was a farce? Unlike his fellow Virtues, he also abstained from comment when I turned back to the party line and suggested we are ever-evolving."

"He is sympathetic, yes. His reaction was there for anyone looking at him to read. But jockeying for information among gossipmongers seems a grim and dangerous way of filling our database."

"That is the dance, Ahriman. Not everything comes from an informant or a tortured captive. Sometimes, you need these instances to make something up, just to see whether, when, and where it comes back to you. These folks use it as a survival tactic. But you and I can use it to extract information from a willing victim. If you cannot clearly demonstrate your own ability to become informed, you will quickly turn into a target and become easy prey."

"And they will pick your bones dry," I replied, noting the crowd around me.

"And happily move on to the next victim," Jehoel concluded.

He was right. There were many systems I needed to work within. If I wanted to succeed in anything I did, I would need to learn to dance. So I made it a point to attend as many of these social gatherings as possible, forcing myself to be as personable as I could be. I was unhappy to find that I could not master self-control the way Jehoel had. I understood the theory, the importance of playing the part, and all the other things that came along with that. But I had nothing to say, nothing to add to the inane conversations in which these people delighted. They measured themselves by a set of criteria that was different from my own. They collected power by spouting nonsense each day and ranked themselves by it. I considered their nonsense, but could only use it successfully to classify them as some varying form of idiot.

My inability to adapt quickly posed certain very real problems. For the first time, I understood some of the reasons underlying Angra's estrangement from me. He was as skilled a marksman in these circles as any. But having a son who never properly played the game made him an easy target. Now that I was in the thick of it, I could see a father's disadvantages in having me as a son.

I kept telling myself I could take advantage of my neophyte status, if I just learned to play. It was not that the game made any more sense or that I derived any satisfaction from playing it. I was driven. I was bright and shiny new, rising from the dust of a failed first attempt in government, and now looking for favors to make up for lost time. This made me an unknown quantity and the intrigue implied in getting to understand me prompted these sociopaths to show little hesitation in letting me into their circle. I was a changed angel and open to taking a position as someone else's pawn. By doing the rounds, as Jehoel had, I slowly picked up information from one and was expected to share it with all. They treated me like I had always been there among them and feigned astonishment when I innocently hinted at my earlier transgressions. Innocence both amused and amazed them. It was like ringing the dinner bell. By affecting an air of naïveté, I was able to protect myself from speculation that I sought power.

But time was running out. Soon, I would be expected to choose my allegiances and begin launching my personal offensives against the concerned enemies to demonstrate my worthiness to some new master. If I did not take up the fight as I should or waited too long, making it clear I was still in the market for better digs, I ran the risk of blowing myself up all together. I seriously doubted whether I would have another shot at this.

"No amount of work will resurrect you from that," Jehoel informed me. "Ignoring the game is one thing, Ahriman. Playing and losing it is something different altogether."

CHAPTER SIXTEEN

It was about this time that Zoan became ill. While we had exchanged some unkind words when last we spoke, my grandfather had always remained very close to my heart and the thought of him no longer being part of my life saddened me. I hated nearly everything about my father and his nefarious comings and goings. With Zoan, I had always felt free to speak my mind. I wallowed in the bitter truth of having rejected him for his honesty. Maybe he was too old to care anymore. Or maybe he cared about what I said, even if it was misdirected or just plain wrongheaded. Whatever it was, I was determined to work it out with him.

During his illness, he secluded himself in his home, seeing few angels. "When you were young," he said to me one night, when I went to visit him, "you listened with fascination to my stories about the wars in the outlands."

"I know. It made me proud to be your grandson," I said, beaming even then. "My friends would all be jealous, listening to how you had led the City's armies outside the walls to meet the trimmers, beating them back and saving the City from annihilation."

"Ahriman, spare an old angel your expletives," he requested.

"Sorry, Grandfather. I meant 'Outlanders.'"

"Tartaruians," Zoan said, correcting me and returning to his earlier amiable mood. "I remember it well. You and all your friends would cheer and roll around on the floor as I spoke of the battles, the cavalry charges..." He paused for a moment, as if looking back into the past. "And the carnage."

"Your campaigns were the stuff of legend and none of us could wait to be old enough to join the army and fight like you had."

"Yes," he said absently, still somewhere in the past.

"We would suit up in our play armor and re-enact the battles in the estate fields, while the house girls looked on and laughingly whispered about us. We would fight to see who would be you, Grandfather. I almost always won in the end. It was only fair."

"Yes," he said with a laugh, coming back from his daydream. "No one could beat you with a sword or a spear."

"Only Simon, but that was much later."

"Simon, yes."

"He leads large parts of our armies now."

"In the outlands, yes." Zoan looked at a nearby table where, on my way in, I had noticed an article about a recent battle fought and won by Simon. Zoan fell back into his stupor.

"What is it, Grandfather? Why do you seem so distant? Are you still cross with me?"

Zoan snapped back to attention. "No, no. Forgive me, boy. I am not well and when angels begin feeling the time is near, they look back upon what they have accomplished."

"Few have accomplished what you have, Grandfather."

"Yes. Few. I hear you are back in the ministry again."

"Yes. I returned not too long ago."

"Purges? Are there to be more purges?"

He had surprised me.

"Why do you ask? You know I cannot talk about such things with you. Even if I knew."

"The worst is when someone is brought down for corruption or disloyalty. Everyone falls with them," Zoan said, ignoring my words.

"Yes, well, I guess that is so."

"Even the highest strata of those quivering gossip fops dread purges," he said with sudden venom.

"Yes, I guess so."

"God has always used such purges to remove anyone who has fallen from favor," he said, turning in his seat. "Whether they were linked to the supposed traitor or not." Zoan's voice was a little hoarse from his ailment.

"It is my feeling that God allows the circles to operate. Even thrive," I said, testing his knowledge of things.

He still seemed very far away.

"Yes. Well, that is what happens, sometimes." He looked at me straight in the eye. "But at least, they did not find my head stuck on any City wall," he said, laughing. He often said this to Angra, whenever they spoke of his resignation from the Order.

I smiled uneasily in response. He was sick and sick angels say strange things. Not surprisingly, Angra had never felt inclined to laugh when they spoke this way.

⌘　⌘　⌘

I decided I would not press Zoan for information about his resignation from the Order. Whatever had happened belonged to a distant past and there was nothing I could do about it now. My family had acquired some notoriety, but that had its advantages. And no matter what had happened, my grandfather was allowed to retain his wealth, which was more than I could say for many hundreds of other poor bastards. I began to visit Zoan on a more regular basis.

I went to his home one night to find him sitting on a couch, reading in the dim light. He looked well enough, but the house-maid told me he had been seized by frequent fits of violent coughing since I saw him last. "Whatever his illness, it will soon take him," she said apologetically.

When Zoan saw me, his face lit up. "Ahriman," he piped, gesturing for me to sit with him on the couch. "Where have you been?"

"I was here just a few nights ago, Grandfather. You know that," I said, as I approached.

"Ah yes. Forgive me." He coughed for a few moments. "You have been able to visit me a lot more frequently recently. I like that." He was pleased, but quite exhausted.

"Well, I was gone for a while. I took a sabbatical. You knew that too. Grandfather, you look rather tired. Why are you up and reading in your condition?"

"Does a sabbatical mean you cannot call on your elderly grandfather now and then?" he asked, ignoring my last question.

I smiled and sat in the chair right next to the couch. "You always knew me better than I knew myself," I said. "You are right. I should have visited you more often." I dropped the subject of his obvious weariness. It was not worth exhausting him further by arguing with him about it.

"What were you doing while on sabbatical?" he asked, wiping his mouth and unsuccessfully stifling a cough.

"I was doing something on the far side of the City. It required my full attention."

Zoan looked at me silently for a moment. "That is what I love about you, Ahriman. Ever since you were a boy, when something interested you, you gave it your full attention. Working, always working to make things right."

"I guess so. Even as a boy, eh?"

"Yep."

He coughed a bit more. I picked up the book he had been reading.

"What is this?" I asked gesturing toward the book.

"Well, I have been reading this the past few nights," he said, guiding me to the open page from which he had been distracted.

"What is it?" I asked again, turning the book over and over, not seeing its title anywhere.

"It is a story that was written long ago about a great angel who falls under the weight of his own shortsightedness."

I was momentarily confused. "Surely, such a book would have been censored?" I asked.

"Indeed," Zoan said, smiling. "But I am sure you are willing to humor an old, dying angel." He was so frail now. Not like the angel I used to ride with when I was a boy.

⌘ ⌘ ⌘

The Acheron had its roots in the mountains to the north of the City and was, in fact, the City's primary source of water. The Great Dividing River separated Elysium from Tartarus. West from east. Civilization from chaos, we had been taught. With much fanfare, God had ordered the construction of great aqueducts in ages past to feed the City. The first had come up in the south, from a place known as Apsatsus or the Forks of Apsatsus, where the Acheron met the Styx and ran northward, parallel to the Acheron, up to the City. Most of the fighting I had seen as a soldier was aimed at protecting the aqueducts, and the roads and towns that had grown up along its length, from trimmer attack. Much later, the construction of another aqueduct farther north along the Acheron and much closer to the City had led to this older one falling into disrepair. The spaces of Elysium between the City and Apsatsus had decayed along with it.

Zoan would frequently take rides to and around the lower Acheron. Most in the City would never have attempted leisure trips to places so close to the areas where trimmers were active. Tartarus may have been on the eastern shore of the Acheron, but trimmers frequently carried out raids across the Forks. It was part of the reason Apsatsus itself as a City colony had diminished. It was just too costly to protect. But Zoan felt comfortable enough there and had told me on many occasions how it reminded him of his greatest feats, those for which he had become so well known and loved.

Though he had shocked the citizenry when he stepped down from the Order of the Seraphim, Zoan had remained an easily recognizable figure throughout the City. He had spent time as a professor in the City's university system and was often seen in quiet restaurants and cafés, meeting with up-and-coming army officers. But he had avoided the throngs of God's minions. In a world where *who* you knew was almost as important as *what* you knew, he had made himself an outsider, spurning the pageantry of the well-to-do and their perennial gaggle of hangers-on. Statuary, depicting Zoan as "Lord Protector" of the City of God, had cropped up around the City. No one had failed to notice when God took no action. Those in the sinful circles of gossiping power mongers would take this to mean that Zoan's split from God did not imply a fall from grace. Still others believed the schism had personal significance for both. Both Angra and Mastema had shared their perceptions of the matter with me. Something very crucial must have been at stake for God to let such an affront go unchallenged.

But back to Zoan. I recall a day from my childhood, when Zoan and I had ridden down the western banks of the Acheron on our way to Apsatsus. I was still in primary school and being able to tell my friends I had ridden down so close to the Styx was enough to confer on me the mantle of celebrity. It had made me nervous and proud at the same time.

We had ridden down through a small town several miles to the north of the Forks, just off the main road. Towns such as these tended to be dangerous. So close to the river and yet so far from the City, they were frequently prey to trimmer forays across the river. But trading through these towns could also be profitable, if luck was on your side. Large crops of ambrosia, both legal and illicit, were grown around and moved through these places. City currency was generally not used, unless locals had recently been in the City to do business. Most City dwellers looked down on townspeople, regardless of whether the latter were colonists or not. Sure, they would do business with them, but townspeople were invariably perceived as either country bumpkins or thieves. Or both. To people of the City, colonists and tradesmen were not trimmers, certainly, but they were outlanders. And that was enough to brand them as undesirables. Zoan did not seem to have any such preconceived notions about these people.

As we approached this town's main square, looking for a place to water our horses and quench our own thirst, we had stumbled upon a ruckus. A mob of angels stood collected around a group of what were clearly City tax collectors.

"You dare tell me you won't pay your rightful levy?" the leader of the tax squad had shouted at what turned out to be the town's portly mayor.

Other angels, gathered around the mayor, had carefully eyed the tax collectors' sheathed swords and stood there oafishly. They were simply incapable of providing any real support.

"It is not that we don't want to pay the levy, Captain," the clearly terrified angel had pleaded. "I swear. But if we pay now, we won't be able to feed ourselves next season."

The captain's sweat-stained armpits had especially caught my attention. I had never seen anyone like him. So much accumulated rage at his disposal, at the tips of his fingers. Townspeople, caught up in the tumult, had looked on anxiously at the exchange. Their lives would depend on what happened next.

"I see," the captain had said, stepping back from the mayor. He had folded his arms across his chest, striking a theatrical pose. "Let me understand you. I'm to report to our Lord that your village, unlike all the other Acheron villages, is too poor this season to pay His levies? Why? You didn't run enough brois this year?" he had asked mockingly, suggesting the town operated as an illegal ambrosia conduit.

The mayor had looked around as the angels beside him inched away in fear.

Raising his voice, the captain had continued, "Am I to tell Him that this village is special and should not have to pay? Are you telling me that I should go to Him and tell Him that I cannot perform my job because of you, you fat dung pile, and your wretched town?"

The mayor had winced. Clearly, this was not how the conversation was meant to progress.

"Are you so inept at governing your people properly in the eyes of God," the captain screamed, now foaming at the mouth, "that you have eaten your levies for the season?"

In an instant, the officer had translated his fury into a much-too-well-practiced punch. Floored in one shot, the mayor had not had the strength to defend himself, as the captain's brute squad sprang into action and began kicking him everywhere their steel-tipped boots could reach. The anxious townspeople had cowered away, covering their eyes and reeling at the sudden onslaught of violence. No one had come to the mayor's aid. They had slinked away from the shame of their impotence as they failed to put a stop to the many blows raining down on the hapless target's legs, stomach, and face.

Witnessing this scene, Zoan had spurred his horse forward, quickly catching the thugs' attention. The captain must have taken my grandfather for nobility, because he had immediately called a halt to the beating, stripped his voice of its earlier harsh tones to a mellowness so uncharacteristic as to be unrecognizable, and shouted out a merry "Good day, sir!" as Zoan reigned in his horse.

"Good day, sir. What is happening here?" Zoan had asked, looking down at the bleeding angel writhing on the ground in pain.

"We are collecting levies this afternoon," the captain had replied with just the slightest hint of impertinence in his voice, before adding, "my Lord." He had smiled and, in more hushed tones, confided, "And this lot seems to think the market price of brois dropped this year." He had sniggered to himself.

"I see," Zoan had said coolly. "Tell me, Captain, is it the policy of the House of Levies to have angels beaten when they are unable to pay their levies?"

A little taken aback by Zoan's perceived effrontery, the captain had taken the reins of my grandfather's horse and stepped up to ensure that his words could not be overheard by those standing around them. I remember feeling suddenly anxious when I saw this. While I had witnessed my share of fights in the schoolyard, this was something completely different. I had felt sure I would not be able to defend Zoan, if things got out of hand. There were many more of them than I could handle and it was clear these angels were experienced hands. Fear had seized me, yes, but not cowardice. I was armed. So I had spurred my horse up to Zoan's.

"Indeed, sir," the captain had retorted, eyeballing me as I approached, "it is the policy of the House of Levies to offer recalcitrant taxpayers, how shall we put it, incentives to pay their taxes when they fall due. In addition, this lot has plenty of black-market brois to go around."

The captain had come ever so much closer to my grandfather. I could now get a whiff of his odor, as sweat seeped through his garments.

"It would be wise, sir, in order to avoid any incident," the captain had continued, one hand on the pommel of his sword, as he gestured in my direction with the other, "if you and your young companion refrained from interfering in such affairs and moved on." He paused for effect. "That is, unless you prefer to come with us and explain why you interfered in official state business," he sneered, flicking a look at his brutes, still huffing from their exertions after the beating they had inflicted on the stricken mayor.

"I see I was misspoken," Zoan had said loudly, ensuring that his words would fall farther than just upon the ears of the leering captain. "I initially showed my respect for you by using the moniker of 'sir' while addressing you. A mistake I will not make again."

Shocked at what he took to be Zoan's insolence, the captain had, momentarily, been dumbstruck. I do believe he would have ordered my grandfather to be taken into custody, had the latter not issued a command at that very same moment.

"You will release that angel now," Zoan had declared, gesturing to the mayor. He had then pointed to the crowd of onlookers. "You there!" he had shouted, picking a dumbfounded onlooker out of the crowd. "Come and help this angel to his feet. Then bring him for medical attention!"

The captain's shock had grown exponentially in an instant. His brutes stood looking around sheepishly as the bleeding, but thankful mayor was dragged up from the ground.

"You, Captain!" Zoan had shouted.

The captain had shuddered with the sudden shock of realizing it was he who was being summoned.

"Move on to your next site. You or your master can meet me this evening at the House of Levies, where I will pay this town's taxes in City currency."

The captain had stood there, mouth agape. The gaps in his rows of teeth had sickened me even more than his sweaty armpits. It was the first time I had looked real malice in the face, I think. And I had felt ashamed of myself for initially allowing the power of that malice to intimidate me. I was ashamed about doubting myself. About doubting Zoan. It would have been the easiest thing in the world to continue on our way, past that town, leaving it and its mayor to whatever end God's providence had in store. But not for Zoan. It was the injustice of God's system of justice that had stirred him to action.

For the captain, payment of the town's levies in currency would not only save him the trouble of having to negotiate in the barter for specie payments, but would also land him a fatter commission.

"How do I know you have it?" he had asked my grandfather, rubbing the bottom of his chin whiskers.

Zoan had pulled out a moneybag and dropped a single talent of gold onto the floor under the hooves of the captain's horse. "If you are willing to risk being pissed upon, the talent is yours," he had declared.

No one in the crowd had uttered a sound. Even the brutes had stood by anxiously, as if trying to judge how difficult it would be to wash piss out of their uniforms.

Clearly an angel of deep moral fiber, the captain had laid aside his public taunting. "If this is what you wish, sir," he had said obsequiously, "we will oblige," he had said as he stooped down and picked up the talent. A month's worth of pay and he had not even gotten pissed on.

"That is the spirit, Captain!" Zoan had shouted. "Let us hope this town will be more obedient in the future to our master, the Lord God, and have the proper levies prepared for our good captain's impending return."

The villagers were now as shocked as the captain had been a few moments earlier.

"Let us also hope that other towns and villages along the Great Dividing River have more foresight than this one," Zoan had continued, looking down at the steadily recovering mayor, "in paying their levies and trafficking in contraband. My family does not, after all, have at its command the sort of resources required to pay the levies of every town and village in the region."

The crowd and even the tax collectors had laughed, now that Zoan's lightheartedness had resolved the matter.

The image of those people—standing there, thanking Zoan for his generosity and his willingness to confront angry and dangerous angels on their behalf—is something that drives me even today. These townspeople had been total strangers. Probably smugglers. Outlanders, even. Someone else would have walked away. Someone else might have extracted payment from the townspeople for intervening on their behalf. Zoan had done neither and, as a result, had achieved something no one else would have. Zoan had never feared God's angels as I did. Through his deeds in that nameless town, he had both honored God and belittled Him in His work. He had looked evil in the eye without flinching. And had done the right thing against all odds. At least, that is how I see it.

⌘　⌘　⌘

"Why are you reading such a book, Grandfather?" I asked Zoan as I came back to the present. "You knew I was coming here tonight?"

"Why could your father not see things as you do?" he asked, ignoring my question.

"What do you mean?"

"I think you do," he replied, crinkling his eyes at me.

I continued looking at the book and ignored him in turn.

"My boy," Zoan continued, "since the day you arrived, your father and I have had philosophical differences over your upbringing. Knockdown, drag-out differences. From the beginning, he wanted you to go to the finest schools, do your mandatory service in the army, come out with fitting decorations and achievements, and act as the savior of our family by undoing the damage he perceived I had done. I, on the other hand, was keen that you should go the way you wanted, do the things that you wanted to do, and get there at a tempo you felt best suited you. It is a bitter irony that your father wanted you to grow up to do what I had done, without actually wanting to know who or what I was."

"But you were all those things, Grandfather. That description you just gave of father's vision of me fits *you* perfectly."

"That is where you are both so very wrong." His last few words were veiled in an inexplicable sadness. "I am not the angel you and your father imagine me to be. In fact, if anything, I have been quite the opposite."

"I do not understand," I said, genuinely confused.

The nurse had explained earlier that my grandfather was becoming disoriented, but this was something more.

"Well, tonight is the night," Zoan said now, his voice deep and firm with resolve. "We will have the conversation you have sought from me for so long. That your father has sought from me his whole life. My parting gift for you, Ahriman, will be the truth. About me. For the first time since the City was refounded."

⌘ ⌘ ⌘

"Everything you know about me is a lie," said he started.

It was not the best way to start a conversation, but it certainly got my attention.

"Okay. Explain." I had been waiting for Zoan's explanation from the time I could understand the word "Seraphim." I believed myself prepared to expect anything.

"The City, God, His people. Things were not always the way you see them today. The way your schoolbooks read. The way God wants His people to see things now."

Of course, I immediately thought of Jehoel and began to sweat.

"I was one of God's angels. One of God's greatest angels, but I am not the war hero the City believes me to be. Wars were wars of power and control, not the way they are portrayed now as struggles for survival." Seeing the question in my eyes, he said, "But I need to be clearer. I have considered these things for so long in my own mind that I forget the story remains only in my head and known to only a handful of angels."

"Try again, Grandfather. It is important to me, because it is important to you."

He smiled and I think I was able to put him somewhat more at ease.

"Trimmers, as God calls them, constantly threatened the City. You know this. They harassed us constantly. Not like it is today, with them hiding on the far side of the Acheron. They would carry out their assaults on the walls, but quickly dissolve into the Elysian grasslands that had once surrounded the City. As one of God's greatest angels, it was my duty to pursue these rogues into the outlands. But the army and, especially, Gabriel frowned on long patrols, particularly anything that involved foraying into Tartarus, where our supply lines could easily be cut and transmission of intelligence rendered difficult."

"That is nearly as true today as it was then."

"Yes, but as you know, Ahriman, attacks against this City no longer take place."

He was, of course, right.

"Our citizens live in fear of Tartaruians, but it is God Who creates these fears and fuels them. Trimmers!" Zoan said with disdain.

Again, I thought of Jehoel, but quickly put my thoughts aside.

"That may be so," I said, "but even today, we are limited in what we can do in order to take the battle to the trim...Tartaruians. In my years in the army, hardly ever did we cross the Acheron. When we did, it resulted in losses."

It was in the marshes of the Forks that Simon and I had been ambushed and wounded.

"As you say, it is not so different now. At least, in that regard. But Gabriel and I saw things differently. He did not believe in taking the battle to the Tartaruians. He feared defeat in foreign lands, leaving the City without protection, even if I organized and ran that protection. Do not misunderstand me. We were friends, Gabriel and I, but we were also rivals. He preferred to think of the Tartaruian threat as a disorganized one, represented by nothing more than a discontented rabble. I disagreed and told God as much. In the end, Gabriel was more persuasive."

"You waited," I surmised.

"Yes. And no. The south wall was constantly under attack. A war council was convened. In the presence of God Himself, Gabriel and I were involved in a dispute over my idea of hitting the Tartaruians where it hurt. I argued that simply being engaged in skirmishes to defend the wall would never actually secure us as a people. We had to take the plunge, going on the offensive, and take the fight right into Tartarus. I assumed Gabriel resisted the idea of venturing into the outlands, because he knew God would give me command of the army. Gabriel is a proud sort of angel. Straight to your face, but has no compunctions about going behind your back to get what he wants the most. Always more interested in fame and power than in the substance of the efforts." Zoan looked at me very closely. "You have to be careful of angels like that. Sometimes, people substitute action with words about action, not knowing or not willing to see that one does not equal the other."

I nodded in agreement, thinking of the last eternity I had spent working in the ministry.

"God eventually called me to Him and asked me to quietly take the army outside the walls. To reconnoiter those areas where we had been too 'weak,' He said, to tread before. I remember His word so clearly: weak. I had never heard Him use that word. Weakness is not something God suffers lightly. Weakness is not a word He utters in public and uses only sparingly, to say the least, even with His most senior trusted counsel."

Grandfather repositioned himself on the couch. Pain caught the muscles of his face in a spasmodic grip, then passed in seconds.

"Are you all right?" I asked, deeply concerned. "We can stop, if you are uncomfortable."

"Do not worry about me, Ahriman," Zoan said. "There is little left for me now. God and the Gabriels of these heavens may be everlasting, but I will remain mortal among the many." He coughed.

"You are sure?" I asked.

Sensing his pain, the nurse came into the room. She was anxious for me to stop exciting him.

He smiled a thin smile at me. "Perhaps it was a little too much to tell you in one evening," he said, acknowledging he had pushed himself to the limit. "Can you come back again soon?"

"I will be back as soon as I can. I promise."

CHAPTER SEVENTEEN

But my time had run out. Shortly after I had been to see Zoan, Mastema came calling. I guess I should not have been surprised. It had been quite sometime since we had last discussed my progress. My return to the PID was public knowledge. I was certain he knew more.

"I assumed you would have made more thorough inroads into the organization by now," he said, as we sat in one of the City's many nondescript drinking establishments. The veneer of this part of the City may have been clean, but its guts were as dirty as any common wretch's hovel. The wine was of poor quality, but there were not too many interested ears there, and I am sure Mastema was not intent on wasting good wine on the likes of me.

"I told you when we last spoke," I replied. "They 'picked' me to spy on the government. They knew I was not the person I had presented myself as. You did not get me 'in.' *They* let me in."

"What difference does that make? You're in and you're now supplying the cell with intelligence. You've been at it for quite some time now, Ahriman. Enough time to start taking some risks," he said mockingly.

"Risks? You are lecturing *me* about risks? Let us remember something here. I am the one on the knife's edge, Mastema. Let us take a quick tally. If I get caught, I am dead. If you get caught, I am dead. Let us not fool ourselves on that one."

He made a mock-childish grimace of innocence.

"If the cell decides I am expendable, I am dead. Where are you in all this? Where exactly is your risk?"

"You have no idea what you're doing, do you?" he asked. "I had figured your grandfather would have explained it to you by now." He uttered the words with a straight face. No emotion at all.

"You leave my grandfather out of this," I said quietly, but through tightly clenched teeth. "One hair on his head out of place, and you will be begging me to kill you before I am done."

Mastema leaned back in his chair and smiled. "A few months in the underworld and you think you're a gangster now. No, my friend. I'm not making threats. You've got it wrong. The book, Ahriman. The book. You've been looking for it, but it's your grandfather who knows about the book."

"What are you talking about? I infiltrated the cell to find the book. What does Zoan have to do with it?"

"If the cell has the book, they got it from your grandfather. You say they targeted you for information about the government, what they're doing, where they're sending troops, blah, blah, blah. Don't you see? You're the scion. We both targeted you, because you are the only one that everyone can trust." He shifted in his seat, lighting a cigar.

"But I..."

"Don't waste any more of my time," he interrupted. "I've given you ample space to build a relationship with the cell. Get the book. Ask them for it and they will give it to you. Ask them and they will *have* to give it to you. Because you are your grandfather's grandson."

⌘ ⌘ ⌘

"Time is running out, my boy," Zoan said, as I returned to his house the very next day.

I had left work early to meet with him. No one knew I had left early. But it would not matter to anyone whether I had, indeed, done so. I had left word with my department that I was going to meet with someone in another department on some issue of minor consequence. I had said nothing to the department where I claimed to have the meeting, and they believed me to be working in my own department. If either office called the other, I was, invariably, in transit.

"I do not have time for games, Grandfather," I said, coming to the point. "I need to know something."

"Yes, I know."

"'Yes, you know' what exactly?"

"Why you are here, of course. You know your father came to me in much the same way, many years ago. I did not give him what he wanted. I have hardly seen him since. Funny that now I have no choice. Even though I do not believe you to be entirely worthy, I will give you what I withheld from him. I have to give it to you or it might be lost."

"Give what to me? What is 'it'?"

Zoan was propped up in his bed. He had grown a sickly gray overnight. His cough had worsened and while he hid his sickness well, I could see specks of blood on his sheets. And hands. Both our hands shook, but for entirely different reasons. His was the end, but mine was the beginning.

"You want to know about the outlanders," Zoan said. "You want to know about the book."

"Do you know Mastema?" I asked somewhat frantically. "Has he spoken to you? How do you know him?"

"I know *of* Mastema. He means nothing here. He is just a cheap treasure hunter. A tomb raider. Just like your father and the reams of other angels who came to me asking for it." He broke off into a cough.

"What does he want with this book? Why has he come to me?" I paused, as Zoan coughed again. "Grandfather, I have put myself in a really difficult position."

He seemed to take interest in these words as he wiped his mouth. I had to come clean. What did it matter if I came clean to an angel on the verge of death?

"I have agreed to use my position at the PID to provide information to a rebellious cell within the City. But my real motive is to lay my hands on a book that outlines their plans. I have promised this book to Mastema in exchange for political standing. I get him the book; he gives me a leg up. He turns me in; I die. Do you understand?"

Zoan broke into a prolonged cough. I could tell from the way he nodded his head that he was listening and understood.

When he could draw breath again, he said, "Then you have been played a fool. And so have I. I had hoped that you would develop more noble goals than your father ever had, but it seems that two successive generations of our family have sought the same ends. Fame. Power." He coughed lightly. "These things are temporary. There is a big difference between becoming a legend and being a hero. In the end, all things are temporary with God. He will never let you get close enough to kill Him."

"No, Grandfather, I don't want to kill God." I could not understand why he had come to this conclusion. "I want to be His Seraph, like you were once." I choked on this last part. All of this was for power. Power to show my grandfather how he had done things wrong. I had done it all wrong, it seemed.

"It does not matter now, Ahriman," he said, shaking his head. "I will never know your true purpose. I will not live long enough to see it. I can only hope that in the end, you do the right thing." My heart dropped. "What is the right thing, Grandfather?" Tears were in my eyes now.

He coughed some more. Blood, this time.

"Tell me how to do the right thing," I persisted.

He wiped his mouth again. Blood smeared his handkerchief. "I cannot tell you how to live your life, Ahriman. It seems you are the best I have to offer. So I will share this with you."

⌘ ⌘ ⌘

"When God made me His First Seraph, Gabriel was livid," Zoan said. "All his conspiring, all his machinations, had gone up in smoke. We had both been Cherubim for so long. It was impossible for me to now outrank him. God knew Gabriel did not have the tactical experience to lead an army, but I also knew I did not have the strategic foresight to outmaneuver Gabriel. God sensed all this and took advantage of it. If Gabriel and I focused our attacks on each other, we would not focus our attacks on Him. And believe me, fear is something He lives with every day. Fear of losing His position. Fear of the truth.

"So I finally got what I wanted. I led the army out the City's walls. Your grandmother, bless her, waved to me from the walls, walls that were burned black at the gates by the fires of outlanders. Those walls had been built off the backs of God's slaves. Well, angels whom He had basically turned into slaves. Angels whom Gabriel had used to build His castles. Angels I had used to throw down the gauntlet in a losing war."

He was clearly grieving over his memories.

"But is it not important to achieve what you desire? Is there something intrinsically wrong in doing what we are driven to do?" I asked.

"No," he said, without blinking. "So long as you are doing the right thing."

Again. The "right" thing.

"Our first engagement was on the western banks of the Great Dividing River. You and I have visited that spot many times since you were a boy."

A smile of recognition came across my face.

"I pulled our armies into their weak center, mindful of the dangers of envelopment. Many an army had been swallowed by this move before. Many City soldiers butchered by the blunder. But we held the line, moving ever farther outward to avoid the envelopment. I moved at the opportune moment and crushed their right. They fled. Simple victory."

"The victory we have all read of," I said.

"Indeed." He surrendered to a coughing spell, before regaining his composure. "But then we crossed the Acheron."

He noted my surprise, as this was not part of the history I knew.

"We replayed this same battle two or three times. Each time, they would collapse in the center and flee to the right and the left. We would lose a few angels. They would lose a few hundred. We celebrated as they pulled us farther and farther away from the river. Until we crossed the River Cocytus." He gagged a little. "I laugh now. Gabriel was right. I still think he was a coward, but in the end, it does not matter. He was right. I was wrong.

"When I say we were outnumbered, Ahriman, I do not exaggerate. We were a few tens of thousands. They must have been at least a hundred-thousand strong. Outlanders from all parts of the wilds. Brought together by whom I did not know. They fell on us and tore us to pieces. My angels died, as wave after wave of outlanders came at us from every direction."

Zoan rubbed his eyes and continued. "I had made the worst tactical mistake of my entire career."

I could see tears welling in his eyes.

"I was so sure of my successes, I allowed myself to be lured out like a novice and be taken by surprise. For two days, we were trapped and cut off from our supply and communications lines. At night, they would probe the outer defensive lines in one direction, but make a full-out attack along another end of our position. They were many, but they were disorganized. The constant drilling and training were the only things that saved my armies from total annihilation."

Zoan stared off into space now. He was in pain. What would it be like to have the fate of thousands of angels' lives in your hands? I had known war, but it had consisted of minor battles in comparison to those my grandfather had fought. I might have been handy with a sword or a spear and seen a few skirmishes, but I had never led angels as Zoan had. All through my military career, I had wanted to lead angels into that desperate fight, into that breach that would make or break the battle. Those breaches, where Zoan had felt at home. Comfortable. Or so I had thought. Is this what happened if you made the wrong decision? Were you doomed to live in pain like this? How had the old angel maintained such a cheerful disposition all through my life, when he had seen such things?

"As we fought desperately to break our way out of our encirclement," Zoan continued, "we managed to capture a senior outlander field commander. Leading the charge into our flanks, she was thrown from her horse."

He could see my surprise. "Yes, I said 'she.' After a brief, but bitterly fought struggle, we managed to recover her behind our lines. The ferociousness of the outlanders' fight over this woman was clear. Her capture enormously impacted their ability to coordinate their fight. Suddenly, they were unable to mount a sustained attack. They milled around the peripheries of our few remaining soldiers, looking over the lines to catch a glimpse of her, but were afraid to make another attempt at recovering her.

"She was wounded when she was brought to me. In fact, she was nearly dead. Looking at her, you could tell she was an older angel, but in great physical shape. She locked eyes with me when I approached her. Asked me who I was. I told her. She asked me if my heart was pure. I said yes straight away, without breaking eye contact with her. She looked at me for a moment, as if trying to make a decision. She said one last thing before she died: 'Then all is not lost.'"

"All is not lost?"

"Yes. That is what she said. For many years, I have wondered what would have made her say such a thing in her final moments. I wondered what I would say in my last moments."

Zoan reached over and squeezed my hand. "When this angel died, the outlanders broke off the fight altogether. My army had been reduced to but a few handfuls. No more than a few hundred or so. But when this outlander died, they fled. I stood there in disbelief. I had been robbed of a glorious death on the battlefield. The outlanders could have wiped us out altogether, if they had persisted with the fight for just a few more minutes. My army had taken many outlander lives, but not nearly enough to call this anything other than an utterly humiliating defeat. As we pulled out, it was not possible to attend to the many wounded. We had to put down as many angels as we could."

⌘   ⌘   ⌘

"It was the worst military defeat in the history of the City. And I was responsible for it," Zoan said. "Without much food or water to sustain us, we had little chance of making it back. No City army had ever strayed that far east. No good maps to guide us. And even if I made it back to the City, I would face a court-martial and be sentenced to death. The few remaining angels knew they would be branded traitors. Sensing anonymity was better than the torturer's lash, what was left of my once magnificent army melted away into the outlands. I never saw any of them again. None, to my knowledge, ever made it back. But I did.

"Looking through the heaps of gore on the field for something to sustain myself, I came back upon the outlander commander lying on the stretcher. But something had happened to her. In the heat of the final moments of battle, I had not noticed. Now, where she had fallen and died remained only her clothes, as if she had slipped out of them, leaving them untouched, just as they had lain upon her body. The blood was still there, but the body was gone. She had worn no armor. Only a white robe and a belt made of silver and gold thread. Hanging from her belt was a small clean dagger, a bag containing a single, plain-covered book, and the scabbard for what must, surely, have been a magnificent sword."

"They came back for her body, then?" I asked.

"It would seem that way. Why they left her clothes and utilities, I cannot say. But I took the belt and strapped it to me. I placed my own notched sword in the scabbard. I would have needed to find a sword maker of incomparable skill to fill that scabbard with a worthy companion. The dagger was razor-sharp and with it, I cut meat from a dead horse that lay nearby. Looking for something to wrap the meat in, I pulled out the book that was in the bag attached to the belt, and loaded the bag with the meat. But I was not interested in reading anything then and there," Zoan said, noticing my excitement. "I found water and several other essential supplies strapped to the bodies of many of the dead soldiers. I tried to get my bearings. Bodies were everywhere and the sickly smell of battle filled the air. It took me the better part of an hour to weave my way through to clean grassland."

Zoan shifted, coughing and wiping his blood-flecked mouth with his handkerchief. I could see his one hand shaking, while the other lay still on the bed. I said nothing and waited for him to continue.

"I expected the outlanders to pick off stragglers like me. I did not see a single living thing in the many hours I walked back through the fields that, just the day before, had been thick with the soldiers of my army. I felt I was being watched. When I made camp that night, I noticed the pain in my wrist for the first time," Zoan said rubbing his right wrist. "I examined it and assessed that it was either badly sprained or fractured. During the fighting, my head had also absorbed the better part of a blow from a descending axe. I had not been too seriously hurt. Mostly stunned, as the axe split my helmet and gashed my scalp. It had bled more than I would have liked, given my situation.

"I mended myself as best I could and considered what my end would be like. But no one came. No one. In the freezing cold of the night, I used the book as a pillow for my beaten head." Zoan looked at me closely now. "I cried that night. And I will always regret that I cried that night for myself, not for my angels. I cried that night, wanting your grandmother, may she rest in peace, and a warm place to be, where politics and war and maneuvers and strategy meant nothing. I cried at how complicated life had become. But each tear was for myself. Selfishness may be our program, but the greater good should always take precedence."

I remained silent.

"I got an early start the next morning." Zoan laughed and coughed at the same time. He scratched at his head, the spot,

I imagined, where he had sustained his wound. "I was practically an icicle by then. So getting a move on was almost a lifesaver in itself." Zoan stared at his shaking hand, the bloodied handkerchief smearing blood into his worn palm. "I walked and walked and walked. I kept a sharp eye out for anyone coming from any direction. But I saw no one. No one at all. I stopped at midday, cursing the blazing sun and trying to find some shelter from the heat. There was nothing. Anywhere.

"That night, I risked a fire, as otherwise, I would have frozen to death. An ignominious end it would have been. As I sat there, warm before the fire, I basically accepted the fact I would either die or be captured." Zoan smiled at me now. "I did not cry that night, Ahriman. But sitting staring at the fire, I pulled out the book that I had found on the outlander commander. I inspected the belt too. It was beautiful, but simple. Silver twined with gold, but strong.

"I had bled on the book a bit the night before," Zoan continued, as if oblivious to my presence, "but luckily, had not ruined it. It was simply bound in leather. It was written in a strange script and in the flickering light of the campfire, it was difficult to decipher the words. Several times, I put the book down, assuming it was written in a language I did not recognize and could not read. But boredom got the better of me and I picked it up again and leafed through it late into the evening.

"As I chewed the sinewy horse flesh, I suddenly recognized the script. It was as if the firelight had rearranged the letters and now, suddenly, I could understand. I wondered to myself whether the blow from the axe had been more damaging than I had first assumed. Combine that with the effects of having walked for the better part of two days now with little food and water," he said proudly. "But mustering some concentration, I could understand what it said.

"It appeared to be a book of laws. It spoke of court process and rights of defense at trial. Other sections mentioned voting for representative government. It referred to freedom of the press, of speech, of assembly, and of worship. But most of all, it endorsed the sanctity of the individual's rights. I did not know what this meant." He reached out with his shaking hand and touched my face. "All these years have passed and still the ideas written in its few hundred pages continue to affect me. It was a book that described a society that had existed before the City of God came into being. A democracy. The book contained its codification of laws."

More importantly to me, it was the book Mastema was looking for. It had to be. But I could not understand the connection between Zoan, of all the angels of the realm, and the cell.

"The next night, I read through the book again," my grandfather went on. "I may not have understood it clearly, but I was excited by the very idea of it. I began to consider why this outlander had been carrying the book. What made it so important that she would strap it to her belt, along with her weapons of war? She had cherished it as much as she cherished her weapons. As if it meant as much. Or even more. Why had the outlanders disengaged, when they saw her fall? They had all but beaten us. Had they taken her body with them, when I was elsewhere on the battlefield? Why would they have left her clothes and other effects sitting there? Especially if the book was so valuable? None of it made any sense.

"But reading the book made me feel better. Maybe because I had found something so rare and so heretical in such an unexpected place. But, more likely, because it gave me something else to focus on. Other than my ignominious defeat." Zoan wiped more blood away from his lips.

"As I began walking homeward the next day, I came upon a stream. It saved my life. I drank as deeply as I could and replenished my water supply. I washed my head in the cool water, getting the dried blood off my face for the first time in days. I began to think I might actually make it back to the City. To see your grandmother one more time, before I was put to death. As I stood there, thanking my good fortune, I began to think. Maybe this book could help me. I sat by the stream, watching the water bubble slowly by. I could have been sitting next to any stream in the realm. But I was in the outlands. A place where angels of the City had never been. Ever. Looking over a landscape no angel had ever seen. It was beautiful to be alive. The outlands were beautiful. So how could I use this book to my advantage?

"Later in the day, after I'd trapped a hare, skinned it, and made myself some lunch, I opened the book for the first time in the daylight. 'All are equal in the eyes of the people. All are equal in the eyes of the Council,' it read. What did it mean? What had become of these people? Where had they gone? Were these outlanders all that was left of them? More importantly to me at that moment, how could something so blasphemous be used as a tool to keep me off God's torture rack?

"I stayed by the river. Thinking. Animals came to drink, which meant food for me. The water was clean and clear, which meant I would not become dehydrated. I sat and thought of a plan to keep your grandmother and myself alive. If the book were true, I could use it, shall we say, to persuade God that killing me was not worth letting a secret as dangerous as this one out in the public domain. It was a terrible bet. Something told me that the book was a true relic. God, both directly and through Gabriel, worked very hard to keep the City and its inhabitants as uniform, non-threatening, and docile as possible. This could be the reason why."

Zoan looked down into his lap, sputtering a shallow cough.

I tried to suppress my excitement.

"No," he said to himself, "I must be fair. God used me. I was the brute force that kept the citizens in line. But what if that brute force knew something no one else did? What if my brute force was now fortified by knowledge that could undermine God's Heaven and sow discontent? What would it be worth to Him to keep that from happening? Keeping me alive seemed a small price to pay, I reckoned. God would have to take the book and kill me to keep me silent. And that would not do. Not in this city."

"An insurance policy, then?" I asked.

"I guess you might say that," Zoan replied, seemingly happy to have stumbled upon another angle from which to view his sordid history. "About a week later, I was found by a City reconnaissance party out looking for the army. Weeks out in the wilderness on my own had taken its toll on me. The stream had sustained me and my hunting forays had proved successful enough to keep me from starving to death. But with little shelter from the elements, I was a bit ragged. One of the senior non-coms of the party recognized me, luckily, and I was taken back to the City. He was a young sergeant named Jehoel."

⌘　⌘　⌘

I guess I should not have been shocked. But I was. If I had ever doubted the truth about the cell, about Jehoel himself, and his role in the conspiracy, such doubts were now dispelled. I expected lies from my fellow bureaucrats. Zoan was telling the truth. Or, at least, I thought he was. Unlike those blood-sucking bureaucrats, my grandfather had nothing to lose in telling me the truth. He would be gone soon and it would be up to me to determine what I should do with the information he had divulged.

He sat there in silence for a while again, watching me work it all out in my head. He seemed more at peace with himself, having got something that had long been bothering him off his chest. But I could tell that narrating the tale had taken something out of him. So many years ago. So painful a memory. So difficult to relive it all now, at the end of his days. His greatest failure. He had stretched back into his mind to remember it, compounding the pain of what was soon to be his passing.

"I honestly do not remember everything that happened in the following weeks, Ahriman." He stared into space, searching his mind. "Suffice it to say that it was one of the most terrifying times in my life. I was taken into custody, charged with sedition. I did not know what had become of your grandmother. I was not allowed to see her. They wouldn't tell me anything about her. They tortured me for information. All I could tell them was the truth. That I had made a mistake. That I had miscalculated the strength of the enemy and my army had suffered for it. I was guilty. What they didn't know was that I was *actually* guilty as charged. My sedition in accepting the book. In accepting the 'Word.'"

Zoan broke his unfocused stare into space and looked at me. "But they didn't find the book. Jehoel had taken it from me when they found me in the wilderness. As we moved closer to the City and I recovered something of my old self, he had come to me, asking where the book had come from. I was trapped. If he read it and understood it, I was really in trouble. But something totally unexpected happened. He told me he had read the book. He told me how his father had related such stories to him when he was young. He had not remembered those stories until now, but he wanted to know more. Alone in the outlands, I had had nothing to do, but think. In that time, I had been unable to come up with a constructive way to save myself. And now, suddenly, I had something.

"I made him a proposition. I had nothing to lose. Jehoel knew who I was and he knew what would happen to me, if they found the book on me. I offered him the book in exchange for my life. He would take the book and when the time was right, I would make it known that if any harm came to my family or me, the existence of the book would be made public. The plan was risky, of course. I had to trust in too many things. The book was real. The story was real. God could not afford to let the book get out. Jehoel would act for me. He would not betray me. It had to work. I convinced myself." Zoan's eyes were clear. "What choice did I have?"

He had asked that question as if he really expected an answer. I scrambled to think of something. If it came down to it, would I betray God for my own life? For the lives of my family?

"That time came soon," he continued. "I had no choice, but to let it be known to God's torturers that I had found the book. The torture stopped. I was moved from the City dungeons and brought to a suite in one of the City's most luxurious retreats. I was attended by a doctor who treated my torture-induced injuries. A message was brought to me from your grandmother that she was fine and with her family in the mountains, north of the City. She would be joining me soon. I was confused. How could I have known that a simple mention of the book would have such impact?"

"You were lucky," I said.

"It was not luck, I think. God came to me that evening. We spoke together in privacy."

"'No guards will be posted to the room,' He said. 'You are free to stay or go, once we've concluded our discussion. Either way, we are to be friends for eternity.'

"I said nothing. I was a traitor. What could I have said to make my situation any better?

"God said, 'You don't know how lucky you are that we share this relationship, my friend. My deal is simple. You will retire. You will be allowed to keep your wealth, your family, and your life. You are to be celebrated as a Hero of the City. You will receive a Triumph. Promise not to play in City politics. I give you my word that you and your family will be protected. All of this in exchange for the book. I will only make this offer once.'"

Grandfather shifted now in his bed, obviously uncomfortable. "I didn't know how Jehoel had done it, but my feeble plan saved me. I had a way out." Zoan looked relieved for having made his confession.

"'After this week,' God said, 'we will never be seen together again. All the power of the army will be now be placed in Gabriel's hands. He will not be allowed to touch you or your family. In exchange for the book. What say you?'

"Of course, I agreed. I could not have expected a better offer in a million lifetimes. God was no fool. He had offered this deal for practical, not personal reasons. I was a well-liked figure among the populace. God's public-relations machine had made me a star and even if He charged and convicted me with sedition, the people would still be sympathetic to me.

"More worrying, I am sure, would be the reaction of the army. I may have caused the deaths of ten thousand angels, but the army was still my child. I had built it from scratch and had treated it with the utmost care. The soldiers would not have been happy to see someone else in command, unless they were certain that my successor had risen to his position with my blessings. I had to appear to be committed. My death would also have rung out among the wealthy sections of the bureaucracy. The army ensured the prosperity of many an angel with its budgetary allocations. Allocations that I was responsible for. Interfering with or, even worse, cutting off their funding would have put thousands of the City's wealthiest and most influential families in a decidedly awkward position, provoking an outcry. Killing me would have invited far-reaching repercussions. By letting me go, God was saved a bloodletting that, perhaps, even He could not have controlled."

Zoan settled back down, as if the burden he had borne for so long had been lifted off his shoulders. The burden of the souls of ten thousand dead angels. The truth was finally out. The truth he had not been able to disclose to Angra. The truth that he was now forced, in the end, to divulge to me. He sighed.

"And so I became the hero you know today. The hero that each schoolchild is taught had vanquished the enemy and come back to tell the tale. I never spoke directly with God again. The deal was done and we both kept our part of the bargain."

"What happened to the book?" I asked excitedly.

"I arranged for Jehoel to return it. Though I said nothing, I could tell he had given me a copy, rather than the original. I did not ask Jehoel about his motives. God had accepted what I had given him, no questions asked. He did not seem to know it was a copy or, alternatively, expected it to be so. As for Jehoel, I made sure that he remained safely anonymous, wealthy, and successful for the support he had provided me and my family. I never spoke with him again either. I did not even think of him again, until you came to me and mentioned his name. My life has been one of celebrity and riches. Had Jehoel decided to trade in the book as I had, had he tried to use the information contained in it as I had, I would have been dead. He sacrificed something important to him to save me. And I will never understand why."

Zoan's story was done. "I have never shared this story with anyone, Ahriman. It would be a breach of my agreement with God and such a breach would not have been worth the risk to your grandmother. The risk to your father, even, as much as we hate each other now. Act carelessly with what I have just told you, and you will put everything in jeopardy." He coughed a long, hacking cough and reflected on his last words.

"I have lived a long lie. Now, at the end, I am split. I regret my decision to suppress what may very well have been the truth. But at the same time, I am happy that my decision allowed you to become the angel you are. There will always be a struggle between what is right and what is merely acceptable." He grasped my arm with his cold, clammy hand. "Doing what is right is simple. Doing what is wrong is even easier, since there are an infinite number of 'wrongs' and precious few 'rights.' Do what I was not able to do." He dropped off now and closed his eyes. Finally, with peace upon him. He murmured to himself, "Do what is right...for once in our lives."

He was asleep. He was at peace, his wheezy breath sputtering in and out.

He died a few days later. He was laid to rest in a splendid mausoleum erected for him in the City's central cemetery. Mourners came from all quarters. Gabriel was there. Checking, no doubt, to make sure his enemy was truly gone. He did not seem happy, but like Zoan, he did seem at peace.

CHAPTER EIGHTEEN

I cannot say I regret what I did next. For if I regretted what I did, it would be implying I regret standing before you today. Where would we all be, if I had done things differently? I do not know. But what has happened since my grandfather's death, in many ways, had to happen.

As Jehoel had requested, I started teaching angels about the way. The Fallen started me off simply enough, in essence, acting as a mentor for newly initiated members. Showing them the ropes, as it were. After a while, I started teaching from the prescribed texts, building a curriculum, and even doing some research of my own. I did not feel the same way about all this as I had before Zoan died. Earlier, I had viewed it as an exercise. Something I needed to do in order to get what I wanted. Such is the life of a spy. With Zoan gone, it was now a personal commitment. I was enthralled with what I saw and heard, each new discovery striking me as the kind of revelation you embraced with a resounding

"Of course!" It was not the truth of the matter that prompted my response so much as the flood of greater understanding as to why certain government bodies were formed the way they were, why certain groups within the City were suppressed or raised up, why our soldiers were trained the way they were. I was a Fallen now. I guess. But unlike the others, I was the only Fallen not satisfied with the depths into which I had fallen.

I approached Jehoel about the book. I told him it was Zoan's dying wish that I see the object that had saved our family and sustained the movement. I walked him through the story that my grandfather had told me before his death. I kept the purpose of Zoan's disclosure to myself.

"The book," Jehoel said, "was always here for you."

I had expected him to balk, even refuse. But he was so natural in his response to my request. As if he had always expected me to get to this place. I did not quite know what he meant and I could feel my ears turn red with embarrassment.

"Well, I did not quite know how to find it" I explained. "I could not just come out and ask for it now, could I?"

"The book was always here for you," Jehoel repeated.

He gave it to me. No questions asked. It was a true testament of his character. The book looked much like Zoan had described it, down to the bloodstains. I do not know whether Jehoel ever believed me and in the end, I did not have the guts to ask him.

⌘ ⌘ ⌘

Mastema did not know I was already in possession of the book when he came calling one night.

"I'm sorry to hear about your grandfather," he said.

I no longer cared whether he was being truthful or not. Zoan had told me all I needed to know about angels like him, like Angra. Like me.

"Yes, it has been difficult for me, though not for my father. I have not heard from him and I do not think he attended the burial."

"Did he give you what we need?" Mastema inquired.

"What *we* need?" I asked. I found it hard to understand why I had once believed Mastema to be an angel of importance. He seemed so small now. So insignificant. Like a bug you step on, when it crosses your path in the street. You do not give it a second thought.

"Yes, what *we* need, Ahriman," Mastema persisted. "You get what you want and I get what I want. We don't need to cover this again, do we?"

I could see he was genuinely irritated. He could choose to wait for me and get what he wanted or kill me and start from a completely different angle.

"No," I lied. "I do not have it yet, but Jehoel has all but admitted to the truth of the matter. He will give it to me. He will give it to me soon."

"Good," Mastema said. He looked relieved. "We're running out of time. Too much longer and it will truly matter for us both."

I left it at that. I did not care. He would be gone soon and I would watch as he died, hanged from the walls of the City, a common criminal.

⌘　⌘　⌘

A fortnight later, I dipped my toes, if you will excuse the expression, into the stream of information passing through the PID. Things began to pop. Using a code name derived from an old Secret Police mole hunt, I intercepted a regular communication between informants and the Secret Police, referring to an angel looking for a prohibited book.

This, in and of itself, would not have raised many eyebrows. But I had to build the story and start somewhere. I could not plop it right down for all to see. It was too loud. People would begin to scramble for cover, and start assigning blame indiscriminately. No, I could not do that. So I continued to attend the cell meetings. I secreted away all my written records. I prepared myself for one of two eventualities: unmasked by Mastema or betrayed by Jehoel, I would die a horrible death; or I would overcome. I put the former possibility out of my mind and focused entirely on the latter.

Every so often, I would introduce further communications into the stream. "Secret book"; "trimmer book"; "dissension among the ranks." That is not to say I was always consistent. Sometimes, it would be the truth. And sometimes, it would be pure fiction. I knew the Secret Police would never catch on. Even if they did, it would take even longer for them to identify a source. They were good at bashing in heads, but their own heads lacked vital matter indispensable for lucid thinking. No. I was waiting for someone else. And it did not take too long for the person to make his presence felt.

I had ensured my comments about the book were obscure enough to suggest that I did not know what it represented or even whether it actually existed. I needed to convey the impression that I was fishing. So I was surprised when this contact wanted a meeting right away. While I was hopeful that I had just snagged the right person, I was also concerned that I might actually just be talking to Mastema or his agents. The contact wanted to know where I was getting my information. I let him know I would not talk to anyone in the Servitude. I was sure I had managed to convey the impression that I was in earnest. Any meeting, I said, had to be face-to-face. The contact cut off communications immediately. I was ready. It was not Mastema.

⌘   ⌘   ⌘

I held off further communications for a while, wanting it to seem as if I had realized that I had taken the matter a step too far.

When I came back into the stream, I acted as if the contact had not occurred at all, as if I were shopping for a new buyer. There were a few takers, but none expressed as keen an interest as the earlier contact.

I dangled a more enticing bait by suggesting a link to rebellious cells within the City. Nothing happened. I made a reference to multiple connections within the bureaucracy. Still nothing. And then I mentioned the death of the source. The earlier contact came right back to offer a fee. It was Gabriel, I was sure of it. I turned it down. The contact returned, agreeing to my original request for a face-to-face. How could I be sure they would come through this time, I asked. Though they did not name him, I was certain Gabriel wanted the meeting. I was allowed to choose the place. It was now or never, I told myself. Sometimes, living itself is an act of bravery.

⌘   ⌘   ⌘

"Why am I not surprised?" Gabriel asked, when at last we finally met.

We were in an obscure, but public place where, I was quite confident, he had never been. Gabriel did not spend much time in the Southwest Quarter. I had just spent what felt like a lifetime there.

"I guess we were destined to meet, you and I," I said, with a bit more gusto than I should have shown. Pointless to observe the formalities, when you have thrown all caution to the wind with God's only Seraph. "Thank you for paying your respects to my grandfather, by the way."

"Your grandfather was a great angel. I hated him, but he was great, all the same." Gabriel laughed a little. "What can I do for you, then?"

I knew it would only be a matter of time before he had had enough of my game and enough of me.

"My window of opportunity is growing narrower by the day," I began. "I give you the book, the cell, and all the rest of my findings. You put me where you are. You put me in front of God. I want a chance to convince Him that while my grandfather was a dangerous angel, I am an angel with an infinite love for Him. I am tired of having to bear the consequences of what my family did. Of what Zoan did. It is time I came home to you and to God."

I had finally said it. All the things I had worked for. Training for education, education for information, information for power, and power for glory. All summed up in one simple demand, made to Heaven's most powerful angel.

"Direct, aren't you? You seem an angel with nothing to lose." He smiled. "That's the worst kind."

He looked around the place I had chosen for us to meet in. Wretched, with the wretched people of God's City. I was not fool enough to think I was anything other than on my own.

"Why would I agree to share God's love with you?" he asked. "Book or no book, the risks aren't what they used to be since your grandfather came back waving that book. God's grip is firmer, His control more direct, His..."

"His need for closure more urgent, now that my grandfather is dead, than at any time since the beginning," I interrupted. "All those years, you knew Zoan would keep his word. You may have hated him, but you knew that he would keep his secret—and God's—until the day he died. But now that he is dead, you have lost control of the information. You do not know who owns those secrets anymore." I looked around the room too. "I am the only one with enough contacts, enough knowledge, and enough ambition to have taken that mantle up successfully." I looked back at him now. "Now *that* is the worst kind of angel."

He smiled at me again. "We're going to be friends, you and I. Yes, we'll be hated, but we'll be good friends." Gabriel appeared as he did the day Zoan was buried. Peaceful.

⌘　⌘　⌘

Mastema was taken the very next day. Charged with conspiracy. I am not sure if he knew I was behind it. He had crossed so many angels. He had no show trial. It had to happen that way to avoid an uprising. It had to happen that way so as to prompt his organization into an internecine war to see who would next reign. I chuckled at the idea that it might even be Angra. No one attended Mastema's execution, but Gabriel and me. He was disemboweled and hung from the City walls, like a common criminal. Just as I had visualized it.

⌘ ⌘ ⌘

The cell headquarters were raided at the same time that Mastema was taken into custody. Gabriel's agents took it in a well-executed operation. The Secret Police were left out of the loop. Everything was confiscated and the entire block burned to the ground. Those ancient statues, their faces frozen for what the cell had thought would be an eternity, were destroyed. Those not killed on the spot were taken to the dungeons. For all I know, their bones still lie there, among filth that rots below God's City. They were my friends and I had betrayed them for the love of God.

⌘ ⌘ ⌘

Gabriel's angels took my proscription lists. In every government department, at every level of the administration, angels of all ranks and social status were taken in one fell swoop. Like a bolt of lightning. Taken before anyone could do anything. It could have been chaos. But it was not.

"The precision of the operation adds to the aura," Gabriel told me. "People like these expect an inept and stumbling Secret Police. This is partly by design and partly because of the nature of the boobs that fill its corps. Either way, it works to God's benefit. The fact that these angels were cut swiftly, surgically from the bone will be a warning far more sinister than anything we could concoct on our own."

He was happy with our success. I was too.

⌘　⌘　⌘

Fear raced across the City. "The Great Purge" was how it became immediately known. Everyone knew someone who had been taken. Fathers, mothers, brothers, sisters, neighbors. People disappeared, suddenly and without trace. My lists were long and the rot they reflected, pervasive. No official explanation was released. The Great Purge took several days to carry out. It took Gabriel another three days to find Jehoel. He was apprehended as he tried to reach Phanuel. I knew he could be found that way. That Jehoel surrendered without a fight haunts me to this day.

CHAPTER NINETEEN

One week later, I had my first audience with God. I approached the steps of the cavernous throne room located in the Seat of God, flanked by my new bodyguard and Gabriel. God looked down upon me. I had never seen Him at such close range. He was so beautiful and He smiled upon me when I knelt before Him.

"You have done well for yourself, Ahriman," He said.

Though everything swirled around me, forever will I remember His first words to me.

"Please, rise and speak with me." He gestured with His hand.

I looked at Gabriel for a moment. God flashed him a look too.

"Go and do what you have wanted to do your whole life," He said to Gabriel.

Looking down at the book I had delivered to him, Gabriel bowed to God and strode out of the chamber.

"Come, come," God said again. "We have much to discuss."

⌘   ⌘   ⌘

"Thank you, Lord, for your gifts," I said as we sat in one of God's select private rooms, connected to His throne room.

"Nonsense, Ahriman," He quickly said. "It is I who owe you a debt of gratitude. You have rid me of the most terrible threat to my kingdom since its foundation, I dare say."

His compliment overwhelmed me and I could not help but think of my father for a split second.

"I will be forever thankful for the work you have, so Gabriel tells me, undertaken on your own."

He smiled at me, relaxed in His chair. I tried not to appear too stiff.

"It is for the Kingdom, Lord, that I have always fought. My grandfather was my model, but you were always my light."

"Yes, yes, your grandfather," He said. "A terrible and wonderful angel, if you do not mind my saying so."

I shook my head silently. I was in the presence of God. Finally.

He looked upon me and smiled again. "I am sure that we will get on like old friends from the beginning," He said with the firmest of assurances. "Gabriel tells me you have taken measures to protect yourself, just like your grandfather had." It was more of a question than an observation.

I was uneasy. God could afford to be blunt. I could not.

He recognized my hesitation instantly. "No, do not take this the wrong way. 'Love' and 'faith' are things that are earned. You were smart to think ahead and I appreciate that. Gabriel appreciates that too. This kingdom suffers from a dearth of intelligent angels. People who understand the way things work. The way you are supposed to love your God. You understand," He said, His brows furrowed in a frown, "though you have only watched from the sidelines." The frown seemed to envelop His entire face now. "Amazing, really."

I did not quite know what to say. I was not sure I had understood.

"Learning is accumulated through experience, but thinking demands intelligence," I said. I did not know why I uttered those words.

"Quite right, quite right," God said dismissively.

He got up and walked to a table nearby. Several servants ran from each end of the room to pour Him a glass of ambrosia.

"Two," He said under His breath.

A second glass quickly appeared and was filled immediately.

He gestured for me to sit down. "Ambrosia?" he asked, handing me a glass.

"Thank you, Lord." God had just served me.

"What shall we do with you, then?" He asked rhetorically, or so I hoped. "Gabriel tells me you want to 'sit' with him, I believe he said. What did you have in mind?"

I waited for Him to sip His ambrosia. My throat was parched.

"I want to start by reorganizing the bureaucracy," I began. "While I recognize that its cumbersome nature can work to your advantage, my Lord, I am concerned that it is not achieving what you need to get done."

I took a sip. So did He.

"That is where I would ask you to let me start, Lord."

"Interesting," He said. "Interesting," He said again under His breath.

He stood up and I bolted to attention. He walked back to where He had been standing a moment ago. Servants refreshed His glass. He motioned for me to walk with Him onto a balcony overlooking the City.

"Let us speak in the open air, Ahriman," He said. He leaned in to me, as if to impart some secret. "Even God's walls have ears, you understand," He said with a wink.

"Yes, Lord."

"There are times when the body accumulates too many impurities," He said, looking out over the City, "which act to restrain and limit the work it must undertake. It is in those times that nature acts to purge the body of what it doesn't need, bringing back equilibrium so that the entire system is able to work at maximum efficiency again."

He looked at me. I became mesmerized by the focused intensity of His gaze.

"You, Ahriman, have played well the role of nature this day. The evils of these angels you exposed were like a cancer on the soul of this City. Motivated by nothing but self-interest and the spirit of anarchy, they were sapping it of its strength. The cleansing, we feel, will bring things back from the brink. You have done well in hastening the natural course of bringing balance back to the City. And, for this, I will reward you."

I must have looked a bit uneasy.

"You have something to say, then?" He asked.

"Something distresses me, Lord."

"Speak freely. I insist, Ahriman."

"Well, Lord, it seems to me that we should be more wary of those given great favor. Angels in such favored positions, it seems to me, Lord, have more opportunity to do evil."

God laughed mightily. "I like you already, Ahriman," He said, once He had caught His breath. "I will be sure to keep a close eye on you so that any 'favors,' as you say, I may bestow do not morph into evil deeds."

He looked back out over the City. Wisps of smoke rose from the factories and markets and the clatter of horses' hooves was distinct, along with the distant roar of all that made up its populace.

"You will soon come to understand that a leader never trusts any of his lieutenants," God went on. "He cannot afford to. If you expect a leader to keep his faith in you, you need to ensure that either he adheres to your beliefs, only more firmly, or, alternatively, your power over him is overwhelming. One should never take loyalty for granted, even if it is manifested in deeds.

"Of course, I naturally assumed that the first thing from your lips today would be a request to be elevated to Seraph," He said, looking at me in what I interpreted as mock consternation.

"Given Zoan, I mean. But you want a job in the bureaucracy, you say."

"Yes, Lord," I repeated.

He pondered to Himself for a moment. "Interesting."

We walked back into the apartment.

"You want to work *for* Gabriel, then, rather than *with* him?"

"Yes, my Lord. I have seen things from the bottom up, the inside. But I do not presume to know better than Gabriel how the administration works."

"Yet," He interjected, as He sat back down in a couch that was not the one He had lounged in earlier.

I waited for His signal, before sitting down myself. "Perhaps, Lord," I agreed. I wanted to graciously ignore His comment. "I wish to reform the bureaucracy, but I want the Secret Police to..." I paused for a moment, "help."

"I see," He said. "The army to Gabriel, but the bureaucracy and the Secret Police to you."

"Yes, Lord."

"It shall be done, then," He said without a moment's delay. "You are now Captain General of my Secret Police."

He drank down His ambrosia in nearly one gulp. This time, servants came running.

"What else can I do for you?" He asked.

I flushed. "I ask for a specific captain for my bodyguards."

"Yes. I assume someone from your time in the field?" God asked, uninterested.

"In a manner of speaking, Lord."

"Who, then?"

"His name is Azael. He sits in one of the City's many prisons."

"Who is this Azael and why is he incarcerated?" God asked, suddenly interested.

"A trimmer who had wounded me, one day, as I fought with my regiment near the Forks on the far side of the Acheron." I was nearly tempted to call him a Tartaruian, bless Zoan for his heresy.

"That is a bizarre request indeed," He said. "Very interesting. Though I must say I need to know why you want an enemy to protect your life."

God signaled again for more ambrosia.

"I led a troop of your good soldiers, Lord, through the marshes of the Forks. This young outlander attacked our troop on his own reconnoiter and, with a single arrow, took my horse out from under me." It was my nod to Zoan.

"Hmm," God said, listening now.

"Not before he plugged an arrow into me and several others with me." I added, rubbing my shoulder, as if the pain of my wound had returned. "He was captured and imprisoned. I learned his name later and demanded that his life be spared."

"Why?"

"The extinction of someone with such fortitude would be a loss to all angels." I tried my best to parrot Zoan.

God thought over it for a moment. "I do not understand," He said, "but consider it done."

He was anxious to conclude the interview and I did not want to delay Him.

"What else?" He asked.

"I will tell you in time," I replied. I did not know how well a show of nerve would go over at this point, but He did not take umbrage.

"Good, then. Later, it will be." He stood up.

I quickly stood as well. The servants went scrambling. They did not know what He would do next.

"I have some conditions of my own," He said, smiling. "They will not be too onerous for you, Ahriman, I am sure. I want you to attend Jehoel's execution. Then we will celebrate a triumph in your honor. The whole City will be witness to the ceremony where I name you one of my Seraphim."

I bowed as deeply as I could. It was done and I had not even asked for it. Not directly, at any rate. My life's work, completed in a moment. The life of the closest thing I ever had to a friend taken in the same moment.

"You will move into a royal residence of your choosing, except for the Seat of God, of course," He said, smiling, "and begin your training with Gabriel. How is that for a place to start?"

"If it pleases you, I will take the Northeast Quarter."

"Fine, fine," He said, again, dismissively.

"Thank you, Lord." I did not quite know what else to say.

"Again, Ahriman," He said, waving a pointed finger at me, "it is I who am grateful to you, my bearer of light." He thought for a moment. "My Lucifer. But remember, my young Seraph, it is not the title that makes the angel, but the angel who makes the title."

"Yes, Lord."

"It is settled then, Lucifer."

That was my first meeting with God. Power and death would become the bread and butter of our relationship.

CHAPTER TWENTY

They did not torture him. I made sure of that. Well, wait. I should not lie to you. While I probably wielded enough power to ensure that Jehoel was spared torture, I did not exercise that right. The completeness of my betrayal had ensured that he had nothing else to surrender. There was no point in torturing him, because not torturing him was torture enough.

"May the Lord watch between me and thee when we are absent, one from another," he repeated over and over to himself, when I visited him in prison. "Eternal love," he said, as he looked up at me.

"When we are absent, one from another," I completed. I looked at him.

"I do not blame you, Ahriman," Jehoel said.

He was shackled to the wall. Dirty and tired he looked, but not really much the worse for wear.

"Power is seductive," he went on. "You have always wanted it. To do more. You have always wanted to change things. That you could not do it from where you were, being a member of the family you came from, was something forever out of your control." He shifted in his chains.

"I did what I did, because I was tired of working my way to the top. I worked and worked and never got anywhere. It is exhausting, working so hard in order to stay in one place. Look at you, Jehoel."

Our eyes met.

"Evolution is not a plan. We cannot wait for things to evolve. We have to make things happen ourselves."

"Ahriman, I told you that you always had the power. Angels will change when they have a leader they can believe in. Who will believe in you now? Tell me? No one will trust you. No one will love you. There will be no faith in you from this day on. People will follow you out of fear. They will follow you, because they know suffering is the only alternative. 'Will' is something God has no time for. Well, not in his subjects, anyway. And now you will become an agent of suppression. Suppression of 'will,' suppression of our very nature. 'Evolution' is the only way to earn the trust, the love you need to 'will' angels into action."

"You are wrong," I said. "Power is the only means to fix Heaven. We can sit and talk for a million years and never get any closer to success. How successful you are is dependant upon the degree of risk you took to achieve it. This, more than anything else, is what you have taught me."

I am not sure I meant it, but I felt compelled to defend myself, if only to pacify my guilty conscience. "Teach people for the sake of imparting knowledge? What is knowledge compared to power? Power can remake knowledge, but knowledge cannot remake power."

"I have lost, then." He dropped his gaze to the floor of the prison cell. "And, not that you would understand, but so has your grandfather. He did not do the right thing when he had the chance. But he did not do the wrong thing either. Where will you go from here?"

I was growing angry now. "I will go where I was destined to go. I will fix things and your purism, your devotion to 'will' and 'love' and all that crap will not matter in the end."

I had weakened for a few moments, but now hardened my heart.

"It matters, Ahriman. It always matters."

"Not now, it does not."

"Do not let it get to your head, Ahriman. I have always found that those most lusting for power are least equipped to deal with it. And I have always tried to teach you that those who consider the exercise of power to be their duty, rather than their job, are the best at making power mean something."

"I will use my newfound power to do what I think is right."

"There are others that will take up after me," Jehoel said, quite sure of himself. "Others who will make sure it all matters in the end."

"I will find them too," I retorted.

"No doubt you will."

He did not seem sad or defeated. It was strange.

"Keep Phanuel safe, would you, Ahriman? Your power will keep him safe."

I tensed up. And thought.

"I will keep him safe," I said finally. "But I will make him in my image."

Jehoel thought about it for a few seconds, as if he had a choice.

"I am okay with that," he said, "so long as my son does not meet a fate he did not deserve."

I guess that is how fathers are supposed to feel for their sons. The way Zoan had felt for his family, perhaps.

"Okay, then. I will keep an eye on him." I agreed.

⌘　⌘　⌘

I was grateful to God for the quiet affair it was. Jehoel was brought to the prison yard. He placed his head on the block. In a few seconds, it was separated from his shoulders. No one was present. Except Gabriel and me. And the executioner, if you choose to see it that way.

"You passed," Gabriel said, patting me on the shoulder.

I stared down at Jehoel's headless torso. The blood continued to flow for what seemed like forever.

"How is that?" I asked.

I was comfortable with Gabriel now. What could he do to me? I felt like throwing up.

"That angel saved your grandfather's life. You have undone what your grandfather did. Now we can be friends."

"I thought you said we would be 'hated friends,'" I retorted in a jocular tone, never really having considered too closely that I had also just betrayed by grandfather's savior.

"'Hated,' I said, but not 'hating.' We'll finish the work that your grandfather and I had started all those many years ago."

I did not understand.

They threw Jehoel's head into a basket and tossed his body into a cart standing nearby.

I was in.

3

CHAPTER
TWENTY-ONE

I became only the third Seraph in the Order of the Seraphim in the City's history. I had come from nowhere to become instantly famous. My service, my sacrifice, was flashed across every corner of the City, through every newspaper, by every town crier. As I rode through the center of the City, mounted on a great charger, God spoke from the apex of His castle steps to the crowds of angels attending my triumph.

"Praise him above all the City's saints!" He cried, pointing to me as I rode ever closer to Him.

Thunderous applause erupted with His words. Gabriel stood by His side. Michael, Gabriel's acolyte, stood close by.

"He saved us from certain doom!" God thundered across the crowds.

Boisterous applause again.

"His deeds will be remembered forever in the annals of the City. He brought light to the darkest of places."

More cheers and screams from every corner of the City.

"Ahriman, the Angel of Light. Now, our Lucifer!" He shouted.

My Seraph name. Lucifer. Bringer of Light.

God presented me with a great war sword of incomparable quality. It was not a display sword, worn for ceremony only. It was the type of sword, I imagined, that had dwelt in the scabbard of that dead trimmer Zoan had encountered all those years ago. It was powerful and in my day, I would have wielded it with authority.

Everywhere, people rejoiced. From the top of palace towers to the burned-out hulks of the Southwest Quarter. I, Lucifer, Seraph of God, author of the Great Purge.

Now, you may ask yourselves, did they care who I was? They did. With absolute apprehension, I am sure. They knew of my grandfather. Who did not? My rise had come so soon after his death, I suspect many of the more connected social elite considered my sudden elevation as having something to do with it. They were right, of course, but not in the way they suspected. They came crowding around me, attracted like scavengers to a carcass. I suddenly had "friends" coming at me from every direction, all offering something and praising me for what I had done. Subtle promises of favors for influence peddling became part of my daily routine.

My mother died just before the triumph. I attended her funeral and mourned her loss, though I did not feel I had known her well. I thought it strange that my father did not come to me and since I was so busy, I did not summon him either. He was, most likely, afraid. I had not involved him in Mastema's fall, but he must have been worried that I would turn on him. That the bad blood between us would manifest itself in ways he rather wanted to avoid. The whole affair must have been gnawing at him from within. I had achieved what he had wished for his entire life, but not in the way he had hoped. Zoan had saved it for me. For some reason. I gave orders to contain Angra, to limit his ability to continue his nefarious activities, but also cautioned that he should not be harmed. He was to be told directly of my orders. Angra was not to approach me, unless he wanted to be tarred with the infamy of Mastema's transgressions.

"You have forgotten the favors you've received and imagine you've earned your success on your own merit," was all he said in reply.

It was to be the last correspondence I would ever have with my father.

⌘　⌘　⌘

I was instantly popular with the people. They saw me as someone who had risen from among them. God's elaborate public-relations machine went into overdrive, selling me as the model citizen. Someone who had served the City, both as a loyal soldier and as an innovative member of the Servitude. Someone who, when confronted with evil, had taken a personal initiative to bring villains to God's justice. My popularity enhanced His own. "Why did I not think of it before?" He joked with Gabriel and me one night, while we sat dining and drinking at one of His private residences. I was sure He considered anything to do with me very clearly before He made a move.

It was almost as if I were in a dream. Gabriel and I became what I can only call friends. To be honest, I could not see what Zoan had disliked about him. He was cruel, yes, but then, so was I. He played politics with more nonchalance and self-composure than I ever could muster and I willingly became his mentee, listening and learning as much as I could from his steely demeanor in public and his egotistical focus when operating behind the scenes. Unlike Zoan, whom he had viewed as a rival, he did not consider me a threat. I assumed my position as Seraph with the understanding that Gabriel was still first in the Order. He tutored me in private on the workings of the City's social and political circles. Not the circles I had seen as a saboteur. The ones I saw now were the real social circles. The real politics. Involving people who ran the City. People who had private one-on-one meetings with God, the substance of which only Gabriel knew. People who became my friends and my enemies, all at once.

⌘　⌘　⌘

"I am having a hard time of it," I admitted to Gabriel one day, when he asked me how things were going. "I know what is right and I can see it before me. But I cannot get these oafs to understand."

"And it makes you mad," Gabriel concluded.

"Yes. I regret my anger later, especially when I can see these reprobates in the back of my mind, making fun of me. Making fun of me," I said through gritted teeth, "the overwhelmed and under charming superior they believe to be their inferior."

"Don't let those who resist your power distract you from your purpose," Gabriel replied. "And never pretend you are just one of the many. You are separate and apart. The people know that. God has made you that. To play to them in a bid to convince them that you consider yourself one of them and gain their confidence may have benefits in the short run. But eventually, they will see through your ruse and resent you for what you have and they do not. It is better to be distant. Aloof. And outwardly aware of your power."

"How can I control them, if I keep my distance from them?" I asked. "I feel compelled to get right in their faces."

"Absolutely no," Gabriel said quickly. "Do not waste your breath trying to convince people with your words. It is only deeds that move people. Most angels don't think about the ideas and values they hold. It's just not something they think about from day to day. But they do have strong emotional attachments to those ideas and values. So when you challenge them directly through your arguments, they resist your attempts to remold their habits of thinking. They become hostile. Every angel has his or her own point of view. Sometimes, there are those who can be swayed. Sometimes, there are those who will not be swayed, no matter how right you are about a particular issue. You must change your style and your approach to suit each one. You can make them yours, without them ever knowing they were persuaded into changing their views."

"Draw your sword when you meet a swordsman," I added. "Do not debate philosophy with someone who is not a philosopher."

"Yes, I guess that's one way to put it," Gabriel said. "Doing all this deliberately can seem time-consuming, but remember, there is no substitute for proper planning, Lucifer. You need to devote time to the endeavor of being successful." His tone was grave. "Or you will become one of them yourself."

"I have always prided myself on being able to make it up as I go along," I said. "I must say that I have been fairly successful too, up until now."

Gabriel grew grim at this. "Being able to make fast and judicious decisions is a skill, no doubt. But as I said, most angels are ruled by their hearts, not their heads. Their plans are vague and, as such, they are forced to improvise when they bump up against life's obstacles. But improvisation will only take you as far as the next crisis," he said, poking a warning index finger at me and tapping it on the table before us. "It is never a substitute for thinking several steps ahead and planning through to the end."

Gabriel could see the gears working in my head. "Don't misunderstand," he went on. "I am not suggesting that you do all the work you are now responsible for yourself."

I sighed at the thought.

"That is not the right response either," he said, noting my reaction. "The truly powerful never appear to be harried or overburdened. Truly powerful angels always keep their hands clean and get others to work their fingers to the bone. Powerful angels surround themselves with only good things and the only announcements they make are of their achievements."

"That's easier said than done."

"Maybe, but you only make yourself look ugly, when you 'roll up your sleeves' and take on the dirty work," Gabriel cautioned.

"No one will respect you, if you do not appear to be above all the little things."

I felt overwhelmed.

"This is the game you've opted to play, Lucifer," Gabriel said very seriously. "You either learn how to play that game or you die. It's that simple."

I was suddenly reminded of Jehoel. How he had tried to teach me the same thing. How to deal with these very same issues. I was suddenly racked by guilt as I thought of Jehoel and Gabriel clearly knew something was amiss.

"Not what you bargained for, Lucifer? I am surprised at you."

"It is not that," I replied, a bit indignantly. "I knew there was sloth and deceit and ignorance where I was going, God forgive me. But, perhaps, I was not prepared to face the evil that seems to motivate these angels in nearly everything they do."

"I wouldn't say that's it. This life, what we do, necessarily makes it impossible to be direct. You simply cannot be so straightforward. Go see the Great Northern Forest. The straight trees are cut down and the crooked ones are left standing."

"What does that mean?" I asked, getting annoyed. But before Gabriel could answer, I continued, "No, you are clouding the situation. They are evil, these angels we deal with. Their corrupt lives, their corrupt business practices," I sneered.

"Listen, Lucifer," Gabriel interjected, his tone earnest, "if God had created Heaven without evil, He would have created a place devoid of the alternatives which make things possible. God created the cosmos and, with that, angels who have true freedom."

"Freedom seems a little bit of an overstatement," I blurted out.

"Listen," Gabriel continued, ignoring my blasphemy, "if angels were not created with this freedom, Heaven's creatures would be incapable of good. But such freedom offers the option of also doing evil. No free angel can consistently be compelled to do good. Otherwise, his freedom and, therefore, his nature and the very purpose of his existence would be relegated to pointlessness. Destroyed."

Gabriel clearly had reflected on and set up a long line of arguments about this subject. It was not the first time he was having this conversation. "Puppets, no matter how skillfully designed, cannot be morally good or evil," he went on. "They cannot be imbued with the idea of freedom. Therefore, evil is necessarily wired into creation."

"I grant you that any angel, who comes into Heaven with the notion that he is really going to instruct its inhabitants in matters of the highest importance, can thank God if he escapes with his skin intact," I said matter-of-factly. "I have served in our Lord's armies and His government. I am no fool. But from my point of view, good or evil either does not exist at all or exists only in the mind of God. It cannot be understood by mere angels...or puppets, as you say. It will be forever hidden from our eyes. Those of us close to God understand this and understand that evil results from angels' misuse of this freedom you mention."

"Angels corrupted by the heavens around them?" Gabriel asked knowingly. "Be careful how you proceed," he warned.

He had ignored my previous blasphemy, but suggesting that God had created anything other than a perfect universe was treading on dangerous ground.

"That is not what I meant," I replied, a little unsure as to how big a hole I might have just dug for myself. "It is just that by nature, I am direct. In my experience, if, in a first encounter, you reveal a willingness to compromise, back down, or retreat, you bring out bloodthirstiness in your opponent, even if he is not usually aggressive. I am just saying that for me, everything depends on perception. Once someone gets it into his head that you tend to adopt a defensive stance in all situations and are ever-willing to appease, to bow to consensus, you will never be respected."

"I don't disagree with that, Lucifer," Gabriel responded. "But don't misunderstand my point. I'm not suggesting you seek consensus or even that you back down. I'm merely suggesting that you apply the force of your power more judiciously. Power, riding on the back of potential force, is unlimited and not exhausted through its implementation. But power born of direct force is finite and, by its very nature, expended when used. Why waste your power when you can, through a simple expedient, put it to use over and over, until you have completed what you needed to get done?"

It sounded logical to me and I nodded silently. Impatiently. I knew I had a lot more learning to do, before I could truly be the Seraph I wanted to be.

⌘ ⌘ ⌘

I was given a bodyguard. Actually, a retinue of bodyguards. From the most well-trained ranks of the army, I was offered a selection of angels who constituted what I could only describe as an elite troop. Far superior to any I had known in my time in the army. They would provide the protection I needed. My newfound wealth and power automatically made me a target. I had always belonged to the upper class, but as a mid-level bureaucrat, I had never really considered the risks to which the powerful and the rich were vulnerable. As the Seraph of God, I was a commodity, a prized catch, something worth stealing, torturing, or killing.

God had been true to His word. From some remote soldiers' camp in the outlands, He had Azael summoned to me.

"I do not understand," Azael said, when I offered him the position of Captain of my bodyguard.

"What is there to understand, Azael? I want you to lead my bodyguards. To protect me."

He mused for a moment. "I have no experience with this," he said.

"Confined as a prisoner for years and suddenly snatched up to lead the personal security contingent attached to one of the most powerful angels in Heaven? Who has experience with that?" I quipped.

"You saved me from death, when all I wanted was to kill you. I may be ragged, but I do remember the service you rendered me."

"Then I can trust you?"

He mused for another moment. And came to a decision.

"I am Azael, my Lord," he said saluting me. "I will be your Captain."

"Then you will also be my friend," I said, extending my hand in friendship. He looked at it for a moment and then took it.

"My Lord."

"'Lucifer' will do."

⌘　⌘　⌘

As part of my new responsibilities, I became an honorary member of the Senate and Protector of the Senate Council, a senior group of select senators whose purpose, ostensibly, was to advise God on the most serious and pointed issues of state. Senators were nominally elected, but in reality, appointed by God. As a senator, the only real power at your disposal was invested in your name alone. It was a farce, meant to placate the common angel and act as an avenue for up-and-coming angels in the higher social and economic classes to build the relationships that would come in useful in generating and maintaining their wealth. As Protector, I had the power to call Senate Council meetings at leisure and end them in much the same manner. This club of old angels struck me as bloated and pointless. So with Gabriel's help, I purged it of some of the more ossified and blood-sucking cliques. Gabriel warned me not to meddle too deeply in the power struggles that permeated the Senate but, as always, I did what I thought was right, even if it meant finding myself more bodyguards to consolidate my security detail. As it turned out, Michael's uncle was one of those removed from the Senate Council. Michael already hated me for taking so much of his master's attention. Insulting his family in this way did little to mend the rift.

Funny, how you graduate from being totally petrified to be-ing deadly cool, when you become accustomed to assassination attempts. I responded in kind with my own reprisals. With my reformed Secret Police at my disposal, the Senate Council quickly found I was not an angel to be trifled with. God dismissed their appeals for retribution against me. For that, I have to give Him considerable respect. I am sure He got a kick out of ruffling the feathers of all those old birds. God was loyal to those loyal to Him. At least, He was loyal as long as He needed someone. I was Zoan's grandson. A second-generation Seraph. God wanted to need me.

CHAPTER
TWENTY-TWO

I did not expect to meet Amee. Then again, who expects to find love? It just happens, right?

She was Gabriel's niece. Her father had been killed in some battle years ago and Amee had come into her uncle's care as a child. Gabriel had a particular affection for her. She was the most beautiful angel I had ever seen. To this day, the image of her, as I had seen her on that first occasion, burns in my mind. I was in a meeting with Gabriel and a number of senior ministers, discussing matters pertaining to water access for the City. She came in to speak with him. He did not give a hint of recognition when she entered and, maddeningly, did not introduce her. I did not know who she was. She whispered something in his ear, to which he nodded in acknowledgement, then handed him a note and left. And that was it. She left the room. I could not concentrate on anything for the rest of the meeting, which was unfortunate, as I was the one who had called the parties together to discuss the issues at hand.

"You called the meeting, but you weren't there," Gabriel observed with an amused look later. "Ministers may be more annoying than useful, but even then, Lucifer, it's not wise to irritate them for no good reason."

I could not tell if he was serious or having fun at my expense. Michael skulked somewhere nearby, eyeing Azael, but always keeping one eye on his master. We walked down one of the great halls of the central administration building, our respective bodyguards in tow.

"What's with you?" Gabriel inquired.

"You are going to laugh when I tell you," I said hesitantly.

He smelled blood. "What?" he asked. He stopped abruptly, watching me closely as I continued to walk on. My bodyguards continued to move along with me, but Gabriel's had stopped in their tracks.

"What is it?" he wanted to know.

"Damned annoying. Really," I said to Azael, as his sharp gaze swept over the hall's pedestrians. I came to a halt and turned to look at Gabriel.

"Come on!" Gabriel yelled in schoolboy anticipation.

"All right." I gulped.

I had known Gabriel for many years now and we had shared many personal experiences. He was my friend. In many ways, he was still a mentor to me. But this was a little more personal than anything I had shared with him before.

"That angel who came in to speak with you," I ventured.

"Ah ha!" he laughed and began walking again.

Now I was the one left standing rooted to the spot.

"What? What 'ah ha'?"

"Oh, nothing."

He walked past me, forcing me to quicken my pace to catch up with him. The jangling of swords and breastplates reverberated throughout the hall as my bodyguard now hurried to catch up with me.

"Come on, what? She was beautiful, do you not agree? I have never seen her before. Is she one of your servants?"

"Lucifer, honestly! Would I have a servant come into the room in the midst of a meeting, especially one interesting enough to have water usage as its focus?" he asked sarcastically.

"Look," I said in sterner tones, "that is an important issue. You can only withhold water from the City for so long, before you have a general uprising on your hands. You know Melchom was making a play just to get His audience. And you would let him speak to God. I know you, Gabriel."

"Indeed I will. God needs to be reminded that He has you and me for a reason. He will see through Melchom and the water will flow at full volume again. Amee told me God had agreed to the meeting."

"Who is Amee?"

Gabriel shook his head as we walked out onto one of the sun-lit porticos surrounding the core of the building. The echoes suddenly resounded with far deeper tones, as the sounds were unable to bounce their way out onto the courtyard below us. It was quieter here, but it seemed as if the walls were listening.

"Lucifer, for someone who has worked his way up the ladder and then leapfrogged over ninety-nine percent of the rest of the City, you don't really think too deeply, sometimes. Amee was the angel you noted. She is my niece."

I gulped again, but for different reasons this time.

"Amee is your niece. I did not know."

"Obviously."

"Why have I never seen her before?"

"She spends most of her time in the Great Northern Mountains. She works for the Ministry of Ecology, running one of its millions of inane projects on woodland and water distribution. As I know from one of your own reports, that project is partially responsible for the current water 'crisis,' as you say."

I did not know what to say. So, as I usually did when I did not know what to say, I said the most direct thing I could think of. "I have never seen a more beautiful angel."

Gabriel frowned. "She'd eat you alive."

I could hear Michael stifling a laugh from many paces away. I really could not bear him.

"Not an entirely unappetizing thought, really," I said, only slightly under my breath.

"Are you sure you want to try this? She's my niece. She'll tell me everything you say, do, breathe, eat, think, wear. Everything! And when she's done, she'll tell you to get lost."

I thought for a moment. "Why not? If she is not interested, she is not interested."

"She will not be interested."

"Why do you say that with such conviction?"

"She is involved." Gabriel looked down to the courtyard below us, a bit irritated, I thought. "Let's walk."

We moved back into the hall, making our way back to the other side of the building, to the street where our respective carriages awaited us.

"I am involved," I finally said, hoping that would remind Gabriel of our conversation.

"Well, then, why would you even want to meet her?" Gabriel wore the faintest of smiles.

Emerging from the building onto the steps of the precept, several of his bodyguards ran ahead to the porters in order to get his carriage prepared. We made our way down the steep steps of the building's façade.

"I have never seen an angel so beautiful before," I said.

I knew Gabriel to have several mistresses, some of whom were very senior married angels of standing. Of course he had servants too.

"You are repeating yourself, Lucifer." He chuckled to himself, as he stepped up into his newly arrived carriage.

Mine was right behind it.

"She will be at the party I am throwing in a month's time," Gabriel said. "You will be there. She will be there. Her lover will probably be there too. I am offering you an excellent opportunity."

"She is coming with her lover? Who is he?"

"Not fair, Lucifer." He wagged a mocking finger at me, as his bodyguards closed the carriage door and took up their positions.

Gabriel leaned out the window. "If I am going to have any fun with this, you have to leave some open ends."

"It is Melchom?" I asked with a degree of sickened conviction. "Is it not?"

"Why do you think I entertained today's meeting? Uncles have soft spots too."

He waved a signal to his escort and the carriage pulled away.

⌘ ⌘ ⌘

Now you may ask: "What does Lucifer's relationship with an angel have anything to do with the fall of the Devil and the establishment of Hell?" It would not be an entirely unreasonable question, given what you have been raised to understand about good and evil. Allegorical stories have their usefulness, but reality is more direct. Amee made me who I am today. Women may not be equals in the eyes of men of the Earth and may even hold inferior status in the lands controlled by God in Heaven. But here, in Hell, among Gehennites in the City of Dis, they are held in special reverence because of my relationship with Amee. All forms of being are equal in Hell. We are all fallen, outside the sight of God. And we are doomed to be that way, in part, because of a woman who made all the right choices, when I could not.

⌘ ⌘ ⌘

I finally met Amee the night of Gabriel's party. Gabriel had many villas around the City and even outside its walls. Each was spectacular in its own way. The villa he chose for this party was designed to capture the many-splendored beauty of the Great

Northern Mountains. It was thus fitting that it should be located in the Northeast District, so close to the mountains themselves and not very far from my own residence. Open expanses of rooms, cleared of their regular furnishings, were highlighted by islands of soft leather couches and candelabras cut in the shapes of the most well-known mountains in the range. Ravines of running water cut through the house, spanned by bridges. The floors were littered with ponds located in cool grottos, where angels could relax with others. Hot springs represented some of the more far-flung areas of the Great Northern Mountains. Whole rooms were filled with forests, where people could sit and listen to birds singing over babbling brooks. The villa was vast and it could, especially when filled with hundreds of the City's wealthiest and most influential citizens, take you the better part of an hour to maneuver yourself from one end to the other. I suspected the lingering issue of water rights had been on Gabriel's mind when he chose his venue. The power of suggestion was certainly clear to Melchom, when he arrived with Amee.

Amee was a vision. I know it sounds comical, but the image of her entering the meeting room several weeks ago had endured in my mind. I had found it downright difficult to concentrate on work in the interim and my distraction proved to be the source of many wisecracks from Gabriel. But we never spoke of her directly. I regretted having mentioned my interest in her, as Gabriel could now use my weakness as a bargaining tool, whenever I needed to address an issue that required his support. If he had noticed my distraction, others would too, and I could not afford to be absent-minded when dealing with the scheming rabble that featured on my daily calendar.

She wore stark white pantaloons, fitted tightly on her smooth body, and a light blue blouse that, while certainly not revealing, aroused me so unexpectedly, I must have flushed in public. She was not tall, but certainly of a reasonable and noble height. Her dark brown hair flowed down to the small of her back and white flowers placed in her hair highlighted her exquisite profile. Such soft skin and such a luminous smile that even now, I struggle to find words to describe her mesmerizing power over me. All these years later, I remember her face so clearly, more clearly than I do any of the details of my first meeting with God. Or even the last time we faced one another.

Gabriel, as head of the house, was the first to meet Melchom and Amee as they entered and, as decorum demanded, lead them through the throngs of people to the area where some members of the Senate Council stood socializing and scheming. I watched like a hawk from a balcony above the entrance room, leaning over and straining to see. I got strange looks from the many who walked by, wondering what I was doing and why I was doing it. Azael's vicious scowl was enough to prompt them to move on. I could see Michael standing with a group of well-connected Senators, always eyeing me. I resolved to take a deep breath and do what most attendees knew was not my strong suit: I would introduce myself and try not to be too overbearing.

When I made it down the long stairway, Melchom was still in the midst of complimenting Gabriel on the magnificence of the villa. "It must be quite a chore to maintain all these inner gardens, considering their size and the diversity of species they harbor," Melchom said, his retinue nodding in absolute and expected agreement.

"Truly a wondrous place," I said, as I approached.

I looked directly at Amee. I was so transparent.

Gabriel noticed me right away and smiled as he said, "Yes, it was a designing curiosity that prompted my architect to suggest that like any Great Northern Mountain meadow, the house wouldn't be complete, unless it had its own running water."

He shot a look back at Melchom, whose eyes narrowed ever so slightly at the implication.

"The water acts as a sort of automatic source for most of the villa's vegetation," Gabriel explained. "Without it, the house would be an empty chamber."

To his credit, Melchom managed to keep his cool. He bowed ever so slightly in acknowledgement to Gabriel. "Thank you for sharing your home with us this evening," he managed. "I'm sure everyone will have a wonderful time."

"Oh, no doubt," Gabriel said, as Melchom and his minions continued past into the rest of the party.

Amee stood planted where she had been since I entered the circle of the conversation. Preoccupied with suppressing his anger, I am not sure Melchom had even noticed I was standing there.

"Uncle, you are a rascal!" Amee said, with her arms crossed. "I wouldn't be surprised if you had planned that from the beginning." She smiled for a moment and then broke her pose to give Gabriel a warm hug.

Gabriel was pleased with himself, almost childlike, and certainly behaving in a way I had never seen him behave before.

"Given that our young Lucifer had just joined the conversation, I thought a subtle reminder of our differences wouldn't be too out of line," he said, nodding toward me.

Amee turned her gaze in my direction. Her eyes flashed across me. I immediately doubted if she had formed the same first impression of me that I had had of her. She looked back at Gabriel.

"Yes, devious you are, Uncle!" She held his arm coyly like a young girl.

"This, my dear," Gabriel said, motioning to me, "is Lucifer, Third Archangel of God, Lord Protector of His Senate Council, and Captain General of the Secret Service. This, Lucifer, is Amee, First Secretary to the Minister of Ecology and my niece."

Both Gabriel and Amee looked at me expectantly. Seconds of silence followed, as I struggled to think of something, anything to say. Gabriel cocked his eyebrow in a silent gesture of exasperation. Perhaps, disgust?

"Ah...hello?" Amee finally said, looking at me as if I might be slightly unhinged.

I was still rooted to the floor, not unlike one the many trees that grew tall among Gabriel's guests. "Mmm, yes. Sorry," I sputtered. Suddenly, I came to with a small cough. "Sorry, but I have not been feeling myself today." I took her hand in mine, bowed, and said, "Very pleased to make your acquaintance. Your uncle has told me much about you."

"Funny," she said, "he told me quite the opposite."

"Indeed, but one could hardly come to such a lovely gathering, hoping to be introduced to the most beautiful angel in the room, and open a conversation by sputtering incomprehensibly and following up by saying that he knew not the slightest thing about her!" I came back upright from my rather deep bow. "That would just be rude," I smiled.

Gabriel laughed. "Oh, my!" he said, drinking down the last of his ambrosia. "I must get another drink." He turned away to look for a steward.

"You are an odd one, you are," Amee said.

At least, she had not moved off with Gabriel, I thought to myself.

"How do you mean, ma'am?" I ventured. "Do you refer to my lack of language skills, my lack of wit in being unable to decide what, precisely, to say after such a prolonged display of interest, or to the fact that I continue to look so directly into your eyes?"

"Well, to be honest, all three. You know I am here with the Minister," she said, throwing Melchom a glance. Her lightheartedness disappeared and was replaced with an unmistakable expression of indignation.

"I am direct with what I want. I always have been," I said. I looked down for the first time since we began speaking. "I will, most likely, always be."

She surveyed me again. "Yes, I've heard that about you. Tell me, what do you expect to happen from this conversation, Lucifer?" Her use of my name was a bit unexpected, but now it was difficult for me to determine whether she was playing or had actually taken offense at my advances.

"Only that I would get to know you."

"Your intentions are that clear?" she asked, almost interrupting me.

"My intentions are that clear. I want to get to know you. I think you are the most beautiful angel I have ever seen and I want to get to know you."

Now it was her turn to be embarrassed. Her ears turned red.

"Would you excuse me?" she asked and walked away.

I bowed as she left, but made sure I continued watching her as she moved through the room. She turned, almost imperceptibly, and noticed that my eyes were still on her. She continued into the crowd.

Gabriel came up from behind me. "Smooth you are not, Lucifer." He patted my shoulder and handed me a glass of ambrosia.

"No, actually, I have never been smooth, but you know that." I was still looking through the crowd at Amee.

She was speaking animatedly with some senator or minister or someone.

"Jehoel didn't know that," Gabriel said.

He stepped around in front of me, cutting off my view and breaking my gaze. I looked at him. I had not really thought of Jehoel for what must have been several years at that point. His name and the memories it suddenly conjured up created a painful confusion in my mind. I bowed my head, partly, to disguise the flare of anger within me and partly, to conceal the surge of totally unexpected grief that overwhelmed me. Gabriel knew where to hurt me when he needed my attention.

"Why do you say that?" I asked.

"Keep your eyes on what's important, Lucifer. You are here for a reason and it is not for Amee. God has seen to it that you take up the work left by your grandfather and that Amee makes the necessary inroads with Melchom."

I looked up, clearer now in my mind. "Why?"

"You do not question God, Lucifer."

"Do you?"

"Do not change the subject. Do what you are told to do and you get to keep what you have. I tell you this as a friend. Keep your focus or you could lose everything that you have worked so hard to accomplish."

Gabriel did not seem angry, although questioning God's will as I had so blatantly would have been a punishable offense for any citizen. He was stern and focused, as if to bring me back.

I willed my expression to soften. "I am sorry," I said. "Perhaps I was not lying. I am *really* not myself today."

Gabriel put his arm around my waist and turned me toward a servant holding drinks. Handing me another glass of ambrosia that Michael had handed him, Gabriel said, "I understand. Drink up, Lucifer. This is a party and the ambrosia is flowing. Tomorrow is another day."

That night, I drank my share of ambrosia and several other angels' shares as well. Azael had to carry me home, probably cursing that he had not properly lined me up in his aim all those many years ago in the swamps of Apsatsus.

CHAPTER TWENTY-THREE

"You see, Lucifer, I remain aloof from the people for good reason," God said, as we walked the halls of the Seat of God.

We often strolled in this manner, talking. For me, it was a learning process.

"For one, it infers upon me a sense of greatness without having to say a single word. They know I am up here, somewhere," He said, gesturing around the grand halls, "looking down on them. Watching them. Taking care of them. That mystery sparks the imagination and inexorably leads the people to believe in an almost supernatural power hidden away, invested in me."

God was pleased by His own logic.

"By withholding myself from the people, my power grows, without me having to do anything at all. I am not a mere ruler. I am all-powerful God."

It was not the first time God had taken me into His confidence in this way. It was not just that I was an outsider with an unadulterated view of Heaven, though I am sure that also inured me to Him. I think it was my unabashed urge to change everything all at once. My innocence. My unrelenting drive to pull His bloated bureaucracy apart and straighten it out.

"Yes, my Lord," I replied.

Once I was made Seraph and given my charges, speculation had been rife among the angelic ranks as to what I would do. I had been determined not to waste any time. Not long after my ascent to Seraph, hundreds of angels were turfed. Once well-positioned angels now found themselves on the street, their access to God totally cut off. God must have loved it. I could do everything He had always wanted to do, without Him having to face any of the political heat for it. I had welcomed the heat and it made me instantly hated.

"Now," He said, changing gears, "what is this I hear about your efforts to upend work on the northern aqueducts? There seems to be no end to the bellyaching of that Interior Minister."

"The work is poorly planned, my Lord," I replied, quite pleased to report the successful outcome of my endeavors. "In reviewing the books, I have come to understand that some within the ministry feel it necessary to overpay thousands of angels who, my sources tell me, are not even licensed to do the work."

"Hmm," God replied noncommittally.

I was suddenly worried I might have stumbled upon something He had some personal interest in. Gabriel had warned me that could happen from time to time. God liked His little secrets.

"Put bluntly, my Lord, it is a scam. Just another way to further bloat the bureaucracy and take from your City," I said with the fervor of a true patriot.

"In our world, Lucifer, the bureaucracy is everything," God said, speaking deeply again. "Angels spending all of their time vying for power, making backroom deals, dispersing the power they have across the length and breadth of the apparatus. Everything ends up a mess, a quagmire of inconsistencies that defies translation."

"That is why I have taken a personal interest in this work, my Lord. It is, as you say, a 'quagmire.'"

"Yes, but you do too much, my young friend," He said. "This is akin to what I was referring to just moments ago. Appearances, or a lack thereof, are everything."

"I am sorry, my Lord," I said, a note of inquiry in my voice. "I do not understand."

"You are so right, Lucifer. You really do not understand," God said quite seriously. "Sometimes, it is the thing you do not do that speaks the loudest. That makes you the most loved. The most followed."

"Yes, my Lord."

"And never forget that if you ignore the hearts and minds of others, they will grow to hate you. Your actions will be revisited upon you by those you have offended."

"Yes, my Lord," I said dejectedly.

I did not care if a bunch of well-manicured angels hated me. The project must have been of some importance to God, as Gabriel had warned. Something, for reasons indecipherable to any of us, God wanted to happen His way.

"I see you are displeased," God observed.

I straightened up right away. "I am pleased to serve *you*, my Lord," I said. "It is not for me to be pleased or otherwise, but for my services to be useful to your rule."

"Bullshit."

"My Lord?"

"You heard me," God said, clearly annoyed now. "Bullshit. We have these discussions, you and I, Lucifer, because I can trust you to tell me the truth. Always. When you lie to me, it makes me mad. Makes me concerned about having placed my trust in you."

I had shot way past the mark now and had not even seen it coming.

"Do not patronize me, like you do those sodden senators you torture every day."

"I am sorry, my Lord. Of course, you are right," I said, hoping I did not sound condescending. "I am disappointed. I do not like to see the City taken advantage of, its resources strained because of the bilious villains who run it."

"They are bureaucrats, Lucifer. They do not know any better."

"Why do you stand for it, then?" I asked.

"Lucifer, my friend, I don't 'stand for it.' I created it!"

God saw the blank look on my face.

"How else do I get anything done?" He went on. "I let the people believe that power remains in their hands, that they have a say in what happens here." God paused for a moment, contemplating His next sentence. "To turn their focus on anything other than the fact that I run Heaven. And that all power flows from me and to me."

"I see it now, my Lord," I said, though somewhat dismayed by a strategy I perceived as inherently laced with downside risk. "But I also see contempt and ambivalence, which breeds malevolence against your rule."

God laughed. "That's what you're here for, Lucifer."

"It all seems too risky to me," I said. Hurriedly, I continued, "But I am a neophyte in such matters."

"Do not spend too much time worrying about it," God said, waving me off.

I seethed a bit at the insult. I had meant to be self-deprecating.

God took it one step farther. "One must be careful at all times as to what one says to the people. It is why I spend so much time doing and so little time being seen. One wrong word and suddenly, the people's perceptions are shattered. Why would I put myself at their mercy in such ways?"

"Yes, my Lord."

"These angels are not like the hags that run the Senate," God continued. "You need not navigate so carefully with that bunch. The bureaucracy is another creature altogether."

"Yes, my Lord."

"The powerful know how to judge who is best positioned to further their interests," God went on. "In all situations, Lucifer. You must learn to control your desire to take sides. If you allow yourself to become involved in their problems, in time, you will find that their problems have become yours."

"Yes, my Lord."

It may not have come naturally to me and even if I did not necessarily agree with the logic behind it, I knew it important to remind God that I recognized and respected His strength. If He was so monstrously insecure, I could not risk inadvertently out-shining Him in any way. My only real task was to make sure God looked better than those who surrounded Him.

"An angel is always dissatisfied. He is always tormented by the feeling that there is something more out there. Something else that he is destined for, beyond his sight. Beyond his own control. Would you agree?"

The question was heretical. What do you do, when you are one of God's greatest angels and He asks you to reaffirm your faith?

"Yes," I said. "I have felt it, my Lord."

"Good," God replied, clearly pleased that I had not "bulls-hitted" Him this time. "That feeling gives you a greater sense of purpose. Does it not? Gives you hope, even, that as an in-dividual, you have more control over your destiny than you really do?"

"Yes, I suppose so," I replied.

"Well, that is the answer," God said.

"My Lord?"

"Faith, Lucifer. I control them through faith."

"There is nothing, then, to this feeling we all have?" I asked.

"I have given all my angels the ability to dream, to will them-selves in directions. Or so they perceive. These directions are nat-urally curbed, this faith they have in themselves, curtailed. Their beliefs, their faith, can be no greater than that which I have given them."

"So, You allowed us to believe we have a freedom we do not really possess?" I asked again, considering the thought.

"Freedom cannot live without faith."

"But your rule can?"

"Yes," God said, happy that I had understood. "Quite right. Faith is necessary in any ordered society. If faith were not allowed, if angels were not able to have some free rein, all that energy would be directed elsewhere. Angels are immoral creatures. You've considered this before, Lucifer. And it rips at you, as your faith in me does not allow you to consider the possibility that I may have created something so imperfect."

"So evil," I interjected.

"Yes. Faith is so important, because it is so much more powerful than reason. One cannot find moral guidance in reason. It is only in faith that a good or, as you say, evil life can be lived. Faith brings with it a feeling of greater purpose. Without faith, angels are directionless in a Heaven totally outside their control. They begin to doubt their purpose and when those two elements combine, it creates in them an unwillingness to bow to those with power. This cannot be allowed to happen."

"So by relaxing the reins a bit and permitting a controlled faith," I interjected, "to inspire angels with a feeling of greater purpose, You offer us a chance to blow off the steam that would, if it were allowed to build up, lead us to confront and, perhaps, to even resist your rule."

It sounded so contrived. Too complicated to make sense. So elaborate, that if it were true, its many moving parts would need to operate in constant unison and achieve a refined degree of synchronicity to work perfectly. In short, a dangerous cocktail easily thrown out of whack.

"Precisely."

God's secret to His rule, then. Fool angels into believing something that makes them compliant with the tyranny that actually keeps their lives on a tight leash.

"Now you are one of the very few who truly understands"

"Thank you, my Lord," I replied. "I will take your wisdom and use your angels to further your rule."

"That's a good boy," God said, slapping me on the back.

We retired to dinner, but in the middle of the first course, God was called away to some important business, leaving me to myself. In an empty dining room. In some empty hall. To contemplate that all my life's work was done under God's direction, rather than for His benefit. The implausibility eating at me.

⌘　⌘　⌘

"You do not call. You do not write. I wonder if you meant what you said," Amee teased me one day, as I happened to walk past her in the halls of some ministry building.

Gabriel may have gotten me drunk that night, but what he said had certainly cleared my head of any notions I might have entertained about her. You do not question God's will. I was not exactly taken aback by her unexpected interest in talking to me, but I was surprised by the remarkable change in her demeanor. I waved her through the circle bodyguards.

"In the inner circle already, I guess," she said, poking fun at the trappings of my position.

"I am afraid they are necessary."

I looked at Azael and he moved the rest of the guard farther off.

"Many angels would much rather be looking down at me than through to me," I said.

She smiled. "Perhaps you insult too many people at parties. You should really consider attending a class on what is accepted as seemly social conduct."

She appeared dead serious now.

"Well…I…I guess I could do that, but…" I fumbled, before noticing her smile. "I see. Yes, perhaps a class would make it easier for me to pick up beautiful angels at parties. Maybe even not-so-beautiful angels."

"See? There you go again! Should I be offended by your advances or should I be embarrassed that you choose such ways to manifest them?"

"Neither. I mean, both." I looked hard at her.

She tilted her head with a smile. "So what, then?"

"So what, then?" I repeated.

"Hmm. You are not who I thought you would be. "

"And who is that?"

"Well, selling your friend down the river, taking down half the government bureaucracy, and jockeying yourself into such an invincible position next to God. Frankly, I had assumed you would be a pompous old bore."

"Well!" I sputtered again.

"Instead, you are only pompous."

I did not respond. I never really spoke of Jehoel. While certainly a topic of gossip around the City, the intimate details of his involvement or of my relationship with him, were not commonly known. Gabriel must have told her what had happened. Hardly a major breach of state secrets, but still enough to make it hurt.

Suddenly, her expression turned grave.

"What is it?" I asked.

"For a minute, you weren't there at all. You were somewhere else. I hit a nerve. And the pompous left hand of God is as easy to read as any child."

"Responsibility comes with power," I said. "I guess I did not really learn that, until I met your uncle. Had I understood it earlier, I might have made different decisions."

I was not sure I was speaking the complete truth, but discussing Jehoel had a way of making me see things differently. Though I had placed Phanuel under my protection, he and I spoke little of his father. Phanuel was willing to pretend that I had had nothing to do with his father's death.

"A hint of modesty. I guess I won't know until later whether you are a fool for doubting yourself or whether I am the fool for believing you."

We smiled at each other.

"I want to see you again," I said, quite serious now. "Can we have dinner?"

She considered this for a few moments. "Are you not involved with someone?" she asked. "You know I am."

"Sometimes, we have to do what we have to do."

"We will see each other again, I am sure."

With that, she bowed and walked through my line of bodyguards and back into the flow of pedestrian traffic. She did not look back this time. She already knew I would be watching her.

CHAPTER TWENTY-FOUR

It took a few years, but eventually God Himself came to me about His project. The project Gabriel and Zoan had begun so many years ago. The one I had no notion of, but was now supposed to complete.

"I built this city from nothing and we rule it with consideration for the important things. The things that make a difference," He began.

Servants ran from several directions to fan Him as we strolled, as usual, along the lengths of one of His enumerable terraces overlooking the City.

"Yes, my Lord."

As Protector, it was my privilege to speak with God about the running of the City, the progress on the collection of taxes, the building of the City's walls, and the status of the operations focused on tracking down and bringing to justice evildoers and all those who would do the City harm. I was revered by all and feared by most. I was at the peak of my power when I stood next to Him. I felt as if we were one. One of his two sons, Lucifer and Gabriel, bringing His power to bear on the City and its inhabitants. I was unstoppable. I was a god.

With time, I had become more accustomed to the directions God's conversations often unexpectedly headed. But despite those tangential paths, what He had to say usually made sense. He was a genius. And when you are a genius, talking to the little people can be taxing. He would say three separate things nearly at once, and only after you had thought your way carefully through the conversation in retrospect would you realize that everything He had said at the beginning closed out what He had said in the end. You had to hope you could make sense of it all, in time to prevent Him from getting really testy. God certainly kept you on your toes.

"Lucifer, I have a project on which I need your help."

I bowed in acknowledgment of the opportunity He was offering me.

"It is something I started a long, long time ago, but was unable to complete."

"Yes, my Lord. Tell me how I can serve you."

"I had an idea. It came to me once, when peace was eluding my kingdom. Not what it is now, under your supervision and Gabriel's."

"We live to serve you, my Lord."

"Well, now, that is exactly it. You came from the outside, Lucifer. Tell me truthfully: what was the attitude of the people of the City when they spoke of me?"

"They love you, my Lord. You are their protector. You are..."

"I DON'T WANT TO HEAR THAT NOW!"

His vehement words took me completely by surprise. I actually cowered, as the boom of His voice hit the air. The servants fell to the floor and lay there, trembling with fear. I stared at Him, not knowing how I should react.

"I am sorry," He said.

The expression of intense displeasure immediately left His face. As if He had not just screamed out in anger without any provocation. I had never heard Him apologize before.

"You do not need to apologize to me, Lord," I sputtered. "I am sorry I angered you so."

"I know, Lucifer, I know." He smiled now, picking up where He had left off.

The servants got up and began fanning Him again, as if nothing had happened. I stood stock still, as He turned to look at me.

"I chose you, in part, because of your noble lineage, Lucifer." I did not react.

"I loved your grandfather and was so saddened by his passing. I know you loved him too. I remember your father as a boy. A nasty little sot, if you don't mind my saying so. But I never knew you, and my falling out with your grandfather caused that.

"I chose you," He continued, "because you have been there, where I have never been." As He turned His back on me, I thought I heard Him say, "At least, not where I remember."

The servants fanned away. He waved them away.

"Now tell me how I am perceived by the City, Ahriman," He said, turning to me and looking me hard in the eye. "Tell me the truth. Speak as a loving son speaks to his father."

Thoughts swirled through my mind. It was a calculated and unnerving question to ask. And He knew it.

"I..." Was it a test? "...think..." What would I pay to know what to say? "...they..." Where do I go from here? I cannot know. "...hate you."

I gulped. I knew He could see the shimmer on my face, but I did not break out in a sweat. So that was good.

"They hate you," I repeated.

He smiled again. "I knew I could trust you, Ahriman."

Now the sweat came. I felt the sweat beading on my feet. I had not known you could sweat from your feet. Where else could I sweat from?

"You see," God went on, oblivious to my state, "you and Gabriel are the only two angels in this kingdom with enough courage, enough toughness of character, to actually look me in the eyes and tell me the truth. I live a strange life here, Lucifer. I rule this land, as I always have, from the time I created this City. But it is full of vice and greed and avarice and the City thrives on this. You have seen this. You know what I mean. It makes me the ruler that I am. Do you understand?"

"You rule as you see fit to rule, my Lord. If you did not rule this way, we would have no order and no order means chaos."

I did not hesitate now. Apparently, I was one of only two angels in the universe.

"You are looking at the circle, my Lucifer, but coming from the other direction. That is why I needed you." He thumped His fist on the balcony ledge in emphasis.

The servants jumped.

"My Lord?"

"You can see with the eyes of the common angel. I do not mean this to be an insult. Believe me."

"Yes, Lord."

"The City hates me, compelling me to rule with an iron fist and my iron Seraphim. How many angels have you removed from office, Lucifer? Ten? Twenty? A thousand? How many have gone to the gallows for crossing you? For crossing me?" He looked at me.

The question had been asked, never to be answered.

"Has Gabriel done any such thing?" He asked, rhetorically, I hoped. "No. He keeps that sycophantic leech, Michael, and has allowed the rot to spread."

I was rather surprised to hear Him speak of Gabriel in such a way. They had a history I could never share.

"Since you came to me," He continued, "you have revamped the City's entire bureaucratic structure. You have modernized everything. You have reformed the Secret Police. You have removed the worst elements from the Senate. You have promoted those who follow your orders through the ranks to the point where they will follow you anywhere. You are a leader of noble blood, but from humble origins."

"I am not noble, my Lord. Regardless of my origins," I said solemnly. I thought of Zoan and Jehoel.

"Do not let feelings of guilt overwhelm you, my friend," He said, immediately recognizing the reference to my awkward rise to power. "You are right to act in concert with the character of the times. Infrequently, I should say, do people of low rank acquire positions of power and influence without using force. Deceit is your business, Lucifer."

I winced at His words.

"No, no," He said. "Do not shy away from what you are good at. I've read through your many reports and have inquired into your activities at the Ministry of Information. Fraud, lies, treachery—these have been the focus of your life's work. Without them, you would not be standing here today, if you know what I mean. It is in the vices of angels that we realize how good we really are," He said, looking directly into my eyes. "It is in the vices of angels that you have learned an important lesson of governance, Lucifer. A leader must achieve mastery in deceit in order to do the great things he must do."

He turned and strolled on, with me beside him, matching his stride.

"Learning that lesson now, learning how to make the most of these attributes and use force to attain the goals in hand. That is a great gift."

He patted me on the back. God had touched me.

"Use your gifts, Lucifer, and do not forget the lesson you have been so wise to teach yourself."

"What has this to do with anything?" I omitted my customary "my Lord". Why not? I was experimenting, trying out avenues I had not explored before. He wanted something from me and was taking His time in getting to the point.

"You put your people into places to support you, but how long before you must reshuffle them?" He asked, apparently deciding to overlook my intentional faux pas. "How long will they last, Lucifer, before the next generation must sweep away the filth your once trusted angels deliberately spewed?"

"I do not know, Lord. I am a manager of angels. I rule them in your name. If I need to remove them or promote them or kill them, it is because I need to rule in your name to bring your greater glory to the City."

"Exactly! Exactly, Lucifer!" He said excitedly.

He looked at me with what I could swear was love.

"You're so much like Zoan," he went on. "I can see it in you. I can see it in your heart."

We walked back into His apartments and He waved a servant over for ambrosia.

"I sat in this room..." He said. He looked around, a confused expression on His face. "No, maybe another. I sat with your grandfather so many years ago and talked with him like this. Like you and I are talking now."

We sat down together.

"It warms me to see some of him back here now."

"Lord?"

"I will continue where we left off. You will continue where your grandfather, before you, left off."

Then, without warning, He sprang to His feet. In a rage, His hand came crashing down on a servant's neck. The angel fell to the floor, sobbing. I stood suddenly. I was at a loss as to what had happened. Other servants appeared from the walls in a split second. Heavily armed, with swords and bows. Not servants. Bodyguards. His bodyguards. I had not even known they were there. They pounced on the stricken servant.

God's eyes flashed molten fury. "Take this away!" He thundered, pointing to the servant.

The bodyguards grasped the servant under his arms, flipped him over, and dragged him from the room. Other servants ran up to take his place and continue pouring ambrosia. God watched as the angel was taken from the room. He waited as another servant provided Him a towel to dry the drops of ambrosia that had apparently spilled on His hand. He straightened His robes and sat back down.

"Sit," He said to me sternly. He was still irritated, but there was a smile on His face again. A disingenuous smile, this time.

"Yes, my Lord," I said, relaxing my grip on the pommel of my sword, but still feeling the tension rippling up my back.

I slowly sat down, trying not to glance at the doorway through which the whimpering angel had just been dragged away.

"I will make a new universe, a new world," God said, quite pleased with Himself and completely at ease in picking up from where He had left off so abruptly. "I will make a new race," He looked at me with what now struck me as a painted smile, "that obeys my commands. He will be called 'Man' and he will serve me like the angels you have chosen to serve you. Man will be my creation."

He took the glass of ambrosia from the new servant. The angel, I could see, was clearly nervous.

"And you, Lucifer, will help me build him."

CHAPTER
TWENTY-FIVE

Angels of the City were dirty, whether you spoke of them literally or figuratively. I had to agree with God. The lower classes hated Him. The middle classes hated the lower classes and God. The upper classes hated the middle classes and God, and didn't care a wit about the lower classes. It was a mess. How did you trust in angels who all hated each other and were unified in nothing other than their hatred for you?

But if you could create a whole new order from dust, build it the way you wanted to, impose your chosen restraints on it, and make it subservient to one master and one master only, what force could topple you? From where would they summon the urge to pull you down? An army of a million trimmers could not subdue an army of automatons that were devoted to you and willing to sacrifice whatever they held dear. For you. It was brilliant. But was it possible?

"Your grandfather and I came quite close in the years we dedicated to building Man," Gabriel told me later, when I went to him to discuss my conversation with God. "Your grandfather was passionate about it. He saw it as an answer to our problems in the outlands." He hesitated. "But he did not see it as God does. God's visions of the City, filled with the devoted Man, far outstripped what your grandfather had ever seen."

He could sense my tension as he brought up Zoan in his discussion.

"Lucifer, I loved Zoan." He put his hand on my shoulder. "We were like brothers. And now, you and I are like brothers. I mean no disrespect." He looked my eyes. "You know this."

I smiled. "I know it, my friend." I smiled more broadly. "I know it."

"Now where to start?" Gabriel said, more to himself. "Or more accurately, where to pick up from?"

"Gabriel," I asked. "What did you do with the book?"

He stopped cold. His expression had not really changed, but even his breathing seemed to come to a standstill.

"Don't be tempted by it, Lucifer." He came back to me, but this time, there was no love in his eyes. "Don't be tempted by it. It took your grandfather, and it will take anyone who touches it. It's evil and it's not something we should discuss."

"Yes, but does that not just make you want to discuss it more?"

"Listen to me. You have read the book. You know what it says. You know the laws of His kingdom. You have served His kingdom with the greatest of distinction and you have done what no others ever could. Don't be temped by it, Lucifer."

"Have you ever discussed it with Him?"

"Enough!" Gabriel shouted. "Enough! *Enough*!" He was enraged.

I made a quick mental note. "Sorry," I said.

"Are you insane? Would you take everything you hold important and throw it away? No. Of course, I've never discussed it with Him! And I never will. The book is evil. I'll say it one more time and if you make me say it again, we shall not be friends any longer. Don't be tempted by it."

I averted my gaze. In a weird way, I felt ashamed. When I had studied the book, I had felt as if the world made sense and answers were almost within my grasp. I never did get quite all the way there, but at that time, I felt as if I were approaching an answer. But now, having infuriated Gabriel, I was ashamed. Ashamed, but still interested.

"I am sorry," I said again. I meant it. I really did.

"We shall start from where I left off," he continued, with what I was sure was the pounding swell of blood in his ears. "And this time, I won't fail."

⌘　⌘　⌘

I saw Amee as often as I could. We would meet for lunch or a stroll in one of the Seat of God's many gardens during the workday's off-hours. I would tell her about some of the things I was doing. Doing so violated the confidentiality I so strictly enforced among my many staff members, but, strangely, I did not feel in the least bit conflicted sharing it all with her. She was Gabriel's niece and, clearly, he told her things above and beyond what the Ministry of Ecology should be concerned with. How would it hurt to tell her about Man and our plans to create a new race of beings? What a blockhead I was!

We spent so much time together, I began to refer to her as "my love." It was true to the extent that I could understand feelings of love. I wanted to be with her, and I did not want her to be with anyone else. Most particularly, not with Melchom. At first, she was surprised and even embarrassed that I would refer to her in such a way. Later, she became accustomed to it and would even tease me about it. She never said she loved me in return. She asked how I could use a word so easily when I understood it so little.

"How could it mean anything?" she asked quite sensibly.

My personal staff was rather confused by the sudden change in my schedule. There had been a time, when almost nothing could take me away from my official work. Since being elevated to the Order, I had taken to task all the items I had not been able to change during my tenure in menial, mid-level positions. Lines of communication were centralized, intermediate staffing removed, policies on escalating important issues immediately, and honors and promotions conferred on those who deserved it. Gabriel joked that I had taken out the middleman. Even now, I am proud to say that is exactly what I did. The City of God harbored a collection of angels looking for a handout and struggling to get past and on top of the angel directly above them. They were not interested in the betterment of the system. They were interested in making their way, in whatever way they could. Like me, I guess. But different, somehow. There would always be backstabbing and politics, but I had made sure that nothing happened without my knowing about it. Heaven would not help those who crossed me.

But now, I left the office whenever the impulse took me. I would call upon Amee and even make appearances at her office. She often expressed unhappiness with the rumblings of rumors around her office. It was plain that Melchom was not particularly happy to see me as interested in his ministry projects as now I evidently appeared to be. Despite her complaints, Amee would come with me.

"I want to see you in some condition rather than simply for lunch or a walk," I said one day, as we sat in one of the more secluded palace gardens.

Waterfalls and streams whispering through the grounds and worn paths to and from the more private glens latticed the area. People walked there to be in each other's company, away from prying eyes, inquisitive ears, and the general noise of City life. I had fooled myself into thinking my meetings with Amee were more than they actually were.

"I don't think that's smart, Lucifer," she replied. "I'm involved. You're involved. What are we going to do?"

"I will call off that relationship. It means nothing. I want to be with you."

She did not smile, though I really hoped she would consider it.

"What will that accomplish?" she asked. "I am still with Melchom. I couldn't get out of it, even if I wanted to."

"Do you want to?" It was a reasonable question, I thought. This was the frankest conversation we had had yet.

"I do not know. You are great and I like being with you, but you are involved in things I do not want to be a part of. I may be Gabriel's niece, but I am not interested in the life you deliberately decided to take on, one to which politics and hatred and internecine conflict are integral. That is not me and I don't want *it* to be a part of *my* life."

I was at a loss for words. We sat together on a simple bench, looking at a simple pond. Why was it necessary for life to be so complicated, so murky?

"I do not know about all that," I said. "I am what I am and it is something I have worked for my whole life to be. But in many ways, chance got me where I am today. That same chance brought you into my life and it is not something I can pass up." I paused to think. "I take my chances when I can and I think we would be worth the chance."

"In your world or mine?"

"Anywhere. I can talk to God. I can ask Him to let us be together. I do His work for Him and I am running His great plan for Him. He can surely give me the one thing I want most."

"Want most?" She seemed upset now. "The one thing you wanted most you've already achieved. You rule this City like a tyrant, brooking no argument and making God's Word your rulebook for everyone else to follow. You are second only to my uncle and the three of you together blow hot fear into the heart of this City."

I was shocked. This was heretical talk and certainly dangerous enough to invite arrest. My expression must have betrayed me. Again.

"You see?" she observed. "You even think like one of them, though you think you're special. You *are* one of them, something I don't want to be. Lucifer, you may call me your 'love,' but you love yourself above all else."

She got up and walked away. I wanted to follow her, but did not. She was right. I knew it, because Jehoel had told me the same thing, years ago.

That evening, I ended my relationship with the other angel I was seeing.

⌘   ⌘   ⌘

"I am telling you, the simplest way to do this is to take what we have now. That is, use our own bodies as the model, rather than starting from scratch," I insisted.

Gabriel was still skeptical.

"Sometimes, the easiest answer is the right answer, all the same," I said with great earnestness.

"Listen to you!" Gabriel said mockingly. "A budding philosopher. Perhaps you should head down to the Temple, later today, and turn in your Seraph's wings."

Gabriel and I had spent what seemed like an eternity working to create God's Man. Entire ministry departments were now dedicated to creating the world that Man would live in. Animals, plants, atmosphere, biology. All of it planned by God's titanic organization. It was the secret I had never been able to piece together, sitting at my desk in the PID. A project so secret that Heaven's most gifted spy had not known about it. But to add Man to the mixture? It required what I hated most. More bureaucracy. God was thrilled. Our new bureaucratic creation ate up huge amounts of angelic resources. The more angels there were on the payroll, the more information could be gathered and the more control exercised. Moreover, busy angels are not as prone to dissent and revolt. It was as if the whole of Heaven had been mobilized to create Man.

"Do not get carried away," I retorted in response to Gabriel's quip. "You see the logic in what I am saying."

"Yes, there is logic. I admit. But Zoan and I had already created something from nothing, a whole new being, long before you got here."

"What you're suggesting is a deviation from the original plan," Michael interjected, aiming his words at me.

It was unlike him to say anything without a prompt.

"And where has that gotten you?" I snapped back at Michael. "Nowhere. Why are you even here?" I growled.

"He's here, because I need him to be here," Gabriel said quietly.

"All the original plan did was pose all sorts of developmental problems," I continued, turning back to Gabriel. "Once you created Man's 'Earth,' the whole thing went awry."

"We've tried many different forms and models."

"Yes. And what have you got to show for it? Earth, filled with vicious and threatening creatures, unable to respond to even the simplest of commands. Legions of them."

"They started from scratch and the process was very long and slow, with little useful development," Phanuel piped in.

He was now a premier scientist in the City's armies and God had allowed me to bring him in as project manager. Gabriel was convinced the son would fall prey to the same evils as the father had, but I had prevailed with God.

"Several times, you have had to wipe the slate clean and start from scratch," Phanuel said

"Yes, Phanuel. We don't need a history lesson," Gabriel snapped.

Phanuel backed down. Michael was pleased that his master had taken the young angel down a peg or two at my expense.

"I am sorry, my Lord," Phanuel said dutifully.

"Listen, we are getting away from the point," I said. "Phanuel has brought simplicity to the table and I think we should pay attention."

When Phanuel first arrived at the laboratory, he had taken one look at what we were doing and suggested a completely different approach to the problem. An approach I fully endorsed. Instead of evolving creatures over time, as Gabriel and Zoan had attempted to do, Phanuel modified the physiological form of an angel. Cloning. Of sorts. It was not perfect, but it worked. In the laboratory. These specimens could procreate a great deal faster than we could and while their development was slow in Earth terms, it was a mere drop in the bucket from Heaven's perspective. This approach also resulted in their brain being basically the same as the angel's brain. This posed a serious problem, as the compliance God demanded of Man could not be guaranteed. By introducing certain modifications, these specimens were prevented from fully utilizing their brain capacity. We only needed what God needed. A new, but intelligent beast of burden.

"It is at Apsatsus that the transition can be made without interference," Phanuel said. "Biologically. Anatomically. Sub-atomically. Lord Lucifer and I have taken all the samples we need. The tests prove it."

"The Styx, then?" I asked. "At the Forks?"

"Yes."

"We must make the necessary preparations at the Forks for this," I said turning to Gabriel. He was lost in thought. The mistakes he and Zoan had made during past attempts could not be completely eradicated. As a result, there were many factors that could easily shorten Man's earthly lifespan. These viruses, diseases, and other issues could be sorted out after they had made the transition from Earth to Heaven. Angels were far less prone to illness. And alarmingly, Apsatsus proved to be the best place for the transition from Earth to Heaven. But more of that later.

"Once we establish appropriate conditions at the Forks, by using our command of the natural processes, we can transition whole groups of individuals into Heaven at one go," Phanuel said.

"But how can we develop such a center of activity on the very doorstep of our enemies? How can it be financed?" Michael asked.

"The transitions can be done in bulk?" Gabriel asked, ignoring Michael.

"Yes," Phanuel said, answering him. "Apsatsus it must be. With the modeling down and the facilities in place, we could simply generate an Earthly earthquake, for example, to take in whole groups that were deemed to be ready for transition and further study."

"All this needs to be carefully planned," Gabriel said, looking back at me.

"Yes," I responded, giving Phanuel a knowing look.

Gabriel had been mostly pushed from the equation with Phanuel's arrival and his resentment of the young scientist was evident.

"The mental inhibitor," Gabriel continued. "Our Lord is very keen to have it in place. Simple minds are necessary to prevent disorder later. The notion of these beings having angelic brains is a bit difficult to swallow."

We have enough disorder already, without the introduction of a foreign species, I thought to myself.

"Yes, Gabriel," I said in agreement.

"And God wants only a certain kind of mental predisposition. He sees an early indoctrination as the best way to get these creatures working the way He wants them to."

Something as simple as fear of the dark went a long way toward getting someone to believe in otherworldliness. But there was more. My conversation with God about freedom and faith had possessed me to push Phanuel to develop a suppression system. The free will of angels would be buried in Man, but genetically disabled. A patch of sorts on the fundamental weakness of the angelic brain. God had already explained to me His problems with angels.

"Yes, Gabriel," I repeated.

He was in a daze.

"Let us keep focus," I said, slapping his arm lightly. "Phanuel has done great work here. The science is indisputable. We should follow his suggestions. Monitor the results. Let me order the building of the facilities at the Forks," I pleaded. "I can handle it."

He thought about it for a minute. It was strange to me how pliable Gabriel now seemed. Someone so implacable, when I had observed him as a youth and revered him as an angel, was now, and often, nothing more than a pushover.

"We will do it your way, then," Gabriel said. "But it will not be easy."

He had addressed the words to me, as if I did not already realize what I was getting myself into.

I nodded. He shot Phanuel an ugly look and walked out.

"Scurry along," Phanuel said, shooing Michael away.

I laughed under my breath. Sometimes, I tended to forget Phanuel was not actually my son.

"Go ahead," I told him once Michael had gone. "Bombard the Earth, as we discussed, and get rid of those monstrous lizard-like creatures that scurry across its surface." I smiled at him. "You got it right, Phanuel. Again."

"Thank you," he said with a slight bow. "But how are you going to build up our position at the Forks? There's no budget." He was looking through his papers. "It could well be easier to set up a facility in the middle of Tartarus than to build out those near ruins at the Forks," he said, only half-joking.

"I have a plan," I said. "And Phanuel, I am Ahriman. Always Ahriman to you." I could not hide the love in my voice.

So, you see, every blade of grass, every molecule of water, every type of quark—everything was designed, created, tested, and put into production by God's bureaucratic apparatus. Man was Phanuel's brainchild and mine, with God acting as the not-so-innocent bystander. He may have put things into motion, but He was happy to watch from the sidelines, so long as He got what He wanted. You are all here today because of the argument we had that day.

⌘　⌘　⌘

War had always existed in Heaven. War, it seems, will always be part of Heaven. To this day, the blood of more angels and men has been spilt on the fields of Heaven than all the grains of sand on all the beaches of the universe. Man's wars on Earth are nothing by comparison. Understand, that when war breaks out in Heaven, it is of a scale hardly imaginable by earthly standards. There are no nuclear missiles, no VX gas, no weaponized smallpox viruses here in Heaven. There is steel and flesh and bone and blood. It is raw and it eats your soul from the inside out.

War broke out with the trimmers again at about the same time that my second varietal of Man was making his way onto the Earth. Even now, I cannot recall what had prompted the fighting. The usual things seemed so usual. Suffice it to say that this time, the trimmer armies were more organized and better outfitted than anything the City had seen to date. Gabriel had been in charge of the armies of the City since Zoan's abdication, and while there were good serving angels in our armies, the overall quality of our fighting forces was not what it had once been. Victory was declared to be the natural outcome of any conflict. Those of us in power knew a little differently.

God did not mind war. He enjoyed being a chief executive in times of strife, so long as the strife did not impact Him personally for too long. He never took to the field. He never felt the need to. He did not go to visit His troops or offer words of encouragement. He expected total obedience to the City and He expected victory. Only later did I come to understand what He was willing to do in order to secure those victories.

"Will you need to go?" Amee asked me one evening, as I walked her home.

Eventually, she had agreed to let me take her to dinner. What had, possibly, prompted her decision in my favor was that I had, in fact, ended my previous relationship and was not pursuing her simply out of lust, though, I must admit, I had plenty of that too.

"I do not know. I do not think so. God has asked Gabriel to consider a course of action. Strangely, He has not asked me to participate at all."

"That doesn't seem so strange to me," she remarked. "You were always a troublemaker in the army, you've told me. That cannot be something God would desire. And besides, you have not been a soldier for quite some time. What do you know of war now? When was the last time you drew a sword in anger?"

"I know more than Gabriel does. That is for sure."

"Why are you so sure? He's led the City's armies since your grandfather stepped down. God is still in His kingdom."

"And look what has happened to our armies. Their organization. Their morale." I felt a little exasperated. "God should have recalled Zoan," I said. "If He were smart," I muttered under my breath.

"Your grandfather left to fight a trimmer army and came back with his army missing and in possession of something God fears," she said.

Now this was interesting! Amee seemed to know as much or more about my grandfather, God, and the "book" than I did.

"I guess," I replied as casually as I could, not wanting to give anything away, "but why would that stop Him from placing His faith in one of His most trusted servants?"

"Superstition? Fear of the unknown or, in this case, the known? God doesn't need you running off and finishing *that* part of your grandfather's work."

I still was not sure what she meant, but wanted to understand.

"You do not want me to go, then?" I asked coyly.

"No."

She looked away up the block toward her home. It was a modest place, given the prestige and wealth her family commanded. But it was her home. My retinue of bodyguards followed me now, alert, but never approaching close enough to overhear my conversation with Amee. Azael saw to that.

"What is the matter? What are you thinking?" I asked, trying to revive the conversation.

"I am thinking that Simon is perfectly capable of leading the army."

"That is what I recommended to God. Simon is a soldier, through and through."

"I want to be with you," Amee said.

It was too sudden. Was something wrong or had I not heard right? I stopped in my tracks. She kept walking, then slowed her pace and turned around to face me.

"You what?" I asked.

"I love you, Lucifer. You forced me to love you," she trailed off, "somehow." Her eyes were tearful.

I walked up to her and kissed her. She did not shy away from my kiss. In all the time we had been together, I had never tried to kiss her. When I stepped back, she looked at me, her expression unchanged.

"You forced me," she said.

"I forced you," I repeated.

I had totally forgotten what we were talking about. Today, some people call it "chemistry," and it is something even I cannot explain. She tasted so good. From that point on, we met nearly every night, making love and enjoying each other. She cried from time to time, but then again, so did I.

CHAPTER
TWENTY-SIX

"The time has come for Gabriel to go out to meet the threat," God said one evening, when He had assembled His senior staff, Senatorial and bureaucratic officials, and generals. "We face something so unusual this time that I will only be at ease with Gabriel leading our armies." He looked at Simon expectantly before uttering the last word, "Personally."

On my recommendation, God had elevated Simon to Grand General of the City's Armies. He had risen through the officer ranks and shown great personal courage on countless occasions. More problematically, however, Simon had quickly garnered the admiration of the army, something God both needed and distrusted. In that way, Simon was very much like Zoan.

"I am sure this is no reflection on your confidence in Simon's leadership, my Lord," I said, also looking at Simon, perhaps more expectantly.

Simon bowed ever so slightly in my direction. From our time together in the army, we saw many things in much the same way, even if we were no longer the closest of friends.

God spun around, looking at me, and paused. "Of course not." Walking up to Simon, He continued. "You know that I have the greatest affection for you and your family, Simon. You have served this city and me, personally, with the greatest distinction. I trust you, as a father trusts his son." He put his hand on Simon's shoulder.

"Thank you, Lord," Simon replied, his face expressionless, as any soldier's was expected to be.

"This time is different," God continued. He turned and looked at the crowd of angels gathered in the room. "This time is very different. They threaten our strategic position at the Apsatsus Fork, posing a risk to the City's newly repaired water supplies. We do not know how they organized themselves so efficiently or how they came to be so well armed." He paced the room, looking each angel in the eye.

Michael appeared particularly worried.

"It seems they have had help this time and it worries me." God turned to look at me once again. "We all know that Lucifer broke the back of the rebels those many years ago. But that was *in* the City. They were insurrectionists, but not trimmers. I had incorrectly assumed that they would melt away in the outlands when they were obliterated here. But this has not proven to be the case."

Every angel was shocked in his own way to hear God admit a mistake. It would be dangerous *not* to talk Him out of His opinion.

"Are they still receiving help from inside the City?" Melchom asked rather clumsily.

God glared at him. "No. No, they are not. I am confident that Lucifer's work was complete," He said, throwing me a glance. "In addition, Lucifer's Secret Service has cleared anything else that has come up since then and Lucifer retains my full confidence."

"Thank you, Lord," I said with a bow, a purely reflexive gesture.

Michael scoffed under his breath.

"All you need be concerned with, Melchom, is providing my army with the provisioning it needs to succeed."

Melchom cringed in agreement.

"Gabriel will take the armies into the outlands with Simon. Into Tartarus. They will find the trimmer army and destroy it, once and for all. We have been dealing with this threat for far too long."

There was a murmur of agreement. God looked at me again. That was three times in as many minutes. Clearly, He had some issue with me and the rest of the room could sense it too.

"My Lord," Gabriel said, "our reconnaissance has already skirmished with the trimmer army and reported back some possible positions of the main fighting force. We will find them and defeat them."

I chortled.

"Good, good. Find them and destroy them all. That is all."

The room began to empty.

"What was that about?" I asked Gabriel, as we left the room. "He was looking at me as if I had been the one to organize, train, and arm them."

"That's exactly what He's considering. You came to power in a rather unconventional way, don't you think, Lucifer?"

"Yes, I suppose so, but I am not sure that translates into my having assisted enemy troops against someone I have served with nothing but the greatest of reverence and obedience."

"No need to give me a pep talk, Lucifer. I know you're not smart enough to try something like that." Gabriel smiled. "But if you're crafty enough to pull off what you did, you're crafty enough to consider it, don't you think?"

I thought for a second. "And that is why He is sending you out there?"

Instantly, Gabriel's good humor vanished.

"Gabriel, when was the last time you strapped on armor and drew a sword?"

"Farther back in the past than you have, certainly, but not too far back, I suppose."

He had considered the question carefully and given himself away. He looked to Michael, as if he were a crutch. I had not realized he was actually worried.

"It will come back to you. No doubt," I said, changing tack. I had not meant to alarm him with my jocularity. "Besides, Simon is the best-regarded general of this age and I have served with him and can vouch for his reputation. His networks provided me good intelligence in the past and he is a thinking warrior, not just a talker."

Gabriel continued to look at me seriously. "Keep work going on the project," he said. He looked over his shoulder. "Michael, please leave us."

"Yes, master."

I knew it had been a blow. I even felt a little sorry for Michael, seeing his master this way.

"What is it?" I asked.

"The project. It means everything to Him. Depending on how this war goes, it could mean everything to the City."

I had seen anger in Gabriel many times. But never before had I seen fear in his eyes. I shot a look over at the departing Michael.

"I will. Focus on the moment, my friend," I said, looking back at him, slapping his arm.

We left each other and I went to see Amee.

⌘　⌘　⌘

"My uncle isn't prepared for war," Amee said.

She was worried too. She was putting her clothes back on. When I arrived, we had had the short, obligatory talk and then got right to it.

"He hasn't been in the field for an age and even when he was there, he never showed a great deal of, shall we say, courage under fire," she said.

"That is nice of you to say. I hope you have more encouraging words for him when you see him off," I scoffed. She did not look amused.

"I am not kidding. He may be a skilled bureaucrat, but he is no soldier. It is not as if Michael will provide him any help. Why would God want Gabriel in the field?"

"To be honest, I do not know," I replied. "God said something about being surprised by the organization and armament of the trimmers this time around."

I paused to look at her. I could not see Gabriel in her at all. She seemed expectant.

"God and I have grown close over the years," I said. "I only slightly hesitate to say that He sees me as a son. But God and I do not speak about Gabriel in any way that I can describe as significant. He keeps His relationship with Gabriel entirely separate from His relationship with me."

She turned and looked at me in astonishment. "Well, of course he does. He cannot afford to have you both link up against Him. He knows He is too weak to overcome you both at the same time."

I was a little taken aback at the bluntness of her words. What did she mean by speaking of God in such a way? After all, He was God. "Are you saying that God is weak, Amee, because if you are, you are treading on very shaky ground."

"Lucifer, what have you been working on with Gabriel these many years?"

She stared at me. She was only half-dressed, so it took a great deal of effort not to say something inappropriate, given the seriousness of her question.

"I have been working on fixing the City and building Man. What does this have anything to do with it?"

"You put yourself in, arguably, the second most powerful position in the entire kingdom and you can't see that God's power is eroding? You scoff at people like Melchom, whom you see as nothing but a thorn in your side, seeking petty objectives. But he makes himself well loved by the people. He's one of a thousand, a million, maybe, who don't see God's rule as eternal or enlightened or all the things that you work so hard to sustain for him. You work to maintain God's power, while the people grow more and more disaffected."

She turned back to getting dressed. I could tell from her choppy movements that she was really mad.

"People are dying every day in this kingdom to undo the things that you do," she went on. "I am one of them and it has been hard for me to feel this way about you, when I stand to undo almost everything you work for."

"Amee, I do not mean to be thickheaded, but what are you talking about?" I myself was angry now. "We have talked about marriage and children and now you tell me you are some sort of subversive?"

"'Subversive' is exactly what I am. But more to the point, I am shocked at your lack of understanding about the things you are doing." She turned to look at me again, this time very much ready to leave. "God is creating Man to build an army. He's building Man to reconsolidate his power base. He has no altruistic aims of making Heaven a better place, Lucifer. He's looking to take back the ground he's lost over the years. You're making the drones he needs to help him regain his power." She walked to the door and opened it. "He's using you to get rid of you and you can't even see it."

She walked out.

I lay in that bed for a few hours more. I smelled her on the pillows and could see her silhouette against the window in my mind's eye. She was more powerful than I had ever imagined and she had more power over me than I cared to admit. But I dismissed the idea that she saw something I could not.

God had explained the reason for His project clearly. He needed angels He could trust in the system. The bureaucracy was a necessary evil. I knew that. I had worked hard over the years to fix those problems. I was His servant. I lived and worked for Him, because it was God Who had made me who I was. Who gave me what I had. If God had problems, I was happy to build Man to fix them. I was His servant. Obedient. Intelligent. Fine. No longer would God have to depend on an inherently flawed and over-complicated system to keep His angels loyal to Him and on the right path. Out of my love for God, I wanted Man to fill the hole that the City's angels could clearly not fill. What did Amee know? About God's power or lack thereof? Power did not strike me as something God lacked in Heaven.

History. The City's history. I thought about that more as I got up and dressed. I had read the City's history a thousand times. It was available at the City's libraries and in books to be found throughout the kingdom. On every posting and advertisement. God had created us. Not that tripe the cell peddled to bend converts to their cause. God was. We owed Him our allegiance and we paid the price for malice against Him.

It was years since I had really thought of the book I had taken from Jehoel. The cell's end-all-be-all book. I had, in fact, not thought of it at all, at least, not since I had begun working on Man. Gabriel had seen to that. But some of it came back to me now. If God had created us, it argued, how was it that we had the power to think for ourselves, to revolt against Him? How did we have freedom of will, if God had, indeed, created us? Wouldn't God have created us to obey Him? As He was having me do now with Man? Had He made a mistake in creating angels? These were very pertinent questions. Questions to which God Himself provided only unsatisfactory answers. But it was just a book and when I was reading it, my will to succeed in exposing the plot had blurred my intellectual curiosity and my natural inclination to see beyond the printed word and read between the lines. Zoan had called it "the Word." Would I think the same, if I read it again? But for Gabriel's dire warning, I might have, to see if I could channel, once again, what I thought I had understood so many years ago.

I went back to my office and began reading the intelligence wires coming in that day. I did not see anything of interest. Nothing at all.

⌘ ⌘ ⌘

I did not say anything about Amee to Gabriel. She was his niece. I did not see her after our last meeting in anything but an official capacity. I was sure he had noticed. But Gabriel did not bring it up. Besides, he was busy preparing himself and his entourage for the movement of the army out of the City. From my exchanges with Simon during this time, I deduced that while the army was ready to go, Gabriel was delaying its departure.

"How are the preparations going, General?" I asked Simon, while visiting his barracks one evening.

He did not seem surprised to see me. "Very well, my Seraph," he replied, standing to attention. "In fact, better than I had anticipated."

"Simon, we are old friends," I said in earnest. "Let us just talk, shall we?"

This time, he was surprised. "Yes, well, okay," he sputtered out.

I laughed. "What is the situation?" I asked.

I had my reports, but wanted to hear it from my angel on the inside, not boiled to a pulp by some censor.

"The angels are ready and waiting. We could leave today. If the order came through."

"And what of your intelligence? Hopefully you have someone in that position now who does a far better job than I ever did."

Simon smiled. "In many ways, Ahriman, it is you who made me what I am today," he said. "Your reports helped lead my armies to great victories."

I was, of course, very interested to hear this, but kept my feelings to myself.

"I would like to say, 'Those were the days!' But they were not really, were they?" I asked.

Simon thought to himself. "They were not."

It seemed rather final.

"Remember that time we were routed through that swamp with the baggage train?" I said lightheartedly, as I sat down, uninvited, in the chair across from his campaign table.

He had sat down at the same moment. I quickly glanced at the mass of papers and maps strewn across the table. He did not seem to notice the direction of my gaze, as he looked across the room at the tent opening, where his guard stood watch. And then back into his memory.

"Yes, I do," he answered. "You were wounded in that skirmish."

"As were you."

"You were worse off than me."

"Yes," I said, lowering my voice. "What was that other soldier's name...?"

"Nicor." The name was still fresh in Simon's memory.

"Yes!" I shouted gleefully. "Nicor."

Simon realized I was reading over his papers on the campaign.

"Only you, me, and Nicor made it out the other end," I said. "The rest succumbed to the harsh conditions of the swamp. The three of us had the baggage train for the entire regiment stuck in that quagmire."

"Meanwhile, the General was expecting us to reinforce him," Simon added. He put both hands out on top of the table. "I seem to remember it was you who suggested demolishing the cart and using the planks to lay a kind of temporary road across the marsh."

"Actually," I said, leaning forward across the table and lowering my voice, "it was Nicor who first suggested it. I was the one who first started hacking the carts to pieces. Remember, you thought I had lost my mind?"

We both laughed.

"Yes," he said. "I was prepared to tie you up until I saw what you had in mind."

In all, we had only spent a few years together in service, but fighting together forges a bond between all soldiers, even if they shared nothing else.

"Any swamps in these plans, Simon?" I joked, pointing to his many maps.

His smile disappeared. "Nicor was killed when we emerged. Do you remember?" he asked. "I remember the arrow shot. Three to the chest, through the armor. Very suddenly. He was struck in the middle of a sentence. He sank into the swamp under the weight of his armor."

Simon was suddenly years and years away from me, sitting there in his tent.

"Yes, I remember," I said, leaning back.

"Azael," I said, looking out the barracks door to my bodyguards.

"Azael," Simon repeated.

One arrow had hit me right after Nicor went down. Simon had pulled me and the rest of the baggage train out and was wounded himself in the process. We had won the battle, but without my help and, at least, in part, because Simon had got the supplies through to the rest of the army. When I was elevated to Seraph, it had not surprised me to learn of Simon's rise through the ranks. But in all that time, I had not thought of Nicor. I can say, quite assuredly, that I had not thought of Nicor even once since being brought to the hospital, wounds bleeding.

"No, no swamps this time, Lucifer," Simon said, finally answering my question. "And this time, thankfully, Azael is on the right side."

We smiled together.

"But to be honest," he went on, "I am not sure it will matter."

That piqued my interest. "What do you mean?"

Simon realized he had said too much. "Is this soldier to soldier or are we speaking officially?" he asked after a long pause.

It was strange question, but I guess I had started it.

"You recommended me for this job," he observed. "It's as much your ass on the line as mine."

"Soldier to soldier," I said, only half-lying.

Simon got up and walked to the tent flaps. He poked his head out and asked the guard to leave. Sitting back down, he said, "We are going to be smashed."

It was very blunt, even for a general.

"Do you not generally plan to avoid such things?" I asked. I thought he was joking.

His expression did not change a bit. "We have, shall we say, too much interference in operations."

"What do you mean? You have the largest standing army the City has put together in an age."

"That is not the issue, Ahriman," he said, reverting to my given name.

"Well, what do you mean, then? Speak clearly."

"I mean that God has instructed me on where to go and how to form up the army when we engage."

"What!"

"I have been told how to lose the battle. On purpose."

"That cannot be so. You must have read the orders wrong."

"I have fought in many wars, Ahriman, and while fate has seen fit to grant me incredible luck, in both my actions and my own commands, never once has God," and here, he hesitated quite clearly, choosing between equally dangerous words, "interfered in my battle plans. I have not read my orders wrong."

"Simon, explain yourself." I was not angry, but stern.

"Gabriel will have command of the army. I am to be his lieutenant. I know he is your friend, but his orders are from our Lord God himself. I have seen them. The instructions are to abandon the unit formations I devised and, I might add, led in the past to victory, in favor of a plain frontal attack." He broke eye contact by looking away. "We cannot win by brute force of arms. And with this approach, we will be throwing out the last million years of tactical advancement." He looked up again. "We will be enveloped, overwhelmed, and cut to pieces."

My head spun. Too much information in so short a span of time. In less than a week, I had had one person whom I loved with all my heart tell me I was being used as a pawn in a plot devised to enable God to throw the entire City into disorder and another person, whom I trusted with my life, inform me that God was working to destroy the City.

"Was it Gabriel or Michael?"

"Would it matter?" Simon asked.

"It could."

"It was Gabriel. Michael will not be attending him in the outlands."

That surprised me. It was surely the will of God. Gabriel had always looked to Michael as though he were his novice. Some strange relationship, this.

"What are you going to do?" I asked, pushing my thoughts of Michael aside.

"I'm going to follow my commands, Lucifer," he said, going back to my formal name. "I shall go into the swamp and get my soldiers killed."

"I see." It was all I could say.

I could not criticize Gabriel or God in front of Simon. That would be treason and it certainly would not help Simon in planning what was clearly to be the end of both his career and Gabriel's. We sat in silence for a few moments. Then I got up and looked closely at him. He was worn. Much more so, than I remembered him. He stood up too.

"All Praise to the Lord in the highest," he said.

I reached out and put my hand on his shoulder.

"All Praise to the Lord in the highest," I replied and walked out of the tent.

⌘　⌘　⌘

The City saw off the departing army with much fanfare. It was a farewell to be remembered. The Senate billed it as major spectacle and almost the entire City turned out to see the many soldiers and horses parade through the central thoroughfares and out of the main gates in the Southeast Quarter. Angels of all ages threw garlands in their path and music was played across the City to serenade them and inspire them with patriotic fervor. Many minor officials made rousing speeches and even God was seen from the lower ramparts of the Seat of God. The citizens did not know what they were happy about, but they were happy, all the same. There is nothing quite like an army marching to war to get your blood pumping.

I wished Gabriel good luck on the eve of his departure. He had organized a small party at one of his more modest homes, inviting some of the most senior bureaucrats and government officials. Amee was there too, but aside from exchanging some pleasantries, we did not speak. Melchom was with her. Gabriel did not seem to notice or care. I was sour.

Afterward, I sat with him in the study. We quietly drank wine. Michael waited outside for his master. As Seraphs, we had access to the City's best ambrosia. Expensive as anything in the City, it was difficult to come by for the common angel. God's monopoly over it had caused many controversies within the Senate. Taxes and tariffs were always an issue. So it had fallen to the ultra-powerful to demand that the libation be made available. Gabriel preferred wine and always drank it when he was alone. Tartarus was said to have some of the best crops of ambrosia and the trimmers did not even drink the stuff.

Silently, we both watched the fire, small as it was. He was deep in thought and I hesitated to interrupt him in whatever conversation he was having with himself.

"You all right?" I finally asked.

He looked up, but did not seem dazed.

"Fine. I noticed that Amee was with Melchom tonight."

I had expected him to bring up the subject sometime, but had not expected him to do so now. "Yes." I replied.

"As it should be, I guess," he said, looking back at the fire.

"Yes. That is what you told me."

He knew more than he had let on. I did give him credit, though. My relationship with Amee, while not expressly forbidden by God, was against His instructions. Gabriel had known it, but had not taken any action against me. It could have been that he was protecting his favorite niece. Or me. I do not know which.

He smiled now. "You know what to do with our project?" he asked for the eleven-hundredth time.

"Yes, it is all taken care of."

"I'm serious, you know. There's nothing more important to God than the successful completion of Man."

"I am not so sure of that," I said.

He looked at me with a flicker of a question on his face, but it was quickly smoothed out into a smile. "You speak, though you don't know what you say. All the good in the universe is concentrated in God. He cannot be moved by greed, as he alone possesses everything and so is uniquely able to dispense justice evenly and in ways no one else could. In this way, God shows us the correct path, the best way to live our lives as angels," he said and looked back at the fire, the smile lingering on his face. He had that same look of peace he had worn at Zoan's funeral.

We were friends. He knew I would look after things for him.

Unlike Gabriel, I sat a little uneasy, knowing what was before us was not of our making and that the greater purpose might never be made clear. Gabriel did not need a purpose greater than that of serving God. I resigned myself to his vision that night. For my friend. In that way, for that moment, we were brothers.

⌘   ⌘   ⌘

News of the army's massacre reached me two weeks later. I remember standing in the main courtyard of the Seat of God, just having finished one of my innumerable meetings. Michael came to me with the ill tidings. From his demeanor, it seemed as if he blamed me for his master's misfortune. I could not really blame him. I had been forewarned, yet had done nothing to prevent the predetermined outcome. I wept. I wept for my soldiers. I wept for my friends. I wept in shame over myself.

⌘   ⌘   ⌘

It was not long before God summoned me. But I had expected to be called and in preparation for the meeting, had an intelligence report ready, containing every bit of information we had at our disposal up to that moment. Given that the scope of the loss was yet to be gauged, it had not been easy to draw up the report. A token few soldiers had managed to flee the battle alive and were being held in villages along the western shores of the Acheron, up and down the river. Their days were, most likely, numbered. Zoan had faced a similar situation all those years ago. If I were to believe his version of events, only that book, Jehoel, and luck had saved him. Now, as likely then, jailors waited along with the disgraced soldiers' families, the former with high expectations of profit and the latter with little or no hope at all.

I also prepared a report on the status of Man. Things were coming along nicely in this area. With Gabriel more than preoccupied with preparations for his departure, Phanuel and I had taken over most of the remaining responsibilities involving day-to-day development and testing. Phanuel oversaw the slow reconstruction of the Apsatsus facilities. Too slow, it seemed, by comparison to the leaps we were making with Man.

The proto-men were getting increasingly coordinated. I would not describe them as "intelligent", but they were able, at least, to understand rudimentary commands. The transition from Earth to Heaven, however, proved to be more of a problem than I had expected, as it frequently left us a mess of organic material, rather than any viable subject for testing. We needed to complete setting up the proper facilities at the Forks to get it right. The specimens who made it through the whole process were either genetically changed by their transfer to Heaven or too "wild" to be considered viable and certainly not worth the feed we needed to maintain them. These were messy, but necessary initial steps in the process and up until now, God had seemed rather pleased with my progress. The final completion of the Apsatsus complex would move all that gory stuff away from the City and its prying eyes.

The night I was summoned by God, however, was a different story altogether. That night, I saw God in a way I would only ever see Him once more. Entering His chambers, I noticed the room was in shambles. I quickly drew my sword. The servants and bodyguards were nowhere to be found and for a split second, I considered the real possibility that someone might have broken in and assassinated Him.

I quickly stalked around the room, looking for signs of life and shouting God's name. A moment later, I noticed Him sitting slumped in a leather chair facing the fireplace. The chair was turned away from me and all I could see from behind was its back, with the very top of God's head visible above it, and His arms slumped over the armrests. The only illumination in the room was the glow from a dying fire. No lighted candles or candelabras, as was usually the case when God entertained or met delegations. The room smelled of smoke, but not of tobacco. Papers were strewn everywhere, curtains wrenched from the eves of the large windows. Books lay where they had been flung, pages torn from their bindings. Several casks of ambrosia were open, one tipped over, leaving a large puddle that stained the cold white marble floors like golden blood. Shards of broken glass lay scattered across vast expanses of the floor. With the curtains ripped from their moorings, the room was entirely exposed to the evening, which violated its privacy with ever-so-subtle shadows. The room gave off an eerie feeling, filling me with the kind of dread I would experience as a boy, when entering my father's study with the knowledge that I was about to interrupt him in his work and likely to suffer the consequences for my intrusion.

"My Lord?" I asked cautiously, as I made my way in, my hand, sweaty though it was, gripping the pommel of my sword firmly.

There was no answer. He did not stir.

I tried again. "My Lord?"

Some movement this time. Grumbling too. "Ergh."

It was all that I could make out. I continued moving cautiously around the edge of the room, looking intently into each dark corner and scanning the room for an intruder who might be hiding or listening. God infrequently stayed far from His servants, but that night, there were none to be found. Where were his bodyguards?

"My Lord, are you all right?" I came around to face Him.

He stared blankly into the drizzling fire, not even acknowledging my presence.

I gripped my sword more forcefully.

"Lord, are you all right?" I asked again, this time in a very firm voice, leaning in closer to see Him properly.

"Mm," He murmured. "Mmm, yes."

It was not much of a response, but I could tell He was not injured. I relaxed my grip and sheathed my sword. I had not unsheathed my sword in anger for many years so now I stroked the soft skin of my hand with my thumb. It ached from the weight of the sword. It betrayed weakness. Approaching closer, I knelt before God and waited. He said nothing, continuing to stare into the fire. Any response at all, I felt, would have been better than this silence, this seeming numbness. I turned and poked the fire, adding some wood, until it produced a bit more light and warmth.

It took some time, but, eventually, He turned to look in my direction. His eyes were hollow. Not even the flickering flames of the fire were reflected in the cold glassiness of His soul, if He had one. He looked searchingly at me, but did not, apparently, see anything I did not want Him to see. If he had, it might have been for the first time. To tell the truth, He could not see me at all.

"Gabriel," He said, His first really decipherable word.

"No, my Lord. It is Lucifer."

"Have they found Gabriel?" He asked.

"No, my Lord. Your generals are preparing a relief force to reconnoiter the area, but it will take time to put it together," I said with a wince of muted anger. "Few soldiers remain in the City and your remaining generals are mere shadows of the angel Simon was."

God looked back into the fire. "Michael will do his job correctly. I have foreseen it."

That took me aback, but I regained my focus when He again asked, "Have they found Gabriel?"

I did not know whether this was meant to express His annoyance at my long-winded answer or if He simply had not understood me.

"No, my Lord," was all I said.

"Mmm."

The marble floor was hurting my knees. My feet began to tingle in pain.

Finally, God stirred from His inert position. There was now a semblance of purpose in Him, as he rubbed His temples with His right hand, while groping at the table next to Him for His empty ambrosia glass. I quickly got up, found the carafe, and refilled His glass. He did not seem to notice, but drank down the contents of the glass in nearly one swallow.

"I want a battle plan on my desk by sunrise tomorrow," God said. "I want a full accounting of all stores. I want an intelligence report on the current status of all heightened security sectors of the City." He looked right at me now. Fire, this time, in His eyes. "I want to know where the project is situated."

It was a powerful look, more so than I had seen in an age. I avoided meeting that look by filling His glass once more.

"Yes, Lord," I said. "I have a preliminary intelligence report with me now. I can also give a status report on the project."

I pulled the report from my bag. He looked at it disinterestedly. So I put it on the table next to the ambrosia.

He smiled. "Why am I not surprised?" He asked, ignoring the report, but taking up the full glass again.

"I am here to serve you, Lord. As best I can." I was beginning to lose my patience.

"You serve your Lord well, Lucifer." He smiled and looked back to the fire. "Tell me. Where are we with the project?"

"We are almost there, my Lord. Praise be to God in the highest. The work I have done over the last several weeks, the work Phanuel has done, have all but solved the problems we were encountering in our efforts to place appropriate curbs on mental development. Apsatsus is almost complete. We should be but a few more weeks, I think."

"More than Gabriel ever produced," He said, sipping at His glass. "Thinking about it now, you were able to make more progress in just a few million years than Gabriel and Zoan made in many billions." He continued sipping. "Gabriel," He repeated. "When did you say you expected to get forces there?"

"It should be a few more weeks before they can leave." It was almost comical the way I had to keep repeating the same things, again and again.

Then something even more unexpected happened. He began to sniffle. It was not quite crying, but whatever it was seemed very emotional. It surprised me, but I did not feel any pity. This was my beloved Lord God, creator of the universe, before me and He was vulnerable. I felt, instead, a surge of aggravation rising up inside of me.

"I did this," He said. His hands were trembling.

I watched the ripples of ambrosia splash His face as He tried to drink from His shaking glass. Choking, He said, "I did this. And do you know why, Lucifer?" He looked directly at me again.

I rose and came back to a kneeling position right before Him. "No, my Lord," I managed, unsure as to whether I should have responded.

"He disobeyed me."

"Who, my Lord?"

He choked on more ambrosia. "Gabriel. He disobeyed me. And this was his punishment." He said it, as if to explain something to Himself.

I did not quite know where to go from here. So I tried for the truth. Looking back on it now, I am still surprised I had it in me. "How did you do this, Lord? Explain it to me. Everything." I was very firm and quite serious.

He looked at me. Like a scolded child.

I grasped the front of His robes. "Explain it to me!" I shouted.

"I told Gabriel to take the force out," He sniffled. "I gave him orders to lose the battle. Gabriel had to pay for his disobedience." He sniffled louder this time. "I did this."

"You killed all those angels?" I growled.

Simon had been right. God had commanded it. And His soldiers had obeyed.

"You killed all those angels for this?" I persisted.

This was not duty. This was...I did not rightfully know what this was. This was ridiculous.

"How could you do that?" I went on. "How could you take the lives of all those soldiers? So callously?"

God began to whimper.

"What did he do? What did Gabriel do to deserve this? What did any of them do to deserve this? How will this help us, Lord?"

But at that, He snapped out of it. "Gabriel disobeyed me!" He shouted.

Roused now, He got out of His chair and began to pace lopsidedly in front of the fire. "I told him what to do and he ignored me!" He shouted, the ambrosia in His glass sloshing from side to side as He paced. "I did this, because it needed to be done. He had been with me for eternity, but when I say I want something done now, I want it done now!"

"You are a petulant child!" I shouted, getting up off my knees.

The words had just slipped out. Castigating. Uncontrolled. I do not know why. I had always worked to do what I thought was right by God. In this moment, something had changed.

"You murdered our soldiers over something like this? And look at you!"

He stopped and looked. At me. Standing in front of the fireplace, I could not make out His expression exactly. I could see Him swaying from side to side, a victim of the ambrosia He had clearly consumed too much of.

"He disobeyed me," He responded, quieter now, but without evident malice.

He stood for a few more seconds and then slumped down on the marble before the fire. Its flames leapt up into the cavernous fireplace as He threw in the rest of His drink. He sat and watched for a second as the flames died down. He dropped his glass and it went rolling in a semicircle until it had come to a standstill behind Him, leaving a thin trail of ambrosia in its wake.

I got up and straightened out my uniform. "I will find Gabriel and bring him back here. Dead or alive, you will honor him! You *will* honor the soldiers that come back from that field!" I shouted, pointing out the window toward Tartarus. "They will not suffer any of your wrath from this defeat, the horrors you willfully inflicted."

God looked up at me. He was like a child, tears streaming down His face. Snot dangling out of His nostrils.

"Yes," He said. "Yes, yes, you're right."

"Yes, I *am* right." It was all I could think to say.

I left the room. Servants were at the door, waiting anxiously.

"Where have you been?" I shouted with all the hatred burning in me.

They shrank from my words.

I turned and pointed to God. "Take Him to bed."

They nodded, their heads wobbling in unison.

"Give Him water and be prepared for a long night."

Another collective nod and off they scurried.

I walked home that night. I rubbed the soft skin of my palm with my thumb. I had torn a bit of the flesh in holding my sword for the first time in an age and it stung. I was weak. Weak, the way He was. Amee had been right. He was weak. I realized how quickly I was walking and slackened my pace a bit. Azael was right beside me. Keeping the pace I set.

"Without enemies around us, we grow lazy," I said under my breath.

"Master?" Azael asked.

"Oh, nothing," I replied.

Azael maintained his pace.

"Do you find it hard working for me?" I asked, thinking of my conversation with God just now.

"No, master."

"Why is that?" I asked.

He thought for a moment.

"Because no matter what, you always try to do the right thing."

"How do you know that?"

"I have firsthand experience." He smiled thinly.

"How do you know I will always do the right thing?" I asked again.

Azael seemed confused.

"What if I am wrong?" I persisted.

"There is no absolute 'right' and 'wrong' in Heaven, master. All that matters is that we be true to ourselves and do what we think is right," he mused to himself as we went on our way.

I looked at him. "Very philosophical answer for a soldier," I said.

It was something Zoan would have said. Something Zoan probably did say.

"My Father taught us well," Azael said, making his first snide allusion to God since I had met him.

"Indeed," I said out loud. Indeed He did, I thought.

CHAPTER TWENTY-SEVEN

I prepared myself to go into the outlands looking for Gabriel and the survivors of our defeated army. I was prepared to negotiate with the trimmers, if need be, for the hostages that I hoped would be spared. Before speaking with the useless gaggle of leftover generals, I took my host of bodyguards aside and advised them of my intentions.

"You are sworn to protect me, but I cannot ask that you go with me this time." I told them. I looked at Azael.

"We have sworn an oath," he said. He looked to the others, who nodded in agreement. "That oath holds no bounds," he went on. "It does not cease when you cross the gates of the City, tread the dust of the outlands, or even navigate the waters of the Styx. To the ends of the universe, our oaths we hold."

"I have already recruited a small band of soldiers. Elite."

Azael looked incredulous.

"Not as elite as you all, my friends," I added.

Azael smiled. It was the first time I had ever seen him really smile.

"If you insist on accompanying me," I continued, "each of you will command your segment of the contingent and receive an enhanced stipend."

"That is, if we return, master?" Azael joked.

He was happy to be heading out to the outlands again. I fleetingly thought that while I had saved his life and given him another of comparable luxury, I had taken him from his home, all the same. I had never actually seen him happy until now, as he considered the prospect of returning to Tartarus.

"If we do return, you will be allowed to choose whatever position you like," I replied.

They were all satisfied.

"Do not overestimate our chances, boys," I said lightheartedly. "Even if we come back, we still have God to face."

"I like our odds," Azael quipped.

"A stupid angel you are," I remarked.

We all laughed.

⌘　⌘　⌘

I rounded up my soldiers directly from their barracks. I did this as unobtrusively as possible so as not to tip Michael off about my intentions. I did not know whether or not he now had the ear of God, as his master had once had, but I was still pondering the significance of God's comment about Michael being involved in the City's defense.

I had grossly exaggerated to Azael and my bodyguards the quality of the "elite" force that was to accompany us into the outlands. It was, in fact, elite, only to the extent that it largely consisted of those few soldiers who had already made it back to the

City from the battlefield and were now awaiting court-martial. Many were recuperating from wounds sustained in combat. I still considered them fit for my purpose. Stirred by both my assurances that they would be safe from official retribution for the military defeat they had suffered and the chance to go back out and find their missing comrades, none turned down my offer. They were anxious to exonerate themselves. We would find more of their fellow soldiers in the villages along the Acheron. If fortune smiled upon us, we would find even more in trimmer hands. All would be happy to clear their names. For the God who had abandoned them to the wilderness, yes. More so for the sake of their honor and that of their lost comrades.

I was careful to recruit no one who expressed avid support for God and I double-checked the political affiliations of each volunteer. I did not need politics following me out into the outlands. My problems were going to be difficult enough to deal with without having to worry about who was sneaking off messages to someone within the City. All individual goals needed to be wholly and consistently in line with my own.

I was only a few days away from departure, when Amee came looking for me. When the servants brought her in to my study, I was surprised by my immediate response to her. It had been a long time since we last met, but she was just as beautiful as the first time I had laid eyes on her as she leaned over to speak with Gabriel.

She was solemn as she spoke. "You're doing this on your own, aren't you?"

"Yes."

The intensity of my longing for her was painful, like a stone pressing down on my heart, but I tried to convince myself it was little more than a passing twinge that time would heal. It was midday, but she was not wearing the clothes she usually wore to work.

"Why are you doing this, Lucifer?"

"Treachery is the gravest of sins, Amee. It not only hurt its targets, but attacks the very ties that bind society together. It threatens the entire social order."

"What treachery?" she asked.

"Never mind," I said. "It does not matter."

"What chances do you have of finding Gabriel?"

"What does it matter to you? I am doing this for myself, not for you. You stopped caring about what I did a long time ago," I said indignantly.

I may have wanted her naked in my bed, but I was immediately tired of the wrangling that had come to characterize my relationship with her. She had released me and I did not feel like explaining that what I was doing was stupid for the right reasons.

"I never stopped caring about what you did," she said, "but I did have to stop caring about you. I needed to see if Melchom was the angel I was supposed to be with. I no longer think he is."

I busied myself with organizing my paperwork. "Well, I am glad you were able to sort things out." I continued with my papers as she looked at me in silence.

"I miss you," she finally said, so faintly I hardly realized she was speaking.

"Hmm?" I asked, now actually absorbed in my work.

"I miss you," she said, clearly and distinctly this time. "You may be the biggest bastard I've ever met, but you cared about me in a way no one ever has. I missed you, though I wasn't the most valuable thing to you."

I stopped what I was doing and looked at her. It was not sadness, exactly, that I saw in her, but a certain remoteness, as if she were far away, looking back over a long life that she had not actually lived yet.

"I could do what I'm supposed to do," she said, "but now that you're headed out there, what I'm supposed to do doesn't seem like the right thing anymore."

"Melchom asked you to marry him, did he not?" I asked.

She may have been far away, but there was also intent in her eyes. She had come here for a purpose. Not to tell me that I was a fool, but to convince herself of something else.

"Yes," she replied.

"Well, I guess that is what you wanted, right? He is moral and upstanding. You will get what you need out of it, I am sure."

She began to weep. I had not meant to make her cry. She had left me for reasons I could do little about. For reasons I was unwilling to change. She did not like my politics. She did not like my devotion to God and the City of God. She saw God in a cold, passionless way that, to me, seemed carried over into our relationship. "Calculated" is perhaps a better word for what I mean. But she was the one with the most at stake. I was a Seraph of God. She was a powerful bureaucrat, yes, but while I had eternity with nearly unlimited powers, she had to deal with the day-to-day, the ins and outs of the bureaucrat's life. That was something I had rejected and she did could not. That was where she was stuck.

"I need you," she said, weeping now. "I came here to tell you this."

I was annoyed again. "Why now? Why do you come to me now? And in this condition? You know who I am. I am God's Seraph. His Protector. His Captain General. Creator of Man. I am the author of those untold things you hold despicable, consider the worst of the worst. Or so you tell me. You are gone for years and now, out of the blue, you come to me, just hours before my departure, to tell me this?"

I should have been glad to hear her make her confessions. There was a time when that was all I had wanted to hear. I had got what I wanted, but I did not seem to want it as much anymore.

"I love you and I am sorry," she said. "I am sorry I treated you the way I did, but I am not sorry about the way I see this City. Its corrupt politicians propped up for political gain by you and Gabriel. God's tyranny over the citizens, ruling without accountability, killing any rival He chooses to, and wielding absolute power, unquestioned. And while I hate all these things, I still love you."

"Well, I am not changing."

Even as I said it, I knew this was a lie. In the last several days, I had taken my life in my hands by yelling at the Lord our God and, for the first time in a thousand millennia, had started thinking about the righteousness of what I was doing. Maybe what I thought as right was not the right thing, after all.

"I'm not asking you to change, so long as you don't ask me to change," she said.

"What does this mean, Amee? Does this mean we stop all the games and start a real relationship? Because if it does not, then you are just wasting my time."

"I want *us*," she said.

"Even if that means that *you* cannot be who you thought you were?" It was a reasonable enough question.

"Lucifer, if you are heading out into the wastelands looking for Gabriel and you are doing this with less than a cohort of angels and in defiance of God's laws, you are not who you think you are either."

I guess I had not considered it quite that way. What had the book said? It is what we do that defines us, not the power we wield. I put the papers down and placed both hands on the table to support my weight. Suddenly, I felt ten times heavier. I looked at my hands for a few seconds. When I was younger, my hands used to be calloused from wielding sword and spear, from holding the reins of my horse for so many hours a day, from working out in the fields with the house staff, clearing brush. Sometimes, my hands bled from the work and I remember thinking how it showed I was an angel of substance, like my grandfather before me. What was I now? My hands were smooth, not manicured like those of many rich angels, but clean and soft, nonetheless. Injured easily, simply from the act of picking up a sword. What would my grandfather have thought of me now? What would he have told me to do?

"I do not know," I said. "We are very different. I may not be the angel you walked out on, but I am flawed, all the same."

"Everyone has his flaws, Lucifer. You may seek power, but you're not looking for power for power's sake. You want to change things and while your aims may not be mine, at least they're noble."

I chuckled. "Noble? Noble."

"Noble," she repeated.

I looked up at her again. "What happens if I find him?" I asked. "What happens when I come back and am no longer noble, but just who I was before?"

"I don't think that will happen," she replied.

I did not understand.

"You've already seen things you haven't seen before. You will do the right thing, because that's what you always do."

I thought for a second. It was all wrong. Somehow.

I walked out from behind the desk and took her face in both my hands. And we kissed.

She stayed with me that night. We blended our hearts and talked about all the things we knew we would not be able to have. We were blessed in finding each other, each, maybe, for the wrong reason, but with the right result. Where would we go, when I came back? How could it work? We considered these things, seriously, for the first and the last time.

⌘   ⌘   ⌘

I did not speak with God again before I left, though I knew protocol demanded that I should. I did not get the feeling that He was afraid of me, exactly. I had treated Him that night as I would a child, as He rolled around on the floor, whining about not getting His way. Maybe He was embarrassed. Besides, it simply was not possible to get rid of both His Seraphs at the same time. He had no discernible contingency plan. I ignored His message to me, wishing me a safe journey and success in my mission. I also ignored a message from Michael, delivered to me by his new novice, Raphael, requesting a meeting before I left the City walls.

I spent time thinking about what I had and what I stood to lose. I decided to benefit from Zoan's experiences and though I think Phanuel knew it, took the genetic code for Man with me. It was the only thing I could possibly use as leverage with God when, and if, I returned. If He did not have the genetic code, He would not be able to conclude the project properly. He could not do away with me without risking everything. All the good work we had done over the last sixty-five-odd million years would be in jeopardy. And if He was in as precarious a position as Amee suggested, it was not something I could imagine Him willing to bet on. It was not a foolproof insurance policy, but it was all I had to hold over Him. The Lord our God. In the end, I was not even sure it was necessary. The Apsatsus reconstruction was not yet complete and while Phanuel had the scientific knowledge and ability to bring Man to fruition, he lacked the know-how indispensable for navigating bureaucratic hurdles and bringing the project to conclusion. God needed me to come back.

⌘　⌘　⌘

There was no fanfare to mark our departure. No one tossed garlands in our path; no one cheered. People averted their gaze from the sight of my bodyguard and the small contingent of troops that followed me. They probably thought we were tax collectors or some other form of brute squad. Armed angels always carried an implicit threat and keeping a distance from them was the best option. My angels had set expressions, though the task they were embarking upon was a thoroughly unsettling one. There was no precedent to fall back on for what we were doing. I was making it up as I went along. I did not even know what I would do when we got there. Wherever "there" might be. Would we find them or would they find us?

Amee watched us from atop the City walls. She stood over the portcullis of the City's main gate. Thick and strong, the gates had never been crossed by an enemy, the wall never breached. But my heart acknowledged no barriers as it leapt easily over the ramparts to her, when I turned back and saw her perched there. She did not wave. That would have been too pedestrian. But she waited there, intently watching the small group of angels and horses until they were out of sight. Our return seemed unlikely, our success impossible.

⌘ ⌘ ⌘

The first few days out, we traveled the well-known roads without fear. I had chosen to wear the battledress of a common soldier. It was Amee's idea and, for the first time, Azael was in agreement with something she had suggested.

"You do not like her," I stated plainly, as we rode along.

He looked ill at ease, if that were, indeed, a mental state Azael could be capable of.

"Go ahead," I said. "Speak freely. We ride to our deaths, my friend."

"She distracts you. And someone in your position cannot afford to be distracted." He was so matter-of-fact.

"Yet you keep these concerns to yourself?" I asked.

"My role, my Lord, is to protect you from harm. Not to protect you from yourself."

"Even if I do myself harm?"

"I am with you now, am I not?" Azael countered, without skipping a beat.

"Good point," I laughed.

Azael shifted in his saddle, before he continued, "But she got it right this time." He kept his eyes focused on a distant point, looking straight ahead. "Dressed as a common soldier as you are, we," he said, indicating the troops following us, "may take offense at your demotion in rank, but we silently smile at the idea that you were once like us. A common soldier, doing his duty..." he stuttered, "...for our people."

I could sense conflict within him. He was returning home. He had been my enemy and I trusted honor would keep him bound to me.

"Whatever may become of us, Azael, we will be together. We may have started out belonging to different peoples, but we will be together in the end."

"And that is what makes you different from Him," he said, before lapsing into silence.

We rode for many hours straight. We made our way through scattered villages during the daylight hours and camped in secluded locations at night. The villagers feared us. Soldiers were God's agents. Plain and simple. They belonged to no one else and followed His orders. As we rode through each village, I remembered the terror in that poor mayor's eyes, as he looked up at Zoan from the dirty ground where had been thrown, bleeding and pleading for his village and his life. Was that how these rural people saw me now? Was I the bad guy? God's soldiers were not there to protect the people. They were there to serve God. In the highest. And woe to those who interfered when His will should be done! I may have been Zoan's grandson and God's Seraph, but I was no Zoan. I was God's servant.

It was this fact that had made trimmer attacks on the City walls such a bone of contention. The army may have grown soft under Gabriel's command, but anyone with an inkling of power knew that no trimmer army had come within a stone's throw of the City walls for ages. It was not that they were incapable of doing great damage. They simply did not engage that way. Trimmers preferred the open ground, where they could steel themselves against the might of our advancing armies, before making their headlong onslaughts. All who served in the forward units knew this to be true. And while our many generals feared the massive trimmer frontal attack, Simon held his own, recognizing the tactic as an essentially flawed one that left the enemy vulnerable. Trimmers fought with brawn, rather than brains and Simon had quickly learned to turn this to his advantage. It was why he had fared so well and been promoted so rapidly. No, God needed trimmers to provide the people with a common focus. To maintain His grip on power. And as a people, we were willing to believe and even perpetuate God's falsehoods.

Trimmers might not attack the City of God, but they had no compunctions about launching offensives against smaller settlements in Elysium or Apsatsus itself. With the refurbishment of the old aqueducts leading up from the Forks, City soldiers once again patrolled the length of the Acheron. That said, chances to disrupt God's ambrosia monopoly did tempt the enemy. A patrol like ours could signal the availability of ambrosia nearby and that meant we were deemed a target. Outfitted as we were as a common City patrol and unencumbered by baggage, we held our breath and hoped we would reach the Forks unmolested. Once we emerged on the far side of the periphery forest, we would trek down the alluvial plains leading to the Acheron's convergence with the Styx at Apsatsus.

We reprovisioned at the last village on the northernmost edge of the forest. The City soldiers stationed there were very happy to see us, assuming we were their relief. They were soon disheartened to know we were simply making our way south and had nothing to trade. They did not recognize me. How could they? The simple angels that they were, waiting forever for someone to take their place in this nowhere post. How I empathized with them!

We picked up several more veterans of the battle, before we moved on. These angels had been languishing in the jail of this last-ditch village, waiting for the City's bounty hunters to earn their fat fee. My decision to pay more than they had hoped for by way of bounty and a few threatening words from Azael were enough to empty the jail cells and add numbers to our small troop. These soldiers were only too happy to accept their freedom in exchange for allegiance. My bodyguard of twelve angels and the corps of angels I had rounded up in the City now swelled to eighty.

"Less than a century of angels, but good enough for my purposes," I thought, as we plunged into the darkness of the periphery forest.

⌘　⌘　⌘

Riding among my angels, I recalled my earlier days in the army and how greatly I had enjoyed the soldier's life. The stories related by my warriors helped me to know the angels I would, in all likelihood, die with. Soldiers' stories. Stories about the battles they had fought, the officers they had bested, the women they had been with, the families they had not seen in years. Soldiers may be trained for war and taught to be fierce in the face of battle, but they never forget the tenderness of the loved ones they leave behind. We sat around the campfires at night, listening both to the rhythm of the forest and the long tales of adventure. We became comrades there in the outlands.

Some of my angels were career soldiers. They bristled at any suggestion that their sacrifices might have been in vain. They were fiercely loyal to the City and their families, but not to God. To them, He was just a leader, not unlike their sergeant, or their lieutenant, or their general. He paid them and they fought. He paid them and they followed. But it was not love of God that drove them. It was their homes they were fighting for. God had told them their way of life was under threat and they fought to protect what was theirs. They had little faith in Him and no trust in His system. "Still," as one of them said, quite rightly, "as a politician, you don't have the benefit we soldiers have of always knowing who's trying to kill you."

Others in my contingent were farmers from outside the City's walls. The City's population had waxed and waned over the years, but was always, seemingly, on the brink of starvation. The need for food remained a desperate one. Food for families, food for livestock, food to trade. The farms were both the City's backbone and home to members of its lowest class. Their City-slicker brethren were menial laborers, criminals, or thieves who gravitated to violence. But farmers were forced to take up the sword to support their families. Between Zoan's time as Seraph and my elevation to the Order, the City's farms had metamorphosed from small, independent, family-run businesses into the lucrative large-scale operations of big business, with profits going to the City's wealthy landowners. One young angel named Ariel complained the loudest.

"It doesn't make sense!" he whined. "We constantly hear the City is suffering from food shortages, right after our wheat has been stolen by God's tax collectors."

"It is the way things are, young one," Azael said mockingly.

"God consolidates and consolidates," Ariel continued, ignoring the taunts, "until we can no longer live on our own plots of land. The 'greater collective' required us to share resources with our fellow farmers, and while that drove down prices, it destroyed us! Millions of families murdered off the back of a depreciating commodity. It was a crime, no less!"

"Watch your tongue!" Azael snapped, thinking it was an attack on me and my policies.

Ariel remembered his place and fell silent. I watched their faces in the flickering campfire light. I felt compelled to speak.

"God works in mysterious ways," I said. "Not everything we see has ends that make sense to us. We can only do our best and hope for the best."

"How do we know what is best?" Ariel asked earnestly.

He was young, but intelligent, I thought to myself. Azael was clearly angered by his outbursts.

"Someone far wiser than me had once said that we must search our hearts to answer that question. But there is no one correct answer. You joined the army to support your family. It may not be the best for you, personally, but it is the best you can do for your family. Your wife, your sons and daughters, will be blessed for your efforts. If anyone asked me, I would say you did the right thing, if that was, indeed, your motivation."

It was a lame answer and I knew it, but Ariel smiled in response.

"What motivates you, my Lord?" asked another young angel we had collected from one of the villages' jailors.

"Family," I said thinking of Zoan. I thought again for a moment. "Yes, family is what motivated me. But somewhere, I learned that, all along, I had been driven by the wrong motivation. I did not listen to my heart. I did not even want to hear it. I listened only to my head, happy to mistake the source of the message and assume it was coming from my heart. But I have made the right choice now and now my motivation is simple."

I looked around the circle of intent eyes. Even Azael, the gruff angel of virtue and discipline, looked at me expectantly.

"To keep you alive!" I finished.

They all laughed and I knew I had successfully evaded the question.

"What about the rest of you?" I asked. "You are from the City, if I am not mistaken," I said, pointing to the one who had spoken. "Tell us your name and what motivated you," I requested.

"My name is Orobas and I don't know about hearts or heads. I took up the cause when I was drafted," he said.

We laughed again.

Azael looked at me and I nodded approval.

"You don't fight for the cause, when you fight that way," he said. "You fight for the cause when, as our master says, you do so because your heart tells you to."

Orobas appeared confused.

"Azael is right," I said. "There was a time when our City's armies were filled with landowners. The cause was clear. These were angels who had a stake in something, something to lose, if their City were defeated. But when the Lord Gabriel took over the armies, the quality of the soldiers, the efficiency of operations, the general morale seemed to deteriorate. Serving in the City's army was no longer a rite of passage, the honor it had been when Zoan led us to victory," I said, with only the slightest hint of hesitation. "It became just another bureaucratic setup to deal with. To mistreat, disrespect, and take advantage of."

They were surprised by my sudden bluntness.

"Master," Azael said, leaning forward and speaking to me in a whisper. "Do you think this is the time to be discussing such matters?"

"There should be no denying the truth," I said curtly.

Azael leaned back, a little embarrassed.

"Lesser angels may run His city," I continued, "but it is God who allowed this to happen. He has never served with you, shed His blood with you. Has He?"

I felt the sensation of heat on my face, but it was not from the fire by which we sat. In my mind, I saw Simon looking at me. All the work he had put into his life and career—for God. Only to be spat upon as a reward and led to slaughter.

"He allowed the quality of the angels under arms, dedicated to the City's protection and domination, to decline. Orobas's forced conscription in the army is but a symbol of what we have become. Our mission today is evidence enough of that."

They exchanged looks, unsure as to how they should respond to my blasphemies. Orobas was silent, but I hoped my tone had made him realize he should not take his military duties so lightly.

"There is no point in denying it," I continued. "Trimmers have been relatively silent for many years, but our Seraph Gabriel did the City no service by allowing the army to wallow in this pitiable condition. Since the threat was not perceived as imminent, it gave us an excuse to allow the army to weaken and rot with the rot of the City. Simon was aware of this, when he took the army into the field. Think about that, as we move on."

They were all silent. I was Zoan's grandson, Seraph of God. Now they too, knew what I had come to know about God. And any good son who recognizes his father's limitations has little to speak of, but much to ponder.

⌘ ⌘ ⌘

The ground opened up before us as we emerged from the southern end of the forest. We were on our own until we reached Apsatsus, as the long stretch of road leading from the periphery forest down to the Forks was relatively unprotected. There was safety in numbers, something we conspicuously lacked. We were on our guard.

"It would be a shame to get killed accidentally," one of us said, as we eyed the eastern shoreline. "If they come, we will never go home."

The thought stayed in my mind, as we continued on our way to Apsatsus.

Though we were in greater danger now, I must admit that after spending so much time under the forest's canopy, it was nice to be out in the light of day once again. The closer you got to the frontiers of the periphery forests, the more obvious the City's inept land management became. Unlike those parts of the Elysium nearer the City that had been raped and robbed of their natural resources, these areas were open and lush. This was, in part, what Amee and Melchom were working for in relation to the Great Northern Forest. The City could not afford to destroy those northern lands in the same manner in which it had ravaged the southern lands. Water management, in particular, was a double-edged sword. Not only did it impact the City's inhabitants in their homes, but took the fight to the City outside its walls. Saving the water meant saving its source that, in turn, meant saving the mountains and the forests. Politicians did not care about the forests or the mountains, but they did care about the possibility of unrest when the citizenry could not access clean, uncontaminated water. I may have disliked Melchom as a politician, but from a strictly objective point of view, he was one of the few genuinely concerned about the long-term viability of the living conditions afforded to the City's inhabitants.

Man gave the southern lands new impetus. Below the point where the Acheron mixed with the Styx stood my revitalized Apsatsus. It had been there for eternity and was rumored to be the City's first site. As a colony, it had died when the northern aqueducts were completed. It just was not an important place anymore. With Phanuel's discovery, however, that Apsatsus was the best of all terminuses for the rendering of Man into Heaven, its status changed once again. The aqueducts were rebuilt, the roads refortified. The old Apsatsus was reborn from the ashes. All in secret. Our work at the Forks had become *the* most closely guarded of state secrets.

What gave this place on the Forks its special qualities was unclear, even to Phanuel and me. We did not know what, specifically, about this area made the transition from Earth to Heaven possible. We knew even less about the headwaters of the Styx, far in the east. But in the course of carrying out some of the most daring and confidential work done in the history of the City, Phanuel and I had surveyed spots all along the Styx for the optimal transition locus. We had hoped we would find something farther downstream, away from the Apsatsus and its proximity to the largely trimmer-controlled Forks. But Apsatsus proved to be the most stable, which meant that in order for God's plan to work, it would take a large contingent of angels to garrison the heavy fortifications needed to hold the spot. To achieve His Man, God readily sanctioned our operations at Apsatsus, though it required us take residence before the very teeth of the enemy.

I was initially very hesitant to reinforce the Forks. Even before Gabriel voiced his objections, I had given Phanuel the same guff. It was a serious practical problem, regardless of the science involved. If the site expanded to take up too large an area, it would only be a matter of time before trimmers attempted to overrun the place. But Phanuel's results proved to be the solution that had eluded our scientists and bureaucrats, Zoan included, for billions of years. As cover for my actual objectives at the Forks, I pushed Melchom to rebuild the existing waterworks, aqueducts, and pumping stations all along the southern lands and even increase their number by constructing new ones. Of course, that entailed a corresponding strengthening of our fortifications. In effect, I used water as a diversion from my real purpose at Apsatsus. It proved a simple solution for keeping the true nature of the encampment a secret. My fights with Melchom over water management in the north were really fights about provisions for my operations in the south. Apsatsus had to be protected at any cost. It was the state's top priority to keep its operations a secret. Few angels knew about its existence and the rest—including Melchom—had to be kept in the dark. In fact, when Simon's army had passed this way in order to cross into trimmer lands, none but God, Gabriel, Phanuel, and I knew how close they were to one of the most daring and dangerous projects He had ever undertaken.

Apsatsus was the key to God's plans for Man. Yet I had not set foot in our reconstituted encampment there. Had He known Apsatsus was the first destination of my officially unauthorized trip into Tartarus, God would, no doubt, have directed Michael or maybe his Raphael to arrest me. Thereby focusing more attention upon His prize. But we needed to reprovision and Apsatsus, through the marshes of the Forks, was the best place to make an undetected crossing into Tartarus. Really, for me, it was all about seeing the product of so many years of my work and toil being born from the brewing and mighty Styx.

⌘ ⌘ ⌘

When, at last, we came upon Apsatsus' fortifications, it was almost three weeks since I had been informed of Gabriel's disastrous defeat. I deemed it better to inform Azael about our destination in advance. He needed no reminder of what Apsatsus had once been to the City of God. To my bodyguards, the sudden appearance of City-like walls, albeit significantly smaller in scale, was a surprise. What difference could it make in the end? What were the odds any of them would ever return to the City, anyway?

"They did not come by here," Renegol, the commander of Apsatsus, advised me that night, as we sat in his quarters.

My angels were taking rest in the officers' quarters and had been cautioned about keeping our true purpose a secret.

"Simon would not have," I said, sipping at the tea the commander had offered me. It was not of very good quality, but certainly a nice change from the canteen water I had been living off of over the past weeks. "It is unlikely he knew this place as anything more than a decrepit water-pumping station. He was not among those cleared for that level of information."

"Yes, but Gabriel was," Renegol said very matter-of-factly.

"Gabriel would not have brought the army here. God would have forbidden it. But Gabriel would definitely have flown here, had he survived the battle."

"In my experience, Seraph, trimmers don't take captives. They'll kill any prisoner they take. And more than once, I've been a witness to cornered trimmers taking their own lives."

Renegol looked at my half-empty teacup. I could tell he did not want to part with any more of his precious tea.

"A strange bunch," he mused.

"You have been in the fighting corps, then?" I asked absently.

"Yes. For many years. But I have seen few battles, Seraph."

"What about this encampment, Captain? The walls showed no signs of attack."

"There have been no attacks, Seraph. We've seen trimmer scouts, but they do not come close enough to make it worth our while. In fact, I'm not sure they know we're here, something for which, I must admit in all candor, I'm quite grateful."

He continued to watch me sip my tea.

"Perhaps they have taken the bait," I suggested. "There are many such places farther west along the Styx."

"Perhaps, Seraph, but trimmers are fairly wide-ranging in their movements. So it seems a happy mystery to me that they've not made a closer inspection of this place that lies so near their domain."

It might have been a mystery to Renegol, but to my mind, it was not a happy one.

⌘   ⌘   ⌘

I toured the outpost, as I was obliged to do. It was made up of a defensive wall still under reconstruction, several barracks and armories, and holding pens for the newly arrived Man. At the moment, almost all Men were being exterminated on arrival. "They are 'Man-like,'" Phanuel explained before I left, "but not quite what we need."

"A few more years," one of the herding soldiers told me, as he poked and prodded a bunch of the newly arrived through the various chutes. One of Phanuel's scientists stood next to him, writing in his log with an odious expression.

"Sergeant!" the scientist barked, not looking up from his writing.

"Yes sir."

"Move them along, please."

"Yes sir!" There was clearly some sort of animosity there, but I was not interested in knowing the reason.

"Why do you say 'a few more years'?" I asked the sergeant, happier to be speaking with him than with the ill-tempered scientist.

"They're loathsome and brutish. They know you're there and they know you're a threat, but they don't seem to notice too much else, sir."

I glanced at the irritated scientist.

"Not that my wife would approve of me saying so, sir," the sergeant went on, "but they remind me of my children when they was young."

"My Lord Seraph," the scientist interrupted, "the processing is going according to schedule. I don't expect there to be any further delays at this point."

"I am happy to hear that," I said. But looking back to the sergeant, I asked, "What do you mean by 'children'?"

"I mean," the sergeant said with a cold look at the scientist, "I knew when my kids were really 'there,' once they were happy to see me come home in the evening, sir."

"Or, more likely, afraid to see you at all," the scientist muttered under his breath.

The sergeant ignored the scientist's comments and continued. "Sleeping, eating, shitting..." he said, suddenly embarrassed. "Beggin' your pardon, sir, but you know...those things, that's just nature. Learning makes the difference, if you ask me. How many times will a kid touch fire, before he decides it hurts and don't touch it again? Once. These things here," he said, poking at one the passing men, "they don't learn. They know what's natural and all, but they don't know me." He smiled.

The scientist piped back up. "My Lord Seraph, the subjects have responded favorably to the required protocol and meet the standards set out in the procedures. We are having some issues with their behavior, but I think it's something that can be worked out in the next phase of the protocol."

The sergeant sneered. "Fear is in every animal's gut, but it's knowing and calculating the risks that will make Man a Man."

I reflected on that for a moment. Man had been programmed with fear. It was necessary to keep him subservient, willing to do only service to God. But perhaps too much fear had spiked the formula. God had been very clear on Man's mental-capacity issues. Learning beyond a certain basic level was not permitted, though Man had the same brainpower potential of angels. Man's basic purpose was simple. Obedience. But if God wanted creatures that could function on only the most basic levels, there was always the risk that those basic emotional responses would not allow for any positive feedback. If the choice was 'attack' or 'run' only, Man would always be a fifty-fifty shot. We would fail, if we continued to follow this design, I realized. Man had to be able to learn.

"What if we upped the brain capacity on Earth, but only allowed full capacity upon transition to Heaven?" I asked, addressing the question more to myself than to anyone else.

"It'd keep 'em safe enough to handle," the sergeant said. "With a bit of intimidation, we could keep control of 'em," he added, nodding in agreement with his own words.

"Yes," the scientist said, finally agreeing with the sergeant. "And the risks of shock may actually be reduced with a more significantly developed brain, depending, of course, on the nature of their transition." He wrote something down. "Yes," he repeated to himself.

I came away from the conversation with an uneasy thought: God wanted these creatures to be docile, servile, but able to fight, when properly motivated. Enhancing the complexity of the brain, basically, removing the inhibitors we had put in place and putting them on par with angels in Heaven, would allow them to transition more smoothly and fulfill God's requirements. But giving Man a bigger brain or, more accurately, the ability to use more of his brain, could be considered a direct violation of God's orders. I had no doubt Phanuel could engineer it, but it would need to be handled very, very delicately to avoid issues. We had no slaves in Heaven. People may have been poor, or destitute, or subject to the whims of an uncaring aristocracy, but they were not really slaves. They were disenfranchised, but for the most part, they could make their own decisions, even if those decisions conflicted with the laws of God. God called that "free will." But as it stood, these new creatures would be slaves in every sense of the term. Mentally inhibited and genetically designed to suppress angelic free will. They would do God's bidding. Support God's infrastructure. Make a loyal political base even more loyal. Totally subservient, in fact. Fighting God's constant wars. What kind of life could Man hope to have here in Heaven?

The sergeant and his squad of soldiers took the group of newly arrived from the river's edge. Watching this Man and his kind, freshly plucked from the Styx, I could clearly see their extreme disorientation. Some were falling to the ground, some simply screaming. Others were belligerent and downright dangerous. Clearly, they did not know their fate or that there was any such thing as fate, but the small dose of brains we had given them had at least made them aware of being in unfriendly hands. The fear we had engineered was working well. The sergeant picked out the healthiest-looking of the bunch and had his soldiers bundle her off.

"This is the part I love," he said, unsheathing his sword. His remaining soldiers followed his lead and proceeded to hack the remaining specimens to death. They wailed in response to the sudden onslaught, but could do nothing as the swords cut down upon them. Their blood, red like angel's blood, seeped into the river and vanished in its quickly moving currents. I remembered Nicor's blood in the swamps. It had mixed with my own before seeping down and disappearing into the muck.

"This is how it will be," I said to myself, turning away from the carnage. "This is what I have done."

Amee was right. I was working for a monster and I was His most loved disciple.

⌘　⌘　⌘

I prepared a report to be sent back to God, before we left Apsatsus. I did not want word getting back to Him that I had been here and had not informed Him about it. That would appear subversive, given our parting words. It had to seem business as usual. Man was my project and I was making an inspection. I advised God that all was going as I had planned and the project would, most likely, be completed without delay. A few more tweaks and maybe a few thousand odd years and we would have the right mix to satisfy His requirements. We could always add further refinements later.

A thought struck me as I wrote. There was nothing to stop me from locking the formula in its current place or, indeed, changing the parameters. God had given Gabriel the power to lock the final designs in place. But with Gabriel out of the picture, God had seemingly forgotten to provide for a backup. By default, Phanuel and I had inherited the formula and I was the sole angel with power. If I locked Man's formula, there was little anyone, short of Phanuel, could do about it. Even God Himself would be helpless. He would have to start all over. It was just the nature of the science. God would try to start from scratch. Again. He would have the lab work, yes, but He would, basically, have to start all over again. Millions of years of work were in my control and my control alone. God had overlooked this. He had never been one for details. He had left that to His subordinates. And to the bureaucracy. I could report back to Phanuel about brain performance at transition. And there was precious little God to do about it. I blushed at the thought, considering it no more than fleetingly.

I mentioned nothing but the status of Man in my report. I certainly made no mention of the way I had liberated and adopted soldiers encountered along our route to the Forks. God might have been distraught the night of our last meeting, but He was not someone to be underestimated. There was a reason that He alone ruled Heaven. Still, I was unable to rid myself of that image of Him rolling around on the floor like a child, whining about Gabriel's insubordination. I had to admit that for the first time since being elevated to the Order, I had questioned my trust in Him. Doubted the Word. He had never lied to me before. At least, I had never known Him to lie to me. But every day outside the City walls, that thought, that image of Him in His petulant and spiteful state had continued to eat at me. My time at Apsatsus had only added to that irritation.

But this period of time also fortified me. I had to get across the Acheron and find those He had treated with such malevolence. Find Gabriel. I kept telling myself I was God's Seraph, perhaps now His only Seraph. My job was to serve Him, regardless of my personal feelings. That was what it meant to love God and be His servant.

"Be loyal to *something*, for God's sake," I blasphemed to myself in irony.

I reconsidered my plan and decided to leave Apsatsus with only my original escort of bodyguards. The soldiers we had encountered along the way were veterans and now, my loyal adherents, but they were an unknown quantity, with more fear and vengeance in mind than I was entirely comfortable with. I did not quite know what I would do, when I encountered my first trimmer, but I was certain it should not include cutting them down in revenge. Not, at least, unless it was imperative. I thanked these soldiers for their service and comradeship. I put Ariel in command. He was young, but I liked his passion. As my personal retainers and new members of my personal bodyguard, I instructed them to support the garrison, as Apsatsus would need their help. Sooner or later, when the importance of this place became clearer, the walls of Apsatsus would have to withstand assault. God had gambled on Man to make sure all threats to His rule could be crushed. A gamble I was willing to make too.

⌘　⌘　⌘

Twelve. I do not remember why twelve was the number of bodyguards assigned to any Seraph, but it was ordained by law and that was good enough. Senators often traveled with bodyguards, but these were personally hired, rather than provided by the City.

God was a different story. He never left the Seat of God with anything less than His bodyguard of twenty-four. Not that He left the Seat of God too often, anyway. As Protector, I was also entitled to a bodyguard, half the number allotted to Seraphim. As I held both positions, I defaulted to twelve. These twelve rode out with me from Apsatsus for, what we were all sure, would be the final leg. They did not flinch. They did not complain. They just rode on.

We made our crossing under cover of night, making our way through the swampy delta of the Forks. These were the very swamps where I had been wounded, the very place I had first encountered Azael. I asked him to lead the way and watched him for telltale signs as we crossed. He was, after all, living in captivity as my servant. But he quickly found the main artery of the Acheron from among the weave of tributaries. I did not know where, precisely, Gabriel had made his crossing, but based on what Renegol had told me, it was north of Apsatsus. We hooked back around to the north and began looking for signs of the routed army. They were not hard to spot and it did not take too long to find the army. Or, at least, what was left of it.

CHAPTER
TWENTY-EIGHT

Soldiering had never wanted me as much I wanted it. The drilling, the marching, the routine. All in preparation for the real role of a soldier: to kill. Ironically, for most soldiers, killing is the last thing they want to do. It is most unnatural. The smell of a freshly cut angel is almost indescribable, but instantly recognizable. A cut through the stomach releases an odor that is different from that which a cut through the chest gives off. For obvious reasons, the smell from the stomach is bitter and rancid, while the chest smells almost like a wet cave. A blow to the head is, on the other hand, quite different, as the brain has almost no smell at all, but putrefies quickly in the open air. However, while each of these has some unique features unto themselves, all of them share one element: the same sweet smell of blood. Not quite death, but, maybe, escaping life. It is why killing is so addictive, why the smell of blood lures us into killing again and again, why we will always be hounded by the lust to kill, no matter how civilized we believe ourselves to be.

Long dead. Well, that is a wholly describable smell. Revolting. Rotting. Acrid. After my time in the army, I could smell something dead from miles away. Even the faintest hint of it could not elude my nostrils. I would walk through the City on my way home from somewhere and smell death in the streets. It could have been anything. A rat, a working animal, an angel. It was illegal to leave these things to rot in public. They caused plague and other diseases that could wipe out whole neighborhoods. Many parts of the City had been put to the torch to rid them of the filth that would just not go away on its own. It was one reason why angels like Mastema had vaulted to power. Being responsible for the removal of that smell had brought angels like him a disproportionally high level of popularity. It was amazing what someone would do for fresh air. The smell of rotting corpses was something no sane angel had a nose for. It did not sicken me as it did other angels. I would wrinkle my nose and know that something somewhere was dead. Across the Acheron, into Tartarus, I did not need an acute sense of smell to know we were heading in the right direction. The smell reached us first. And then we saw the birds.

They circled endlessly. From far away, their mass appeared like black wisps of cloud dancing in the wind. They rose and fell in some sort of invisible rhythm. As we got closer, the sound of their beating wings pounded the air with such frenzy, it seemed as if they had created their own wind. Their collective shrieking made me wonder if the battle still raged. But the only battle on now was the fighting among the crows for their fair share of carrion.

I had fought in the army. I had seen my share of fighting. I had witnessed carnage and watched cavalry charges and the flights of a thousand arrows. Shields cracked with the battle mace, war dogs tearing into angels and trimmers alike. Lines of heavily armed soldiers barricaded against each other, pushing and hoping the other side would buckle first under the weight of it all. Spears aloft, marked against the sky as points of death. It was part of the job.

In the service of the Lord. And when we retired, we appreciated the fact we had made it through and mourned our dead comrades.

This was different. I was not sitting in my tent with the officers, reading battle maps and wishing I were plunging into battle. I was not checking on the wounded. I was not even supervising the required burials. This was so very different.

⌘   ⌘   ⌘

Bodies on bodies. Piles of them. Legless horses rammed into the dirt from the force of their fall. Hacked-off limbs and the agony of horrendous wounds. Bodies trailing through the field's carnage, as angels crawled in unknown directions to their ends. Weapons broken and cleaved, littering the ground soaked in blood. What I saw that day was all of that, and more.

Fire had consumed a large strip of ground, from the top of the nearby ridge to the edge of the Acheron below. Everything in its path had been devoured. Whatever trees were growing on the spot before the clash of arms had either been cut down to stumps by the fierceness of the battle or burned to their very roots. Wisps of black smoke drifted up into the air, before being caught in the afternoon breeze and the whirl of circling birds. Everywhere, little sticks poked out of the smoking earth, remnants of barrage after barrage of arrows that had struck the ground and were now burnt low. We could see patterns of them like wavy fields of grass, as we circled the periphery of the scene. Bodies pulled into a fighter's stance, as the muscles shrank and contracted in the heat of the ravaging fire. Animals had eaten what was left of some of them, roasted as they were.

On the un-burnt sides of the field, chaos reigned without end in heaps of what looked like a crawling brown mass. What had once been angels and horses were now swarms of flies, ants, and every type of bug that lived for miles in every direction. The ground literally crawled with insects, ferrying their meals back and forth to their nests from the battle. Bodies bristling like pin-cushions. Bloated torsos of angels, their ribs sticking up or broken in piles. It looked like moving dung. My angels and I rode through the burnt-up sections of the field for fear of being consumed like our dead comrades by these voracious insects. No traces of blood. It had all been consumed.

I could imagine nothing worse. The horror of it all. Like nothing I have seen before or since. The wars that followed my fall from God's grace were gruesome, to be sure. But after all those battles? Nothing could be as horrifying as that day in the burning fields along the serene Acheron.

All this meant I would now have to do something I had hoped, all along, would be unnecessary. I set myself to meet the trimmers head-on, though in truth, my heart wavered at the idea. I ordered Azael to set fire to anything and everything not already burnt. The fire would purify the ground and the remains of the army. There was nothing else I could do, the carnage was so great. There was no way I could identify Gabriel or Simon from the mess. Simon, my friend, gone. Gabriel, my fellow Seraph, gone.

It took us all day to set ablaze what was left of the battlefield. Fresh fumes of smoke billowed up into the wind. Black, ugly smoke. The birds fled and the ground crackled with the scorching bodies of insects and their feast alike. We erected a marker of spears once we were finished, memorializing the place where so many angels had been lost. We stood by and waited for the trimmers to find us.

⌘　⌘　⌘

We did not need to wait for long. If the billowing black smoke had not sent a signal for miles in every direction, the fire raging across the fields and lighting up the evening skies made up for the lack.

The first trimmer patrol arrived at the burning fields early the next morning. Surprised by the reality of what they had considered a virtual graveyard suddenly bursting back to life, the trimmer patrol had come prepared, larger in numbers than the usual reconnaissance patrol. It must have appeared strange to them to arrive on the scene, only to see thirteen angels on horseback poised in full regalia beside the smoldering field, holding high the standard of the City of God. My own Seraph's standard fluttered in the warm wind beside me, atop those of the City. The patrol stopped just short of effective bow range.

There were around one hundred mounted trimmers. Both men and women, it appeared. They wore lightly fitting armor and carried only bows and quivers of arrows. There was uniformity in their attire, but many were also outfitted with weapons and armor, recognizably of the City and recently come by, no doubt.

"Who are you?" came a shout across the field from what appeared to be the leader of the group. "Why are you here?" He wore a clean white fitted robe with a single rope belt. He did not appear to be armed.

"I am Lucifer, Seraph of the City of God in Heaven," I replied. "I come to find my comrades who fought upon this spot. If there are any left among you, I am here to parley for their release. I wish to speak to your commander."

I had not practiced a speech and I immediately regretted not having had the foresight to prepare myself more meticulously for my first encounter. I resigned myself again to certain death.

There was no immediate reaction from the line of mounted trimmers. Horses whinnied and trimmers shifted on their mounts. The leader was unable to understand why we were there, but seemed to be considering my request. He gestured to the two trimmers flanking him. They, in turn, signaled down the line. Both ends of the line of trimmers slowly peeled off and came around our flanks. If they were concerned about the possibility of an ambush, the burning fields precluded the chance of such a trap being set. With the river to our backs, it quickly became clear that we thirteen were alone in the wilderness.

After the trimmers had signaled each other that all was clear, their leader spoke again.

"We already have a Seraph's standard in our camp," he said. "I repeat: who are you and why are you here?"

"I am not here to discuss flags," I replied. "I am here to find my soldiers, those of them who survived. I repeat: I wish to speak with your commander."

Trimmer horses began to rear up. My bodyguard began to reach for their arrows.

"Hold steady," I said to Azael.

Even he had tensed up.

The trimmer leader gestured to his horsemen to remain calm and they fell silent again. He moved forward, taking with him the two trimmers he had signaled to before. They trotted across the open expanse, their faces alight with the rays of he rising sun behind me.

I leaned over to Azael. "I will go alone."

"Yes, my Lord," he replied, clearly uneasy with what I was about to do.

I urged my horse forward and met them in the middle.

The leader was young, but confident. His hair was long, but not unkempt. His flowing robe was a pure white. The rough belt of rope he wore held little but a small dagger and a leather pouch. I was immediately struck by the sight, by the memory it had triggered. And the look on my face gave me away. The trimmer followed my gaze down to his belt.

"You've seen someone like me before," he said matter-of-factly.

We were only a few meters or so apart.

"No, but my grandfather did meet a trimmer of your kind once. He had described how she was dressed. As you are now."

"We are angels, as you are, though we are of Tartarus. Not of Elysium. We do not use the word 'trimmer' to refer to ourselves."

"Tartaruian," I said through clenched teeth.

The young trimmer was satisfied. "You say you are Seraphim. You wear the clothes of a City soldier. I don't understand what you are doing here. Where is your army?"

"I have no army. Just the twelve angels who have sworn to protect me. I am here to find Gabriel and to arrange for the release of my angels."

"You have said so already," the young trimmer retorted. "Why are you really here?"

"I am telling you," I repeated with as measured a response as I could muster, "I am here to find Gabriel and take my angels back with me. I am prepared to pay for their release and promise that they will never be used in the service of the City's army again. If that will not do, I offer myself as a hostage for their safe release."

The young trimmer looked to the two others flanking him, apparently unsure of himself. This was going a whole lot better than I had imagined. The older and more battle worn of the two trimmers reined his horse forward until he was very close to me. We looked at each other, nearly nose to nose. I motioned back to Azael, silently urging him not to react.

"You said 'grandfather' just now, didn't you?" he asked unexpectedly.

"Yes. What of it?

"You are Lucifer," the older trimmer said, pleased with himself. I did not recognize him.

"As I said, yes," I confirmed, looking back at the leader who seemed a bit annoyed now. "I have no ulterior motive. I am here to arrange for the release of my angels."

The older trimmer squinted a bit and reined his horse back. "Crocell, go back to the camp," he said to the leader's other lieutenant, "and tell the General that Lucifer, Seraph of the City of God, has come to speak with Maalik."

The other trimmer rode off immediately. The leader continued to look annoyed, but the older trimmer turned back to me.

"You will be granted safe passage to speak with our leader Maalik," he said. "You may retain your personal standard, but the standard of the City, along with all your weapons and those of your angels must be handed over."

The leader reared his horse around and signaled to the line of remaining trimmers. Some peeled off from the main formation and rode into the outlands, while several others moved forward to meet us in the field.

"My angels will not be mistreated," I said matter-of-factly.

Both the older trimmer and his young comrade nodded in agreement.

"I insist," I said.

"Your soldiers will not be harmed, if you disarm now and follow our directions," the older trimmer said.

"What guarantee do I have that you will keep your word?" I asked, still a bit skeptical about whom I was dealing with. "What assurance do I have from you that you will respect my parlay?"

"You have my word," the older trimmer said, glancing at the young leader.

He nodded again and reined his horse to join the approaching trimmers. The older trimmer opened his leather satchel and removed a book.

"If you are who you claim to be, you know what this is. I swear on the laws of the city of our forefathers that neither you nor your soldiers will be harmed while in our company." He looked at me gravely. "Behave, and you may be released unharmed."

Of course, I recognized the book. It was the same as my grandfather's, which had gone to Jehoel and then come to me. Which had subsequently gone to Gabriel and was now in God's possession.

"I understand," I said.

I turned and shouted to Azael to have my angels all hand over their weapons, along with the City standard. I could sense Azael's reluctance.

"Do it and you honor my grandfather and my family," I said.

They looked at the trimmer horsemen approaching and then at each other.

"Trust me," I said.

The older trimmer looked at me, clearly pleased.

"Lucifer," he said, "we Tartaruians have been waiting for you for a long time."

We moved off, past those hills of abysmal death, the smoke, and the stench. I had not understood what the trimmer meant when he said they had been waiting for me, but I had the strangest feeling, as I eyed the leather satchel slapping against his side in rhythm with his horse. Then suddenly, Zoan was with me. He had been gone from me. For an eternity, it had seemed. Since before the time I had risen to the rank of Seraph. He was very welcome back in my heart now, even if that heart warned me of the consequences of my rash actions.

⌘ ⌘ ⌘

We travelled for several days, making our way eastward without much haste. The trimmers shared their food and water with us, as if we were one of them. In the evenings, when we set up camp, they provided us spare tents and arranged for a fire to cook our meals. The trimmers showed us no apparent malice. My bodyguards and I sat around our campfire and ate silently, our initial fears reduced to a more manageable state of alertness. We did not know where we were going, with whom we were about to meet, or whether we would be released alive. But at least we were traveling easy.

They did not really speak with us, until I asked the young leader where we were headed. The older trimmer was no longer traveling with us, having gone ahead somewhere to prepare for our coming.

"You will speak with Maalik and Maalik alone," he replied. He refused to tell me who exactly Maalik was or why I was meant to speak with him.

I hoped I was headed where I needed to go. The thought that I might have surrendered myself and my angels to some random group of outlanders, intent only on our capture to take us hostage, crossed my weary mind.

On the third day, we came upon a city of white tents. It popped out of the horizon, hidden, this far, in the swirling warm air rising off the ground before us. The circumference of the tent city was massive, accommodating what turned out to be tens of thousands of people. Angels, children, horses, and other animals. White flags fluttered in the breeze sweeping across the camp.

Positioned as it was in the plain, the many sweet and foul smells of the tent city were blown farther east, away from their enemies in the west.

The tent city was ringed by temporary palisades and fortifications, impressive obstacles that could easily frustrate even the most ferocious of cavalry charges. Patrolling the perimeter of the camp were well-disciplined riders, keeping an eye on the horizon in every direction. We encountered several large groups of riders coming out of the tent city as we approached. Each of the riders, clad in light mail armor, was armed with bows, arrows, and short, curved swords. Their horses were clearly bred for speed, given their impressive gait, and each unit had a leader clothed in white robes, similar to those of the young leader of our group. Some of these white-robbed riders were women, a fact that surprised me. Women leading patrols of soldiers. Just like Zoan had described to me. Each white-clad rider carried a leather satchel, draped over a breastplate of silver. A jeweled dagger was attached to each rider's rope belt.

We passed through the first protective screen and to the gates of the tent city. They were temporary gates, but strong and certainly formidable. Once through the gates and past two guard stations, a long boulevard stretching into the tent city's center lay before us. A thousand meters of open causeway for horses, carts, people, and all manner of animals. Merchant stalls selling everything possible lined the boulevard and the many narrower branching alleys. Loud exchanges, as trimmers bargained and sold goods. Congregations of people, all talking. Trimmers sitting out in front of establishments selling food and drink. The smell of cheap wine and roasted meats. Ambrosia even, something I had not expected to smell outside the tight circle of God's innermost sanctuaries. The sudden mass of trimmers and their society hit me hard. What I saw here was no different from the thousands of markets that lined the many streets of the City of God. The only real difference was the absence of refuse and soldier patrols. The area outside the camp swarmed with armed horsemen. Inside, not a single weapon did I see, as we made our way up the lively boulevard.

When we reached the center of the tent city, I realized the boulevard along which we had just traveled was just one of several spokes. Similarly, trimmers and animal-packed boulevards ran in three other directions, making the spot on which we stood the hub of the massive encampment. I marveled at the sheer size of the place and watched as a single trimmer directed horse-cart traffic around the central hub. The young leader was pleased as he noticed my astonishment.

"Your God portrays us as bloodthirsty monsters, interested in nothing but destruction and mayhem. This city can move in an hour all its angels and animals and baggage. We've become experts at moving, a necessity, when you're hunted like animals. Tell me, Lucifer, do you still think we're animals?"

I thought about it for a second. We had all been raised to think trimmers were simply marauders, looking to take our City from us at every convenient opportunity. We had been brought up to fear them, their nomadic ways, their existence in the outlands. That we seldom saw a trimmer did not seem to matter. That, in the few instances where we actually clashed in combat, they were seldom victorious did not seem to matter. They were the enemy and we were at war.

"God's ways can be mysterious," I replied, still marveling at the activities around me. "But we live in faith, faith in our way of seeing life and faith in the way God leads us. Faith in the Word. You say you are not animals, but I have seen the way you attack our walls, cut off our City's supplies, abduct and murder our citizens."

I looked intently at him now, with a fire that had not flared within me from the time preceding my discovery of God's betrayal of Gabriel.

"You slaughter our armies," I added.

The leader's expression immediately changed. "We have the right to defend ourselves," he countered. "Your God took everything he could from us. And when he couldn't take any more, he resorted to killing us. We do what we need to do for survival and you, your City, and your God are the reasons we live the way we do. You have no one to blame, but yourselves."

"You and your people walked away," I retorted. "We did not chase you. You chose to disobey and you paid the price. It is not my people's fault, nor our Heavenly Father's, that you chose not to live within the system. God provided you with shelter and you shunned it. God provided you with nourishment and you threw it in His face. God provided you with everything you needed to survive and you pushed Him away. What do you know about living on the edge? You live the way you do, because it was easier to be selfish than smart." I looked at the bustle of trimmers and animals around me. "You have all this, because He made it so. You live in the wilderness, because you wanted to take more than you were given. You are foolish. You are selfish. And you will never stop to see what you have done to yourselves, because you look only into yourselves, your selfish little desires, while the rest of what is good could be yours. Selfishness is what drove you here. Shunning the face of God. Shunning the love of God. Shunning the Word."

The young leader was really angry now.

But I was unstoppable. "Selfishness is what has made you. Not God," I sneered.

My bodyguard was pleased. Azael remained expressionless. The trimmer horsemen around us were clearly enraged.

I was not used to arguing this way. In the City, this trimmer's blasphemies would have warranted instant death and as a Seraph of God, I had both the power to preserve life and the power to impose death. While I used those powers sparingly, I did use them. As I sat upon my horse, watching this young trimmer fume, I found myself in a place I had never been before. Someone had criticized God and I had not struck him down. Though I had not used it in an age, it felt strange not to have my broadsword strapped to my side. I felt the void where its weight should have lain. And instead of taking this trimmer down for his blasphemies, I argued with him. A wave of self-doubt, unlike anything I had ever experienced before, hit me. I fought for what I assumed was the truth, but did not really know if I was right.

"We'll see," is all the young leader could say. He suddenly seemed strangely satisfied.

"I guess I was right," I murmured under my breath to Azael.

He seemed ill at ease in this tent city.

My mind switched gears immediately. "Do you have someone to go to?" I asked him, realizing, for the first time, that Azael had probably once been a resident of this city. "It has been a long while, but perhaps worth a look," I suggested, feeling for him. I did not know if he had a family I was keeping him from.

"I don't know," he said earnestly. "It's been so long."

"Then it is all the more important that you look," I said.

"I will think about it, master," he replied, still shifting uneasily in his saddle.

"I think you should," I replied, as the young trimmer beckoned us on. "I think you should," I repeated, thinking of Amee.

⌘ ⌘ ⌘

We left the roundabout, made for the far boulevard, and shortly afterward, turned down one of the tent city's many teeming capillaries. The tent city was surprisingly clean, certainly a contrast to the pungent odors of Heaven, filled with the excrement and trash of its citizens and animals. Eventually, we came upon a barn at the mouth of a particularly wide alleyway. It was a simple wooden structure. Though one of the only solid ones I had seen so far, it had been cleverly designed to be mobile. The young leader told us to leave our horses and assured us they would be properly watered and cared for. We left them, fairly certain that no matter what happened to us, the horses, at least, would be well tended. We continued on foot down one of the nameless alleys nearby. I was completely lost at this point and quite certain I would never be able to find my way back out. The clusters of people on the street began to thin out. Suddenly and unexpectedly, it had become eerily quiet.

We were led up to a tent like any other, except, perhaps, for its slightly larger size. Its only notable feature was its intricately woven tent flaps, made of very fine threading. The motif on them appeared to be that of an ancient city, distinctly powerful and strangely welcoming. Embroidered across the top and bottom of the weave were words formed from letters belonging to an alphabet I did not recognize. It was a beautiful script, worked out in golden thread, surrounded by ornate and unique designs. It was hard to believe I was looking at tent flaps. Our party, trimmer escort included, was utterly mesmerized. Simply clothed, but well-armed guards stood around the tent.

The old trimmer we had encountered on the burning fields stepped out of the tent, looking much as he had when we had last seen him. His name was Haures and he flashed me a friendly smile.

"My Lord," he said, greeting me as if we were old friends. He did the same to Azael. "Maalik will speak with you, Lucifer. Your bodyguard," he went on, looking at my angels, "are to be taken to another tent, where they will stay until such time as it is proper for you to return to them."

"I cannot accept that," Azael said, stepping forward.

No one moved. Haures did not seem in the least bit alarmed.

"No harm will come to your master, Captain," he said reassuringly.

"I have your word my angels will not be harmed," I reminded him.

Nothing had befallen us so far and I was beginning to hope we might actually be able to make our return journey home in one piece.

"Your angels will be unharmed." The affirmation came from someone inside the tent.

From beneath the tent flaps stepped an old man. Well, actually, at first I had thought he was old, but in some strange way, another look convinced me that my eyes had been playing tricks. I could not really tell how old he was. I was immediately taken with him. About my height, he was thin, but not wasting. Dressed all in white, his robes had clearly been made by far more skilled hands than our young escort's. Around his waist was a golden belt from which a single small, sheathed dagger hung. His face was open and he had a full head of wavy silver hair. He held his hands before him, clasped together. They were clean, strong, capable-looking. He was barefoot, but his feet seemed well cared for. "Noble" was the word that came to mind. It was all I could think of at the time. He looked so damned noble. Azael stepped back.

This trimmer and I looked each other in the eye. I immediately felt he was reading me, but at the same time, I felt I could read him too. I just did not know what he was reading and it unnerved me.

I turned to Azael. "Follow our escorts where they take you. I order you to obey their commands. You will be safe and we will see each other again shortly."

My angels were restless, but reassured by the tone of command in my voice. Azael looked at the gray-haired trimmer again, then looked at me and saluted. Each angel then saluted me in turn and walked off in the company of the escort, Azael out in front. The young leader and Haures followed them. I eyed the city standard, still in the leader's hand.

"They will be returned to you before you leave," the gray-haired trimmer said, gauging my concern.

I turned back to him. We were alone in the small courtyard before the tent. The guards had disappeared during our exchange. I could hear the wind in my ears, but the surrounding tents did not flap. I could smell the earth around me. My senses were suddenly wide open. I could find no explanation for this sensation.

"Are you Maalik?" I asked.

"Yes." He looked at me quizzically, studying me.

"Do we know each other?" I asked. It was such a strange feeling. A strange thing to say, I thought, once I heard my words. "I feel we have met before."

Maalik smiled. "We have, Ahriman, but you were very young then. Only an infant at the time. I knew you before everything."

"You know my given name?"

"Yes."

"But I do not remember you."

"That's true."

Before everything, I repeated silently. 'Everything' covers quite a lot of ground. *Before* I had come to power. *Before* I had sat and pondered my lot in life. *Before* I had plotted how to get what I wanted. I turned back again to watch, as my bodyguard disappeared into the city's maze of tents, not sure how I would find them, if I needed them.

"You and your angels will not be harmed," he assured me again.

"My captain," I said, indicating Azael. "He was a trimmer... outlander, when he came into my service," I stuttered. "I would ask your protection for him, in particular, while we are here. He is a good angel."

"No doubt," Maalik said, searching his mind for something. "No harm will come to him."

"I know it is an unusual request," I interjected cautiously, "but I would also ask that he be allowed to seek out his family. It has been more than an age since he has seen them."

"I will consider it," Maalik said sincerely.

"I believe you," I said. I think I actually did.

"But you do not know why you do," Maalik said, completing my thought. He seemed very sure he knew me. "Come inside," he invited, gesturing into the tent, "and we can speak comfortably. You had a long trip and I wager you did not expect to meet me today."

"No. No, I did not," I said, feeling inexplicably humbled. I chastised myself for not having adopted a more imperious stance with this trimmer the moment we met. "Okay, then," was all I could say.

With a gesture, he silently invited me to precede him into the tent, looking at me and smiling as entered.

⌘　⌘　⌘

"We have been waiting for you, Ahriman, hoping you would come here looking for answers one day. If I understand Haures correctly, it seems you came looking for answers to questions I had not intended you to ask, but that is all right too." Maalik poured us both water and handing me the goblet, said, "I will give you answers, even before you know you have questions." He gestured toward some chairs. "Sit down. Please."

I remember thinking there was no point in telling him I had no clue what he was talking about. I sat, my arms draped over the chair's armrests, and looked around the tent. My head was spinning. The wind had been in my ears, as I stood outside the tent, but now my ears were ringing of their own accord. I felt a bit nauseous. My pulse raced and my eyes darted from one corner of the tent to the other. There was not much to see. A small, but comfortable-looking bed, a desk holding a single unlit candle, burnt low, a few more comfortable-looking chairs, two or three candelabra, a small table with the remains of a meal and a glass pitcher of clear water, and a collection of overlapping rugs that covered the entire floor of the tent. This was certainly no throne room.

"Are you the leader here?" I asked, having completed my survey of the place.

"No," he replied simply.

I nodded in acknowledgment, not sure what, precisely, I should say next. Then I noticed the wall hanging.

It was as if my feet were suddenly planted on the ground, fixed and motionless. I cannot explain with any degree of clarity how moved I was by this simple decoration. It struck me at the very core of my being. It was a long tapestry, with several scenes carefully and meticulously woven into it. It read from left to right and stretched the entire length of the tent's backmost flaps. I had not noticed it when I first entered.

It featured a city of people, flanked on either side by winged guardians. Around the city stood verdant lands, with animals and birds carousing. Naked angels prayed to an adjacent forest. Above the city floated twelve angels. Each held a book in one hand and the index finger of the other hand aloft. They were clothed in white robes with golden belts, just like my host and my young escort from the battlefield. The city was abuzz with all sorts of activities, but each person and animal looked up to the Twelve with an expression of recognition. Not quite of love, but certainly of comfort. Some tended to their market shops, selling their wares—breads, meats, bottles of wine, manuscripts, trade tools. Others herded animals outside the city, seeking the shade of trees and resting by streams of clear water. The city itself was clean and white, towers topped with flags waving in the wind. The day around them was sparkling, light pouring down from the sky, embracing all in its warmth.

As my eyes traveled to the next panel, the same city seemed to lose the clear light of day; it had a gray and sullen look to it. Flags still fluttered from the tops of the city's towers, but the people were no longer settled and content. Instead, they appeared wretched, crushed by anxiety. The guardians who had flanked the city in the previous panel were shown, in this one, to be distracted from their duties and engaged in heated argument. The animals and birds of the forests were gone and the naked angels sat on the ground, covering themselves in shame and looking pensively up at the Twelve.

The Twelve were no longer standing together, overseeing the city as they had been before. There was now a stranger among them. On the far left stood one of the Twelve, book clutched in hand, but head bowed. Four of the Twelve were standing around him, heads also bowed, each holding their books closely, lost in thought, their expressions solemn and tense. On the far right stood this foreign figure, not one of the original Twelve. In his hand was not a book, but, rather, a rod aimed at the others across to the left. Around him knelt six of the Twelve, looking up at him in admiration. Around this group, at their feet, their once-revered books lay discarded. Each of these figures wore swords on their belts where, before, they had worn none. They did not appear angry, but determined and set. They were also focused, like the others on the left, but for entirely different reasons. Only one of the Twelve stood in the middle, apparently trying to decide in which direction to go, right or left. While his book was still in his hand, with his other one, he now clutched a sword. The sword had notches broken into the blade's edge and he wielded it in the direction of those with bowed heads. The book had been turned to face those surrounding the figure with the rod in hand. Confusion covered his face.

Looking at the next panel, I was bewildered by what I saw. The Twelve were no longer over the city; only the foreign figure who had been holding the rod stood there. His followers were putting to the sword those who had stood to the left in the previous panel. Blood flowed across the city. Fire licked the walls from out the windows of the once majestic towers. The scene was terrible to look upon. Angels were killing angels. The winged guardians no longer protected the city, but were now engaged in its plunder. The city's inhabitants were united only in their efforts to kill their fellow citizens, burn down the buildings, steal whatever valuables and goods they could, or flee the place. The surrounding lands and forests were also aflame. The confused one of the Twelve, who had brandished both sword and book in the previous panel, could be seen running away from the burning city. Around him were animals in flight, chased by fear of the hoards of dreadful folk streaming from the city's crumbling edifices. The people themselves were covered in burns and wild-eyed, as if possessed by some uncontrollable hunger or anger or fear.

⌘ ⌘ ⌘

"You find this interesting, do you?" Maalik asked.

"Yes," I said, unable to tear my eyes away from the scenes of destruction. "To be honest, I do not know what to make of it."

"It is history, Ahriman. Your history, though you may not know it."

I looked at him now.

"It is our history," he said. "Yours and mine."

"The City of God has never been sacked, if that is what you mean. It has withstood many attacks, but never have its walls been breached," I said, both pride and indignation in my voice.

I had worked my whole life to ensure that such a situation never came to pass.

"You are correct," Maalik said. "Indeed, the City of God has never been sacked. But you assume this is the City of God, Ahriman. It is not."

"What is this place, then? And how do you know me as Ahriman? I am Lucifer to you, trimmer."

"My name is Maalik and I do not offer you anything other than respect."

"Then why do you refuse to recognize my name?"

"Because Ahriman is your name. It is who you were." Before I could respond, he looked at the last panel. "What you see here, Ahriman, is a depiction of something that happened almost fourteen billion years ago. Before the universe came into being. Before almost everything you know...but it is not before your time."

"I am not that old! And I have always lived in the City of God."

"You have not always lived in that city and it has not always been the City of God."

"I have heard this before," I said, exasperated before I could even listen to the rest of this trimmer's story. "It was the language of the cell, if you know what I speak of, and I suspect you do. But never in all my time with them were those traitors able to show me proof of their claim being anything other than fiction. To their doom, they fabricated a story, a convenient story in support of those who would construct as broad a foundation as possible in order to gather the dispossessed and unite them against our Lord. It is the only way to put up a unified resistance, because there are few means as effective to bring disparate people together under one banner, to have them share something in common *other than* the Word. It is a fraud. A false path. A fallacy. And I am disappointed that the leader of my trimmer enemies has not sought to advance a more powerful argument than this one."

Maalik smiled. "As I said, I am not the leader here. And your reaction betrays you, Ahriman. You argue these things more to convince yourself than to make your point. Though you do not know why, you have felt for a long time that something was wrong with the picture your family, your army, your bureaucrats, your

God painted for you. You drove yourself to achieve. Your grand-father was driven too, but he never spurred you on himself. Your father is a self-serving coward and while that may have impelled you to achieve something utterly different, it was never he who urged you along that path. Your army wanted your time, your strength, and your blood, if need be, but it gave you little in terms of motivation. Your government ground you down, pushed you in the opposite direction. It wanted nothing more of you than for you to obey, to do what you were told, when you were told to do it. And since you became God's Seraph, what has God driven you to do? Root out sedition? Organize the unorganizable? Is this motivation, Ahriman? I ask you, have you ever been motivated by anyone other than yourself?"

"What does this have to do with why I am here? It has noth-ing to do with my soldiers or Gabriel." I should have stopped there. "It has nothing to do with the convenient stories you trim-mers, you traitors spout in order to support your seditious cause." I had blocked his thrust, but now moved to parry. "But to answer your question, what you say makes no sense. This is my existence. Those are the angels in my life, those you spoke of. The people I have. The organization or, rather, the civilization I live in. These people, these things, did not have the responsibility to move me in one direction or another. That is not how it works. They are driven by their base needs and in answering them, drive other an-gels to their own needs. My grandfather did not force or impel me in any direction, no. But he did inspire me to move forward by the examples he set. My father, the army, the bureaucrats. All the same. The examples they set or did not set motivated me. That is why I am where I am today. You are the sum of all the parts and none of this gets me closer to my purpose here now."

"You are right. I knew Jehoel," he said, ignoring my arguments. "Better than you could ever know him."

I was sure he could sense my guilt.

"You are here now for the same reason that you had delved deep into Jehoel's rebellion," he went on. "You want to know. You want to know why things are as they are. Of course, these angels and circumstances set you on a path, but you alone make your path. Your path is knowledge and with knowledge, Ahriman, you sometimes discover that what you stand upon was never really there to begin with."

"Let us stop skirting around the main issue," I said, growing more and more annoyed, "and focus back on why I am here."

"Go on," Maalik said.

"I am here to secure the freedom of any City soldier you may have taken prisoner and to take Gabriel back with me, if he is your prisoner," I said brusquely. "Assuming you have not already killed him."

"Okay," Maalik said, bemused. "You are right. I am too anxious to teach you what you came to learn. Let us talk of this first, then. Those City soldiers we captured will be released on your command." He looked at me for a moment. "If they wish to leave at all."

"Why were they not released before?" I was sure it was another game.

"They will be released, now that you are in our company. If it makes you feel better, think of it as suiting our purpose to keep them here until you arrived." He was pleased with himself. "Besides, it is more than an even trade, I think. Would you not agree? A few thousand soldiers for a Seraph of God."

I was struck by his mention of "a few thousand" and he anticipated my next question.

"You will know when they are free to leave," he assured me. "Believe me."

"Where is Gabriel?" I asked, now putting aside my concern for the prisoners. "One of your riders said you have his personal standard."

"We keep his standard safe here with us, yes, but Gabriel is not here among us. He was not taken prisoner and as far as I know, he was not slain on the battlefield, though not from any want of effort on our part. If you are missing your fellow Seraph, it is not of our doing."

He finished his water and began to pour some more. "Would you like some more?" he asked, gesturing to my full goblet.

"No," I mumbled, picking up the goblet. Having learned that Gabriel was not a prisoner, I felt the need to down the contents all at once. But as the liquid touched my lips, I realized immediately that it was not water after all.

"It is ambrosia," Maalik said, noting my surprise. "It used to grow wild throughout much of Heaven, even in Elysium. When God came to power, however, he saw to it that no common angel could have access to it and stole ambrosia from the city. It's availability has been restricted by his monopoly ever since." He checked himself. "Well, to put it correctly, I should say, it has been his monopoly for the residents of *your* city ever since. Ambrosia continues to grow wild in many places in Heaven. In Tartarus, especially." He looked harder at me. "But you know this. Your armies forage for it and die protecting it." He looked at his goblet. "God makes a simple flower worth the lives of many armies in order to stock his personal cellar."

He was right, but I was not really listening. My mind was abuzz. If I were to believe this Maalik, the prisoners would be released, Gabriel had neither been captured nor slain, and my own soldiers would not be put to death or mistreated. If Gabriel had escaped capture, why had he not returned to the City? He had had ample time to get back before I left. Where was he? My stomach began to knot. I had just delivered myself, a Seraph of God, into the hands of the trimmers in a fit of self-righteousness, in order to find our people, only to learn that Gabriel was somewhere out on his own. Whose trap had I fallen into? God's, Gabriel's, or my own? In leaving the City, I had assumed I would die either getting here or once I was taken. But that clearly was not going to happen. I was to be a hostage. Maalik could see me turning the possibilities over in my mind.

"So then," I said, ignoring his last comments altogether. "What is left? What will you do with me, seeing that I have already achieved everything I set out to?"

He sat down and looked at me. "Just what we have been discussing, Ahriman. We will give you a history lesson. We will give some true meaning to that drive that has motivated you all along. Soon, you will see that coming here has been the single, most defining moment of your entire life. Up to this point, at any rate."

Haures came into the tent. "Maalik, everything has been prepared."

"Good," Maalik said, rising to his feet. "Come, Ahriman. Haures will see you to your quarters. I am sure you will find everything you need there. Haures," Maalik said, turning to the other angel. "See to it that Ahriman's captain...his name...?" he asked, looking at me.

I hesitated.

"I promised you he would come to no harm. You believed me, remember?"

I huffed. "Azael. His name is Azael."

Maalik turned back to Haures. "See to it that Azael is permitted free movement throughout the city."

Haures's expression gave him away.

"So that he may search for his family," Maalik concluded.

"Yes, Maalik," Haures said obediently.

Turning back to me, Maalik continued, "Tonight, you will dine with our governing members. The rest of the Council is as anxious to meet you as I was. Of course, you can see your bodyguard before dinner, if you like. Haures will be your guide while you stay with us. Simply ask him for anything you may need."

I got up and looked from one trimmer to the other. I looked at the tapestry once again. Then silently, I followed Haures out. I am sure I overheard Maalik muttering his gratitude as I left the tent.

⌘　⌘　⌘

Haures led me to my own tent. It was not large, but more than sufficient for my needs. A single table, upon which sat several candlesticks, a box of candles, and some matches, stood at the center of the space inside. My bed was comfortable enough and essential toiletries had been provided. I had never been taken prisoner, but the hospitality shown me in this place was truly amazing by any standards. A young trimmer was stationed right outside my tent, with orders from Haures to follow my commands. Later, once I had cleaned myself up, Haures came back to fetch me.

"You've been provided fresh clothes, my Lord, yet you continue to wear the soldier's dress of your city. Might I suggest you change?" Haures said.

The young trimmer guard looked at me expectantly.

"I am Lucifer, Seraph of our Lord God," I declared. "I do not wear trimmer garb. You are my enemy and I am your prisoner. I will continue to wear this soldier's uniform, until I am released."

I could see frustration rising in Haures, but before he could get another word out, the young trimmer spoke.

"I will be most pleased to wash your uniform, my Lord," he said. He looked at Haures. "After he has returned from dinner, that is," he followed up apologetically.

Haures thought about this.

"Thank you," I said to the young trimmer. He smiled, but noting Haures's annoyance, resumed his position in front of the tent.

"It is unusual, but so be it," Haures acceded. "Let's not be late. First, I will take you to your bodyguard."

I followed him to the tent where my men had been accommodated and Haures left us together to share a few moments in private. "Do not be long, my Lord," he advised, before stepping out and leaving us alone. "They are waiting."

Azael and I stood outside the tent, watching him go. When he had disappeared, I turned to him and asked, "Have you been mistreated?"

"No, my Lord," Azael replied. "They've provided us with food and water. They allowed me to find my family," he continued. "They are well."

It was a bit awkward. He was not a slave, but he served me, bowing to my will.

"I...I..." I started.

"Thank you for allowing me this time. For asking them to help me. You were right. It was worth the look. But it is you I serve, my Lord. On my honor."

"They seem to be true to their word. So far." It was all I could think to say. "You are a good angel," I added.

"Yes, my Lord," Azael replied with a smile, as we stepped into the tent.

The rest of the bodyguard looked pensive, but seemed to be well taken care of.

"They say they have at least a thousand of our troops," I told them.

"What about Lord Gabriel?" Azael asked.

"They say he was not taken or killed."

The group stirred.

"Where is he, then?" Azael asked.

"Good question. I do not know." I let my gaze travel from one angel to the next. "What I do know is that I have put you all in terrible danger for no reason."

"The lives of your soldiers is no trivial matter," Azael said sternly.

I looked back at him and smiled. "I am glad to hear you say that, my friend," I said. "True, it is no trivial matter. They say the prisoners will be released, if I give the word."

"That's not likely," one of the angels said.

Azael shot him a look.

"Why do you say that, Jeqon?" I asked.

He was immediately unnerved.

"Go ahead," I encouraged.

Azael stared at him.

"If it is, indeed, thousands, my Lord, they are thousands that will be pressed back into the Lord's service."

The rest of the angels agreed.

"Letting them go means more death and destruction." Jeqon looked around to the others. "Why would these trimmers let that happen?"

"I cannot dispute that," I said. "But I looked into this trimmer's eyes as he made that promise and thought I was seeing the truth."

No one said a word.

"How have you been treated, then?" I asked, changing the subject.

Haures popped his head into the tent. "One more minute, my Lord."

"All right," I replied. I looked back at my angels. "And?"

"Everything is fine, my Lord," Azael said, clearly annoyed at Haures for addressing me as "my Lord". "They provided us with ambrosia."

"Yes. That point was brought to my attention too," I said, wiping my lips. "Maalik, the chief trimmer I spoke to, made it a political issue."

"We are fine, my Lord," Azael reassured me again. "We will wait for your return."

"Yes. I am to meet their governing body. A 'Council,' he called it, but somehow, I doubt it will be anything like the proceedings of our own Senate Council meetings."

Haures came into the tent. "It is time, my Lord," he said, bowing ever so slightly.

My angels watched him.

"Yes. It is time," I agreed.

CHAPTER
TWENTY-NINE

I walked out of the tent feeling comforted by the knowledge that no harm had come to my angels. I was even more relieved that Azael had returned to me. I was odious, compared to him, this trimmer who had become an angel, when doing so meant losing himself. But it was how things were and I had not been in a position to do anything else at that point. Azael was my captain. And he, along with my other angels, was genuinely concerned about the safety of our City's captured soldiers. They had extended their support to me, realizing our journey had not been in vain. Their trust in my mission was matched by Amee, the only other angel who seemed to think I was doing the right thing.

As I followed Haures through the maze of tents, I thought again about my attire. In my common soldier's garb, I was not dressed as a Seraph should be. I had cleaned myself up as best

I could before leaving my tent, but I would still not be presenting myself at my best, as I should in the capacity of our Lord's emissary. The clothes the trimmers had offered me were simple, but practical. There was nothing demeaning about wearing them. They were the same garments nearly everyone else seemed clad in that day. And to be honest, I could not recall an instance in the City's history, when someone had been put to death for being inappropriately attired, though I certainly would not have put it past God to issue such an order. Had I accepted the trimmers' offer of clothing, I might have put them more at ease for suggesting a certain open-mindedness on my part. Perhaps they would have been more inclined to lower their guard. Open resistance was not likely to get me very far. Resistance to their overtures was what they expected from us and I chastised myself for not having considered welcoming their gesture when I had the chance. It would have put them off-balance. Frankly, I did not know whom I was about to meet, but if Maalik was as senior in the hierarchy as he seemed to be, I would have to be as sharp as I could be and keep my mouth shut long enough to learn something.

I felt ready, but not quite sure what I was ready for. My whole life had been built around order. Order in my schoolwork, order in the army, order in my job, and order in the City. The central focus of that order had been beaten into my brain from childhood: love of God and preservation of His society. The trimmers were the single biggest threat to the safety and security of our society. They raided our lands, attacked us, and killed our animals and our people. From the earliest times, our City had lived with the fear of what was out here in the outlands and what the trimmers were planning. Their threats forced us into a constant state of preparedness, influenced how we organized our armies, and dictated how we managed our economy. God saw to the City's defenses and its armies. And we were told our armies had always been victorious. But what of that? Zoan had spoken to me about the massacre of his soldiers and the routing of his army, but you could find no mention of that military disaster in any of our history books. During my own time in the army, I had been involved in many skirmishes, but nothing that matched the magnitude of the battles Zoan had described. Nothing that came close to what I had witnessed out on those scorched plains. How many times had we met trimmers in battle? How many times had City soldiers fallen in battle? No one knew. Even I did not know and I was God's Seraphim. What did that mean? Was God actually the nasty little sot I had seen that night in the study? Was He anything less than what I had been brought up to believe? That night, that wretched night in His chambers was burned into my brain now. The God who protected the people, whom we all loved, who made us what we were, curled up in a slobbering ball, whining like a child on the floor!

I had to be careful. I was in their power now. Those very same beings I had been raised to despise and hate. Those who, given half the chance, would tear our City down, brick by brick. I kept repeating, "Preserve our society," in my head, as we wound our way around. If things were as the trimmers wished them to be, the order I had striven so hard to preserve would break down and give way to chaos. All that I had worked and lived for would be swept away forever.

But I was here now. I had gone into the outlands to face our enemies. Into Tartarus itself, looking for them. God had not stopped me. No other citizen had ever done what I was doing now. Parlaying with trimmers. Bargaining with them for the lives of ordinary angels. Why had He allowed me to go? Was it because He suspected that I was not likely to return? If what Amee had claimed was right and God needed me to finish Man, before even considering disposing of me, He could not afford losing both Gabriel and me at the same time. With both of us gone, Man would never be completed and the fulfillment of God's dream would be indefinitely delayed. I was that necessary to His purpose. So why had He let me go? For all He knew, Gabriel might be dead. Or did He know something with greater certainty than I did?

My short time in Apsatsus had proved to me that the formula was still flawed. As I became disoriented in the maze of tents through which I was led, I kept hearing the words of that dirty sergeant in my head: "Fear is in every animal's gut, but it's

knowing and calculating the risks that will make Man a Man."
He was right. Mere brutes would not do. But that was what
God wanted. Intellect, free will—these were gifts to which
only angels were entitled. But denied those complexities in
his composition, Man would be nothing more than a beast of
burden. A most cleverly designed beast of burden, no doubt,
but nothing more than that. Automatons built for political
purposes.

Either way, I thought, these trimmers are looking for information and they know I will be doing the same. I must not let on
about anything. I must be wary at all costs.

Finally, we halted before a giant tent. Bewildered by the tent
city's labyrinth and deep in my own thoughts, I had not noticed
it as we approached. It stood much taller than the surrounding
tents, with thick wooden columns supporting its massive circumference. Thick ropes tied the tent down, each secured to the
ground with large silver spikes. A spire rose from the tent's lower
awning, pushing up into the night sky. From a flag post atop the
spire fluttered a banner emblazoned with an image of the city I
had seen on the intriguing tapestry in Maalik's tent earlier in the
day. Around the main entrance of the tent milled white-robed
trimmers, talking animatedly with each other. Each wore a silver
belt from which swung a small dagger. None wore armor or carried the leather satchels I had noticed on just about every other
trimmer in the camp that day. When they noticed my arrival in
the courtyard, a sudden hush fell upon them. In unison, they focused their attention on me. We stared at each other for the long-
est of moments, crowds of hundreds at one solitary angel. One
staring back at hundreds. I did not know what to do, so I nodded
an acknowledgement. The mass of trimmers all bowed together
in response.

"Come. You are a most welcome guest this evening," Haures
said, motioning for me to move on and enter the tent.

"No doubt," I said, looking away from the crowd of trimmers
to the tent's lofty spire. Dangerous, however, was the word that
crossed my mind, as I proceeded inside, ever so slightly acknowledging each individual in the crowd as I passed.

⌘　⌘　⌘

Inside, it was wonderfully warm and inviting. Casting a quick glance around, I could see garlands draping the walls, giving the tent the feel of an outdoor garden. Though considerably less ornate, it immediately reminded me of Gabriel's house, where I had first met Amee. Hand-woven rugs entirely covered the earthen floor. Candelabras of varying heights and sizes radiated light across the expanse of the tent so that no spot was obscured in darkness. Behind a long table sat a group of trimmers, cleanly dressed and quietly talking among themselves. I felt as if I had just arrived in the polar opposite of my first encounter with the cell; here, the trimmers bathed in soft light, there, the Fallen shrouded darkness. The table was covered in fine linen and set with exquisite silverware and glass. I judged they would soon be eating well. A number of servants stood close by. Facing the long table was a much smaller table, suited to accommodating one guest. Me.

Everyone immediately rose at my entry. Their faces were wiped clean of all expression and again, there was an uncomfortable moment of silence as we eyed each other. I noticed Maalik standing among them. Haures motioned for me to sit at the small table. I broke off my gaze from the assembly and strode over to the table.

How many trimmers had I killed, I pondered. How many of these people's friends and families had been affected? Had the young leader of trimmers from the burning fields been right? Was I not largely responsible for their situation, the very reason they were "trimmers" and not "angels"? They were rebels and outlaws, because I had helped God make them so. And now I was before them, their prisoner. Their willing prisoner. I stood at the table and turned to look back at the assembly. In my tent, I had tried to prepare myself for this moment. I had tried to prepare myself for any inquisition prompted by my bold and reckless actions. I doubted myself, though, when it came to pain. My mind suddenly flashed back to the angels I had ordered broken over the years.

How could it be that I had never once considered the possibility of facing torture myself? I cursed myself now. It was a lapse on my part, but that failing was also symptomatic of a certain arrogance that I silently swore never to forget. Assuming, of course, I had the opportunity to live up to my oath.

One of the assembly spoke.

"We have no leader here," he said. "We have this Council, as we did in the old days. When you speak to us, know that you are speaking to everyone in this camp. Know that your actions and words tonight will define how we, as a people, deal with you in our midst. You will be treated as you treat us. It's a simple rule, really, the only rule we live by."

"Who are you?" I asked. It was a simple question. I looked at Maalik expectantly. "I came here of my own accord," I began. "Do not forget this. We have each other's mutual audience this evening, because I wished it so. You know who I am. If we are to treat each other the way we rightly should, it seems fitting that you tell me with whom I am speaking."

"You are right, of course," the speaker said, without introducing himself. "We all know who you are, Seraph. Protector. Captain General. The one who stands above all of God's angels."

His sarcasm did not strike me as a propitious note on which to begin our interview, but Maalik interrupted this trimmer before he could continue.

"We are the Council of Twelve, the governing body of what you, in the City of God, call the 'trimmers.' My brother, Matel, here means no disrespect," Maalik said, shooting Matel a clearly offended glance. "It is as difficult for us to speak with you, as it must be for you to speak with us."

"I doubt that," I said.

"Have no illusions, Ahriman, and let me be clear. We live, as Matel has just described. We treat others as they would treat us. You and your people have hunted us down for billions of years. You serve God, who chased us from our homes and made us outsiders. You built walls to keep us out, raised armies to keep us on the run, passed laws to brand us as criminals. For no reason, other than the fact that we live unto ourselves, unbeholden to the Word of God. We committed no crime, other than to do what we think is right rather than what he demands of us." His tone was stern, but gave no hint of apparent condescension. "And now you are before us," he went on. "But you are right. You are before us of your own accord and, as such, are protected here and will be treated in the same fashion as anyone of this city would be. You will, of course, be subject to our laws and our ways while you are here."

"While I am here? Do you mean to suggest that I may leave?"

"You will be allowed to leave when we are both content with our mutual learning. We have much to learn from each other."

"That I do not doubt. You say we have known each other, though I have no memory of you. What are you people? Why are you here?"

Matel sat down, his gaze moving back and forth along the length of the table as if trying to ascertain if others had understood what I meant. Even Maalik was confused by my question. The assembly members began to murmur to each other.

"As I said, we are here because of you. We are what we are because of you," Maalik repeated.

"Because of me? I have nothing to do with your treachery. Your rejection of God's Word. Do not blame me. I did not put you here."

"Indeed you did. With every breath you take, you send us farther and farther away," Matel said, clearly astonished by my protestations.

"You did this to yourselves," I persisted. "I am not to blame for your plight, though I admit to having expended much of my energy hunting you down."

"We are here because of you, Ahriman," Maalik said once more. "Certainly, you must know this. You, of all angels."

"Me, of all angels? What do I have to do with *your* choices? I sit here tonight, a Seraph of our Lord God, but no different from any other loyal citizen of the City of God."

My words provoked a fresh outburst of murmurs.

"And if you are to treat me with respect," I carried on, "it might be better for you to address me by my chosen name. I am Lucifer. 'Ahriman' is a name I no longer go by."

"You were Ahriman to us. We do not mean to be disrespectful, when we use it. In a way, it is meant to bring you back to us."

"What are you saying, trimmer!" I blurted out, already losing my temper. This was certainly not what I had expected.

The Council began to collectively grumble in their seats.

"If you wish to treat me with respect, as you say, then you will address me by my proper name."

"Fine, then," Maalik conceded, exhaling audibly. "It is because of you, Lucifer, that we live as outlaws, as trimmers. Yet you deny any knowledge of this reality?"

"What am I to know? I am the son of Angra, grandson of Zoan. I am God's Seraphim, Lucifer. This is who I am and everything I have done in my life was done in one of those three capacities."

"You do not know," Maalik said matter-of-factly. He looked at the rest of the Council with a stunned expression. Then he shook his head in sudden understanding, while the rest remained confused. "He was never told," he muttered. He looked back at me. "You are a loyal citizen of the City of God, then?"

"Of course I am. Everything I have done has been for the greater glory of the City and the greater glory of God, the One."

Maalik walked up behind Matel and put his hand on his shoulder. "See, we have already learned something from our brief encounter. He has never been told. And why would he have been? Why would God have told him the truth?"

"What are you talking about?" I asked in furthering agitation. "God is the One. He teaches all His children what is right and good. He teaches us to love Him and our greatest glory is praising God and His holiness." Though I had been assailed by doubt in the time following the massacre of our army, my loyalty suddenly flared with a violence that shook me, flooding my entire being. "It is your lack of faith that defines you," I continued, looking around at the confused table of trimmers. "It is your lack of faith that makes you outlaws. God loves all His children, but punishes the disobedient, the faithless, those who would do Him and His children harm."

"We are saved, brothers," Maalik said, ignoring me.

The Council's murmuring stopped. Everyone looked at him. Of all the people present in the tent, stomachs grumbling, he was the only one unperturbed by our short, confusing exchange.

"We are saved," he repeated. "He does not know. In keeping the truth from him, God has given us an advantage we had never even considered. He needs to be taught. He needs to be turned."

Suddenly, a trimmer to the left of the table spoke out. "That's impossible!" he exclaimed. "This angel is our enemy. He's always been our enemy. He's done nothing but bring death and destruction on us for millions of years. And now we coddle him and treat him like an honored guest. Even if he does learn the truth, there is no assurance that he will take up arms against God."

His words shocked me, but Maalik chimed in, "He came to us."

"So what? We have a chance to stop things right here, right now. You know that the only other competent angel among them is Gabriel. And we've just given him the bloody nose that no one will forget in a hurry. God has no backup plan. He's too self-centered, too narrow-minded to think of something like 'succession.' There's no succession with God. There is only power. And obedience."

"That might be true," Maalik conceded, "but you speak as if this will solve everything. We do not know what He is thinking. We do not know what He will do with Gabriel. This has happened before and we were wrong. We have another chance now." Maalik looked at me again. "Fortune has given us Zoan's grandson. What could be more fitting?"

I was lost. I stopped listening too closely and sat down at my table, eyeing the ambrosia. Was it this lot I gave myself up for, I thought shamefully. I had exploded in rage at my Lord, blasphemously, in what appeared to be a moment of His weakness. I had come here, only to be lectured by a bunch of nonsensical and ranting fools, teetering in the face of their first real military achievement in a hundred millennia. Whatever fears I had harbored about torture or pain disappeared. This is why they are trimmers, I thought. They are directionless, leaderless, and stupid.

After several more minutes of argument, Maalik was able to regain some calm. "Ahri..." He corrected himself. "Lucifer, your life has been the start of our existence and will be its finish too. We are guilty of misjudgment. We misjudged you and we misjudged God. This was meant to be a cordial dinner, not a venue for one combatant facing the other, exchanging venom, while we decided how to profit from your surrender. But in light of this extraordinary revelation, I perceive the first weakness in God's plan. It is a weakness we can exploit—together."

"Maalik, or whatever your name is," I butted in. "We are enemies, as you say, and we will remain so. I will not help you exploit anything at all. I will be your prisoner, as long as it suits you and your rabble here," I said, pointing to the table of trimmers. "Remember this, because it is very important: I serve God and I will remain His faithful servant to the end. Meanwhile, I will drink your ambrosia and eat your food and consider what is best for me and my angels."

"You are a faithful servant of God. I can see that, Lucifer," Maalik responded. "Your title and your name say it all. Your faith is admirable and, frankly, I am not in the least surprised at your loyalty. But ask yourself a simple question: why did you come here?"

"For my angels."

"No. No, you came here because of weakness. God's weakness." Maalik looked at me intently. "Yes, you hear the blasphemy in my words, but what's different this time is that you've felt the blasphemy, because you have considered this truth yourself."

"God has no weaknesses!" I shouted. "He is all good and all powerful. Only I am weak and I will always be His loyal servant."

"No, Lucifer. You are here *because* of his weakness. His grand plans. His stab at personal glory. You did not come here to glorify God. You came here out of mercy. Mercy for your angels. That is your weakness. And you well know God has no mercy like that."

"I came here for my angels and for the glory of the realm..."

"Please!" Maalik shouted, his expression suddenly changing to one of anger.

I could tell I was doing something right.

"You know this makes no sense. If you are God's weakness, then God has a weakness. You came here, because you are different from God. You seek something different, just like your grandfather did before you."

"What do you know of my grandfather?" I said venomously. "You are a liar!"

"We do not lie here. Zoan and I were friends."

"That is not true!"

"It is true. Billions of years ago, he sat there, where you are sitting now."

"That is impossible! That never happened." Suddenly, I was doubting myself again.

"You know it is true, Lucifer. Surely, your grandfather had told you stories. You heard stories from Jehoel. You have..."

"You knew Jehoel?" I asked, a strange feeling of anticipation rising within me.

Maalik smiled. "We were brothers," he replied, a fleeting expression of pain passing over his features. "You have heard stories from God himself about your grandfather. How great an angel he was."

"What do you know about it, trimmer?"

"I knew Zoan, because I led the army that defeated him," Maalik replied, ignoring my insult. "And I brought him here. And he listened to what I had to say. And he cursed me and praised his God. And he listened. And he learned. And he led us. Holding us together and keeping you safe. But when he left us, our plans died."

"He never told me that. He told me of his defeat and of his relationship with Jehoel and how he had kept books he had taken from the enemy he escaped." I knew I was letting too much of the truth leak out.

Maalik smiled again. "Zoan was always a good storyteller. He told you partial truths, Lucifer. I do not claim to know why. Maybe he came to truly reject the faith he had received from us. Or maybe his love for you made him unwilling to risk your life for a political movement. Whatever it is, *you* have clearly never been told the truth. And you need to know the truth. That will be our mission while you are here. You will listen. My brother, down at the other end of the table, advocates killing you," he said, pointing to the portly trimmer who had recommended my execution. "This would weaken God for sure, but not enough to make things right again. You would become a martyr, another rallying point for God, more powerful than the one he had made by exploiting Zoan. We will not play into God's hands again, for he may be ruthless and cruel, but very rarely makes the same mistake twice."

"You can talk and talk and talk all night, trimmer, but you will not confuse me with stories or overtures about my family."

"No, you are right, Ahriman," Maalik said, reciprocating my lack of courteousness. "We will not try to persuade you with stories. We will show you. Show you how the City of God used to be a government of the people, ruled by the people, for the benefit of the people. How the Council of Twelve ruled the city as the people's representatives for billions of years. How your arrival forever changed things, before the rise of Yahweh and the destruction of the City and our exile."

"You dare speak His name!" I said in a hiss.

I was truly shocked to hear God's name spoken aloud. Even during my own blasphemous outbursts, I had never once considered speaking His name. In fact, I had never once considered saying His name to anyone. Anytime. Ever.

"It is just a name, *Ahriman*," he said. "Like you, God shed his true name when he came to power, as if by doing so, he could hide his evil acts. Once he had overthrown the city and slaughtered its rightful rulers, he was not Yahweh anymore, but 'the Lord God.' How a simple trick of psychology can be so effective! But we endured. Now our Council is run by beings of lesser stature than those who had once ruled the city, but they have equally stout hearts. Ruling in the place of the true and rightful beings. God's true name is sacred to you, but to us, your name is sacred. You and Yahweh are brothers. You and I are brothers. But now, we are the only ones left."

"Blasphemer!"

"Yes. In Yahweh's eyes."

"Blasphemer!"

"What else do you have?" Maalik asked, taunting me. "Is that it? Is that all you really think? That is not the brain of someone thinking, Ahriman. The brain of someone capable of thought would realize that God had sacrificed an army and that you had the power to save those who could be saved. Ahriman. Lucifer. You can save everyone. Everyone. And you do not even know it."

"I call you a blasphemer, yes. There needs to be order in the universe and God offers that order. What can *you* offer? Dinner? A glass of ambrosia? A tent city of straggling trimmers? What does any of that amount to, when compared to the greatness of God?"

"The 'greatness of God,' you say. Tell me, what has God done that is great? Tell me, what have you seen? Has he saved your people from starvation? From poverty? Has he kept the people happy? Has he waged war and killed hundreds of thousands of angels—children, many of them—in the process? Has he ruined your water, your forests, your City? Tell me, Lucifer, what makes God great?"

"Faith. Faith makes Him great."

"Faith does not put food on the table, Lucifer," Maalik said gravely. "You know that. You had faith in God, when you ran your miserable government office. And where did it get you? Faith did not put you where you are now, Seraph. Deceit, lies, transgressions. Murder," he said pointedly. "That is what got you where you are now. Faith is something you can believe in. Tell me, what do you believe in?"

I was silent. An image flashed in my mind: Jehoel's head falling into the executioner's basket. Impaled on a spike on the walls of the City, along with those of the rest of the conspirators. Blistered in the sun. Stinking and covered in flies. All the remorse I had tucked away so many years ago. It was for the best. I had made it. I had become a powerful angel and made things better. The words seemed to fall from my lips, as if of their own accord. "I made things better."

"Maybe. *You* made things better. Did God?"

"I am His instrument."

"You are your own. You are as beautiful as God."

"Because He made me so."

"No, Ahriman. You are unique and you are as God is."

"Blas..."

"Yes, yes, 'blasphemer.' Give me something more. You have brains. Use them. What does your head tell you, because I bet, if you let it, it will offer you a smarter version of the message your heart gives you."

"I do not listen to my heart anymore," I said dejectedly. But I should not have done so.

"If that were true, it would be a shame. But I know that to be wrong. Your head did not tell you to go into the outlands and give yourself up to your enemy for the safety of your angels. There was no benefit in it for you. No accolades to win in making such a sacrifice. Your heart told you to come here."

"It was my mistake, my weakness."

"It was God's weakness and it is your salvation. And I am betting it will be our salvation too."

"I do not understand." Though our conversation had lasted for only a few minutes, I felt worn out.

"You are one of us. You, me, Yahweh are the last of our kind."

"I still do not understand."

"And you will not. At least, not right now. Suffice it to say that when the Council of Twelve came to ruin at the hands of God, you were meant to lead us. And because God did not let that happen, the City of Heaven came to ruin. It became the City of God."

I had nothing further to say. I felt weaker than I ever had. I had not endured pain. I had faced a challenge to my faith and was not sure I had come through successfully. I knew God. I knew what He was. I do not like to admit it now, but it was that chink that would open me later. Once I had doubted God, I doubted everything. My only consolation was that the doubt I had experienced was of my own doing, only deepened by the words of these strangers. At the time, I had hoped that my doubt would be dispelled, that the hole in my faith would be filled, making me strong again, like I used to be in the beginning, when it had all made sense. Strong in my faith, in my devotion to my Lord, the City, and my family.

We spoke no more that night. I ate in silence, as the Council members spoke animatedly among themselves. I did not understand it then, but I must say, as I look back now, it is a happy recollection. Maalik was right. As it turned out, my doubt would lead to my ruin. And my salvation.

⌘ ⌘ ⌘

"You spent your whole life trying to get to God. Why do you think that is?"

It was the hundredth day of questioning. Or at least it seemed that way. It was not painful so much as annoying. It was as if I were back in primary school again, learning how to read, write, respect my elders, and love God. Only now, the curriculum was entirely about how to hate God. And it was interminable. I did not want to believe what was being taught. In truth, I could not believe it, even if I wanted to, for it would be tantamount to admitting my whole life was a lie. And that was something I could not bear to consider.

"You know, I was speaking literally, when I said I was prepared to face torture," I answered mockingly.

Maalik just looked at me. Other trimmers silently transcribed everything that was said. I could hear the scratching of their quills against the parchment. When I stopped speaking, they paused. When I spoke again, they would scratch, scratch, scratch away. It was maddening. Every now and again, I would say something completely off the wall, just to see if they would transcribe it. They did. If I could just talk and talk, I would not have to hear the scratching anymore. I leaned back in the chair and pushed the palms of my hands into my eyes and rubbed.

"Oh," I sighed. It was all I could get out.

"I want to know, Ahriman. Only parts of your life are known."

"It seems to me your spies are nearly equal to my own," I quipped. "So how could that be?"

"Anyone can get to know the angel who uncovered a plot against God after shrugging off the yoke of the bureaucratic ranks," Maalik continued unabated. "It has been written. You struggled so long for change. It is a great headline. God is great, if at nothing else, in the creation and perpetuation of propaganda and lies. Anyone can know that you took the reins of government and streamlined the city. Anyone can know that you and Gabriel are God's greatest angels. Blah, blah, blah. But not just anyone can know the angel you are. How do you expect to inspire and raise the generations of citizens, when the questions everyone is interested in asking remain unanswered? Even worse, unasked?"

"Maybe it is the mystery of it all that makes them believe," I said, continuing to rub my palms into my eye sockets. "Maybe if I pushed hard enough," I thought, "I could knock my brain out and end my suffering."

Scratch, scratch, scratch.

Maalik sat quietly for a moment, thinking. When I finally unglued my hands from my eyes, his face wore another of those enlightened expressions.

"That's it, Ahriman! You put your finger right on the crux of it all. 'The mystery of it all,' is exactly the impression God wants to convey in all his doings. He makes us want to believe, so that we'll do his will."

"His will is all that matters," was my reflexive response.

"Yes, but why do you think that? Why have you spent your whole life trying to be closer to God?"

"It just is."

"That is that 'faith' talking again! But you are a rational angel. You believe what you can see. Why else would you have bucked your way out of the bureaucracy and made your own way in the world? Do you not see, Ahriman? That is why God needs you. You are too dangerous not to be on his side."

"Lucifer," I said exasperatedly. "My name is Lucifer and I am no different from any other citizen."

"You do not actually believe that. Think about all the angels you encountered who made a dent in your life. Your father. He is not the 'average citizen,' is he? Long before you rose to power, the city's elite knew your father was a criminal who fed on the system."

"He is no different from you or me," I said sadly. "He just has fewer natural inhibitions."

"Again, you do not actually believe that. You would not have spent so much time trying to be so like your grandfather, if you truly believed that about your father."

He had a point. I must admit that even today, I admire the effort Maalik went to in torturing me with that truth.

"My grandfather was a great angel."

"I know," Maalik said. He looked at me. "I know."

He believed it. Without another remark, he motioned to the scribes and left. The session was over. The scribes collected their articles and hurried out after Maalik.

I leaned back in my chair, a sigh of relief inadvertently escaping from the depths of my chest. I laughed to myself. "I guess I *am* being tortured," I said out loud.

I looked at the top of my hands as I considered my exchange with Maalik. Though I was a prisoner of the enemy, my hands were clean and well cared for. I was treated with nothing but the greatest respect. I looked down at my boots. Also clean and well tended. I had the young guard outside my tent to thank for that. I looked around my tent. It was warm and well stocked with anything I needed. Lamps were properly wicked and trimmed. The couches and tables I had requested had been brought immediately and arrangements had been made for adequate reading light. Many parchments and quills had been provided for my personal use. I had written a little, just to see if anyone would examine what I had written. Nothing. In many ways, I felt more at home than I had in years. More at home than in my own palace. The attendants here were polite and attentive, motivated not by fear, but devotion. Servants in my own quarters, in Gabriel's quarters, in any senior angel's quarters in the City lived and died at the whim of their lord. I had watched God sentence many a servant to death for nothing more than looking the wrong way. They did your bidding, but solely out of fear, though that did not stop my own servants from snooping around my home, looking for information to take back to God. I may have been in the Order of the Seraphim and Captain General of the Secret Police, but God's fear of intrigue and dissent held no bounds.

I looked at the young trimmer standing in my tent's entranceway.

"Do you need something, my Lord?" he asked immediately, noticing my gaze.

"No." I thought for a moment. "No, thank you. Tell me, how old are you?"

"Seventeen, my Lord."

"How did you come to be my porter?"

"It is my honor, sir." He hesitated for a moment. "I am the son of Haures, my Lord, and he is at your disposal."

"I see. Son of Haures. What is your name? I have been here for what seems an interminably long time and yet I have never asked you your name."

"It is no matter, my Lord," he said hesitantly.

"It is not much of a matter, but a matter, all the same," I replied.

"Ukobach, my Lord."

"Are you not a soldier, Ukobach? Have you not been trained to kill the soldiers of God?"

My question clearly compounded his uneasiness and he looked around the tent, as if seeking safety.

"Yes, my Lord," he finally replied, "but I have not fought in any battle. We are forbidden from engaging with the enemy. From fighting, my Lord, until we are adults."

"Why is that? Do you not want to fight?"

"That's the law, my Lord, and yes, I do want to fight. Young angels should respect each other first and only then should they consider how to resolve issues of life and death."

The answer was both perfectly reasonable and totally unreasonable to me.

"I want to fight, my Lord," he said, looking me straight in the eye for the first time. He paused. "But I don't look forward to taking another angel's life."

"Are you afraid for your own life?"

"No sir." He was resolute and speaking the truth. "It would be an honor to die to protect my people."

"Would you kill me, if you had the chance?" I gave him a stony look.

"No, my Lord."

"And why is that? Does it not contradict what you have just told me?"

"On the field of battle, we would clash and fate would determine who came away victorious. But when we sit together, face-to-face, we are one. Even if you don't agree with me or with what I'm saying."

It was too deep for a such a young angel. By Ukobach's age, I had already finished secondary school and was preparing for my first tour in the army. I had looked forward to killing. Zoan's reputation had, indeed, been a big one to live up to. But this boy was thinking of possibilities, not reactions. At his age, I had done what I was told. This angel, but a boy, was thinking for himself.

"Interesting," I replied.

Ukobach bowed and stepped out of the tent.

I put my hands behind my head and looked up at the eves of the tent. Why did I believe in God? It was a good question. It was a nice tent.

⌘　⌘　⌘

I spent a lot of time walking around the tent city. I was allowed to go wherever I pleased, so long as I had trimmer escorts, one of whom was almost always Ukobach. I was at leisure to see Azael and my angels. They were well looked after and received the same care that I did. No better and no worse. I gave Azael permission to see his family when he was not on duty.

When I walked the tent city, I encountered many people, but no one ever intruded on me. Nor did anyone ever speak to me unless I spoke with them first. Everyone was polite and answered any questions I had. They were, in fact, pleased to see me. Pleased to speak with me, though it may only have been my inquiring into the cost of an apple or street directions I had sought. I noted riders coming in and out of several gates around the tent city. Most were soldiers, but not all.

For the most part, trimmers went about their daily business. They did not seem the ferocious beasts or even the scared rats we had been told they were. They were people, "citizens" of a ragamuffin city, yes, but clearly dedicated to the preservation of their livestock, their families, and their way of life. They ate, drank, spoke, and relaxed as any angel might. Any angel of the City of God.

I spoke with Ukobach often, though he was never completely at ease with me. We spoke of his growing-up years and my curiosity as to what the younger generations of trimmers were being taught never flagged.

"Freedom is the highest of all our virtues," Ukobach said frequently. "We would die to defend the rights of our fellow citizens."

We strolled through one of the many markets that dotted the tent city.

"To answer your question, my Lord," he continued, "it is what we all hold most dear."

"To whom do you owe this 'freedom'? Is it because you defy the rule of the Lord or is there some other meaning?"

Trimmers did not often speak of God. That was understandable, given His determination to wipe them out. But this omission stood in stark contrast to the words used by the inhabitants of the City of God. "God" was part of our daily vocabulary. So much of the City's life was built around the threat of trimmer invasions, trimmer attacks on our settlements, the protection of the City against the threat of destruction posed by trimmers. The City's defenses were there to protect us, we were told. The

City's armies were constantly conscripted to defend us, we were informed. The City's natural resources constantly farmed to sustain us, we were persuaded to believe. These were our Lord's words. The "Word." He had put these things before us and so we spoke of Him often.

"We owe it to ourselves," Ukobach replied. And then he seemed to become a bit uneasy. "We take pride in our freedom, when compared to the tyranny of your city. We live by our own rules and are not beholden to any single ruler. Our rules are simple. We do what is right to our fellow citizens, because that is what they would do to you."

"But 'right' is not intrinsic. It is not an objective reality. Are there not instances of injustice here? It cannot always be as you describe."

"There is injustice everywhere, but the injustice perpetuated upon our people by the likes of your people unifies us and make us stronger."

"Stronger? How so?" I asked, testing him.

"Stronger in that we've learned to depend on ourselves. Stronger in the bonds of brotherhood we share with our fellow citizens, knowing that the angel to the right or left of you will defend your freedom, as you would defend your own."

He paused in his stride and I turned to look back at him. He called himself an angel.

"Much as you yourself have done, my Lord," he went on. "You came out here to protect your angels, even if those angels are dedicated to the evils of your lord. You sacrificed yourself so that others would live. Hence our interest in you. You did what we have only seen our own people do. And it makes us wonder where we all went wrong."

Before I had a chance to ask him what he meant, Haures and Maalik came up through the crowd. Both looked grave. Haures summoned Ukobach with a gesture and the boy went to him immediately. A good son, I thought, as I watched them together. They spoke quietly, as Maalik approached me.

"We need you to return to your tent now, Ahriman," he said. "The city must move at once. You will be met at your tent shortly with a new escort. You will cooperate in this now." His tone was urgent and I could sense fear in him.

"I understand. I will do as you ask," I said. I had no intention of resisting his orders.

"You did not tell us anything about another offensive being planned," Maalik said, looking at me earnestly.

He seemed to think that I would tell him of our armies' movements of my own free will. For a moment, I felt shame. The feeling took me by surprise, because it implied a kind of guilt on my part for not having shared information with him that I was, rightfully, expected to withhold as a soldier of God.

"After the defeat we just suffered," I said, "I did not think God had the resources to mount an offensive, whatever be its scale."

I thought about it for a moment. I looked at Haures and Ukobach. The older trimmer was looking at his son with a kind, but grave expression. Ukobach's head was bowed. Clearly, he was disappointed about something. Haures slapped him on the back and Ukobach made a quick bow in my direction. Then he made his way through the crowds, taking with him the contingent of trimmers who had been escorting me.

I looked back at Maalik. "They are not planning to launch an offensive against this place," I told him. "It is too far out in the wasteland to be deemed safe. Too far from their lines of communication and supply." I pondered over it again. "And even if that were not the case, the burning fields would make them think twice about advancing without reinforcements." No matter who was leading them, Michael or someone else, fear would grip them as they came upon the scene of our military disaster and witnessed what was left of the carnage. "They are headed for the Forks at Apsatsus." I was sure of it.

"Why?" Maalik asked. "It is nothing but a watering hole. You have little provision there."

I did not flinch. I had trained myself not to, when talking about Apsatsus.

"I do not know, but if you have detected any movement, that is where they are heading," I only half-lied. But I had given way too much away already. "I am sure of it."

Maalik looked at me. He believed me. I was telling the truth. Sort of. It felt good.

"Get ready," he said. "We are moving."

CHAPTER THIRTY

I hurried off to my tent and began my preparations to leave. It was exciting and frightening at the same time. I had only been here a few weeks, but in that time, I had witnessed a great many extraordinary things that had touched me to the core. I had been exposed to a bit of history I had never known of or otherwise rejected as an outright lie. I had seen a fully functional, but divided Council, debating the future and granting me nearly complete freedom and a certain respect, despite my status as a Seraph of God and my history of violence against these people who were now my hosts. I had been allowed to rescue what was left of my City's army and guaranteed their safe passage home.

With God's armies moving toward Apsatsus, the City of God would be nearly undefended. God had seen to it that Gabriel's destruction was complete. Who else was left to defend the City, but His personal bodyguard and some miscellaneous troops? By moving His armies to the Forks, He would be depleting the City of the rest of its active troops. Yes, there were some legions on the City's far northern side and one or two in the mountainous areas, but united, they could not have amounted to more than ten thousand angels under arms. Clearly, God had been led to believe that trimmer forces were weaker than they truly were. But how was that possible? It made no sense that He should send the City's best troops to slaughter, if He thought there was even the remotest possibility of trimmers mounting a counteroffensive in force. He was too afraid of that happening. Something, obviously, had gone wrong. And now, Apsatsus was vulnerable. God had magnified His own weaknesses tenfold by His drive to take down Gabriel. Pride was an evil failing.

As I rushed to put my few personal items in order, I considered the reality of the situation. God was now without an army to speak of. He was moving most of His remaining troops to cover His secret of all secrets, Man, while leaving the City dangerously open to attack. Maalik wanted me to step up and accept what he believed, justifiably or fancifully, was my rightful place among them. Absurdly, it seemed, I could command an army, if only I wanted to do so.

"I could take the City," I thought. "If only I could tell them to do so."

⌘ ⌘ ⌘

In the time it took me to pack all my personal effects, the tent city had been dismantled and organized into one long column of people, baggage, and horses. In fact, I had ducked out of my tent into the daylight to find that it was the only one left standing. The servants who normally ringed my tent were dancing around anxiously and, at a signal from me, immediately set about taking my tent down.

What only an hour before had been an immense city of tents, people, and life was now a moving procession of beings and goods, with not a stick left on the ground to indicate anyone had ever been in the area. Hardly a shred of evidence remained of anyone having camped there so comfortably. The innumerable flags carried by this moving mass fluttered in the breeze like a flock of white birds silhouetted against the sky. Along the ground, a great snake seemed to be inching slowly to the northeast. To the southwest, I could see huge dust clouds, the size of which indicated the presence of a force of trimmer horsemen, maybe thirty thousand strong, protecting our rear. If God's army was, indeed, making another foray across the Acheron, they would wheel left to hold the eastern bank of the river, nearly within sight of the burning fields. It would take a good deal of persuasive charm to get the remaining soldiers to cross the Acheron and hold enemy lands so recently the site of a massive defeat. It had to be Michael, I thought. No one else would be so bold—and so arrogant.

As I watched, surprised and dazed at the sight, a familiar voice I had never expected to hear suddenly said from behind me, "Incredible, isn't it, Lucifer?"

I spun around. It was Simon. Alive! I was elated. Then I noticed his uniform. A trimmer officer's uniform.

"You old dog!" I shouted, embracing him so warmly that I think I genuinely surprised him. "How is this possible?" I asked, then, holding him at arm's length.

He looked at me with what I thought was a smile of relief.

"I have been here for weeks and only *now* do you come to me?" I jested.

"It's been a long and unexpected trip," Simon said. He seemed to be at a loss for words.

"Understated as ever," I quipped, looking at his uniform. "No one told me you were alive." And now I felt a bit ashamed. "To be honest, I came looking for Gabriel. I assumed you had been killed." I took his hand. "I am sorry, old friend."

He was surprised. I had always tried to treat Simon as an equal. He and I had endured the fire together. It had scorched us both a bit, but in different ways. He had retained Nicor's memory as a keepsake, something to spur him on. For me, our time together had marked part of a path I needed to traverse before I could start making my political moves. We had both been affected by our time together, but I suspect he had always believed himself to be a subordinate, whereas I had seen him as a friend.

"There's no reason to apologize, my Lord," he now said. "We were always about the City, first and foremost."

"And where exactly are you now?" I asked more seriously, pulling at the folds of his trimmer uniform. "It seems to me that the last time we spoke, you were a general of the City of God. You appear to be a traitor now."

He did not flinch. "I am," he said gravely. "A traitor of the City of God." He said it so matter-of-factly. "Now I serve the true army of Heaven, though few of our City compatriots would understand."

"Compatriots? You should include me in this mystery, for I still do not understand what I see before me. Though I must admit that I find myself frequently lacking in understanding these days."

He smiled. "I am to accompany you while we make our move. You are a guest here and are accorded the rights of a citizen, even if you mock the citizens you see around you."

"You have really gone over to them?" I asked, smiling back.

My joy in seeing him again had overshadowed any anger or resentment I might have felt at his betrayal. God had chosen to sacrifice Simon, after all. If he had turned, I surmised, it was a natural reaction. Not everyone could appreciate what it meant to be God's servant. Simon was alive and that alone made me feel that what I had done by coming out to seek the trimmers had not been entirely in vain.

"Well," I said, with as much sarcasm as I could muster, "now that we are enemies, shall we spend this time together getting to understand one another?"

"Yes. Yes, I think that is a good idea, but one, I must say, that is decidedly not fitting for a Seraph of God."

"Indeed," I replied. "If I had a cohort of soldiers at my disposal…"

We grasped each other's hands. His grip was strong, his hands hardened by the sword he had wielded for the City. My hands were soft. It had been a very long time since I had stood and fought for anything or anyone, other than God. And myself. The toll upon Simon had clearly been greater than the toll events had taken upon me.

"Your horse, my Lord," he said, as an attendant came up with a mount.

It was a beautiful animal.

"What is his name?" I asked, as I seized the beast's mane, swung my leg up, and mounted him.

"His name is Morello. He is named after a loyal servant of these people." Simon mounted his own horse. He was suddenly thoughtful. "Thinking about it now makes me laugh," he said, unsmiling.

"Why is that?"

"It was, most probably, one of our own reconnoiters that caused Morello's death. Funny, that you should now ride a mount named after him." He adjusted his reins. "No matter. I doubt if anyone thought of it." He looked at me wryly and whirled around to face the north. "Giving this particular animal to an enemy of the people."

"Thank you, General," I said, not sure whether the mood had turned. "Though we are now enemies, it will be good to ride alongside you, if only for a while."

"My Lord," he said, bowing atop his mount.

"Call me Lucifer. At least for this short time, we are friends."

"Lucifer, then," he said, kicking his mount into a gallop and following the snaking line of people and animals.

I fell into line behind him.

⌘ ⌘ ⌘

"You will have noted that each soldier carries a bow and several quivers of arrows," Simon said, pointing in the direction of our cavalry rearguard. We had been riding for several days, generally northwestward, switching direction from hour to hour, almost as if we were, in fact, a snake moving through the grasslands. I hated serpents, but by moving this way and that in a single column, we made it more difficult for unseen enemy scouts to gauge our numbers. Not that any army of the City of God would ever venture that far eastward beyond the Acheron. Beyond even the River Cocytus. Not since Zoan, or so he had told me.

As I listened to Simon, I became possessed with the thought that God was leaving the City unprotected in His unexpected race to Apsatsus. Perhaps it was the soldier in me that made me ask as much about the disposition of the trimmers' troops as Simon was willing to divulge. Perhaps it was the burgeoning idea of conquest.

"They are masters with these weapons," Simon continued, "and can discharge a great many arrows in the course of a single minute. Even riding at full gallop, they seldom miss their targets."

"And yet you survived, Simon," I observed. No sarcasm was intended.

"I was taken prisoner." he said with a low growl. "They never execute prisoners."

I was surprised to hear this.

"Never execute prisoners? Why, then, do so few, if any, of our soldiers ever return from Tartarus?" I asked.

"They don't return, because they opt to stay." Jostling left to right and back again in his saddle, he was quite serious.

"Is that what they tell you?"

"That is what I know," Simon replied, looking at me now. "The prisoners you ordered released as we broke camp? Only those who opted to return left us. Of their own free will. The rest stayed."

I was not sure I believed him.

"And what of your bodyguard?" Simon continued. "How many are here with you?"

I looked around us.

"All twelve?" Simon asked. "Were any of them put to death? Are they not a liability in this time of risk?"

He was right. I had not really thought about it in our rush to evacuate.

"No prisoner is ever executed," he continued. "Most of the angels who survived the burning fields are now among us, as soldiers of these people." He was quite serious. "Look around you, Lucifer. You would know your own troops, if you had taken the time to know them. Before sending us to our deaths."

"You know I did not send you," I said defensively. "I did not give the order. We spoke frankly that night. It was God…"

I caught myself. It was blasphemous to blame God for anything.

Simon did not seem to care. "You knew angels were being sent to their deaths."

"I had no idea. I knew God was looking to punish Gabriel for reasons I am still not sure I understand. I knew He had given command to Gabriel and that you had reservations about His military plans. I had no idea what would happen. And, really, neither did you."

I was not sure I believed myself.

Simon remained silent. The dust kicked up by the column billowed around us, making him disappear and reappear, though we rode right next to one another.

"Why else would I have come out here?" I said, continuing the argument.

"Maybe you are looking for something."

"Oh, Simon! Not you too? I am not what these people think I am. I do not think even they themselves know what they think I am! If they can agree on anything at all."

"The Council debates, Lucifer. That's what it does. What you've witnessed is the way things get done. Ideas are shared. Opinions considered. Soldiers do what they are told, yes, but they only do what the Council wills."

"Can you tell me with confidence that it works?" I countered. "Can you tell me this system, as fair as you consider it, is what will save these angels? Bring them to the end they seek?"

I did not even notice at the time that I had referred to trimmers as "angels."

"Maybe yes, maybe no. But they've lived this way their whole lives. They have lived this way since the founding of the City of

Heaven. It wasn't until God that their way of governing, their way of protecting what is right, was washed away. And it has persevered out here. No, it may not be the answer to all things and no, it may not be the most expeditious way to legislate. But it is the will of the people that rules, not the whims of some tyrant."

"He was no tyrant to you. God made you master of our armies."

"God made me what I was. It was 'He' who decided I would command. Lucifer, do you know how I came to be a general in this army, the army of your sworn enemies, with which you now ride?" he asked.

I rode on, shielding my face from the dust.

"The people asked me. The Council voted to make me a general. It was the people and their vote of confidence. A people against whom I had led troops. A people I spent my whole career hunting and killing. Ordering others to hunt and kill. They gave me a second chance to make a difference." He looked out onto the train moving forward. "How many second chances has Yahweh given anyone?"

"He gave me a second chance and, if truth be told, He gave Zoan a second chance too," I said, not even noticing that God's name had been so blasphemed. I had become so accustomed to hearing it now.

"You don't believe that," Simon retorted. "That's what Maalik has told you and what you've rejected out of hand. You can't use it as an argument now."

"Oh, please! Maalik? He longs too much for the answers he wants. In that way, you can make him believe anything you want."

"No, Lucifer. Not anything I tell him, but anything *you* tell him."

"But why? Why is this?" I asked, getting upset now.

"Because he believes you are one of them. You are like him. More to the point, you are like Yahweh. You share the spark that has kept this civilization alive for billions of years, against all odds. There were once twelve. Now there are only three."

"You believe this? You believe that I am one of these...things? Why? How can you know?"

"Because Maalik knows. And the Council knows, though its members don't want to admit it. Because I know. You came out to find us, which means that you doubted God. Something happened between the two of you that you're not sharing. Something else you know about what Yahweh's been doing."

"You do not know what you are talking about," I said, finished with the conversation.

"No? How many troops has Yahweh sent to Apsatsus?" Simon asked.

I shot him a quick look. He knew. He knew what I knew.

"Gabriel conspicuously avoided the Forks. He was too obvious." Simon's face was set. "Don't you see? He fears you. God knows what you can do. Yet he'll risk his entire city to make sure you don't get what you need to succeed. Whatever that is."

"There is little risk in sending troops to Apsatsus," I lied. "The City of Heaven is not like this rabble, these people who live off the backs of horses, people who do not even have true walls to protect them."

"These people have been on the back foot for the last thirteen billion years. Their existence, in many respects, is premised on their ability to conduct an orderly retreat," Simon said, looking at the moving mass of people, animals, and equipment. "Progress cannot be measured by the thickness of your walls."

We rode on a little longer in silence, before he continued. "Sadly, the City's defenses have largely been abandoned."

"Why do you say this?" I asked, more out of frustration now than anything else. "I have personally spent a great deal of time shoring up vulnerable spots along the lines."

"You would know better than me, Lucifer," Simon said a bit soulfully. "But from my point of view, God's generals, myself included, constantly worried that any attempt to strengthen the City's defenses would be construed as an attempt to consolidate power. An effort to resist God. In his paranoia, God would misconstrue our actions. Have you ever known someone with unequaled and absolute power to be in the habit of nurturing his ambitious and talented juniors?"

"He has helped me," I said. "He gave me everything."

"Has he?" Simon asked, looking away from me and squinting into the bright day around us. "I'd think carefully about what God has given you, Lucifer."

We rode on without speaking. Simon did not know what Apsatsus meant, but he was smart enough to know that whatever it was, it was more important to God than the City itself. Put differently, it was more important than anything ever had been.

⌘　⌘　⌘

I did ask Simon once about Gabriel. But he didn't answer. Finally, days later, unexpectedly and unsolicitedly, he broke his silence.

"Gabriel panicked when he heard that an outlander army was already pinning down our lead elements across the Acheron," he began. "He thought a quick movement across the river, so far north of the Forks, was imperative. An unexpected move. Something that would, at least, give us enough time to get the entire army across, unmolested. Bringing the fight to the outlanders. Zoan's strategy, to be put into operation for the first time in an age. But when I, along with about half of the troops, made landfall on the eastern bank of the Acheron, outlanders appeared on the ridge, a league or two away from us. They were waiting for us to get halfway across. I signaled Gabriel to wait for the entire army to make the eastern shore before ordering us out. 'Dig in,' I said. 'Create a beachhead for the rest of the army.' At least, this would allow me and the soldiers who had just made it across and were emerging, sopping wet, from the water to establish a solid perimeter. In continuing our landings in force, I knew we risked being pinned against the river, but at least, it would be our full fighting force pinned against the river." Simon looked down at his saddle, as if dredging up memories he would rather not have shared. "At least, we would be more motivated to fight forward, when we had nowhere to retreat backward.

"But others must have been more eager," Simon continued, "and managed to convince Gabriel in their favor. He signaled that I was to attack with whatever troops I already had at my disposal. We were to use the rest of the army, still on the Elysian shore, as a reserve. I couldn't understand what had motivated Gabriel to issue such orders. There was no place to maneuver, the element of surprise was gone, and our forces were divided across the river. Meanwhile, outlander forces had massed in an ill-defined formation at the top of the ridge and I knew, with our limited range of view, that we couldn't see what they held in reserve. I signaled Gabriel that I would reconnoiter up the bank of the river as far as I could safely get, before meeting resistance. I needed to fortify this end of the line to avoid being rolled up on our left flank. I thought I might even be able to get around them, as they focused on our landings."

"You left the command?"

"I felt I had to."

"With Gabriel in overall command?"

"I was satisfied Gabriel knew what to do. I gave him my advice and though he had his orders from God, I could tell he was looking to me for finding a way out of the situation."

I was a bit skeptical about this.

"Anyway," Simon continued, "Gabriel signaled a 'go' and I led a cohort of horses north along the river. But Gabriel must have panicked when the first mounted outlander archers started harassing our front line. He ordered a redeployment, as I made my way north."

"'Must have'? What do you mean?"

"I was only a few hundred meters upriver and probably still within bowshot of our left flank, when I turned to see the far left elements of our line reforming in the center. In fact, the entire left wing had collapsed and merged with what had become one side of a giant hollow square. My troopers and I were suddenly much farther off the line than I had ever anticipated. While we turned to race back to the main body of the army, outlanders came over the ridge and clipped us, pushing us right into the river."

He paused, his expression bleak, staring blankly into the mass of people moving ahead of us. He did not blink, though the dust caked up around and into his eyes.

"I lost many troopers," he continued, "and horses. We were washed downriver, past our own army, trying to get across to their Tartaruian landing sites, and into the rear of the outlanders' left wing. I was taken prisoner and forced to watch from their command post along the ridge, as the rest of my army was torn to pieces.

"I was immediately brought to Maalik," Simon continued. "He knew who I was. I was treated with respect. My troopers, those who made it, anyway, were treated properly. I sat among the outlander commanders and watched helplessly."

Simon finally blinked the dust out of his eyes and shifted in his saddle.

"They do have effective ways of torturing you here," I said in jest.

"Gabriel must have thought a square formation would afford protection against the risk of being outflanked," Simon continued, ignoring me, "now that I was clearly out of the picture. I'm sure he cursed me for the traitor he probably suspected me to be for having fallen out of it so soon."

"There are no certainties in war, Simon," I said. "You know that better than most."

"Yes, but this was preventable. I had been rash. And I watched as he set his square, with the river to his back acting as the fourth wall. He continued to get soldiers across the river, but it cost him almost all his mobility. While the mounted outlander archers made their strafing attacks, the rest of the outlander army beat their shields with their spears along the ridges. Over the other side of ridge, and out of Gabriel's view, the reserve beat drums, making a deafening and menacing noise. It must have given Gabriel the feeling that the outlanders had more soldiers than, as I saw from my new vantage point, they clearly had. Outlanders on the ridge also had mirrors and flashed the morning sunlight into the eyes of the still-forming City soldiers.

"The mounted archers focusing sustained attacks on the two points where the square touched the river, to the north and the south simultaneously. City cavalry elements sent to drive off the mounted archers were forced to retreat under heavy fire. They swirled around at the river points, leaving the front of the square virtually unhit.

"As the first skirmishes started, Gabriel reinforced the front line," Simon continued. "But as the northern and southern attacks developed, he moved more troops to the weak points at the river's edge. The mounted outlander archers made murderous progress on the river points, compelling Gabriel to order these positions to be further reinforced. But with the density of the City's formation slowly increasing, as more and more troops came ashore, the square could hardly be contained. Nearly every arrow fired from the back of an outlander horse found its mark. Many angels fell. Panic soon broke out. As soldiers disembarked from across the Elysian shore, they saw the deluge of arrows taking out their comrades and began to flee back and even into the river. They were swept up in the confusion of the landing boats behind them and shot down, as they stumbled along the shoreline.

"Slowly, meticulously," Simon said, "the outlanders were able to peel our soldiers off both the northern and southern river points so that they could now intercept the flotilla of soldiers coming across the river. Cut off from the river, Gabriel was forced to reform, now in a complete square. Much of the rest of the army was mid-river, trying desperately to reach the Tartaruian shore to save their falling comrades, now trapped. The outlanders slammed showers of arrows into the boats. Oarsmen were taken out. If a boat didn't founder from the panic on board, it was knocked hopelessly off course by the flowing river." Simon paused again. "It was a terrible sight."

I looked out over the wide expanse of the outlands. I had not seen that part of the battlefield when we crossed so many weeks ago. Apparently, the river had done to half the army what trimmers had done to the other half.

"'What is Gabriel thinking?' was all I could ask myself," Simon continued. "What *was* he thinking? Who was advising him? How could I have failed so? Why did I care, when I had been ordered to help him fail?" Simon gripped his reigns harder and shifted again in his saddle. "With one wing of his cavalry already taken out and his army either boxed up or drowning downstream," he continued, "Gabriel moved east in an attempt to get the fight hand-to-hand."

"Uphill?" I asked. "Even Gabriel must have known that was a tactical blunder."

"The mounted archers didn't fall for it," Simon replied. "They weren't about to trade their mobility and effectiveness to mess with heavily armed City foot soldiers. They just swarmed in circles, firing as they approached, strafing the line as they turned, and firing behind them as they cleared off. At some point, Gabriel gave the order to lock shields overhead to protect the infantrymen from the intense arrow fire from the ridgeline. But the outlanders were anticipating this too. As soon as the shields were locked, they threw their own heavily armored foot soldiers down off the ridge and into our front line. The City's line panicked, weakened from reinforcing the now-collapsed river points and struggling in an awkward defensive position that effectively prevented them from fighting at close quarters. Unable to unlock their shields, many City angels were cut down. When finally, they were able to break shields, the outlander infantry withdrew and the archers resumed their work."

"Gabriel gave no order to move back across the river?"

"He had already sustained heavy casualties and must have decided digging in was better than being sunk fleeing back across the river."

"He followed your advice, only too late."

"Yes, I guess. At some point, he must have realized the mounted archers were being resupplied with arrows from the top of the ridge. He dispatched what was left of our cavalry to drive off those archers. The outlander horsemen began a running retreat up the ridge and our cavalry began to charge farther on, heartened to see some progress made for the first time that day. But when the mounted outlander archers stopped and turned around, their arrows cut down the front line of our cavalry charge. Simultaneously, the outlander heavy infantry moved back down the ridge, through the mounted archers' positions and the now faltering cavalry charge was hit again, this time from the ground. The mounted archers reformed, while this was happening, and proceeded to flank our cavalry, cutting them off from the square and from any hope of retreat. They were slaughtered to the horse." Simon reined in his horse and checked his stirrup momentarily. When he looked back up, he said, "I'd never seen anything like it before."

"And no retreat was signaled?"

"Gabriel must not have seen this happen. He ordered a general advance. Whatever protective positions they'd actually been able to build were now abandoned, as the square tried to move up the slope and onto the ridge. The outlanders let them advance, over the dead bodies of their comrades. Having reached the apex of the ridge, they realized they were completely surrounded. Sitting there, perched upon the ridge, they could, for the first time, see their complete encirclement. They got hit from every side at once. Gabriel was left perched on a ridge, watching his reinforcements drown in the river, with no cover and with bloodied, cut off, and worn-out soldiers.

"As night fell, all outlander attacks ceased," Simon continued. "In the dark, Gabriel fled back down the ridge, unaccosted, though Maalik certainly had the power to finish the whole thing then and there. Gabriel abandoned thousands of wounded angels on the ridge. The outlanders spent much of the evening picking up his wounded from the surrounding fields. I know this, as I was still in Maalik's tent. There was no celebration among the senior outlander officers, but many of their troops howled into the night. And could you blame them? Their strategy had worked to perfection. Some got too carried away. The fire started when some rolled large metal balls, filled with grass, covered in pitch, and lit as incendiaries, down the ridge into Gabriel's bloodied positions on the river's edge. It caused great confusion and destruction. Maalik immediately halted further attacks and, in fact, removed the offending troops' officers immediately."

"Unbelievable."

"The fields continued to burn for hours. Maalik had to move his command to a different ridge, as the wind began to whip the fire in all directions. I slept little that night. The moaning and wailing of the wounded prisoners rent the air. But the outlanders treated them as if they were their own. And now those same soldiers...angels, ride with us as outlanders. As 'trimmers' and forever grateful for their fate," he said cynically.

The dust cleared and, suddenly, I could see green fields off in the distance. We were moving into a lush valley at the foothills of a mountain range I did not recognize.

"They are beautiful," I said, trying to change the subject and gesturing toward a glacier hanging from the end of the range.

Simon was still lost in thought and did not hear me.

"Maalik sent Gabriel a message the next day, offering to negotiate" he said. "There was no answer. Gabriel must have slipped back across the Acheron in the night with some of his senior officers. At first, the remaining soldiers and cavalry had tried to make it back across the river. But after a single attack from the outlanders' mounted archers, they began surrendering. Ten thousand or so in all, from both days of battle. I estimate that about twenty thousand of our angels were killed. Among the captured, those whom you traveled so far to find so that you could secure their release, only a handful opted to return to the City. Most, it seemed to me, were middle-ranking officers whose families would suffer, if it became known they had betrayed God and stayed among us voluntarily."

"You spoke to them, then?"

"Yes," Simon said ruefully. "I tried to convince them to stay. They would not."

"What about the trimmer casualties?" I asked, still looking up at the beautiful glacier before me.

"I don't know the extent of their casualties, but I have no doubt that their losses were minimal. I counted no more than twenty or thirty funeral pyres that night in camp."

"A resounding defeat," I commented.

Morello snorted a bit to get the dust out of his nostrils. The air was clean and clear now.

"In every way," Simon affirmed. "They separated the officers from the soldiers, weeding out the diehards from the rest. The diehards were released into the outlands. Unarmed. The rest were offered sanctuary, as long as they didn't cause trouble. Maalik came to me later and, astoundingly, offered me a command, if I stayed with them. I declined, saying that I didn't understand how such an honor could be bestowed on me, following such a dishonorable defeat. 'We are all equal in the eyes of the universe,' was all he said. Since then, I've spent time learning the history of this conflict. The real history. I took command of five thousand horsemen, many of whom were cavalry from the City. At one point or another. I lead them as an equal citizen. I have not led them in battle. At least, not yet."

"Not yet," I muttered to myself.

How did every person who came in contact with these people seem to become one of them? Was I missing something? Some mystical power about these stories that was lost on me? These were not the monsters God had warned us about. These were just people. Angels. Angels like those I had got to know in the cell. The laborers, the bakers, the nobodies. They brandished swords out of fear and a desire for self-determination, not for destruction. They had no grand scheme to wash themselves in the blood of the City's inhabitants. If their lives were a struggle, it was because someone else made it so. I, for one. They carried those swords, because I had made them do so. I was a soldier of God. I did His work for Him. I had helped make the City what it was, but what was it, really? A tyranny cloaked in the guise of something else? It was great. No one could argue that point. But what constituted greatness? City armies had been fighting these people for as long as I could remember and even earlier, but all that "greatness" had failed to dull the glow of these people's spirits, on their conviction about what they felt meant the most in the universe. The idealization of the individual. It was wrong to kill before you were an adult. It was proper to treat everyone, even your enemies, with respect. What was greatness, when compared to compassion? Greatness had an ancient and invincible city. Compassion had the run of the outlands. I was not sure I knew what meant the most.

We pitched camp that day. Days and days after retreating from the dustbowl that lay east of the burning fields. Trimmers had, indeed, set fire to the field of battle. But those responsible had been punished for it. What would happen when Apsatsus began turning out Man, loyal soldiers of God, dedicated to His cause? How far would the burning fields creep? A hundred leagues? A thousand? Would the mountains I now saw before me become the same graveyard I had ridden through to get here? An army of slaves created for the purpose of destroying compassion for no reason other than to be great?

⌘   ⌘   ⌘

"I'm telling you," Simon said, winded from our morning workout, "don't get too comfortable. We may have set up camp here, but we will move back west as soon as we can assess the situation."

Every morning, for the next few weeks, we fenced for several hours. Though members of the Council saw my desire to hone my martial skills as a dangerous sign, Maalik allowed it, as long as Simon was my partner. Azael stood nearby. Watching, as always. It was an age since I had wielded a sword and a shield, a spear or a staff. My hands bled the first few days. I took a beating. I think Azael was more amused than anyone else.

"I have become soft," I said the first morning, after Simon entered my tent without warning and roused me.

"This is what you asked for, right?"

"Yes. I guess I had forgotten just how much work it takes to be a soldier. I will be no challenge at all."

And beat me he did, morning after morning. But with time, the spear began to feel comfortable in my hands once again. Even Maalik noted, one morning, that my skills with a spear were returning.

"Even if the rest of God's propaganda is a lie," he felt compelled to add.

"Why would we leave this place, Simon?" I asked, as I threw my weight behind a sword thrust and missed my mark.

"This is not where the Council says we belong."

He swung wide and missed my back, as I jumped out of the way.

"But it makes no sense, I tell you."

Again, I lunged forward, but too slowly for Simon, who quickly stepped away, twirled around, and came down with an overhead swipe. Rolling aside, I jumped up and we faced each other again, wooden swords in hand and both of us out of breath.

"Keep moving your feet!" Azael shouted gruffly.

Apparently, time with his long-lost family had done little to quell his exasperation with my awkward style of combat.

"This isn't as much fun as it was only a week ago, Lucifer," Simon said, smiling. "I enjoyed myself much more when I could cut you down in five moves."

"You won't cut him down so easily, if he just moves his feet!" Azael grumbled, annoyed that I was ignoring his advice.

"You are a good teacher, I guess, Si..." I tried to say.

Before I had a chance to finish, he had come across from the left, always my weak side, and smashed his wooden sword across my right arm. I yelped in pain, as Simon laughed heartily. Azael spat into the grass.

"Not so good, it seems," Simon said, completing my thought for me. He was clearly pleased with himself.

I rubbed by arm, which was already starting to swell, over and above the swelling from the earlier beatings I had suffered at his hands. Simon was good.

"You're too prone to losing your focus when people are insulting you, Lucifer. Seems it's the weakness of a angel, no matter how much you practice."

"If we are headed back west, why are your armies not preparing for an attack? You cannot run forever," I said.

The thought of an undefended City of God was still knocking around in my head.

"It seems to have worked so far and, besides, it is the will of the Council, something they haven't seen fit to make me a part of."

I switched my sword to my left hand now and lunged at Simon's legs. Quickly, he moved and we parried a number of reciprocal thrusts.

"God's armies are moving to Apsatsus, leaving the City wide open," I said.

Simon had already known this. He had admitted as much. So I did not feel I was divulging anything that should have remained confidential.

"Yet they do nothing?" I persisted.

Another swing and Simon's sword crashed down on top of my shield.

"Why are you so interested, Lucifer? You do not speak as I would expect a Seraph to," he said slyly.

More parrying back and forth. We were both getting tired.

"Watch your footwork, my Lord!" shouted Azael, yet again.

"You are so slow!" Simon taunted, dancing out from another of my failed swings.

"It just makes no sense," I went on. "You have an opportunity and you do not take it."

"It's not *my* opportunity to take, Lucifer. It is the will of the people who govern us and I am but one voice."

"Ah, so you *have* suggested something, then?"

"I've suggested that they give you command of the armies," he said.

I froze. Simon cut down hard on my left shoulder and I collapsed to the ground, pain peeling me in half. Azael huffed, spat again, and walked away, grumbling.

Simon stood over me. "These angels are yours to lead, if you but take the opportunity in hand." He looked at me gravely. "The soldiers trust you. You were a good leader. You made yourself an example. You led by example. We are not the only ones to understand that God's power is a false power, propped up by angels like you."

In anger, I swung hard at his legs, but missed.

He came down hard on my back. "You may wish to deceive yourself, but you hold more leadership qualities in that poorly exercised hand of yours than exists in the whole of God's body."

I took another swing and managed to get myself up onto one knee in the process. But Simon anticipated the move and jumped away, while rapping my helmet with the tip of his sword.

"I am a Seraph!" I just barely got out. "I cannot betray my God!"

I was mad now. I swung again and got back up on two feet. I switched the sword back into my right hand, damning the pain. Charging at Simon, I knocked him off his feet, but not fast enough to stop him from thrusting his sword into my stomach, knocking the wind out of me.

"I do not mock you, Lucifer," he said, getting up and brushing himself off. "Lucifer," he said again. "I knew you when you were Ahriman. I know the stuff you are made of. I tell you the truth. These outlanders have watched you as you defied God, took a handful of angels, and rode out here alone to bargain for the lives of your soldiers. What faith has God shown in his soldiers? What love? What compassion?"

I was still gasping for air, but he hit me in the back again as I tried to get up.

"Stay down, Ahriman. It is a position you know well as the mongrel of that mad fake. You are smarter than this. But you refuse to accept it."

Simon took a few steps back and relaxed.

On my hands and knees now, I looked up at him. "What would you have me do?" I asked, wincing in pain. "Lead an army of deserters against my City?"

"It's not *your* city, Ahriman. It never was. That's the point. It's his. Everything in it. And it always will be. Unless you become something more."

"What more? What more can I become?"

I thought of Zoan. How hard I had tried to be like him. To live up to his reputation. To make things right.

"You can take this army and end this war."

Simon broke his gaze for a split second.

I went at him, dashing him down with my sword. Anger radiating from my brain and coursing down to my hand. But it was anger with myself. For having been fooled for so long. No. For having fooled myself for so long. Simon crumpled on the floor, trying to parry my blows, but not well enough. As I hit him, I thought again of that night with God in His chambers. How He had led His angels to their deaths for His personal amusement and revenge. He had done it, though. Got His revenge. At the expense of thousands. Including poor Simon, now bleeding from the face. I stopped.

Simon looked at me, wiping the blood from his nose.

"What are you doing in Apsatsus?" he asked unfazed. He didn't seem to notice his wounds. "What's so important that God would leave the city open?" He looked at me, unflinching and determined.

"That is enough," Maalik said, as he and Ukobach approached.

Ukobach, his sword drawn, was standing anxiously next to Maalik. Maalik stood unarmed.

"No one doubts you are a great angel, Ahriman. God's Lucifer," he said. "Your services to the city are well recorded. But it is time you wrote another chapter in the book of life. It is time you learned the truth."

I turned to them and dropped my sword. My wooden sword. "The 'truth,' you say. You have been threatening me with the truth ever since I got here."

"And those have not been idle threats. You fight for what you believe in. It is both your greatest strength and your greatest weakness. You fight, but you have always been told what to fight for. Imagine, for a moment, if you fought for what you know is right, rather than what you have been told is right?"

"Right is what God tells us."

"No, Ahriman. Right is what we feel in our hearts," Maalik replied.

I snorted, then turned around and held out my hand to help Simon to his feet. He looked at my hand for a moment and then quickly at Maalik. I knew, without looking, that Maalik was nodding his acquiescence. Simon took my hand and hauled himself up.

Slowly, he cracked a smile. "Azael is right. You need to move your feet," he said.

I managed a smile too. "I think we both need to move our feet."

We walked past Maalik and Ukobach, the boy still with sword at the ready, and went to clean up. As we walked by, I heard Maalik whisper to Ukobach, "It is time to get the books."

CHAPTER
THIRTY-ONE

Maalik came to me that night as I sat outside my tent, watching the fire I had made, rubbing my sore limbs, and lost in thought.

"How are you feeling?" he asked with genuine concern.

I looked at him, smiled, and then looked back at the fire. "You are lucky to have such an angel leading your armies," I said, rubbing the thin sheen of heat from the fire off my arms. "He is a good soldier...and a loyal angel."

"Funny you should use the word 'loyal,'" Maalik remarked.

"Simon is loyal to his beliefs," I said, quickly shooting a look at Maalik, "and loyal to his friends." I looked back down at the fire. "He knew God was using him. He knew God was sending them to their deaths." I sighed. "Yet he did his duty. Such angels are few and far between."

"Not here, they aren't," Maalik observed.

I ignored him. "God knew what He was doing," I said, thinking for a moment. "Your infiltration must be very deep for you to have known where and when to strike Gabriel," I surmised, looking up at him again.

Maalik smiled, but not out of contempt. "We had intelligence, yes, though we did not know how accurate it was. We are a good people, but soldiering is not what we are best at," he sighed. "We took a chance and it paid off."

"Well, it was quite a good guess," I acknowledged.

"Any rule, God's included, is a slave to existence," Maalik said.

I looked back up at him, but before I could get a word out, he continued. "I see your eyes, Ahriman, and know your doubts. But hear me out. Though a ruler, any ruler, may make a thousand efforts to direct change in the universe, he will exert only an indirect influence over the course of events. If he proves successful to an extent, he will regard himself as mighty and powerful. But the impact he assumes he has created will not be truly of his own making. It is to existence itself that anyone would properly owe this change. The geographical position of his domain, which he may or may not have any real power to shift, the state of society that has developed largely on its own without his help, the nature of the people he rules, though he may not know their origins. Existence happens without him, whether he is willing to accept it or not. Life moves irresistibly on and he struggles in vain against it, deluding himself when, quite fortuitously, he turns into the proper current. And succeeds."

"You mean to tell me you guessed the 'currents,' as you say?" I asked incredulously.

"Like I said, soldiering is not what we're best at."

"What are you best at, then?" I asked.

"We are best at living. At prospering. At governing. The very things that Yahweh took from us."

"That He took from you? What did He take?" I asked wearily. I had grown tired of Maalik's constant proselytizing. "God has ruled since the beginning, creating the heavens and the universe. He is our Father and He has taken His children into His arms and protected those who loved Him. For those who reject His love, He has nothing but contempt. He must protect His loyal children. And I am one of them," I said.

I looked around me. Ukobach stood by in the quiet night.

"Simon was one of His loyal children," I finished.

"Yahweh has no children," Maalik said with unexpected vehemence. "He has only those who do what he says and those who do not. We are no lesser beings for wanting our lives to follow the path we have forged for ourselves," he said, looking at the tents around us. "Not as *he* wants them."

"I am in no mood to fight with you this evening, Maalik," I sighed, my arms still throbbing from Simon's thrashing. "I am your prisoner and by my terms of war, at least, that leaves me at your mercy. I sacrificed myself for my angels, but do not expect me to sacrifice myself for you. These interminable debates cannot end well. Surely, you see that?"

"Simon had a question for you this morning," Maalik said dryly, ignoring my plea.

"Simon knows more than he should," I sighed again. "And I am not surprised. An angel in his position, an angel who leads the armies of God, is always in need of information."

I instantly regretted saying it.

"Something that will shift the balance of power in this war?" Maalik asked cautiously.

"Yes."

Another moment of instant regret.

"Something that you know well?"

"Yes."

And another.

"Well, then. Tonight shall be our last interrogation. Your last night as a prisoner."

I looked at Maalik, imagining he was jesting.

He was clearly serious. "There will be no more questions. I promise. Only answers, from now on."

"What do you mean?"

Maalik sat down next to me. "Over the ages of this universe," he said, eyeballing Ukobach, "a city was created. The City of

Heaven. You know it as the City of God. We have no records to tell us how or when the City of Heaven was established. We only know that it was an ancient city, conceived in liberty by free angels. From the time of its founding, it was ruled by angels who treated each other as if they were brothers and sisters. They ruled through a council, the Council of Twelve, and wanted nothing but the greatest of things for their people. They lived in harmony, ruling with a firm, but fair hand. Opinions were shared in an open forum, points debated on all issues. But in all things, a majority determined the end. It was fair. There were no winners or losers. There were just citizens."

"Yes, I have seen all this here."

"We preserve the old ways, not in the same form, but adapted to our purpose," he said. "Pay attention," Maalik said emphatically.

I was a bit surprised. "Yes?"

"The Council that runs our people today, outlaws and vagrants as we are," he continued, now eyeing me, "on the run and desperate to live our lives as we wish, is much like the Council of Twelve that ran the City of Heaven in those days. But unlike our Council, the beings who ran the City of Heaven were immortal or, at least, shall we say, less mortal than most. They were born, they were children, they grew to adulthood, but they seldom died. At least, not from natural causes. They were called 'the Ones,' for lack of a better description, and in them, the glory of the cosmos resided."

"I heard such nonsense from the cell," I said. "You have suggested a connection here. It is nothing but an old legend, designed to recruit the weak-minded."

"No. It is the truth," Maalik said with conviction. "It was that way for thousands of generations. Eternity, as all the people knew it. It was peaceful and tranquil. Until Yahweh came. Together, with a small band of followers, he came from the deserts beyond the rivers. No one knows from where, precisely. But he came as a distant traveler and was greeted in the city by both the people and the Council rulers with great interest and courtesy, as was their custom. He was brought before the Council whose members, inspired by a yearning for knowledge, questioned him, all the while, giving him respect, as he was a visitor to their land. The Council wondered how he had come to them from so far a place, about which they had no knowledge. Where were these lands and what other secrets did they hold?"

"Are you claiming God was an outlander?" The idea was beyond ridiculous.

"Yes. Yahweh told the Council of a fabulous land, a land where clean, clear water flowed from the mountains, the animals were abundant, and the land so verdant and beautiful, it stung the senses. He described a place that was nothing short of a paradise, where he had been born and raised. 'Gehenna,' he called it. And with the magic he wove with his descriptions, he bound the Council, as if with a spell.

"When he left the Council chambers," Maalik continued, "he and his followers walked among the people of the city, a celebrity. Telling them of the great things he had seen and experienced. Telling them that he and his followers were the last of his people and that a powerful clan of nomads he referred to as 'trimmers' had attacked and slain the rest. Warning the City's inhabitants that their own time would soon be at hand. He spoke of an apocalypse to be visited upon them. The trimmers were on their way to the City of Heaven and only he could lead the city to overcome the threat. He had fought these trimmers before and survived. He told the people they could have untold riches in exchange for swearing allegiance to him. He became both a well-loved figure and the herald of impending doom."

"We have such subversives in the City now," I said. "But they are just that: subversives. And God deals with them accordingly."

"Through you, Ahriman. Is that not so? Through you?"

"Yes, I guess so," I conceded, reflecting momentarily on what I had done in the name of God.

"Well, the once peaceful citizens of the City now began to clamor, prompted by fear. Fear of the impending attack and fear of how they would face it. For the first time in the history of the City of Heaven, citizens were unsettled, full of questions for their government in which they had, all along, placed such abiding faith. How, they asked, could the Council not have known of these places from where Yahweh had come? How would the Council protect the city against these trimmers who had slain his people? What was the Council prepared to do for their protection?

"What Yahweh accomplished in so little time is debated even today," he went on. "He split the people from their government. Even worse, he split them from each other. Never before, in the intractable history of the city, had there been what then became a reality: vicious political factions. Yes, politics had lived in Heaven from the time of the city's founding. But it had been nothing like the beast it would become with the arrival of Yahweh." Maalik sneered. "He was a 'creator' all right!"

I watched Maalik as he sat looking into the fire. He was venting his anger and frustration in a way I had not seen him do before. It was a life he was describing. A life he had lost. And I believed him. Or rather, I believed he had truly believed in it. I thought of Jehoel. Wrestling within a system he hated, with angels he hated, and yet managing to hold his own so well and so convincingly.

"There were no laws against lying, and that is exactly what Yahweh was doing," Maalik said, returning mentally from the edge. He picked up a few pieces of wood and threw them onto the dying fire. "Well, not entirely, I guess," he added. "You see, now that we have been out here in the outlands, in Tartarus, now that we are outlanders ourselves, we can see the 'paradise' Yahweh had described." He looked up into the darkness where the glacier slept on the mountains. "And all of that was true. We live off the land and it gracefully sustains us. In that respect, Yahweh was, indeed, our guide. But the true measure of the city was the bond that tied its citizens to it and to each other. And that is what Yahweh preyed upon. He and another." Maalik paused, suddenly ill at ease. "The other's name was Zoan."

"Now wait a minute...!" I began.

Maalik waved me off. "No, you wanted to know the truth, Ahriman, God's Lucifer!" he shouted, his eyes flashing fire. "You can choose to listen or you can leave! You came all this way, Lucifer, and still you refuse to hear our story? What is your purpose, if not to understand us better? We do not lie here. Lies are the exclusive domain of your master! Which is it going to be? Will you listen to me and to my story or will you deny the possibility that truth is never entirely what you are told it is?"

He was right. Much as I hated to admit it, Maalik had never lied to me. Simon had never lied to me. Jehoel had never lied to me. But Gabriel had and so had God, Heaven help me.

"Go on, then." I had composed myself.

"So, yes, there was a paradise out here. And yes, there was a horde of nomads making its way across the Acheron toward the city. Yahweh had not lied in this regard. And when they appeared on the horizon, as Yahweh had predicted they would, it seemed to many that he was the only one capable of dealing with the situation. Anyone could see them there, camped not far from the edges of the then unwalled city. They sat there, waiting, and the city fell into a panic. Yahweh's word for them, 'trimmers,' had been chosen, he said, because they supposedly fed off the edges of society, killing indiscriminately, destroying anything not theirs, and stealing anything they did not destroy. Looking back to that time, Yahweh's trimmers had, in fact, been precisely as he described them. Not as we are now." Maalik was clearly saddened by the comparative picture he had just drawn. "And now, with Yahweh established as a political power, pounding the pavement of the city with fear, doom was no longer impending, but right there before them. Camped outside the city walls. In the pristine fields of Elysium. Unprepared to deal with Yahweh's machinations, the Council did not know how to proceed. The city fell into chaos."

"Who were they?" I asked, forgetting myself.

"I will get there in a moment," Maalik said, happy, no doubt, to hear a note of anticipation, rather than rancor, in my voice. "When the city began coming under trimmer attack, Yahweh convinced the people that if the City of Heaven was to endure, they must confront the invaders. The citizenry agreed and without the consent of the Council, Yahweh publicly named himself the city's commander. The Council members were furious, but given that Yahweh seemed to be the people's choice, they ruled in favor of the decision, after the fact, as it were. By doing so, the Council proved itself weak and fell in the people's estimation. It would prove to be the beginning of their end. In the meantime,

Yahweh had appointed one of his followers as the general of the city's army. His name was Zoan."

"You are saying that Zoan came to the city from the outlands with God?" I asked, desperate now for clarification. Again, the very possibility was preposterous.

"Yes," he answered in measured tones. "When the trimmers attacked, Yahweh told the people that Zoan had been their general in Gehenna. He had defended Gehenna to the end and he would do the same for the City of Heaven. On Yahweh's instructions, Zoan set to work, creating the first army of the City of Heaven. It was composed of the city's most influential people, its leading residents. Those with property. Those with the most to lose."

I squirmed. Maalik could tell I was about to interrupt again.

"I told you there was equality among the citizens of the City of Heaven, Ahriman. And that was true. All citizens had equal power in the state. But not all citizens were equal in their personal and private power. 'Equality' is not always a measurement of economic or even social status. It was not an egalitarian world about which I speak, Ahriman, but it was one where the citizenry shared political power in all the right ways."

"It seems rather convenient, Maalik," I replied. "And inconsistent with what I came to know from my experience in dealing with subversives. And trimmers." I was unsatisfied with his explanation, but willing to let it go for now.

"Be that as it may, that was the way things were," he said. "Zoan's army was meant to take the fight to the trimmers. Defend the city. Simultaneously, Yahweh began to call for the construction of the city's first walls. Led by Mizpah, the most vocal member of the Twelve, the Council balked at these developments. They moved to prohibit construction. There had never been a wall, they said. There will never be one, Mizpah added. But as the city was increasingly subjected to attacks from this mysterious enemy camped just outside it, Mizpah's position, and the Council's along with it, became untenable.

"Perhaps it was the people's backlash against the Council's effete rubberstamping of Yahweh's creation and control of the city's army," Maalik went on. "Perhaps it was naïveté on their part. Perhaps it was an erosion of faith in the crumbling system of trust between a government and its citizens.

"Whatever it was," he continued, "piecemeal construction began in direct contravention of the Council's pronouncements. Yahweh played it up. The Council was ineffective, he said. Mizpah was blind to the city's plight. Only he, Yahweh, could lead the city to preserve its sovereignty. Mizpah objected, declaring that the defense of the citizenry was foremost in the Council's thoughts, but that circumstances should not be allowed to destroy the city's character, its history. But it was too late. Mizpah was losing Council members every day. His calls for Yahweh's removal fell on deaf ears, as the Council became irrevocably divided, embroiled in infighting while the trimmer attacks continued unabated.

"Yahweh seized the opportunity and pocketed several Council members who, seemingly no longer constrained by the rules of the Council, moved to push the legislation through. Instinctively attuned to the power of rhetoric, Yahweh blatantly played to the gallery, asking the citizens if he alone, among so many, could see the threat for what it was. Here he was, busy building an army and erecting marginally effective defenses for the city without proper financial support, while Mizpah's faction of the Council prevaricated. But he was not above the law, Yahweh said. He would work within the system to move the legislation along, if that was what was needed. He worked both sides astutely and ground them down from inside as well. Promises and lies.

"Things turned very much for the worse when trimmers breached the ramshackle defenses one night and ransacked part of the city, killing citizens and dragging people from their beds and out into the outlands. You must understand. In a place where there had never been any record of violence, the horror of that night was beyond anyone's reckoning. The city was defenseless. It was clear that the Council and, more particularly, Mizpah were to blame. Leading a mob of citizens, Yahweh occupied the Council chambers and forced the Council to vote. Enough was enough, he proclaimed to the city, and with all the heavy-heartedness Mizpah's faction could bear, legislation for building the city's walls was formally passed."

"I do appreciate your story, Maalik," I interrupted. "Truly, I do. But you are guilty of the same folly as Jehoel's. There is no one, other than those who would see God dethroned, who believes these yarns. You have no proof. Do you not see that your story is indistinguishable from every other story that every other lunatic who has opposed God relates? Do you not see that what you tell me has no more substance or validation than the ramblings of mad angels? Our history is our history and no amount of storytelling will change the will of God. He has made us and He will not be undone."

Maalik sat quietly, staring steadily into the fire.

"Even if I accepted that this story was founded on a grain of truth, how can you prove it? You cannot possibly," I said in utter exasperation.

"I can," came his quiet reply.

"What was that?" I asked.

"I can," he repeated. "I was there. I was one of the Council of Twelve, a celestial being who ran the city." He looked up at me now. "I am of the One. There were always only twelve of us, until Yahweh showed up."

"I do not believe you."

"I was there. Whether you believe it or not."

"I do not. Even if what you say were possible, that would make you older than the very foundation of the universe."

"Nearly," he said with a smile.

"Okay, then. How old are you?"

"Only ever so slightly older than you, in the reckoning of *our* people."

"Speak sense, Maalik. What do you imply by 'our' people? What do you mean?"

"I told you this would be a night of answers, Ahriman," Maalik said with the gravest of expressions. "Yahweh was one of us. One of the Ones. Like me. Like the Council."

He could see me winding up for another retort.

"Now, before you start arguing with me," he went on, "I know I told you that I do not know where Yahweh came from. But he had the same nature, the same power, the same light that we did. We, the Twelve. There were only supposed to be twelve of us at any one time. That was how it had always been. Power was managed among us and none among us had more power than any other. But Yahweh changed all of that. From wherever he came, so must the twelve of us have come."

"So using your logic, then, He was meant to be of the Council of Twelve?" I felt somewhat pleased with this notion.

"Yes. But this was only part of the problem. Wherever Yahweh came from, he brought more than just Zoan and a few followers. He brought you."

"I do not understand. You are trying to tell me that I am not who I think I am?" I laughed out loud.

Ukobach shot us a quick glance from the shadows of his guard post.

"That I too, am One?" I scoffed.

I was growing quite tired of Maalik's story. I had endured years of similar gibberish while hunting down members of the cell. Never once had *this* crazy story raised its wooly head.

"In a manner of speaking, yes," Maalik said. "You see, when Yahweh came before the Council that first time, he did not come as an interesting stranger. He came as a threat. Yahweh brought you to us as a baby. He said he had found the place where Creation had been born. The place where he found you. You were One. And he was One. He said our time was at an end and that a new time was rising. A time when he and you would rule in our stead. His threats led to the first cracks in the Council. Pushed Mizpah into the opposition. Spawned two factions: those who supported Yahweh and his consolidation of power under this new order and those who remained wed to the old ways, following Mizpah, refusing to allow power to be concentrated."

"As a baby? He found me and brought me here?" My mind was overwhelmed by a mix of frustration, confusion, and exhaustion.

"To break the stalemate, Yahweh offered you up as a sort of insurance policy. If the Council did what he wanted, Yahweh would instruct Zoan to take you into his family, raising you as his son and later, as his grandson, but never making you any the wiser as to your power. We, the opposing Council members aligned with Mizpah, petitioned you to be given to another family, any other family, given Zoan's allegiance, but Yahweh would not budge. We reckoned that at the very worst, we might, in accepting this offer, be able one day to wrestle you from Zoan and restore the balance of power. Yahweh's offer would not be the end of our problems, but at least it left us with some options. We were naïve in thinking we could play the game the way Yahweh did."

Maalik looked at me. "I know this is a lot to swallow all at once, but I think somewhere inside of you, you're not that surprised."

"You have no idea what makes me tick, Maalik," I said, shaking my head. "You might just as well have told me that I had popped from the head of one of those statues we broke into a thousand pieces in that dank dungeon in Jehoel's headquarters."

"Well, it's not too far from that, in fact," Maalik replied, only half in jest. "But let us not get lost in fantasies. As I said, Yahweh gave us an ultimatum. If Mizpah and his faction on the Council rejected his offer, Yahweh would order Zoan to use the new army to directly overthrow the Council. He would make it appear as if he were saving the city. The Council, he would say, was unwilling to protect the city from trimmers and had been removed in order to protect the City of Heaven in this, its most desperate hour. Then he and his general, Zoan, would ride out and defeat the trimmer armies, validating Yahweh's actions and making him an unprecedented and enduring hero. There could be no possible return for the Council. Either this, or we could accept his terms. In essence, Yahweh threatened the Council and the stability of the City of Heaven by using *you* as a bargaining point."

I remained silent, listening and thinking quickly.

"Though we had little choice," Maalik continued, "we who opposed Yahweh could not decide. I could not decide. I wanted what was best for the city, but here before me were two beings with powers like ours and an enemy army hovering virtually on our doorstep, not much farther than a stone's throw from our homes. Maybe Mizpah was wrong? Maybe the Twelve had been wrong all along? Maybe there were not just twelve, but more out there? More like us, with the power to rule? Equally important, no matter how we considered ourselves and viewed our rule, was the fact that the citizens *wanted* Yahweh. They *wanted* an army. They *wanted* the walls. Were we not a Council bidden to rule by and for the people? What argument did we have in support of withholding our consent, when our citizens were clamoring for us to accept Yahweh's conditions? If we purported to represent them and they wanted a wall, who were we to deny them? When Yahweh stormed the sacred chamber, with the citizenry behind him, we had no choice. We agreed."

"God frequently negotiates at the end of a sword," I said.

"At the end of your sword, Ahriman. Your sword."

"Indeed."

"With the walls under construction and the army in training, the trimmers finally attacked the city in force. But Yahweh ordered Zoan to hold back, until it was clear that the citizens themselves would no longer support Mizpah and his Council. The city was sacked. I fled in the fighting, along with many citizens. Mizpah was killed on the floor of the Council chambers. What could we do? The city was set alight, the sign, it seems, for Zoan to enter and defeat the invaders. Even then, his army sustained remarkably high casualties, not surprising, when you consider that the fighting force was made up of the city's leading citizens, not soldiers. But what better way for Yahweh to rid himself of what would, most probably, become unruly opponents later? Fighting and dying to protect their beloved city, they did it willingly. Fighting for the very person who was stealing their freedom from them."

"It was a ruse," I said, more to myself than to Maalik. I looked up from the fire at him. "It was a lie."

"Yes," he said with a heavy heart. "Yes, it was. Trimmers attacked the city all right, but at Yahweh's command. Zoan had created an army for Gehenna all right, but it was the trimmer army that now attacked the city."

The fire crackled, as the last burnt embers fell in.

"The Council members were mere children, compared to Yahweh," Maalik continued. "We did not understand that kind of malevolence. We simply could not conceive it. And so we played into Yahweh's hands. He threw down our own rule. From the inside out. Together, he and Zoan made the Council members look like fools. To the point where the citizens finally rose up and destroyed their own government. Looking back on it now, it seems that having considered all points of view, we were truly idiots."

A tear came to Maalik's eye. It ran down his face and onto his white robes. He made no effort to wipe it and I watched as the path traced down his face by that first tear was followed by others. He was a strong angel and yet his emotions, his love of his people and his way of life, moved him to cry before his enemy. The one, perhaps the One, who had killed his family, chased his herds, and robbed meaning from his life. All in the name of God.

⌘　⌘　⌘

"Sometime later, Zoan grew a conscience," Maalik began without warning, after a long silence. "No one knows why he defected, but it was widely believed that aware of the prophesied power of what was then his new grandson, he wanted power for himself. Or maybe Gabriel had eclipsed him. Knowing Zoan, I prefer to think something changed within him. He saw an opportunity to do some good, when all he had done before was evil. Something in his relationship with Yahweh changed. Something made him give up what he had so fervently believed before and make a fresh start. Like you, he came to the outlands on his own account, driven by something deeper than he could identify."

"I have a question," I said.

Maalik was surprised by the change he perceived in my attitude.

"Of course, Ahriman. What is it?"

"How did you know Yah...I mean...God was One? What made you believe Him? No matter what you say, and I have only known you for a short while, I doubt you were 'idiots,' as you suggested."

Maalik laughed and seemed pleased to have moved past his sadness. "It is just a feeling. A feeling like no other you have felt before. I cannot explain it. You just know and in knowing, you feel a sense of peace. Peace that comes from being with someone so close to you that you are almost one." He snickered. "One."

"I think I know what you mean."

Maalik did not appear surprised. "I hope so," he said.

"When I first saw you, I felt I knew you. I did not know why. I do not know why. I have no recollections of seeing you before I came here. Yet in meeting you and speaking with you, I sense a connection that I cannot explain."

"You do know, then."

"I have felt that way before, though."

"In the presence of God?" Maalik asked knowingly

"Yes." It made sense now. "In the presence of God."

"You thought it was just love of God? You thought it was your faith in him that brings you together."

"Yes." I thought a moment more. "It feels like being home. Like I was in the right place."

"And you experienced this only with him?

"Yes."

"Not even with your grandfather or Jehoel?" he asked.

I swallowed hard. "Zoan was not imbued with this special power you speak of? Like God?" I swallowed hard again. "Like me?"

"Neither he nor Jehoel were One, as you and I are. No. Zoan was just an angel, like most. Brilliant? Yes, as he had helped Yahweh conceive his scheme to come to power. But it was not that he had just helped Yahweh build his army. He alone knew where Yahweh had found you."

"I am not sure I follow."

"When Yahweh came to the Council with you, he told us he had found the site of Creation. But he did not share its location with us. Why would he? It was the source of his power and could, if disclosed, be taken from him. Wherever you were created, wherever Yahweh came from, was a secret to all, but Zoan."

"How is that?"

"Sadly," Maalik sighed, "he never told me. But if you came from the same place Yahweh had come from..."

"You are suggesting that God and I are related? That the three of us are brothers?"

"In a way. There were twelve, for as far back into the past as existence can go. And then there were more. You know in your heart that you are not like most of those around you."

"Yes, I think you are right."

I may not have wanted to admit it, but it felt right.

"You and he are of the same stock, no matter where you came from."

"What of Jehoel?" I asked, the guilt welling up in me. A taste I had forgotten but of late. "He was a citizen. Like any other. But he was loyal to the true Council. To Mizpah. When the city fell, he stayed, outwardly loyal to Yahweh, but inwardly dedicated to the restoration of the City of Heaven. It was hard on him. Leading a double life, as you well know, makes for difficult living. Always looking over your shoulder for signs that someone has caught onto you. Always fearing for your loved ones, for your own neck, and feeling guilty for what your double life leads you to do. Betraying comrades, on both sides, in order to do something you never really know whether you can achieve. Sitting on the sidelines, as you watch what you loved and dedicated yourself to wither and die. Watching the havoc Yahweh next wrought. Truly and fantastically horrific."

"Zoan told me before he died that he had met Jehoel in the outlands," I said. "A young officer in the army. He never mentioned any connection with God."

Maalik was confused for a moment. "No, that is not right. Not as far as I know, at any rate."

"That is what Zoan told me before he died."

Maalik thought hard to himself. "I cannot guess what Zoan's intentions were when he told you this. It is possible that even after everything else I have to tell you, he did not know Jehoel's allegiances and his role in the flight of the remaining Council from the city."

"'Everything else,' you say?"

"Yes, Ahriman. It gets worse. So prepare yourself."

I was skeptical.

"When Zoan overcame the trimmer army in the fight for the city, the menace was over. The Council had fled, Mizpah was dead, and large parts of the city were ruined. The Council chambers had been burned to the ground. The city's army was shredded in the fighting, but the City itself had been saved. The captured trimmer soldiers were rounded up by Yahweh's personal guard, led by an angel named Gabriel, and imprisoned. Once the flames had been doused and the city restored to calm by Yahweh, Gabriel publicly executed the remaining Ones, along with all the trimmer soldiers, who believed to the end that they were still playing a part in Yahweh's plan. Gabriel's guard butchered them all, as the city's few remaining citizens roared their approval."

"God deceived them."

"Yes. The trimmers enlisted in Yahweh's plan, believing they were taking the city for themselves and would continue as part of his army."

"But God had other plans," I said.

God had built two armies, destroyed them both, and become more powerful than any other being in existence. That felt about right.

"Yes. That same day," Maalik continued, "Yahweh had Gabriel post a list of those who were to be sentenced to death for their betrayal of the city. The list included everyone on the Council of Twelve, their families, and anyone important in the city who had not rallied to Yahweh's side. In one fell swoop, Yahweh sentenced to death nearly the entire upper stratum of the city. Blood ran through the streets, as whole families, an entire generation of angels, was murdered. Angels who had fled were hunted down, their heads brought back to Yahweh for inspection and payment, if the victims had been of some import. By confiscating all the properties of those who had found their way onto the lists, Yahweh amassed untold wealth. Villas, castles, cropland outside the city walls, forests, and rivers—whole sections of the city and its en-virons became his, as nearly the entire adult population was now dead, either in combat or by his executioners' sword. The City of Heaven had truly ceased to exist."

"The City of Heaven," I repeated to myself, poking at the em-bers and stirring sparks into the air before me.

"It was evil like we'd never known," Maalik said with great sadness. "Yahweh brought the people into his fold, made them believe they were part of something bigger than they had ever understood before. He integrated them into his group, unifying them under his tutelage. He showed them the way. And offered them protection. But them alone, those individuals who shared his goal, now the common goal. A phantom, actually, but some-thing real enough for us all to believe him. Yahweh's followers be-came all the more zealous in their steadfastness, willing to destroy anything that threatened him, because if he were threatened, so were they. Anyone who spoke out against him, whether it was true or false, became a target."

"Where was my grandfather in all of this?" I asked, hating to do so.

"Unlike now, Yahweh had one Seraph and he was busy building the army."

"Zoan was God's Seraph before Gabriel?" I asked.

This too, was inconceivable.

"Yes. But unlike his grandson, Zoan was not the engineer, the administrator, or the politician. He was a soldier and Yahweh knew it. And both Yahweh and Zoan knew that in order to stabilize the new regime, there had to be some external threat. Yahweh's new administration needed something to unify the new city."

"That phantom you spoke of," I said.

"Yes. Yahweh needed another common enemy. But by then, Yahweh was no longer Yahweh. When he had finished killing off the populace, he ceased to be 'Yahweh' and became 'God' instead. And God wasted no time in setting out to reconstruct the city's government so as to make sure no one would ever be able to undo what he had done. Or more to the point, to ensure that no one could ever do what he had done. God was blameless, or so this new order said. The problems that necessitated his rise to power, inherent in the Council of Twelve and their flawed rule, had been eliminated, it added. Yahweh became God, in whose sight, all citizens could rejoice in his love for them. Those whose loyalty to him was not deemed absolute were condemned as enemies of the true faith and eliminated."

"Like you," I said.

"Yes. Me. And all the people who would flee into the outlands, all of us who had suddenly switched places with the tyrant now wielding absolute power over our beloved city. But God was smart. He realized that if he wiped out all our history, he would be eroding the very foundations of his own legitimacy. So he did not destroy all the old ways, but refashioned them to suit his purpose. Not so much changing the language in which they had been written, as changing the context in which they could be read. And thus did people come to believe they were following the old ways when, in reality, they were following God's way."

"And what became of you?" I asked, as if I did not already know the answer.

"We became the new trimmers. *Your* trimmers," Maalik said, referring to my efforts as Seraph to destroy all resistance to God's reign. "Yahweh and his Seraph, Zoan, decided we were the threat the city needed. A common threat that would bind the city's survivors together. The dogma grew and was perpetuated by the likes of Zoan and Gabriel, each of whom profited from the power God gave them."

"Jehoel came to me when my grandfather was first struck by illness," I revealed.

"Yes. He was afraid that you'd been told the truth, by someone not good at telling the truth."

"What do you mean? You said something about Zoan giving up God."

"Zoan defected. For whatever reason, he fell from Yahweh's graces. You, above all people, know that no one can just walk away from God. Zoan did. And when he did, he took you along. You were too young to remember your time here. In the outlands. But when Yahweh threatened to kill his family, Zoan broke down. He may not have loved his son the way he loved you, but he could not let Yahweh kill his family."

"That does not make sense. My father hated Zoan."

"For having lost his title as Seraphim. It makes complete sense. Zoan fled with you, but left your father in the city. Your father had every reason to hate Zoan. He was Yahweh's hostage."

"This is not what Zoan told me before he died. He wanted more than anything that I do the right thing, whatever that was, but you are suggesting he lied to me with his dying breath?"

It was an idea that truly angered me.

"I do not know his reason for lying to you. He eventually left the outlands and returned to the new City of God. Ironically, he used you as a bargaining tool in much the same way Yahweh had used you, years earlier, with the Council. In exchange for his life and that of his family, Zoan did two things: he gave you back to Yahweh, though only for you to rot away quietly as a private citizen, and he vowed to devote his efforts to discovering the secret of your creation. From the place only he and Yahweh knew. He bargained with Yahweh so that as long as he lived, you would be protected."

"But I remained untouched, did I not, when my grandfather died?"

"Because you took his place. Like your grandfather before you, you became Yahweh's lieutenant, doing his dirty work for him. Gabriel had become too set in his ways. Too complacent in his positions. Too much of a liability. And though Gabriel has Michael to support him now, you had the fire, the drive, to make God's tyranny really complete."

I rubbed my head. The embers of the fire had flickered out. It was all too much. My life a lie. Powers I possessed, but did not know of. Lies and betrayals from the people I knew, loved, and respected.

"You see. You could not go out with Gabriel's army. Yahweh needs you for something else. Otherwise, he would have killed you by now. He needs you to finish what Zoan started for him." Maalik stood and looked down upon me. "Tell me about Apsatsus."

It was the end of the torture. The end of my imprisonment. Maalik was right. I looked up and met his gaze.

"I will only tell the Council," I said. "Assemble them for tomorrow."

Maalik smiled, pulled out a sleeve of papers from inside his robes, and placed it on the ground before me. "You know," he said, "to succeed someone great and not be eclipsed by his aura, you have to outshine him. And to do so, you have to accomplish twice as much as he had. It is easy to get lost in his shadow and get stuck in a rut that was not of your making." Maalik looked at me and then at the sleeve on the ground before me. "Make your own way and make your name. Step out of Zoan's shadow. Discard his legacy and make your own way the way of Heaven."

He left me to my thoughts.

Ukobach stood quietly in the shadows. Listening. Watching.

CHAPTER
THIRTY-TWO

I opened the sleeve of papers and began reading.

YAHWEH SAYS THAT ALL DIVINE THINGS STAY ETERNAL AND THE SAME. BUT IF THAT IS SO, WHY DID HE NEED TO OVERCOME? YAHWEH OVERCAME THE PANTHEON OF GODS, BUT IF HE CREATED IT, WHY DID HE NEED TO PREVAIL OVER THEM? HOW CAN SOMEONE SO BEREFT OF AWARENESS HAVE CREATED THE WORLD OF WHICH HE PROCLAIMS HIMSELF THE MAKER?

It was Zoan's handwriting. I could tell right away. How many times had I read his letters to me, guiding me with his advice on my way through university, the army, the city bureaucracy? Just like me, he capitalized all references to God. It came from rigorous training. And I had copied him from the time I could read and write. The papers were incomplete and in scraps, but I read on, anyway.

> MARLA USED TO ASK ME WHAT I HAD DONE TO CURRY FAVOR WITH HIM. I BELIEVED. THAT'S ALL HE NEEDS. HE NEEDS ME TO BELIEVE AND IF I BELIEVE, THEN I'LL DO ANYTHING FOR HIM, EVEN IF IT IS THE MOST DESPICABLE DEED.

Marla was my grandmother, though I had not thought of her in ages. In fact, I never knew her. She died when I was young, but I have faint recollections of her arguing with my father. My grandfather always refused to get involved. An angel with such a fierce reputation for combat, Zoan, strangely, had never fought with my grandmother.

> WHAT IS THE TRUTH? I HADN'T KNOWN. I USED TO BELIEVE THAT EVERYTHING HE SAID WAS THE TRUTH, EVEN IF IT WAS A LIE. I WATCHED, AS HE KILLED ALL THOSE PEOPLE. I WAS THERE, WHEN HE BURNED THE CITY DOWN. YET WHATEVER HE SAID, WHATEVER HE DID, I SUPPORTED HIM, BECAUSE SOMEHOW, IN SOME WAY, HE MADE ME BELIEVE.
>
> YAHWEH WANTS US, ABOVE ALL, TO BELIEVE AND HE'LL STOP AT NOTHING TO

MAKE SURE THAT THE TRUTH DOESN'T GET IN THE WAY. HE WOULD HAVE US BELIEVE THAT WHEN YOU LOOK INTO THE FACE OF YOUR NEIGHBOR, YOU LOOK INTO HIS FACE, THE FACE OF GOD. WHEN YOU LOOK OUT TO THE ENDLESS HORIZON, YOU LOOK INTO THE FACE OF GOD. WHEN YOU LOOK AT THE HORROR, THE AFTERMATH OF BATTLE, THE DEAD STREWN ALL AROUND, YOU LOOK INTO THE FACE OF GOD. GOD IS THE REALITY AROUND YOU, SINCE HE CREATED ALL THINGS.

YOU LOOK TO ME TO ANSWER YOUR QUESTIONS. "IF NOT GOD, THEN WHO? IF NOT GOD'S WILL, THEN WHOSE WILL?" I CANNOT PASS ON KNOWLEDGE IN ANY PURE FORM. I CAN ONLY CONVEY TO YOU MY OWN INADEQUATE UNDER-STANDING OF THE DIVINE. BUT WE WERE MADE IN SUCH A WAY THAT WHEN WE CONTEMPLATE THE ABSOLUTE MEANING OF THINGS, WE ARE DRAWN TO THE EASY ANSWERS, BECAUSE WE SHARE A COM-MON UNDERSTANDING OF EXPERIENCE. IT'S EASIER THAT WAY AND GOD FEEDS ON THAT. HE TELLS US WHAT'S DIVINE, BECAUSE HE CAN SEE HOW WE'RE ALIKE IN THAT WAY. BUT WHEN IT COMES TO SELF-DETERMINATION, WHEN IT COMES

TO UNDERSTANDING THINGS ON OUR OWN, WE RISK STEPPING INTO DANGEROUS TERRITORY. HE FEARS THIS. THE THEOLOGICAL SPECULATION HE FEEDS US IS NOTHING MORE THAN SELF-INDULGENT GUESSWORK ABOUT THINGS NO ONE CAN PROVE. IT'S JUST THAT HE'S TAKEN CREDIT FOR IT!

REASON IS THE POINT WHERE WE CAN DRAW THE LINE. WE MUSTN'T GET TOO WRAPPED UP IN THE ETHEREAL AT THE EXPENSE OF THE REAL. ONLY BY BEING GROUNDED IN WHERE WE ARE AND COMING TO AN UNDERSTANDING OF HOW THAT WORKS CAN ONE BECOME AWARE OF DIVINITY. NOT GOD HIMSELF, BUT THE PLACE WHERE ALL ANGELS LIVE. JUDGMENT IS A STRICTLY SELF-IMPOSED MISTAKE. THEOLOGICAL SPECULATION, THE KIND GOD WOULD HAVE US BELIEVE IN, IS NOTHING MORE THAN THE SELF-INDULGENCE OF AN INTOLERANT BEING, LOOKING TO PREACH "THE WORD" FOR HIS OWN ENDS, WHETHER THOSE ENDS—OR THE MEANS—ARE UNDERSTOOD. GOD HAS SUPERIMPOSED HIMSELF BETWEEN US AND REALITY. HE'S A GO-BETWEEN, MEANING TO APPLY A MYSTICISM THAT DOESN'T ACTUALLY

EXIST. IT'S HIS MEANS OF CONTROL, HID-
DEN IN THE GUISE OF A MORAL LIFE.

I had read things like this before. In the cell. Much of the study I had undertaken was on such matters. To be honest, reading and thinking about these things had made me happy at the time. Life and existence were more than simply God. They were also about me.

REASON IS NOT THE SIN GOD WOULD HAVE
YOU BELIEVE IT IS. REASON IS THE ONLY
WAY TO UNDERSTAND HIM. IT GIVES US
UNDERSTANDING ABOUT GOD, BUT NOT
OF GOD. THAT'S WHAT HE WANTS TO
WITHHOLD FROM US. THAT'S WHAT HE
DOESN'T WANT US TO LEARN. BUT GOD'S
MESSAGE IS WRONG. LEARNING IS THE
HIGHEST FORM OF UNDERSTANDING
AND WE SHOULD NOT DISCRIMINATE
AGAINST ITS SOURCE OR DISMISS WHAT
IT OFFERS OUT OF SELF-IMPOSED PREJ-
UDICE OR BECAUSE OF THE MACHINA-
TIONS OF A TYRANT.

It sounded so much like my grandfather. So much so, that I could almost see him standing out in front of a crowd, speaking these words. At the same time, they were so far removed from what I knew of him. What I had been taught in my textbooks and classes. True, I had read more about his life's exploits than we had ever discussed face-to-face. In fact, one of the few times he had talked to me about himself was during our last conversation. At the time, I had been glad for that, as his story was so fantastical and convenient that it was easier to believe it was just a dying angel rambling on. He may have known Jehoel. That I could get. But his story then had been nothing but a lie. A lie to protect me, yes, but a lie, all the same. Why was everyone always lying to me?

⌘　⌘　⌘

I sat before the Council the next day. They looked at me solemnly, but expectantly. I had finally made my choice.

"I have been here in the outlands with you for what seems like an eternity," I began. "I listened and learned and gave you information about things and you did the same. You gave me the opportunity to see how you live and tried to explain to me why you live the way you do. For this, I am grateful."

"You are welcome," Maalik said.

Only some of the Council nodded in agreement.

I continued. "There is no easy way to put this. So I will come out and say it. God has created a most powerful weapon." I paused for a moment and reflected. "No, well, actually, I created for God a most powerful weapon. It is called 'Man' and it will destroy all that you know."

No one moved. The only audible sounds came from the newly laid tent-city streets outside.

Finally, someone spoke. "We must destroy it, then." It was Matel.

There were no questions from them. Only belief in my words. They knew.

"You cannot," I said. "Not, at least, without throwing out one of your most coveted beliefs."

"And what is that?" asked Corpens, the Council member who had, so many months ago, called for my immediate torture and death. He was just as fat and red in the face as he had been that first night, when he recommended I should be put to death.

"Compassion," I said grimly.

This time, there was a murmur.

"If you claim compassion as one of the hallmarks of your people," I went on, "you cannot exterminate Man. He is a living, rational being, though not yet perfected. He can feel, he can sense, and he can think. He is primitive, yes. But though I have made him that way on God's orders, he is no less animate than any of you."

"How has this come to pass?" Corpens asked.

Matel nodded his approval of the question, looking at me with great concern. Maalik sat in pensive silence.

"I picked up from where Zoan had left off, though I did not understand the implications at the time. When I took the title of Seraph, God instructed me to complete Zoan's work. I know you all respect him for reasons I may never fully understand. And for that, I respect you. But whatever he may have meant to you, here in the outlands, his bargain with God led to the creation of Man." I looked around the tent. "You taught me that. You told me Zoan had shared secrets with God that gave him the kind of power almost equal to His or, at least, enough for God to consider him His most trusted advisor."

"What proof do you have of these things?" asked Corpens, referring to Man.

"I have no absolutes. You will have to trust me. But what I have learned, while in your company, fills in some interesting pieces of the apparent puzzle. Pieces I have to take on faith. Zoan knew of God's birthplace and that place seems to be the Forks at Apsatsus. On the Styx. While in God's service, Zoan had started working there and...well...experimenting."

"God made this possible?" Matel asked.

"Yes. My guess is that even God did not know the full significance of the site. Somehow, Zoan did. And lorded it over Him. Zoan did not tell me of his involvement in this matter before he died. Maybe he hoped I would never find out, because if I did, I might complete his work. Maybe he had some other motivation." I mused. "I do not know."

"What is this 'Man' then," Matel asked over the murmur of exchanges between the Council members.

Maalik alone, remained silent.

"I do not quite know how to explain it," I said. "Before my time, Man had been a mishmash of many elements. Zoan's experiment had gone terribly wrong. He had created a host of biological monstrosities that required immediate extermination and, therefore, our prompt intervention. But when I became involved, I asked myself, what better way to succeed than to make Man in God's image? It was a proven model. You asked what Man is? Man is you and me. He can think, breathe, see...whatever. Like you and me. He is almost a perfect copy."

"Where is this 'Man,' then?" asked Corpens.

"On Earth."

"Earth is nothing but a rock in the mess that is the universe. There is nothing there, but rock and ash."

"Your intelligence is not as good as it ought to be, then," I countered. "God's many ministries have been working for billions of years, making Earth a place where Man can live, propagate, and come to us here, in Heaven."

"How is this?" asked Matel.

"Millions of angels doing God's good work. Surely, that does not surprise you?"

The Council fell into murmured discussions again.

"Man is an Earth-bound angel, formed in our image. Well, your image, at any rate."

Maalik perked up at this. "So you have come to believe, then?" he asked, breaking the silence for the first time.

"That's convenient," Corpens said sarcastically.

"I have come to believe that I do not have all the facts, and that while God has shown me infinite mercy, He has shown little of the same to most. As you said, He seems to need me for something. Maybe this was it?"

"How could this have happened?" asked a councilwoman named Margaret.

"I do not have these answers, madam. As you all knew after my first night here, I have not been provided all the facts. God never fully trusted me. He has secrets He will never share with me, with anyone. If that be the case, we are all working in the dark. All we have is what our hearts tell us."

Maalik stood up. "Call Simon in here!" he shouted to the guards at the tent flaps.

"This is why He moves His troops now," I continued. "It must be. I suspect He fears I have done what my grandfather did, so many years ago, and taken up your cause. And maybe I have. The doubts I fostered for a lifetime have come down hard on me during my time with you here. There is more to this than I know. This is the first time I have been out of God's sight and what I see, staring back at Him, is disturbing."

Simon entered the tent and stood at attention.

"Simon, how many of the city's troops have moved into positions near Apsatsus?" Maalik asked.

Simon was unprepared to answer the question, but quickly composed himself. "Our best guess is that he has sent at least four legions."

"Has there ever been such a concentration of city troops at that location before?" Margaret asked.

"No madam, never before."

The Council looked back at me in unison.

"No, never before," I agreed. "Until the last few days, we have never had more than a battalion at that location. We could not risk tipping the trim...tipping you off that anything more than an aqueduct was being maintained there. This concentration of forces is unprecedented, as far as the number of troops deployed is concerned and as a manifestation of God's fear."

Maalik managed a smile.

"When will this 'Man' be ready?" asked Corpens, the fat in his cheeks quivering in barely controlled anger.

"God could use these beings now, if He wanted. They would be undisciplined and difficult to maneuver, of course, but He could throw a mass of them in any direction and see what sticks."

"Ahriman, please. Give us some idea of the dimensions here," Margaret implored. "Is this an organized attack, as you suggest, or is Yahweh just 'seeing what sticks'?"

"Well, Earth was created many billions of years ago, along with billions of other planets. This is widely known. God calls it Creation, but you and I know that means something else."

The Council did not seem to entirely agree.

"In the final analysis, though, Earth simply had the best environment. It worked best for what God had in mind. I am guessing a bit, but I suspect that once Zoan identified the locus of God's Creation, he must have determined he could also create something himself, almost in reverse. It took years, but my grandfather was able to get a rudimentary beings developed. Large and lizard-like, they were not what God wanted, exactly, but the progress made over the millennia seemed, at least, to keep Him interested in Zoan's project. But looking at the data, it is my feeling now that Zoan may have intentionally thwarted each of his apparent attempts to achieve the results God desired."

I shot a look over at Simon. His eyes swiveled back and forth between the Council and me.

"What do you mean?" asked Matel.

I looked back at the Council. "There are many possibilities. For a certain period of time, for example, Zoan had the oxygen levels on Earth so high, it artificially created beings that were well beyond the dimensions God had specified. These things were entirely uncontrollable and simply not usable. They were nothing but animals, really. Zoan seems to have put it down to trial and error. Rather than use matter from his own created environment, he started from scratch."

"And?" Matel persisted.

"He started from a blank slate and, as a result, fooled God into believing He needed Zoan for a longer period of time than He actually did. My grandfather was, after all, producing results. Just not the results God wanted. He was deliberately stalling."

There were no comments from the Council this time. Everybody was lost in thought.

"When I took over, I did not continue his work. Or, at least, not his approach. I pummeled the Earth with debris, knocking out almost all life, and started again. This time, I took our race or, rather, your race of angels as the foundation of Man's evolution. In the sixty-five million years since then, I have been able to develop something that looks and feels like one of us. An angel on Earth. Man. Man is still brutish, as I said, but on my way here, I stopped at Apsatsus and had a remarkable thought. If I change the inhibitors I have currently placed on Man, that is, give him the ability to think as we do once he reaches Heaven, rather than continue as the stunted version of an angel that God has demanded, Man could be a blank slate. On Earth, he would be God's intellectual slave. In Heaven, for all intents and purposes, he would be an angel. But this change in the genetic coding could only be made by someone who has the formulas."

"And?" Maalik asked, with a glimmer of insight into what my next words would be.

"I, alone, have the formula."

"What about Gabriel?"

"He may think he has it, but as things evolved, my work moved well beyond the scope of his understanding." Under my breath, I murmured, "I can thank Phanuel for that." I refocused on what I would say next. "No one has as detailed an understanding of these creatures, their abilities, their strengths, as I have. No one can control Man as well as I can."

"Again, convenient!" Corpens shouted this time.

"I find it decidedly inconvenient!" I snapped back. "The only way I can make these beings rational is to get back into the City and make the necessary changes."

"Ahriman, how will that help us?" asked Maalik.

"If I can give Man the ability to reason, I can make him rational."

"I do not follow," Maalik said earnestly.

"Did you not read the scrolls you yourself gave me last night?" I asked him, a little exasperated by his obtuseness.

"He means Man can be made to follow us, instead," Simon interjected.

"Yes," I replied. "Simon has it right."

"Can't we just destroy it?" asked Margaret.

"Do you not see?" I said in exasperation. "God will do anything He can to prevent that from happening. He left His beloved City open and unprotected in order to protect Man. What does that say to you? Do you think He would do such a thing simply by chance? Of course not! Man is *that* important to Him. He must suspect I have already shared this information with you and is willing to sacrifice His beloved City just to protect what I have done for Him."

"Ahriman, is there any other way to make this formula change you refer to?" Maalik asked.

"No," Simon said.

"How do you know this?" asked Matel suspiciously.

Even I was surprised at Simon's response.

"Lucifer can get back into the City and do what he's suggested," he said, ignoring the question.

He looked at me and I nodded in acknowledgment. He felt comfortable making a decision for the Council. He might be one of their generals, but he was not one of them.

"He is right," I continued, looking back at the Council. "If I can get back into the City, back to my laboratory, I can make the necessary changes. There is no one there who would even know I made them. Not Gabriel, not even God."

I decided it would be better not to discuss Phanuel at this point. It was simply too complicated to explain and I would deal with that, somehow, when the time came.

"Without me, God would either have to work with the unstable and less-than-ideal prototype He has now or start from scratch. Again. He knows Man is not ready. His only hope is to make Man work. Even if He knows I have switched sides, He is still dependent on me to make it work. I will still be valuable to Him for a little bit longer."

"How many such beings can be produced?" Matel asked.

Only Maalik had understood the significance of what I had just said.

"As many as needed," I replied. "As many as desired. Such men will arrive at the Forks in the same condition they were in earlier in their lives. But they will not be able to reproduce here in Heaven. In that respect, they will not be angels. Only their souls will survive the transition from Earth. But God made Earth a fertile place for them. His bureaucracy worked for as long as I can remember, making the universe what it is so that Man could overcome the teetering balance that has come to mark Heaven. God made Man to win the war and God did His work well."

"*You* did His work well," Corpens shot back.

"I am giving you God's greatest weapon," I went on, as if he had not spoken. "I am offering to give you all the knowledge you would need to use God's weapon against Him. You might not approve of what I did, but you succeeded in doing what you had all wished to, since the fall of the City of Heaven and the creation of the City of God. You made me yours and only I can make this happen."

Even Simon, still standing at attention, always the good solider, winced a bit at this.

"What is this plan, then? To make Man rational? That seems a rather precarious place for us to focus our hopes on. Besides, how do we know this is not some elaborately concocted ruse meant to lure us into a trap!" shouted Corpens.

"All he has told us is true," Maalik said.

I looked at Maalik.

"I can sense it," he insisted.

I was not sure even I believed him.

"I have done a great many things I am now ashamed of," I continued, still looking at Maalik. "But believe me when I tell you that your world will end when God has Man at His side. It is only a matter of time before He brings all His forces to bear on you and your people." I looked back at the rest of the Council. "Jehoel had an inkling of this. Otherwise, he would not have come to me. God changed the game and realized that I was the one who could put things back in place. I was God's advantage. I was the One. Jehoel took a huge risk in coming to me, because he knew it would mean facing the real possibility of my rising to this cause." I looked back at Maalik again. "The conflict within him must have been substantial."

"You will not be taking over any cause," Matel shot back in anger.

"Really?" I asked, looking at him slyly.

"Lucifer is the only one who can do it. We all know this," Simon said, relaxing his posture so that he now stood at ease. "He is the only one who can lead this cause and have the slightest chance of being successful. Do you honestly think you will sway people, bring them back into the fold, sitting here as you do, debating with each other?"

I looked again at Simon and felt strangely proud.

"This is madness!" Corpens exclaimed loudly, ignoring the truth of Simon's words. "Surely, all of you can't be seriously considering making *him*," he went on, pointing at me, "the leader of our armies, of the cause so many of us have fought so hard to further? Should I remind you all that only a short while ago, both these angels were commanding armies with the sole purpose of killing everyone in this room!" The words were shouted out as he pointed to both Simon and me.

"He has a point," I said.

Everyone shot me a startled look.

"He has a good point," I admitted. "For the last seventy some odd million years, I have dedicated my life to the service of God. So has Simon. We lived and breathed God and did what He asked us to do, with no questions asked. But if you truly believe in yourselves and in what you have taught Simon and me, then you would know we have no choice, but to do this. No choice, but to restore that which God wrongfully took from your ancestors." I looked at Maalik. "What Yahweh took from you."

I had never uttered His name. In all my life. It was as far as I had ever been from God. He had been the central focus of my life since the beginning and now, for the first frightening time, I did not feel Him near me. I was free and facing a direction I had never faced before.

"Otherwise, you are all as false as God," Simon chimed in.

"This situation with Man changes things in ways I had not considered," Maalik said, shaking his head. "Things are happening too fast."

I was losing them. I stood up and began to pace along the length of the Council table.

"Jehoel knew this would happen," I said. "Not Man, I mean, but the choice we would have to make in moving forward. Do we stick it out or do we grab it by the horns? It is a difficult decision, I grant you, but Jehoel did not dread it for the possibilities it held. He dreaded it for the very reason Maalik just mentioned. It would be too fast. And the change would not be based on evolutionary principles, ideas, and attitudes," I looked at Corpens, "but on revolution. You say I am risking the cause you fought so hard to further? Where was that battle fought, Corpens? Where were you, when the standards of the City of Heaven met the standards of the City of God on the field of battle?"

Corpens cheeks grew redder.

"I was not at that battle either, because it has never been fought. Jehoel believed too much in the ideals of an old republic to regard this movement as one of sudden and violent change. If the sovereign rules at the will of the people, the people must put the sovereign in his position. But do you not all see it now? That is precisely what caused you to fall before. A republic will forever be stronger than an autocracy. That is true. But the transition from tyranny back to your sacred little republic cannot, by its very nature, be a peaceful one. Jehoel's evolutionary approach will never work under the circumstances and if you sit here and wait for it to happen, you will be chased across the plains of Heaven, until the last of you is hewn down by God and His Man."

The Council watched me intently. So did Simon. And Ukobach, standing outside the tent flap.

"Your approach," I continued, "will never work in a place ruled by such fierce and feared leaders. You are going down the same path your predecessors took those many billions of years ago, when God first presented Himself on the outskirts of the City of Heaven. You do not know it, but you are still under the sway of God."

The room reverberated with gasps of anger and exasperation.

"Listen to me!" I shouted. "You stay hidden, far from God's eyes. Yet you continue to subjugate yourselves to His will. He tells us that we serve Him, if we surrender to Him and remain subservient to His wishes and averse to change. So, as His subjects, we neither take action nor raise our voices, because our submission to His commands is held in the highest regard. Taking a step forward and being bold is a sin. We wind up living a life where we are expected to be strong. Yet that very strength is the cause of our suffering. We would rather suffer than take the steps necessary to do what is right!"

"And what is right, Ahriman?" Maalik asked.

It was not the first time I had faced this question. A question that had haunted me since Zoan first posed it, those many years ago.

"If you do not act now," I continued, "you will lose the opportunity to act. Do not think that such action, revolution, is evil. Revolt motivated by violence alone is evil, yes. But rebellion inspired by the desire for betterment of all? Now how can such a revolution be evil? If there is violence, it is for the sake of sudden, nearly spontaneous change, directed by one, powerful central figure willing to give up his gains at the end of the day. That is what I am talking about. Those willing to follow will follow. Those not willing to risk freedom? Well, those people will be left out of the new order."

There was silence. For a while, nothing but silence.

⌘ ⌘ ⌘

Maalik finally spoke. "You must understand that what you propose is anathema to everything we stand for. How can we claim to be the guardians of liberty, custodians of the will of the people, and justify our willingness to invest everything in a single leader?"

"You make a point, Maalik. The Council makes a point," I said, with a slight bow to them. "But has not the past given you any insights at all on the path to the future?"

I marveled at the sclerosis in the room.

"Destiny is not written," I went on. "God would have us believe so, but it was you helped me come to understand this is not the case. You showed me how His words held no substance, that they were uttered not for the sanctity of their meaning, but to deceive and entrap the free spirit that belongs to each of us. If the future has to be the way we envisage it, we must be bold enough to try and shape it. You cannot sit here, millennium after millennium, and simply hope that justice will prevail. You will need to take it in your hands and make it a reality!"

"When you speak from a philosophical perspective, you make sense," Margaret said. "Admittedly. But when you think in real, practical terms, based on what we have here on the ground today, your arguments don't justify the risks you're suggesting we take."

"You are wrong!" I said excitedly, feeling the heat rising within me. "It is the only reason to risk everything! You cannot cling to the middle ground forever. Sometimes, it makes sense to take the middle ground, yes. But those who choose to linger there indefinitely are fools, doomed to failure. God has changed the stakes here. He has upset the balance to which you were accustomed. But by changing the game, He has ensured that you can no longer risk wavering between the 'philosophical,' as you put it, Margaret, and the 'real.' There is nothing more real than death."

"You know nothing of death, except what you wrought on us," Corpens grumbled.

I must be getting to him, I thought. At least, he was not shouting at me.

"That does not help," Maalik said, annoyed. "He came here of his own accord," he reminded Corpens, pointing to me, "as it was prophesied he would. He has taken up our cause, as it was prophesied he would," he said, bowing slightly to me. "We should not doubt the truth of his words."

"It is not the truth of his words that's the issue here," Margaret said. "It is their wisdom." She looked at me. "Launching boldly into action has a way of hiding your real deficiencies."

"With all due respect, Maalik, this has happened once before," Matel interrupted. "Zoan had stood right here and said many similar things. Perhaps he wasn't suggesting we devolve rule to him personally, as Lucifer now is, but look where that got us."

"I conceal nothing from you," I interjected. "I speak to you plainly. Give me the power. The only way to take the City from God is by taking the fight to Him. To bring about the radical transformations needed to make this mission successful, you cannot invest your hopes in mere discussion. It is action you should invest in, led by the One. I am One. The One. One, whose mind and methods will mold and transform the highly ordered, but insidious existence God created, shaping that blasphemy, a blasphemy in its true sense, into the liberty you hold dear. I come to you, not to fulfill my personal ambitions, but to attain the dream of all. That I swear to you. Allow me to do what you will not. I will do what you cannot. My deeds, whether you consider them moral or not, will be justified by the results."

"It's too risky," Corpens said.

"Risk is not the same as uncertainty. Risks are calculable. Uncertainty is not," Simon said. "If the only way someone can impel people into following his path is through violence and threats, is that being powerful?" Margaret asked. "Yahweh doesn't seek power now. He seeks domination."

Both Simon and Maalik shifted at this.

"There is a difference, you know," she said.

"We cannot advance in life following the road of the past, Margaret," I replied. "We can learn from the lessons it teaches, yes, but we can only follow that road as long as it makes sense and is relevant. Once we find a new path, a new way, we should have the moral courage to forge ahead and follow it. The truth is open to everyone."

"But how is your truth relevant to us?" Margaret asked. "Should we give up what we believe in order to win? What kind of power is that?"

"Power can only be measured in terms of someone else's weakness," I replied.

Simon nodded his agreement. Maalik was less enthused.

"God has betrayed His weakness and we should do everything in our power to exploit it, even if it means giving up some of our convictions to achieve what we must for the greater good."

"I guess my concern lies in the suggestion that the only way to make things right, using your argument, Lucifer, is to trust *you* in all things," Matel said. "We risk our very liberty. And none of us are willing to trade one tyrant for another."

The Council agreed with him. Simon remained silent, but I knew he agreed too.

"We are familiar with the evil we face now. What evil will we face, if you are our friend?"

"I cannot believe what I am hearing!" I said in exasperation.

"You are missing an opportunity that may never present itself again," Simon said, coming back around to support my argument.

"How can you claim to want change, but be unwilling to undertake the challenge of making it a reality?"

I nodded in agreement.

Maalik stood expressionless. For some reason, it struck me as the same face he must have worn when he heard of my betrayal and Jehoel's death. Of Yahweh's ultimatum.

"Ahriman may believe what he is saying is the truth," he now said to no one in particular. "But most, either deceived by what they think is right or motivated by their own ambitions, allow themselves to fall into a trap, where they find themselves again making whole what they have fought so hard to destroy."

"I understand your concern," I said. "I really do. Many have, indeed, caused more harm than good for the reasons Maalik has just cited. But look at me. You know me. Better, it may even be said, than I know myself," I laughed. "I am singularly driven and I tell you now what I know in my heart: if we prevaricate in this manner, if we remain so irresolute at such a crucial moment, we will fail in the end."

"Your impatience could get everyone killed," Margaret said.

"Patience is worthless, if you are unwilling to fall ruthlessly on your enemies at the right moment," I said. "This is that moment."

The Council sat in silence. Simon stood to attention again.

"Hope is not a plan," I said, closing my argument.

Heaven seemed to have folded in on itself. Again.

⌘   ⌘   ⌘

I sat in my tent that night, thinking about what I had said. It defied logic that they should treat a prisoner as fairly as they had treated me. Yet they had. It equally defied logic for them to trust me, yet they wanted to. At least, Maalik and Simon did. And I knew it certainly defied logic for them to accept me as their leader when I, until so recently, had been their most dangerous foe.

"The faith they displayed in making me a general in their army was astonishing," Simon said, as he came into my tent, unannounced. "Handing you control of the movement doesn't seem to me like that much more of a leap of faith."

He settled himself in a chair after pouring himself some wine. He was at ease, but distracted.

"It is not a matter of failing in the field anymore," I said. "It is a matter of failing altogether."

"Yet it would be foolish not to deliberate, wouldn't it?" Simon asked. "You are who you are. That's why they move so carefully." He sat forward and rested his elbows on his knees. "Their faith, in a way, revolves around you coming to accept what you now have. But they weren't prepared to deal with the situation once they had finally achieved their aim."

"And what have I come to accept, Simon?" I looked at him mournfully. "I become a traitor, if I do the right thing. And remain a villain, if I obey the will of God."

"You will die, if you do the will of God," Simon replied, rubbing his eyes. "Death is the only thing God knows how to dispense."

"And who should they trust now?" I said, feeling more tired than I had in a long while. "Me? You? They do not know what they want, though they make speak otherwise."

"It is not what they want that happens to be the problem. It is what Maalik wanted. It is what Jehoel wanted. Most of those people are so far removed from the core of what they claim to believe," Simon said, straightening up in his chair. "They have had to devote so much time to mere survival that they have forgotten how to live."

I was reminded of Amee suddenly.

"Maybe so," I said "but to delay any longer would be madness. Michael has surely been given orders both to secure the Forks and send reinforcements back to the City as soon as he consolidates his position. God will be working furiously to fortify the City. If these people do not act, God will sense their weakness. He will gauge the dissension in their midst and exploit it to His advantage. Again."

"You are right, of course, but consider it from the Council's perspective for a moment," Simon said. "They can keep running, but at least they would be running. Taking on what we're proposing would turn the last thirteen billion years into a giant gamble."

We sat in silence for a few minutes. I wanted wine, but was sure I would regret it later.

"Do not forget one of the most important factors in this situation," I said, doubt lacing my own words. "Even if we succeeded in taking the City, we would have to hold it long enough to win its inhabitants over to our side. They may be chafing under God's boot, but there are, and will, most likely, always be strong elements in the City with a great deal more to lose with God's ouster. My family, the families of many others of the nobility, will not take kindly to an egalitarian government being set up in Heaven." I looked at Simon. "Regardless of what the true history may be." I poured myself some wine, but did not drink it. "They may not like God," I said emphatically, "but they profit from His rule."

"The city is accustomed to a tyrant," Simon said. "Why should the citizens care whether the tyrant himself remains in power or is ousted by another, if their expectations, spawned under the rule of the first, have no chance of changing under the second?"

"That is not the way of it," I replied, surprised by his suggestion. "Under the kind of government we propose, how do we keep the City strong and at peace, when its most powerful elements oppose us in principle?"

"Perhaps by following God's example," Simon said without hesitation.

"Simon, I warn you against such ideas," I said, after studying him carefully for a few moments.

"You are right," he replied.

I laughed. "A year ago, if you had said that to me, I would not have twitched at all," I chuckled. "'Kill them all. Set things on the course we want,' does not seem in keeping with your style these days, Simon."

"But isn't that what you're really proposing?" he asked. "To overcome God, you need to become as God is?" He was not laughing.

"No, though it saddens me you think so," I said. "Threats of that nature will do us no good. Not only does it bring us down to God's level, it does nothing to weaken Him and His cause. Moreover, it may provoke the angels we will need on our side, when the time comes."

Simon averted his gaze. Maybe there was still too much of God in him.

"If we act the way God does, we become what He is," I said. "The Council was right. Heaven cannot afford another tyrant. There is no point in making so great a sacrifice, if 'Lucifer' is simply another way of saying 'God.' If we are the light bearers, if we are, indeed, 'Lucifer,' we need to bring light. If we cannot, by the strength of our arguments and beliefs, convince the people that our way is the right one, there is no point in establishing our rule." Begrudgingly, I added, "We should accept that, no matter what it ultimately means." I thought about it for a moment. "Those who cannot be made subjects should be made free."

Again, we sat in silence for a while.

When Simon got up to leave, he said, "I hope you are right. No matter what happens, though, I would rather bring the fight to God than wait for him to bring it on us."

"Yes," I agreed, gulping down my wine. "But when we no longer fight for a cause, we fight for the sake of ambition. That, perhaps, more than God, will be a far greater challenge," I said. "If we win, that is."

We both laughed, though I am not sure why.

⌘ ⌘ ⌘

"We have voted," Maalik advised me, as I sat before the Council the next day. "You will be given sole command over all our forces and granted complete executive and administrative power. This power will last only as long as the City remains in Yahweh's hands. If, or when, you succeed in overpowering him and bringing the

Council back to the City, you will surrender your power and it will return to the Council. Only if you accept these terms will we have an agreement."

It was more than I had anticipated. Corpens sat quietly, but stared steadfastly at me. Margaret sat with head bowed. Matel's face was expressionless. The rest of the Council sat waiting for my response, almost as if they hoped I would decline the offer.

"I am honored," I said truthfully.

"This decision has not been made lightly," Corpens spat out. "There are some of us who don't agree with this course of action." He looked at Maalik. "We are placing a great deal of faith in Maalik's estimation of you. If you fail or deviate even slightly from what we have agreed upon, Maalik will suffer the same fate as you do."

"More blood on my hands," I said.

Corpens had never shown me the least bit of civility. Why should I expect any different now? His son had been killed fighting City soldiers. Unable to bear the loss, Corpens's grief-stricken wife had taken her own life. My life had touched so many more angels in so many more ways than I could ever have imagined, as I sat in my bureau office during my years as a young angel, scheming on how to rise in the ranks.

"I understand and I do not take this appointment lightly," I replied.

Corpens clearly did not like the snub.

"That said, we need to move quickly, as we have already spent far too much time considering a course of action," I declared. "The City may already have organized its defense by now and I have little time in hand to make the necessary adjustments to my formulas." I stood. "For the time being, this Council is adjourned. I will need no more than two angels to remain with me here. They will share power equally, though in different spheres."

The Council members looked at each other, indecisive and befuddled. I had dismissed them. That had never happened before.

"Go to your families and prepare them for what lies ahead," I said, trying to strengthen their resolve. "The path we follow will not be a pleasant one, but if we remain united and are successful in our quest, you will be rewarded with something that has been denied you in most of your lifetimes: freedom."

The tent emptied of its occupants. All, I could sense, were reluctant participants in the mission I had outlined for them. Even those whom I had directed to stay back with me.

⌘　⌘　⌘

"Simon. You are now my Archangel of the Armies. You will command all outlander armies. Get them equipped and ready to move out tomorrow."

"Yes sir," Simon replied automatically. A wisp of dust kicked up, as he clicked his boot heels together.

"Let us not slip into that old habit," I said, smiling at him. "We agreed we would remain on a first-name basis as long as we were riding together. We will ride together now."

Simon smiled.

"Yes, Lucifer."

"Ahriman."

"Yes, Ahriman."

"Maalik," I said, turning to him. "You are now my Archangel of the Realm. You know more about the history of Heaven and have more status among the nobility here than anyone else."

"There is no nobility here. We are all one," came his spontaneous reply. At least, he was consistent. I had to give him that.

"Maalik, there is no time to parse political philosophy. Your job is to keep the aristocracy happy. Keep the Council members happy. Without their support, we risk losing the support of all the people."

He seemed pleased that I had now embraced what he assumed to be the truth. "Much as I may fall short in my understanding of your republic or its governance, it is vital that it remain united as one to overcome the challenge ahead of us. Even if I can modify the formulas and give Man rationality, and even if we can take the

City, we have a hard road ahead," I said. "A hard road, in all respects. Simon," I said, turning back to him. "Your preparations for the offensive should not only focus on an assault on the City, but include a stratagem for holding it, should we succeed in breaching the walls. I need not remind you that God will urgently recall His forces from Apsatsus when He sees an approaching army intent on launching an all-out attack. I do not know how you will do it, but I rely on you to find a way."

Simon saluted.

"And without delay," I said to that, completing my instructions.

Simon nodded, already pondering the problem.

"Maalik. Once we take the City, we will need to sequester its nobility. It will not be safe for us to allow them free movement. You must prepare to impose martial law throughout, until our position is secure enough to engage in the delicate dance of politics and power."

Maalik seemed discomfited by the idea.

"All rights will be restored to the citizens in time," I assured him. "Not to worry. But we cannot afford to betray any weakness inside the walls, once we take them. We can deceive our enemy about the actual strength of our armies, but we cannot do so where the resolve of our citizens is concerned."

Maalik smiled now.

"Also, you will need to figure out how to supply the City for what may turn out to be a long siege. Simon has been entrusted with the defenses and the tactics. You are responsible for the supply and the logistics."

"I understand," Maalik replied. "What do we do first?"

I thought for a moment. "I need to get back to the City as quickly as I can. But it must not seem as though you voluntarily set me free. It will need to look like an escape. Simon, you will need to send out patrols to create the impression that the trimmers are looking for me—a fugitive."

"I will circulate a rumor that you have escaped," Maalik said. Turning to Simon, he continued, "If it is spread in the right circles, news will get back to the City quickly," he said confidently.

"Right, then," I said. "Simon, when I am away, you will need to work out some kind of diversionary tactic to mislead enemy scouts so that the bulk of the army can cross the Acheron before word gets to Apsatsus. If Michael is forewarned about our moving toward the City, the whole plan may collapse."

Simon thought about it for a moment. "I will send a raiding party south to the Forks to create the impression that this is where we intend to engage. Meanwhile, I will lead the rest of the army on a wide swing to the north. Outlanders almost never go there, as the area is mountainous and the forests are dense along that part of the upper Acheron."

"Fine, fine. You will have to wait for me to give the sign, though." I thought furiously, but did not know at that moment what form it would take. "You will know," I said. "You will have to know when I give the sign."

"Understood," Simon said. "But it should not be so obvious as to be too widely understood. Never before has an outlander army approached the City from the north, which may be reason enough for God to anticipate that very strategy."

I slapped him heartily on the shoulder. "You and I are together again. If He is smart, He will expect something unexpected."

"Let us hope for all our sakes that that is not so," Maalik said, clearly nervous.

"Do not look so worried, Maalik. Simon will not fail."

"And what about you? How will you get back into the City?" Maalik asked.

"I will walk right through the front gate," I said, after a moment's thought.

Neither Simon nor Maalik seemed to have expected that answer.

"As I said, do not look so worried."

"You take too much risk, master," Azael said, speaking up for the first time.

Maalik had seen fit to have him summoned when I requested the Council be convened.

"You are with me, then?" I asked Azael cautiously.

"I will always be with you, master. To help you do the right thing," he said firmly.

We grasped arms in a show of brotherhood. He had always been far too good to me.

"Then it is you who will risk too much, my old friend," I said.

Maalik, Simon, and Azael all seemed confused.

"You must sneak back into the City without being detected," I told Azael. "I will need you when the time comes."

His countenance changed. "You have taught me all the good ways in," he said with a smile.

"Pray that I have and that you will know when the time is right."

"I need not pray to have that faith, master," he said, smoothing down his clean, but now slightly tattered City uniform.

"Ahriman, my friend," I said to him. "I will be known as Ahriman once again."

"Yes, master," Azael said with a smile.

"All right, then," I said, clapping my hands together and looking around the empty tent. "If I am supposed to have escaped from the outlands, it must look like I escaped from the outlands. I will receive a hero's welcome from the City and a very guarded reception, if at all, from God. He will suspect, but not know for certain, that I have turned against Him. In every way, it must appear that I am still His Lucifer." I thought for another moment. "Perhaps Corpens can help me."

4

CHAPTER THIRTY-THREE

I raced my steed through the cold night, maintaining as swift a pace as I could manage. Due west, until I hit the downward leg of the Great Northern Mountains and then southward and around its foothills. Each of Morello's vigorous movements made my sides and shoulders sting more fiercely than ever. Simon and Maalik had been shocked by my request that Corpens beat me to a bloody pulp, bringing to bear in every blow all the strength and fury he could muster. It had taken a moment for them to understand my real intentions. Corpens, of course, had understood immediately and taken to his task with all the zeal I expected of him. Clearly, he wanted nothing more than to execute his new dictator's orders with zest. Azael, leaping to my defense, had needed to be forcibly restrained, but had eventually understood the necessity if my ruse was to be successful.

Morello moved with all the speed his sturdy legs would allow him. Back through the green lands, now as dark as the night, and back through the scrublands I had called home for so many of the last several months. I had no armor. I wore the ripped and dirty uniform I had worn out into the outlands. I brandished my chiseled sword, the sword God had given me when I ascended to the Order. Notched now by the further abuse I had requested of Corpens. I had to look as though I had fought my way out of captivity. I also carried with me something else that would give God great pleasure. He treasured the law books of the outlanders and Maalik's original would complete His collection. It was the only remaining book of the only remaining member of the Council of Twelve of the now truly dead City of Heaven.

"Would you rather have an old musty book or the return of your lost city?" I had asked Maalik as he argued vigorously, putting up a fierce resistance to my command.

He could not give up the old ways, no matter how staunchly he now supported me. Perhaps none of it would matter. I could only indulge in speculation as Morello and I made our way through the darkness. Even if the City welcomed me as a hero, it would not take long for God's paranoia to take over and prompt Him to cast me into a dungeon as a traitor.

"Couldn't hurt," Simon had laughed out, as Maalik gave in with the greatest reluctance and handed over the sole remaining ancient text.

"I will let you know when they are done stretching me on the rack," I joked.

It was a joke to cover up my nervousness, though my faltering courage did not, thankfully, show through. It had taken all my courage to go into the outlands alone. It was now taking more than mere courage to return home.

By morning, I was across the Cocytus and at the foothills. I turned southwest and made for the Acheron. All through the next night I rode, until I had come to that Great Dividing River. Morello and I were both exhausted, but we rested only briefly. Morello seemed to sense my urgency.

It took me a good deal longer than I had expected to find a suitable crossing. I had not realized in the dark how far north I still was. When I hit the river, I needed to head far south, down the banks, to get past the cataracts, until I could make a straight shot for the City. Once across, though, I knew I was really in harm's way. The odds of encountering a City patrol were quite high, once I crossed over. And while it would be convenient to be "found" in order to lend plausibility to my story, I would be losing valuable time, if I were intercepted too far from the City walls or worse, found by the wrong type of angels.

As the fields flew by and the night air chilled me to the bone, I reflected on everything I had done and seen. What was important to me? I had fought for years to be someone important. When I had finally achieved my goal, I was happier than I had ever been. I liked being a Seraph of God. The power, the awesome power in being so close to God. Knowing that anything I said would be worshipped. Any order I issued would be carried out immediately. It was intoxicating and I wanted more and more of it. And God always obliged. He had always been there for me. Yes, He had told me what to do and, often, how to go about it. But I had never thought what He had said or done was evil. It just was. What was evil about wanting absolute power, if you were prepared to use it wisely? Most people do not know what is best for them. God knew and He had instructed me, His best pupil, accordingly.

But how many had suffered so that I could enjoy that power? Thousands? Millions? These questions had never come up in my mind as I locked horns with the City's politicians and turned things the way I thought they should be. The way God wanted them to be. Looking back on it now, I do not know how the thought had never struck me that I might be doing wrong in the name of right. People had died each and every day at my command and never had I really considered the consequences of my decisions. How such decisions might have affected their stricken families. Compared to me, who were they? Nonentities. Nobodies. It had just never mattered until now. Now they were everything. I was the One. Chosen for reasons—fate or destiny or whatever—that eluded me, to redress the injustices of God and restore the balance that had prevailed before He corrupted it all.

In my blindness, I had made it all far worse. I had rooted out the subversives who would have seen the old order restored. I had streamlined the bureaucracy to make the City and God's twisted universe function as efficiently as possible. When it became clear to Him that His city was no longer as easily governable as it once had been, I had facilitated a way for Him to build an army of believers. His "children," as He was once so fond of calling all angels, would take on a whole new meaning with the arrival of Man. He would not need to corrupt an entire race of beings, as He had with angels. Man's corruption was already built into his system, making him ready to do God's bidding as and when He saw fit. Best of all, Man would never rise up against Him. Denied the necessary programming on God's order, Man would lack the resolve to rebel against his maker. Even if treated by God with the utmost contempt, Man would never be the wiser, loving Him because it was obligatory to do so, fearing Him, as He was the creator. He had made Man His slave. He would love Man above all angels, precisely because such a creature could not reason or judge. And I was responsible for this state of affairs.

I seethed at the way I had been manipulated all along. I railed at my shortsightedness. Jehoel had warned me of it before I had him killed. Zoan had warned me of it before he died. They may both have lied to me here and there, but both had detected in me the very thing God Himself had seen. A way to make it all happen. They had both been right. I was, indeed, willing to sacrifice everyone else to make my way up. I was selfish. I had allowed, willingly allowed and encouraged God to corrupt me. Whatever history had been there before me or around me, I was willing to sell myself for an illusion of glory. To be God's Seraphim.

I spurred Morello onward. Running like the wind.

⌘　⌘　⌘

I was slumped in the saddle and barely awake when I approached the walls of the City of God. I had not eaten but a mouthful or two in the last week of travel. Broken ribs had made the ride torturous. My face swollen from the beatings I had requested from Corpens, the cold outland wind that lashed at my torn skin, and the sun burning down upon me. I had survived on leather from my saddle, cut up and eaten after boiling, the odd bits of scrub, and even the carcasses of dead animals that had lain on my path. Had I not known better, I would surely have believed that I had, in fact, escaped from tormentors across the miles of outland.

No one noticed as I approached. The watch was out, but clearly not watching. I was very groggy and certainly weaker than I could ever remember being. As Morello trotted across the outward end of the City gateway, the alarm was finally sounded. I sat upright and secured the reins in a tighter grip. Soldiers came pouring out from their barracks and took up position before me under the portcullis. Citizens coming in and out of the gate, being checked by the City's censors, were pushed aside in the onrush. Some ran for cover, while others stood there and watched as I tugged at the reins and brought Morello to a stop.

"Who goes there?" yelled an officer, stepping out from among the wall of wary soldiers.

Morello whinnied, as if telling me to take courage.

"I am Lucifer, Seraph of God and His loyal servant." It was harder to get those words out than I had imagined. "I have returned," I said in utter exhaustion.

Citizens and soldiers stood there together, shocked. No one said a word. Just the wind blowing through the opening of the great City's gateway.

The officer finally spoke. "Show yourself, if you are who you say you are."

They were bold words, indeed, if he truly believed me to be who I was.

I drew my sword and urged Morello forward. The group of soldiers jumped at the ting of my sword leaving its scabbard.

"Do you not recognize this sword?" I yelled, roused from my lethargy by the affront, and urging Morello forward into the wall of pointed spears before me.

The crowds moved back in fear.

"It is the sword of our Lord God, given to me on high, to protect and defend this City and bring it everlasting glory."

I came within nearly an arm's length of the officer. The soldiers behind him, grim of expression, were frightened at my unexpected move. I swung at the officer, letting my sword crash down on his helmet and knocking him to the ground. He looked up in terror, as I sat astride Morello, glaring down at him with all the fire I could muster in my eyes. All the angels cowered.

"These great walls have stood here for as long as this City has. And yet I passed into this realm unmolested by any patrol, unimpeded by any guards, until I set foot in the gateways of God's inner dominion?"

My words echoed off the walls of the colossal gateway. Citizens began running in fear and the troop of soldiers fell back into the City. The officer feebly held up his arm to shield himself from me, bleeding and shocked at my sudden blow. He could muster only a few whimpers.

I looked around, burning my gaze into each angel's eyes. "You fear me!" I screamed.

More soldiers came running up behind their quaking comrades, but they too, stood astounded.

"You fear me!" I screamed again. "Get out of my way!" I swung my sword through the air as a gesture for people to move. I spurred Morello on. To the next officer I passed, I shouted, "You there! Get a message to our Lord's palace that I have returned. You are now in charge of this wall." Pointing back with my sword to the officer bleeding on the ground, I said, "Take that one to the dungeons and let him reflect on the disservice he has done God."

This is how I returned to the City of God. It did not take long for word to spread across the City that Lucifer had returned from the outlands. I do not know what happened to the soldier put in the dungeon that afternoon, but he was, most likely, the first casualty of my revolt.

⌘　⌘　⌘

"Still alive?" The voice came from somewhere inside my apartment.

I was out on the terrace, looking over the City and nursing my bruises. I turned to find Gabriel standing there, solemn, but amicable.

"Gabriel!" I was genuinely surprised. "You old cock! They told me you were killed."

I was lying. Everything I said now would be a lie. Everything I had said had always been a lie.

"And you believed them."

We hugged each other like old brothers. This was the angel who had killed all those people and helped God to seize power. I clutched my ribs in pain, but looked him squarely in the eye.

"I did not know what to believe. I just hoped," I said. At least, the pain was real.

"Sit down. Let's sit down. You need to tell me all that has happened since I last saw you," he said, genuinely interested or, at least, feigning it superbly.

We moved back to a table in an alcove on the balcony. Many times, he and I had made plans or just talked in that place. Now it would be for show. Wincing as I sat down, I hoped I could pull it off.

"He sent you here?" I asked.

"No." Gabriel became suddenly serious again. "I am no longer of the Order of the Seraphim. I was demoted to Archangel. God punished me for my defeat by taking my position away. Michael has replaced me."

"I did not know." I was a bit annoyed. I was, after all, God's senior Seraph now. "When did this happen?"

"Right after I returned to the City. He made the announcement that I was in need of recuperation and that Michael would be taking over my responsibilities."

"And that was it?"

"That was it."

"He always was a snot," I said, patting Gabriel on the shoulder. "Michael, you mean?"

"Of course." A crude form of test, I thought.

"God had hoped I would die leading that army out there. But after I returned, He could not risk suggesting that the defeat was any more than a minor blip. I have been discredited and, for all intents and purposes, the City knows that I am out of the picture."

"I guess He got what He wanted in the end."

"Not exactly. You leaving for the outlands put Him in a very delicate mood."

"'Delicate,' you say?" I asked. "We did not part on good terms. That I must admit."

"God does not like disobedience, even if it's clothed in righteousness."

"I had to find you. I had to protect the soldiers." I paused. "I needed to find Simon," I said, looking down at my hands as I wrung them. "I sent him there and he knew you were all doomed."

"Did you find him?"

"No. The field was strewn with the dead. Even if he were there, there was no way I would ever have found him. Burned down and wiped out."

"And then you were taken?" The tone of Gabriel's question, slightly off-kilter, instantly put me on guard.

I looked at him. "Always playing the game," I said with a bit of implied malice.

We had both been players for a long, long time now. It was just that the servant had become the master.

He smiled thinly. "No. No. Just old habit, I guess."

"If He wants to know, I am His servant. I await His command."

"He'll call for you in time. He is happy to know you are back. I am sure of it."

"Why has my fellow Seraph not come to visit me? I have been back in the City for two days now."

Gabriel seemed uneasy with this query. "Michael will come," he assured me. "He has many new responsibilities to undertake."

"I am sure you have been an excellent teacher."

Again Gabriel seemed ill at ease. "He has made Raphael his lieutenant."

"I really only know *of* him," I replied. I struggled to place a face with the name.

"He was one of mine. Michael will do well with him."

Gabriel seemed not to care. So neither did I.

"Well," I said, trying to bring the conversation back around to Michael, "he will have much to learn from you."

"He leads our armies, yes, but now with you back, I don't know what else I can teach him." Gabriel sighed. "Michael has been my lieutenant for many years. There is little I know that he does not."

"Yet it seems there is much he knows that you do not." I could afford to make veiled insinuations.

"That may be so," Gabriel replied with an insincere smile. "But enough of that. You must tell me what happened to you." He looked me straight in the eye again, as if searching for something he needed. Desperately. "You gave up everything to find me. No one has ever done such a thing for me. I thank you and I embrace you now like a brother."

He extended his hand and I took it. He made a face and looked down at my palm.

"Your hands are so hard," he said, studying both my hands intently. "These are not the hands that left the City."

I guess he could afford to make veiled insinuations as well.

"They condemned me to manual labor," I said, thinking quickly. "Breaking down tents, lifting bails, breaking ground with a pickaxe. Like a servant."

I had not prepared myself to explain the condition of my hands. Honestly, the thought had not occurred to me. But it had not escaped Gabriel's notice.

"It must have been backbreaking," he said, looking up at me intently.

"Actually," I said, clutching my side again, "it was rib-breaking."

We both laughed. It hurt to laugh, but I do not think Gabriel cared. We talked into the night, but I think he got all he really needed in those first few minutes.

⌘ ⌘ ⌘

I was called before God the following evening. Much as it hurt to do so because of my injuries, I dressed in my finest clothes and donned a simple, but ceremonial silver armor breastplate. I carried my notched sword with me. Maalik's book of laws hung from a loop on my belt.

After dismissing my servants, I stood looking at myself in the full-length mirror for a long time. We did not have many actors in the City of God. They were considered too liberally inclined in their political views.

"Maybe He was right," I thought to myself, as I stood there.

I addressed my reflection in the mirror, as though it were God Himself, repeating, with as much conviction as I could muster, those parts of my story that I suspected I might be questioned about, and simultaneously observed if there were telltale changes in my expression as I trotted out my well-prepared lies. I had to look sincere and sound utterly convincing as I spun out my story, and derived some small comfort in knowing that thanks to the measures I had resorted to in anticipation, I would not have to feign pain in my ribs. As a spy and a leader of spies, I had made a thorough study of people's faces and believed that I had sharpened my instincts sufficiently in this area and obtained enough insights to detect someone's lies simply by the way he or she looked at me or away from me, when speaking. In the world of a Seraph, almost everyone with whom I interacted lied, whether servant, cabinet minister, or God Himself. My time in the outlands, I worried, may have dulled those hard-earned insights. More disturbingly, I feared my time in the outlands might have affected by own ability to lie in the very complicated ways I would need to.

"Keep it together," I said to myself out loud.

I looked around the room to satisfy my growing paranoia of unwanted eyes and ears. It was quiet, but for the wind through the windows and the sounds from the streets below.

I boarded my carriage and made my way to the Seat of God. I looked out onto the City's streets as I rode by. These angels were no different from the outlanders. They lived and died under the rule of their sovereigns, be it the tyranny of God or the disorder of the Council. All any of them wanted was to live in peace and know their government had their best interests in mind. But where the outlanders continued to possess that fire, that passion for self-determination, the people I observed now were beaten down, no more than servants to their government and their Lord. Those unwilling to submit to Him became fodder for His rule. And my responsibility. I punished, I took away, and I gave to whomever I wanted. Sometimes, at my own discretion and, sometimes, at the will of my Lord and master. As the streets rolled by, becoming cleaner and better maintained as we drew closer to His Seat, I realized that in both worlds, in two rather dissimilar ways, I was the real difference between these two kinds of people. The City of God professed to love me, because I was the bringer of order, the rod of God's wrath. The outlanders professed to trust in me, because I was the leveler, the One to strike down God's tyranny with the same rod He Himself had given me.

Through the gates and past God's guards, the carriage made its way up the driveway, until we had come to a stop at the foot of the stairs. Guards were posted all the way up the stairs. At the top, God stood waiting for me with His entourage. As I climbed down from the carriage and looked up at Him, I noticed that among the many there stood Amee.

God is smarter than I thought, I sighed to myself, as I began the long climb up the stairs. I walked tall, my hand resting on the pommel of my sword. The host of sycophantic hangers-on could not fluster me, but God knew my guard would be down, even if it were ever so slightly, in the presence of Amee. I strengthened my resolve in anticipation of a much longer night than I had prepared myself for.

"We welcome you home, Lord Lucifer," God said warmly, as I reached the top. "Our City has been ever so much on edge during your time away and your exploits and the details of your escape from the trimmers have already made the greatest news in the City."

I knelt on one knee before Him and bowed my head.

"Heavenly Father," I said, "it is I who am happiest returning to You, the most Holy of Holies. I have suffered greatly at the hands of our City's enemies, but I bring You a gift that is intended to show You, my Lord, that our armies' sacrifices were not in vain."

Given that Gabriel stood nearby, unharmed by the entire ordeal, no one missed out on the irony of my mission. I presented Maalik's book to God.

There was a moment of silence no one had expected. Not even God. I smiled inwardly, knowing I had shifted the momentum back in my favor. He looked at the book very carefully. It was real. He knew it. He carefully wiped the expression of annoyance from His face, though I think only I may have noticed it.

"While escaping from my captors, I managed to wrest this token from the leader of the apostates," I said. "Though I do not know for certain, I hope that during the struggle, my blows landed in the right places and with enough force to kill him. I know, my Lord, that such trophies are nothing compared to Your glory, but I hope You will accept this gift as a sincere expression of my love and gratitude. To Your kingdom, the power and the glory, from this day to the end of all things."

The crowd around us all knelt as well and whispered their own prayers. I looked up at God, but could not help shooting a quick glance at Amee. Her head was bowed in reverence.

God put His hand on my shoulder. "I cannot express more clearly how happy it makes me to accept this gift from you, of all my servants. Many millions of years ago, you had presented me with another such token and it had elevated you to the Order of the Seraphim. I am afraid there is no higher order to which I could promote you, Lucifer," He said, without a trace of sarcasm. "With your gift tonight, we will celebrate your return and pray for the destruction of all our enemies."

God looked around to all as our Father. "Rise, all of you, and let us retire to banquet. Lucifer has much to tell us."

Before we could go, however, God stepped forward and removed my sword from its sheath.

"I just had a thought," He said. "This sword is old and beaten, my friend." He swung its notched blade in the fading light. "It has seen much service in my name," He continued. "In celebration of your most recent exploits, I will have a new sword forged for you. A sword representative of the many great services you have rendered to our great City."

I realized with lightning swiftness that without a weapon, I would be nearly defenseless. Quickly, I responded, "I have killed many foes with the sword you gave me so long ago, my Lord. My gratitude for your generosity is boundless. I would like to keep this sword, though, if it pleases you, my Lord, as a reminder of the greatness of our City and as a personal memento of your wise rule."

God looked at the sword and then turned His gaze to the law book in His other hand. Those around us seemed uneasy. It was one thing for me to speak to Gabriel in such a way. But to flout God's wish, that too, in public, was unthinkable.

"Indeed," He said. "This sword is a treasure, to be sure. You shall keep it, but it will be put on display in the City's great museum for all citizens to appreciate and study."

"Yes, Lord," I replied. What else could I say? My sword had been taken from me. I was already on the defensive.

We made our way into the palace, God and I walking together.

"I hope your wounds are not too painful this evening, Lucifer?" He said, as we walked through the palace.

"No Lord. Mere pain could not have kept me from Your presence."

"Good. Good," He said, more to Himself than to me. "We shall enjoy ourselves tonight and later, you and I will speak alone. Like we have so many times before."

"Yes Lord."

"You are my favorite son and I have missed your counsel and good advice."

"Yes Lord. As You wish."

"Good. Good," He repeated.

⌘　⌘　⌘

"So how have you been?"

It was, admittedly, a rather feeble way to open a conversation with the angel I had once thought could be my wife.

"That seems to be a more appropriate question for me to ask you," Amee smiled. "You're the one who's been far away for so long."

"Yes, but is not the story getting old and worn now? Everyone thinks I am a hero, when all I did was go out into the wilderness, get myself caught, get my angels killed, get myself beaten within an inch of my life, and escape. What is all that, when compared to what others have done?"

"No one cares about this. It is you they care about. You are who you are, after all."

I frowned, but Amee merely looked exasperated by my response.

"Don't pretend you don't like the attention, Lucifer," she said with some impatience. "Time among the trimmers will not have changed you in that respect."

"So I take it you have been fine, then," I stated, ignoring her comments.

She smiled again and looked down at her plate. The room was filled with angels. Talking, drinking, carousing, celebrating my return. Michael was not there. God seemed to be enjoying Himself, though He was not drinking. He was speaking with some minister or the other, I could not remember who. But when He noticed me glancing in His direction, He immediately nodded in acknowledgement.

"I'm sorry," Amee said, taking up the conversation again. "No, actually I haven't been that fine. With my uncle having fallen from God's good graces, it's taken a toll on my life as well. Our project funding has suddenly dried up and interest in the state of the northern forests and the City's drinking water seems to have gone into hibernation in some random bureaucrat's office. God, it seems, is not interested in ensuring that his people are well provided for, now that Gabriel is no longer his Seraph."

It had totally slipped my mind that Amee's work took her into the northern forests. My mind ran wild for a moment, but I pulled it back in time.

"You should be careful about the way you speak, Amee." I cautioned, genuinely concerned. "I know we have never seen eye to eye in matters involving our Lord, but to adopt such a tone, especially in public, is not wise."

"It didn't seem to stop you earlier this evening."

"That is different. I was not being outwardly disrespectful. I was simply hoping to keep my sword."

"You don't understand, Lucifer. It doesn't matter."

She looked down at her plate again, playing with her food. She was sad. She looked irrepressibly sad. Then it dawned on me.

"Since when?" I asked, masking my anger.

"Since you left. He came to me. He told me that with Gabriel out of the picture and you out in the wilds, I was alone. Either I would submit or I would suffer." She looked up from her plate with tears in her eyes. "What should I have done?"

I relaxed. She was right.

"I am sorry," I said. "I would have done the same thing, because that is all anyone can do."

"Knowing that doesn't make me feel any better," she paused for a second, "but thank you." We sat silently for a few minutes. Angels swirled around us. So many things I could have done differently with Amee. What might have been possible had we met in different circumstances? But there were no circumstances other than those of God's making. And Amee was trapped in them now. God watched us. Amused, I think. It was just the type of game He liked to play.

"He will want to know what we discussed," she said, finally breaking the silence between us and regaining her composure.

"Tell Him the truth." What else was there to say? "He knows we are both in pain over this matter. Telling Him the truth is the only way to get back at Him. He cannot have fun, if we are not playing His game."

Amee looked at me with interest now. "I've never heard you say anything so close to blasphemy before."

"That is what He wants? Right? He told you to find out what I am doing. You can sense His fear, can you not?" I asked.

Her smile disappeared. "Okay, the truth. The truth? The truth is: yes, he wants me to find out whether you broke down under interrogation. To find out how much the trimmers know about the work you were doing for him."

"He wants to know whether I betrayed Him," I said matter-of-factly.

"Yes. And he thinks you trust me."

"I do not trust anyone here," I said, looking around.

She looked interested again. "And again. You warned me not to speak so openly. Yet you seem not to mind speaking openly yourself. Now."

"Look. God always gets what He wants. I have no intentions of telling you anything I am not telling Him."

"You're lying."

"I am telling you the truth."

"Well, I guess we're at an impasse, then." Amee put down her fork and wiped her mouth with her napkin. "Same old Lucifer," she quipped, starting to get up from her chair.

"Can you come tonight?" I asked.

I had always been good at ignoring her anger. And looking at the bigger picture.

"Yes. That is what he expects," Amee replied, throwing down her napkin on the table. "And we all must do what he tells us to do."

"You know where to find me," I said.

She looked at me. Strangely, she seemed to have the same empty expression Zoan had worn when we last spoke. I realized it was the look of hopelessness. It burned more than the pain in my ribs. She walked away and I could see God smiling through His first drink.

⌘　⌘　⌘

"Lucifer, I am going to dispense with the pleasantries and get right down to it," God said, as His servants poured us ambrosia. He waited for them to finish and waved them away. "A lot has changed since you left. I know you spoke with Gabriel yesterday. He has informed me you have been told of Michael's elevation."

"Yes Lord, though I missed Michael tonight. I wished to congratulate him."

"Do you agree?" God asked, ignoring my last words. He took a sip of His ambrosia and looked intently at me.

We were in His private chambers, the same place where He and I had last spoken in privacy.

"If it makes sense for Michael to lead the armies, you could have done that in a far less orchestrated way," I said.

God put His glass back down on the table.

"You see, that is what I am looking for," He said with a grimace. "Direct and arrogant answers to my questions."

He had set Himself against me.

"That tone of insolence I have never known in you before. It is the same tone you had assumed when Gabriel was sent out into the wilds. You should be thanking me for his fall from grace, rather than speaking to me in so chastising a tone. His demotion has made you Number One. Like your grandfather before you."

I kept my face empty of expression and gave no indication that I intended to respond.

"Gabriel had been with me forever. Then you had to come along with that little insurrection. Shook everyone's faith in you, did it not? Turning them over, turning...what was his name... Jehoel over to me and walking on all their backs to get to where you are now? I thought it so," and here He paused, as if to savior the memory, "enjoyable." He picked up His glass again. "But you chose to take offense at my plans and threw yourself into a world you were not prepared to understand."

"Lord, what I understood was that our soldiers were being used in a game. I am sorry, my Lord, for my insolence," I said, bowing in reverence, "but I could not find it in me to sit idly by. I had to do something."

"Yes, I guess I know that about you. You are not one to believe in doing nothing, even if doing something is the wrong thing to do," He lectured. "You have no idea what I intend to do." He leaned forward.

I could sense the edge of the envelope I was pushing.

"You made Man for me," He said. "You succeeded in doing what your grandfather could not, what Gabriel could not. You made things work." He took a sip of ambrosia. "But you do not see the whole picture."

It was a test. He thought He knew where to push me, to see if I would slip. If I would blurt out even a word that might indicate I actually knew more than I should.

"I have made Man," I replied, "because you asked me to. I worked for everything I have in order to please you. You are right. I have no idea what you plan to do. What I do know is that while you did remove Gabriel from his position, I have not replaced him. And, frankly, that was not on my mind the last time we spoke. My Lord."

"What did you tell them?" God asked plainly. "Tell me what you told them and know that I will know if you are lying."

"I have never lied to you, Lord, and I do not intend on starting now."

God laughed to Himself, but then suddenly, His entire demeanor changed. "Come on!" He shouted, looking me straight in the face. "What did you tell them?" His cheeks were flushed red.

I was startled by the suddenness of His outburst, but had been anticipating something like this would happen.

"I told them that our armies were weakened after the defeat at the burning fields," I replied. "I told them that if ever you were weak, it was now, with both Gabriel and me gone. I told them they would never succeed in taking the City and theirs was a lost cause. I called them apostates. I called them traitors." My tone of voice remained flat, unwavering. I stared right back into His eyes. Unflinching. "I told them you were a coward."

Nothing happened. I could not believe it, but nothing happened. The God I had lived for and loved. God who was feared, our loving and terrible Father. Nothing. He leaned back into His couch and seemed almost pleased, as He sipped at His ambrosia again.

"You are a much stronger angel than I gave you credit for, Lucifer."

He stayed there for a moment, thinking. Then putting His glass aside, He stood up. Instinctively, I stood too.

"I have always thought of you as something of a cretin," God said. "Slinking around. Looking to get information on everyone. Looking for a way to sleaze yourself into the right position. But when you were suddenly overcome by a burst of self-righteousness, I was not entirely prepared for it. It was not a trait your father had ever revealed. It was something Zoan had showed me only once." God straightened out His robes. He was clearly preparing to leave. "The formula for Man will be moved into my personal residence here. You will retain your position as Seraph, but you will no longer work on Man."

"My Lord?"

"Yes, you have done quite enough. When I thought you were nothing but a little shit, it was fine for you to work on Man. You are smart enough and organized. You know. Able to bullshit with the bullshitters. But seeing that you are something more, something that might prove dangerous to my plans, I no longer need you there."

He noted my silent rage.

"You have something to add?" He asked aggressively. "Choose your next few words carefully, Lucifer," He said, dead serious now.

"With all due respect, Lord, I am the only one who can complete Man. You know Gabriel cannot and..."

He cut me off. "Man is done, quite as he is. He will serve my purposes well enough in his current form."

"Lord, he's little more than an animal. Horses and oxen can help us build stronger, larger walls. But what you want is intellect and that is something Man cannot yet manage. Please, Lord, let me finish the project."

"No," He said without hesitation. "You will be on administrative leave from the project. Oh, but do not go too far. We have a public triumph planned for you," He said with a self-satisfied smile, "and you will be watched."

"Yes Lord."

"You can go now." He waved me away in the same manner that He dismissed His servants. "You have come far these many years, Lucifer. But the good traveler knows when it is time to end his journey."

We were done.

⌘　⌘　⌘

When we were finished, we lay together for a while.

"It's been a long time," she finally said.

"Yes. I guess it has."

"We were good together," she said.

She was right. I never felt more at home than with Amee. With her, here.

"I suppose we always were."

There was a pause, a suddenly very uncomfortable pause.

Then, "What are we doing now?" she asked.

"Well," I started, "you are here to gauge how I am taking the fact that God has taken Man away from me. You are spying."

Amee's expression did not change. No reaction, no surprise.

"Ah, yes," she said.

"You see. Truth is a lot easier," I chortled.

She turned to look at me and I at her. She was beautiful. I had almost forgotten how beautiful. When we were last together, I had been at the height of my power, it seemed. I had something that only power could have achieved. But the more time I spent with her, the clearer it became to me that she was not attracted to the power I wielded. And that scared me. But lying there in the dark with her, her body outlined in the evening glow, I remembered what had driven me to her in the first place.

"And what should I tell Him?" she asked.

"The truth. Always the truth."

Amee sat up. "What is it with you?" she asked exasperatedly. "You've never acted this way. Something clearly happened to you out there. I know you too well. You're saying 'truth' and for the first time since I've known you, I think you actually mean it."

"I do."

"Yes, but why?" she blurted out.

"Take it easy, Amee."

She backed down a bit.

"Can I assume you are more interested in an honest response from me, because you genuinely wish to understand me, than in going back to Him with something to report, even if that something is inconsequential?"

She gave me a cross look.

"Okay, fine," I said.

"Tell me," she repeated, but this time, her voice was gentle.

I could see tears rolling down her cheeks. I wiped them away.

"God forced Gabriel to take those soldiers out there to die," I began. "Your uncle could have shown his mettle and actually won the battle, but God knew Gabriel did not have it in him. He stacked the deck against him and Gabriel fell. And our soldiers died. Gabriel had told me everything before he left. He knew he was riding to defeat. God had grown tired of him. Your uncle did not know why this was so and God had got His pleasure out of forcing Gabriel to his death. As it turned out, your uncle did not die, but God got what He wanted out of him in the end."

"I know, Lucifer. You have already told me all this."

"Yes, but I ignored God's commands and went out into the outlands to find Gabriel. I had spoken to God in the admonishing tone a parent takes to scold a naughty child and He had sat chastened by my words. Tonight, He told me outright that He had never respected me, that my defiance of His orders and my arrogance made me more dangerous than He had ever imagined possible. He admitted tonight that He feared me. I spoke my mind and that made me more powerful than Gabriel. Tonight, I was more powerful than God Himself. And He knew it. All because I had told the truth."

She looked at me. Her tears had stopped. "That's astonishing."

"Do not tease me," I said, rolling back to my side of the bed. "I am not in the mood."

"No, I'm serious. When has anyone talked to God this way?"

I so wanted to explain to her the history I had been taught by the likes of traitors and outlanders. But I could not trust her, especially if she was also sharing a bed with God.

"I do not know if it has ever happened before," I said, rubbing my eyes. "And I am not entirely sure I can stop myself from doing it again."

"We broke up once, because you couldn't stand my insolence to God. Now you've done things, said things to His face that no other angel would dare to." She paused for a moment. "And we're apart."

"Amee, that is not the only reason we split up."

"Tell me, then, what was it?"

"Look, it does not matter now. We have to deal with the real here and the reality is that no matter how I speak with God or what He does to me, He will always be God. Things will never change."

"Things have already changed, Lucifer. Gabriel is no longer God's first angel. You are. Simon is dead and Michael leads our armies now. Michael is weak, not as an angel, but because he hasn't had the time to build the relationships he needs within the army. The army was behind Simon. Michael is seen as an outsider imposed upon the soldiers against their will." Amee grasped my arm. "They might be far more eager to follow you."

"Come on!" I said, pulling away. It was something I had not included in any calculation. "Simon and I were friends, yes, but the army would not follow me on the basis of that alone."

"I agree, but even if that is true, God has never been as weak as he is. Right now."

"That is what I told Him," I said.

"You told Him what!" she gasped.

"I told Him I had told the trimmers that He was a coward."

"How is that possible?" she asked, incredulous.

"It is easy. It is what I did. That is why He took Man away from me. I am not joking with you. He genuinely fears me." I looked into her beautiful brown eyes. "He said so Himself."

"Lucifer, don't you see what you've done?"

"I do, absolutely. I have just dug an early grave for myself. Well not, at least, before the public celebration of my triumph. Only then will He allow me to fall."

"Lucifer, there are people in the City who want another life. There are people..."

"Amee, do not say it," I warned, my voice stern.

"But surely you want to know!" she shouted.

"No!" I felt as if I had been thrown back to our last fight. But this time, I was fighting both Amee and myself. "What you are talking about is very dangerous and I will not be a part of it. I went too far. Both earlier and tonight. Nothing is worth losing everything for."

Amee got up abruptly and started putting on her robes. Her movements were brusque, angry.

"Lucifer, it is you who are the coward," she said. "Sometimes, there are things out there, bigger than we are, and they can only be achieved through real sacrifice."

"There is nothing bigger than God," I said, feigning absolute determination.

She sighed. "I will be sure to tell Him."

"Be sure you do. Tell Him what I told you."

"What? About the truth?" she shot back in anger.

I looked at her for moment. "Tell Him what I told you."

She was gone. Again.

CHAPTER
THIRTY-FOUR

I had no time to waste. For all I knew, Simon was already positioned and waiting for my signal. God clearly suspected me of something. I had always been prepared for that. But I had seriously miscalculated His intention to humor me and keep me on until Man was complete. It defied all logic, unless He was merely waiting it out, playing a long, tantalizing game to force my hand, to see whether I would make a move. With Tartaruian armies sitting in the northern forests, waiting for my signal, and the City's armies commanded by a new and untested general, miles and miles away from home, I had no time for God's little maneuvers.

I had no one in the City to speak to. No one I could confide in. Gabriel continued to come to my apartments and speak with me. It was almost like old times. I ignored the fact that

I outranked him now and he ignored the fact he had been entrusted with the task of organizing my triumph. That slap in the face must have been hard for him to deal with. Though I had sought his friendship again, I reminded myself that he, personally, murdered for God. I bore no personal grudges against him, but thousands of others would certainly have felt very differently.

Amee was another problem. I wanted to trust her. She had always been nothing but honest with me, while I had always held her at arm's length. How could I not confide in someone who had always told me the truth? And even if I did tell her I was now God's sworn enemy, a spy, a saboteur, and the commander of the enemies' armies, I might not be able to revive her from the laughing fit that was sure to seize her. What would I get out of telling her anything, anyway? It would serve no purpose, other than to put her in harm's way. What could she give me that I could not already take for myself as Seraph?

And that left me with Man. God quickly saw to it that the laboratory was moved from its original location in my offices and into His own. With all contact severed, I could not tell what sort of work was going on there. Had God found someone else who could complete my work? Why would He trust Phanuel, given his background and relationship with me? I had brought Phanuel up to be God's faithful servant, but he was, after all, my son, if ever I had one. Short of Phanuel, there were no understudies, no staff from whom I drew my brainpower. It had all been locked in my head and my heart. Until I could change that formula, there was no point in sending a signal to Simon. Even if we took the City and held it for a while, Man would come to God's aid eventually. The confrontation would be brutal and savage and Man would be my end.

I had no time to waste and I did not know what to do. I thought of Mizpah and Maalik, sitting in council all those billions of years ago, trying to figure out what to do with Yahweh. And me. Should they submit or should they deliberate more? Or should they fight? I consoled myself by thinking that at least I did not fear the fight. But it had to be the *right* fight in order to work. I could not just launch a flurry of blows and hope one of them landed where I needed it most to land. I had to land the right blows in the right order at the right time and with the right force.

"I have built myself this perfect mess," I said to Gabriel one day.

He seemed surprised. "What do you mean?"

"I should never have spoken to God in that way. Look what I have ended up doing to myself."

"Lucifer, you are God's favorite angel. Don't be an ass! You've taken my position in the hierarchy and yet you're worried about Man? What is Man, other than a dirty image of us? What will God use Man for? Man is a beast like all others and will only ever be God's plaything."

"Gabriel, after all our work, you still do not understand. Man is not built that way. God can mold Man into whatever He wants. Man can be God's army. Man can be God's builders. Man can be God's angels. And Seraphs, if that is what He wants Man to be. Man can be anything, because that is the way I designed him."

Gabriel sat quietly for a moment. "I didn't know." He seemed hurt.

"I am sorry, old friend, but God had instructed me to do the work myself. Man has had the capacity to replace us angels, basically since I first started working on him. I was just doing God's work."

Gabriel did not seem much appeased by my excuse. "God's work?" he repeated angrily. "Well, I guess you were just following orders."

He got up to leave. I got up after him. It did hurt me to see him hurt. The authors of millions of deaths together, now sorry for each other.

"Do not go, Gabriel. Do not be mad at me."

"I'm not mad at you, Lucifer. You were doing what you were told to do. Even if it meant lying to God's first angel."

"It was my duty. I am sorry."

"Sorry? I'm sorry for the whole thing. All I ever wanted was to serve God. And this is how He repays me."

"God works in His own ways. He sees things we do not. You taught me that once. You would be wise to remember it now,"

I said quite seriously, my heart dancing within me in excitement, knowing that Gabriel had just given me an opening. All I needed to do was provoke him.

"Don't threaten me, Lucifer," he said now. "I was murdering for God long before you were in the picture. You've been told you're special and you don't even know why. But there's nothing special about you. You were born this way. I had to work for everything I have."

"Gabriel, I think you have said about enough. If God wants us to fling ourselves over the walls of the City, that is what we must do. That is what all angels do. When they are told to do so."

"Is that what Man will do, Lucifer?"

"Yes, as a matter of fact. It is exactly what Man will do."

"And there you have it," Gabriel said heatedly. "You want to know what God is doing to Man, now that you are out? He is building Man in vast numbers to have as many as He wants fling themselves over the walls. Ask your friend, Phanuel."

I pricked up my ears.

"The son of the angel you killed. Working for you. Working for God. What an existence we have!"

He stormed out.

"That seemed a little too easy," I said to myself out loud.

One of my servants stepped out of the shadows, thinking I had asked for something. I waved him off.

Phanuel looked upon me as a son would his father. Why was Gabriel speaking of him now? We had had that fight many, many years ago. Making my enemy into my enemy's enemy. Phanuel had learned from me about the greatness of God. I had urged him into the army and turned him toward the sciences thereafter. Jehoel might have rolled in his grave to see his son working for God, but Phanuel, like me, was willing to put his father's beliefs aside and take his lead from God instead. But would he help me now? Or would I have to betray him too, to get what I needed?

⌘　⌘　⌘

"You sure you're all right?" Phanuel asked, as we walked down the halls of the Interior Ministry.

"Yes, yes. I am fine. A few broken ribs and a couple of chipped teeth, but okay otherwise."

Phanuel was genuinely concerned. I could sense it. But it was not my physical condition that was bothering him.

"That's not what I heard," he finally said.

"What have you heard, then?"

"You're different." He could not look at me. He was clearly ill at ease. "Something has changed."

"Come on, Phanuel. Talk to me. We have known each other a long time."

I was a Seraph, but Phanuel was not intimidated by me the way almost everyone else was. I was powerful to them. I was a father to Phanuel.

"Why am I watching over Man? You may be God's Seraph, but..." He did not need to end his sentence.

"Listen, I do not know what gossip you have heard. Most of it is probably tripe. You need to realize that once you are in power, your back is never safe. There is always someone out to get you, to take away what you have worked so hard for, and to put themselves in your place. They will do or say anything to insert a wedge of doubt in your mind. A wedge that feeds on lies and grows and festers and can only be ejected by the truth. The only way to deal with it is to be the only one capable of doing what you do. Make yourself indispensible. Entwine the fate of those you work for with yours so that they cannot possibly get rid of you. That is how you deal with it. When you have it."

The boy absorbed what I had said. I say 'boy,' but he was now, indeed, an angel. And he was clearly miserable.

I sighed. "So what is it, then, that you heard?"

"People are saying you have lost God's favor. God himself came to me and asked me to report any conversation I had with you. To keep away from you. To explain why my laboratory was being moved so as to be under his personal supervision."

"I am glad you have caught the eye of God. Few angels have the privilege," I said. It was true, though I was not sure now whether it was a privilege or a burden.

"Ahriman, it's not just that. Other people are coming to me and asking me to approach you with questions." He stopped and looked me in the eye for the first time since we had greeted each other. "I'm not comfortable with that."

I put my hand on his shoulder. I tried to inspire him with confidence and reassurance, directing the full power of my thoughts toward him. "I raised you to love, honor, and obey God. And in the short time since I returned, for reasons I cannot share with you, I have not lived up to those ideals myself. God and I have quarreled and, as a result, He has taken Man away from me." I put my other hand on his other shoulder and looked him straight in the eye.

He did not flinch. Such a good boy.

"That is it," I finished. "That is what has happened. Nothing less and only a little more," I smiled.

Phanuel did not seem reassured. "I don't know what I'm doing, Father," he said, gulping down his emotions.

"Do not call me 'father,' Phanuel. That is reserved for only two angels."

"I don't know what you've done and I don't know how to complete what you've started," he continued. He eased his shoulder out from under my grasp. "There's a lot of pressure on me to finish the project. They seem to think our relationship will give me a greater understanding of how to complete Man. I may be a scientist and your adopted son, but I don't know the chemistry, the biology, the mechanics of what you've done these many millions of years."

And then it came to me. "I will help you."

I thought about it for a moment. Had God expected me to help Phanuel? Had He sent the boy to me for this purpose? Or was it a trap, like so many others He had laid? Surely He, most of all, knew I would never share something so secret with anyone other than Him? Well, I mean, assuming I remained loyal to Him. I had betrayed thousands of angels, seen to their executions, all in the name of God to protect His kingdom. Would He suspect me of scuttling Man? Unless...unless, He thought I would rise to help Phanuel. Or perhaps be motivated by vanity to complete what I, to all intents and purposes, had started myself. Or, more likely, to use Man as my own weapon to supplant God Himself. My mind swam and Phanuel noticed.

"Ahriman?" he asked, watching, as my face betrayed my emotions.

"Sorry, I was lost in thought. I am back." I smiled at him. "Yes. I can help you."

"God will suspect something, if I suddenly begin making the breakthroughs He's been demanding."

"God wants this. I can feel it. It is the only way it could work."

"But what about your disagreements with Him?"

"I do not know, Phanuel, but it seems the best way for everyone to get what they need is for the two of us to work out the last few details of Man. God will get Man, you will be in God's eternal good graces, and I will see my project completed."

"But what will God do with you? After everyone has gotten what they need?"

It seemed a reasonable question, regardless of my motives.

"I do not know, Phanuel." I smiled a reassuring smile. "I guess we will all find out when the time comes."

⌘　⌘　⌘

"Amee, stop and listen to me!" I pleaded.

We had not spoken since that last night together. I had come to her new apartments to speak with her. As one of God's new consorts, she had been allotted a very nice place from which one could gloat over the City's others. Gabriel's fall from political power had had no apparent effect on his niece's social status. Besides, God could keep a closer eye on her from His own apartments. He expected me to be with Amee and try my best to extract information from her about His intentions. I had to do what God anticipated to avoid arousing His suspicions. He expected me to backstab and I would oblige.

"You disgust me!" she shot back, pointedly disengaging her arm from my grasp. "You are the most spineless being I've ever encountered and I curse the day I fell in love with you."

"Amee, that is why I am here. I am here...because...I love you too."

She looked at me blankly. "Didn't you hear what I said? This is not a moment to share, Lucifer. This is a moment of recognition, of acknowledgment that I've made a terrible mistake in ever getting involved with you. Where in this relationship do you see anything worth confessing you love me? How could you, so low a thing, love me, something even lower?"

I had not gone to meet her to tell her the truth, the truth about what I was about to do. It was clearly the wrong thing to do, no matter how you considered it. What I was doing was sedition, yes. But in telling Amee, I was putting not only myself, but thousands of others at terrible risk.

"Amee, I am here to tell you the truth."

"What do you know about the truth?" she snapped back again. "It's a word you bandy around like that notched-up sword you used to swing in the name of God. Taking angels down with it."

I risked everything by telling her anything at all. If God's hunch was wrong and I ended up not confiding in her, He stood to lose nothing. If He was right in assuming I would share my plans with her, He would take me down as publicly as He had elevated me to power. And He could always find another lover.

"Amee, plea..."

"What!" she shouted, spinning around and looking at me, hands on hips.

The house servants scurried about the apartments, fleeing from the heat of her wrath. I could sense their footsteps not far away.

"Please listen to me. I love you."

"What do we have to say to each other? What will love get us? You were right. God put me here to spy on you. He's using me like He uses everyone else. To get information. Tomorrow, none of us may be here, but God always will be. What does our love have anything to do with it?"

"You need to lower your voice. This house is full of inquisitive ears."

"I don't care what He hears. I'm tired of it all."

I grabbed her by the arm, shushing her and walking her farther into the house. "Come out into the gardens," I suggested. "We have to talk."

"No."

"Please?" I implored.

She stopped and looked at me. In that look, I could see, slight though it was, a release. "I don't remember the last time I heard you say that. 'Please.' It sounds so...well...nice. It's sad how you play it on me."

"Come on. Let's go to the gardens and talk." I smiled at her wryly. "Please?"

She finally smiled. "All right." But the smile immediately disappeared. "But not for long. I have more important things to attend to."

⌘　⌘　⌘

"I am telling you the truth," I said, as the magnitude of what I had just told her began to sink in. "I gave myself up to the trimmers. The Tartaruians. They showed me the true history of God and this City of Heaven. It has suffered under Yahweh for billions of years. We simply do not know it." Hearing myself say it, it sounded absurd, fantastical. "He erased all history of His deeds. He killed nearly everyone who was involved in His rise to power. Those He has not been able to kill, He hunts down like animals. He threatens us each and every day and uses the people as His slaves. The true people of this once great place, their liberty ground under His feet, reside as virtual hermits beyond the rolling plains, the great rivers, and in the mountains of Heaven. They were there. Waiting for me. Waiting for me to come and lead them back. God keeps them there in order to maintain His power in the City, but is burdened by the fact that they know the truth. They were there, doing His bidding, unknowingly, until I arrived. And now I have taken it upon myself to wrest back the City of God and return it to the City of Heaven once again. God's Seraph leading the revolt. God's Seraph liberating Heaven from His tyranny." I paused. "It is so much bigger than you think."

She sat looking into one of the garden ponds. Spellbound. I swear, I was more afraid looking at her then, lost in contemplation, than at any other moment in my life.

"You couldn't tell me," she said.

It wasn't a question or an accusation. It was an acknowledgment.

"I could not tell you. I should not have told you. I have so little time to plan."

She sat so still. The fear swelled in me. Was she with me or did she see an opportunity, the same way I had seen an opportunity those many millions of years ago, sitting in that café with Jehoel? Of the two of us, at least, she hated God more than me. Or so she made me think.

"You shouldn't have told me." She looked at me. "For so many years, I've wanted you to tell me what you've just told me. That you'll be a leader. That you'll protect the people of this city. And yet now that you have, I find it hard to believe."

"It is all true. I swear to you. I read the true history of Heaven. I spoke to the last remaining angel, the one who had been there before all of this," I said, waving my hands around. "God lied to us, stole from us, killed indiscriminately, and crushed us under His heel. He used me to do His dirty work for Him. He used your uncle, my grandfather—His own people. I told you it was so much bigger. What I should have said was, it is so much worse! Worse than we could ever have thought."

She continued to look at me. She said nothing.

"What?" I asked.

"Only a great fool believes there to be singularity in truth, Lucifer."

She shook her head, as if to wrestle out the thoughts colliding violently in her head.

"What?" I asked again.

"How?" Her expression did not change. "How do you intend to do this?"

"I cannot tell you. But I could use your help."

"That makes sense," she said to herself. She looked back into the garden pond and then back up at her apartments. "That makes sense."

"Amee?"

She stood up suddenly, her spine straight, her posture erect.

"What can I do to help?" She asked. There was complete sincerity in her voice.

At least I hoped there was.

"I need you to go to the Great Northern Woods."

⌘　⌘　⌘

I did not tell her about Phanuel and my plans for Man. It would have been simply too much to absorb, and she did not need to know everything. I only needed a few more days to get Phanuel to alter Man's genetics, and I would permanently reset the way I needed Man situated. The way we needed Man to be. The way the City of Heaven needed Man to be. Built in God's image, yes, but with all the capacities of angels.

Amee did not tell me whom she would send, but I guessed it had to be Melchom. I might not have liked him, but he clearly had no love for God and a great deal of love for Amee. He would not be told anything specific. Only that he had to provide a signal. To whom that signal would be sent, neither Amee nor Melchom knew. All they needed to know was that it would initiate my coup d'état. I could only hope Simon and the army had made it there in time, and he would recognize the signal when the moment came.

⌘   ⌘   ⌘

"You must be getting excited," Gabriel said, as we ate together a few nights later.

He had invited me to dinner at his main residence and seeing that our relationship had been strained since our last conversation, I felt it incumbent on me to accept. While once I would have spent all my days with him, I had hardly seen him in the month since my return. His invitation had come without warning.

"Your triumph is but a few days away."

I tried to look interested. "Yes, of course," I said. I was clearly preoccupied.

"Your last triumph was quite a spectacle. I only hope I'll be able to do something to match it in the minds of the people."

"And God," I said.

Gabriel smiled. It was a patently disingenuous smile. He ignored my comment and sat quietly for a moment.

"Michael will be returning for the festivities," he observed.

In that one second, everything was lost. I was dead. The City of God would not fall. Simon and his army would walk into a well-defended trap.

"At the head of our army, no doubt," I said, in as nonchalant a tone as I could muster. I had hardly skipped a beat.

"Mmm," was all Gabriel was willing to acknowledge.

My mind spun. Gabriel looked at me. I felt faint. He knew. Maybe not about my precise plans, but he knew.

"You seem uncomfortable, Lucifer." He had said it with the deliberate intention of expressing his satisfaction.

"What have you done?" I asked. It was a stupid thing to say.

Gabriel put his napkin on the table and leaned back in his chair.

"I've done nothing. Nothing but wait for you to do what God has always expected of you."

"I have always been loyal," I lied.

"Oh yes. Very loyal. So loyal, in fact, that you were willing to kill your friends for your personal advancement. So very loyal that you would throw your grandfather's work out the window, take up God's most important project ever, and keep it from me."

"You are so very small, Gabriel," I growled back at him. "So loyal that I ensured the continuation of His rule for the last sixty-five million years. What have *you* done?"

He clenched his jaw. I could see the muscles of his face pulsating with hatred. This must have been the way he looked, those many millions of years ago, when he had put all those trimmers to the sword. Evil. Vengeful. Happy.

He leaned forward. "I put God where He is today. I sweated and bled for Him, long before you arrived. I protected Him from everything and I will continue to protect Him forever. You are nothing but a flash of lightning. Strong, powerful, fearsome. Yes. But momentary. Expelling all your energy in one uncontrolled punch, unable to see how that same energy can be harnessed for greater things. Well, you caused your damage and now that you're done, I will see to it that all is returned to its original state."

"If only that were true!" I snarled.

The blood boiled within me. This was not the angel I had grown to love. This was an angel seized by greed and anxious to regain God's goodwill.

Gabriel signaled. Instantly, guards strode into the room. Gabriel's bodyguards.

Gabriel stood. "Lucifer, Seraph of God, I arrest you in the name of God, our Father, for sedition and conspiracy to commit sedition."

"You cannot arrest me. You have no proof of anything. And you have no authority over God's Seraphs."

"Sedition is sedition in God's eyes, my friend," he said in a veiled reference to Zoan and his betrayal. "And when did we ever need proof in order to dispose of someone?

"Surely, you jest? This is nothing but the outcome of your naked jealousy and God will see through it."

"God knows all," he said with something akin to sadness. "By choosing a great opponent, you have created the semblance of greatness for yourself. That just won't do. For that," he said, "may He have no mercy on you." He forced a smile once again. An empty smile. "It is for the greater good of the City."

And in that moment, I was lost. Everything was lost.

CHAPTER THIRTY-FIVE

I was taken from Gabriel's home, hands and feet bound together, to be transported by carriage not to the City's dungeons, but to the Seat of God itself. Jehoel's face came to me. All the guilt I had felt for so many millennia. At first, I was afraid. I would die, most likely, a horrible death.

But the more I reflected on the matter, the more I realized that I was not really afraid. If there was fear within me, it was not of death, but rather, of missing out on all that was waiting to happen. What would become of Amee and my father, of Gabriel and Michael? Would Simon ever get the signal? Would he able to win without me? Would he and our armies come down into the City and be caught in an unsuspecting trap? Would I be blamed?

I also feared I would never have the chance to retrospect as an old angel, to reflect on the mistakes of my youth and learn from them in preparation for what lay beyond. God had always maintained that Heaven was the first and the last. Nothing had preceded Heaven and nothing would follow it. I had pondered over that as I worked on Man. Would Man also come to believe that Earth was the first and last, that he was nothing but intellectualized dust, mixed with astonishing luck in the blend that was the universe of God's creation? Or would Man recognize that Earth was just the springboard, not totally devoid of all merit, as this was where he would learn to socialize and build in the ways that God had intended?

In that moment, I realized that while I feared these two things, I regretted something even more intensely: I would never actually see Man. I would be denied the triumph of witnessing that moment when he reached his full potential. The people of Heaven, be they God-fearing, law-abiding inhabitants of the City of God or outlanders eking out an existence on the scrublands, mountains, and forests of Heaven's vast expanses, might remember me later in whatever way they saw as most just; but I would never be known to Man. He would hear stories from his master and His minion. But Man's creator, Man's real creator, would die before his creation was complete.

"I have always known that one day, I would take this road," I said to myself, as the carriage trundled along. "But yesterday, I did not know it would be today."

Years later, those would be the words of a man, in his own time. But his inspiration, in that particular moment, would be far different from my own now.

⌘　⌘　⌘

In the next moment, everything changed. Again. The carriage suddenly lurched upward, throwing me, along with my guards, to the back of the compartment. Explosions ripped all around us, as the carriage keeled over sideways and was dragged along the dark, empty street. I could hear the shrill, frightened screams of horses and sparks flew, as the metal of the carriage ground into the pavement and was dragged along it. More explosions and the carriage jumped up over the road on which it was being dragged. In a split second, everything seemed to come apart. Smoke and fire and debris and angels. The carriage slammed into a building bordering the street. Everything slowed down again. I felt my body being hurled in one direction and then the cold, wet pavement. Angels running in every direction, as I tried to look up, vision blurred, sounds muffled, distanced. The acrid smell of burning flesh. Mixed with the odor of fresh blood and wet streets. The smell was overpowering. And then everything ceased.

I remember thinking, just before everything went black, I must be dead.

⌘ ⌘ ⌘

But I was not dead. Not yet. When I came to, I was lying on the street. My vision was blurry, at first, but I could make out some sort of light. Fires burned all around me and looking down at my arm, I could see that I had also been on fire at some point. My face stung and when things came into focus, I saw Phanuel patting me down with a wet rag.

"You're alive!" he shouted.

I thought for a moment. "I think so," I murmured, looking around me.

Azael stood before me. Somehow, he was there. With him were my smiling bodyguards and many angels I did not recognize.

"What is it?" I asked. "What is happening?"

"You have been rescued," Phanuel said, as if it were obvious to everyone. "These angels are here to help you. Help the City. Finish the work that you set out to do."

I looked at them all. "I do not understand."

So often, in the last few years, had I felt this way. So often would I have to go on faith, it seemed.

"Always several steps behind," Azael said quietly.

"We have to move you off the street, Lucifer," Phanuel said. He almost never called me by that name.

Azael turned and issued a few short, but direct orders. "Move this debris off the street quickly. Kill any of Gabriel's remaining angels. Bring up the carriage and be sure that we have medical treatment at hand."

He looked down at me as I tried to sit up with Phanuel's help.

"He should at least appear to be seriously injured," Azael said, "or people will wonder."

The angels around us went off to do his bidding. Azael and my bodyguard remained close by, swords drawn. There were only eight of them, I noticed. It seemed angels had already died in defending me.

Phanuel seemed to guess what I was thinking. "Some of them didn't make it," he said, tending to my injuries. "It's the price we'll have to pay to get you out of here."

I looked at my bodyguards and shook my head.

"At your service, my Lord," Jeqon said, as if understanding the reason for my hesitation.

"Can you move, Lucifer?" Phanuel asked.

"Yes, I think so."

He helped me to my feet. My head was still swimming from the percussion of the blast.

"How did you know what had happened to me?" I asked, gingerly touching the burns on my face and arm.

"Azael came to me. He explained everything."

I looked at Azael, furious with him for the first time since he had come to serve me. "That was a terrible risk," I said sternly.

"One we had to take, my Lord," he said matter-of-factly. "And I was running out of options."

I was not satisfied with his explanation, but Phanuel interrupted me before I could get another word out. "Let it go, Lucifer. Azael did the right thing. And as it turned out, his timing was right too."

"What do you mean?"

"I received word from someone that Gabriel had invited you to dinner," Phanuel said, now inspecting my injured arm. "It seems Gabriel's personal bodyguards had been ordered to his residence. This messenger assumed you were compromised and asked for my help."

"From whom did you receive word?" I asked, more confused than ever.

"Amee," Phanuel said.

My heart nearly stopped. "You saw Amee? Is she all right?"

"She was fine when we parted, but I have not seen her since. She came to my laboratory and told me that if I truly loved and cherished you, I should hasten to meet the angels she had posted at a point on your expected route to ambush your carriage and its escort and that I was to take care of you, regardless of the circumstances."

"You set this up?" I asked Azael, looking around at the rapidly clearing street.

"Yes, my Lord," he smiled. "It seems Amee and I have more in common than I had originally assumed."

"You are not part of this...resistance?" I asked Phanuel, grasping his arm.

"No," he replied, looking around. "I do not know these angels." He looked at my burned face for a moment. "But when Amee said you needed me, I didn't hesitate. Azael came to me and it all made sense."

I had never had a son. I will, perhaps, never have a son. In those few moments, Phanuel was more a son to me than any flesh and blood of mine could ever be. I had taken his father from him. Yet he loved me. I did not deserve him, but cherished him all the same. I do, to this day.

"Lord, we cannot wait any longer," Azael reminded me.

"I agree," Phanuel chimed in.

"Azael, you never cease to amaze me," I said, smiling at him. "If we live through this, you have to tell me how in the name of God you got here."

He smiled back at me. "You can ask Jeqon, my Lord. He seems to know the city even better than you do."

I shot a look at Jeqon.

He smiled in acknowledgment, but instantly moved forward as Azael shouted his orders.

They led me from the street, my bodyguards taking up position all around us. Angels were still busy putting out the fires, taking bodies away, and generally restoring the street to its former orderliness. I was still rather woozy from the blast. I needed to be helped into the carriage that was brought up. An angel I did not know quickly cleaned and bandaged my arm, as my bodyguards took position on and around the carriage. I winced at the pain as he tended to my face.

"This will leave a scar, no doubt," said the angel, as he applied salve.

"Where are we going?" I asked absently.

Week after week, I had been intently focused, at least in my own head, on what I needed to do, wondering how I would go about it. Ironically, the blast seemed to have emptied my head of all thought, all concern. I did not know where I was or where I was headed. All I knew was that I was safe.

"The Seat of God!" Phanuel shouted to the driver.

His words shocked me back into the moment.

"What!" I shouted.

Phanuel looked at me. "There's one last adjustment I need to make to Man. And if your plan is to work, you need to take God prisoner." He paused for a moment, as if what he was about to say pained him. "Or kill him."

"I thought we were through with that," I said, an imploring note in my voice. "It will never work. There is just too much at risk." I was babbling.

"Get a hold on yourself, Ahriman," Phanuel said firmly.

Azael looked at him in surprise.

"Whatever is happening here, you are the catalyst," Phanuel continued. "A leader of angels. It is what you have always been. So get yourself together."

I felt ashamed.

He looked out at the streets. "I've listened to your advice on Man since your return from the outlands, but it was clear to me that you were not carrying out God's will. Out of love for you, I kept my suspicions to myself. God does not know any better and neither would anyone else. But others in the lab could. Acceding to your requests meant changing what I knew to be God's express demands and while you would not tell me the truth, I held back. Now that I understand your purpose, out of love, I will obey you, though I don't know where this will end."

I looked at him mournfully. "I killed your father, Phanuel. I killed him to succeed in the existence God has seen fit to make for me. All for a damned promotion!" Tears rolled down my cheek and burned into my scorched face. I was not acting this time. "Only now, at the end, do I see the truth in what your father had stood for. And now that I see what God is, what He has done, what He intends to do, I cannot sit idly by and merely let things take their course."

"I know, Ahriman," Phanuel said. "You taught me to believe in God, but all along, you always taught me to believe in myself."

I had not thought of it that way. From the moment I had taken up the cause, the cause of the City of Heaven, its overthrown and dying Council, Maalik, Simon, the thoughts and angels that made up the outcast trimmers, I had only thought in terms of what they had told me. Could that be called "belief"? No. But in those few moments, Phanuel made me believe.

"Yes," I murmured to myself, "believe in yourself."

"What?" he asked.

"I am sorry. I am so sorry. I wish Jehoel were here now to help me. To help us. It is I who have put you in this situation."

"I need no tears from the loss of a loved one, Ahriman. Not as I see it. We cry to prove to ourselves the feelings of loss we suffer. We show them off, share them with others. Make them feel sorry for us. But as soon as we take our eyes off of ourselves, the pain goes away."

I looked at him proudly. He was a better angel than I could ever be.

"Should I fritter my life away fearing the loss of a friend? A father? Even if they are gone from me, aren't they still with me where they were when I was able to see them before me?" He looked at me again. "Get yourself together, Lucifer. Whatever it is you need to do tonight, do it right. Make things right. Here's your chance. And in what small way I can, I will help you."

I was back. Back in my head.

I banged on the roof of the carriage. "The Seat of God! As quickly as we can!" I looked at Phanuel. "They are expecting me," I said. "God is expecting me."

I pulled a sword from Jeqon's scabbard. He quickly unsheathed another. Azael pulled his own sword.

"And we should not keep God waiting."

⌘　⌘　⌘

Amee had betrayed my confidence, but she had not betrayed me. As my mind whirled with all that I needed to do in the next few moments, I considered how she had found Phanuel. Had found Azael. Had offered to help me directly, an offer I had refused. And because of my refusal, she had had to take certain measures to make it all work, despite my resistance. I had calculated on her either betraying me or holding her tongue, but I had not calculated on her saving me.

The streets sped by. It was early evening. Dawn was many hours away, but as I looked east, I could see the coming day, filled with strange portents. A strange light. But it did not matter. Gabriel still believed I was a prisoner in custody, on my way to God. To face His wrath. God knew I was on my way to Him and He was preparing to place me under His complete control. His palace was well guarded and His personal contingent of guards hardly insubstantial. How, with a handful of angels, could I hope to take God prisoner and hold Him as long as I needed to before

Simon's arrival? Assuming, of course, that Simon would arrive at all.

"If nothing else, I must set an unequivocal example for the people. For all angels. They must know, before God's paranoid propaganda machine intervenes to distort facts and spread misinformation, that I stood up against Him. That I took a chance, not for my personal benefit, but for the benefit of all." I said it more to myself than to anyone else.

"You will die a martyr?" Phanuel asked.

"Exactly," I agreed. "Otherwise, all my efforts will have been in vain. Not just what I have done for your father, my grandfather, or the people of the City of Heaven. If I fail, I have to fail the right way."

"Somehow," Phanuel finished.

"Yes."

"How?" Azael asked.

I did not know. For someone who prided himself on strategizing, I had no master plan. How could I lead a revolt against God and not have a strategy?

"I need to get Maalik or Jehoel's book first. The book of laws," I said.

It was hardly definitive proof of anything at all, but it seemed to me as good a place as any to get the word out.

"God's collection of these books of law is a kind of trophy wall," I said. "It is the law book for each of the heads of the Council of Twelve. It is a means of keeping the true Word hidden from the people. It is His way of ensuring that every angel, all angels, believe in Him and Him alone." My mind was spinning. "If I can get one out and give it to the people, somehow, maybe that will be enough."

"Somewhat ironic, then, that you yourself are the one who gave them to God," Azael said.

I thought about that for a moment. "Indeed. I have sown my own doom in more ways than one." I cursed my shortsightedness.

Phanuel looked out the window. "We are nearly there."

"Okay, my angels," I said, looking at Azael and the rest of my bodyguards. "Change now."

Quickly, they changed out of their uniforms and donned the ones taken off Gabriel's dead soldiers. Phanuel followed suit.

"Are you sure you are ready for this?" I asked him.

"I am," he replied. It was all he needed to say.

"When was the last time you wielded a sword in anger?" I asked.

"More recently than you, I would wager," Azael said.

He was probably right.

"Keep an eye on him," I whispered to Azael.

I left it at that. Things would not be as before.

"Be ready," I said. I looked again at Azael. "And may the glory of the Kingdom of Heaven be with you."

With a shout, they all responded, "And also with you!"

"And also with you, my Lord," Azael said.

CHAPTER THIRTY-SIX

The carriage pulled into the quiet, but tension-filled entranceway of God's residence. How many times had I been there? A thousand times? A million? A small squad of soldiers was waiting there for us. The gates closed behind the carriage, though the waiting soldiers had clearly been expecting the second escort carriage.

"Where is the other carriage?" shouted the captain.

Azael spoke. "We were ambushed along the way. The other carriage was blown to pieces. We managed to escape with the prisoner, though he is injured."

The captain seemed concerned, but not surprised. "There are reports of uprisings all over the City," he said. "What soldiers we have at our disposal were sent. All four quarters." The captain looked up at the sky. "The northern forests are burning and the eastern sky is filled with strange lights."

We all looked up. Even me. The light I had seen from the carriage was not the light of the coming day. It was an eerie, unnatural glow, emblazoning the entire northern sky. It had not even occurred to me that Heaven's sun could not possibly be rising in that direction!

"Get the prisoner out of the carriage!" shouted Azael.

The door was sprung open. I walked out and down the steps with as much bravado as I could manage. I said nothing. My presence alone was enough to make the soldiers nervous and unsure of themselves.

"Return to your post," the captain told Azael.

"No. We have strict orders to escort the prisoner to God Himself."

The captain eyed him suspiciously.

Azael met his stare with suitable ferocity. "Who are you," he barked with supreme confidence, "to deny Gabriel's orders?"

"You will all pay dearly for these insults!" I shouted. "I am of the Order of the Seraphim. Protector of the Lord's Senate. Servant to the Lord God Himself! You dare feel free to bandy words before me!"

Even Azael was a little startled by my outburst.

The captain thought quickly. "You there!" he motioned to his lieutenant. "I will take six soldiers and escort this crew to the Lord's Chamberlain. You will remain here at your post and keep an eye out for the second carriage or possible stragglers."

The young lieutenant was nervous.

"And make sure no one else comes through that gate!" the captain shouted.

Phanuel leaned over to me and whispered, "Apparently, whatever uprisings Amee was able to instigate have severely strained God's remaining troops. We may be in luck."

"I do not believe in luck," I said.

"Funny you of all angels would say that," Phanuel remarked.

"Quick, now!" shouted Azael. "Let's get a move on it. We are late already and our Lord must not be kept waiting."

We moved out of the driveway and into the palace proper. Soldiers were visible throughout, but Phanuel seemed to be right about the chaos engendered by the insurrections. Angels ran here and there. Disorder and panic seemed to prevail. The household battalion appeared to be at half-strength. With all of His power, how could God have so underestimated His needs?

We passed through many familiar rooms and hallways. Soldiers and bureaucrats of all kinds ran about, carrying valuables, papers, and boxes. In some of the larger rooms, small fires had been set up in wide-lipped cisterns and documents of all sorts were being burned. Smoke billowed into the luxuriously-appointed rooms and even with the windows open, I could already make out growing soot stains on the ceilings. God would be more than furious when He saw the total mess and the utter lack of regard for order and cleanliness. It was absolutely unprecedented. Either something I could not quite fathom was happening or God was more paranoid than I had ever expected Him to be.

We made our way up several private stairways. Given our hurried pace, I found myself out of breath. As I began to sweat, my face and arm started stinging intensely, the burned flesh already oozing into my bandages. I truly looked a mess, with blood all over my robes, some of it my own and some of it from Gabriel's now-dispatched angels. The higher we ascended, the more deserted the residence became. Rooms lay empty and whole hallways were stripped of their furnishings. It seemed the evacuation had progressed from top to bottom. Some paper debris lay strewn in the passageways, but other than the occasional guard or two, the place was almost completely empty of angels.

At last, we came to the quarters of God's Chamberlain. Another squad of soldiers stood in the hallway, all of them talking nervously among themselves.

The captain escorting us spoke. "Make way. We have our Lord's prisoner with us."

The captain of the other squad stepped forward.

"Show him. Show him to me."

Shaking off the restraining hands of my disguised bodyguard, I stepped forward. "Who are you?" I demanded.

The second captain stood in silence, apparently at greater ease than his counterpart from the driveway squad. "What difference does it make to you, traitor?" he shot back.

"It will make the greatest difference to all of you," I countered.

He grasped my bindings and pushed me to the floor. My bodyguards, betraying their loyalty, all drew their swords and quickly moved forward. Azael stopped them.

"Enough of this. This is God's prisoner and we shall not wait around for you and your games," Azael said quietly, but very firmly to the captain.

"Who are you to tell me what to do?" the captain shouted back.

The captain of the driveway squad watched nervously. I tried to stand up again, but the captain pushed me back down.

"In the name of the Lord," bellowed Azael, "I demand that you step aside!"

As the captain was about to draw his own sword, the door behind him opened. Everyone seemed to stop breathing at once. God stepped out. All instantly dropped to their knees and bowed their heads. I rose to my feet, as if to emphasize that I was not one of them.

God looked at me. He seemed taken unawares by the shouting and noise rising up outside His door. His servants must have been beside themselves, as He had clearly opened the door on His own accord. I was about to speak out, but then something about Him caught my eye. God seemed disheveled, confused. He looked at all the angels bowing before Him, as if He were surprised to even see them there. Gone was His arrogance and anger. Before me stood someone small, almost meek. The way He was the night I had come to Him after Gabriel's defeat. The night I had first defied God and all that He stood for. I almost wanted to ask Him if He was all right, but He cut me off before I had the chance.

"Where is Gabriel?" He asked, His voice a croak. "Where is my greatest Seraph?"

We all looked at Him, bewildered.

"I am here, Lord," I said, before I even realized what I had done. "It is I, Lucifer, your Seraph."

He looked at me and squinted as if He did not recognize me. "You are not Gabriel. You are an impostor."

Azael raised his head. Something had to be done.

"My Lord, I am Sraosha, Commander of Gabriel's household troops," Azael said.

I could only hope Azael knew what he was saying.

"I bring you the traitor Lucifer, Seraph of the Realm, as you ordered my master to do," Azael concluded.

God looked at him. "Do I know you, angel?" He asked.

Azael bowed in acknowledgment of the question. "No, my Lord," he answered. "But I bring to you the prisoner, as you had requested."

God seemed to struggle with this for a moment, but then suddenly snapped to. "Ah, all right, then. Bring him in."

With that, He turned on His heel and walked back into His apartments. Everyone looked at each other, dumbfounded, even those who, only a few moments ago, had been about to come to blows. Azael sheathed his sword, took me under the arm roughly, and walked me into God's chamber. The two captains just stood there motionless, as the door closed behind us, still reeling from their expected and confusing audience with God.

⌘　⌘　⌘

"Leave us," God commanded.

Azael bowed and directed the angels back out into the hallway.

"Sit," He said to me.

I did as I was told.

"You know, Lucifer, I truly thought you would have more brains than to try something like this so soon after returning from the outlands."

He stood silhouetted against the window, the night sky a glaring yellow from the burning forests of the north. He seemed to have regained His faculties.

"Insurrections broke out across the entire city earlier this evening, nearly at the very moment you were summoned to Gabriel's home," God continued. "I loved Gabriel like a son, but when he failed to carry out my orders in the project involving Man, I had to get rid of him." God turned to me. "Once I sent him off to the outlands, I expected you to let him go, but I underestimated your affection for him."

He walked over to a nearby table and poured Himself some ambrosia. Never once had I seen Him pour His own drink.

"Instead, you headed out to the outlands, defying my commands, to find him. To find the armies." He looked at me. "It seems you found something else, instead."

"I found out something, instead," I confirmed, "Yahweh."

God did not flinch. He simply took a sip of His ambrosia. "Only Gabriel has called me that these many years," He said thoughtfully. "It sounds strange to hear that name now. Almost as if it is not a part of me."

"Perhaps *that* is your problem. Whatever you were, whatever you intended, you created a horrific version of the greatness this place once possessed. You killed, murdered thousands, millions of angels for your glory, if that is what it ever was. You betrayed friend and foe alike to make yourself the most powerful being in Heaven. You sowed nothing but fear and discord in the people you call your subjects. And for what? All for your adoration."

"Do you know what they did, that Council of fools?" God asked, ignoring my question. "They blinded themselves. Sitting there, day after day, doing nothing but prevaricating on any issue that was presented. Unable to make a decision. Unable to deal with change. Heaven changes and I was the only one willing to show them the truth. They were failing their people. Failing all angels. All of Heaven. Carrying on without the vision, a silly, senseless bunch, who were undermining the very fabric of the society they claimed to champion. What had they done to promote justice or equality? Nothing, the hypocrites! They just sat there, as they always had, squabbling and doing nothing, proving to anyone willing to see the truth that they had become obsolete and needed to be replaced." He seemed pleased with Himself all over again. "Oh, what I did saved this City! What I did was the first good this City had seen in its existence."

"You are a sad being, Yahweh," I said, shaking my head. "You speak of the 'good' you have done, but you do not know what 'good' is. In fact, you have deliberately confused good with sin and brought about the absolute destruction of our liberty."

"Hmm," was all He said.

"Do you not get tired of it, Yahweh? Not being anything other than 'God'? Not even being Yahweh, whatever he was, before he became God? Did there never come a time when you said to yourself, 'Enough is enough?' Or do you simply not become tired of honoring yourself?"

"Do you become tired, Satan?" He asked.

I was a bit confused. I was not sure to whom He was referring. Perhaps He was deluded again?

"You and I are from the same stock," He went on. "You know this now. You have been fighting for years, not just our enemies or the enemies I have told you to fight, but me as well. Have you not come to see the futility of it all? Have you no common sense?"

"A proper angel's reliance on common sense is proportional to his reliance on intuition and reason," I replied.

"Intuition? Reason?" God asked with a disdainful laugh. "This is what you have for me? What difference does any of that make? Things are as they are, because that is what I tell you they are. Only that is real."

"And in an existence where you are God, our sovereign Lord, creator of the universe and father to us all, that might be true," I replied. "The problem, Yahweh, is that none of that is true. You are a usurper. A destroyer of the natural order. You fooled people into believing you and then you forced them to believe *in* you. But you never believed it yourself. You realized that only by creating something wholly 'else' would you have a real sense of the divine. You seek to make Man and create nature because you fooled yourself into believing your own story. Zoan knew. He knew you, where you were from. Where I was from. You saw your chance to live our your fantasy in Zoan and that is why you could not kill him. You had to hope that he could make you what you wanted to be. 'The Lord, God.' And that is what you saw in me. You were willing to overlook Zoan's betrayal and the fact that I was following in his footsteps, because you knew that only we could make you truly immortal."

"You have power, Satan, I give you that."

"Why do you call me '*Satan*?'" I finally asked, not knowing what He meant.

"You oppose my order, my rule. You are no longer my Lucifer. You are an enemy: Satan."

"You think names will hurt me?" I asked, finally recognizing the ancient angelic word. "*Satan*": adversary or foe. "I am not afraid of a name, Yahweh," I said with as much of a barb in my words as I could muster.

"You do not know the power I have," God said, returning to His point. "The power you have. To rule. To bring order to these heavens and any other world we create. No one knows how great we are."

"You think what you have created here is real power? There is no power in itself. There is only the perception of power that I helped build for you." God *had* come to believe His own propaganda. "We are nothing alike, you and I. You used your powers to deviously establish your cause as the cause of the City. You hid behind the City's most ancient institutions, while acting, all the time, to destroy those very same institutions. You used your power to deceive people into believing your way was the time-honored and true way," I said breathlessly. "My power is different. I refuse to make you immortal. No, I know you. And you know now that I will do everything in my power, whatever power that is, to thwart you."

God sighed. "Yes, yes. This is something I have always known, Satan. But let's get down to what we're really talking about: Man. He is but a shadowy reflection of what I really need. But Man will invigorate me in ways that will bring me as close to my goals as anything you or Zoan or anyone has ever done. Man will spend his time on Earth, preparing, so that when he gets here, he will have no doubt that the institutions of God are imbued with absolute authority. A simple appeal to his common sense will discourage any perilous criticism of my rule. I need not fear angels any more. Their absolute obedience will make angels redundant, unnecessary."

"Again, only if things were truly the way you think they are, Yahweh."

I had got His attention now.

"What do you mean? Speak up!"

"Has Man been completed?"

"Yes. The final version was approved not a day ago."

"And who championed this final version?"

"Phanuel, your most favored angel," He smiled. "Somewhat ironic that your own minion would do my bidding. Perhaps you are not the angel you believe yourself to be?"

"Are you sure? You should be sure of that," I said with a smile.

God stood thinking for a moment, as if to double-check the many lists in His mind and confirm things were as He had directed them to be.

"I am sure," He said, but without conviction.

"My 'most favored angel,' you say?" I asked.

God's face began flushing. "Yes," He said through clenched teeth.

"I would check that if I were you, Yahweh."

"What have you done?"

"I guess I have lived up to my new name," I said, almost chortling.

His face was bright red. I wondered, momentarily, whether it burned as much as the burns on my own face did.

"I did only what you expected me to," I continued. "So says Gabriel, anyway. Your Man will not be as you planned. As I had reported. As Phanuel had reported. As even Gabriel had reported. The formula is set. The science is done. Unless you wipe out the last sixty-five million years of work and start from scratch, assuming you can find another one of 'us,' you will be stuck with Man as I designed him. Man will not be the automaton you wished him to be. He will be thinking, rational, like we are. With all the faculties we have. And all of this by the time he arrives in Heaven. Only Man will be better than God and His angels. Man will be able to learn, to improve his world by improving himself, making himself equal to God in many ways." I paused for effect. "Really, if you think about it, you will be inferior to Man, for you have your armies, your rule, to thank for your immunity from fear. Man will have to use his brain. He will have to develop his mind and body, succeed on his own, in overcoming fear. Oh, Man will arrive in Heaven prepared all right. He will come to Heaven with the capacity to see through the 'bullshit,' as I believe you once called it, able to access the intuition you would have denied him. The same intuition you delude yourself into thinking we angels have been willing to put aside for you."

I had never seen God as angry as He was at that precise moment. I derived a certain perverse pleasure from the knowledge that it was I who had provoked that fury. It felt so good. So inexplicably, unutterably satisfying. I would have made a worthy adversary, I thought.

I continued, "You know, it is funny. Even if I die here tonight, even if the City of God never reverts to the City of Heaven, even if everything I hoped for fails, I will still have won. You once wanted me to complete Zoan's work. I think...no, I *know* now that tonight, I have."

From across the room, God exploded into a rage. "*Curse you!*" He screamed, flinging His glass at me.

Though surprised at the outburst, I stepped out of the way and the glass hit the floor behind me, splintering into pieces. Then He did something I had not entirely expected. He started laughing.

"It doesn't matter," He laughed. "Ah, you are so blind!" He laughed more heartily.

"What do You mean?" I asked.

He picked up another glass and poured Himself more ambrosia, as if nothing had changed. "You do not even realize the gravity of your mistake, do you, Satan? In your race to unseat me, you have managed to do for me that which I would, most likely, not have been able to do on my own. On Earth, Man will personify me—all the good in the world, all the bad in it too. The power of reason you gave him will not operate beyond the limits of his mind, as you seem to think. He will look at himself and see me and he will see no error in himself. He will see no error in himself, precisely because he can reason, justify...no...*rationally* justify himself. Instead of inspiring and developing the world, he will judge it, condemn it, and bring it to ruin." God laughed out loud again. "You have just made Man more a part of me than I could have ever done on my own. You will be cursed, Satan, and I will be loved. You will be blamed and I? I will be the light of the universe."

"Reason will prevail in him," I said, suddenly unsure as to whether I believed myself.

"It is no matter," God said, far more assured of the strength of his statement than I was of mine. "Man, reason or not, will create us himself. Reason or not, he will not understand his world and will look to the divine for answers."

"Answers he will never receive," I retorted.

"On the contrary," God said, almost surprised. "Without a divine light to guide him, Man will be uninspired. There is no spirituality in reason. Reason is too complicated to address the common good. We have spoken of this before, though it seems to have escaped your attention. He smiled a ferocious smile. "No, no. Man's questions on the infinite, all the gifts he finds waiting for him, will only be answered in the divine. And his spirituality will bring him closer and closer to me."

"Man will come to use his reason to better understand the universe," I retorted. "There is no unbridgeable gap between the absolute rational and one's faith. One will find the truth in the other. Man will see that in preparing for the divine, he will be preparing for the truth of Heaven."

"Reason will not give Man what you think it will, Satan," God countered. "He may use it to understand the world he lives in, but it will give him no greater understanding of his ultimate purpose."

"The things of their world," I said, "will be the predecessors of what men can expect in this world. Reason will give them an entrée into the Heaven you have shaped. They will come to understand that by questioning God, like I have," I said defiantly, "the only truth they will find in their quest for you is that you exist."

"You are an egomaniacal fool, Satan. Your vision is flawed. With his vision of me, Man will be unwilling to see anything else. His lack of understanding will feed his inability to consider the universe of possibilities, the ideas others have to offer, thereby reinforcing tenfold his belief in his own views. It will drive him close to his own faith, even if that faith doesn't make sense in a logical or rational way. This shortsightedness, this lack of understanding, will compel him to wield 'God' as his sword against all who do not see the world as *his* God does. You have done me a favor, Satan. By polarizing Heaven, you have driven Man closer to me. All men will perpetrate their evil in the name of God, dying to the last to protect me from their perception of what you are." He said it with a sneer.

"Man can become more," I said, doubting myself now.

"But he will not. Your mistake will prepare Man for me. I will represent for him a warm homecoming, as opposed to what you and your real world stand for in his eyes."

"I will help him."

"And push him ever closer to me. But by giving Man reason, you have given him multiple ways of understanding existence. This will compound his confusion and uncertainty, leaving him to face what lies ahead with awe, rather than confidence. It renders him more malleable, easier to bend to my will." He finished His drink and poured another. "The more I think about it, Man, without reason, would be too sloppy for me."

"I know what I made for you, Yahweh," I said with conviction. "Maybe you are right. Maybe Man will cherish faith more than reason. But for how long? Faith may be a necessary step in his evolution, but no more than that. There will come a time when faith in God will no longer provide the solace or protection you seem to think it will. You will be replaced and Man will no longer labor under your yoke on Earth. You will be labeled a fraud. You will be deemed evil." It was all I could say.

"I do not think so. Think, Satan," He said. "I have ruled this City for the last thirteen billion years. Where was the revolution? Eh? Where was my ouster? I am still here and willing to wait another thirteen billion years for Mankind to come around to accepting the validity of your arguments."

"Your overthrow is in the making, Yahweh. Look out that window," I said, pointing. "That is your City, rising up against you."

"That is nothing," He said, His glass held to His lips. "It is no different from any other uprising. Uprisings, may I remind you, which you helped me put down. You are the hypocrite here, not I."

"A hypocrite? Me? Where is your Gabriel, Yahweh? You cut him down to nothing. You divested him of his power and relegated him to the position of a spy. Your spy. Where is Michael? In Apsatsus? With most of your army? To whom will you now delegate the responsibility of slaughtering the apostates now rising up throughout your city? You are nothing more than a bad angel's vision of what a good angel should be."

"Gabriel had enough power to bring you here, did he not?" God asked waspishly. "I think you will find that I am more powerful than you and your fellow instigators imagined."

"I think when you open those doors," I said, pointing at the doors of His chambers, "you will discover that things are no longer as you had left them."

God stopped in His tracks.

"You lie," He said.

"Not any more."

"Open the door!" He yelled out to His servants.

"But my Lord..." one of them whispered.

"*JUST DO IT!*" He roared.

The servant complied at once. Azael, Jeqon, and the rest of my angels walked calmly in, wiping the blood of God's soldiers from the blades of their swords. Phanuel was among them, looking a bit shaky, but clearly in command of his faculties. Had he ever witnessed bloodshed?

"My Lord," Azael said to me, as he approached.

Jeqon began rounding up the frightened servants. They fell into furtive and hushed exchanges between themselves as the rest of my bodyguard posted watches in the hallway and, with Azael's help, began searching the room for any remaining soldiers from God's retinue.

Phanuel walked up to me and removed his helmet. "My Lord," he said, lightheartedly mocking Azael.

God looked at him in disbelief. "How can you defend this angel?" he asked, aghast. "This Satan? He had your father killed! For his own profit!"

"This is how it ends," Phanuel said. "In obeying you, God, we all became your victims." He turned to me. "Now that we have him, what should we do with him?" he asked.

It seemed the right question. What do you do with God, when you have Him at your mercy? I looked to Azael.

"Do the right thing, Lucifer," he said, sheathing his sword.

I smiled.

"*SATAN!*" God screamed.

"You are consistent and wise counsel," I said to Azael, ignoring God's outburst.

But before I could utter another word, from the crowd of servants emerged a solitary figure, a drawn bow in hand. The arrow was released in a moment. I could see it clearly. I can still see it now. But I said nothing. Felt nothing. Did nothing.

Phanuel had seen it too. He pushed in front of me. With a clang, the arrow found an unintended mark. I looked at him with pain in my eyes. Phanuel seemed surprised, as if he had always doubted himself and now the answer had come. All too quickly. With me unarmed and Phanuel stricken, the servants saw an opportunity and charged at us. Azael turned into them and cut them down. Jeqon fell, a stiletto in his side, up under his armor. I held Phanuel close to me, as God slipped out in the confusion. It was over. Phanuel spat up blood as he tried to say something. He grasped my burnt arm. He wanted to speak, but could not manage the words. There was just too much blood in his lungs. It lasted for only a moment. Then he was dead, robbing me of the chance to say I loved him. I slumped to the floor with him, holding his body close to me.

Azael finished dispatching the servant who had killed Jeqon and hurried over. He looked down at us, at my tear-filled eyes. "God must have hidden an assassin among the servants," he said.

Obviously. I did not respond.

Azael shot a look over at Jeqon's lifeless body. "We must not linger," he said, realizing that I did not sense the urgency of the moment as he did.

I held Phanuel's head in my lap, stroking his hair. I had failed both Phanuel and his father.

"I am a fake. A fraud!" I spat out. "I take power from the sacrifices of others." I choked a bit and my head spun. "That is it. It seems all I am capable of doing. I change myself and those around me suffer." I looked down at my poor, dead angel. "All those around me."

"Lucifer, we have to go." Azael seized my arm. "There will be more troops here soon. We haven't any time!" Azael picked me up off the ground.

"I cannot do it," I said.

"Come on!" he shouted, pulling the sword from Phanuel's sheath and handing it to me. "Let his death not have been in vain. *We have to go now!*"

Azael dragged me from the room. I tried to look back. Look back at the angel who had been the closest thing I had ever had to a son. My bodyguard, now depleted by one, immediately surrounded me. They had always surrounded and protected me. Jeqon no longer would. No one in my presence seemed safe. Yet someone was always there to protect me. The adversary. Satan.

⌘ ⌘ ⌘

The palace swirled with confusion. Angels fighting angels, though I could not understand why. I heard screaming and shouting. I could see blood. Smell it. Yet everything seemed remote, at once removed, as if I had cotton stuffed in my ears. In my mouth and in my eyes too. I blush to think how unprepared I was for the loss of Phanuel, knowing as I do now what was to come afterward.

"Where are we going?" I finally managed to get out, realizing that we were in a carriage racing away from the palace.

"A meeting place. A safe place, from where you can lead the fight," Azael answered, scanning the streets as they flew past.

"What place? Where is it?"

"Phanuel told me about it as we were finishing off the soldiers in the hallway. He said Amee had directed him to take you to that place. He made me swear that I would take you there, if something happened to him."

"I see." It was all I could get out.

"I failed you, Lord," Azael said, witnessing my profound grief. "I did not protect Phanuel."

"You could not. You were protecting me."

I melted a bit, thinking of it. But the fierceness of Azael's gaze brought me back to the urgency of the moment. Whether I planned it out or not, things were moving. And, as they were moving fast, I needed to be in a place where I could quickly evaluate the situation and take charge. The right decisions had to be made. There was little room for error.

Amee had seen to it that I would be given the right tools to make it happen. Somehow, she had managed to get word out that I had been summoned to present myself before Gabriel. I have no idea how she anticipated my arrest, but that did not matter. She had known I would be brought directly before God instead of being taken to the dungeons.

Whatever her role had been, the City was now rising up against God. I could not be sure if it had anything to do directly with me, but it was, nonetheless, keeping the remaining soldiers in the City occupied. If I could have an idea of how widespread the rebellion was, I might have a better understanding of how to organize it. With Michael still outside the walls, even a token force of outlanders might be able to take control of the City. Had Amee arranged for a signal to be sent to Simon? Would I even have anyone to lead? The more I pondered over the matter, the more probable it seemed that the blaze in the northern forests was a sign that Simon was on his way. But where were they now? I knew Michael was approaching the City with the four legions of God's remaining armies, but there was no way I could know how far out they were or whether the soldiers would stay loyal to God or rally to Simon's side, when and if he arrived.

I did not know where God had gone. The City, though markedly smaller than it is today, was still a big place. And God surely had strength. He held some sort of reserve, about which even I knew nothing. Could I really claim to have overthrown God, when I could not lay my hand upon Him and either dispatch Him or force Him publicly to surrender His powers?

Where was Amee? This last concern was really my primary one. My father. In those flashing moments of panic and exhilaration, I had not spared him a thought. He had been a stopover or, more aptly, a kind of caretaker for me, while I traveled the roads set out for me by God, Zoan, Jehoel, and Maalik. No one had considered the road I wanted and I had resented that. But now that the road I had chosen was littered with the bodies of those who had meant the most to me, the paths Angra had chosen for me did not seem so bad, after all. The only road I had rejected outright was Amee's. Ironically, it had been the only road from which I was meant to benefit. She had wanted only good for me. She had wanted to love me and have me love her in return. The lust for power and, afterward, my desire for righteous power had blinded me to that love. When everything came down, when the heavens came crashing down around us, the sole remaining thought in my mind was focused on Amee.

When we pulled up to the safe house at last, I recognized it immediately, though I had not been there in millions of years. It was the burnt-out remains of the temple. Where Jehoel had taken me to learn about the true history of Heaven. The neighborhood had been burned to the ground with my rise to Seraph. The heart-shaped door had been ripped from its foundations, while I received effective command of the City's bureaucracy. The carved columns of the temple had been hacked down and hauled away to be put to use in repairing the City's walls, as I stood witness to Jehoel's execution. And now, I was back at that place. Its books long gone and its knowledge long departed from the City of God. But I was back, this time, not as a follower-turned-spy, but as the leader of the very movement I had worked so hard to crush.

What, indeed, is "right" and "wrong," when the universe has infinite possibilities? So many possibilities, in fact, that by their very definition, choosing only one path is the "wrong" decision, no matter how much thought and deliberation prompted it.

My mind cleared for the first time since Phanuel's death. My grief would have to wait. Amee would have to wait. I would no longer hold back my feelings for her when next we were together. But now she would have to wait.

"I need a situational report, now!" I shouted, walking down the dusty stairs of the dilapidated temple.

Angels looked up at me. The chaos brewing a moment before had suddenly ebbed. All looked upon me. All seemed astonished. Me, strutting down the stairway, my face and arm, burned through my bandages, blood-soaked. All seemed relieved. Azael ordered my bodyguard to spread out.

"Who is in charge here?" I demanded.

Angels began to return to whatever matter I had interrupted them from.

"I am," Melchom said, striding up.

I reached the bottom of the stairway and looked around. It all seemed so familiar, but so far away. Something akin to déjà vu. I looked at Melchom. I had hated him from the first moment I met him.

"What is the situation here?" I demanded.

He bowed. "My Lord, we have managed to spark fighting in all four of the City's quarters. We are weakest in the Northwest and the Southwest Quarters. We've taken the Northeast Quarter's principal fortress, but reports have already come in that it may be surrounded by God's soldiers."

"How long will it hold?" I asked.

"There may only be a few soldiers in the City, my Lord, but they are soldiers. We are not prepared to fight trained killers. We are only trained to think," Melchom said, his words clearly insinuating his disgust for me.

"We will have to hope for the best. Meanwhile, we need not worry about the Southwest Quarter," I said, walking across the ruins of the great hall to a table strewn with maps of the City and its surrounding areas. "I sincerely doubt God will consider these slums the most significant of His objectives. He will concentrate all efforts on gaining control of the City down here," I said, pointing to the farthest southeastern corner of the City's walls. To the City's main gates.

"We took the Southeast without difficulty," Melchom said. "We hold it now. There have been no reports of significant resistance since the fighting first erupted."

"That makes no sense," I said, thinking about it.

Azael looked concerned.

"God needs to re-establish control over those gates to get Michael back into the City."

"Well, we hold the gates, my Lord," Melchom said. "It is our position here that worries me. If our position is overrun, we will not have a command post from which to direct operations. Not until your armies arrive."

"You got the signal out, then?" I asked. I was relieved.

"Yes, my Lord. We were able to get a signal out through the aqueducts that feed the City in the Northeast Quarter."

I smiled at Melchom and slapped him on the back in approval. "In the final analysis, I have to acknowledge how glad I am that you disobeyed me in every way," I remarked, referring to our years of arguments over the Great Northern Forest and the City's water supplies.

As usual, he did not seem too concerned with decorum, at least as far as I was concerned. "It was my pleasure to ignore you at every turn, my Lord." He looked at me quite seriously.

"Then we understand each other now?" I asked.

"We do."

"Where is Amee?" I asked.

As Melchom thought about this for a moment, his expression gave him away. "I do not know, my Lord," he admitted. "She has not come back from the Northeast Quarter and I fear that she may be trapped in the fortress."

"Are you sure that Simon was alerted by your signal?"

He was surprised at my question, but shook it off.

"I did not know your general was Simon, but I am certain he received the message. Shortly after we set the forest ablaze, we detected movement in the forests, running parallel to both the river and the northernmost parts of the City walls."

"Good," I said with great relief. "If we could spot them from the City walls, Simon will reach the southeastern gates soon." I looked at Melchom again. "How long can we hold that fortress?" I asked.

"My guess? We can hold until morning, if nothing else fails."

"Good," I said. If nothing else fails.

Azael, looking at the maps, spoke up. "He will allow the fortress to be held only as long as it takes for Michael to move up from Apsatsus."

"What do you mean?" I asked, looking at the same maps, but not quite understanding his point.

Azael pointed to the City's main gates. "God will wait until Simon reaches the City, then pin us between the walls and Michael's army."

We all looked at the maps.

"God's reserving the Southeast Quarter for our retreating fighters. Then He'll crush us from both the inside and the outside at once," Azael said.

It certainly seemed possible. "We have no way of knowing when Simon will reach the gates?" I asked.

"No, my Lord," Melchom replied. "We hold certain parts of the eastern walls, but whatever movement was detected out of the forests did not appear to be enroute toward the gates."

"Simon must be trying to avoid Michael's armies moving up from the south," Azael said, tracing a direction on the map.

"He is betting on us to hold the City walls, in the same way that God is gambling on us to surrender them," I said.

"What do you mean?" asked Melchom.

"Simon will loop around east before coming back in and pinning Michael against the City walls," Azael said, before I could reply.

"Exactly." I was disheartened. Will we succeed in holding the walls, I asked myself, rubbing my temples and feeling the sting of my burns. "I led Simon to rely too heavily on my ability to hold the City," I said. "If I had captured Yahweh, when I had the chance, things might have been different. The City soldiers would have stood down and we would have had a chance to hold the walls until Simon pulled up behind Michael."

We stood staring at the maps. And waited. The reports began coming in. They poured in all night.

CHAPTER
THIRTY-SEVEN

Request reinforcements to hold NE Fortress. Completely encircled. No word of rebel activities in NW Quarter.

<u>*Tartaruian soldiers spotted in NE Quarter*</u>*. No further info. Reports suggest they branched off into two groups, but no info on which direction they took.*

NE aqueducts blown up. Water supply to city cut off. Tartaruian army spotted approaching eastern walls. Concerted counterattack now being launched to wrest NE Fortress from our control. Heavy fighting. Uncertain how long we can hold.

SW Quarter on fire. Reserves ordered to put out fire and protect citizens.

All available SW reserves to commit to NW Quarter. Tartaruian artillery hitting eastern wall and siege towers seen pulling up. <u>Forces do not...repeat...do not appear to be main army group</u>. Need to hold fortress long enough for Tartaruians to breach eastern walls and link up.

Tartaruian forces earlier reported in NE Quarter reported to be wiped out. <u>No survivors</u>.

Simon's main force whereabouts unknown. Tartaruians reported to have originally entered City through aqueducts before blown up. <u>All scouts tasked with getting tactical details to Lucifer killed</u>.

Tartaruian siege machines have hit eastern walls after heavy bombardment. Some Tartaruians made it across walls, but most siege machines knocked out by God's reserve forces coming in from NW Quarter. Still no reported rebel activities in NW Quarter. Cannot hold NE Quarter much longer.

City forces reported rising up in SE Quarter. Rebel positions coming under sustained attack. Positions fortified by rebels and Tartaruians who made it down the eastern wall expected to hold for now.

Rebel reserves pivoting from SW to NE Quarter failed to break through. NE Fortress has fallen. God's standards seen flying on the Fortress again. Not clear whether any remaining rebels can break out of NE Quarter.

Uncontrolled fires in NE Quarter. Entire quarter appears to be on fire.

Remaining rebel reserves in SE Quarter now under sustained attack. Cannot control fires SE Quarter fires. City troops pouring in from NW Quarter. Greater number of God's troops than originally estimated. No rebel activity reported in NW Quarter. Impending attack on SE headquarters. <u>All strategic reserves either committed or destroyed</u>.

Rebel reserves have linked up with few remaining rebels fleeing NE Quarter. Linked up with Tartaruians who made it across eastern walls. All rebel troops now falling headlong into SE Quarter. SE Quarter fighting has resided after repulsing initial counterattacks by City forces.

Fires in NE and SW Quarters now out of control. NE Fortress reportedly abandoned by City soldiers due to fire. <u>More City troops heading out of NW Quarter into SW Quarter</u>. <u>Bug out! Bug out</u>! <u>You are about to be overrun!</u>

⌘ ⌘ ⌘

Citizens fought bravely. They used the element of surprise to their advantage, but as Melchom suggested, they were little match for trained soldiers, when it came down to it. God had calculated correctly. He had enough strength hidden in and around the Seat of God to hold the City.

"We need to leave this place now," Azael said to me. "We need to hold the southeastern gates long enough for Simon to arrive and relieve us."

"If we hold them and Michael arrives first, we are as good as dead," Melchom said. "If we hold them and Simon arrives first, we'll all be pinned down together."

"And if we do nothing, we will die right here!" Azael shouted.

"Wait," I interjected.

The two angels looked at each other angrily.

"Fighting among ourselves will do no one any good."

Both backed down.

"Good," I said, though I was not sure why.

Nothing looked good at that moment. Earlier, we had held three-quarters of the City. Within six hours, we had lost the whole Northeast Quarter and were about to evacuate the entire Southwest Quarter.

"We simply do not have the means to hold so large a section of the City without Simon," I said.

Everyone agreed.

"We should have focused our efforts on one quarter, rather than trying to defend three."

Melchom was about to say something, but I cut him off.

"It is no matter. What is done is done, Melchom. There is no blame to be assigned, but that which rests with me."

All angels looked at me solemnly.

"We leave here now and set up a headquarters in the Southeast Quarter. Alert all forces to retreat to the Southeast Quarter and hold their positions as long as possible."

No one argued. There was nothing to argue about. Many good citizens had died that night, because I was unable to capture Yahweh. And why was that? Because I had refused Amee's help when she offered it. And why was that? Because my pride had led me to take command of the outlanders and believe I could wrest control of the City away from a monster who had held the City of Heaven in His grasp for the last thirteen billion years.

"Where will we take up your new headquarters?" Melchom asked.

"We will position as many units as possible, rebel and Tartaruian alike, as close to the City's main gates as possible. We may need to evacuate the entire City. At least, then we will be able to see whether enemy forces or our comrades approach first. My guess is that even with the losses we have sustained, our fight in the Northeast has taken some of the punch out of God's troops. If we are forced out of the City, I cannot see how God would have enough soldiers to follow us out. He will sit on His walls and watch us go and hope that Michael arrives in time. He has no generals left in the City. No real leaders. They will not leave the safety of the walls without Michael."

"What if what Azael said is true?" Melchom asked. "What if we are pinned against the walls of the City by Michael's forces?"

"Then we will fight the noble fight." I stared into his eyes, those eyes I had loathed all these many years. "But we will fight."

"Yes Lord," he said.

It was the bravest thing I had ever heard him say.

"Besides, we will need to whittle down Michael's armies as much as we can so that when Simon finally does arrive, he will have less of a force to reckon with."

All seemed to agree.

"Remember, I may be leading this rebellion, but a victory is not for me. The cause is more important than any one angel. It may have taken me a long, long time to understand that, but it is true." I looked at Azael. "It is right."

Azael nodded.

"Okay, then," Melchom said. "Get all these papers burned," he ordered his staff. "Take only what you need."

Angels scampered off in a show of model efficiency.

"And be sure to take a sword or a spear!" shouted Azael.

"Always the pragmatist, my friend," I said, patting him on the back.

"I completely forgot, my Lord," Melchom said, surprising me. "Amee asked me to give this to you."

He produced a long rag-covered object and handed it to me. I uncovered the rags to find my sword, notched and beaten, as it had been the day God took it from me.

"She took it from the Central Museum, just before she headed off to send the alert. She said you would need it." Melchom looked embarrassed at having forgotten about it until this moment.

Quietly, I strapped it to my back. I already had Phanuel's sword strapped to my side. "Thank you, Melchom," I said. "It seems I misjudged you all these long years. I am sorry."

He looked at me and shook his head. "Well," he stammered. "Get us out of this mess and we can call it even."

It was the first time we had ever smiled at each other and meant it. It would also be the last time.

⌘　⌘　⌘

I wish I could say our retreat was tactical. It was not. It was a free-for-all. Defenses that had been set up along the North-South axis road were already under attack when we got there. Actually, we fell on God's forces from behind, as they clearly had not realized we were still in the Southwest Quarter. It was the first time in many years that I killed angels with my own hands. I did not know them. I did not know where they came from. But since they wore the uniform of God, the Almighty Father, I took pleasure in killing them. Curse me for saying so, but I did. Once through, we continued to move as quickly as we could, until we were only a few blocks from the City's great gates.

"Take fortified positions across the top of the wall and be sure to take as many artillery pieces as we can manage up there," I ordered. "We will need them for bombarding both God's forces in the City before us and, perhaps, Michael's forces behind us."

It was a grim order, but one that seemed to me to make the most sense given the circumstances. We could not afford to be flanked from atop the walls.

"We will maintain a semicircular defense with the walls of the City holding us in," Melchom suggested.

"Yes. Then the only way they can come around us is over the top of the walls. The walkways are narrow and their numbers will count for nothing, if we properly defend those positions," Azael said.

We stood in our new headquarters, the morning's light now coming up over the horizon. I looked up into the sky. "It is good to see the sky. Its blue spells encouragement."

"Yes, my Lord," Azael and Melchom said in unison.

"My Lord, my Lord!" shouted a runner making his way up to our bombed-out position.

My bodyguard would not let him through. There were only four of them now, including Azael.

"My Lord," the runner said breathlessly, standing outside the ring of fierce angels, jumping up and down.

"Easy, lad," I said. "Get your breath." I looked at him. I knew him! He was covered in dirt and blood, but I knew him! "Ukobach!"

"Yes sir," the boy choked out.

"Let him through!" I shouted roughly.

He was dressed in a City soldier's uniform, but it was Ukobach.

"How did you get here?" I asked, utterly astonished.

Melchom looked at Azael inquiringly.

"Where is Simon?" I asked tentatively.

"He is still in the outlands," Ukobach said, still out of breath. "I came through one of the aqueducts before they were blown."

"And you fought your way down here?" I asked, still unable to get over my surprise.

"Yes sir."

"Where is your father?"

"Dead, sir." Ukobach did not even bat an eyelid.

"No." It was all I could say. I looked down.

"Yes sir. He was killed coming over the eastern walls. He was meant to reach you last night but..." The boy paused, trying to come to grips with what he was saying.

"I am sorry. Your father was a good soldier."

"He was a good angel," Ukobach said.

"Yes. You are right. He was a good angel. Can you tell me what happened?"

"Simon put him in charge of our feign. We were meant to hit the eastern walls as a distraction to pull more forces away from this position. But it didn't work. Simon underestimated the number of City troops holding the fortress. It just wasn't enough to do the job, I guess. Father died leading charges of angels across the walls in an attempt to break the siege. It worked, but he is dead."

"And what about you?"

"I was scouting the farthest reaches of the northern forest, when I saw the messenger from the City emerge from the aqueduct and light the signal fire."

"Your father finally gave you soldier's work to do, eh?"

"Yes sir. When I came back to report to Simon, I asked him to allow me to lead a contingent of angels back the same way I had observed the City angel come out. He agreed."

"Very brave of you."

"Thank you, sir. I was able to get only about fifty or so angels through the pipes before they were blown. Many angels were still in the pipes when they went up."

"Many good angels have fallen today," Azael said.

"What news do you have for me, Ukobach?" I asked, bringing the conversation back around to what was most pressing. The fact that Tartaruians were in the City changed everything. Of course, I had been receiving reports throughout the evening, but now, looking at one and seeing Ukobach, it lightened my heart.

"I was not given too many details, sir. Simon knew of your fondness for me, but thought I was too young to carry messages to you. The angels through whom he did send word were killed trying to make it to your position last night."

"Yes, we did receive reports, but did not know what to make of them," Melchom said.

"So what, then?" I asked.

"It is my guess, sir, that seeing the City on fire, Simon will wheel back west to the river and return here this morning," Ukobach said. "He had intended to wait for Michael in the open fields, where our cavalry could swallow them as it had done earlier."

"Right again, you are," I said, looking at Azael.

"Yes, my Lord."

"Do you have any idea of the size of Michael's forces?" I asked Ukobach.

"No sir," he said, but there was a note of hesitation in his voice.

"Yes?"

"Well, it's my guess that we maintain superior numbers."

"Your guess?" asked Melchom.

"Yes sir."

"My Lord," Melchom said to me, "we cannot depend on this boy's conjecture. Who knows how many angels Michael has with him?"

"Not all angels, perhaps," I said, looking around at the carnage. "He had enough soldiers stationed here to practically knock us out of the City." I thought for a moment. "It must be Man."

"What, then?" asked Azael.

"Man," I repeated. "Man was about done, when I left for the outlands. Man was all but done, when I returned. God had told me the final solution was approved but a few days ago. With Phanuel's work and my input, Man is ready to go in a format God could use right now."

"What is 'Man'?" asked Melchom.

"There is no time to explain now. Only that Man may well be among us angels already."

"And he intends to use them in battle?" asked Ukobach.

"That is my guess," I replied. "God sent out a weakened army to protect Apsatsus. But His approaching army will be His new army, its ranks filled with Man. Unknowing, unthinking, and willing to fight for his master."

There was a silence like no other. The battle continued to rage around us. Artillery had been falling on us all morning. For those of us who understood the pattern of things, no good end was in sight.

"What do we do?" asked Melchom.

"I do not see how anything has changed," Ukobach said.

"Boy!" Melchom began, but stopped when he saw my expression.

"Ukobach is right," I said. "But there is something we can do. Simon is unaware that his adversary's army is many times larger than he anticipates." I looked back at the boy. "Ukobach, take a horse and go intercept Simon without delay. He must be warned that God now wields His powerful new weapon. Simon must not be drawn into a fight until he can assess God's true strength." I thought for a moment. "No good," I said. "No good answers." I looked at Ukobach again. "Stop Simon from making his way here. Tell him we are aborting. We will evacuate the City and make our way to him. Simon will use our army to cover the citizens' retreat."

Everyone around me began to speak at once.

"No!" I shouted interrupting their clamor. "I built this creature and I know what it can do. There is no point in destroying every last hope here today, when we can live to fight again tomorrow."

"Lucifer, when again, if ever, do you think we will hold the City's gates?" shouted Melchom. "From within the City. Nearly the entire quarter!"

"I do not know," I replied. "But justice will prevail. Man will rise up against God one day and on that day, we will retake this City and return it to the citizens of Heaven, from whom it was usurped."

Not one angel agreed with me. But I was in charge. As it turned out, it did not matter. A few moments later came a call from the lookouts posted on the gates.

"Our army approaches! Simon approaches!" The shout went up, but only the few around me knew that this likely meant the end.

⌘　⌘　⌘

Out in front of the army rode Simon and Maalik. Riding the way they were, neither appeared to have a care in the world. Observing them, you would never have imagined a war had broken out the day before. It seemed as if Phanuel's work on Man were still in progress. That angels were not killing angels. That Haures was alive and all was right in Heaven. As I watched them approach, I felt anger consume me. Our angels were fighting and dying, but Simon and Maalik rode as if nothing untoward had happened. Through the gates I strode, arrows and projectiles firing and landing all around me. Through the gates, into the outlands, and right up to their horses.

"Explain yourselves!" I shouted as I approached. "Angels are dying in there and you approach the City as if it were already yours!"

"Lucifer, Michael has been defeated," Simon said, his air nonchalant, his voice ringing with confidence. "We defeated him early this morning. We present you with the prisoners we took: one thousand City soldiers. They hardly put up a fight."

Even Maalik, normally circumspect in revealing his real feelings, seemed pleased with Simon's response.

"You fool!" I shouted. "What you conquered was not Michael's army!"

"No, Lucifer," Simon responded. "There were two legions of God's troops. We took them swiftly and by surprise."

"They were God's legions, yes. But they weren't Michael's army."

Now both looked perplexed and not a little bit worried.

"Ahriman, what do you mean?" asked Maalik.

"It was a trap!" I shouted. "Michael approaches from Apsatsus with an army of men! What you encountered was not his main force. Our angels in the City have been all but obliterated. We will be crushed against the gates of the City by Michael's real army."

Suddenly, another shout went up. "Look! *Look!*" screamed the lookouts from the gates.

We all turned as one. Several miles away, a large mass of troops could be seen kicking up clouds of dust. The soldiers moved slowly, as if lumbering forward. Before them fled two angels, riding like mad. Coming to warn us. Riding out in front of Michael's army of men. I knew them in an instant.

"It is Ariel and Orobas!" Azael shouted in astonishment, his gaze scanning the distance out into Elysium.

"Damn it!" I yelled, running back toward the gates.

Simon spun on his horse and began shouting orders. The hordes of men coming down on the rear of his army seemed unending.

"How were they not spotted?" I asked myself loudly, running under the portcullis of the City gates. "Quickly!" I shouted to my angels. "Set the defenses alight! Burn the rest of the City down! It is the only way to get distance between us and the City's armies!"

It was a rash order and one I knew would only delay God's soldiers for a while. By the time they worked their way out, they would see us below them, pinned to the walls by Michael.

The fires were lit. Our artillery opened up in all directions. Both into the City and at the advancing soldiers of God. Into the outlands, where Simon's army was quickly turning about and forming up to prevent its total rout. Both Ariel and Orobas had made it through to our lines. But what of it? As the Southeast Quarter began going up in flames, the remaining rebels and Tartaruians fled from the City. I stood at the edge of the gates, looking up into their eves. It was probably the last time I would ever gaze upon the City itself. Most of it was aflame already. Whether I would go down in history as a savior, a usurper, or a destroyer seemed far less certain now. Whatever I had done, I had done for the greater good and the City was suffering for it. Even those of the lower classes, those who might have stood by me, had I succeeded in commanding the City, would never support me again. I was responsible for burning most of their homes to the ground. My concerns and my many earlier conversations with Maalik about maintaining continuity while consolidating power seemed so rash at this moment. I had made a terrible mess of everything. And as always, Heaven's angels were paying for my errors.

CHAPTER
THIRTY-EIGHT

B y the time the sun set over the walls of the City, fighting had broken out on the Elysian fields before the City's main gates.

"Michael's forces are disorganized," Maalik commented, as he, Simon, Melchom, and I looked over the most recent reports coming in.

Azael stood outside the tent with a dutiful-looking Ukobach nearby. Seeing Ariel and Orobas return, Ukobach had asked to be made a member of my bodyguard. And after considering the request, Azael had consented.

"His forces have moved up to just within range of our artillery positioned on the City walls. But he seems to have totally discounted the possibility of our moving those pieces onto the field. If we can get catapults even within a few feet of the entrance to the gates, we would have enough range to take out several hundred of his men in a matter of minutes," Simon said.

"If we take those pieces off the wall, we will be unable to hold our positions in the City," I reminded him. "The firepower on those walls is the only reason we have not been run out completely."

"Yes," Simon mused to himself. "There is something else." He scratched at his chin. "Scouts tell me Michael is using angels as field commanders to direct the battalions of men."

"This is correct, my Lord," Ariel affirmed, stepping into the tent behind Azael and Orobas. "The men are not good fighters. They have had no training and were collected by Michael and Raphael in haste."

"They reacted to our attack with fear," Simon agreed. "They were being held in place by the old soldiers. Angels."

"That is correct, my Lord," Orobas chimed in.

"And what of it?" asked Melchom.

"We can do significant damage to Michael's army in rather short order," Simon replied.

"Yes, but Tartaruians are accustomed to fighting on horseback. Pushed up against the walls as we are, we cannot maneuver," Maalik said.

He had a good point.

"We will stampede some of the horses through the ranks of Michael's armies. Even angels will be in fear of their lives," Simon said.

"Excellent!" Maalik said. "Following through the fracas, our mounted troops will make short work of all those who have not fled the field." He paused for a moment, rubbing his hands together. "And then we can turn into the City. We could be at Yahweh's main fortress by nightfall."

"More importantly," I interrupted, "we have a means of escape."

They all stood quietly and looked at me.

"Simon said it himself," I said, compelled to defend myself. "Our forces are superior. If we need to evacuate the City, we should be able to fight our way out into the outlands."

"Why do you speak in this way?" asked Maalik. "Of defeat?"

It seemed a strange turn of events, indeed, that had me speaking of defeat and Maalik of victory.

"As its leader, I look to preserve the movement," I said, somewhat indignant now. "Not twenty-four hours ago, we held three-quarters of the City. Now we sit outside its walls, only a few hundred yards from God's soldiers and even closer to an army larger than our own."

"But not an army that matches our own in strength," Simon added.

I looked at him while rubbing the palms of my hands. Blood had soaked into their new roughness.

"Now is the time, Ahriman," Maalik interjected. "Upon the main gates of my city, God placed solid bronze doors, never to be breached, holding in everything that would be his new City of God, my beloved City of Heaven. Standing here now, right here, is the closest I have been to my City of Heaven in over thirteen billion years." His face caught in a grimace of pain. "Think about that. Do you understand the sense of loss I feel standing here? How many of my friends have died so that I could stand here in Elysium right now? How many years have been lost to a mad tyrant who runs Heaven and its citizens into the ground for his pleasure? Some setbacks in the city today? Perhaps. But look what we have at our command!"

His passion was moving. It strikes me even now, thinking about it in retrospect. An angel without a home. Deprived of his home for so long. It was, indeed, a desperately sad plight.

"We have an opportunity now to make things right again, to take back what was stolen from us," Maalik went on. "We have the will to do it too. And your angels are behind you."

My head ached. What was the right thing to do? Waste everything? Salvage what was left? Melchom remained silent. He seemed pensive, as if he were actually having difficulty disagreeing with me.

"Take heart," Simon finally said to me with a smile.

"Take heart," I repeated to myself.

I had seldom doubted myself. It was an egotism I had grown to love and trust in. But now, even God's rebellious angel, his Satan, had a difficult time seeing the right way. God had a way of clouding our judgment of what was right.

"I appreciate your good counsel," I said, shaking off the feeling of pessimism that had seized me. "All of you. You are right. Let us take the fight to them."

They smiled and we all clasped hands in brotherhood.

"Now we fight army to army, angel to angel," Maalik said. "We will fight on, until we seize what was taken from us."

I returned to my tent and slept not a wink. But not before I had ordered all units to prepare to be surrounded.

⌘   ⌘   ⌘

Maalik's arrival was announced in my tent in the early hours of the morning, before the sun had come up.

"Did you get any sleep?" he asked.

"No," I said.

"You worry for Amee."

"I do, yes. But I worry more for the day," I replied.

Maalik smiled. "Ahriman, there is nothing to worry about. We will do what is right and we will have no regrets. Today will be a great day, no matter what happens."

I sat on the edge of my bed, toying with my armor. I looked up to him. "How do you know?"

He sat down next to me. "It was told. And I believe. There would be a great rent in the fabric of the universe and there was. It was told. The tear would separate the world into darkness and light and so it has been. We Tartaruians wear the white that, to us, represents the light of the universe. But as much light as we think we carry, never really have we used that light to bring order. Until you came."

I blushed. "I have done nothing."

"On the contrary. In both our adversity and our union with you, you nurtured us. As Yahweh's Seraph, you drove us to survive. When you came to us, as we believed you would, you listened and learned. And in what you learned, you took up our light. You lead us now. You carry the light on you and we, as a people, have followed you to this point. For billions of years, we have been outcasts in our own lands. Content to run and hide and fight, when necessary. But your coming, your light-bearing has brought us farther than ever before."

I huffed, "You trust in me, when what I do could get us all killed?" I strapped my shin guards to my legs. "It will kill the movement and everything that many angels before us have stood for."

"They stood for an idea, Ahriman, yes. But you stand before us as a leader. Someone who is willing to put his beliefs and his very life on the line." Maalik patted me on the back like a father. "Do you not see that you have given us the courage to take all our political philosophy and translate it into reality? What is theory, if it is never practiced? Empty and meaningless."

"Yes, but..."

"There is nothing left to discuss."

Maalik was happier than I had ever seen him. A worrywart, now happy to charge into battle.

"Before these walls," he went on, "we will show Yahweh that he is not 'God,' but just like any other being in Heaven."

"And what is that?" I asked.

"Just another angel."

⌘ ⌘ ⌘

I walked to the edge of my tent flap and looked out onto the field. I must have heaved a heavy sigh, because even Azael noticed while he was speaking with Ariel and Orobas. Before I stepped out, though, I looked at a spot on the field where the rising sun's light had already taken root. Joined in battle with the darkness of the dying evening. I walked out and stopped just short of the battle line, remaining surrounded by the cool darkness of shadows around me. With an inexplicable sense of hesitation, I faltered, as if something were preventing me from walking farther, from stepping onto the sunlit patch of ground. It surprised me, this hesitation, as I looked upon the line drawn before me. What was holding me back? What prevented me from touching this first light of day? There was something about this swath of light that dazzled me. In all my endless years, I had witnessed, without any similar thought or concern, untold projections of sunlight, cut and shaped by any number of features or edifices. I had passed them, without notice, just as I passed most normal things in the course of my day. In each of those encounters, never once could I recall having stopped to look at such a display with so much interest, introspection, and concern.

Then it came to me. This light before me had traveled untold millions, maybe billions of miles, through transected space and dense atmosphere. And despite whatever odds the mathematicians could muster, it had landed on the very spot before me, its journey suddenly halted by a substance whose structure did not, quite by chance, permit translucence. This energy, generated by the sun's brilliance, had landed, of all the trillions of places in the universe, at my feet. For me alone to admire. I had no say either in its generation or in its termination. Yet, despite my powerlessness to control its destiny, it was there—for me alone. Now. Only I would see this battle take place upon this spot and watch as the light, yet again, won its battle with darkness. I looked at the forbidding City walls.

"How utterly delightful!" I said to myself, as I looked back down and stepped into the light.

⌘　⌘　⌘

I received an update on our situation. Reports indicated that Melchom might have been killed during overnight skirmishes in the City. Never a soldier, he had, nonetheless, lived through eons of God's rule. There was something to be said for that.

"We cannot hold our positions in the City too much longer, my Lord," Ukobach reported, as I strode across the ground toward the command tent.

"Where is Melchom's body?" I demanded.

"We do not know, my Lord. We do not even know if he is dead," Ariel said, his hushed conversation with Azael now taking on a new significance.

"He was in the midst of ordering our angels to pull whatever artillery pieces could be salvaged from the walls into the field, when a shower of arrows came down upon him and his angels." Ukobach sighed. "We no long hold the position."

We entered the tent. Simon stood by with the gravest of expressions. "Lucifer, we have all but lost the City," he said. "It is foolish to continue the fight there. We have to take what we can and face Michael directly on the field."

"We will be compromised from the rear, then," I said, thinking as quickly as I could.

"What do you propose?" Simon asked.

Here was a great leader and military thinker. Asking me what to do. It brought home to me as nothing else could the exigency of our situation. I looked at Maalik and then at Ukobach. My mind raced.

"We cannot hold the City," I announced. "Pull all our people back to this spot. I have already ordered two lines of fortifications to be built, one facing the City and the other facing Michael's army."

"Michael will try and thwart any efforts we make," Simon said.

"That is why you will make that bloody cavalry charge into their ranks and follow up with a few battalions of horse," I said implacably. "You will decide whether Michael's undisciplined men can withstand a real fight. If you are lucky, you will split them." I turned to Orobas. "Slay as many of their officers as you can. At the very least, it will give us the time to complete our fortifications."

"And how will that happen?" asked Maalik.

"You," I stated simply, "must remember that Simon is the army. You, Maalik, are the bureaucrat. The organizer. Apply your skills to the job and finish erecting those defenses. Fortifications facing the City must be far enough away to prevent us from getting hammered by their artillery, but close enough for us to wheel backward, if and when we break Michael's army." To Ukobach, I said, "Meanwhile, burn those damned gates down. If we can pull back around, we do not want to be locked out and have to fight our way back in."

"Yes, my Lord," everyone said in unison. Their words were bereft of spirit.

"Heads up, boys," I said encouragingly. "We may yet make this thing work."

I looked at Ukobach again. He was strong, but afraid. In the last two days, he had endured his first experience of combat, lost his father, and was now among my inner circle.

"Not bad for two days," I told him.

He stood straighter and saluted. The world must surely have seemed to be collapsing around him.

I looked at all of them. "Know that whatever the outcome, we have made a good go of it. We did what was right in the face of evil. Somewhere, someone will know and understand the sacrifices we make here today."

A sudden shout interrupted my words. God had appeared on the walls of the City. My sacrifices were about to come screaming home to me. In ways I preferred not to imagine.

CHAPTER
THIRTY-NINE

"Where is the great Satan?" God yelled across the outlands.

Accustomed only to hearing Him speak in rational times, extolling the virtues of some angel, crowing to the crowds about His own achievements, or haranguing them about the deviousness and ruthlessness of the City's enemies, all angels, even those among His own forces, stopped fighting to gaze up at something they had never seen before: God in what appeared to be a wild, frantic state. On the wall He stood, smeared in blood. In one hand, He held a sword. With the other, He held Amee by the neck. Around Him stood his bodyguard. Gabriel stood nearby. On his face was an expression of utter devastation. God's manic demeanor left all of us, myself included, transfixed.

"Where is he? My most favored angel? Higher than high among my most trusted?"

God's eyes swept the field, as if He had not noticed the pitched battle halted below Him. Had He truly been our father, His rage at the scene should have known no bounds. All His children fighting and killing one another on the fields before His sacred City. He should have been ashamed at our conduct. But His face wore no such expression. He seemed to feel no such concern. All we saw was that look of utter madness, scraped together with anger and hatred. He hated everything. Most of all, He hated me.

I stepped forward. "I am here, Lord," I said.

The wind blew around us. The City was burning behind Him, the wind blowing the ashes all around. His burning City and the last vestiges of His supposedly insuperable power, splayed out before all, in total chaos.

"Yes, there you are, Satan!" He yelled, His eyes picking me out from the crowds of thousands.

Maalik shouted from the tent behind me, "Watch for snipers, Ahriman! You are too bold in showing yourself!"

I did not listen.

"What would you have of me, my Lord!" I shouted up to the walls.

In that same instant, the last of our troops and citizens fled through the City gates into our lines and behind the rudimentary defenses already being set up.

"I would have your allegiance again!" He shouted. "I would have you bring this rebellion to a close and come back to our family!"

I looked at Amee. She was shaken, but unafraid. My heart ached to see her.

"I cannot do that, my Lord. You know this. I know too much."

"Today was supposed to be your triumph. You were to be celebrated as a hero of the City."

"That's a lie!" Amee screamed.

Gabriel moved to pacify her.

"You would have publicly sacrificed him in front of everyone!" she shouted.

Gabriel's efforts to calm her down were in vain.

"The Lord your God does not lie. I am all powerful and only I wield the power to decide what is right or wrong."

"You are a megalomaniac who has lost His grip on reality and His grip on the slaves He calls His people!" Amee shouted.

Enraged, God struck her down so that she was lying prostrate at His feet. No longer able to see her from my vantage point below the walls and looking at Gabriel's expression of horror and helplessness at witnessing his niece's suffering without being able to help her, I felt the breath sucked out of my body as though I had been hit myself.

"*Yahweh, let her go!*" I roared, trying to divert His attention. "This will not solve the problems between us!"

God looked at me with a murderous expression. "I will take everything from you today, my adversary. Satan. I will take all your ambition and your righteousness and rob them of meaning! You will be dust before me and you will beg for death!"

"Yahweh," I said. "This City is yours no longer. These people do not belong to you." I pointed across the fields to Michael's army. "Those men do not belong to you. You may have created them, but you have no love for them. No love within you at all." I looked around at everyone across the expanse. "These angels and men deserve more than this. Unquestioned devotion is no longer to be expected in Heaven. We have seen your weaknesses, your inability to understand what love really means. You speak of love as if it is something square and obtuse, but it is not. If you could really see, you would know that love is flowing and unending. You cannot claim to love us as your children, when all you wish of us is to surrender all our power to you."

"What do you know of love?" He shouted, holding a bleeding Amee in His grasp. "Love drove me to make this City a grand place. Love has made me the most powerful being in existence."

"Love is what moves our hearts, my Lord. Lord, love is not a means to an end, though you treat it as such."

Shaking Amee by the hair, He shouted, "*This* is your idea of love?" Then He pointed into the burning City and out to the carnage on Elysium's plains. "*This* is your idea of love? Bringing destruction to my City?"

"It is not *your* City anymore, my Lord. It belongs to the people. To the angels who suffered under your rule. To the men who, if you are not stopped, will also suffer, though they were built to love you!"

"End this now!" God shouted. "End this at once, turn yourself over, and I will let her go," He said, shaking Amee by the hair again.

Suddenly, His face was wiped clean of its maniacal expression. His glance swept over Gabriel weeping at the sight of Amee as she bled from her nose and cut lip. Then He looked down at me, our eyes meeting again for the last time.

I was shaking as I looked at Maalik. He ran toward me, as did Azael and Ukobach.

"Do not do it!" Maalik shouted. "Do not be taken in by it."

I looked at Amee. Bleeding though she was, she seemed at peace. I would lose her, I thought. I spoke of love. In a few crazy moments, standing on a field of death, with nothing but anger and betrayal driving me, I spoke of love.

"Don't do it!" Amee yelled.

"For the love of God!" yelled Gabriel. "Do *not* let this happen!"

I looked once more at my angels. Heartbroken. And then I turned back to God.

"I will not. I am." It was all I could say.

Without a moment's hesitation, God dragged Amee to the edge of the walls and threw her over. I watched her fall, as if in slow motion. I thought of all we had meant to each other, all the time we had spent together, and everything she had taught me without my even realizing it, blinded as I was my by own self-indulgence to the depth of her faith in me. Dignified to the last, she made no sound as she fell. Whether she still loved me in those fleeting last moments I will never know. She was everything to me. And I did nothing as I watched her hit the rocks that lay up against the walls' foundation and lie in a crumpled heap. It was I who screamed out in pain and watched God walk off the walls, shouting orders as He went. Arrows rained down upon me. But once again, I was protected. Azael and Ukobach's shields covered me, but Ukobach fell as he slid in to protect me, taken down by the hail of darts meant for me.

Azael dragged me back through the fortifications. Never again would I see Amee or Ukobach alive. The City burned as never before, but it was nothing compared to the way the image of Amee's face in those last moments burned into my brain. Defiant to the end and willing to die on the chance that God might be overcome.

⌘　⌘　⌘

The fortifications saved us. Simon led a reconnoiter with Orobas into Michael's lines. Ariel, fulfilling my prior orders to Ukobach, set fire to the City's gates. Maalik had the time he needed to put enough wood and dirt between us and the hordes surrounding us. It was becoming increasingly clear that more time and effort was required to develop Man into a truly useful instrument of war. I watched as men slammed against our hastily, but well built palisades in waves. Men driven by the whips of angels behind them. God may have slapped some armor on them, put a sword or a spear in their hands, and pointed them in a direction, but they were not soldiers. It was interesting to witness the fights that broke out among them and for a time, we all watched, as Michael's forces turned on each other and fought among themselves.

We thanked our good fortune that Man had turned out to be the floundering rabble he was, as God threw the rest of His army through the burning gates and into our other flank. Ariel and the angels under his command made short order of those first soldiers who made it out. It was only a temporary victory, though. Before long, more soldiers had come over the walls in a concerted attack on our defenses. Caught between two advancing armies, we fought with the desperation only the insane are capable of. I rode Morello through the ranks, calling out encouragement to Tartaruians and citizens of the City alike. To those who were left, that is, after the long, unyielding hours of battle. They fought admirably, with everything thing they had. Azael was there, as Morello was shot out from under me. My bodyguard was now reduced to three angels. I was no longer the privileged angel I had been. I fought on foot, wielding sword and shield and spear. Cutting down any City soldier I came across, fighting with my angels against the minions of Yahweh. Many fled before me, knowing who I was. Others were anxious for a chance to engage me in single combat. I thanked fate for having brought Simon to me, for had he not retrained me during my time in Tartarus, I would, no doubt, have fallen within the first hour. My spear and sword served me well, as they once had when I was an idealistic follower of God, though now I used them upon His angels.

Simon returned through the newly built palisades as the evening descended again. He was wounded, as were most of his horsemen. Orobas did not return. Thankfully, Simon had lost few riders in comparison to the destruction wrought on Michael's forces. That said, the charge had been unsuccessful in breaking Michael's army in two. There were simply too many men.

When Simon was brought to the surgeon's tent, I could see the horror in his eyes as he gazed upon the many thousands of citizens' heads impaled on spikes along the walls of the burning City.

"They are our angels," I said.

Simon could not speak.

"My father's head is over the eves of the burnt-out City's gates," I said.

Maalik remained silent.

"I cannot be sure, but I think God may have unearthed Zoan. A skull sits besides my father's decapitated head."

The arrows sticking out from Simon's armor were slick with blood.

"Take him in and do the best you can for him," Maalik said to the litter bearers.

"Attend to his angels as well!" I shouted, pointing to the rest of Simon's weary cavalry. "They fought like monsters today." I meant it. "They fought like no one has ever fought before," I said, looking at the City's burnt-out gates, now adorned with the heads of my family.

⌘ ⌘ ⌘

"How bad is he?" I asked the surgeon, as he hovered over Simon in the dim light.

"I am with you, Lucifer," Simon said. He grasped at my hand as I stood next to his bed. It was cold and weak. I looked at the surgeon.

"Satan," I said in jest.

"He will not be able to get back on a horse to fight," the surgeon said. "He's done for now."

He wiped his bloody hands with a towel. The arrows had been extricated from the wounds, but the surgeon had not been able to stanch the bleeding completely.

"Nonsense," Simon gurgled, blood bubbling up in his mouth. He spit the froth on the floor, angry, but determined.

"Rest easy, Simon. You have done well. Your fighting today will give us another day at it," I said half-heartedly.

"At least," Maalik concurred, shaking his head.

Simon settled back down. "How did we do?" he asked weakly. We both looked at Maalik.

"Well, we lost many angels today for sure," he replied. "But because of you, Simon, Michael's army made no significant headway against our defenses."

"Me and Orobas," Simon said dejectedly.

"Where did he fall?" I asked, looking back at Azael and Ariel.

"He died fighting Raphael, when he happened upon Michael's command post. Orobas carried out your orders well, Ahriman, before his fall. Many an officer was dispatched before Raphael's sword met its mark."

"He was a good angel," Ariel said, standing quietly behind Azael.

"Ahriman kept our exposure to the City well in hand," Maalik said, trying to inject some good cheer back into all of us. He patted me on the back. "Without Ahriman, we would not have been able to complete those defenses."

I had not realized how sore I was from the fighting.

"He bested sixteen angels, is what he did," Azael said light-heartedly, cleaning the blood from his sword.

Simon mock-taunted me. "Sixteen is all?" He coughed up more blood, but waved away help. "I'm fine. I'm fine," he sputtered.

"It was very nearly fifteen," Azael said.

"How is that?" Simon managed to get out.

"Lucifer had turned away from the fighting momentarily to help one of our soldiers nearby who had been wounded. He had disengaged from the battle and torn off his sleeve to use as gauze to staunch the angel's bleeding," Maalik said, almost in a triumphant tone.

"If I had thrown my two stilettos a second late," Azael said, "Lucifer would have taken an axe in the head." Maalik frowned and turned to me. "The wounded angel was evacuated, Ahriman. You need not worry," he reassured me.

"The decisive moment will come tomorrow," I said.

Simon seemed as pleased to have heard the story as Maalik was to relay it.

"The fighting has all but stopped tonight," I said. "Both sides are exhausted. But you can be sure that God will get more troops out of the City tomorrow."

"Did the angel make it?" Simon interrupted, getting back to Maalik.

"Yes," Maalik said, taking great pleasure in his efforts to lighten my serious mood with these conversational diversions.

"Angels," I said, putting an end to their exchanges.

They stood up straight and looked alert, as they sensed my gravity.

"Our defenses may hold for a while, but we do not have the advantage of winning a fight of attrition here. We need to focus!"

The residual smiles that had remained on their faces faded as they all silently agreed with me.

"Michael's army of men may be disordered and clumsy, but they will inevitably take their toll on our forces, if for no reason other than their sheer numbers."

Orobas is proof of that, I thought to myself. That was not all. In such a short time, I had lost Phanuel, Amee, Ukobach, my father, and now, if what I suspected was true, my grandfather as well. Not to mention Morello.

"Even I underestimated the speed with which Man would be able to reproduce. And the impact he would have on the battle," I said.

"God has no mercy," Maalik said. "Did you see how those creatures were thrown headlong into the fighting without any real hope of success?" he said referring to Man.

"Man will succeed," I said, pushing thoughts of lost ones to the background. "Do not be deceived. God built him to succeed. What we saw today was nothing but a taste of the potential Man has for destruction. Man is not weak. He is just inexperienced. In time, he will be very dangerous. Perhaps even more so than you angels."

"Well, at least not anytime soon," Azael correctly noted, slapping Ariel on the shoulder.

We all nodded, acknowledging the truth.

"How can we use their weaknesses to our advantage, though?" Maalik asked. It seemed an almost reasonable question, considering we all thought we would be dead by then.

I looked at Simon. "I have an idea," I said.

⌘　⌘　⌘

The late evening was cool and relatively quiet. Minimal and sporadic fighting had been reported here and there, along both sides of our lines. During the night, a great noise rose from Michael's camp. Men were being put to death on his orders.

With all that God had at stake, Michael was now exterminating elements in his own army.

Whatever the situation, I prepared myself again for battle. Sitting on my bed, as I had sat the night before while discussing strategies with Maalik. A time when Amee had still been alive. Alive, somewhere in the City. Now gone forever. That moment, as she fell from the walls, her body smashing into the rocks below and breaking over them, would not stop replaying itself in my mind. The eyes of the angels I had cut down appeared again and again to haunt me, some fearful, others full of anger, and a few surprised. Amee's eyes had been calm, as if she knew something the rest of the universe did not. As if she were being released from her pain. My armor was battle-scarred from the day's skirmishes. I wondered what Zoan's armor must have looked like after years of combat. I wondered about Gabriel's armor, back when he was Yahweh's sword-wielding henchman. Amee had worn no armor. She had fought for what she believed in with nothing to protect her, but faith in herself. Driven to fight, in part, by her disillusionment with me.

In my mind, I saw her fall over and over again and could only hope that in witnessing, during her final moments, how I led an army against all of God's hegemony, she had felt her sacrifice was not in vain. Like the many other angels I had slain, I had killed Amee too. I had caused her death. Through the efforts she had made to rouse the City to rebellion, the work she had undertaken in its cause. And for the first time, it dawned on me. She may have loved me. Possibly, she had. But it was by no happy coincidence that she had become my lover. I had been God's spy chief. She had sought me out deliberately with a hidden purpose: to safeguard her rebellion. I did not know how I should feel about this. Whether to be happy or sad. I considered the choices before me as I felt the tears stream down my face. I prepared myself now for what lay ahead. Without her.

CHAPTER FORTY

Waves of God's soldiers, pouring out from within the walls, hit our defenses facing the City. At the same time, swarms of men rushed in toward the defenses facing Elysium. The battle had begun in earnest. Although our arrows cut them down by the thousands, the enemy forces were relentless in their onslaught, each wave of soldiers so densely packed that it became increasingly difficult for our angels to get close enough to engage them individually in combat. But eventually, they were able to move in. As Michael's army of men pulled down the palisades, they screamed and cheered with a newfound hope. The Tartaruians were just barely able to prevent a total rout. But as they looked up from the mass of flailing arms, they began, without warning, to counter Man's cheers with their own. Something unexpected had occurred.

Positioned now behind Michael's army, I attacked from the rear, leading a charge against Man. While Michael's army squabbled all night long, I had been able to sneak many hundreds of horses through our lines unnoticed, pull around the southern edge of Michael's army, and move up behind him. I wished I were astride Morello again, as I led the ferocious offensive. But my mount would brook no comparisons and earned himself honors that day. Driving into the rear of Michael's forces, I slashed and cut.

"Come now!" I yelled, egging my angels on, as we sped as one toward their lines. "Show them what you are made of, my champions of the righteous and the good! Let the swiftness of your swords and spears and arrows drive home your message! That you have returned to reclaim this hallowed ground from the forces of darkness! That you have returned to retrieve the light and restore it to its rightful place—in the souls of all angels!" Pointing my sword straight at our onrushing enemies, I shouted, "Follow me! They are no stronger than we are! They are soldiers of God but our swords and our spears pierce them no less surely than theirs do ours!"

And so into their ranks we plunged. Slashing and slaying anything and everything in sight. Slaughter. Slaughter, just like I had dreamed of as a young angel. Finally I was its author.

Disordered and disoriented, Michael's army broke ranks. And began to flee. In their moment of triumph, I had been able to break them. Break Man.

In the chaos, I unexpectedly came upon Michael in the field. An angel I assumed to be Raphael stood before him, protective and defiant. As the rest of my cavalry rode down what remained of Michael's command post, I reined in my horse. Both angels stood utterly still, shocked at my sudden appearance, quite unable to understand what had set off the carnage around them. As they watched everything in sight being cut down, Raphael pulled his own sword from its scabbard. With one swipe, I knocked it out of his hand. He stood his ground, nonetheless, shielding Michael. At least he was loyal.

"You are God's Seraph now!" I shouted at Michael.

He stood there, looking at me from behind Raphael. Not really afraid, but overcome by shock.

"You are no soldier and these men are no army," I declared, wheeling my horse around. "Tell God I will take Mankind away from Him. I will use the power God gave Man to overthrow His tyranny. I will use His own weapon against Him and I will not rest, until God is dead."

Michael nodded, dazed. Glassy-eyed. I could only assume he had understood my words. Raphael stood straighter, his stance more resolute than ever.

"As for you," I said, pointing God's sword, now in my grasp, at Raphael, "we will meet again. You took an angel from me yesterday. I will not forget it."

Raphael sneered, but said nothing as I turned my horse away.

Many days since that moment have I regretted not cutting them both down, then and there. For in the years that followed, Michael would grow into a successful leader and Raphael, a formidable soldier. Slaying many of my angels. Many days have I regretted riding away, back into the fray, killing anything I could find, when the heads of the two angels who mattered most had been mine for the taking. I felt no mercy for the Man I had created. I would go to any lengths to ensure that God was toppled from His heights. Michael belonged to the Order of the Seraphim and so, on that fateful day, I let them go.

⌘ ⌘ ⌘

My surprise attack worked beyond all hopes. Our troops poured out of our defenses and made short work of the men and their angel taskmasters. Once before had the City witnessed such carnage and death. Only then, they had marked Yahweh's overthrow of the City of Heaven. What we did that day on the Elysian fields before the old City of Heaven was retribution. Retribution for billions of years of tyranny. We were the righteous. I truly believe it. Angel and men fell before our swords and spears and while many were innocent in their own right, we had to sacrifice them for the greater cause. It was the right thing to do.

Seeing Michael's army being cut to ribbons, the City's soldiers began to flee back to the City walls. In their panic to reach the safety of those walls, many trampled over their comrades or went down in the melee themselves. Residents of the City, ordered out to the walls to witness for themselves what had been proclaimed as the unqualified victory of God's angels over their new Satan, were horrified to see the straggling remains of His armies running haphazardly in all directions, with my angels in pursuit, cutting them down as they went. It was on that day that my trimmers, my outlanders, my Tartaruians became divine. That day, they were no longer angels. They became demons.

The shout went up as our troops scampered through the fortifications in pursuit of the enemy.

"Ten heads for each of the those God has stuck on the walls of the City!" Azael shouted, leading his soldiers through.

Our troops were only too happy to comply as best they could.

When it was all over, the field lay littered with the wounded and the bodies of the dead. Writhing angels and men, vanquished and in pain. Victorious angels, my demons.

"None of the survivors shall be put to the sword!" I ordered. "The fight is over. All City angels and all men who can walk will be taken prisoner. They are not to be mistreated. All City angels and men who are wounded and cannot be transported will remain on the field!"

Maalik looked at me with what I perceived to be admiration. "You have learned," he said.

"These angels are our brothers," I replied. It was a true enough statement.

As evening settled in, the City was still alight and sections of the walls abandoned to the few citizens who had risked venturing a look out into the outlands.

"What will you do, then?" Azael asked, as we settled down before the fire to eat whatever remained of our meager provisions.

"I will speak to them. Try to bring them down and join with us here, in the depths. Far removed from the sight of God," I said solemnly.

⌘　⌘　⌘

I ventured out from behind the refortified palisades once again, flanked by Azael and Ariel, my good, brave bodyguards. Snipers were nowhere to be seen along the wall this time. Only those who wondered what was to come next.

"Angels of the City of Heaven, for that is the true name of the City in which you live!" I shouted. "I, Ahriman, Lucifer, Seraph, Proctor, Captain General, and Satan, your adversary, have risen up against our God. An apostate. A usurper. God has taken everything from me, just as He has taken it from you. Your lives are His. Your families are His. Everything you own, say, or do is subject to His approval, His judgment. But there is a different way. The way it used to be, before God threw out the venerable City of Heaven and replaced it with this," I said, pointing at the now-scarred walls around us. "The way it is with us, down here. I am your humble servant, much like I once professed to be God's. And the devotion I gave Him these many years, I swear to give you now. My people. Join me now and let the righteous prevail."

I came back into the fortifications.

"Good speech," Azael said, with the hint of a jest.

I raised my eyebrows and laughed. It was unexpected.

"What now?" Maalik asked, as the four of us walked into Simon's tent. He lay very still, but was awake.

"We have won the battle," I said to them all. "We have seized the decisive moment and made the best we can of it. But we cannot hope to win the war. Not here. Not now."

No one commented.

"We will retreat from here. Leave the walls of the City of Heaven. God has won. This time."

"We cannot continue to fight forever," Maalik said, reluctantly acknowledging the truth of my words.

"For whatever reason, call it fate or fact, Yahweh has the City," I said. "Try as we might, we may never succeed in handing it back to its rightful owners. The majesty that the City of Heaven once stood for may never be resurrected again. I think we really have to consider that possibility now."

Simon sputtered, "What, then? What do we do?"

"Our angels will go back to the way things were before," Maalik said, looking up at me. "You have done a wonderful thing here today, Ahriman," he said, standing straight and at attention. "You, their most favored son, have shown the citizens of the City that God is not what they think him to be. You have shown them there is another way."

"I agree," Simon whispered. "They have watched as God killed. Before the very eyes of Gabriel. They have watched how you defied him, standing up not simply against his rule, but against everything he stands for." Simon broke into a gurgling cough.

"Rest, Simon," I said. "What I say and what I do are two very different things. Someone once told me what matters more is the example I set, rather than what I claim to stand for."

I thought of Amee, again wondering what had brought us together—love or purpose—and which of those two had sustained our relationship till the end.

"Amee died demonstrating that resolve and she was right. What I do now may impact us more than any battle we fight. The only way to win this war is to show the universe we are right. All this time, we were congratulating ourselves for doing what was right without knowing what that really meant."

"What does it mean, Ahriman? No one knows," Maalik said.

"No one knows, because righteousness is in the eye of the beholder," I answered. "Following God is right, unless you are Maalik, leader of the Council of Twelve of the City of Heaven, now a trimmer and an outlaw of the wastelands. Unless you are Simon, former Archangel of God and general of His armies, now a traitor, an apostate, and the leader of the enemy armies. Unless you are Lucifer, of the Order of the Seraphim, now Satan, flung down from the heights of power as God's favorite out of sheer jealousy, fuelled by nothing but the spite and revenge in His heart. Would following God seem right to you as a citizen?" I asked. "Not to me, it would not."

"In circles we go again," coughed Simon.

"What, then?" asked Maalik, wiping the blood from Simon's lips with a cloth. "What do you propose?"

"We will leave this place," I said. "Take our dead and wounded. Take the prisoners and educate them in the way you educated me. Convert those we can and release those who wish to remain faithful to Yahweh."

"Where will we go?" gasped Simon.

Before Maalik could reply, I said, "We will go far away from the City of Heaven, toward the distant mountains in the east. Yahweh called them Gehenna. We encamped at their foot not long ago, I think. We will take refuge in the mountains and build a new city. A city, where all the elements that had once given the City of Heaven its greatness will serve as the very mortar of its foundations. Where we can begin again. We cannot continue to be wanderers, trimmers, outlanders, moving from place to place in fear and living out of tents. The fortifications that Maalik had built for us there on those battle grounds were strong enough to hold back God's soldiers and Man. The walls we build around our new city will surpass the walls of the City of Heaven in strength," I said. "Until the day comes, when no walls need separate all the peoples of Heaven."

"And what of Man?" Maalik asked.

"Man will have his own time," I said, worrying to myself now. "Even God does not know Man's true potential. Built in His image, Man will be able to elevate himself to a level where he manifests all that is best in us. But he will also be capable of manifesting all the elements that constitute God's worst persona. God will work hard to gather as many men as He can around him. His City is burned to the ground. His armies are depleted. Man will be God's slave. So we must strive to take as many men from God as we can and whenever we have the chance. We will save Man from the fate God laid out for him. We will use Man for everything he has to offer, but his kind will be an equal partner with angels in our new city."

I turned to Azael, ever faithful and my most cherished protector. "I need you to find Amee's body. There is nothing I can do for my father and my grandfather now. They will, no doubt, be treated with all the disrespect God in His vengeance is capable of. But Amee's body must not suffer the same fate."

"I will find her, my Lord." Azael saluted and quickly left the tent.

"Keep Ukobach's body with Amee's," I said to Maalik. "He was young and dedicated and protected me, even when I was his enemy. He died saving me and for that I will remember him always."

"It will be done," Maalik said solemnly.

"We have not retrieved the bodies of Melchom, Phanuel, or Orobas, then?" I asked hopelessly. I did not bother to ask about Jeqon.

"No, my Lord," Maalik replied, his tone as solemn as before. "We cannot find Orobas. And Melchom and Phanuel could not brought out before we lost the City."

"Before *I* lost the City," I said, correcting him. "Their names will also have a hallowed place in our new city. I did not know Orobas well, but he served me loyally when I went into the outlands, unsure of my objectives. He continued to serve me, faithful unto death. Melchom was my enemy, when he should have been my friend. And whatever he may have done earlier to antagonize me, he helped Amee make this fight a good one. He may not have believed in me, but he died believing in our righteousness. Phanuel was my son, when he should have been my enemy. I was responsible for his father's death and yet he looked to me with the hope that one day, I would see the error of my ways. I failed him in almost all respects, but his sacrifice will never be forgotten. Not within our new city."

"I will give the order for preparations to move," Maalik said.

"And what do I do?" Simon asked.

He reached for my hand. His clasp was heartbreakingly feeble. The yellow tones of his face worried me.

"You will recover quickly," I said, smiling. "No matter how thick and how high we build our walls, God will come after us, anyway. You will rebuild our army." I looked at Maalik. Simon managed a tortured smile. "All right, then," he said. "That is something I can do."

"Call all the angels out," I ordered. "Under cover of darkness, we will retreat into the outlands."

Maalik looked worn and a bit despondent.

"Do not worry, my friend," I told him. "One day, we will take this City back. It may be beyond our years, but it will be ours one day."

"I believe you, Ahriman, but like you, I worry for the day," he replied.

I smiled. "Sometimes," I said, "just living is an act of courage."

CHAPTER FORTY-ONE

I do not know what the inhabitants of the City thought when dawn broke: we—the invaders, outlanders, apostates, and destroyers—were no longer there. We left nothing but the dirt embankments and the littered battlefield. Were the citizens appalled by the fact that we had taken away prisoners? Those prisoners might have been fathers, husbands, brothers, or sons. I do not know for sure. Were they surprised to find that we had helped those wounded as best we could and left them there for the City to provide further care? I do not know for sure. What did they think of me, their Lucifer, who had been for many millions and millions of years the star of the City, now fallen and forging such an unexpected path. What did they make of it all? That I do know. They had seen living proof of my righteous message.

Riding next to Simon's litter, I looked at the open fields. Here and there lay corpses of the enemy. Picked off by our troops some-time during the fighting. Maalik rode with me. Azael, as always, near at hand, with Ariel behind him. Azael was the last of my original bodyguard, the only one to survive. Looking up into the air, I watched the birds circling here and there in concentrated flocks. Focused upon Elysium, seeking out the carcasses they would soon pick apart and consume. Above the still-burning City they also flocked. Ever circling, ever focused. Miles away, one could see the smoke rising into the sky, a relentless stream fed by fires. Up and up it rose. The once white walls were stained black in so many places now. Thankfully, the wind blew in from the east. Smells from the Acheron we would shortly be crossing. Across and into more fields of burned-out madness, where the City's armies had met one of their many defeats, not at the hands of trimmers, but engineered by God, their own master.

As we rode on, I tried not to look to the north. My memories of Amee were too powerful, though, and my gaze turned, despite my best efforts, to the forests smoking from their deep and penetrating burn. How Amee had loved those forests! Her entire life's work. What must she have gone through to put them to the torch? Or had the forests just been another cover for her true goals. Like me? A necessary expedient? I cared not to think of it. I glanced over at the horses drawing her covered body, along with Ukobach's. Azael had found her on the spot where she had fallen to her death. Molested no more by God. I looked at my horse. Felt his size. Morello was dead. But this horse had served me just fine.

"I will call you Ukobach," I said to him, patting the side of his neck. I meant it with the greatest of respect.

"What's that?" Maalik asked, thinking I was speaking to him.

"Oh, nothing. I was thinking that Morello had been a good horse. Named after a hero who died fighting God."

"Yes," was all Maalik said.

He swayed back and forth in his saddle, looking ahead. Toward the outlands, the river, and our new home in the mountains. Beyond our range of vision for now.

⌘ ⌘ ⌘

We crossed the river on the third day. I looked down along its bank to the south as our angels, men, and horses were ferried across. Down to where Apsatsus sat at the Forks, into the Styx. We would be going there quite often, I expected. Looking for men. In the years to come, God would dam up and divert the Acheron, the Great Dividing River, and the whole region would turn into a giant desert. The Styx would continue to flow. God could not afford to choke off the Styx. It was from there that Man had emerged. It was there that Zoan had found me those many, many years ago. Somewhere along its marshy banks. It was the source of all good and all evil in Heaven, it seemed, regardless of whether you were one of my angels or an angel of God.

I felt good when the tent city came into view. Of course, the outriders spotted us in advance. We came through the barricades to find the streets lined with eager families, anxious to know what had happened and how their loved ones had fared. I rode silently through the streets. People looked at me with questions in their eyes. They gazed at my uniform, the uniform of their people, my face and arms burned, my armor scarred from hard combat. They looked at Maalik, who reached out to touch the outstretched hands of the throngs as he passed. The throngs holding garlands and bouquets of ambrosia flowers that they now understood would serve to commemorate rather than celebrate. As word spread that the City had not fallen and that many had died in the vain attempt to seize it, the camp fell into mourning. Prisoners were properly quartered and Maalik saw to it that they were entitled to all the rights enjoyed by a Tartaruian. Just as I had been.

I retired to my tent that night. The same tent in which I had once been held prisoner. In the very same place I had left it. I half-expected to see Ukobach as I came around the corner to the tent flaps, Haures coaching him about something or the other. Being a good father to his good son. There was no one. I did not need to be guarded now. New aides reported to me that evening, but I never took the time to learn their names or anything about them. They were young and happy to be my valets, though I had failed their predecessor so badly. Nothing had changed. Everything seemed the way it had been the day I left. The day Corpens had beaten me to within an inch of my life. Books, candles, chairs, bed. All the same. As if nothing had befallen us in the interim. As if that one slice of history did not exist at all.

Simon mended, though it took a while for him to be restored to even minimum mobility. His injuries limited him physically, but not mentally. He scoured the camp for angels of intelligence and skill to replenish the army's depleted ranks. With my leave, Ariel became his second. A spirited and faithful angel, he deposed the many prisoners, converting them to our cause. He even managed to enlist some men into the ranks, though they continued to be difficult to manage. Ultimately, Simon managed to rejuvenate and restock the ranks of the army. Unfortunately, I use the term "rejuvenated" quite literally, for I had lifted the ban on younger Tartaruians engaging in combat. It was only out of necessity, of course, and just for those first few years. Thankfully, the Council saw fit to leave me to myself.

I lay in my bed every night, staring at the roof of the tent for hours. It was a comfortable tent. At least as comfortable as any place I had ever lived in. Not as comfortable, of course, as the places where I had spent many hours with Amee. I spent a great deal of time thinking about all the things I had done. I was responsible for so much destruction. Destruction of lives, of peoples, of cities, of movements. Though there was no way of quantifying the devastation I had wrought, I figured I was probably guilty of greater destruction than God Himself. That had not been my intention when I set out. Had it really been worth it all? Was there any real meaning to anything I had done? My family had been destroyed. My position within society destroyed. My love destroyed. The armies of these people, so devoted to the cause, destroyed. Would another city, something we built ourselves, make up for the inconceivable anguish I had put so many of Heaven's occupants through? Maybe Maalik was able to see the good in the things I had done, to justify them as right, but I was not so sure I could.

Saving Man was the only other thing I could do. Who knows who created the universe? It was not God, as He would have everyone believe. But it was God who created Man. If by saving Man,

I could make up for some of the evil I had perpetrated, maybe in the grand scheme of the universe, I could make amends for all that I had done wrong. But I knew there was more to it than that. Maybe by saving Man, I could save myself.

⌘ ⌘ ⌘

Eventually, the Council called me.

"That was not our intent!" Corpens shouted, the blood surging into his face as usual.

"You granted me power only as long as the City remained in God's hands. Well, the City remains in His hands. I retain all power over our people."

"Our people? *Our* people?" Corpens shouted. "These aren't *your* people, Lucifer. They are my people! They are Matel's people! Margaret's people!" he roared, pointing down the table to the other Council members. "They are the Council's people!" He stood up, his hands working violently, as if he were dying to get them on me. "*They are their own people!*"

"Shouting is not going to get us anywhere," Margaret interrupted unexpectedly.

"Who says it won't?" Corpens yelled back.

"Lucifer, the army is loyal to you," Margaret continued, ignoring him. "They love you and Simon and would, in all likelihood, follow you, when and wherever you direct them. Our people," she said, shooting a sharp, forbidding look at Corpens, "both admire and fear you. Your attempt to take back the City of Heaven was both brave and miscalculated. But Corpens is right," she sighed. "The power you were granted was meant to help you deal with a crisis situation. That situation has passed. What you now suggest was never part of our agreement."

"Margaret, I understand," I said wearily, but relieved to sense some degree of support. "We never spoke of founding a new city. We spoke of taking the old City. But that is where you should focus. It is the 'old City' and whether we take it by storm or it falls under its own weight, it will never again be what you all want it to be."

Even Corpens was silenced by this.

"What I suggest," I went on, "is to start afresh. In a place protected from God and His armies. In a place where we can compete with God on His level, rather than fight with Him on His terms."

"I truly believe this is the right thing to do," Maalik said to the rest of the Council.

"You are of little use to us now, Maalik," Corpens retorted, now doubly incensed. "Since the day this...this demon came into this tent, you have reversed yourself on nearly everything this Council had stood for over billions upon billions of years!"

"Well, maybe that is because this Council has been deceiving itself into believing something that will never come to pass," Maalik said, his voice perfectly steady. "You are right. We sit in council. Year after year after year. Moving from one place to the next. Taking what victories we can manage and harkening back to the good old days when we governed the City of Heaven with the help of this good book." He held aloft his newly copied book of laws. "Has any of that gotten us any closer to bringing the City back to us? Has it really? Think about it. Has anything we've done brought us one real step closer to ending Yahweh's tyranny?"

Again, the room was silent.

"I would say, no, it has not." Maalik put his book down on the table. "That angel there," he said, pointing to me. "In the short time he has been with us, he has absorbed all our learning, demonstrated a change of heart, matched, possibly, by no other angel, and bravely stepped into the void of *this* Council. In very little time, he has rallied all our greatest hopes and led us to the very walls of the City from which we were once driven out. True, our campaign did not culminate in absolute victory, but it has put God on the defensive." Looking back at Corpens, he continued, "When was the last time anything *you* did brought us closer to our restoration?"

Margaret interrupted again. "Let us not get personal in this debate. Many things, beyond our control, have taken place and we must deal with the facts as they are."

"Indeed," I observed. "The facts are, that despite our most valiant efforts, we could not overthrow God and banish Him from our City." I quickly looked at Corpens. "From *your* City. All our efforts have made it clear that God is just too entrenched to be so easily ousted. Effort after effort, made from within by those loyal to the cause, has failed to convert the mass of citizens. God has succeeded in wiping the memory of liberty clean from their minds. Their overriding feelings are only of fear and the hope that God and all His henchmen will leave them alone. They have no alternative. Do you not see? Founding a new city, one where citizens' liberties are codified and respected, will do more for the cause than one hundred cells sneaking around and engaging in clandestine subversive activities. It will be less bloody than all the battles we would need to fight just to breach the front gates of the City of God." I looked around the room to observe their expressions. "For the first time in their lives, citizens will have a choice: either live in fear under God's rule or live in harmony with us and out of His sight."

"He has explained it better than I ever could," Maalik said, sitting back in his chair and crossing his arms, a look of satisfaction on his face.

"And what of Man?" asked Matel.

"He will become our symbol," I said. "Man, as conceived by God, had been the emblem of slavery. He was created to perpetuate an unholy and unjust rule, where His absolute power would be accepted without question. I almost helped make that situation a reality. Man, now reconstituted, will have all the abilities with which you and I are endowed. All he needs is time to develop. What I changed in Man transformed the nature of the equation that God sought to use to His advantage to vanquish us, once and for all. Over time, Man's brain will go through the necessary process of development enabling him to share our capacity to reason. It will take a while, but eventually, that goal will be attained. We must be patient. Man will demonstrate in the foreseeable future a level of intelligence, strength, and cunning that rivals the attributes of angels like us. What more poignant expression of compassion on our part than to save Man from God?"

"What will we do with this Man?" Margaret asked.

"We will treat them as we treat all citizens here. Like the prisoners who sit in re-education now. They will learn the true history of the universe and be made a product of those who have chosen to remove themselves from God's sight. They will be both our allies and our brothers and sisters."

"To the greatest end," someone said.

I looked around in the direction of the voice. It was Corpens.

He looked up, breaking away from his thoughts. "To the greatest end," he repeated. He seemed to be asking me for confirmation.

"To the greatest of all ends," I replied. I did not share my own thoughts with them.

I sat for several minutes in silence while the Council members conferred with each other. As I waited, Azael came in, with Ariel trailing him.

"My Lord," he said so softly that I could barely catch the words, "we've completed the reconnoiter you requested. And I believe we've found the best spot possible."

"Where is it?" I asked with a level of excitement that startled even me. I looked up at the Council members who were now aware that I was engaged in an unrelated conversation.

"It is on the rib of a great mountain far to the east," Azael replied. "The plains immediately before it are nothing but swampland, but the foothills themselves, situated the way they are, will be perfect for fixed fortifications. For located within the foothills are six smaller hills surrounding a seventh central hill, which commands a view of the entire area stretching over hundreds of miles. By connecting the ring of hills, we would be protected at least from three of the four directions by the very character of the topography."

"It sounds perfect. Except for the swamp," I said.

"It can be drained, my Lord," Ariel intervened, stepping up from behind Azael. "By damming the mountain streams. The supply of water that feeds it could be diverted into the city. That will yield fertile land, excellent for the cultivation of crops."

The Council, unable to overhear our whispered exchanges, was now beginning to show signs of impatience and frustration.

"What is this about?" asked Margaret, clearly having lost interest in the discussion between the Council members.

"Azael has just reported that he has identified a perfect location for our new city."

"We have yet to decide," Matel said, exasperated.

"I have decided," I said defiantly.

"Another rash decision that will lead us all to our deaths?" Corpens asked, evidently not entirely swayed by my arguments.

Ignoring the bickering, Margaret asked, "Where is this place?"

"It is in the vale of the eastern mountains," I announced.

Azael looked at me. I motioned for him to go on.

"It is Gehenna, in a place called Dis," he said.

CHAPTER FORTY-TWO

S tanding on the mountain summit and looking out over the lands that would become the new City of Heaven and be more commonly known as the City of Dis, I knew Azael was right. To my back stood a sheer mountain, up the face of which we could continue to build when the need arose. In front of me lay six large hills, not quite mountains in their own right, but surrounding my hilltop perch in a semicircle from north to south and forming natural lines of defense to the swamp plains before them. A large lake lay within the confines of this natural border of hills, fed by the water coming down from the mountains behind me.

Azael came up behind me. He stood gazing at the view.

"Heaven is a beautiful place," he said.

I smiled to myself. "The most beautiful of places, I think."

"This will make a good home," Maalik said, coming up the hill.

Simon, still suffering from his wounds, but well enough, at any rate, to make the journey stretching over several days from the tent city's location to the foot of the mountains, brought up the rear, with Ariel aiding his ascent up the hill.

"That forest to the south will give us the wood we need to start," Simon said, panting a bit for air.

"The mountain is made of good, sturdy rock too," Azael added. "We will have strong walls."

"We will need them," I said, already thinking of the times to come. "We gave Yahweh a bloody nose," I said, taking His familiar name from that time on, "but the first time we poach men from the Styx, He will come after us with everything He has. It is true that this new City of Heaven will draw Yahweh's faithful away from Him and convert them to our cause. It is just as true that the best test of our morality will be our efforts toward the salvation of Man. It is equally true that this city of ours will be a living and breathing reason for Yahweh to continue His campaigns against us. We may no longer be known as 'trimmers,' but He will continue, for the purpose of self-perpetuation, to rail against us and try turning His remaining citizens against all that we stand for."

Having made it to the top, Simon could not help but add, "And we will be ready for him."

The five of us stood in silence, looking across the plain where our new city would rise. The City of Dis. Hell.

⌘ ⌘ ⌘

Not long afterward, our people moved to the vale of Dis. Immediately, we began work on building the city. Maalik and Azael began mining the stone we would need to build our first walls. Initially, they would be thin and low, like the walls that immediately surround this temple. But they carried out the job. My comments proved prescient; it did not take long after our first lightning raid into the Forks at Apsatsus for Yahweh to find His courage again. We still controlled the lands to the east of the Acheron, but the longer Apsatsus worked, pumping out men, the more developed the outlands became. Yahweh's armies were no longer as timid as they had been in the years I was Seraph. They now moved easily on the east side of the river without us being able to provide much by way of impediment. We became used to the constant fighting that went on in the Tartarus, where the blood of many angels and men was shed. And continues to be shed. Blood that turned once fertile land into wasteland. Sure, Yahweh would refer to all outlands as wasteland when I had been Seraph, but now the numberless years of battle had, indeed, reduced everything to dust.

In time, the walls of Dis rose higher and grew thicker. In time, more men, women, and children were taken from the Styx or from Yahweh's soldiers, contributing to a population explosion. Yahweh's City was also growing considerably. But whereas His walls were built to mark His wretched City's expanding social status, our own would increase in number over the years to withstand the repeated attacks of Yahweh's armies. Man doubled and then tripled His fighting force. Left with only the men and women we could find and round up, the erection of more walls would prove increasingly necessary to protect the teeming masses who collected around us: refugees from Yahweh's City of Heaven who, at first, had decided that Dis or Hell was not the place for them, only to discover subsequently that it was the only place in the end.

Heaven is in a constant state of war. For generations, Yahweh's soldiers have fought the angels and men of our city. It will never end, until one of us is taken down. I hate this war. The knowledge that I created Yahweh's nearly inexhaustible supply of soldiers eats at me as nothing else can. So if you find yourself suffering, it is, indeed, I who have caused your pain. I have made this world the way it is and I cannot help feeling regretful over my role.

I hope that one day, this war will be over and we will live in peace as once we did, or so I am told. Until that time, it is our sworn goal to bring to this place, this hallowed ground, as many who strive for freedom and are willing to fight and die for it as we can. Do not get dismayed or disillusioned when you find us being portrayed as the epitome of evil. For what is evil but a mere perspective and one that differs from one angel to another, one man to another, one leader to another. Hell may be evil, but we are the only evil that provides salvation. We are the only form of grace left in Heaven.

5

CHAPTER
FORTY-THREE

Satan closed his book. "There is much more to our history than I have related to you," he said, patting the tome before him. "But there is enough time in this place," here, he smiled, "for you to read and study everything you need to know. Do not take my word for it. Stay here, among us, and learn. Learn from those who have been here a thousand years, a million years. Learn from those men and women who have been in the teeth of battle, recruited to join Yahweh's forces as slave soldiers, and seen their angel masters whipping them onward to clash with the enemy. Learn from the scars that deface our walls and from the crowds of people who stake out those very same walls for their protection from the universe's real evil."

Satan looked at Gazardiel. The latter looked away in disgust.

"Yahweh will never accept peace, unless He has the power to dictate its terms," Satan went on. "If you intend to strike at such a tyrant, the only way to succeed is to deal a fatal blow." For the first time, he bowed his head, averting his gaze from his audience. "We have tried, but failed. We fight on, nonetheless." He took a deep breath. "To bring to Heaven the only city truly based on merit. Here, those whom Yahweh had once kept under His heel now have the same rights as any other angel or man. Stay here and learn and you will see it with your own eyes. Yahweh's citizens, the tears of the dead crying out for death once again."

The room remained utterly silent. The sky had taken on its late afternoon colors, as warm and inviting as the early morning, but now filled, somehow, with a more solemn sense of purpose. The hall was no longer filled with the innocent, Satan thought to himself, but with the possessed.

"In ways Yahweh had never considered, He made me His prophet. Through me, His Word is transmitted to you, His people. Though now, they may not be the words He wishes to relay."

There was light laughter in the hall.

"Yes, indeed," Satan continued, "it is the irony of the situation that should make you laugh. You believed Yahweh's Heaven, the afterlife, Nirvana, Valhalla, whatever, to be something it is not. Heaven is not a place that encourages independent thought, a place of personal liberty where ideas can be tested in an incubator for Earth. It is rigidly structured and bereft of the personal initiative that is indispensable for social progress. For such initiative is seen as a threat to Yahweh's absolute rule. Looking back on it now, I realize I made a terrible mistake. Yahweh's City was one where power reigned supreme at the cost of all else. Personal ambition was the same as political ambition. The only way to garner power was to insinuate oneself into Yahweh's good graces. And the only way to be in His good graces was to accumulate power. In so invidious a system, my efforts to bring about change could not, therefore, have been construed as anything other than an attempt to wrest Yahweh's tyranny from Him and keep it for myself to use to my advantage.

"But Man and angels have freedom here in Dis, in Hell," Satan said with renewed spirit. "Away from Yahweh's prying eyes, your personal initiatives are nearly universally seen as directed toward the greater good of our society. For free men and angels will always overcome those whose motivation originates in the lash of the whip and whose passivity derives from fear. Free men and angels have more to lose than those who are little more than slaves, and they understand that teamwork and perseverance are the key to a happy existence.

"I can say no more," Satan concluded. "Perhaps I have said too much already. Only you can decide what course to take. I beg you to choose the path I am offering you. I will not hold it against you if you reject it. Such a decision would not be entirely unreasonable on your part. In fact, it would, perhaps, be almost natural. It is what you know. But hear this: Dis was founded, in part, on the premise that it is healthy for every citizen to be empowered to dispute the decisions of his or her government in an open, fair, and fearless way. This applies to any citizen. For if the individual is stifled, so is the community. It is the common good that must be sought in everything you do, for it is from the common good that the majority benefits. Therefore, the decision lies with you and you alone. Take what I have offered you today and make your decision."

Satan looked at his escorts once again. It was his signal. "I am done," he said, shuddering in exhaustion.

His angels flanked him, as they carefully descended from the stage. Without prompting, many in the crowd rose to their feet, their eyes on Satan as he was led away. Down the rows of newly arrived.

"Is everything arranged?" they could hear him ask one of his guards, as they made their way.

"Yes, my Lord," the angel replied.

It was Azael, for sure. Satan left the hall. But to those who had heard his Word, he was no longer the same being who had entered.

⌘ ⌘ ⌘

The statue that stood in the Negates Hem gardens was nearly as old as the foundations of the temple itself. It had been erected there, among the quiet cherry trees and fragrant jasmine bushes, to honor the loss of Satan's Amee and, for a time, it had been consider some of the most hallowed ground in all of Dis. But time had weathered both the Amee's statue and the City's devotion to the woman that it recognized, her sacrifices for a better Heaven.

"My master first brought me here," Gazardiel said out loud when he heard the approaching footsteps he had for many hours anticipated. He looked up into Amee's eyes. Eyes he imagined Satan had looked into and foreseen the foundation of his beloved city. "Her memory inspired him to build this city. To make Heaven what it should be. Why wouldn't I worship as they did once? As he does now and forever?"

Azael stepped up from out of the brush, behind Gazardiel, and rested his hand on the angel's shoulder.

"I never really liked her," Azael said, looking up, into the same eyes Gazardiel gazed in to. "You never knew what she was thinking."

"That's a strange thing to say," Gazardiel replied as he stood and turned to face Azael. Azael's guards flanked him. It made no matter.

"Not if you knew her," Azael said. "It is time to go."

"I don't suppose," Gazardiel said calmly, after thinking for a moment, "that I can convince you to change your mind?"

Azael shook his head slowly but with no observable malice.

"It is the way of things," he said.

"The way of things," Gazardiel repeated. "Man overcomes."

"That is not for me to decide," Azael replied. "I am a good soldier and I do what I am ordered to do."

"Spoken like a true convert," Gazardiel sighed, resigning himself to his fate. Again.

"I have never been anything but," Azael said knowingly.

"It is a beautiful place," Gazardiel said, changing the subject and looking around one last time. "It reminds me of how I was born a citizen of Dis. Born an angel of the City of Dis."

Azael thought for a moment. "If it is any consolation, you will die an angel. An angel of the City of Dis."

With that, Gazardiel was taken. But not before Azael winked at Amee's statue and saluted.

⌘　⌘　⌘

Upon the outermost wall's ramparts they stood. One bound. The other two standing free and clear. The city's guards had been dismissed. There would be no attack on the city that night. Two of the three knew this to be true. With all their hearts.

"You are too predicable, my friend," Satan said, looking down at the angel kneeling before him. "And until now, I had been proud of you. But you have become too much of a liability."

Gazardiel's head was bowed, but neither from shame nor in deference. Droplets of blood speckled his robes and the ground below him. His face was bruised from the beating.

"We cannot afford this kind of disobedience," Satan continued. Azael stood next to them both. He gripped and released the pommel of his sword repeatedly.

"This isn't right," Gazardiel said softly.

"What is that you say?" Satan asked, gently clasping Gazardiel's chin and lifting his head up. "Right, you say?"

Satan released his chin and Gazardiel's head dropped back down.

"You think debate is the answer to our questions? You think we should stutter on and on, waiting and hoping that Yahweh does not strike a blow as we sit and argue, point and counterpoint? The Senate has fooled itself into thinking it is the true power in Dis, just like those fools in the Council before it. But the people know, Gazardiel, that I am the real power. And I will not let that change on account of foolish political machinations."

"This isn't right," Gazardiel repeated.

"What do *you* know about righteousness?" Satan snapped. "Were you there when everything that ever meant anything was taken from me? Was that right?"

"That is what you created," Gazardiel retorted, coughing and wincing as a pain gripped his chest. "That is what you teach us. What you taught us. Freedom."

"Freedom?" Satan asked incredulously. "Freedom is the problem, my young friend. You and Maalik are both fools. The divergent views freedom throws up are the constant cause of instability. I tried to teach the Council a hundred thousand years ago. I tried to instill the Senate with the same knowledge after we built this city. But they dithered and were too stupid to understand that with so many points of view comes an equal, if not greater, number of ways by which to proceed!" Satan said flamboyantly. "Freedom deprives us of central authority and in the absence of such authority, a kind of nihilism is born, with everyone entitled to his or her individual point of view, no matter how grotesque or abhorrent that point of view may be. Freedom protects those individuals' points of view, blind to their inherent absurdities and weaknesses, bestowing on them the same status as those ideas with true and objective merit!" Satan looked back to his battered former student. "Freedom breeds idiots like you."

"Freedom only allows for equanimity, if the power of the arguments underlying individual points of view holds true in the eyes of the people," Gazardiel mumbled. "What you taught us," he repeated.

"If that is what you think I teach then you have failed in your lessons. What I teach, my friend, is that war has been and always will be our lives until we defeat Yahweh," Satan said. "The particulars are not important, Gazardiel. Not important." Satan got down on one knee and looked at the beaten and bleeding angel. "You have not thought this through, Gazardiel. *That* is certainly not what I taught you. What is the point of dreaming for great things, if you sit idly by and allow others to take the credit?" Satan stroked Gazardiel's hair, now matted with blood. "I thought you had learned. I thought you understood. You cannot lose your head in idyllic and nebulous dreams." Satan looked intently at the angel's head and, without warning, slapped him hard on the side of the head. "You must plan to the end!" he shouted into the beaten angel's ear.

Satan stood up and straightened his robes. "No, I am afraid compromise only breeds opportunities for your enemies. And that is something we just cannot have, Gazardiel." Satan looked at Azael. "Something that led to our defeat more times than I care to remember.

"The Senate will not hear your bill but will, no doubt, mourn your loss. After tonight, there will be no stomach to move your ridiculous notions forward. Whether they were for or against you makes no difference. Whether they believed in excluding Man from our city or not is of little consequence. A politician's will is only slightly less steadfast than his interest in his constituency. And the constituency is with me. Have no doubt," Satan hissed.

Reaching out, Satan slowly removed Azael's sword from its scabbard. "No, I work from boldness and I say that Man will continue to fill our ranks. We have no choice."

"They pollute our ranks," Gazardiel said, more forcefully this time. He looked up at his old master. "They are not the men you made, Satan. They are worse. Far worse than you ever imagined! They're not God-like. They *are* God. And they will bring destruction upon us."

"I applaud your resolve, Gazardiel. I really do." Satan looked at the sword, knowing it was unnecessary to test the blade's edge. "But there is no getting around the fact that Man is our only weapon. He has more resolve in his little finger than either you or I could muster, even if we drank from the Styx itself." Satan turned back to the broken angel.

"Lord, Yahweh uses you with Man," Gazardiel said. "Surely you can see that. By assuming the role of his antithesis, you do nothing but perpetuate God's rule. You are doing God a favor by being this idealist. By elevating Man the way you do. By saving him to save yourself. That's what you're really doing, isn't it? Your idealism has blinded you and will lead you to your downfall."

"That is my problem, not yours. And the Senate will see things as I do. I will not allow you to instigate the removal of Man from the equation."

Satan looked out over the walls. They stood high above the squalor of settlements below them. This is what Yahweh had made them do. Where He Himself had put them.

"I will miss you, Gazardiel," Satan continued. "I regret that things have come to this. But we must not lose sight of the end game. We will not be distracted. And we will win and make things right in Heaven once again. Man need only be a temporary tool."

"My Lord," Gazardiel said, looking up.

"Yes," Satan replied, as he carefully raised the sword over his head.

"What of my son?" There was genuine grief in Gazardiel's eyes.

Satan paused. And thought for a moment. "Azael," he said, looking at the stern-faced angel next to him. "You will take care of things?"

"Yes, my Lord."

"Good."

The end was swift. There was no basket for the head to fall gently into. Those below the walls simply pushed the mangled corpse that had toppled down from the top of the ramparts into the drainage ditch. It was not the first. It would not be the last.

⌘ ⌘ ⌘

Satan stood on his balcony once again. A long day's work behind him. He regretted what he had been forced to do. Once again, there were shades of ambiguous gray, where he had hoped for nothing but the reassuring, unequivocal clarity of black and white. But his message would be heard. And understood.

The sun dipped beneath the city skyline. Like it had so many times. The plains appeared as they had a thousand times. The colors gone. Stamped out in the muddle of the city he had created. He felt relieved to see the darkness descend again. "For as the contest between light and dark unfolds," he thought to himself, "both contestants seem unconcerned with their audience and un-knowing that with every victory, inevitably comes another defeat until the end of time. There can be no victor. No one can prevail. But that does not stop them and the battle swings now in favor of darkness once again. And darkness, spurred on by yet another victory, seems content to settle and become more comfortable in the space it has carved out for itself."

The land could now release its pent-up heat from the day.

THE END